PENGUIN CLASSICS 🐧 DELUXE EDITION

IN THE SHADOW OF
YOUNG GIRLS IN FLOWER

MARCEL PROUST was born in Auteuil in 1871. In his twenties, following a year in the army, he became a conspicuous society figure, frequenting the most fashionable Paris salons of the day. After 1899, however, his chronic asthma, the death of his parents, and his growing disillusionment with humanity caused him to lead an increasingly retired life. From 1907 on, he rarely emerged from a cork-lined room in his apartment on boulevard Haussmann. There he insulated himself against the distractions of city life and the effects of trees and flowers–though he loved them, they brought on his attacks of asthma. He slept by day and worked by night, writing letters and devoting himself to the completion of *In Search of Lost Time*. He died in 1922.

JAMES GRIEVE, sometime Reader in French at the Australian National University has published a translation of the first part of Proust's work (*Swann's Way*, 1982) and two novels for young adults, *A Season of Grannies* (1987) and *They're Only Human* (2001).

Marcel Proust

In the Shadow of Young Girls in Flower

Translated with an Introduction
and Notes by James Grieve

GENERAL EDITOR:
CHRISTOPHER PRENDERGAST

PENGUIN BOOKS

PENGUIN BOOKS
Published by the Penguin Group
Penguin Group (USA) Inc., 375 Hudson Street,
New York, New York 10014, U.S.A.
Penguin Group (Canada), 10 Alcorn Avenue, Toronto,
Ontario, Canada M4V 3B2 (a division of Pearson Penguin Canada Inc.)
Penguin Books Ltd, 80 Strand, London WC2R 0RL, England
Penguin Ireland, 25 St Stephen's Green, Dublin 2, Ireland (a division of Penguin Books Ltd)
Penguin Group (Australia) Ltd, 250 Camberwell Road, Camberwell,
Victoria 3124, Australia (a division of Pearson Australia Group Pty Ltd)
Penguin Books India Pvt Ltd, 11 Community Centre, Panchsheel Park, New Delhi–110 017, India
Penguin Group (NZ), cnr Airborne and Rosedale Roads, Albany,
Auckland 1310, New Zealand (a division of Pearson New Zealand Ltd)
Penguin Books (South Africa) (Pty) Ltd, 24 Sturdee Avenue,
Rosebank, Johannesburg 2196, South Africa

Penguin Books Ltd, Registered Offices:
80 Strand, London WC2R 0RL, England

First American edition published in 2004 by Viking Penguin,
a member of Penguin Group (USA) Inc. 2004
Published in Penguin Books 2005

3 5 7 9 10 8 6 4 2

Translation, introduction, and notes copyright © James Grieve, 2002
Note on the translation © Lydia Davis, 2002
All rights reserved

THE LIBRARY OF CONGRESS HAS CATALOGED THE HARDCOVER EDITION AS FOLLOWS:
Proust, Marcel, 1871–1922.
[A l'ombre des jeunes filles en fleurs. English]
In the shadow of young girls in flower / Marcel Proust : translated with an introduction
and notes by James Grieve ; general editor Christopher Prendergast.
p. cm.
ISBN 0-670-03277-8 (hc.)
ISBN 0 14 30.3907 5 (pbk.)
1. Villages–France–Fiction.   2. France–Social life and customs–19th century–Fiction.
I. Grieve, James, 1934–   II. Prendergast, Christopher.   III. Title.
PQ2631.R63A97313 2004   2003058912

Printed in the United States of America
Set in Berthold Garamond
Designed by Francesca Belanger

Acknowledgments

Jeannie Gray, for all the loving care she took—of me and with Proust—and for the King of the Barbarees!

Madeleine Haag, who relieved my sick arms of some of the typing.

Jean-François Kleiner and Jacqueline Mayrhofer, upon whose power to construe Proust I sometimes had to call.

Kevin Windle, who was always ready to taste a phrase.

Contents

Introduction, by James Grieve   *ix*

A Note on the Translation, by Lydia Davis   *xvii*

PART I: *At Mme Swann's*   *1*

PART II: *Place-Names: The Place*   *219*

Notes   *535*

Synopsis   *549*

Suggestions for Further Reading   *558*

Introduction

To win the Goncourt Prize seldom requires literary genius. Cronyism, Parisian faddery, and petty intrigue usually weigh more. Flimsy nets are for catching small fry: since the first award in 1903, close on a hundred novels have won the Goncourt, and very few survive. One is *In the Shadow of Young Girls in Flower*, this second part of Proust's novel, the winner in 1919. Some said he was too old, at forty-eight, to have a prize intended for young writers. Inclined to see this volume as a "listless interlude," Proust was surprised that "everyone is reading it."[1] As happens each year, the award, which he affected to see as "a poor thing,"[2] made the book a nine-day wonder; and Proust was briefly a household name in households that were strangers to books. Despite the Goncourt, however, the nine-day wonder has long since, as Proust says of masterpieces such as Beethoven's last quartets, created its own posterity.

This second section of *In Search of Lost Time* is in two parts: "At Mme Swann's" and "Place-Names: The Place." In Proust's original conception, the book was not split after *Swann's Way*. Grasset, his first publisher, required him to make more than one volume of it. Proust transposed some pages from a later passage, to round off what thus became the first major section of the novel as we know it. This is why, at the end of both *Swann's Way* and "At Mme Swann's," we find Mme Swann with sunshade in an avenue in or near the Bois de Boulogne. The consecutiveness of the original text remains visible, despite the division of the book: at the beginning of this section of Proust's work, the narrator is still moving into the vicinity of the Swanns, as he was at the end of *Swann's Way*. In "At Mme

Swann's" the narrator continues to be infatuated with Odette and besot-
ted with her daughter, Gilberte. She is the first of the adolescents with
whom he dallies here. The others he will meet at the seaside, at Balbec,
in "Place-Names: The Place." The cast of Proust's great and memorable
characters is now enriched, especially by the advent of Albertine and
(briefly) of Charlus, who will both figure largely in the later volumes, and
by Bergotte and Elstir, who complete the trio of artists begun in *Swann's
Way* with Vinteuil. Proust's characters are, be it noted, the work of a cari-
caturist: he gives to each a distinctive voice and mode of speech, most
noticeably here Norpois and Charlus.

As for place-names, many are those of real places, some of them relocated on the map of Brittany or Normandy. Others, invented, borrow
evocative syllables from real ones, like Balbec itself: it looks like Bolbec,
near Le Havre; and, as the town with an "almost Persian" church, it ap-
propriately sounds rather like Baalbek in Lebanon.

Largely devoted to the narrator's attempts to love and be loved by a
series of girls, and to his serious acquaintance with love as a source of
pain, this section also expands three other worlds he will explore further
in later volumes: art, society, and friendship. In the world of art, he goes
to see La Berma act; he meets both Bergotte, the writer he read in the garden at Combray, and Elstir, a painter (whom the reader has met before, in
a different guise). In a lowly level of society, he makes personal acquaintance with not only the Swanns, but also Mme Verdurin. He next meets
members of the exalted Guermantes family: Mme de Villeparisis, Robert
de Saint-Loup (who is to be the main vehicle of the theme of friendship),
and the Baron de Charlus.

Love, art, society, friendship: these are the major realms of experience
to be explored by the young protagonist. From the narrator's encounters
with these great enigmas and temptations, Proust distills his lengthy medi-
tations, variations on some of the most structural themes of his novel: the
disparities between cognition and thing, theory and practice, desire and
discovery, appearance and truth, imagination and reality. For the narrator
is now coming to an awareness of life as mystery, full of passions that baf-
fle, appearances that conceal, illusions that seem to promise, impressions
that tantalize. He has inklings of the sheer unpredictability of beauty, the

inability of words and names to capture the essences of things, the contradictions with which life replaces expectations, the discrepancy between impression and memory, his own sentimental fatalism. In "Place-Names: The Name," the last section of *Swann's Way*, the narrator longed to see Balbec, its Persian church, its perilous tempest-thrashed shore; and here, in "Place-Names: The Place," he sets eyes at last on all three, to his dismay. None of them resembles the fancied version of itself. Wishes never come true. The expected revelation of a transcendent truth becomes the disappointing "tyranny of the particular." But this in turn will be redeemed by an understanding of truths about beauty and reality: that impressions, our only access to these, are inadequate to their conscious capture, that they are individual, irreplaceable by any generality, untranslatable in any word, accessible only by a freak of memory or through art. In his variations on this theme, Proust transmutes epistemology into poetry. And all the time, as the narrator, persuaded by Norpois of his lack of talent, strays apparently further and further away from his lost "vocation" to become a writer, frittering his life into pastimes as futile as Swann's before him, the irony of existence will slowly secrete in these very pastimes the only subject he can write about: perception, and the states of consciousness that translate the world into an individual's experience, those shallow and transitory states in which, without being fully conscious of them, we mostly live. Proust is never more original as a novelist, never more Proustian, than when examining a momentary awareness of which we are barely aware: a glimpse of something possibly glimpsed long ago, the sight of a building we have heard of, a close-up of a face first loved at a distance, appearances as affected by sleep, erotic arousal, or drunkenness, the nature of things imagined from the sound of a name, subliminality as unexamined memory or impressions barely remembered. For vivid impression fossilizes into habit, a trance from which only chance memory can release it. Once released, only simile can capture it. Awareness of the world is an optical illusion, in other words metaphor: the figures which describe things as other things are as organic in the style of Proust as in the paintings of Elstir.

Lack of forethought in devising some of the book's major divisions, imposed on Proust by his ignorance of the technicalities of publishing, can also be seen in smaller aspects of his text, inconsistencies, improvisations, and discrepancies, which reflect as much his mode of composition as French publishing practice of that time. Among the great novelists, as a bungler of basics Proust has no equal, save perhaps Henry James—think of chapter I of *The Portrait of a Lady*, where James has tedious difficulty in getting his story under way, in defining the point of view of his narrator. Is the latter a know-all or a Flaubertian deducer from appearances? The man seems unskilled in introducing his characters to his reader, and in enabling characters to converse. In similar things, Proust too seems incompetent, or perhaps an improviser. Both James and Proust were of at least two minds. James was unsure whether he was American or English, whether he was writing for American or English readers, whether he was to yield to the temptation to be French. Proust was intermittently unsure whether he was writing an essay or a novel. Here is a novel written by a critic and literary theorist, both a novel in the form of an essay and an essay on the novel. Proust must not only show but tell, tell rather than show, tell at the expense of showing; he must make the reader, who may wish only to revel in the fiction, admit the truthfulness of its fictionality. Proust's reflections, his enunciation of philosophical and psychological truths, his aesthetic theories, his opinions and system of thoughts are often more important to him than his verisimilitudes. His composition was often not linear; he wrote in bits and pieces; transitions from one scene to another are sometimes awkward, clumsy even. He can make heavy weather of simple movements: characters get stood roughly into position so that the next demonstration may take place; action must be performed perfunctorily, so that protracted analysis of it may ensue; the narrator seems to say farewell to Elstir at his front door, yet two pages later is walking him home. Proust shows, it has been said, "utter nonchalance" about "loss of fictional verisimilitude."[3]

Some of this shows Proust's disdain for Realism and its tenet of observation of the physical world. But other features of this work, quite analogous, cannot be so explained. The narrator's presumed age is at variance with the events in which he occasionally participates (Norpois's table talk, for instance, with its naughty allusions to cuckoldry, emotional blackmail, the indelicacies and delightful improprieties of Mme Swann). This may be one reason why Proust never divulges how old the narrator is: it enables him to fudge, to have it both ways, in disquisitions on the appreciation of art and music, on human behavior and experience of life and love, well beyond the narrator's assumed years. It may be to assuage this impression that many characters remark on the narrator's precocious intelligence and sensitivity.

Another main uncertainty for the reader is Proust's conflation within the one text of two narrative viewpoints, first person and third. Whereas in *Swann's Way* the two are largely kept apart, first person in "Combray" and "Place-Names: The Name" and third person in "Swann in Love," in this second section Proust never resolves his indeterminate narratorial point of view. On one and the same page the narrator's subjectivity, aptly blinkered in the face of a character's hidden qualities, becomes a disconcerting omniscience. We learn of the motives and emotions of characters frequenting Mme Swann's at-homes, of Dr. Cottard or of the Swanns themselves, from a narrator who, as outsider and (presumably) callow youth, should know them as little as we do.

The translator can have a similar uneasiness from an indeterminacy in Proust's use of the imperfect tense: though it is normally reserved for repeated or continuing happenings, he will use it for events that appear to be single and preterite. This feature of the writing can be bothersome; the translator may be (justifiably) tempted to clarify what Proust has left ambiguous and unsatisfactory: did this act take place once or more than once? Such ubiquitous symptoms of the text, inseparable from major structural features of it, suggest that the latter were improvised rather than planned, then persevered with rather than revised. Jean-François Revel, though admiring Proust, says the writing is not improvised, only slipshod: "he makes endless additions, rewrites without rethinking, overwrites, forgets, repeats himself, muddles the design."[4] Originally vanity-published, Proust's manuscripts never received the attention that Maxwell Perkins gave to Scott Fitzgerald's or the devoted Bouilhet to Flaubert's. It has been said that Proust's contract with Grasset "rid him of all editorial constraints."[5] His novel is one of the few masterpieces never properly edited before publication and containing to this day infelicities which some may be surprised to find in a masterpiece. The translator wishing to make a seamless text for his reader is often thwarted by Proust's seams, which tend to be rough. His paragraphing often seems idiosyncratic.

Smaller discrepancies abound. In "At Mme Swann's," Bloch tells the narrator all women are "always on the lookout for opportunities to make love" (p. 150), a revelation he had already made in "Combray." In "Place-Names: The Place," with every air of reminding us of something we know, the narrator says Mme de Villeparisis once gave him a duck holding a box of chocolate (p. 335); yet, though he has been telling us much about her for many pages, not only have we heard nothing of this surprising event, but in the accounts of his grandmother's first meetings with Mme de Villeparisis at Balbec, much tends to contradict it. Near the end of "Place-Names: The Place," the narrator seeks to contrive an introduction to Mme Bontemps (p. 506). But hundreds of pages earlier, in "At Mme Swann's," her fellow guest, he seems to know her well enough (pp. 173, 180). In the Miss Sacripant episode, the flowers are first roses, then twice (or is it thrice?) carnations (pp. 428, 429). Mme Swann's white furs, Proust says, are of *zibeline* (= sable), which I translate as "ermine," since white furs made from a black animal seem to indicate that here (p. 210), as occasionally elsewhere, he used the wrong word. Having decided (belatedly) that Saint-Loup's garrison town shall be called Doncières, Proust later wrongfoots us by seeming to have left it unnamed (p. 365). The sudden and disconcerting appearance of Nissim Bernard (p. 354), then his disappearance, are symptoms of this same makeshift mode of composition: again the translator is tempted to make things easier for his reader by smoothing over an afterthought which breaks up the Blochs' conversation about Bergotte and makes some pronouns problematical. The narrator is twice introduced to Andrée (pp. 461, 464). The mention of "doubts" on p. 510 is odd, there having been no doubt in the narrator's mind up to this point. These examples and others, some of which I mention in footnotes, show the unedited and unrevised nature of some of Proust's text.

In translating, it is sometimes necessary to edit. For example, the French has a strange parenthesis in "*la reine de (Naples)*": had I faithfully translated this, it would have given "the Queen of (Naples)" (p. 353); rather than perplex my reader, I edit. Similarly, in a scene where Andrée is absent, she appears to speak. Or, rather, which character speaks the words "I've put up with her awful dishonesty for ages" (p. 466) is in French unclear; in English it must, I believe, be clarified. The unclarity is here compounded by the fact that Proust, having just introduced another of the girls into the scene, has neglected to name her. Or take what looks like a tiny example of defective revision or lack of editing: the words "overhanging the threshold" (p. 500). These words surprise the reader: the narrator is walking with Andrée through woodlands, in a country lane, and there is no building to which this "threshold" might belong. It is interesting to note that, to this little translator's dilemma, C. K. Scott Moncrieff's solution, quite defensible, was to quietly omit the words. Here and there, with other small perplexities, I do something similar.

The Dreyfus Affair is made much of by some commentators on *In Search of Lost Time*. In fact, Proust deals with it hardly at all (in the whole novel, the name of Dreyfus occurs less often than the headwaiter's, a very minor character), and then only in its most trivial repercussions in fashionable society, such as those reflected on p. 91. More important to the novel than Dreyfus is the virulence of the anti-Semitic prejudice generally shared by the fashionable characters, of the sort satirized on p. 345 in a speech by Charlus (and perceptible, if less virulent, in Proust's own ambivalence toward the Blochs). Still, such as it is, it is here that we see the first allusions to the Affair. Early in "At Mme Swann's," there is a comparison (p. 19) that may be a reminiscence of Colonel Picquart, a hero of the Dreyfusards. And the only other mention of Dreyfus (p. 388) may suggest that the summer which the narrator and his grandmother spend at Balbec is that of 1898, one of the Affair's acutest phases. (Despite which, the volume contains passing references to the Russo-Japanese War of 1904–5 and to the King of England.)

I think it is also misleading to speak of Proust's sharp "powers of observation," of "the immensity of his social canvas," to say he has "a grasp of how society works" and gives "a vast panorama of society."[6] Proust's book is much more about the power of covert sexual transgressiveness to undermine a social order founded on class, snobbery, and money. True, his characters include duchesses and scullery maids, ambassadors and busboys. But there is little in between. And they are all seen from a perspective that likens them to one another. Proust needed little evidence in support of his generalizations. He certainly professes a sort of Balzacian expertise in diagnosing the ills of the social body; but his sociology is hampered by the shallowness of his sample and by his prizing of introspection over observation of externals. This should surprise no one: he was a cosseted Parisian whose Right Bank world was narrow, who preferred to live in the past, in bed, in a cork-lined room, who rarely traveled and never did a day's work.

Proust's real strengths lie in his analysis of the ordinary, his close acquaintance with feelings, the pessimism of his examination of consciousness, his diagnosis of the unreliability of relationships and the incoherence of personality, his attentiveness to the bleak truths he has to tell of time, of its unrelenting wear and tear, its indifferent outlasting of all human endeavor, its gradual annulment of our dearest joys and even our cruelest sorrows, voiding them of all that once made them ours. Life, as Proust tells it, is disappointment and loss—loss of time, as his title says, and loss of youth of course; loss of freshness of vision, of belief, and of the semblance it once gave to the world; and loss of self, a loss against which we have only one safeguard, and that unsure: memory.

For the young narrator, it is to be a summer full of discoveries, about art, about friendship, about girls, about love, about the Guermantes family, all lit by the sun, the reflections from the sea, and the almost unnoticed atmosphere of real life passing by, a time in which only the old narrator's searching memory will be able to find happiness. And therein, for Proust, lies bereavement, the source of all his art.

James Grieve

A Note on the Translation

The present translation came into being in the following way. A project was conceived by the Penguin UK Modern Classics series in which the whole of *In Search of Lost Time* would be translated freshly on the basis of the latest and most authoritative French text, *À la recherche du temps perdu,* edited by Jean-Yves Tadié (Paris: Pléiade, Gallimard, 1987–89). The translation would be done by a group of translators, each of whom would take on one of the seven volumes. The project was directed first by Paul Keegan, then by Simon Winder, and was overseen by general editor Christopher Prendergast. I was contacted early in the selection process, in the fall of 1995, and I chose to translate the first volume, *Du côté de chez Swann.* The other translators are James Grieve, for *In the Shadow of Young Girls in Flower;* Mark Treharne, for *The Guermantes Way;* John Sturrock, for *Sodom and Gomorrah;* Carol Clark, for *The Prisoner;* Peter Collier, for *The Fugitive;* and Ian Patterson, for *Finding Time Again.*

Between 1996 and the delivery of our manuscripts, the tardiest in mid-2001, we worked at different rates in our different parts of the world—one in Australia, one in the United States, the rest in various parts of England. After a single face-to-face meeting in early 1998, which most of the translators attended, we communicated with one another and with Christopher Prendergast by letter and e-mail. We agreed, often after lively debate, on certain practices that needed to be consistent from one volume to the next, such as retaining French titles like Duchesse de Guermantes, and leaving the quotations that occur within the text—from Racine, most notably—in the original French, with translations in the notes.

At the initial meeting of the Penguin Classics project, those present had acknowledged that a degree of heterogeneity across the volumes was inevitable and perhaps even desirable, and that philosophical differences would exist among the translators. As they proceeded, therefore, the translators worked fairly independently and decided for themselves how close their translations should be to the original—how many liberties, for instance, might be taken with the sanctity of Proust's long sentences. And Christopher Prendergast, as he reviewed all the translations, kept his editorial hand relatively light. The Penguin UK translation appeared in October 2002, in six hardcover volumes and as a boxed set.

Some changes may be noted in this American edition, besides the adoption of American spelling conventions. One is that the UK decision concerning quotations within the text has been reversed, and all the French has been translated into English, with the original quotations in the notes. We have also replaced the French punctuation of dialogue, which uses dashes and omits certain opening and closing quotation marks, with standard American dialogue punctuation, though we have respected Proust's paragraphing decisions—sometimes long exchanges take place within a single paragraph, while in other cases each speech begins a new paragraph.

Lydia Davis

PART I

At Mme Swann's

WHEN IT WAS FIRST SUGGESTED we invite M. de Norpois to dinner, my mother commented that it was a pity Professor Cottard was absent from Paris and that she herself had quite lost touch with Swann, either of whom the former ambassador would have been pleased to meet; to which my father replied that, although a guest as eminent as Cottard, a scientific man of some renown, would always be an asset at one's dinner table, the Marquis de Norpois would be bound to see Swann, with his showing off and his name-dropping, as nothing but a vulgar swank, "a rank outsider," as he would put it. This statement of my father's may require a few words of explanation, as there may be some who remember Cottard as a mediocrity and Swann as the soul of discretion and modesty in all things social. As regards Swann, it turns out that our old family friend was now no longer only "young Swann" and "Swann of the Jockey Club"; to these personalities he had added a new one, which was not to be his last, that of Odette's husband. Adapting to her humble ambitions all the flair, desires, and industry that he had always possessed, Swann had contrived to construct a new position for himself, albeit far below the one he had formerly occupied, but suited to the wife with whom he must now share it. And in this position he had turned into a new man. Since this was the beginning of a second life for both of them, among a circle of new people (except for personal friends from his bachelor days whom he went on seeing alone, and whom he did not wish to burden with the acquaintance of Odette, unless they themselves expressed the wish to meet her), it would have been understandable if, in judging the social standing of these new people, and thereby gauging the degree of self-esteem that their company might afford him, his standard of comparison had been based at least on Odette's former associates, if not on the exalted individuals among whom he himself had moved before his marriage. However, even when one knew that the people he now wished to associate with were unrefined civil servants, or the sort of dubious women who were fixtures of the annual ball at certain ministries, one could still be astounded to hear this man (who in former days, and even now, could show such exquisite tact in not advertising an invitation to Twickenham[1] or Buckingham Palace) braying out the fact that the wife of an undersecretary's undersecretary had returned Mme Swann's visit. It may be thought that this was because the simplicity of manners in the fashionable Swann was only a finer form of vanity, and that, after the manner of certain Jews, our old family friend had passed through the successive phases of a development observable in the breed he belonged to, going from the most guileless snobbery, the crassest caddishness, to the politest of refinements. The main reason, however, was (and it is one which holds good for all of humanity) that even our virtues are not extraneous, free-floating things which are always at our disposal; in fact, they come to be so closely linked in our minds with the actions we feel they should accompany that, if we are required to engage in some different activity, it can take us by surprise, so that we never even think that it too might entail the use of those very virtues. In his gushing ways with these new friends and his boastful citing of their exploits, Swann was like the great artist who takes up cooking or gardening late in life and who, though modest enough to be untroubled by criticism of his masterpieces, cannot bear to hear faint praise of his recipes or flower beds, and basks naïvely in the delight of hearing them lauded; or who, though generous enough to let a canvas go for nothing, will be put out by losing a few pennies at dominoes.

As for Professor Cottard, we shall meet him again eventually, and at some length, at La Raspelière, the château of the Patronne. For the moment, let the following remark suffice. The change in Swann may well be surprising, since it had already come about, albeit without my knowledge, by the time I had become familiar with him as the father of

Gilberte, at the Champs-Élysées; and then, of course, as he never spoke to me, he could not brag about his connections in the political world. (And even if he had done so, I might well not have been immediately aware of his vanity, as one's long-standing mental image of others deprives one of sight and hearing in their presence—my mother took three years to notice the lipstick that one of her nieces was using; for all she could see, it might have been totally and invisibly dissolved, till the day when either an extra dab of it or some other cause brought about the reaction known as supersaturation: all the unseen lipstick crystallized and, in the face of this sudden splash of color, my mother declared, after the manner of Combray, that it was a disgrace, and all but broke off relations with the girl.) With Cottard, however, the days when we saw him witnessing Swann's introduction to the Verdurins were long past. Honors and official titles come with the years. Also, it is possible to be unread, and to like making silly puns, while having a special gift that outweighs any general culture, such as the gift of the great strategist or the great clinician. So Cottard was seen by his medical colleagues not just as an obscure practitioner who had eventually risen to celebrity throughout Europe. The cleverest of the younger doctors declared— for a few years at any rate, since all fashions, having arisen from a desire for change, eventually pass away for the same reason—that if ever they should fall ill Cottard was the only eminent man to whom they would entrust their persons. Obviously, for conversation, they preferred the company of certain other senior colleagues who were more cultivated or more artistically minded, and with whom they could discuss Nietzsche or Wagner. At Mme Cottard's musical evenings, to which she invited students and colleagues of her husband's in the hope that he would one day become dean of the faculty, Cottard himself never listened to a note, preferring to play cards in one of the other rooms. But he was renowned for his diagnostic skill, for the unhesitating acuity and accuracy of his eye. In addition, in considering the general effect that Cottard's manners made on someone like my father, it should be noted that the nature we display in the second part of our life may not always be, though it often is, a growth from or a stunting of our first nature, an exaggeration or attenuation of it. It is at times an inversion of it, a garment turned inside out. In youth, everyone except the Verdurins, who had taken a great fancy to him, had mercilessly mocked him for his hesitant air, his excessive diffidence and affability. Did some kind friend suggest he adopt an icy demeanor? The eminence of his position certainly made it easy for him to comply. Except at the Verdurins', where he instinctively became himself again, he now made a show of being cold and taciturn; when speech was required, he was brusque and made a point of saying unpleasant things. He first tried his new manner on patients who had no prior acquaintance with him, who could therefore make no comparisons, and who would have been amazed to learn that he was not a man to whom such abruptness came naturally. He aimed first and foremost at being impassive; and even when he made some of his puns doing the rounds in the hospital, making everyone laugh, from the medical superintendent to the newest student, he would always do it without moving a muscle in his face, which, since he had shaved off his beard and mustache, was also quite unrecognizable.

Of the Marquis de Norpois it can be said that, having been a plenipotentiary of Napoleon III before the Franco-Prussian War, he had been briefly elevated to an ambassadorship during the constitutional crisis of May 16, 1877. Despite this, and to the great astonishment of many, he had also been appointed several times since then as an extraordinary representative of France, accomplishing special missions and even acting as Comptroller of Public Moneys in Egypt, where his great financial ability enabled him to render important services, at the behest of Radical cabinets, on whose behalf a mere middle-class reactionary would have declined to act, and to which M. de Norpois's past, connections, and opinions should have made him suspect. But these progressive ministers seemed to realize that, in making such an appointment, they were demonstrating the breadth of vision of which they were capable when the higher interests of France required it—so outclassing the average politician that they might expect to be called "statesmen" by the *Journal des débats* itself!—while basking in the prestige afforded by the man's noble name and title, and in the interest created by a dramatically unforeseeable choice. They knew too that, in having recourse to M. de Norpois, they could enjoy these advantages without fear of political disloyalty on his part, as the Marquis's breeding, rather than giving them grounds to suspect him of any such thing, ensured against it. In this, the government of the Republic was not mistaken, for the good reason that a certain aristocracy, bred from childhood to see their name as an intrinsic benefit which nothing can take away (and the value of which is fairly well gauged by their peers and by those of even higher birth), know they can spare themselves the efforts made by many a commoner to profess only opinions seen as sound, and to mix only with people seen as proper, as these efforts would be of no profit to them. However, wishing to magnify themselves in the eyes of the princely or ducal families which are their immediate superiors, these aristocrats also know that they can do this only if they enhance their name with something extraneous to it, something that, other names being equal, will make theirs prevail: a political influence, a literary or artistic reputation, a large fortune. So they lavish their attentions not on the futile squireen who is courted by the commoner, or on a fruitless friendship that will never impress a prince, but on the politicians who, though they may be Freemasons, can get someone appointed to a plum job in an embassy or elected to a safe seat, on the artists or academics who can pull a string or two in the area they dominate, on anyone who might be able to lend some distinction, or help in the making of a rich marriage.

In the case of M. de Norpois, however, the most important thing was that, through long practice of diplomacy, he had deeply imbued himself with the spirit known as "government mentality," that negative, ingrained conservative spirit which informs not just the mentality of all governments, but in particular, inside all governments, that of the Foreign Office. The career of the diplomatist had given him an aversion, a dread, and a disdain for the more or less revolutionary, or at least improper, ways that are those of oppositions. Apart from some uncouth members of the working and the fashionable classes, who are incapable of making such subtle distinctions, what brings people together is not shared opinion but a latent propensity of mind. Despite his fondness for the classics, an Academician of the likes of Legouvé may still approve Maxime Du Camp's or Mézières's eulogy of the Romantic Victor Hugo more than Claudel's of the classical Boileau. Though a shared jingoism may be enough to endear Barrès to those who vote for him, and who probably see little difference between him and M. Georges Berry, more would be required to endear him to those of his colleagues in the Académie Française who, despite sharing his political opinions, have a different cast of mind, and will thus prefer adversaries such as M. Ribot and M. Deschanel; and the latter pair of Republicans may be favored by staunch monarchists over Maurras and Léon Daudet, despite the fact that these two are also supporters of a restoration of the throne. M. de Norpois was a man of few words, not only by virtue of the diplomatist's habits of prudence and reserve, but also because words have a greater worth, and more subtle shades of meaning, for men whose efforts over a decade to bring together two countries may amount to a single adjective in a speech or a protocol, but in which, unremarkable though it may appear, they can read volumes. At the Select Committee, on which M. de Norpois was one of my father's fellow members, and where the others saw him as very standoffish, they constantly congratulated my father on the friendliness shown toward him by the former ambassador. My father was as surprised as they were by this friendliness. Being himself of a less than sociable disposition, he was used to having few relationships outside his immediate circle, and made no secret of it. He was aware that the diplomatist's good opinion of him was no more than an effect of that personal idiosyncrasy which biases each of us for or against those we like or dislike, against which no qualities of intellect or sensitivity in a person who irritates or bores us will outweigh the straightforwardness and the lightheartedness we enjoy in someone else whom others would see as vacuous, flippant, and insignificant. "It's quite remarkable—Norpois is taking me out to dinner again! It's the talk of the Select Committee! A man who doesn't cultivate personal relations with anybody! I expect he'll pass on some more of his revelations about the Franco-Prussian War." My father was aware that M. de Norpois had been perhaps the only one to warn Napoleon III about Prussia's growing power and warlike intentions, and that Bismarck had a high regard for his intelligence. And quite recently, during the state visit of King

Theodosius, the newspapers had commented on the sovereign's lengthy conversation with M. de Norpois at the command performance at the Opéra. "I must find out whether that state visit was really important," said my father, who was greatly interested in foreign affairs. "I know old Norpois is very tight-lipped. But he has a nice way of opening up with me."

As for my mother, the ambassador's intelligence may not, of itself, have been quite the kind to which she would have been most attracted. I must say M. de Norpois's conversation was such a complete catalogue of outmoded speech forms belonging to the style of a particular career, class, and period—a period which, for that career and class, may not have quite ended yet—that I sometimes regret not having simply written down statements I heard him utter. It would have been an easy way of achieving an outdated effect, rather like the actor from the Théâtre du Palais-Royal who, when asked where on earth he found such bizarre hats, replied, "I don't find 'em—I keep 'em." To tell the truth, I think my mother saw M. de Norpois as rather behind the times; not that this irked her in a man's manners; but it certainly would have been less to her taste in his ways of expressing himself, if not in the ideas he voiced, those of M. de Norpois being actually quite up to the minute. However, she felt that she was subtly pleasing her husband by expressing admiration of the diplomat who had so singled him out. By strengthening in my father's mind the high opinion he had of M. de Norpois, and thereby also fostering in him a higher opinion of himself, she felt she was fulfilling the wifely duty of making life sweet for her husband, just as she did when she saw to the excellence of the cooking and the quietness of the servants. Being incapable of lying to my father, she did her best to admire the ambassador, so as to be able to praise him in all sincerity. She did, in any case, take an honest pleasure in his kind manner, his slightly old-fashioned courtesy (which made him such a stickler for ceremony that, if he caught sight of my mother passing in a carriage while he was striding along with his upright gait, he would even throw away a cigar he had just lit before doffing his hat to her), his deliberate manner in conversation, referring as seldom as possible to himself, and always attending to whatever might please his hearer, and his punctuality in sending off a reply to a letter, which was so striking that if my father, having just written to him, recognized M. de Norpois's hand on an envelope, his impulse was to believe that their letters had unfortunately crossed in the post—it was almost as if the post office arranged extra collections for his special convenience. It never occurred to my mother, who marveled that a man could be so punctilious though so busy, so attentive though so widely connected, that every "although" hides an unrecognized "because," and that (just as the old are always "remarkable for their age," kings never lose "the common touch," and provincials are always "up with everything that's going on") M. de Norpois's different abilities—to have so many irons in the fire yet to be so orderly in his replies, to be all things to all men yet still be nice to us—were rooted in common habits. Furthermore, as with all those who are too modest, my mother's mistake came from the fact that she always ranked her own interests below those of others, and thus saw them as quite separate from others'. In seeing proof of considerateness in the letter dashed off by my father's friend, a man who wrote so many letters in a day, she failed to see that it was only a single one among those many; just as it did not enter her head that for him to dine at our table was no more than one act among the countless acts making up his social life, that the ambassador had long been accustomed by the diplomatic career to seeing the honoring of invitations to dinner as part of his functions, and to displaying to that end an ingrained graciousness which he should not be expected to put aside just because for once he was dining with us.

The first occasion when M. de Norpois came to dinner, at a time when I was still playing at the Champs-Élysées, has stayed in my memory because that very afternoon I had at last been to see La Berma, in a matinee performance of *Phèdre*; and also because, in chatting with M. de Norpois, I realized suddenly and in a new way how different were the feelings aroused in me by everything connected to Gilberte Swann and her parents from the feelings aroused by the same family in all other people.

One day my mother, who had presumably noticed my dejection at the imminence of the New Year holidays, during which, as Gilberte herself had told me, it would be impossible for me to see her, said to me, "If you're still so keen on seeing La Berma, I think your father might allow you to go. Grandma could take you."

It was because M. de Norpois had urged my father, who till then had been quite opposed to my wasting my time and possibly even falling ill just for the sake of what he called, giving umbrage to my grandmother, "stuff and nonsense," to let me go and see La Berma, as it would be something for a young man to remember, that he had almost come to see the outing to the theater, now that it was advised by the ambassador, as a sort of prescribed activity among certain others deemed vaguely essential for anyone hoping to achieve a brilliant career. My grandmother, who had forgone on my behalf the benefit she believed I would have derived from seeing La Berma, and who saw this great sacrifice as justified in the interest of my health, was astonished to learn that, at a single word from M. de Norpois, this interest turned out to be of no significance. Rationalist that she was, she placed invincible trust in the regimen of fresh air and early bedtimes which had been prescribed for me; and, seeing my intended departure from it as a disaster, she said sadly to my father, "How irresponsible you can be." To which he barked, "What! You mean you don't want him to go now? Well, that's rich! You were the one who kept saying how much good it would do him!"

My father's ambitions for me had been altered by M. de Norpois in another particular, of much greater importance to me. My father had always looked forward to seeing me enter the diplomatic corps; and I could not bear the thought that, even if I was to remain in Paris for a while attached to the Ministry, I must risk being packed off one day to serve as an ambassador in capital cities where Gilberte would never live. I would have preferred to take up again the literary ambitions which I had once cherished, then given up, during my walks along the Guermantes way. But my father had constantly opposed the idea of my embarking upon a career in writing, which he saw as far inferior to diplomacy, even denying that it could count as a career, until the day when M. de Norpois, who rather looked down on the newer generation of diplomats, assured him that it was perfectly possible for a writer to enjoy as much esteem, and to exercise as much influence, as any diplomat, while retaining more independence.

"Well, who'd have believed it!" my father said. "Old Norpois's got nothing against the idea that you might make a career in literature." Being himself quite influential, he believed there was nothing that could not be sorted out and favorably resolved by a chat between important men. "I'll bring him home to dinner one of these nights after a session at the Select Committee. You can have a chat with him and he'll be able to form some opinion of you. So just write something nice that you can show him. He's a great friend of the editor of the *Revue des deux mondes*, you know. He could get you in there, he could look after it for you, he's a pretty sharp old fellow. I must say, he doesn't sound greatly enamored of the diplomatic career nowadays."

The blissful prospect of not being parted from Gilberte made me eager, but not able, to write a fine piece that could be shown to M. de Norpois. From sheer boredom, the pen dropped from my hand after a few preliminary pages; and I dissolved in tears of rage at the thought that I would never have any talent, that I was not gifted, that I could not even turn M. de Norpois's imminent visit to the advantage of remaining forever in Paris. The only thing that cheered me a little was the knowledge that I was going to be allowed to see La Berma. But, just as the only storms I longed to see were those that raged along the wildest shores, so I wished to see the great actress only in one of those classical parts in which Swann had assured me she rose to the sublime. When our wish to be touched by nature or art is prompted by the hope of a grandiose revelation, we are loath to let it be replaced by lesser impressions, which might mislead us as to the true value of Beauty. La Berma in Racine's *Andromaque* or *Phèdre*, in *Les Caprices de Marianne* by Musset, these were the stirring things that I had gloated on in imagination. I knew that if I could ever hear La Berma deliver the speech beginning

It is said, Sire, that a prompt departure must take you away, etc.[2]

my delight would be the same as when I could step out of a gondola, to stand in front of the Titian in the Frari or the Carpaccios in San Giorgio degli Schiavoni. My acquaintance with these lines of Racine's was in black and white, as mere print on the pages of books; but now my heart beat faster at the thought that I would soon see them in the warm, sunny glow shed on them by the Golden Voice. A Carpaccio in Venice, La Berma in *Phèdre*, were masterworks of pictorial or dramatic art; and the glamour that surrounded them gave them such vital force, and made them so indivisible into their parts, that if I had had to look at Carpaccios in a room at the Louvre, or see La Berma in a play that I had never heard of, I would never have felt that delight of amazement at being face-to-face at last with the unique and ungraspable object of so many thousands of dreams. Also, in my expectation that La Berma's acting would give me a revelation about nobility and grief, I had the impression that everything great and true in her acting was bound to become greater and truer if she put it into a work of genuine worth, instead of embroidering Truth and Beauty on the coarse cloth of some valueless vulgarity.

In any case, seeing her in a new play would make it difficult for me to appreciate her skill and diction, as I would be unable to distinguish between the unfamiliar text and all the intonations and gestures which, although she had added them, would seem to belong inseparably to it; whereas the classical texts I knew by heart were like broad surfaces, already designated and prepared, awaiting only the fluent frescoes that La Berma would lavish upon them and the unconstrained appreciation with which I would greet the inexhaustible felicities of her inspiration. Unfortunately, she had abandoned the classical stage and its repertoire years before, and was now the star and mainstay of a more popular theater; and however often I went to look at the posters, the only plays they ever advertised were recent ones, tailor-made for her by modish authors. Then, one morning, as I scanned the Morris column for the matinees being given during the first week in January, I saw for the first time a program which, after a presumably insignificant curtain-raiser, whose title seemed opaque because it was full of the proceedings of a plot that was unknown to me, promised as the final item Mme Berma in two acts of *Phèdre*; and for the following matinees, it specified Dumas's *Le Demi-Monde* and Musset's *Les Caprices de Marianne*, titles that to my eye, like

Phèdre, were transparent, full of nothing but illumination, because the works were so well known to me, glowing through and through with the smile of Art. They seemed to add nobility to La Berma herself, once I had read in the newspapers, after the programs for these matinees, a mention that it was she herself who had decided to make a public appearance once again in some of her time-honored parts. Clearly, the artiste knew that in certain roles there is an interest which outlasts the novelty of their first appearances, or the success of their revivals, and that her own interpretation made them into museum pieces, which it might be instructive to display again to a generation who had once admired her in them, or to reveal to another which had not. By having *Phèdre* advertised among other plays, which were intended only to while away an evening, its title neither printed in special characters nor occupying more space than the others, she gave it a touch of the understatement used by a hostess who, as she introduces you to your fellow guests just as you are all about to go in to dinner, includes among the names that are merely names, and in the same tone of voice in which she has announced all the others, "M. Anatole France."

My doctor, the one who had forbidden me all travel, advised my parents against letting me go to the theater: afterward, and possibly for a long time, I would be sure to be ill; the net result for me would be more pain than pleasure. I might have been dissuaded by such a fear, if what I expected from the matinee had been a mere pleasure that could be canceled by the counterbalance of subsequent pain. But what I did expect from it—as from the journeys I had longed to make to Balbec and Venice—was something far beyond a pleasure: it was access to truths which dwelt in a realer world than I did, truths which, once glimpsed, could never be taken from me by any of the nugatory incidents making up my futile existence, however painful they might be to my body. Any pleasure to be had from the performance seemed to me no more than the possibly inevitable form which the glimpsing of these truths must take; and this was enough for me to hope the predicted sickness would hold off until the end of the matinee, so that the pleasure might not be jeopardized or vitiated. I badgered my parents, who, since the doctor's pronouncement, no longer wanted me to go to see *Phèdre*. I kept reciting the speech

It is said, Sire, that a prompt departure must take you away . . .

trying to put all possible intonations into it, the better to enjoy the unexpected one that La Berma would be sure to employ. By day and by night my mind was haunted by the knowledge of the divine Beauty which her acting would be bound to reveal, hidden like the Holy of Holies by the impenetrable veil, behind which I imagined it in constantly changing guises, according to whichever of Bergotte's images recurred to my mind from his little study of Racine, which Gilberte had managed to find for me—"her noble plasticity," "the white garb of Christian penitence," "her Jansenist pallor," "this Princess of Clèves and of Troezen," "this Mycenaean melodrama," "a Delphic symbol," "a solar myth"—and it was the reckless severity of my parents that was to decide whether or not in this mind of mine, where her altar was perpetually lit, the perfections of the Goddess would stand unveiled forever at the very spot where now stood her invisible form. With my gaze fixed on the unimaginable figure, I had to struggle all day long against the obstacles raised by my family. Then, once these obstacles had fallen, and once my mother, despite the fact that the matinee was on the very day of the Select Committee session after which my father was to bring M. de Norpois home to dinner, had said to me, "Look, we don't want you to be sad. If you really think you'll enjoy it so much, you'd better go," now that it was up to me to decide on the outing to the theater which had previously been forbidden, now that I was free of the need to make sure it should cease to be impossible, I began to wonder whether it was desirable, whether reasons other than my parents' prohibition should not perhaps make me choose to stay at home. For one thing, having hated their cruelty to me, I now loved them so much for their kindness that the idea of saddening them saddened me; the point of existence seemed no longer to be the seeking for truth, but the finding of fondness; and life as a good or a bad thing could only be judged by whether my parents were happy or unhappy. "If you're going to worry about it," I said to my mother, "I'd really rather not go." She, however, did her best to scotch the notion that she might be unhappy, saying that it could spoil my enjoyment of *Phèdre*, which had been their main consideration in changing their minds about the outing. But now that I seemed to be under an obligation to enjoy myself, I found it rather irksome. What if I did fall ill afterward? Would I get better by the end of the holidays, and be able to go back to the Champs-Élysées as soon as Gilberte returned? In the hope of deciding which to choose, I weighed against all these reasons the veiled invisibility of La Berma's perfections. On one side of the scales, I put "knowing Mama's worrying, me not being able to go to the Champs-Élysées"; and on the other, "her Jansenist pallor" and the "solar myth." But the words themselves gradually grew darker in my mind, and lost all weight and meaning for me; my hesitations became so painful that the only reason I could have had now for choosing to go to the theater would have been to put an end to them, to be rid of them for good. And by going so as to cut short my sufferings, rather than to seek perfection and derive intellectual benefit, I would have been going not to the gentle Goddess once imagined, but to some implacable, faceless, nameless Divinity who had surreptitiously taken the other's place behind the veil. Then, all at once, everything changed, and my longing to see La Berma act was revived by something that made me look forward to the matinee with joy and impatience. As though turned into a stylite, I had gone to my Morris column, a daily activity which of late had become very painful, and there I had seen the first detailed poster for *Phèdre* itself, still damp with paste, which, though the other members of the cast offered nothing that could help me decide whether to go or not to go, did give to one of the rewards of my contending urges a more concrete form, and a kind of imminence that made it seem on the very point of becoming a reality: as the poster showed the date not of the day when I stood there reading it, but of the day when the matinee would be performed, and even the time when the curtain would rise, I was suddenly inspired by the happy thought that, on that day, at that very hour, I would be sitting in my seat ready to see La Berma; and in the fear that there might not be time now for my parents to book two good seats for my grandmother and myself, I ran all the way home, full of the magic of the words that had displaced "her Jansenist pallor" and the "solar myth" in my imagination: *Ladies wearing hats may not sit in the stalls. The doors will be closed at two o'clock sharp.*

This first matinee was, alas, a great disappointment. My father had suggested giving my grandmother and myself a lift to the theater, which was on his way to the Select Committee. As he left the house, he said to my mother, "You'll make sure it's a nice dinner tonight, won't you? Remember, Norpois's coming home with me." She had not forgotten. Since the day before, Françoise, glad to be practicing the cook's art, for which she had a definite gift, inspired by the coming of a new guest, and knowing she was required to compose, in accordance with methods known only to herself, a dish of beef in aspic, had been living in a flurry of artistic creativity. Like Michelangelo spending eight months in the mountains of Carrara, selecting the most perfect blocks of marble for the tomb of Pope Julius II, Françoise, who attached extreme importance to the inherent quality of the materials out of which her masterpieces were to be wrought, had been down to Les Halles in person more than once to choose the finest slabs of rump steak, the best shin of beef and calf's foot. She threw herself so strenuously into this pursuit that my mother, seeing our old servant turn red in the face, feared that, as the sculptor of the Medici tombs had sickened in the quarries at Pietrasanta, she might make herself ill from overwork. The day before, Françoise had sent down to the oven of the local baker what she called "a Nev York ham," looking like pink marble inside its coating of breadcrumbs. In the belief that the language was poorer than it is, and her own ears less reliable than they were, the first time Françoise had heard of "York ham," she must have deduced that the lexicon could not possibly be so abundant as to allow for both York and New York, that she had misheard, and that the right name was the one she already knew. Hence, ever since, the name of York was always preceded, for Françoise's ears and eyes, by the word "New," which she pronounced "Nev." So it was with total sincerity that she would say to her scullery maid, "Go down to Olida's and get some ham. Ma'am particularly said she wants the Nev York." On the day in question, while Françoise's state of mind was the burning certainty of the great creators, my own was the thankless anxiety of the seeker after truth. To be sure, right up until the moment when I saw La Berma act, I enjoyed the day. I enjoyed it in the little garden outside the theater, where, two hours later, the gas lamps, once lit, would cover the leafless horse-chestnuts in a metallic sheen and illuminate the details of their branches; I enjoyed it in the lobby, faced with the box-office staff, whose selection, promotion, and fate all depended on the great artiste whose word was law in that theater, in which there was an obscure succession of temporary and purely nominal managers; I enjoyed it as they took our tickets without a glance at us, in their anxiety to be sure that each and every requirement of Mme Berma's had been definitely made known to the new employees, that the hired clappers must never applaud her, that windows had to stay open till she was onstage, but that every single door must then be closed, that a pitcher of hot water must be concealed near her, so as to keep down the dust—and sure enough, any moment now her carriage and long-maned pair would draw up in front of the theater, she would step down wrapped in her furs, favor those who greeted her with a moody wave of the hand, then send one of her ladies-in-waiting to check that her friends had been allotted the proper stage box, to see that the house temperature was right, find out who was in the best boxes tonight, inspect the attendants, for the theater and the audience were no more than an outer garment which she put on, the medium of greater or lesser conductivity through which her talent had to pass. I even enjoyed it inside the auditorium; since learning that all the spectators looked at the same stage, unlike what my childish imagination had long pictured, I had supposed that so many people must make it as difficult for each of them to see as it is when one stands among a crowd; but now I realized that, because of the layout of the theater, which is in a way symbolic of perception itself, each person has the impression of being at the center; and this explained why Françoise, having been treated to a seat in the gods at a melodrama, had told us hers had been the best seat in the house and that, instead of feeling remote from the stage, she had been intimidated by the proximity of the curtain, which had seemed a mysterious living thing. I enjoyed it even more when, from behind the curtain, I began to hear sounds as vague and strange as those heard from inside the shell of an egg when a chick is about to emerge; they soon grew louder, until, suddenly, from that world which our eye could not penetrate but which could see us, they became three portentous strokes,[3] clearly intended for us, and as thrilling as a message from Mars. The curtain having risen, my enjoyment continued at the sight of a writing table and a fireplace, both of them quite nondescript actually, which obviously meant that any individuals who might come in would not be actors turning up to speak lines, like some I had once seen at a party, but just people in their own home, engaged in living a day of their lives, on which I happened to be eavesdropping. My pleasure was interrupted by a moment's unease: just as I was looking forward to the beginning of the play, a couple of bad-tempered men came walking across the stage, raising their voices enough for everyone in that thousand-strong audience to make out every word, whereas when two customers start scuffling and shouting in a small café you have to ask the waiter what they are saying; but at that same instant, in my surprise that everyone else was paying polite attention to them, all sitting submerged in unanimous silence, the surface of which was now and then broken by a ripple of laughter, I realized that this rude pair of intruders were the actors, and that the short play called a curtain-raiser had just begun. It was followed by an interval which went on for so long that the audience, having come back in, began to express their impatience by stamping their feet on the floor. I was alarmed at this; for, just as, when I read in a report of a trial that a man of courage and honor was to jeopardize his own interests by giving evidence in defense of an innocent man,[4] I dreaded the thought that people might not treat him well, that his act might not be properly acknowledged, that he might not be handsomely rewarded, and that in his disgust he might even join the forces of injustice; so, equating genius with virtue, I was afraid that La Berma might take umbrage at the bad manners of such an uncouth audience (among whom I would have much preferred her to be able to recognize and draw comfort from a few celebrities whose good judgment she valued) and express her displeasure and disdain for them by

acting badly. I gazed about me as though to implore these stamping
savages not to trample underfoot the fragile, precious impression that
had brought me there. The final vestiges of my enjoyment lasted until
the opening scenes of the performance of *Phèdre*. The character of Phèdre does not appear in those early scenes of act II; and yet, no sooner
had the curtain gone up, and the red velvet of another curtain had been
partly opened, so as to double the depth of the stage, as was done in
all the star's performances, than there entered upstage an actress who
looked and sounded exactly as I had been led to believe La Berma
would. They must have changed the cast! All my careful study of the
part of Theseus' wife was pointless! But then a second actress engaged
in a dialogue with the first one—I must have been mistaken in thinking
she was La Berma, as this newcomer looked even more like the star and
came much closer to her diction! Both of them now enhanced their
speeches with noble gestures—which were clear and recognizably relevant to the text, as they lifted the folds of their fine robes—and with ingenious intonations, fraught with passion or irony, which showed me
shades and depths in lines I had read at home without paying enough
attention to what they meant. Then, suddenly, a woman appeared between the parted curtains of the inner sanctum, standing there as though
within a frame, and instantly—from the fear that filled me, much more
acute than any La Berma might have felt, at the prospect of someone
opening a window, spoiling her delivery of a line by rustling a program,
upsetting her by applauding her fellow actors, or by not applauding
her enough, and from the effort of concentration, also greater than
hers, which forced me from that moment on to sense the auditorium,
the audience, the actors, the play, and even my own person as nothing
but an acoustical medium, of importance only insofar as it might enrich
the modulations of that voice—I realized that the pair of actresses whom
I had been admiring for some minutes past bore not the slightest resemblance to the one I was there to see and hear. But at the same time, all
my enjoyment had dissipated: however hard I strained toward her with
my eyes, ears, and mind, so as not to miss a single scrap of the incen-
tives she would offer me to admire her, I could not manage to find any.
I could not even perceive in her diction or use of movement, as I had

with the other actresses, any sensitivity of tone or delicacy of gesture. I
sat there and listened to her as I might have read *Phèdre*, or as though at
that moment Phèdre herself was saying the things I was hearing, without La Berma's talent seeming to add anything at all to them. I wished I
could arrest and hold motionless before me each of her intonations,
freeze each of the changing expressions on her face, so as to study them
in depth and find out what was beautiful in them; at least I tried, by using all my mental agility, by having my whole attention at the ready
and focused on a line just before its delivery, not to waste in prelimi-
naries any iota of the time taken by each word or gesture, in the hope of
being able, by sheer intensity of attention, to absorb each of them as I
might have done if I had been able to hold them before me for hours
on end. But the time they occupied was so short! My ear had barely registered each sound when it was replaced by the following one. In one
scene, where La Berma stands still for a moment against a backdrop of
the sea, with one arm raised to face level, and her whole figure given a
greenish tint by an effect of the lighting, the audience had no sooner
burst into applause than she changed position and the tableau I wished
I could study closely disappeared. I told my grandmother I could not
see very well, and she lent me her opera glasses. But when you believe
in the reality of things, using an artificial means to see them better is
not quite the same as feeling closer to them. I felt it was not La Berma
that I was seeing, only an enlarged picture of her. I put the glasses
down—but what if the image received by the naked eye was no more
accurate, given that it was an image reduced by distance? Which was
the true Berma? When she reached Phèdre's declaration of desire for
Hippolyte, a part I had been specially looking forward to, because the
diction of Oenone and Aricie kept revealing unsuspected subtleties
in parts that were not as fine as it, I was sure her intonations would
be more striking than any I had contrived to imagine while reading
the play at home: but she did not even rise to the effects that the other
two actresses would have managed; she blurred the whole speech into
a toneless recitative, blunting the keen edges of contrasts which any
semi-competent performer, even a girl in a school production, could
hardly have failed to bring out; and she gabbled through it at such

speed that it was not until she reached the closing line that my mind became aware of the deliberate monotone in which she had delivered the opening ones.

At length I felt a first surge of admiration within me—it was brought on by a sudden outburst of frantic clapping from the other members of the audience. I clapped and clapped too, keeping on as long as possible, in the hope that La Berma might excel herself out of gratitude, and I could then be certain of having seen her on one of her best days. The remarkable thing is that the moment when that storm of applause broke out was, as I later learned, one of those when her acting was at its most inspired. Certain transcendent realities seem to give off a sort of radiation which the crowd can pick up. From the unclear reports of certain great events, such as a danger threatening an army on a national frontier, a defeat or a great victory, the educated man may be unable to make much sense, but the crowd thrills with an excitement which surprises him and which, once he has been authoritatively informed of the military situation, he recognizes as their perception of that "aura" surrounding events of great moment and visible from hundreds of miles away. We learn of a victory either after the war is over, or at once from the janitor's jubilation. A touch of genius in the acting of La Berma is revealed to us by the reviews a week after we have seen her onstage, or by the cheers from the back stalls. But as this immediate communal responsiveness also expresses itself in many mistaken outbursts, here people usually applauded at the wrong moments; and the waves of clapping were often mechanical consequences of previous applause, just as in a gale the waves may go on rising, once the surface of the sea is disturbed enough, even though the wind is no stronger. So, the longer I went on clapping, the better La Berma's acting seemed to have become. "Say what you like," a rather common woman sitting nearby said, "you've got to admit she throws herself into it. She really hits herself, you know. And she runs around! That's real acting!" Relieved to learn of these grounds for believing in the genius of La Berma—though suspecting they were as inadequate to account for it as were the words of the peasant on seeing the *Mona Lisa* or Benvenuto Cellini's *Perseus*: "Well, it's pretty good, isn't it? It's all gold! Good stuff, huh? A lot of work went into that!"—I let the cheap wine of this popular enthusiasm go to my head. Even so, once the curtain had fallen, I was aware of being disappointed that the enjoyment I had longed for had not been greater, but also of wishing that, such as it was, it would continue, and that I was not obliged to leave behind me forever, as I walked out of the auditorium, this life of the theater in which I had just shared for a few hours. To part from it and go straight home would have been as heartrending as going into exile, had I not looked forward to learning a lot about La Berma from the admirer of hers to whom I owed the fact of having been allowed to go and see *Phèdre*, M. de Norpois. To introduce me, my father called me into his study before dinner. When I entered the room, the former ambassador stood up, bowed from his full height, gave me his hand and the careful scrutiny of his blue eyes. During his period as France's representative abroad, with each passing stranger introduced to him (all of them, not excluding well-known singers, being people of more or less note, of whom he knew as he met them that he would be able to say, if he should happen in the future to hear mention of their names in Paris or Saint Petersburg, that he well remembered the evening spent in their company in Munich or Sofia), he had cultivated the habit of making a show of affability, so as to let them see how pleased he was to make their acquaintance; and, in his belief that life in capital cities, where one is thrown into constant contact both with the personalities of interest who pass through and with the customs of the local population, affords one a thorough knowledge of history, of geography, of the ways of different peoples and of the intellectual life of Europe, which no book can give, he also turned upon every newcomer his acute proficiency in observation, so as to see for himself what manner of man he was dealing with. It was a long time since the government had appointed him to a post in a foreign capital; but when people were introduced to him, his eyes, as though they had not been notified of his removal from the active list, still took up their work of profitable observation, while his whole demeanor set about assuring such persons that their names were not unknown to him. So, as M. de Norpois spoke to me with the kindly and important air of the man who is aware of his own vast experience, he examined me with a perceptive curiosity calculated to derive all possible benefit from me, as though I were some outlandish custom, an instructive landmark, or a star on a foreign tour. In this, he treated me with both the majestic considerateness of wise Mentor and the studious curiosity of young Anacharsis.

However, he made me no promise of good offices with the *Revue des deux mondes*, although he did ask me certain questions on my past life and studies, as well as on the things I liked, this being the first time anybody had mentioned such things in a way which, instead of giving me the idea that it was my duty to resist them, suggested they might be perfectly respectable. Seeing that I was inclined toward literature, M. de Norpois, rather than try to put me off it, spoke of it with deference, as though it were a charming dowager whose select company one remembers well from having been admitted to it in Rome or Dresden, and whom one would be glad to see more of, were it not for the unavoidable impediments of life. More favored and freer than himself, I could be sure of having a good time with her, or so a hint of envious naughtiness in his smile seemed to suggest. But the very words he used showed me that Literature was utterly different from the image I had had of it in Combray; and I realized how right I had been to abandon all notion of it. Until that moment, my only thought had been that I had no gift for writing; but M. de Norpois now freed me of the very urge to write. I tried to explain what my dreams had been; I was trembling with emotion, in my anxiety to find the most accurate words to express what I had felt but had never before tried to put into words; and that was why what I did say was so garbled. It may have been a professional habit with him, it may have been the acquired composure of any important man being asked for advice who, knowing that control of the conversation remains in his hands, lets you meander about and exhaust yourself looking for the best words, or it may have been to display at its best the style of his head, which he saw as Grecian notwithstanding his great muttonchop whiskers, but M. de Norpois, while you held forth, kept as straight a face as if you were haranguing an ancient (and stone-deaf) bust in the Glyptothek at Munich or Copenhagen. Then, as conclusive as an auctioneer's gavel or the Oracle at Delphi, his voice as he replied struck you with unexpected force, nothing in his expression having let you guess at the effect you had been making, or what view he would give.

"Quite," he said suddenly, as though the matter was closed, having let me flounder about under his unmoving stare. "I know of the case of the son of a friend of mine who, *mutatis mutandis,* is just like you." (His tone, as he spoke of our shared hankerings after the writing life, was reassuring, as though we had a predisposition toward rheumatism rather than literature, and he wanted me to know it was not fatal.) "So he preferred to leave the Quai d'Orsay, despite the fact that, thanks to his father, his career path was clear, and then, without caring so much as a fig for any views others might have on the matter, he started to publish. He is not likely to repine at having done so, believe you me. Two years ago now, he wrote a book—he's a good bit older than yourself, of course—on the Sentiment of the Infinite on the western shore of Lake Victoria Nyanza, and then, this very year, a work of lesser scope, but still written with a nimble—nay, sometimes a sharp—nib, on the repeating rifle in the Bulgarian army, and these two productions have really put him in a class all his own. So he has already gone a fair way. He's not a man to do things by halves, and I can assure you that, though no firm nomination of him for the Académie des Sciences Morales is yet being envisaged, his name has cropped up once or twice in conversation, and that in a manner far from disadvantageous to him. In a word, though it would be untrue to say he has yet scaled the highest peak, it must be said that, by dint of meritorious endeavor, he has contrived to make a pretty fine position for himself, and that his worthy efforts have been duly crowned by success—for success, you know, does not always go to the muddleheads and scatterbrains of this world, or indeed to the upsetters of applecarts, who usually turn out to be in it for show, anyway."

By this time, my father had no doubt I would be a member of the Académie in a very few years; and his satisfaction was increased when M. de Norpois, after a momentary pause in which he appeared to ponder the consequences of such an act, handed me a card and said, "Go and see him, tell him I sent you—I warrant he'll have some good advice to give you," words which caused me as much heartache and alarm as if he had told me I was to be taken on, the very next day, as a cabin boy on a clipper.

I had inherited from my aunt Léonie, as well as many more objects and furniture than I knew what to do with, almost the whole of her money, the posthumous display of an affection for me which I had never noticed while she lived. My father, who was charged with managing this money until I came of age, sought M. de Norpois's advice on a certain number of investments. M. de Norpois recommended certain low-yield stocks that he looked on as rock-solid, notably English Consolidated and the Russian 4 percents: "With first-rate stocks like those, though the return may not be very high, at least you are sure that your capital will never suffer." My father told him succinctly about the other stock he had bought. M. de Norpois's smile of congratulation was all but imperceptible: like all *rentiers*, he saw money as a desirable thing, but deemed it tactful to restrict his compliments on what anyone owned to a veiled glance of understanding; also, being himself hugely wealthy, he believed good taste required him to appear impressed by the lesser incomes of others, while enjoying a quiet reminder of the superiority of his own. However, he did not hesitate to congratulate my father on the "composition" of his portfolio, "very stylish, very neat, very handsome." It sounded as though he endowed the differences between the market values of shares, and even the shares themselves, with something like aesthetic merit. When my father mentioned one of these securities, quite a new one, not very well known, M. de Norpois, like the man who has read a book that you thought you were the only one to have read, said, "Yes, yes! I enjoyed following it in the Share List—good buy, wasn't it?" And he smiled with the reminiscent appreciation of the subscriber to a review who has read its latest serialized novel, installment by installment. "I would not advise you against buying up some of the issue to be floated in the coming days. It's very tempting, they're offering the shares at attractive prices." My father, referring to certain older stocks but not quite remembering their names, which were easily confused with other, similar ones, opened a drawer and showed the ambassador the certificates themselves. I was delighted by the appearance of them, all decorated with cathedral spires and allegorical figures, looking like old publications from the Romantic period that I had once looked at. All the productions of a particular time look alike; the artists who illustrate the poems of a certain period are the same ones who are employed by its banking houses. There is nothing more evocative of certain episodes of Hugo's *Notre-Dame de Paris*, or works by Gérard de Nerval, as I used to see them displayed outside the grocery store in Combray, than the river divinities wielding the beflowered rectangle that frames a stock certificate issued by the Compagnie des Eaux.

My father's attitude toward my type of mind was scorn sufficiently diluted by affection for his reaction to whatever I did to be, on the whole, blind indulgence. So he had no hesitation in sending me to fetch a little prose poem I had written one year at Combray, on the way home from an outing. I had written it in a state of exhilaration which I felt it must directly convey to anyone who read it. But my exhilaration must have failed to touch M. de Norpois; and he handed it back to me without a word.

My mother, who was full of respect for any of my father's occupations, came in to ask shyly whether it was time for her to have dinner served. She was reluctant to interrupt any conversation in which she was not supposed to be participating. So my father went on reminding the Marquis of some useful measure or other which they had decided to support at the next meeting of the Select Committee, in that special tone of voice used by two professional colleagues (or two classmates) who, though out of their usual element, and in the presence of others who are not privy to the shared experiences of their other life, speak of these experiences, while apologizing for doing so.

The state of total independence from his facial muscles in which M. de Norpois lived enabled him to listen while not seeming to hear. My father, having stumbled through a longish preamble, eventually had to grope for a word: "So I had been thinking I might just ask for, you know, the views of the Select Committee . . ." Whereupon, from the countenance of the aristocratic virtuoso, who had been sitting as still as an instrumentalist awaiting his turn to play, there came, with perfect attack and a smooth delivery, in a sharpened pitch and sounding as though finishing a phrase just begun, but in a different tone-coloring, the words, ". . . of which, of course, you will not hesitate to convene a meeting, given that each and every one of its members is personally known to you and can come in at any moment." In itself, this completion was hardly remarkable. But the unmoving posture that had preceded it gave it the sudden crystal clarity, the almost mischievous surprise of the phrases by which the piano, after its silent rests, makes its punctual little replies to the cello in a Mozart concerto.

As we went through to dinner, my father asked me, "So—did you enjoy the matinee?" so as to give me a chance to shine, and in the hope that my enthusiasm would find favor in the eyes of M. de Norpois; then, with the technical and conspiratorial tone of retrospective allusiveness which he used for referring to the sessions of the Select Committee, he added for the benefit of the diplomat, "He's just been to see La Berma, you know. You remember we spoke of it."

"You must have been delighted," M. de Norpois said, "especially if you were seeing her for the first time. Your good father here was inclined to be anxious about the repercussions your little escapade might have on your state of health—I understand you're rather delicate, not in the best of health. However, I reassured him. Theaters nowadays are not what they used to be, even just twenty years ago. I mean, one has more or less comfortable seats to sit in; and the air circulates a bit—though we still have a long way to go to equal Germany and England, which in that respect (as in many another!) have far outstripped us. I have never seen Mme Berma in *Phèdre*, but I have been told she is outstanding. It must, of course, have been a great thrill for you."

M. de Norpois, being incomparably cleverer than I was, must be in possession of the truth that I had been unable to derive from La Berma's acting! He would be able to reveal it to me. In answer to his question, I was going to beg him to tell me where that truth lay; and in so doing he would vindicate the desire that had urged me to go and see her. I had no more than a moment to take advantage of, to focus my inquiries on the salient points. But what *were* they? Concentrating my whole attention on my impressions, which were hopelessly confused, with no thought of shining or finding favor, but in the hope of getting from him the truth I sought, I made no effort to substitute set phrases for the words that failed me, I made no sense, and eventually, so as to have him say straight out what was so admirable about La Berma, I owned up to my disappointment.

"What's that?" exclaimed my father, appalled at the poor impression my ineptness might make on M. de Norpois. "How can you say you didn't enjoy it? Your grandmother told us you didn't miss a word, that you just stared and stared at her, that nobody else in the whole audience lapped it up the way you did!"

"Well, yes, I was listening as hard as I could, to see what was so great about her. I mean, she's very good . . ."

"Well, then, if she's very good, what more do you want?"

"One of the things which contribute most definitely to the success of Mme Berma," said M. de Norpois, taking care to turn toward my mother, so as to bring her into the conversation and to fulfill punctiliously the duty of being courteous to one's hostess, "is the impeccable taste she exercises in her choice of parts, which always ensures her a clear success, one that is thoroughly deserved. She rarely plays mediocre parts—I mean, here she is now as Phèdre. And one can see the same good taste in her costumes and in her acting. Even though she has made frequent and profitable tours to England and to America, the vulgarity—I won't say of John Bull, that would be quite an unfair thing to say of the England of this Victorian era of ours—but the vulgarity of Uncle Sam seems not to have affected her. Never any colors that are too flagrant, never any exaggerated vocal effects. Just that wonderful voice, which serves her so well, which she uses to such good effect, which she plays on, I might almost say, like a musician on an instrument!"

My interest in La Berma's acting, being no longer subject to the compression and constraints of reality, had gone on growing since the end of the performance. But I felt the need to find explanations for this interest, which, while she was onstage, had sated itself with equal intensity on all the rich complexities of real life, as she offered them to my eyes and ears, but without separating any of them or distinguishing anything. So there was some relief to be had in finding a reasonable cause for it in these praises of her as an unspoiled and tasteful artiste; it attracted them to itself by its own power of absorption; it latched on to them, as the drunken man in his bonhomie is moved to maudlin by the actions of a passerby. "He's right, you know!" I thought. "What a lovely voice, what simple costumes! How clever of her to think of doing *Phèdre*! Of course I'm not disappointed!"

The cold beef with carrots now made its appearance, laid out by the Michelangelo of our kitchen on great crystals of aspic that looked like blocks of transparent quartz.

"You have a chef of superlative quality, madame," said M. de Norpois. "And that is a thing worthy of note. Speaking as one who has had to keep up a certain standard of such things in foreign parts, I know how difficult it can often be to find the perfect Vatel.[5] I see you have prepared a sumptuous repast for your guest."

It was true that Françoise, inspired by the challenge offered by a guest of such quality to create a dinner fraught with difficulties that for once were worthy of her, had taken pains of a sort she no longer took when we dined among ourselves, and had become once more the incomparable cook she had been in Combray days.

"Now, that is something you can't get in any public eating establishment, not excluding the very best: a dish of braised beef, with aspic that doesn't smell like glue, in which the meat has absorbed the flavor of the carrots—quite magnificent! Do allow me to have a little more," he added, with a gesture that requested another helping of the aspic. "I would be interested to see how your Vatel would acquit himself of quite a different dish—beef Stroganoff, for example."

To contribute his fair share to the enjoyment of the meal, M. de Norpois now served up for us several stories which his diplomatic colleagues were familiar with, some of them featuring the sesquipedalianism of a certain politician known for his preposterous utterances larded with mixed metaphors, others featuring the epigrammatic brevity of a diplomat who was a master of elegant Atticism. It was clear that M. de Norpois's judgment of these two types of sentence was based on a criterion utterly unlike the one I applied to literature. I missed many niceties in his stories: I could see little difference between the clumsy sentences, which he accompanied with guffaws, and the others, which he thought were so fine. He was the kind of man who would have said of the books I liked, "So you fancy this sort of stuff, do you? Personally, I have to say I don't see much in it, I'm not one of the initiated." But I could have said the same thing to him: in a statement or a speech, I could not see what he saw as witty or what he thought was stupid, what was eloquence and what was bombast; and the lack of any apparent reason why one was good and the other bad meant that these literary standards struck me as most mysterious and obscure. The only deduction I could draw was that, in politics, it was a mark of superiority rather than inferiority to repeat what everybody else thought. Each time M. de Norpois used certain expressions, which were as trite as the newspapers in which he read them, and which he spoke with emphasis, one could sense that, by virtue of having been uttered by him, they became an act, and that this act would not go unnoticed.

My mother had been expecting the pineapple-and-truffle salad to be a great success. But the ambassador, after spending a moment exercising his penetrating gift of observation on the dish, ate the salad with complete diplomatic discretion and vouchsafed no opinion on it. My mother urged him to have some more; and as he did so, instead of offering the expected compliment, he said, "I cannot refuse, ma'am, since you have clearly issued an ukase."

"We read in the 'public prints,'" my father said, "that you had a long conversation with King Theodosius."

"Quite. His Majesty, whose memory for faces is remarkable, was gracious enough to recall, when he noticed me in the front stalls, that I had had the honor of seeing him over a period of a few days at the Court of Bavaria, at a time when he had no thought of his Eastern throne—as you know, it fell to him as a result of a European congress; and he even had some serious hesitation about whether to accept it or not, as he saw it as not quite up to his lineage, which is the noblest in the whole of Europe, heraldically speaking. So an equerry brought me the command to go and greet His Majesty, and naturally I lost no time in complying."

"And do you find the results of his visit satisfactory?"

"Completely and entirely! Mind you, one might well have harbored some misgivings about how well such a young monarch might comport himself in such difficult circumstances, especially given the delicate times we live in. Personally, I must say I had no qualms whatsoever about the sovereign's political instincts. However, even my expectations were more than borne out. The toast he proposed at the Élysée–which wholly reliable sources have assured me was entirely his own work, from the first word to the last–was in every way worthy of the universal interest it has aroused. It can only be called a masterstroke. A daring one, I grant you, but one which events have fully vindicated. The traditions of diplomacy undoubtedly have their value, but in this case they had managed to create between his country and our own a staleness in the atmosphere, which was unhealthy for both of us. And, of course, one way to get a breath of fresh air–a way which one would obviously be loath to recommend, but which King Theodosius could afford to adopt–is to break windows! He did it with a fine humor, which delighted everyone, and an accuracy in the choice of words which showed he is the worthy descendant of that lineage of highly literate princes to which he belongs through his mother. Certainly, when he spoke of the 'affinities' linking his country to France, he used a word which, though it may not be of common currency in the lexicon of the chancellery, was singularly apt. As you can see," he said, aiming the remark at me, "literature never goes amiss, even in diplomacy, even on a throne. I admit that the state of affairs had been recognized for a long time; and the relations between the two powers had become excellent. Still, it needed to be said. We had been hoping for some such word; the one used was selected with perfect taste; and you can see what an effect it has had. I for one applaud it wholeheartedly."

"Your friend M. de Vaugoubert must have been very happy. He had been working at the rapprochement for years."

"Yes, especially since His Majesty made a point of springing it on him by surprise, the sort of thing he is in the habit of doing, I may add. And it was a *complete* surprise for everybody, not excluding his own minister of foreign affairs, who, as I have been told, did not find it entirely to his taste. He is reported to have said quite unambiguously to someone who broached the matter with him, and in a loud enough voice to be heard by others, 'I was neither consulted nor warned,' giving clearly to understand that he took no share of responsibility for the event. It must be admitted that it has stirred up quite a fuss; and I should not care to wager," he went on with a mischievous smile, "that certain colleagues of mine, who appear to make a virtue of sloth, have not been disturbed in their repose. As for Vaugoubert, you know he had been roundly attacked for his policy of rapprochement, which must have cut the man to the quick—and he's so sensitive, he's the soul of delicacy. I know what I'm saying, you know, for, though he's very much my junior, I have had a great deal to do with him—we have been friends for many a year, and I know him well. Who *wouldn't* know him, I ask you? The man's soul is as clear as crystal. Actually, that's the only fault one could find with him—it's not necessary for a diplomatist to have a heart as transparent as his. Despite which, there's talk of sending him to Rome, which would be a great step forward for him, but also a very great challenge. Between ourselves, I suspect that Vaugoubert, though he's utterly devoid of ambition, would be very pleased if it was true, and has no desire to let *that* cup pass from him. If he does go to Rome, he may well turn out to be very successful. He's the candidate favored by the Consulta; and I for one can see him being well suited, with that artistic bent of his, to the setting of the Farnese Palace and the Carracci gallery.[6] One might think that nobody could dislike such a man, though it must be said there is a clique who are close to King Theodosius who are little more than the creatures of the Wilhelmstrasse,[7] always acting in response to its suggestions, and who have definitely attempted to put a spoke in Vaugoubert's wheel. He has had to contend not only with backstairs intrigues, but with the insults of hired scribblers who, with the cowardice of all stipendiary journalists, and though later they were the first to cry 'Pax,' had no objection to broadcasting the paltry accusations made against our representative by unprincipled men. Yes, for more than a month, the enemies of Vaugoubert were like a scalping party doing the *war dance*," M. de Norpois said, stressing this term. "But forewarned, as we know, is forearmed, and he just kicked the insults aside," he said, with even greater force, and a glare that made us stop eating for a moment. "As a fine old Arabian proverb puts it: 'The dogs bark, the caravan moves on.' " M. de Norpois paused, watching us to see what effect this quotation would have on us. It had a great effect: his proverb was well known to us. All worthy men had been using it that year instead of "Sow the wind and reap the whirlwind," which was in need of a rest, not being a hardy annual like "To labor and to seek for no reward." The culture of these eminent men was of the alternating variety, usually triennial in its cycle. Not that the articles M. de Norpois wrote for the *Revue des deux mondes* would have appeared less than sound and well informed had he not deftly sprinkled these sayings throughout them. Even without the ornamentation which they added to his prose, the lay reader could instantly identify and acknowledge the career diplomat in the other type of expression that M. de Norpois could always be relied upon to place aptly in his articles: "The Court of Saint James was not slow to perceive the danger"; or "At Pevchesky Bridge, where an anxious eye was kept on the selfish yet astute policy of the Double-Headed Eagle, excitement now reached fever pitch"; or "A cry of alarm sounded in the Montecitorio"; or "This predictable double game carries the hallmark of the Ballhausplatz."[8] But what had led some to see in M. de Norpois not just the career diplomat but the man of higher culture was his studied way of using certain quotations, of which the unquestionable paradigm in those days was: "Show me sound policies and I'll show you sound finances, as Baron Louis was fond of saying." (This was before the time when we imported from the Far East "Victory goes to him who can hold out for a quarter hour longer than his opponent, as the Japanese say.") It was this reputation as a man of letters, as well as a real genius for intrigue concealed behind a mask of indifference, that had got M. de Norpois elected to the Académie des Sciences Morales. There were those who became convinced that his rightful place was actually in the Académie Française on the day when, in his conviction that it was by strengthening our ties with Russia that we could reach an understanding with England, he did not hesitate to pen the following sentence: "Let this be well understood at the Quai d'Orsay, let it figure in all school geography books that do not make a point of saying so today, let every candidate at the *baccalauréat* who cannot repeat it be failed out of hand: all roads may lead to Rome, but the road which goes from Paris to London must of necessity pass through Saint Petersburg."

"As a matter of fact," M. de Norpois went on, talking to my father, "Vaugoubert has made a great success of this, one which really goes further than he had been hoping. He had expected a formal toast, nothing more, which, given the coldness of recent years, would actually have been a good sign. Several people among those present have assured me that, if one merely reads the text of the toast, it is not possible to realize the effect it had when it was proposed and so brilliantly expounded by the King, who, being the master he is in the art of public speaking, brought out so well each and every intent, each and every shade of it. In that connection, a rather choice detail has been brought to my attention, one which shows to advantage, yet again, the youthful goodheartedness which so many find endearing in King Theodosius. I have been assured that at the very moment when he spoke that word 'affinities,' which was after all the great novelty of the speech, one which, mark my words, will lend itself to much comment in the chancelleries, His Majesty, foreseeing the joy it would cause our ambassador, who would see it as the fulfillment of his every effort, the realization of his dream, one might say, in a word, his marshal's baton, His Majesty half turned toward Vaugoubert, rested that engaging eye of the Oettingens on him, and carefully enunciated that word 'affinities,' so well chosen, such a felicitous expression, in a tone of voice which let everyone know it was being used quite deliberately and with intent. It appears that Vaugoubert was quite unmanned for a moment; and I must say that, to a certain extent, I sympathize with him. After the banquet, when His Majesty had gathered about him a more restricted circle—I have this from a person whose word is utterly unimpeachable, you understand—it is said the King even approached Vaugoubert and murmured to him, 'Well, Marquis, are you satisfied with your pupil?' It is indubitable that a toast of that sort has done more than twenty years of negotiations to strengthen our two countries' *affinities,* as Theodosius II so vividly put it. You may say it's only a word, but it's certainly one to conjure with—look at the echoes it has awakened throughout Europe, the press everywhere have taken it up, people have sat up and taken notice, it has struck a new note! And that's quite typical of this particular sovereign. I won't pretend that he produces such gems of genius every day, but in his prepared speeches—indeed, even in the most impromptu conversation—it is very rare for him not to leave his distinguishing mark—I almost said, not to inscribe his signature—by the coining of some trenchant phrase. No one can suspect me of bias in this, as I am utterly opposed to innovation in such things. Nineteen times out of twenty it is pernicious."

"Yes, I was pretty sure the Kaiser's recent telegram would not be very much to your taste," my father said.

As much as to say, "That man!," M. de Norpois cast his eyes heavenward: "For one thing, it was an act of arrant ingratitude. It was worse than a crime—it was a mistake![9] And as for the stupidity of it, the only word for that is monumental. For another thing, if someone doesn't put a stop to it, the man who gave Bismarck his marching orders is quite capable of repudiating each and every one of Bismarck's policies. And when that happens, we'll see a fine mess!"

"My husband tells me, monsieur, that you're thinking of taking him off to Spain with you one of these summers. I'm sure he would enjoy that."

"Yes, I must say it's a most engaging prospect, madame, I'm looking forward to it very much. I really would relish such a trip in your company, my dear fellow. But what about yourself, dear lady, have you any plans for the holidays?"

"My son and I may be going to Balbec, but it's not quite certain."

"Ah, Balbec! A lovely spot, I took a look at it not so many years ago. Lots of very smart houses going up. I'm sure you will find the place to your liking. How, may I inquire, did you come to choose Balbec?"

"My son has a great desire to see some of the churches in the area, especially the church of Balbec itself. I had been a little apprehensive about his health, what with the strains of the journey and especially inconveniences of accommodations. But I have been told they've just built a first-class hotel, which will mean he can have the kind of comfort required by his state of health."

"Well, I really must pass that information along to a certain person. She will be glad to know of it."

"The church at Balbec is a fine one, isn't it, monsieur?" I asked, de-spite the displeasure of knowing that one of Balbec's attractions lay in its smart houses.

"Well, it's not bad. But it can't bear comparison with delicately worked gems such as the cathedrals of Rheims and Chartres, or that jewel in our crown, the Sainte-Chapelle here in Paris."

"But the church of Balbec is partly Romanesque, isn't it?"

"Absolutely. It is in the Romanesque manner, which is of course one reason among others why it is so frigid. It's a style which in no way seems to foreshadow the elegance, the delicate inventiveness of the Gothic architects, who could work the stone like lace. No doubt the church of Balbec is worth a visit, if one happens to be in the vicinity—you could while away a rainy afternoon if you had nothing better to do, take a look inside, see the tomb of Admiral de Tourville."[10]

"Did you happen to go to the dinner at Foreign Affairs last night?" my father asked. "I couldn't manage to attend."

"No," said M. de Norpois, smiling. "I must confess I sacrificed that pleasure to a very different way of passing the evening. I dined at the house of a lady of whom you may have heard—the beautiful Mme Swann."

My mother all but trembled. Being of a readier responsiveness than my father, she was often alarmed on his behalf by something that would not affect him until a moment later. She was the first to notice things which would cause him displeasure, much as bad news for France is known sooner abroad than at home. However, she was curious to know what sort of people went to the Swanns', and inquired of M. de Norpois about his fellow guests.

"Well, now . . . to tell you the truth . . . I must say it's a house at which most of the guests appear to be . . . gentlemen. There were cer-tainly several married men present—but their wives were all indisposed yesterday evening, and had been unable to go," the ambassador replied, with a crafty glance masked by joviality, his eyes full of a demure discre-tion that pretended to moderate their mischievousness while making it more obvious.

"To be completely fair," he added, "I must also say that there are

women who go there. But they . . . belong–how shall I put it?–let's say
to the world of Republican sympathies, rather than to the world of
Swann himself." (This name he pronounced "Svann.") "Who can tell?
One day it may turn out to be a literary or political salon. Although
they do appear to be quite satisfied with the present state of affairs.
Swann himself actually makes it rather too obvious, if you ask me. I was
taken aback that a man of such delicacy should be so brash and tactless,
not to say tasteless, about dropping the names of people who've invited
him and his wife to dinner next week–yet I can assure you they were
not people one would be proud to be invited by! He kept on saying,
'We're not free on a single evening!,' as though this were something
to boast about, as though he were a vulgar outsider, which of course he
isn't. Once upon a time, after all, he did have many friends both male
and female, and no doubt not all of the latter, perhaps not even most of
them, but I do know for a fact that one of them–I believe one can go so
far as to say this without risking being indiscreet–who is a very great
lady indeed, might not have evinced total reluctance at the suggestion
of frequenting Mme Swann. And if that had happened, then very likely
some more of Panurge's sheep[11] would have followed suit. However, it
would appear that Swann put out no feelers in that direction. Ah,
what's this, now? What, another Nesselrode pudding! After such a feast
of Lucullus, it will behoove me to take the waters at Karlsbad! Mind
you, Swann may well have sensed that it would have all been far too
difficult. What's clear is that the marriage was thoroughly deplored.
Mention has been made of the wife's money, but nothing could be further from the truth. However, people did think the whole thing was too
unsavory. And not only that, but there was Swann's aunt, a woman
who's hugely rich and very highly thought of, the wife of a man who,
financially speaking, is a force to be reckoned with. Well, not only did
she close her doors to Mme Swann, but she even conducted an all-out
campaign to make sure all her friends and acquaintances did the same. I
don't mean to imply that anyone in the best Paris society actually cut
her dead. No, no, of course not! The husband being, in any case, quite
capable of sending around his seconds! Anyway, the strange thing
about all of this is that Swann, with all his connections in the best soci-

ety, lavishes such attention on company of which the best that can be said is that it is extremely mixed. I used to know him quite well, and I must say I was both astounded and amused to see such a man, a man who's so well bred, so much at home in the most fashionable and exclusive circles, falling over himself to thank the chief undersecretary of the postmaster general for gracing him with a visit, asking him whether Mme Swann might *feel free* to call on his wife! He must feel out of his element. It's so clearly not his world. And yet, you know, I don't think the man's unhappy. It's true that the woman stooped to some pretty nasty things in the years before the marriage, some quite unsavory emotional blackmail—if he ever declined to satisfy her on something or other, she just forbade him access to the child. And poor old Swann, who's really as naïve as he's refined, assumed each time that the disappearance of his daughter was mere coincidence, and would not see the truth of the matter. Also, she made him so miserable with her nonstop scenes that everyone thought that, if she ever had her way and got him to marry her, she would lead him a dog's life, and the marriage would be a disaster. Then, lo and behold, what happened was the very opposite! People take great pleasure in laughing behind Swann's back at the way he goes on about his wife. Not that anyone expects a man who's more or less aware of the fact that he's a . . . (Molière's word, you understand)[12] to go about proclaiming it *urbi et orbi*. Still, people think he's going a little too far when he tells you what a wonderful wife he's got. Yet, you know, it's not as far-fetched as they think. The way she behaves toward him, which is not the way all husbands would prefer—and, mind you, between you and me, it strikes me as improbable that Swann, who's nobody's fool and who had known her for years, didn't have a shrewd suspicion about you-know-what—there can be no denying that she seems fond of him. I'm not saying she's not still a bit flighty, and certainly Swann himself doesn't let the grass grow under his feet in that regard, at least if one listens to what people say—and, as you can imagine, people *do* say. But she's grateful for what he has done for her; and, notwithstanding all the dire forebodings voiced by everyone, she seems to have become as mild as can be." This change in Odette may not have been such an extraordinary thing as M. de Norpois thought. She had never believed that Swann would eventually marry her. Every time she informed him in a meaning tone that a certain fashionable gentleman had just married his mistress, she had been met with an icy silence; and if she went so far as to say to him straight out, "So—don't you think that was a nice thing to do? Don't you think it's the decent thing for him to make an honest woman of someone that's given him the best years of her life?," the most she ever got was the tart reply, "I'm not saying there's anything wrong with it—he can please himself." In fact, Odette had come close to believing that he would do what he sometimes threatened to do in a fit of temper and leave her for good, for she had not long since heard a sculptress declare, "There's nothing men won't stoop to, there's not a good one among them"; and the pessimism of this profound verity had so struck her that she had taken to uttering it in all sorts of situations, accompanying it with a defeated air that seemed to mean, "Well, what would you expect, it'd be just my luck!" As a consequence, all efficacy had gone from the optimistic maxim which had hitherto guided Odette's steps through life: "You can treat men that are in love with you any way you like, they're such fools," to which she always gave the twinkle of the eye that might accompany a statement like, "Don't worry—he's quite house-trained!" Meanwhile, Odette was mortified to think how Swann's conduct must appear to one of her friends, who had recently managed to marry a man whom she had been "with" for a shorter time than Swann and Odette had been together, even though she did not have a child by him, and who was relatively accepted now, receiving invitations to balls at the Élysée Palace. A more perceptive clinician than M. de Norpois could no doubt have made a different diagnosis—that it was this feeling of humiliation and shame that had embittered Odette, that the shrewish character which came out in her was neither integral to her nor an incurable malady—and he might have easily foreseen what had in fact taken place, that a new regimen, marriage, would bring about an almost magical remission of these painful attacks, which, though of daily occurrence, were in no way organic. The marriage came as a surprise to almost everybody, which is itself a surprise. No doubt, few people understand either the purely subjective nature of the phenomenon of love, or how it creates a supplementary person who is quite different from the one who bears our beloved's name in the outside world and is mostly formed from elements within ourselves. So there are few who see anything natural in the disproportionate dimensions we come to perceive in a person who is not the same as the one they see. In the case of Odette, however, it should have been possible to notice that, though she had admittedly never fully appreciated the quality of Swann's mind, at least she was acquainted with the titles and the details of his writings, that the name of Vermeer was as familiar to her as the name of her dressmaker, that she knew by heart certain traits of Swann, the kind which all other people either mock or do not know, the true fond likeness of which reposes only in a mistress's or a sister's heart; and these traits in ourself we cling to so much, even the ones we would most like to see changed, that when a woman comes to have an indulgent and banteringly amicable attachment to them, seeing them more as they are seen by ourselves and by our close relatives, a long-standing liaison can come to have something of the mildness and strength of affections within the family. The feelings we share with another are sanctified when, in judging one of our faults, that person adopts the same point of view as we do. However, there were certain aspects of Swann's mind that Odette had in fact appreciated, since they too were in part outcomes of his character. She lamented the fact that, when Swann did produce a study or some other piece of writing, these aspects were not as perceptible as in his letters or in his conversation, where they abounded. She suggested that he should give them greater scope. Her reason for this was that it was these features she herself preferred in the man; but since this preference meant only that these things were more "him" than others, she may have been right to wish they might be more visible in his writings. Perhaps she thought too that if these writings could have more vitality in them they might be more successful, which might then have enabled her to aspire to the thing which in her time with the Verdurins she had come to see as the greatest of all achievements—a salon of her own.

Twenty years earlier, those who thought such a marriage quite outlandish, people who, if the question had ever arisen for themselves, would have wondered, "What ever will M. de Guermantes think, what will Bréauté have to say when I marry Mlle de Montmorency?," the people who maintained that sort of social ideal, would have included Swann himself: in those days, he had gone to great trouble to be elected to membership in the Jockey Club, and had fully expected that, by eventually making a brilliant marriage, he would consolidate his position and become one of the most notable men about town. However, if they are not to wither and fade, such imaginings of a future marriage must be constantly revivified by external stimuli. Your dearest dream may be to humiliate the man who spurned you. But if you go to live in another country and hear no more of him, your enemy will come in time to have no importance for you. If you have lost touch with all the people because of whom, twenty years ago, you longed to become a member of the Jockey Club or the Institut de France, the prospect of belonging to one or another of these bodies will have lost all its power of attraction. A long-standing relationship can do as much as illness, retirement, or a religious conversion to replace old images with new. When Swann married Odette, he did not go through a process of renunciation of his former social ambitions—she had long since brought him to a state of detachment from them, in the spiritual sense of the word. And had he not been detached from them, it would have been all the more to his credit. In general, marriages that degrade one of the partners are the worthiest of all, because they entail the sacrifice of a more or less flattering situation to a purely private satisfaction—and, of course, marrying for money must be excluded from the notion of a degrading match, as no couple of whom one partner has been sold to the other has ever failed to be admitted in the end to good society, given the weight of tradition, the done thing, and the need to avoid having double standards. In any case, the idea of engaging in one of those crossbreedings common to Mendelian experiments and Greek mythology, and of joining with a creature of a different race, an archduchess, or a good-time girl, someone of blue blood or no blood at all, might well have titillated the artist, if not the pervert, in Swann. On the occasions when it occurred to him that he might one day marry Odette, there was only one person in society whose opinion he would have cared for, the

Duchesse de Guermantes, and snobbery had nothing to do with this. Odette herself was all but indifferent to the Duchesse de Guermantes, thinking only of the people who were immediately above her, rather than of those who inhabited such a remote and exalted sphere. But at moments when Swann sat daydreaming about what it might be like to be the husband of Odette, he always saw the moment when he would introduce her, and especially their daughter, to the Princesse des Laumes, or the Duchesse de Guermantes, as she had become upon the death of her father-in-law. He had no desire to present them to anyone else; but as he imagined the Duchesse talking about him to Odette, and Odette talking to Mme de Guermantes, and the tenderness the latter would show to Gilberte, making much of her, making him proud of his daughter, he could be so moved that he spoke aloud the words they would say. The circumstances that made up this fancied presentation scene were as detailed and concrete as those invented by people who set about drawing up ways to spend some huge imaginary lottery prize. To the extent that a decision may be motivated by a mental image coinciding with it, it can be said that the purpose of Swann's marrying Odette was to introduce her and Gilberte, even though no one else might be present, even though no one else might ever know of it, to the Duchesse de Guermantes. As will be seen, the fulfillment of this social ambition, the only one he had ever harbored for his wife and child, was the very one that was to be denied him; and the veto preventing it was to be so absolute that Swann was to die without imagining that the Duchesse would ever meet them. It will be seen too that the Duchesse de Guermantes did come, after Swann's death, to be acquainted with Odette and Gilberte. He might well have been wise, given that he saw so much importance in something so trivial, not to see the future as too dark in that respect, and not to exclude the possibility that the meeting he longed for might take place, even if at a time when he was no longer there to enjoy it. The mills of causality, which eventually bring to pass more or less all possible effects, including those that had been believed to be the least likely, can at times grind slowly. Their workings can be slowed still more by our own desire, which impedes them while trying to hasten them, or even by our very existence; and they may produce nothing until long after the exhaustion of that desire, or even the end of our life. Swann could really be said to have known this already from his own experience—for, when he eventually married the Odette whom he had not found to his taste to begin with, whom he had then loved so distractedly, but whom he did not marry until he had stopped loving her, until the man who had once longed to spend his whole life with Odette, and who had despaired of ever being able to do so, had long since died within him, did not this mode of post-humous happiness somehow foreshadow what was to happen after his death?

Fearing that the conversation might turn away from the subject of the Swanns, I now broached the subject of the Comte de Paris,[13] to ask M. de Norpois whether *he* was not a friend of Swann's. "Absolutely," M. de Norpois replied, turning toward me and staring at my modest person through the blue of his eyes, in which his great capacity for intellectual toil and his powers of assimilation could be seen floating as though in their natural element. Then he added, turning back to address my father, "And if I may say so, without overstepping the bounds of the respect I profess for His Highness—albeit I do not entertain personal relations with him of a sort which would conflict with my position, however unofficial it is—I permit myself to retail to you a rather choice little incident which, as recently as four years ago, took place in a small railway station in a certain country of Central Europe, where His Highness had occasion to set eyes on Mme Swann. Now, of course, no one in his entourage saw fit to ask His Highness what he thought of her. Such a thing would not have been seemly. But when the vagaries of conversation happened subsequently to bring up her name, His Highness appeared not averse to letting it be divined, by means of certain signs, you understand, which, though they may verge on the imperceptible, are withal quite unambiguous, that his impression of the lady had been far from, in a word, unfavorable."

"But it would surely have been quite out of the question," my father said, "to present her to the Comte de Paris?"

"Well, now, who can say?" M. de Norpois replied. "One never knows with princes! Some of the most illustrious, some of those who are most adept at having rendered unto themselves what must be rendered, are also on occasion those who ride roughshod over even the most inviolable decrees of public opinion, if in so doing they can reward certain good and faithful servants. And what's certain is that the Comte de Paris has always noted with the greatest goodwill the devotion evinced by Swann, who is also, be it remembered, a fellow of fine wit."

"And what was your own impression, Excellency?" asked my mother, as much from politeness as from curiosity.

M. de Norpois's reply, delivered with all the energy of the old connoisseur, was at variance with the moderation with which he was accustomed to express himself:

"Absolutely first-rate!"

Then, knowing that owning up to having been strongly impressed by a woman, as long as one announces it in a waggish manner, is consistent with a highly regarded notion of table talk, the old diplomat laughed quietly to himself for a few moments, bringing water to his blue eyes and a little quiver to nostrils finely veined with red, and added:

"Why, she is quite, quite charming!"

"And was there a writer by the name of Bergotte at the dinner, sir?" I asked, in a diffident attempt to keep the conversation focused on the Swanns.

"Yes, Bergotte was there," M. de Norpois replied, inclining a courteous head toward me, as though in his goodwill toward my father he attached real importance to anything connected with him, including the questions of a boy as young as myself, who was unaccustomed to be shown such deference by men as old as himself. "Do you know him?" he added, gazing at me with the bright eyes which Bismarck admired for their acuity.

"My son doesn't know Bergotte," said my mother. "But he admires him very much."

"Well, now, I'm afraid that's not a view I can share," M. de Norpois said (and when I realized that the thing I set far above myself, the one thing I saw as the highest in the world, was the least of his admirations, the doubts this planted in my mind about my own intelligence were much more crippling than those which usually assailed me). "Bergotte is what I call a flute-player. It must of course be admitted that he tootles on his flute quite mellifluously, albeit with more than a modicum of mincing mannerism and affectation. But when all's said and done, tootling is what it is, and tootling does not amount to a great deal. His works are so flaccid that one can never locate in them anything one could call a framework. There's never any action in 'em, well, hardly any, and especially no scope. It's their base that is their weak point—or, rather, they have no base. In this day and age, when the increasing complexity of modern life leaves one barely any time for reading, when the map of Europe has undergone a profound recasting, and may well be on the point of undergoing another which may prove to be even more profound, when so many new and threatening problems are cropping up on all sides, you will allow that one may fairly claim the right to expect that a writer might aspire to be something higher than a glib wit, whose futile hair-splittings on the relative merits of merely formal matters distract us from the fact that we may be overrun at any moment by a double wave of barbarians, those from within and those from without! Now, I know that to speak thus is to utter blasphemies against the sacrosanct school of what certain gentlemen call Art for Art's Sake—but in our day and age there are more urgent tasks than stringing jingles of words together. I must admit that Bergotte's jingles can at times be quite pretty, but all in all they add up to something that is pretty jejune, pretty precious—and pretty unmasculine, if you ask me! Now that I'm aware of your quite excessive admiration for Bergotte, I can appreciate better that little thing you showed me before dinner, about which, by the way, the less said the better—I owe it to you to say so, for did you not say yourself, quite openly, that it was mere childish scribbling?" It was true, I *had* said so—but I had not meant it. "All sins shall be forgiven, especially the sins of our youth. Many another man could own up to something similar. You're not the only young fellow who has ever fancied himself a poet. But in that piece you showed me, one can detect Bergotte's pernicious influence. Now, clearly, it will come as no surprise to you to learn that it contained none of his better qualities, he being a past master in the art of a certain phrase-making—though one should add, mind you, that it's a shallow art—and you being a boy who cannot be expected to have grasped even the rudiments of that. Still, young as you are, it's exactly the same defect, the aberration of stringing together a few fine-sounding words, and not finding any substance to put into them until afterward. That's what's known as putting the cart before the horse. And even in Bergotte's own stuff, all these finicking futilities, all that rancid and insubstantial Mandarin manner that he goes in for, none of that is to my taste. Nowadays, a chap sets off a few verbal fireworks and everyone acclaims him as a genius. But masterpieces aren't as easy to come by as that! Among all of Bergotte's stuff, I should have to say he hasn't got to his credit a single novel that aspires to anything above the mundane, one of those books that one keeps in a special place on the shelf—not one, if you ask me, in the man's whole output. Though, mind you, in his case it must be said that the work is a cut above the man himself. Believe you me, he's the perfect illustration of the idea of that clever fellow who once said that the only acquaintance one should have with writers is through their books.[14] I defy you to find an individual who is more unlike his books than Bergotte—he's so pretentious, so solemn, so uncongenial! At times he's vulgar, at other times he talks like a book—not like one of his own books, mind you, but like a boring book, for, say what you like, at least his aren't boring. If ever there was a mind that was woolly and convoluted, it's his! He's what an earlier generation was wont to call a trader in fustian. And the things he says are made even more displeasing by the way he speaks. Much the same thing was said of Alfred de Vigny by Loménie—or was it Sainte-Beuve?[15] But, unlike Vigny, Bergotte has never written anything of the caliber of *Cinq-Mars* or *Le Cachet rouge*, whole passages of which deserve to figure in any self-respecting anthology."

I was devastated by what M. de Norpois had said about the piece I had given to him to read; and at the thought of the difficulties I encountered whenever I tried to write an essay, or even just engage in some consecutive thinking, I became once more acutely aware of my own intellectual poverty and of the fact that I had no gift for writing. It was true that, once upon a time in Combray, certain impressions of humble things, or a page of Bergotte, had moved me to thoughts and feelings which seemed important and valuable. But it was those very thoughts and feelings that my prose poem expressed; and there could be no doubt that a mere mirage had misled me into thinking something was good in it, whereas M. de Norpois, who was no fool, had seen through it at a glance. What he *had* done was inform me of the microscopic insignificance of myself when judged by an outside expert who was not only objective but also highly intelligent and well disposed toward me. I felt deflated and dumbfounded; and just as my mind, like a fluid whose only dimensions are those of the container into which it is poured, had once expanded so as to fill the vast vessel of my genius, so now it shrank and fitted exactly into the exiguous confines of the mediocrity to which M. de Norpois had suddenly consigned it.

"The bringing together of Bergotte and myself," M. de Norpois said to my father, "did have its potentially prickly side—though even prickles, of course, may tickle the fancy, if I may say so. You see, some years back, during my time as ambassador in Vienna, Bergotte turned up there on his travels. He was introduced to me by the Princess Metternich, subsequently signed the book at the embassy, and let it be known that he wished to be invited to the ambassador's table. Now, I being the representative abroad of France, and he being a man whose writings do honor in some measure to our country (to be quite accurate, an inconsiderable measure), I should have been quite prepared to forget the poor opinion I have formed of his private life. However, he was not traveling alone; and, what's more, he insisted on not being invited without his . . . traveling companion. I believe I can honestly lay claim to being no more of a prude than the next man; and, being a bachelor, I might have been able to open the doors of the embassy a little wider than if I had been a husband and father. Nonetheless, I vouch that there is a degree of ignominy at which I draw the line, and which is made even more revolting by the high moral tone, or, rather, the frankly moralistic tone, which he adopts in print. For the books are just chock-full of incessant analysis (which, between you and me, is actually quite sickly), with agonizing scruples and morbid remorse and a veritable deluge of preachifying over the merest peccadilloes—and we all know

what that's worth!—when, all the time, in his private life, the man behaves with the most out-and-out cynicism and lack of conscience. So,
to cut a long story short, I did not commit myself. And when the Princess gave me a reminder about it, she got no more satisfaction. With
the result that I must suppose I am in no very good odor with the
gentleman in question; and I can only wonder whether he greatly appreciated Swann's delicacy in inviting him and myself at the same
time—unless, of course, it was Bergotte himself who suggested it. No
way of knowing, though, as the man's ill. That's the real explanation—
indeed, it's his only excuse."

"And was Mme Swann's daughter present at the dinner, sir?" I asked,
glad to be able to broach this matter as we went through to the drawing
room, and thus conceal my excitement more easily than I might have at
the table, sitting up there in full view.

M. de Norpois seemed for a moment to search his memory:

"Ah, yes. A young lady of fourteen or fifteen? Yes, I do recall her being presented to me before dinner as the daughter of Mine Host. I must
say, though, that I saw little of her, and she went off to bed at an early
hour. Or perhaps she went out to the house of a friend, I'm afraid I
can't remember. But look here, I see you are very well informed about
the house of Swann."

"I play with Mlle Swann at the Champs-Élysées. I think she's
lovely."

"Aha! Yes, I see how the land lies! Well, yes, I must tell you, I thought
she was charming. Mind you, I do feel it incumbent upon me to say that
I doubt whether she will ever have the looks of her mother—if I may so
put it without in any way intending to wound your own feelings."

"I prefer Mlle Swann's face, but I also admire her mother very
much. I go for walks in the Bois just in the hope of seeing her pass by."

"Really? Well, I must tell them! They'll be delighted!"

As he spoke these words and for a few seconds longer, M. de Norpois was in the position of anyone else who, on hearing me speak of
Swann as an intelligent man, of his respectable family firm of stockbro-
kers, of his fine house, assumed that I would speak in identical terms of
any other equally intelligent man, of other just as respectable stockbro-

kers, of any other fine house; he was at the stage when the sane man has not quite realized that the man he is chatting with is insane. Also, he was perfectly aware that it is natural to enjoy the sight of pretty women, and that when a man speaks warmly of a pretty woman it is good form to pretend to believe he is in love with her, to share a little joke with him about it, and promise to put in a good word for him. But when he said he would mention me to Gilberte and her mother (which would enable me, like one of the gods of Olympus taking on the fluidity of a breath of air, or, rather, the appearance of the old man impersonated by Minerva, to be an invisible visitor to the salon of Mme Swann, there to capture her attention, be thought about by her, earn her gratitude for my admiration, and stand revealed as the friend of an important man, a worthy future guest at her house, someone who could be admitted to her family circle), I was suddenly so overcome by tender feelings for this important man, who was going to exercise on my behalf the great prestige he must enjoy in the eyes of Mme Swann, that I had to restrain myself from kissing his soft hands, so white and wrinkled that they looked as though they had spent too long steeped in water. I thought no one noticed how close I came to doing this. But it is difficult for any of us to gauge the scale on which others register our acts and words; for fear of seeing ourselves as overimportant, and by magnifying hugely the dimensions to which other people's memories must stretch if they are to cover a lifetime, we imagine that all the peripheral aspects of our speech and gestures make little imprint in the consciousness of the people we talk to, let alone stay in their memory. It is this sort of assumption that makes criminals retrospectively emend statements they have made, in the belief that no one will ever be able to compare the new variant with an older version. However, it is quite possible that, even in relation to the immemorial march of humanity, the newspaper columnist's philosophy that everything passes away into oblivion may be less reliable than the opposite prediction, that all things will last. In a newspaper in which the author of the leading article, a moralist commenting on some event, a masterpiece, or more likely just a songstress who has "had her hour of fame," laments, "But who will remember any of this ten years from now?," page three of the very same issue will carry an account of a session at the Academy of Antiquities concerning something that is of less intrinsic importance, a piece of doggerel, say, dating from the time of the Pharaohs, yet which is still known in its entirety. In a short human lifespan, of course, things may not happen quite like that. Nevertheless, some years later, when I was a guest at a house where among the other guests M. de Norpois seemed to be my surest ally, since he was not only a friend of my father's and an indulgent man, well disposed to our family, but also inclined by profession and nature to be discreet, I was told after he left that he had spoken of an incident long ago "when I had been on the point of kissing his hand." This not only made me blush to the roots of my hair; it also astounded me with the knowledge that both the ambassador's way of speaking of me and the very stuff of his memory were very different from what I would have expected. This piece of gossip, by enlightening me on the makeup of human consciousness, and its unexpected potential for absentmindedness and presence of mind, for memory and forgetfulness, was as much a wonder and a revelation to me as it had been to read in a book by Maspero, the Egyptologist, that the exact names of the huntsmen invited by Assurbanipal to his *battues*, ten centuries before Christ, were known to us.[16]

"Oh, if you would do that, sir," I exclaimed to M. de Norpois when he said he would mention to Gilberte and Mme Swann my admiration for them, "if you did mention me to Mme Swann, I would be indebted to you for life—my life would be yours! However, I should just point out that I don't know Mme Swann and have never been introduced to her."

This final statement I added only out of a punctilious concern not to be thought to be boasting improperly of an acquaintance to which I could lay no claim. But even as I spoke the words, I could sense there was now no purpose for them to serve. The warmth of my thanks was so chilling in its effect that, from the first syllable, I caught a glimpse of hesitancy and annoyance flitting across the ambassador's face, and saw in his eyes that cramped, vertical, averted expression (like the obliquely receding line of one side of a figure, in a projection) meant for the invisible listener one carries within, and to whom one addresses a remark that one's other listener, the person one has been talking to—in this case, me—is not supposed to catch. I realized at once that the words I had uttered, quite inadequate as they were to express the huge rush of gratitude that swept through me, and though it had seemed to me they could not fail to touch M. de Norpois, and must succeed in persuading him to act in a way which would afford him so little trouble while affording me so much joy, were perhaps the very ones (among all the potentially evil words that might have been spoken by people wishing to harm me) which would make him decide not to. And just as when a stranger with whom we have been agreeably exchanging what appear to be shared opinions on passersby, who we both think are vulgar, suddenly shows the real pathological distance separating us by patting his pocket and saying casually, "Mmm, pity I didn't bring my revolver with me—I could have picked 'em all off," so, when he heard me speak these words, M. de Norpois, knowing that nothing was easier or less prized than to be recommended to Mme Swann and to join her circle, but seeing also that for me this represented something of such value that it must be assumed to be out of my reach, decided that the seemingly unexceptionable wish I had expressed must actually conceal some quite different ulterior motive, a dubious intent or the memory of a *faux pas,* which must be the reason why no one had ever wished to offend Mme Swann by undertaking to put in a word for me. I realized then that M. de Norpois would never put in such a word, that even if he saw Mme Swann daily for years on end he would never once mention my name in her hearing. However, a few days after this, he did find out from her some information I had asked for and passed it on to me via my father. He had not seen fit to tell her on whose behalf he was seeking the information. She would therefore not learn that I was acquainted with M. de Norpois or that I longed to visit her house. This was perhaps less of a disaster than I thought; for, even if she had learned of this longing, it would probably have done little to increase the effect of my being acquainted with M. de Norpois, as this acquaintance was itself of doubtful benefit to me. Since the notion of her own life and house caused no mysterious agitation in Odette's heart, she did not see the people of her acquaintance, the people who visited her house, as the fabulous beings they were to one who, like me, would have been glad to throw a stone through the Swanns' front window if only I could have written on it that I knew M. de Norpois—I was sure that such a message, even if delivered in such a startling fashion, would do more to recommend me to the lady of the house than it would to prejudice her against me. But even if I had been able to comprehend that M. de Norpois's unaccomplished mission would in any event have been useless, or that it might actually have biased the Swanns against me, even if M. de Norpois had been willing to comply with my request, I would never have had the courage to withdraw it and forgo the ecstasy, however baneful its consequences might be for me, of knowing that my name and person were, just for a moment, in the presence of Gilberte, inside her unknown house and life.

After M. de Norpois's departure, my father glanced at the evening paper, while I sat thinking over my experience of La Berma. The pleasure I had taken in seeing her act was so far from the pleasure I had been looking forward to, and was in such acute need of sustenance, that it immediately assimilated whatever might nourish it, such as the qualities M. de Norpois had identified in her acting, which my mind had absorbed as easily as a parched meadow soaks up water. My father now handed me the newspaper, pointing to a review of the matinee: "The performance of *Phèdre* given today before an enthusiastic audience, distinguished by the presence of the foremost personalities in the world of the arts and criticism, afforded Mme Berma in the title part the opportunity to score a triumph than which, in the whole course of her illustrious career, she has rarely had a greater. We shall have more, much more, to say on another occasion about this production, which marks a veritable milestone in the theater. Suffice it for the moment to note that the best-qualified judges are as one in pronouncing that such an interpretation will stand not only as a landmark in our appreciation of the character of Phèdre, one of the greatest and the most searching parts ever produced by Racine, but also as the finest, highest achievement in the realm of art that any of us have been privileged to witness in this day and age." This new concept of "the finest, highest achievement in the realm of art" had no sooner entered my mind than it located the imperfect enjoyment I had had at the theater, and added to it a little of what it lacked; this made such a heady mixture that I exclaimed, "What a great artiste she is!" It may be thought I was not altogether sincere. Think, however, of so many writers who, in a moment of dissatisfaction with a piece they have just written, may read a eulogy of the genius of Chateaubriand, or who may think of some other great artist whom they have dreamed of equaling, who hum to themselves a phrase of Beethoven for instance, comparing the sadness of it to the mood they have tried to capture in their prose, and are then so carried away by that perception of genius that they let it affect the way they read their own piece, no longer seeing it as they first saw it, but going so far as to hazard an act of faith in the value of it, by telling themselves, "It's not bad, you know!" without realizing that the sum total which determines their ultimate satisfaction includes the memory of Chateaubriand's brilliant pages, which they have assimilated to their own, but which, of course, they did not write. Think of all the men who go on believing in the love of a mistress in whom nothing is more flagrant than her infidelities; of all those torn between the hope of something beyond this life (such as the bereft widower who remembers a beloved wife, or the artist who indulges in dreams of posthumous fame, each of them looking forward to an afterlife which he knows is inconceivable) and the desire for a reassuring oblivion, when their better judgment reminds them of the faults they might otherwise have to expiate after death; or think of the travelers who are uplifted by the general beauty of a journey they have just completed, although during it their main impression, day after day, was that it was a chore—think of them before deciding whether, given the promiscuity of the ideas that lurk within us, a single one of those that afford us our greatest happiness has not begun life by parasitically attaching itself to a foreign idea with which it happened to come into contact, and by drawing from it much of the power of pleasing which it once lacked.

My mother did not seem very happy that my father had given up all thought of a diplomatic career for me. I think she lived in the hope of seeing my nervous susceptibility subjected to the discipline of an ordered way of life, and that her real regret was not so much that I was abandoning diplomacy as that I was taking up literature. "Oh, look, give it up," my father exclaimed. "The main thing is to enjoy what one does in life. He's not a child anymore, he knows what he likes, he's probably not going to change, he's old enough to know what'll make him happy in life." These words of my father's, though they granted me the freedom to be happy or not in life, made me very unhappy that evening. At each one of his unexpected moments of indulgence toward me, I had always wanted to kiss him on his florid cheeks, just above the beard line; and the only thing that ever restrained me was the fear of annoying him. On this occasion, much as an author, to whom his own conceptions seem to have little value because he cannot think of them as separate from himself, may be alarmed at seeing his publishers putting themselves to the trouble of selecting an appropriate paper for them and setting them in a typeface that he may think too fine, I began to doubt whether my desire to write was a thing of sufficient importance for my father to lavish such kindness upon it. But it was especially what he said about my likings probably never changing, and what would make me happy in life, that planted two dreadful suspicions in my mind. The first was that, though I met each new day with the thought that I was now on the threshold of life, which still lay before me all unlived and was about to start the very next day, not only had my life in fact begun, but the years to come would not be very different from the years already elapsed. The second, which was really only a variant of the first, was that I did not live outside Time but was subject to its laws, as completely as the fictional characters whose lives, for that very reason, had made me feel so sad when I read of them at Combray, sitting inside my wickerwork shelter. Theoretically, we are aware that the earth is spinning, but in reality we do not notice it: the ground we walk on seems to be stationary and gives no cause for alarm. The same happens with Time. To make its passing perceptible, novelists have to turn the hands of the clock at dizzying speed, to make the reader live through ten, twenty, thirty years in two minutes. At the top of a page, we have been with a lover full of hope; at the foot of the following one, we see him again, already an octogenarian, hobbling his painful daily way round the courtyard of an old-people's home, barely acknowledging greetings, remembering nothing of his past. When my father said, "He's not a child anymore, he's not going to change his mind," etc., he suddenly showed me myself living inside Time; and he filled me with sadness, as though I was not quite the senile inmate of the poorhouse, but one of those heroes dismissed by the writer in the final chapter with a turn of phrase that is cruel in its indifference: "He has taken to absenting himself less and less from the countryside. He has eventually settled down there for good," etc.

My father, in an attempt to forestall any criticism we might have to make about his guest, said to my mother:

"I must say old Norpois *was* rather 'old hat,' as you two say. When he said it would 'not have been seemly' to ask a question of the Comte de Paris, I was afraid you might burst out laughing."

"Not at all," my mother replied. "I'm full of admiration for a man of his caliber and his age who hasn't lost that simple touch. All it shows is a fundamental honesty and good breeding."

"But of course! And that doesn't prevent him from being acute and intelligent either, as I know from my dealings with him at the Select Committee, where he's quite different from how he was here tonight," my father said, very pleased to see that Mama appreciated M. de Norpois, and trying to persuade her that he was even more admirable than she thought, for cordiality magnifies merit as gladly as pettiness minimizes it. "How did he put it again: 'One never knows with princes . . .'?"

"Yes, that was it. I thought it was very clever when I heard it. Anyone can see he's a man with a broad experience of life."

"Isn't it remarkable that he dined at the Swanns', though? And that the people he met there are really quite normal, I mean civil-service types. Where on earth can Mme Swann have dug up people like that, I wonder?"

"Did you notice the mischievous way he phrased his remark about 'a house at which most of the guests appear to be . . . men'?"

Both of them tried to imitate M. de Norpois's delivery of this comment, as though it had been a line spoken by Bressant or Thiron in *L'Aventurière* or *Le Gendre de M. Poirier*.[17] But the person who most enjoyed one of M. de Norpois's *obiter dicta* was Françoise: years later, she could still not "keep a straight face" if you reminded her that she had once been called "a chef of superlative quality," an accolade which my mother had relayed to her down in the kitchen, as the minister of war passes on the congratulations of a visiting head of state after the review of the troops. (I had been down to the kitchen before her, having earlier extracted from Françoise, the bloodthirsty pacifist, a promise not to inflict too much pain on the rabbit she had had to kill, and wishing to know how it had met its death. Françoise assured me that everything had gone off perfectly, very quickly: "I never seen any animal like that. It just died without saying a single word. Maybe it was dumb. . . ." Unversed in the speech habits of animals, I suggested that perhaps rabbits do not screech quite like chickens. "Oh, what a thing to say!" Françoise gasped in indignation at such ignorance. "As if a rabbit wouldn't screech as loud as a chicken! They've actually got much louder voices!") Françoise accepted M. de Norpois's compliments with all the simple pride, the joyous and (albeit momentarily) intelligent look of the artist listening to talk of his art. My mother had once sent her to certain celebrated restaurants to see how they did the cooking. I was as pleased to hear Françoise call some of the most famous ones "just feeding places" as I had once been to learn that, with respect to actors, the reputed order of their merits was different from the real one. "The ambassador insisted," my mother said, "that one can't get cold beef or soufflés like yours anywhere!" Françoise agreed with this, as though accepting in all modesty a simple statement of fact, and without being in the slightest impressed by the title of ambassador. She said of M. de Norpois, with the fellow-feeling due to somebody who had thought she was a chef, "He's a good old bloke, just like me." She had of course tried to catch a glimpse of him as he arrived; but, knowing that Mama detested any spying at doors or windows, and being convinced that, if she did try to look out for him, the other servants or else the concierge and his wife would "tell on her" (Françoise lived surrounded by "backbitings" and "telltalings," which in her imagination played the same unchanging sinister role as others believe is played by the machinations of the Jesuits or the Jews), she had been satisfied to risk a glance at him through the kitchen hatch, "so her upstairs wouldn't have a bone to pick"; and in that summary glimpse of M. de Norpois she had concluded he was "the spitting image of M. Legrandin" because of his "nimbleness" (even though the two men had not a single feature in common). "But look," my mother asked her, "how do you explain that nobody can make beef jelly like you—when you feel like it, that is?" "Well, now, I don't know as I know how that becomes about, madame," replied Françoise, who made no clear distinction between the verbs "come," in some of its usages, and "become." This was the truth, of course, at least in part, as Françoise was no more able (or willing) to reveal the mystery behind the superiority of her jellies and custards than a fine fashionable lady would have been to divulge the secret of her elegance in dress, or a great prima donna the secret of her singing. Such explanations never reveal much in any case; and the same held true for our cook's recipes. "They always cook everything in too much of a hurry," she said of the famous restaurateurs whose establishments she had visited. "And they don't do the things together. I mean, the beef has got to turn into a sort of sponge, so it soaks up all the gravy. Though I must say there *was* one of them cafés where I thought they knew a thing or two about cooking. Mind you, I'm not saying they could manage *my* jelly, but it was done nice and slow, nice and gentle, you know, and the soufflés had plenty of cream in them." "Was that at the Henry?" asked my father, who had just come in, and who had a high opinion of the restaurant on the Place Gaillon, where he and his colleagues dined at regular intervals. "Oh, no, sir," Françoise replied, concealing her deep disdain in a mild tone. "I was talking about a little restaurant. At that Henry's, it's all very good of course, but it's not really a restaurant, is it? More like a . . . soup kitchen!" "Do you mean Weber's, then?"[18] "Oh no, sir! I'm talking about a *good* restaurant! Weber's is on the rue Royale, and it's not a real restaurant, it's only a flashy big café. And I'm sure they don't even serve you properly. I don't think they've even got tablecloths! They just bring it along and plunk it down in front of you, just like that." "Was it Cirro's?" "Well, now," Françoise said, smiling, "I'm pretty sure that, as far as cooking, what *they* go in for is ladies of virtue." To Françoise, "virtue" meant "easy virtue." "Well, I mean, it's for the young ones, isn't it?" In her views of famous chefs, we could see that, for all her air of simplicity, Françoise was as devastating a "colleague" as the most envious and self-centered actress toward her peers. But we felt she had a proper sense of her art and a respect for tradition when she added, "No, it was a restaurant where the cooking looked nice, like right and proper, kind of home cooking. But still a big sort of a place. You should see the business they do, the money they make, the pennies they rake in!" The economical Françoise always spoke in pennies, leaving the golden *louis* to the bankrupt. "*You* know, madame, up on the big boulevards, along on the right there, set back a little bit. . . ." The restaurant of which she was speaking with such fair-mindedness mingled with pride and nonchalance turned out to be the Café Anglais![19]

When New Year's Day came around, my first occupation was to accompany Mama on family visits. So as not to tire me, she had my father map out an itinerary for us; and she arranged our calls according to which part of town our relatives lived in, rather than in any order of family precedence. But we had hardly set foot in the drawing room of a rather distant cousin—the lack of distance to her house being the reason why she was first on the list—when my mother was horrified to see, among the bringers of the seasonal offerings *marrons glacés* and *marrons déguisés,* the best friend of the touchiest of my uncles, who would therefore be informed that we had seen fit to make our first visit of the morning to someone other than himself. My uncle would be sure to be offended, as he would no doubt have taken it for granted that we should go all the way down from the Madeleine to his house, near the Jardin des Plantes, then come all the way back to Saint-Augustin before crossing the river again to go to the rue de l'École-de-Médecine.

When these visits were finished, my grandmother having excused us from making one to her as we were to dine with her that evening, I dashed to the Champs-Élysées with a letter for Gilberte, which I wanted to give to our woman in the booth, who would pass it on to the servant of the Swanns' who bought the spice cake from her several times a week. This letter was a New Year's Day message, which I had decided to write to Gilberte on the day when she had made me so unhappy, in which I told her that our former friendship had died with the old year, that I was going to forget my grievances and disappointments, and that, from January 1, we were going to build together a new friendship, which would be so sound that nothing could destroy it, and so wonderful that I hoped she would try to take pride in it, keep it beautiful, and warn me in good time, as I promised to do for her too, of anything that might jeopardize its well-being. On the way home, Françoise made me stop at an open-air stand on the corner of the rue Royale, where she spent her New Year's gratuity on two photographs, one of Pius IX and the other of Raspail,[20] and where I bought one of La Berma. The artiste's face, her only one, seemed a meager gratification to offer to so many admirers: as unvarying and vulnerable as the coat worn by people who have no more than one to wear, all it could ever display was the same soft little groove on the upper lip, the high-set eyebrows, and a few other physical features, always the same ones, always susceptible to a chance burn or blow. It was a face which of itself would not have seemed beautiful; but because of all the kissing it must have had, kissing which its flirtatiously tender looks and archly innocent smile still seemed to invite from the surface of the "album copy," it gave me the idea and consequently the desire to kiss it myself. After all, the desires that La Berma confessed through the disguise of Phèdre she must often experience for young men in real life; and everything, including the prestige of her name, which enhanced her beauty and extended her youth, must make it easy for her to satisfy those desires. In the gathering dusk, I stood beside a Morris column with its posters announcing La Berma's New Year's Day performance. There was a mild, damp wind blowing. It was weather I was quite familiar with; and a sudden feeling and presentiment ran through me: that New Year's Day was not a day that differed from any other, not the first day of a new life, when I could remake the acquaintance of Gilberte with the die still uncast, as though on the very first day of Creation, when no past yet existed, as though the sorrows she had sometimes caused me had been wiped out, and with them all the future ones they might portend, as though I lived in a new world in which nothing remained of the old except one thing, my wish that

Gilberte would love me. I realized that, since my heart yearned in this way for the redesign of a universe which had not satisfied it, this meant that my heart had not changed; and I could see there was no reason why Gilberte's should have changed either. I sensed that, though it was a new friendship for me, it would not be a new friendship for her, just as no years are ever separated from each other by a frontier, and that, though we may put different names to them, they remain beyond the reach of our yearnings, unaware of these, and unaffected by them. Though I might dedicate this year to Gilberte, though I might try to imprint upon New Year's Day the special notion I had made up for it, as a religion is superimposed on the blind workings of nature, it was in vain: I was aware that this day did not know it was called New Year's Day, and that it was coming to an end in the twilight in a way that was not unknown to me. What I recognized, what I sensed in that mild wind blowing about the Morris column with its posters, was the reappearance of former times, with the never-ending unchangingness of their substance, their familiar dampness, their ignorant fluidity.

I went home. I had just experienced the New Year's Day of older men, who differ on that day from the young, not because nobody brings them presents, but because they no longer believe in the New Year. I had received presents; but they had not included the only one that could have brought me any pleasure: a note from Gilberte. However, I was still young, as I had been capable of writing one to her, full of the forlorn yearning for tenderness which I had hoped would inspire the same in her. The sadness of the man who has grown old is that, having learned how pointless they are, he does not even think of writing such letters.

I lay in bed, prevented from sleeping by the street noises, which went on later than usual because of the celebrations. I thought of all the people who would end the day in pleasure, the lover or possibly the band of rakes who must have waited at the stage door for La Berma, after the performance I had seen advertised for this evening. To soothe the agitation I suffered from during the sleepless night, I could not even tell myself that La Berma probably gave no thought to love, since the lines she spoke, which she had studied at great length, reminded her incessantly that love is full of delights, which she knew anyway, as was clear from her ability not only to reproduce its notorious pangs—albeit fraught with a fresh violence and an unsuspected sweetness—but to strike new wonder into spectators, though each of them had felt these pangs to the full. I lit my candle again to gaze once more at her face. At the thought that at this very moment it was being caressed by the men whom I could not prevent myself from seeing with her, from drawing superhuman but imprecise pleasures from her person, the passion I felt was a cruel rather than a sensuous yearning, exacerbated now by the note of the hunting horn one hears in the night at Mid-Lent and often at other public holidays, which, because it is devoid at such times of poetry, sounds more mournfully from a drinking den than when it "haunts the heart of the evening woods."[21] At that moment, a note from Gilberte might not have been what I most needed. Our desires interweave with each other; and in the confusion of existence, it is seldom that a joy is promptly paired with the desire that longed for it.

On fine days, I continued to go to the Champs-Élysées, through streets of elegant pink houses which, because there were a great many exhibitions of watercolorists at that time, were washed by the subdued and variable light of pastel skies. It would not be true to say that in those days the palaces of Gabriel on the Place de la Concorde seemed to me things of greater beauty than the adjoining buildings, or even that they dated from a different period.[22] To my eye there was greater style and even greater age, if not in the Palais de l'Industrie, at least in the Palais du Trocadéro.[23] My adolescence, wherever it walked, deep in its fevered sleep, saw whole districts through the same waking dream; and I had never suspected that there might be an eighteenth-century building on the rue Royale, just as I would have been astonished to learn that the Porte Saint-Martin and the Porte Saint-Denis, masterpieces dating from the days of Louis XIV, were not of the same period as the most recent constructions in the squalid areas that now surround them. Only once did one of the palaces of Gabriel make me stop and gaze for a longish moment: it was after nightfall, and the columns of stone had been desolidified by the moonlight, which, by turning them into cardboard cutouts, and reminding me of a stage set for *Orpheus in the Underworld*,[24] gave me my very first glimpse of beauty.

Gilberte had still not come back to the Champs-Élysées. Yet I very much needed to set eyes on her, as I could not even remember her face. When we look at the person we love, our inquisitive, anxious, demanding gaze, our expectation of the words that will make us hope for (or despair of) another meeting tomorrow, and, until those words are spoken, our obsession fluctuating between possible joy and sorrow, or imagining both of these together, all this distracts our tremulous attention and prevents it from getting a clear picture of the loved one. Also, it may be that this simultaneous activity of all the senses, striving to discover through the unaided eyes something that is out of their reach, is too mindful of the countless forms, all the savors and movements of the living person, all those things which, in a person with whom we are not in love, we immobilize. But the beloved model keeps moving; and the only snapshots we can take are always out of focus. I could not really say what the features of Gilberte's face were like, except at those heavenly moments when she was there, displaying them to me. All I could remember was her smile. Unable to picture the loved face, however strenuously I tried to make myself remember it, I was forever irritated to find that my memory had retained exact replicas of the striking and futile faces of the carousel man and the barley-sugar woman, just as the bereaved, who each night search their dreams in vain for the lost beloved, will find their sleep is peopled by all manner of exasperating and unbearable intruders, whom they have always found, even in the waking world, more than dislikable. Faced with the impossibility of seeing clearly the object of their grief, they come close to accusing themselves of not grieving, just as I was tempted to believe that my inability to remember the features of Gilberte's face meant that I had forgotten her and had stopped loving her. Eventually, she came back to the Champs-Élysées to play almost every day. Each time she came, she left me with new things to desire for the following day, new things to ask her; and this did have the effect of transforming my love for her into a new love every day. But then something happened to alter once again the way in which, about two o'clock every afternoon, I was faced with the problem of my love. Had M. Swann intercepted the letter I had sent to Gilberte? Or was she perhaps alluding to a state of affairs of long standing, meaning that I should be more careful? As I was telling her how much I admired her father and mother, her features started to take on that unfocused look, full of secrecy and unspoken things, which she always put on when anyone mentioned the things she had to do, visits she had to pay, shopping to be done; and suddenly she said, "They don't fancy *you* very much, you know!" Then, slipping away like a water nymph—that was how she was—she burst out laughing. There were times when her laughter was at variance with her words, and appeared to be translating an invisible surface into another dimension, as music does. Her parents were not demanding that she give up coming to play with me; but she thought they would have preferred our relationship never to have begun. They frowned upon my having any dealings with her, thought I was quite untrustworthy, and assumed that I was bound to have a bad influence on their daughter. I could imagine the type of unscrupulous young man that M. Swann thought I was: hating the parents of the girl he loves, flattering them to their faces, but making fun of them when with her, enticing her into disobedience of them, and finally, once he has had his way with her, preventing them from seeing her. Against these characteristics (which are never those that the most hardened villain sees in himself) my innocent heart protested vehemently, alleging the true nature of the feelings it held for M. Swann, which were so passionate that, if he could only know of them, I was convinced he would come to see his assessment of me as a miscarriage of justice crying out to be put right! I went so far as to set out everything I felt for him in a long letter, which I asked Gilberte to take to him. She agreed to do this—but, alas, it turned out that he took me for an even greater fraud than I had thought! He was skeptical about my sixteen pages of protestations and truth! And so the letter, which contained no less passion and sincerity than the words I had spoken to M. de Norpois, met with no more success than they had. Gilberte told me the following day, after having taken me round to a secluded little pathway behind a clump of laurel, where we sat on chairs, that as her father had read the letter, which she had brought to give back to me, he had shrugged his shoulders and said, "This whole thing is pointless. It just goes to show how right I was!" To me, knowing the innocence of my intentions, the purity of my conscience, it was galling that my words had had not the slightest effect on M. Swann's absurd misconception. For at that moment I had no doubt that it was a misconception. I was convinced that my delineation of certain unimpeachable features of my sincerest self had been so accurate that the only explanation of M. Swann's inability to recognize them through my words, as of his failure to seek me out, beg my forgiveness, and admit to his mistake, was that he had never had such noble feelings himself, and consequently that he was incapable of appreciating them in others.

Of course, Swann may well have known that magnanimity is often nothing more than the outward appearance of a selfish impulse that we have not yet seen as such or named. In my protestations of goodwill toward him, perhaps he recognized a mere effect, as well as a resounding confirmation, of my love for his daughter; and he may have foreseen that my subsequent acts would be inevitably governed by this love, and not by my secondary veneration for himself. This was not a view I could share, as I had not managed to isolate my love from myself, to see it as belonging to the same general category as any other love, and to hazard an experimental deduction about its likely consequences. I was in despair. I had to leave Gilberte for a moment, as Françoise had called me. She wanted me to go with her to a little green-trellised pavilion that looked something like one of the disused Paris tollbooths from former times, in which had recently been installed what the English call a *lavabo*[25] and the French, in their misguided Anglomania, "water closets." In the entrance, where I stood waiting for Françoise, the smell of the old damp walls, which was cool and musty, instantly freed me from the worries I had contracted from M. Swann's words as told to me by Gilberte, filling me with a pleasure that was of a different essence from all others; for they leave us more unstable, unable to grasp them or possess them, whereas this one was of a denser consistency, reliable, delightful, peaceful, pregnant with a lasting truthfulness, which was as inexplicable as it was undeniable. I would have liked to try, as I had done before, on our walks along the Guermantes way, to fathom the charm of the impression that had come over me, to pause for a moment's investigation of this old-fashioned redolence, which invited me not just to enjoy the pleasure, offered as a mere bonus, but to see through it to a reality it had not quite revealed. But the woman in charge of the establishment, an old dame with plastered cheeks and a ginger wig, struck up a conversation with us. Françoise was convinced the woman came from "her parts of the country." Her eldest had married what Françoise called "a posh young man," that is, someone who in her view differed as much from a worker as in Saint-Simon's view a duke differed from a man "belonging to the dregs of the people."[26] No doubt this woman, before becoming what she was, had been better off. But Françoise was convinced she was a countess, of the Saint-Ferréol family. The countess urged me not to stand about in the inclement air; she even opened one of her cubicles for me: "Wouldn't you like to step inside? Here's one that's nice and clean—and you can use it free of charge!" This may have been nothing more than the sort of offer I sometimes received from the sales assistants in Gouache's, who, when Mama and I were placing an order, would urge me to have one of the sweets under the glass covers standing on the counter, which my mother, to my chagrin, would never allow me to accept; or it may have been the slightly less innocent sort of suggestion made by an old florist from whom Mama bought blooms for her ornamental flower-stands, who would make eyes at me and give me a rose. But if the fancy of Françoise's countess did run to youths for whom she opened the hypogean portal into her stone cubes, where men crouch like sphinxes, the aim of this kindness toward them must have been less the chance of seducing them than the unrequited pleasure of being indulgent toward a loved one, as I never saw her being visited by anyone other than one of the old park-keepers.

Having taken leave of the "countess," I soon left Françoise to her own devices and went back to Gilberte. I saw her sitting on a chair behind the clump of laurels, so as to be invisible to her friends, with whom she was playing hide-and-seek. I sat beside her. She was wearing a flat toque, which almost covered her eyes and gave them the sly, unfocused, evasive expression I remembered from the first time I had seen it at Combray. I asked her whether there might not be a way for me to talk this thing over with her father. Gilberte said she had already suggested this, and that he could see no point in it. "Anyway, look," she said, "here's your letter back. We'd better go back to the others now, since nobody's found me."

If M. Swann had come upon us before I had managed to retrieve the letter whose sincerity he had been unreasonable enough to doubt, he might well have concluded that his doubt was fully justified. As I came close to Gilberte, who was leaning back in her chair, telling me to take the letter but not handing it to me, I felt so attracted by her body that I said:

"You try to stop me from getting it and we'll see who wins."

She held it behind her back, and I put my hands behind her neck, lifting the long plaits which hung on her shoulders, either because it was a hairstyle that suited her age, or because her mother wanted her to appear younger than she was, so as not to age too rapidly herself; and in that strained posture, we tussled with each other. I kept trying to draw her closer to me; she kept resisting. Flushed with the effort, her cheeks were as red and round as cherries; she laughed as though I were tickling her. I had her pinned between my legs as though she were the bole of a little tree I was trying to climb. In the middle of all my exertions, without my breathing being quickened much more than it already was by muscular exercise and the heat of the playful moment, like a few drops of sweat produced by the effort, I shed my pleasure, before I even had time to be aware of the nature of it, and managed to snatch the letter away from her. Gilberte said in a friendly tone:

"If you like, we could wrestle a bit more."

Perhaps she had obscurely sensed that my antics had an ulterior motive, though she may have been unable to notice that my aim was now fulfilled. However, fearing that she might have detected it (a slight movement that she made a moment later, hinting at restraint or withdrawal, as though her sense of delicacy was offended, made me suspect I was right), I agreed to wrestle with her again, in case she might think my only purpose, now achieved, had been the pleasure that left me feeling no desire other than to sit quietly beside her.

On the way home, I suddenly recognized the hitherto hidden memory of the impression that I had been drawn toward by the cool, almost sooty air of the little trellised booth, but without being able to glimpse it or identify it. It was the memory of my uncle Adolphe's little room in the house at Combray, which was full of the same dampish redolence. I could not understand, and I postponed the effort of finding out, why the memory of such an insignificant impression should have filled me with such bliss. This made me feel that I really did deserve the disdain of M. de Norpois: not only was my favorite writer someone he dismissed as a "flute-player," but I had experienced a moment of genuine rapture, not from some idea of importance, but from a musty smell.

For some time, if a visitor chanced to mention the gardens of the Champs-Élysées in certain family circles, the name had been greeted by the mothers with the jaundiced look with which they might deprecate a mention of a highly regarded doctor who they claim has made too many mistakes of diagnosis for them to place any trust in him—these gardens, it was said, were not good for children, and were responsible for too many cases of sore throats, measles, and different sorts of fevers. When my mother did not forbid my visits to the Champs-Élysées, some of her friends, though not openly questioning her love for me, did at least doubt her wisdom.

Neurotics are perhaps—*pace* accepted wisdom—those who "coddle themselves" the least: they are so used to detecting disorders in themselves, which they later come to realize were quite harmless, that they reach the stage of paying no attention to any of them. Their nervous system has so often cried wolf, as though it is faced with a serious illness, when it has nothing more untoward to contend with than a fall of snow or a move to a new flat, that they come to ignore these warnings, as easily as a soldier in the heat of battle can avert his mind from them and, for another few days, even though he is dying, go on leading the life of a healthy man. One forenoon, with my habitual disorders in their usual state of coordination, my mind paying as little attention to their constant circulation within me as to the circulation of my blood, I ran cheerfully into the dining room to join my parents at the table and sat down, with the customary thought that feeling cold may mean, not that you should try to get warm, but only that you have been chided for something, and that not feeling hungry may mean it is going to rain, rather than that you should avoid eating. As soon as I started to swallow my first mouthful of an appetizing chop, I was overcome by a wave of vertigo and nausea, the feverish response of my body to an illness which had already begun, to which my indifference had turned a blind eye, masking and delaying the symptoms, but which was now adamantly refusing the food I was in no state to absorb. At the same instant, like a wounded man's instinct of self-preservation, the thought that, if I was seen to be unwell, I would not be allowed out, gave me the strength to drag myself to my room, take my temperature (it was 104), and get ready to go to the Champs-Élysées. My smiling soul, through the permeable and sickly body that surrounded it, was already there, insisting on the sweet pleasure of a game of prisoner's base with Gilberte; and an hour later, barely able to stand but happy to be with her, I still had enough strength left to enjoy it.

When we got back home, Françoise announced that I had "had a turn," that I must have caught "a touch of the chill"; and the doctor, who was immediately summoned, announced that he "preferred" the "fierce onset" and the "virulence" of the attack of fever accompanying my lung congestion, which he said would turn out to be nothing but a "flash in the pan," to a more "insidious" or "lurking" form of it. For years I had suffered from attacks of shortness of breath; and our doctor, despite the disapproval of my grandmother, who was convinced I would go to an alcoholic's early grave, had recommended that, in addition to the caffeine already prescribed as an aid to my breathing, I should have a drink of beer, champagne, or brandy each time I felt an attack coming on. The "euphoria" brought on by the alcohol would, he said, "nip it in the bud." Rather than conceal the state of breathlessness I was in, I was often obliged almost to exaggerate it before my grandmother would allow me to have such a drink. Also, as soon as I felt an attack coming on, my uncertainty about how serious it might or might not be became a more acute anxiety because of my grandmother's sorrow, which always upset me more than the fit itself. However, my body, whether because it was too infirm to bear the stress of keeping this secret to itself, or because it feared that someone unaware of the imminence of the attack might require me to make an effort that would prove impossible or harmful to it, made me need to inform my grandmother of my discomfort with a degree of accuracy that I eventually came to invest with a sort of physiological realism. If I noticed within me a bothersome symptom I had never before identified, my body remained distressed until I could let my grandmother know. If she pretended not to pay attention, my body required me to persevere. Sometimes I went too far; and, wincing with pain, the loved face, which was not as skilled as it had once been at concealing its emotions, showed an expression of pity. The sight of her grief cut me to the quick, and I fell into her arms, as though my kisses might take the grief away, as though my love for her could cause her as much joy as my being well and happy. My anxiety being now lessened by the knowledge that she was aware of the discomfort I had been in, my body had no objection to my reassuring her. I told her there was nothing distressing in the discomfort, that she must not feel sorry for me, that she could be sure I was happy. My body had been trying to receive as much sympathy as it deserved; and as long as it was known that it had a pain in its right side, it did not mind if I stated that the pain was neither severe nor an impediment to my happiness. My body did not take itself for a philosopher; philosophy was not its province. During my convalescence, I had fits of breathlessness like this almost every day. On one occasion, when my grandmother had seen me quite well earlier in the evening, she came back into my room much later; and when she saw how short of breath I was, her face was stricken with grief and she moaned, "Oh dear, oh dear! You're so ill!" She went straight out, I heard the *porte cochère,* and she came back in a little while with a bottle of brandy, which, as we had none in the house, she had gone out to buy. I soon started to feel better. My grandmother was rather flushed and looked embarrassed; and her eyes were full of an expression of weariness and discouragement.

"I think I'll leave you, now that it's doing you a little good," she said, turning quickly away. I had time to kiss her and to feel something wet on her cool cheek, which I thought might have been a trace of the damp night air out of doors. The following day she did not come in to see me till the evening, as she had had to go out, I was told. I thought to myself that this showed a fairly indifferent attitude toward my well-being; and I had a good mind to tell her so.

When my attacks of breathlessness went on inexplicably, long after my pleurisy had cleared up, my parents called in Dr. Cottard. A doctor consulted in a case like this must be more than just well versed. In the face of symptoms which may be those of three or four different illnesses, the thing that enables him to decide which of them he is most likely to be dealing with, behind appearances that are very similar, is ultimately his flair, the sharpness of his eye. This mysterious gift implies no superiority in other aspects of the mind, and may be found even in a person of the utmost vulgarity, someone who is devoid of intellectual curiosity and who enjoys the most dreadful painting or music. In my case, what was externally observable might have been caused by nervous spasms, the early stages of tuberculosis, asthma, a toxic alimentary dyspnea with renal insufficiency, chronic bronchitis, or even a complex condition comprising several of these factors. The nervous spasms needed to be treated with disdain, the tuberculosis with great care and a form of over-nutrition, which could have been bad for an arthritic condition like asthma, and possibly dangerous for a toxic alimentary dyspnea, which in its turn requires a regimen quite harmful to a patient suffering from tuberculosis. But Dr. Cottard barely hesitated before issuing the imperious command: "Drastic, violent purgatives. Milk and nothing but milk for several days. No meat. No alcohol." My mother murmured that I really needed building up, that I was high-strung enough as it was, that this draconian purging and such a regimen would be hard on me. From Dr. Cottard's eyes, which looked as anxious as though he were afraid of missing a train, I could see he was wondering whether he might not have behaved with his natural mildness of manner. He was trying to re-member whether he had made sure to put on his mask of frigidity, the way one looks for a mirror to see whether one has not neglected to knot one's tie. In this uncertainty, and so as to compensate just in case, he barked rudely, "I am not in the habit of repeating my prescriptions. Get me a pen. Milk, milk, that's the main thing. After a while, once we've dealt with the attacks of breathlessness and the insomnia, we can start taking some clear soup, then some broth, but always and still with milk—milk, that's the thing! You'll like that, because Spain is fashionable these days—*olé! au lait!*"[27] His students were familiar with this pun, which he trotted out whenever he prescribed a milk diet for a cardiac case or a patient with a liver disorder. "Then we can gradually come back to the ordinary family diet. But if ever the cough and the breathlessness come back, purgatives, enemas, bed, and milk!" With an icy demeanor, he heard out my mother's final objections, saying nothing in return, then took his leave without so much as a word to explain why he had chosen this treatment. My parents, taking a view that it was irrelevant to my condition and needlessly debilitating, decided not to try it. They naturally sought to keep the professor in ignorance of their lack of compliance; and to make sure of this, they stayed away from any of the houses where they might have run the risk of meeting him. Then, my condition having worsened, they decided to follow Dr. Cottard's instructions to the letter; three days later, all the rattling in my chest had gone, my cough had cleared up, and I could breathe properly. We came to understand that Cottard, though, as he said later, he had thought I was asthmatic and especially "not quite right in the head," had seen clearly that what predominated in me at that moment was a toxic reaction, that the liver and kidneys had therefore to be washed out, thus decongesting the bronchial tubes and enabling me to breathe and sleep again, and regain my strength. So it was we realized that Cottard the buffoon was a great doctor. At length I was able to get up. But the talk now was of not allowing me to go back to the Champs-Élysées. The reason given was the unhealthy air. But I was sure this was just an excuse for them to keep me away from Mlle Swann; and I made myself say over and over the name of Gilberte, as though it were a native tongue and I one of those captives in exile who endeavor to keep it alive, so as not to forget the homeland they will never see again. Sometimes my mother would stroke my forehead and say:

"Don't little boys tell their sorrows to their mamas anymore?"

Every day, Françoise would come in and say: "Ooh, young master don't look so good! You should take a look at yourself—you're like death warmed up!" Of course, if I had had the merest cold, Françoise would have been just as lugubrious. Her lamentations were inspired by her "class" rather than by my ill health. At that time I could not be sure whether Françoise was a pessimist more in sorrow than in satisfaction. I decided provisionally that she was a social and professional pessimist.

One day, when the postman had just come, my mother laid a letter on my bed. I opened it, my mind elsewhere, as it could not possibly contain the only signature which would have made me happy, that of Gilberte Swann, because I never had any contact with her away from the Champs-Élysées. Yet there, at the bottom of the page, which was stamped with a silver seal in the form of a helmeted knight surmounting a scrolled motto *Per viam rectam,* at the end of a letter in an expansive hand, which seemed to have underlined nearly all the sentences, because the crossbar of every *t* was dashed above the letter and not through it, thus scratching a line under the corresponding word in the line above, the signature I read *was* Gilberte's! However, because I knew this signature to be impossible in a letter addressed to me, the sight of it, unaccompanied as it was by any belief in it, brought me no happiness. For a moment, all it did was cast an unreal light on everything around me. At dizzying speed, the improbable signature jumbled the things in my room, the bed, the fireplace, the walls. Everything I looked at was wobbling, as though I had had a fall from a horse; and I wondered whether there might not be some other mode of existence, quite different from the one known to me, at variance with it but more real than it, which in the glimpse I had just caught of it had filled me with the hesitancy which sculptors depicting the Last Judgment show on the faces of the awakened dead, who stand already on the threshold of the Other World. The letter said: "Dear Friend, I hear you have been very ill and are not going to the Champs-Élysées now. I've almost stopped going there too, because of everybody falling ill. But my girlfriends come to tea with me every Monday and Friday. My mother wants you to know we should be very pleased if you could come too, as soon as you are well again. We could have nice chats at home the way we used to at the Champs-Élysées! So, in the hope that your parents will allow you to come to afternoon tea very soon, I say goodbye and send you all my best wishes. Gilberte."

While I was reading these words, my nervous system, with admirable diligence, was receiving the news that a great joy was descending upon me. But my inner self, the one most closely concerned after all, was still in ignorance of it. Happiness, happiness from Gilberte, was something I had constantly thought about, something that existed only in thought, something like what Leonardo da Vinci said about painting, *cosa mentale.* And thought cannot instantly assimilate a sheet of paper covered in letters. But as soon as I had finished reading it, I thought about it, and it became an object of reflection; it too became *cosa mentale,* and I felt such love for it that every five minutes I had to read it again and kiss it. It was then that I became aware of my happiness.

Such miracles lie in wait for the lover, who may expect one at any time. This particular one may have been arranged by my mother, who, seeing that for some time past I had lost all pleasure in living, had perhaps had a message transmitted to Gilberte, asking her to write to me, much as, in earlier days, when I was learning to swim in the sea, she would, unbeknown to me, to make me enjoy swimming under water, which I hated, as it prevented me from breathing, give wonderful boxes covered in seashells and branches of coral to my swimming instructor, so that, when I came upon them lying on the seabed, I could believe they were my own discoveries. In any case, it is best not to inquire into how life, with all its contrasting developments, can impinge upon our love: the laws that govern such things, whether their workings are inexorable or just unexpected, seem to be those of magic rather than of rationality. When a woman who is plain and without money of her own leaves a multimillionaire with whom she has been living, a man of charm despite his wealth, and when he in his despair summons up all the powers of his wealth and sets in motion all the influences of this world, but fails to get her to come back to him, rather than seeking a logical explanation, it is better to assume, in the face of the willful mistress's resolve, that Destiny wishes to crush him and make him die of a broken heart. The obstacles against which such a lover has to struggle, and which his imagination, overstimulated by suffering, tries vainly to identify, may lie in a singularity of character of the wayward woman, in her stupidity, in the influence now exercised on her by people whom the lover does not know, in fears they may have put into her mind, in appetites she is briefly bent on satisfying, which may be of the sort that her lover, with all his fortune, cannot satisfy. Moreover, the lover who seeks to know the nature of such obstacles is handicapped: the woman's guile will hide it from him; and his own judgment, biased by his love, prevents him from assessing it accurately. Obstacles of this kind are like tumors that a doctor may succeed at last in reducing without ever knowing what caused them: though temporary, they remain mysterious. However, such obstacles generally last longer than love. And as love is not a disinterested passion, the erstwhile lover no longer strives to find out why, in her need and obstinacy, the flighty woman whom he once loved declined for years to let him go on keeping her.

In love, it is not only the causes of catastrophe that may lie forever beyond our grasp: just as often we remain in ignorance of the whys and wherefores of sudden outcomes that are happier—such as the one that Gilberte's letter brought to me—or, rather, outcomes which appear to be happy, as there are few truly happy outcomes in the life of a feeling, which can generally look for no better reward than a shift in the site of the pain it entails. At times, however, a temporary remission is granted, and for a while one may have the illusion of being cured.

As for the letter itself (on which Françoise refused to recognize the name Gilberte, because the *G* leaning against an undotted *i* was so embellished that it looked more like an *A*, while the last part of the name ran on into a fancy elongated flourish), if it is deemed that a rational explanation is required for the change of heart which it signaled, and which brought me such joy, perhaps it will be said I owed it in part to an incident that I had actually expected would be the sort of thing to damn me forever in the sight of the Swanns. Not long before, at a moment when Professor Cottard happened to be with me—now that I was following his instructions, my parents had called him in again—Bloch had come up to see me. The consultation was over, and since Dr. Cottard, who was staying to dine with my parents, was sitting with me like any visitor, Bloch too was allowed in. In the course of conversation,

Bloch having told how he had heard from someone whom he had met at dinner the previous night, someone who was very close to Mme Swann, that she was very fond of me, I knew I should tell him he was quite certainly mistaken, and thus, in accordance with the scruple that had moved me to speak of the same thing to M. de Norpois, and in case Mme Swann should think I was a liar, have it acknowledged once for all that I did not know her, and had never so much as spoken to her. But I did not have the courage to correct Bloch's error, because I could see well enough it was a deliberate one, and because I knew that, in inventing something that Mme Swann could never in fact have said, he was trying to show himself in a flattering light by saying another thing which was untrue: that he had dined with a lady who was a friend of Mme Swann's. However, whereas M. de Norpois, on learning that I did not know Mme Swann but would very much like to, had been careful not to mention me to her, Cottard, who was her doctor, having deduced from Bloch's statement that she knew me very well and liked me, said to himself that, if he told her the next time he saw her that I was a charming fellow and that he knew me well, he would not be pushing me forward but would be putting himself in a good light, two reasons which persuaded him to put in a good word for me with Odette at the first opportunity.

And so that apartment opened to me, sending the perfume used by Mme Swann down the stairs to greet me, and welcoming me with an even more fragrant charm, which was the specific and forlorn flavor of the life led by Gilberte. Before long, when I asked the once-implacable concierge, now transformed into a benevolent Eumenid, whether I could go upstairs, he took to raising his cap with an auspicious hand, which showed my wish was granted. Soon, when I had spent a whole summer afternoon in Gilberte's room, it fell to me to open the very windows which, from the outside, had once interposed between me and treasures not meant for me a gleaming, haughty, and superficial glance, which had seemed like the gaze of the Swanns themselves; yet now I was the one to let some fresh air in, or even, if it was her mother's at-home day, to lean out alongside Gilberte and see the ladies as they arrived, stepping out of a carriage and sometimes glancing up to wave to me, as though thinking I was a nephew of their hostess. At such moments, Gilberte's plaits would touch my cheek. Her hair seemed to me, in the delicacy of its grain, both natural and supernatural; and in the power of its artful foliations I saw a masterwork crafted from grasses grown in paradise. If I could have had even the tiniest sample of it, a heavenly herbarium would have been the only fitting repository for it. But since I could not hope to possess a real length of her hair, if I could have had just a photograph of it, how much more precious it would have been than any picture of little flowers drawn by Leonardo! To this end, I made compromising overtures to family friends of the Swanns, and even to photographers, which did not get me what I wanted, but made me the victim of not a few veteran bores.

Whenever I stepped into the Swanns' dim anteroom, where the atmosphere thrilled with the perpetual possibility of meeting one or the other of Gilberte's parents, who had for so long prevented me from seeing her, an encounter more awesome but more longed for than a glimpse of the King would have been at Versailles (and where I would trip over a huge seven-branched coatrack like the Candlestick in Scripture,[28] before effusively greeting a footman who sat in his long gray frock coat on the firewood chest, and whom I mistook in the half-dark for Mme Swann), if she or her husband did happen to cross my path at that moment, my hand was shaken, I was smiled upon and spoken to in an unirritated voice:

"Good afternoon! Gilberte knows you're here, does she? Good, good, that's fine, then." Both of her parents, by the way, said "Good aft'noon," pronouncing "afternoon" without the middle syllable, which of course, as soon as I was back at home, it became my incessant pastime and pleasure to omit too.

But the most important thing was that the tea parties to which Gilberte's girlfriends were invited, and which had for such a long time seemed the most impregnable of the many barriers separating her from me, had now become an opportunity for being with her. To these functions I was summoned, as a still quite recent acquaintance, on a variety of different notepapers. One of them was embossed with a blue poodle over a humorous English motto ending in an exclamation point; another was stamped with a ship's anchor. Once, the monogram G.S., hugely magnified and elongated, was bounded by a rectangle running right down the page from top to bottom; on other occasions, it would be the name *Gilberte* either scrawled across one corner in golden letters imitating her signature and final flourish, and sheltering under an open umbrella printed in black, or else enclosed inside a motif in the shape of a Chinaman's hat, on which the name figured in capital letters, none of which was individually legible. And as her range of notepapers, though extensive, was not inexhaustible, after a few weeks I would receive an invitation written on the one she had sent first, with the motto *Per viam rectam* under the helmeted knight on his seal of burnished silver. In those days, I assumed her choice of this one or that one on particular days was determined by certain rites. But now I think she just tried to remember the ones she had already sent, so as to be sure of letting the longest possible time elapse before sending another of the same to any of the recipients, or at least to anyone for whom she did not mind taking a little trouble. Because some of the friends invited to her teas attended different classes at different times of the afternoon, and had to leave just as others were arriving, on my way up the stairs I could hear the murmur of voices from the anteroom; and this, combined with the emotional disturbance created by the awe-inspiring ceremony which was about to be enacted before me, suddenly severed the links that joined me to my former life and, long before I reached the Swanns' floor, deprived me of the ability to remember to take off my scarf as soon as I was indoors in the warmth, or to keep an eye on the time so as not to be late home. The staircase itself, entirely of wood and of the style favored at the time by certain speculative builders who liked imitation Renaissance, so long Odette's ideal but soon to be abandoned by her, was adorned with a notice saying *It Is Forbidden to Use the Elevator for Coming Down,* the like of which had never been seen in the house we lived in; and it impressed me as a thing of such magnificence that I told my parents it was a genuine antique staircase, acquired by M. Swann and brought there by him from somewhere very far away. My respect for the truth was so great that, even if I had known this information to be untrue, I would still have said the same thing, for this was the only

way to have my family share the esteem inspired in me by the dignity of
the Swanns' staircase. It was a reasoning akin to that which advises one,
when dealing with an ignoramus who cannot see the genius of a great
doctor, to say nothing of his inability to cure the common cold. But
since I was very inobservant, being generally ignorant of the names and
species of the most everyday things, knowing only that if they had anything to do with the Swanns they must be quite out of the ordinary, it
did not strike me as a certainty that, in assuring my parents of the aesthetic value and distant origin of this staircase, I was telling a lie. Not a
certainty; but perhaps a probability, as I felt myself turn very red when
my father interrupted me with the words: "I know those kind of houses,
and if you've seen one, you've seen them all. Swann just rents a few
floors—they were all built by Berlier."[29] He added that he had at one
time thought of renting an apartment in one of them, but had changed
his mind because they were not really comfortable, and the main entrance was badly lit. Thus spake my father; but, knowing instinctively
that my mind must make whatever sacrifices might be necessary to the
prestige of the Swanns and my own happiness, I exercised the authority
of my inner self and, despite what I had just heard, put behind me once
and for all, as a true Catholic might shun Renan's *Life of Jesus*,[30] the cor-
rosive notion that the Swanns' apartment was a perfectly ordinary apartment, an apartment that we ourselves might have lived in.

So, on Gilberte's afternoon-tea days, I climbed that staircase, step by
step, divested already of memory and the power of thought, reduced to
a creature of the crudest reflexes, and came at last to the level where the
fragrance of Mme Swann's perfume floated. My mind was full of the
majestic chocolate cake set in the circle of side plates and little gray
damask napkins, required by etiquette and peculiar to the Swanns. But
the workings of this regulated and unchanging arrangement, like those
of Kant's necessary universe, seemed to depend on a supreme act of free
will. That is, once we were all gathered in Gilberte's little sitting room,
she would dart a glance at the clock and say:

"Look here, it's been hours since lunchtime, dinner's not till eight,
and I'm feeling quite hungry. Would anyone care to join me?"

Whereupon, she would show us through to the dining room, which was as dim as an Asian temple interior as Rembrandt might have painted it, and was dominated by the architectural splendor of a cake, as cheerful and familiar as it was imposing, which seemed to be standing there as though this day was an ordinary day, just in case Gilberte might have felt a passing urge to demolish its chocolate battlements and lay waste the slopes of its steep, dark ramparts, baked like the bastions of Darius' palace. The best thing was that, in setting about the destruction of her Ninevite cake-castle, Gilberte was motivated not only by the urges of her own appetite; she inquired also about mine, as she salvaged for me from the crumbling ruins a whole wall varnished and studded with scarlet fruit, in the Oriental style. She even asked me what time my parents dined, as though I knew something about it, as though the emotional upset from which I was suffering could enable any sensation such as lack of appetite or hunger, any notion of dinner or family, to survive in my vacant memory and paralyzed stomach. Unfortunately, this paralysis was only temporary; and there would come a time when the cakes I consumed without noticing them would have to be digested. But that moment was still in the future; and in the present, Gilberte made "my tea." I drank huge quantities of it, although normally a single cup of tea would keep me awake for twenty-four hours. So it was that my mother had come to remark, "It's a worry—every time that boy goes to the Swanns' he comes home sick." But while I was at the Swanns' I would have been unable to say whether or not it was really tea I was drinking. And even if I had known, I would have gone on drinking it; for even if I had been restored momentarily to proper awareness of the present, this would not have given me back the ability to remember the past or foresee the future. My imagination was incapable of stretching to the remote moment when I might feel tired or think of going to bed.

Not all of Gilberte's other guests were so tipsy with excitement that making up their minds was impossible. Some of these girls actually declined the offer of tea! At which Gilberte would say a thing that people said a lot at that time, "Well, my tea doesn't seem to be a great winner, does it?" Then, in an effort to make the occasion look less ceremonial, she shifted a few of the chairs set at regular intervals about the table, adding, "For goodness' sake, we look as though we're at a wedding breakfast! Aren't servants stupid!"

She nibbled her cake, sitting sideways on an X-shaped seat which stood at an awkward angle to the table. And if Mme Swann, having just seen one of her visitors out—her at-homes were usually on the same days as Gilberte's tea parties—should look in quickly, sometimes in blue velvet, often in a dress of black satin covered in white lace, she would say in a tone of surprise, which suggested Gilberte might have had all those little cakes to eat without her mother knowing about it:

"What's this! Doesn't that look scrumptious! It makes my mouth water to see you all sitting here eating cake."

"Well, please join us, Mama," Gilberte would reply.

"You know I can't, my precious. Whatever would all my ladies say? I've still got Mme Trombert, Mme Cottard, and Mme Bontemps—you know how the visits of dear Mme Bontemps are never very brief, and she's just arrived. What *would* these good ladies have to say if I left them in the lurch? But when they've gone, if nobody else comes, then I'll come back and have a nice chat with you all. That would be so much more to my liking! I think I deserve a little rest—I've had forty-five visitors today, and of those forty-five at least forty-two have talked about Gérôme's new painting!"[31] Then, turning to me as she made ready to return to her ladies, she added, "Look, why don't you drop in one of these days? You could have your cup of tea with Gilberte. She knows how you like it, the way you have it at home, in your own little studio." She made it sound as though what I was seeking in this world of mystery was something as familiar to me as my own habits (if my supposed liking for tea could be called that; and as for the alleged "studio," I was unclear whether I had one or not). "So—when will you come? Tomorrow? We'll have *toast* for you that's as good as you can get at Columbin's.[32] No, you really can't? Well, you're a selfish thing!" She delivered this last statement in tones reminiscent of the mincing tyranny of Mme Verdurin, for Odette, now that she was beginning to have a salon of her own, had started to ape some of that lady's ways. Since both "Colombin" and the English word *toast* were utterly obscure to me, her promise could not make her house more attractive to me. As for the eulogy she then delivered of our old "nurse," my momentary inability to understand whom she was referring to may appear somewhat stranger, given that the word is now used by everyone, possibly even at Combray. Despite my ignorance of English, I soon grasped that it meant Françoise. Whereas at the Champs-Élysées I had been so anxious about the bad impression Françoise must have made, I now learned from Mme Swann that what had predisposed her and her husband in my favor was everything Gilberte had told them about my "nurse": "It's pretty clear that she's devoted to you, that she's just perfect!" (My opinion of Françoise changed instantly, one effect of which was that it no longer seemed so essential to me to have a governess equipped with a raincoat and a hat with a feather in it.) I deduced too, from certain words that Mme Swann spoke about Mme Blatin, whose kindness she praised and whose visits she dreaded, that to have been on friendly terms with the lady would have been of less value to me than I had thought, and would in no way have improved my standing with the Swanns.

Though I had begun, full of this tremulous respect and joy, to explore the enchanted domain which had just given me the freedom of its hitherto forbidden avenues, it was only in my capacity as a friend of Gilberte. The realm in which I was now welcomed was itself encompassed by another even more mysterious one, in which Swann and his wife had their supernatural being, and which, if we chanced to meet, going through the anteroom in our different directions, closed behind them again as soon as they had shaken my hand. However, soon I too had access to their Inner Sanctum. For instance, if Gilberte was not at home but her parents were, they would ask who it was at the door; and, having been told it was me, they would have me sent in to see them, with the aim of asking me to influence their daughter toward a certain course of action in some matter or other. I remembered the exhaustive, persuasive screed which I had not long since sent to M. Swann, and to which he had never deigned to reply. I was struck by the impotence of the mind, the reason, and the heart in bringing about the slightest change in people, in reducing a single one of the difficulties which life, left to its own devices and in ways that escape us, manages to resolve so easily. My new status as friend of Gilberte, capable of influencing her for the better, put me in the favorable position of someone who happened to be the school friend of a king's son, as well as being always at the head of the class, and who, because of those fortuitous facts, now has the run of the palace and private audiences in the throne room: with infinite kindness, and as though he was not much occupied with lofty considerations, Swann would usher me into his study and speak to me for an hour about things that my state of emotional turmoil prevented me from understanding a single word of, and to which I could reply only with stammerings, diffident dumbness, and sudden daring outbursts of short-winded incoherence; thinking they might interest me, he showed me books and finely wrought objects, the beauty of which, I was prospectively convinced, must infinitely surpass all the holdings of the Louvre and the Bibliothèque Nationale, impossible though it was for me to view these. At such moments, the Swanns' butler would have endeared himself to me had he asked me to hand over my watch, my tie pin, and my boots, or if he had begged me to sign a deed recognizing him as my heir. The state I was in is described perfectly by a fine colloquialism—"I didn't know whether I was coming or going!"—the coiner of which is as unknown as the author of the greatest epic poems, but which, like them—and *pace* the theory of Wolf[33] — must have had an originator, one of those modest creative spirits who turn up every now and then to enrich the rest of us with a felicitous expression like "putting a name to a face," but whose own face we can never put a name to. However long I was closeted with Swann, all I ever got from these moments was a feeling of surprise at the utter non-achievement they led to, the total lack of satisfying outcome I derived from the hours spent in the enchanted dwelling. Not that my disappointment came from any deficiency in the masterpieces he showed me, or the impossibility of forcing my distracted eye to focus on them. It was not the intrinsic beauty of these things which made it miraculous for me to be in Swann's study; it was that, adhering to the things (which could have been the ugliest imaginable), there was the special, sad, thrilling emotion that I had invested in this place for so many years, and of which it was still redolent. Nor was it Mme Swann's multitude of mirrors, silver brushes, and little shrines to Saint Anthony of Padua, painted or sculpted by friends of hers who counted among the finest artists, that filled me with the knowledge of my unworthiness and her own regal graciousness, whenever she received me for a moment in her room, where three beautiful and imposing creatures, her first, her second, and her third maids, were smiling and laying out wonderful garments, and to which I wended my way, when the footman in breeches and hose had conveyed to me the injunction that Madame wished to speak to me, along a winding corridor that was remotely perfumed by the precious essences wafting the constant current of their sweet scents all the way from her dressing room.

When Mme Swann had gone back to her visitors, we could still hear her talking and laughing; for, even in the presence of only two people, as though commanding the attention of the full complement of "chums," she raised her voice, she held forth, as she had so often seen the "Patronne" do among the "little clan" so as to "keep the conversation going." The expressions we have most recently borrowed being those we most like to use, at least for a time, Mme Swann sometimes chose the ones she had picked up from the few distinguished people whom her husband had not managed to avoid introducing to her (such as the mannerism of dropping the article or the demonstrative pronoun before an adjective describing a person), and sometimes more vulgar ones (for instance, "Isn't it ducky!," which one of her close friends was always saying); and these she tried to work into whatever stories she told, as had been her wont since the days of the "little clan." At the end of her stories, she would sometimes add, "I'm *very* fond of that story," or "Now, you must admit, that's a *lovely* story!," a habit she had acquired, via her husband, from the Guermantes, whom she did not know.

After Mme Swann had left the dining room, her husband, who had just come home, might then look in. "Is your mother alone now, Gilberte, do you happen to know?" "No, she's still got some of her ladies with her." "What? At seven o'clock in the evening! How dreadful! The poor dear must be exhausted. It's quite odious." At home I had been accustomed to hearing "odious" with a long *o;* but both Mme

Swann and M. Swann gave the word a short one, making it into "oddi-ous." "Just think," he went on, turning to me, "she's been going since two this afternoon! And Camille tells me that there must have been twelve of them just between four and five! What am I saying, twelve? I think it was *fourteen* he said! I tell a lie, it was twelve—or was it? Anyway, when I came home just now, I had quite forgotten it was her at-home day, and when I saw all the carriages outside, I thought there must be a wedding in the house! And for the last few minutes, sitting in my study, I've heard nothing but the doorbell ringing. Given me quite a head-ache, I can tell you. Has she still got many of them with her?" "No, just two now." "And who might they be, do you know?" "Mme Cottard and Mme Bontemps." "Ah, yes, the wife of the private secretary to the min-ister of works." "Well, I know her hubby works in a big minister's office or something, but I don't know what he is," Gilberte said, putting on a silly voice.

"Silly girl! You sound like a two-year-old. Works in a big office, in-deed! He's actually the *private secretary* to the minister—that means he's the boss of the whole thing! Or wait, no, what am I saying? I'm as silly as you are—he's not just the private secretary—he's the *principal* private secretary!"

"Well, how am I supposed to know? So a principal private secretary, that's good, is it?" Gilberte said, always ready to show indifference to whatever her parents took pride in, or possibly thinking to enhance the effect of their acquaintance with such an exalted personage by appear-ing not to attach much importance to it.

"Good, is it?" Swann exclaimed, preferring plainer speech to such modesty, which might have left me in some doubt. "I'll have you know he's next in importance to the minister himself! Or actually he's *more* important than the minister, because he's the one who's in charge of everything. I'm told he's a man of caliber, too, a first-rate man, a really distinguished person. Officer of the Legion of Honor. A fine fellow in all respects, and actually very handsome too."

In fact, his wife had married him, against much opposition from within her family, because he was a "charmer." The general effect of this person of superlative refinement may be judged from the fact that he had a silky fair beard, a pretty face, an adenoidal pronunciation, bad breath, and a glass eye.

"I don't mind telling you," Swann said to me, "that it's really quite funny to see people like that in government circles these days. You see, they're the Bontemps of the Bontemps-Chenut family, the epitome of your narrow-minded middle classes, priest-ridden reactionaries. Your late grandfather was very familiar, at least by sight and repute, with old Chenut—who never tipped a cabman more than two cents in his life, though he was wealthy for those days—and Baron Bréau-Chenut. They lost everything in the collapse of the Union Générale,[34] which you're too young to remember anything about, and since then they've had to pick up whatever pieces they can."

"He's the uncle of a girl that used to go to my school. She was in one of the classes well below mine—'that Albertine,' everybody used to call her. I'm sure she'll be very 'fast' one of these days, but at the moment she's the funniest-looking thing."

"What an amazing daughter I've got! She knows everyone!"

"No, I don't know her. I just used to see her about and hear everybody shouting 'Albertine, Albertine' all the time. But Mme Bontemps I do know, and I can tell you I don't like her much either."

"Well, you're quite wrong there, my girl. Mme Bontemps is charming, pretty, and intelligent. Witty too. I'll just pop in and say hello to her, ask her whether her husband thinks there's going to be a war, and whether we can rely on King Theodosius. He's very much in the know, so he must know a thing or two about that, wouldn't you say?"

In earlier days, Swann would never have spoken in this way. But a similar change can be seen in the once-unpretentious princess of royal blood who, ten years later, having eloped with a footman, then tries to re-enter society, only to sense that people are not very willing to frequent her; so she spontaneously adopts the conversational habits of boring old women who, when the name of a fashionable duchess is spoken in their hearing, instantly say, "She looked in to see me only yesterday," and "I lead a very sheltered life these days, you know." Which shows how pointless it is to study human manners; they can be deduced from the laws of human psychology.

The Swanns were not immune from this foible, common to people whose circle of acquaintance is not as wide as they would like. A visit, an invitation, even a friendly word spoken by anyone who was at all noted, they took to be an event that should be bruited abroad. If by some ill chance the Verdurins were in London when Odette happened to hold a dinner party that was at all remarkable, there was always some way of making sure that a mutual friend would telegraph the news to them. The merest letter or even just a telegram that Odette might receive, if it was in any sense flattering, the Swanns were incapable of keeping to themselves. Friends were told about it; the document itself was circulated. The Swanns' salon was reminiscent of those hotels in seaside resorts where they pin up messages on a bulletin board.

Also, the people who had known the former Swann not just in a private capacity, as I had, but also in society, in the world of the Guermantes—where the highest standards of wit and charm were expected of everyone, except duchesses and highnesses, and where even eminent men might be unwelcome if they were seen to be boring or vulgar—might have been surprised to discover not only that the former Swann had turned into someone whose ways of referring to people he was acquainted with were indiscreet, but that his criteria for choosing such people were also quite lax. How was it possible for him not to be exasperated by Mme Bontemps, who was so common and nasty? How could he possibly say she was a pleasant person? His memories of the Guermantes set should surely have prevented it. But in fact they abetted it. The Guermantes, unlike three-quarters of the world's social sets, certainly had taste, and exquisite taste at that. But they also had snobbery, which makes for the possibility of momentary failures in the functioning of taste. In the case of someone who was not an indispensable member of their set—a minister of foreign affairs, say, rather too full of his own Republicanism, or a garrulous Academician—their taste discriminated against him; Swann would commiserate with Mme de Guermantes over her having had to dine with such commensals at an embassy; and the whole Guermantes set infinitely preferred a fashionable man, a man of their own world, that is, devoid of any special talent, but with the Guermantes cast of mind. However, a grand duchess or a princess of royal blood, by dining frequently at the house of Mme de Guermantes, would also be seen as being in the set, although, by virtue of her lack of the Guermantes cast of mind, she was not *of* it. But with the naïveté of the fashionable, since she was one of their number, they did their best to think she was good company, rather than knowing that it was because she was good company that she was one of their number. "She's actually quite a nice woman," Swann would say in support of Mme de Guermantes, after HRH had left. "And she's even got a touch of comedy in her. I must say, I doubt whether she has ever read the *Critique of Pure Reason* from cover to cover! Still, she's not too bad."

"I agree entirely," the Duchesse de Guermantes would reply. "Mind you, today she was a little bit shy. But you'll see, she can be quite charming." "She's much less of a bore than Mme XJ"—this being the wife of the garrulous Academician, a quite outstanding woman—"who keeps spouting books at you." "Oh, there's no comparison!" It was at the Duchesse de Guermantes's that Swann had acquired his facility in saying such things, which he said in all sincerity; and it was an ability he had kept. It served him now with the people who visited his wife. He tried hard to see in them, and to like, the qualities which any human being shows if examined with a favorable bias, and not with the disdain of the fastidious; and nowadays he stressed the merits of Mme Bontemps as he had once stressed those of the Princess of Parma, who would really have been unacceptable to the Guermantes set, had not certain highnesses benefited from preferential treatment—and even if the ones admitted had been expected to possess wit and a little charm. As has been seen, Swann had once enjoyed exchanging his social position for one which, in certain circumstances, suited him better; and all he was doing at present was adapting this practice to a more lasting situation. It is only people who are incapable of perceiving the composite nature of what seems at first sight indivisible who think that person and position are one. The same man, seen on different rungs of the social ladder at consecutive moments of his life, belongs to separate worlds, each of which is not necessarily more elevated than the previous one; and every time a new phase of living brings us into, or back into, a certain social circle that welcomes us with open arms, we quite naturally start to put down roots and become attached to it.

As for Mme Bontemps, when Swann spoke of her in such glowing terms, I think he was also quite pleased by the thought that my parents would know she was on visiting terms with his wife. It must be said, however, that the identity of the people with whom Mme Swann gradually came to be on such terms aroused more curiosity in my family than admiration. On hearing the name of Mme Trombert, my mother said:

"Now, *there's* a new recruit! And she'll bring in others."

And she added, as though Mme Swann's brisk and impetuous conquest of new acquaintances were a colonial war:

"Now that the Tromberts are subdued, the neighboring tribes will not hold out much longer."

If she happened to pass Mme Swann in the street, she would tell us about it that evening:

"I saw Mme Swann today in full battle order. She must have been launching an incursion into the lands of the Massechuto, the Singhalese, or the Tromberts."

When I mentioned all the new people I had seen at the Swanns', a somewhat mixed and artificial society, many of whom had been rather unwilling to belong to it, and who derived from very different backgrounds, my mother could tell at once how they came to be there, and spoke of them as though they were spoils of war:

"Brought back from an expedition to Mme de This's or Mme de That's."

In the case of Mme Cottard, my father was amazed that Mme Swann should think there was kudos to be got from the company of such a dowdy middle-class person: "Even allowing for the professor's position, I must say it's beyond me." To my mother, on the other hand, it was quite clear: she knew that a woman could miss much of the pleasure to be got from graduating to circles different from those she had moved in before, if she could not inform her old acquaintances about the relatively more conspicuous acquaintances with whom she had replaced them. For this purpose, a witness is required, who shall be allowed into the world of new delights, as the blundering insect plunders a flower, then flies off to visit others, to spread the news, or so it is hoped, sprinkling its random pollens of envy and admiration. Mme Cottard, perfect for this role, belonged to that special category of guests whom Mama, who had some of her father's style of wit, called "Strangers to Speak in Sparta."[35] Besides—apart from another reason, which did not come to light until many years later—in inviting this friend, who was demure, reserved, and well meaning, to her splendid at-homes, Mme Swann had no need to fear she might be harboring a traitor or a competitor. She knew the great number of middle-class blooms that this tireless worker, armed with her plumed hat and her little card case, could pollinate in one busy afternoon. She knew how prolific this form of seeding could be; and, allowing for the law of averages, she was right to expect that, by the next day but one, this or that "regular" of the Verdurins' would have heard of the card left on her by the commanding officer of the Paris region, or even that M. Verdurin in person would be told that none other than the chairman of the Turf Club, M. Le Hault de Pressagny, had included the Swanns in his party for the grand ball in honor of King Theodosius. She imagined that these two events, both of them flattering for herself, would be the only ones the Verdurins would learn of, for the particular concrete manifestations of fame which we like to picture and to which we aspire are few, given our penury of mind and our inability to imagine simultaneously more than one of the many blessings of fame, though we still harbor the vague hope of seeing them all descend upon us at once.

Besides, Mme Swann's only successes so far had been in what is known as "the world of officialdom." Fashionable ladies did not frequent her house. It was not that they were deterred by the presence of the Republic's representatives. During the early years of my childhood, all who belonged to conservative society belonged also to fashionable society; no self-respecting salon would have countenanced admitting a Republican. Those who constituted this set were convinced that the impossibility of ever inviting an Opportunist,[36] let alone an unspeakable Radical, was something that would last forever, like oil lamps and horse trolleys. But after the manner of kaleidoscopes, which are turned from time to time, society composes new designs by jumbling the order of elements that once seemed immutable. By the time I had taken my first communion, prim and proper ladies were being confronted, to their astonishment, with elegant Jewesses in some of the houses they frequented. These new designs in the kaleidoscope are made by what a philosopher would call a change of criterion. Another of these was to come with the Dreyfus Affair, at a time slightly later than my first entry into the world of Mme Swann, and again the kaleidoscope shuffled its little tinted shapes. All things Jewish were displaced, even the elegant lady, and hitherto nondescript nationalists came to the fore. The most brilliant salon in Paris was that of an ultra-Catholic Austrian prince. If instead of the Dreyfus Affair there had been a war with Germany, the kaleidoscope would have turned in a different direction. The Jews, who would have shown to everyone's astonishment that they were patriotic, could have kept their position; and no one would have wished to go, or even admit to ever having gone, to the Austrian prince's. Even so, each time society is briefly stable, those who make it up imagine that further change is ruled out, just as, having seen the advent of the telephone, they now wish to disbelieve in airplanes. And the philosophers of the daily press damn the former time, not only in its modes of pleasure, which they see as the epitome of decadence, but even in the work of its artists and thinkers, which they now see as worthless, as though it were inseparably linked to the constant inconstancies of the fashionable and the frivolous. The only thing that never changes is that there always appears to be "something changing in France." In the days when I started frequenting Mme Swann's world, the Dreyfus Affair had not yet happened, and certain notable Jews were very influential, none more so than Sir Rufus Israels, whose wife was an aunt of Swann's. Lady Israels did not enjoy the same fashionable connections as her nephew once had; and he, though he must presumably have been her heir, had little enough contact with her, as he disliked her. However, she was the only relative of Swann's who knew something of his real standing in the elegant world, the others being as ignorant in that respect as my own family had been for years. When one member of a family emigrates to high society—something which at the time seems to him a unique occurrence, but which with ten years' hindsight he can see has been managed by more than one of the young men with whom he was brought up, albeit in a different way, and for different reasons—he lives inside a twilight zone, a *terra incognita,* which is quite visible in its finest detail for all those who inhabit it, but which is dark and empty for all who do not have access to it, who may live alongside it without ever suspecting that it exists. No Reuters news agency ever having informed Swann's cousins about the people he mixed with, these ladies would exchange stories at family dinners about how they had—before the man's wretched marriage, of course—"dutifully" devoted their Sunday afternoon to visiting "Cousin Charles," who they thought was somewhat given to the poor relation's envy of his betters, and whom, with a pun on the title of Balzac's *Cousine Bette,* they wittily dubbed "Cousin Batty." If envy there was, it was on the part of Lady Israels, who knew perfectly well the identity of the people who lavished their friendship on him. Her husband's family, who were as rich as the Rothschilds, had for some generations managed the affairs of the princes of Orléans. Lady Israels, who was hugely wealthy and very influential, had contrived to make sure that no one of her acquaintance would ever be at home to Odette. Only one person, the Comtesse de Marsantes, had disobeyed, and that secretly. One day, as Odette arrived to visit this lady, by an ill chance in swept Lady Israels. Mme de Marsantes, who was on tenterhooks, plucked up the cowardice of those who could just as well choose to be brave, and said nothing to Odette for the duration of her visit. This occurrence did nothing to inspire Odette to venture further into a zone of society which in any case was not the one she wished to belong to. In her utter disregard for the Faubourg Saint-Germain, Odette remained the untutored light-o'-love, quite different from the middle-class people who are minutely informed on the finer points of genealogy and whose longing for aristocratic connections, unrequited by life, can be assuaged only by perusal of an older generation's memoirs. As for Swann, no doubt he went on being the lover who turns a blind and indulgent eye to a former mistress's idiosyncrasies; and I would often hear Odette utter the most flagrant howlers about things social while Swann, moved either by a lingering fondness, or by the low esteem in which he now held her, or perhaps because he could no longer be bothered trying to improve her, sat by and did nothing to correct them. This may also have been a mode of the simplicity of manner which had had us fooled for so many years at Combray, and which, since he had kept up his separate connection with some of the most outstanding members of the Faubourg, made him reluctant to mar the conversation in his wife's drawing room by seeming to attach any importance to such people. In fact, for Swann himself they were of less importance than ever, the center of gravity of his life having shifted. So Odette, in her complete ignorance of society, went on saying, whenever a passing mention was made of the Princesse de Guermantes just after a mention of her cousin the Duchesse de Guermantes, "I see! They're princes now, are they? *They've* gone up in the world!" If people referred to the Duc de Chartres as "the Prince," she would set them right: "No, no, he's not a prince, he's a duke." Of the Duc d'Orléans, the son of the Comte de Paris, she would say, "It's odd, isn't it, the son being above the father like that." Then, like the Anglophile she was, she would add, "All these 'royals'! Isn't it confusing!" And once, when someone asked her which of France's old provinces the Guermantes family hailed from, she gave the name of a *département,* "From the Aisne."

In any case, Swann was blind not only to the gaps in Odette's education, but also to her poverty of mind. Indeed, when she told one of her silly stories, he would listen to her full of an obliging, cheerful, even admiring attentiveness, which could be explained only by his finding her still sexually arousing; whereas, in the same conversation, Odette's inveterate way was to lend a perfunctory ear, bored or impatient, to anything subtle or even profound that he might say, to half ignore and at times sharply contradict him. It must be supposed that, in many marriages, such subservience of the outstanding to the vulgar is the rule, for one need only think of the opposite case, that of the gifted wife who smilingly defers to her crass boor of a husband as he crushes her nicest conceits, then gushes with loving indulgence at the inept buffoonery he thinks is humor. Among the other reasons which at that time prevented Odette from being accepted in the Faubourg Saint-Germain, it must be said that a series of scandals had lately caused another shift in the patterns of the social kaleidoscope. Certain women, with whom people had been mixing without suspecting anything untoward, turned out to be common prostitutes and English spies. For a while, it was going to be expected, or so it was believed, that the only acceptable people would be those who were of unimpeachable respectability. Odette stood for everything which had just been shunned, but which (as people do not change overnight, but seek to continue a former state of affairs in the guise of a new one) was soon going to be welcomed back with open arms, having slightly altered its forms, thus enabling society to fool itself into believing it was no longer the same as it had been before the scandal. However, at that time Odette bore too close a resemblance to society's lately exposed ladies. The elegant are nothing if not shortsighted—at the very moment when, having ostracized all the Jewish ladies of their acquaintance, they are looking about for other ladies with whom to replace them, they suddenly notice a newcomer who turns up like an orphan in the storm, but who happens to be Jewish too; it is the novelty of her that prevents them from seeing in her what they had seen, but chosen to abhor, in her predecessors. She requires no one to have no other gods before hers; and she is adopted. In the days when I was making my first entry into the world of Mme Swann, though the problem was not anti-Semitism, she was of a kind with those who were to be kept at a distance, for a time.

As for Swann, he would often visit some of his former set, all of whom belonged of course to the most elegant society. However, if he ever spoke to us of the people he had been to see, I noticed that his choice among his former acquaintances was influenced by the same semi-artistic, semi-historical sense that informed his taste as a collector. When I realized that the reason why he was particularly fond of this or that great lady who had come down in the world was that she had been Liszt's mistress, or that Balzac had dedicated a novel to her grandmother, just as he would buy a drawing if it was mentioned in Chateaubriand, I began to suspect that we had substituted for the misleading Combray Swann, the middle-class man without social connections, another Swann, who was just as misleading, the man about town who belonged to the best circles. To be on friendly terms with the Comte de Paris means nothing. Plenty of men who are the friends of princes will never be accepted in self-respecting drawing rooms. Princes know they are princes, are not snobbish, and in any case see themselves as being so far above anyone who is not of their blood that those beneath them, the middle classes and peers of the realm, appear to be almost of the same rank.

However, the pleasure Swann derived from his social contacts was not just the straightforward kind enjoyed by the cultivated man with an artistic bent who restricts himself to society as it is constituted, and enjoys his familiarity with the names engraved in it by the past and still legible now. He also took a rather vulgar enjoyment in making as it were composite posies out of disparate elements, bringing together people from very different backgrounds. These experiments in the sociology of entertainment, which is how he saw them, did not have exactly the same effect—or, rather, did not have a constant effect—on all the ladies who visited his wife. He would say with a laugh to Mme Bontemps, "I'm thinking of having the Cottards to dinner with the Duchesse de Vendôme," looking like a gourmet whose mouth waters at the novel undertaking of adding cayenne pepper to a particular sauce instead of the usual cloves. But this design of Swann's, though it would certainly strike the Cottards as entertaining, was calculated to appear quite outrageous to Mme Bontemps. She, having herself only recently been introduced by the Swanns to the Duchesse de Vendôme, and having deemed this occurrence to be as pleasing as it was natural, had found that impressing the Cottards by telling them all about it had been not the least of the pleasures it afforded her. But, like those who, as soon as their own names figure in the latest Honors List, would like to see the supply of such decorations run dry, Mme Bontemps would have been better pleased if, after she had been presented to the Duchesse de Vendôme, nobody else from her circle could be. She secretly cursed Swann for the warped taste with which, merely to satisfy a misplaced aesthetic curiosity, he had wantonly squandered all the kudos she had seen reflected in the eyes of the Cottards as she told them about the Duchesse de Vendôme. Would she even have the heart to tell her own husband that Professor Cottard and his wife were not to partake of the very pleasure that she had assured him was unique to themselves? If the Cottards could only learn that their invitation was not seriously meant, but had been sent just for fun! The fact was that the Bontemps had been sent their invitation for exactly the same reason; but then Swann, who had borrowed from the aristocracy Don Juan's undying gift for fooling each of two commonplace women into believing she is the only one he really loves, had assured Mme Bontemps that, to dine with a woman such as the Duchesse de Vendôme, no one could be better qualified than herself. "Yes," Mme Swann said some weeks later, "we're thinking of having the Duchesse de Vendôme with the Cottards. My husband thinks it's a conjugation that might produce some quite entertaining results." Though Odette had retained from her days in "the little clan" some habits dear to Mme Verdurin, like shouting so as to be heard by all the "regulars," she had also picked up words such as "conjugation," dear to the Guermantes set, which, as the moon does to the sea, exercised its power on her from a distance without her knowing it—and without her coming any closer to it either. "Yes," Swann said, "the Cottards with the Duchesse de Vendôme—that should be good fun, don't you think?" To which Mme Bontemps replied tartly, "I think it's quite preposterous! It's playing with fire, nothing good will come of it, and it will serve you right!" In fact, she and her husband[37] were also invited to the dinner in question, as was the Prince d'Agrigente; and both Mme Bontemps and Dr. Cottard took to describing the event in two different ways, depending on the identity of those to whom they described it. To the first group, Mme Bontemps on the one hand and Dr. Cottard on the other both replied casually, when asked who else had been there, "Oh, just the Prince d'Agrigente. It was very restricted, you know, very select." The other group were those who might be better informed than the first—one of them had even asked Cottard, "But surely the Bontemps were there as well?" "Ah, yes, I'd forgotten them," Cottard replied, with a blush and a mental note to classify this person as a pernicious gossip. For the benefit of this second group, both Mme Bontemps and Dr. Cottard, quite independently of each other, had a version which was identical in plot, but in which their names featured in reverse order. Dr. Cottard's version ran like this: "Well, there were our hosts, of course, then the Vendômes, the Duc and Duchesse, you know, and"—here he gave a smug smile—"Professor and Mme Cottard. Oh,

yes, and there was another couple there too, though nobody could figure out why—M. and Mme Bontemps, sticking out like the proverbial
sore thumb!" Mme Bontemps rattled off exactly the same speech, except that the gloating intonation stressed the place of her husband and
herself between the Duchesse de Vendôme and the Prince d'Agrigente,
while the disreputables who she went so far as to say had gate-crashed
the event, and who were such flagrant outsiders, were the Cottards.

When Swann came home from his afternoon out, it was often
shortly before dinnertime. At six in the evening, which had once been
the hour of such sadness for him, he no longer wondered what Odette
might be up to; he was now almost indifferent to whether she had
someone with her or whether she had gone out somewhere. Now and
again it did occur to him that there had been a time, many years before,
when he had tried to decipher a letter from Odette to Forcheville
through its envelope. But he found this memory irksome; and to avoid
the full sense of the shame it brought, he preferred to twitch the corners
of his mouth, or even give a little shake of the head, as though to say,
"Well, so what?" He had, however, come to see as unfounded the notion he had often entertained in those former days that Odette's daily
doings were quite innocent, and that it was only the dark figments of
his jealousy which sullied them (a beneficent notion, in fact, since it
had soothed his anguish, for the duration of his lovesickness, by whispering that it was imaginary); and he now believed it was the jealousy
that had been right all along, that, though she might well have loved
him more than he had given her credit for, she had also been much
more often unfaithful to him than he had liked to believe. In those
days, wallowing in his grief, he had promised himself that when he had
stopped loving her, when he would no longer care about annoying her,
or making her feel importuned by being loved too much, he would enjoy sitting down with her and finding out, in a spirit of simple respect
for the truth, as a mere point of historical fact, whether or not
Forcheville had been in bed with her on the day when Swann had rung
her doorbell, then banged on her window, and she had not come to the
door at first but had later sent the note to Forcheville saying it was an
uncle of hers who had turned up. But this fascinating problem, which

Swann was looking forward to solving as soon as his jealousy had abated, stopped fascinating him when he stopped being jealous. This did not happen instantly. There was a time when, though Odette herself no longer aroused his jealousy, he could still be plunged back into its throes by the thought of that afternoon when he had stood outside the little *hôtel* on the rue La Pérouse banging on the door.[38] It was as though his jealousy, after the manner of those illnesses that seem to have their seat or source of contagion more in certain places, certain houses, than in certain individuals, had not focused so much on Odette as on that past day, that long-lost moment when Swann had stood knocking at all the entrances of her house. It was as though that single day, or that evening hour, had had the power of fossilizing a few last particles of the loving personality which had once been his, and which he could only ever retrieve at that point in time. He had long since ceased to care whether Odette had been unfaithful to him, and even whether her infidelities continued to this day. Yet, over a period of some years, attempting to assuage those persistent pangs of unrequited curiosity, he had gone on seeking out former servants of Odette's, in the hope of learning whether, at six o'clock on that day,[39] so long ago, she had been in bed with Forcheville. Then even the curiosity had faded; but his investigations continued. He persisted in trying to find out something in which he no longer had any interest, because his former self, albeit now in the final stages of its senility, went on functioning mechanically, at the urge of a preoccupation so extinct that Swann could no longer even imagine his former anguish, though it had once been so acute that he could not imagine ever being rid of it, and the death of the woman he loved had seemed the only thing capable of clearing a way for him through the grief-encumbered years ahead. (Yet the pain of jealousy, as a cruel counterdemonstration will show in a later part of this book, is proof even against death.)

To know the truth of what it was in Odette's life that had caused him such pain had not been Swann's only longing. He had nursed another deep desire: to avenge that pain at a time when, having survived his love for Odette, he would no longer live in fear of her. The opportunity of enjoying this revenge was now to hand, since Swann was in love with another woman, a woman who, though she gave him no grounds for jealousy, made him jealous all the same, since in his inability to find new ways of loving he put to use again with the other woman the way that had once served him with Odette. For his jealousy to revive, it was not necessary for this woman to be unfaithful; all that was required was that for some reason she had been away from him, at a dinner perhaps, and had apparently enjoyed herself. This roused all his old anguish, the sad counterproductive excrescence of his love, and deflected Swann away from the real woman into a compulsion to find out the truth about her feelings for him, the concealed cravings that made up her daily life, the secrets of her heart; for, between him and the woman he loved, the anguish set a solid, irreducible mass of once-harbored suspicions originating in Odette, or possibly in some other woman who had preceded Odette, and which obliged the aging lover to relate to his present mistress through the ancient collective figment in which he arbitrarily embodied his new love: The Woman Who Made Him Jealous. Swann often suspected that this jealousy misled him into believing in nonexistent infidelities; but then he would remember that he had once been misled into giving Odette the benefit of this very doubt. So, whenever the young woman he loved was away from him, whatever it was she happened to be doing came to lose all semblance of innocence. But whereas, long ago, foreseeing a possible day when he might stop loving the woman who he did not know would one day become his wife, he had sworn to flaunt the full sincerity of his indifference to her, to avenge the self-esteem which she had for so long humiliated, now that he could slake this thirst for vengeance with impunity (since what did it matter to him if Odette took him at his word and deprived him of her company, which had once been so necessary to him?), he could not be bothered taking his revenge. When his love for her had ended, the desire to show her that his love for her had ended had also disappeared. And the Swann who, when he suffered because of Odette, had wished for the day when he might let her see him in love with someone else, took ingenious precautions, now that this was possible, to keep his wife in ignorance of his new affair.

* * *

These invitations to tea, to events that had once caused me the sadness of seeing Gilberte leave me to go home early, were not the only way in which I was now included in her life. M. and Mme Swann allowed me to be part of Gilberte's outings with her mother, either a carriage drive or a matinee at the theater, which had prevented her from coming to the Champs-Élysées and so deprived me of her on those days when I hung about alone on the lawns or near the merry-go-round; not only did I have my place in her parents' landau, but I was the one they asked whether I preferred to go to a play, a dancing lesson at the house of one of Gilberte's friends, a social gathering at the house of one of the Swanns' own friends (what Mme Swann called in her English a little "meeting"), or to see the Tombs of the Kings at Saint-Denis.

On days when I was going out with the Swanns, I was also invited to what Mme Swann called "the lunch." As the Swanns' invitation was for half past twelve and my parents lunched at a quarter past eleven, it was after they had left the table that I would set off for the Swanns' luxurious district, which was rather deserted at any hour of the day but especially so at this time, when everybody else was indoors. Even on frosty days in winter, if it was fine, adjusting from time to time the knot in my magnificent tie from Charvet's, and making sure the gloss on my patent-leather boots remained unsullied, I loitered about the broad avenues, in the hope that it would soon be twenty-seven minutes past twelve. From a distance, I could see the leafless trees in the Swanns' little front garden, sparkling in the sunshine as though white with frost. There were only two of these trees; but the untoward hour made it a novel spectacle for me. Such pleasures from the natural world, sharpened for me by the departure from habit and even by hunger, were mixed with the overwhelming prospect of lunch at Mme Swann's; this prospect, though it dominated those other pleasures, did not diminish them; it exploited them, turned them into fashionable accessories. So, although that time of day, when I did not normally notice fine weather, cold air, and winter light, gave me the feeling of having just discovered them, they also felt like a mere preface to the eggs Béchamel, a sort of patina, an icy pink glaze added to the outside of that mysterious sanctum, the house where Mme Swann lived, inside which all would be warmth, perfumes, and flowers.

By half past twelve, I would have plucked up the courage to enter the house, which, like a great Christmas stocking, seemed to promise supernatural delights. The French word *Noël*, by the way, was never heard from the lips of Mme Swann or Gilberte. They had replaced it by the English word and spoke of *le pudding de Christmas*, of the *présents de Christmas* that they had been given, of going away (which gave me an unbearable pang) *pour Christmas*. At home, it would have been beneath my dignity to speak of *Noël*, and I went about talking of *le Christmas*, in the teeth of my father's ridicule.

Once I was inside, my sole encounter at first was with a footman, who walked me through a series of spacious drawing rooms before putting me into a little one that was uninhabited and was beginning to bask in the blue afternoon from its windows; there I was left in the company of orchids, roses, and violets, which, like people who stand waiting beside you but do not know you, did not break the silence, which their individuality as live things only made the more striking, while they looked shiveringly glad of the warmth of a fire of glowing coals, preciously laid behind a pane of clear crystal, in a trough of white marble, into which now and then crumbled its dangerous rubies.

Having sat down, I jumped up each time I heard the door open—but it was just a second footman, then a third; and the only outcome of these pointlessly thrilling toings and froings was a few coals added to the fire or a drop of water to the vases. The footmen went away and I was left alone again, behind the closed door that Mme Swann was bound to come and open soon. I would have been in less trepidation in an enchanter's cavern than in this little anteroom with its fire, which might, I felt, have been working Klingsor's magic transmutations.[40] At the sound of more footsteps, I sat where I was, it must be just another footman—it was M. Swann! "My dear fellow, what's this! All by yourself? Ah, that wife of mine, you know, she's never been very good at knowing what time it is. Ten to one already. Getting later every day. You mark my words—she'll come drifting in here thinking she's got plenty of time to spare." Since he was still subject to neuroarthritis and had become rather ridiculous, the fact of having such an unpunctual wife, who came home inordinately late from the Bois de Boulogne, wasted hours at her dressmaker's, and was never in time for lunch worried Swann for his stomach but flattered his self-esteem.

He would show me his latest acquisitions and explain their interesting features; but in the heat of such a moment, on an unusually empty stomach, my mind, though agitated, was a vacuum, and though I was capable of talking, I was incapable of hearing. And anyway, for me the main thing about the works he owned was that they lived with him and belonged to this thrilling time just before lunch. Even if the *Mona Lisa* had figured among them, it would not have given me more joy than one of Mme Swann's tea gowns or her bottles of smelling salts.

I sat waiting, either alone or with Swann, but often with Gilberte, who came in to sit with us. I was sure that the arrival of Mme Swann, foreshadowed by so many majestic entrances, would have to be a stupendous event. I expected it at each creak of a floorboard. But our expectations are always higher than the tallest cathedral, the mightiest wave in a storm, the highest leap of a dancer; and after all these liveried footmen, whose comings and goings were like those of extras on the stage preparing the climactic coming of the Queen, but thereby making it something of an anticlimax, when Mme Swann did slip in, wearing her short otter-skin coat, her veil lowered over her nose, which glowed from the cold outside, she broke all the promises that the wait had made to my imagination.

However, if she had spent all morning at home, she would come into the drawing room wearing a tea gown in a light shade of crêpe de Chine, which to my eye was more sophisticated than any evening gown.

On certain days, the Swanns would decide to stay at home all afternoon. So, as we had been so late having lunch, I could watch the sunlight quickly dwindle up the wall of the little garden, drawing with it the end of this day, which earlier had seemed to me destined to be different from other days. And despite the lamps of all shapes and sizes, glowing on their appointed altars all about the room, brought in by the servants and set on sideboards, teapoys, corner shelves, little low tables, as though for the enactment of some mysterious rite, our conversation produced nothing out of the ordinary, and I would go home, taking with me that feeling of having been let down which children often experience after Midnight Mass.

However, that disappointment was really only in the mind. I was usually radiant with joy in the Swanns' house, for if Gilberte had not yet joined us she might come in at any moment and for hours on end let me enjoy her words, her attentive gaze and smile, as I had first seen them at Combray. The greatest of my displeasures was a touch of mild jealousy if she disappeared, as she quite often did, up an inner staircase leading to large rooms on the floor above. Unable to leave the drawing room, like an actress's lover who has his seat in the stalls but can only imagine the disquieting things that may be happening in the wings or the greenroom, I sat with Swann and, in a voice that was not without a trace of anxiety, asked cunningly disguised questions about that other part of the house. He explained that the room where she sometimes went was the linen room, offered to show it to me, and promised that, whenever she had to go there, he would make sure she took me with her. With these words and the relief they brought me, he suddenly bridged for me one of those dreadful chasms within the heart, which put such a distance between us and the woman we love. It was a moment when I believed my affection for him was even stronger than my affection for Gilberte. For Swann was the master of his daughter, and it was he who gave her to me; whereas, left to her own devices, she could at times withhold herself from me; I did not have the direct power over her that I could exercise indirectly through him. And since I loved her, I could only ever see her through the confused desire for more of her, which when you are with the person you love deprives you of the feeling of loving.

Mostly, though, we did not stay in; we went for a drive. Sometimes, before going to change, Mme Swann would sit down at the piano. The fingers of her lovely hands, emerging from the sleeves of her tea gown in crêpe de Chine, pink, white, or at times in brighter colors, wandered on the keyboard with that wistfulness of which her eyes were so full, and her heart so empty. It was on one of those days that she happened to play the part of the Vinteuil sonata with the little phrase that Swann had once loved so much. Listening for the first time to music that is even a little complicated, one can often hear nothing in it. And yet, later in life, when I had heard the whole piece two or three times, I found I was thoroughly familiar with it. So the expression "hearing something for the first time" is not inaccurate. If one *had* distinguished nothing in it on the real first occasion, as one thought, then the second or the third would also be first times; and there would be no reason to understand it any better on the tenth occasion. What is missing the first time is probably not understanding but memory. Our memory span, relative to the complexity of the impressions that assail it as we listen, is infinitesimal, as short-lived as the memory of a sleeping man who has a thousand thoughts which he instantly forgets, or the memory of a man in his dotage, who cannot retain for more than a minute anything he has been told. Our memory is incapable of supplying us with an instantaneous recollection of this multiplicity of impressions. Even so, a recollection does gradually gather in the mind; and with pieces of music heard only two or three times, one is like the schoolboy who, though he has read over his lesson a few times before falling asleep, is convinced he still does not know it, but can then recite it word for word when he wakes up the following morning. Except that, in my case, I had heard nothing of the sonata until that moment; and whereas Swann and his wife could make out a distinct phrase, it was as ungraspable to my perception as someone's name that you try to remember when the mind retrieves nothing but a vacuum, into which, without your assistance, an hour after you stop thinking about them, the complete set of syllables that you have been vainly groping about for suddenly leaps. Not only does one not immediately discern a work of rare quality; but even within such a work, as happened to me with the Vinteuil sonata, it is always the least precious parts that one notices first. So not only was I wrong in my belief that, since Mme Swann had played over for me the most celebrated phrase, the work had nothing more to reveal to me (the result of which was that, for a long time afterward, showing all the stupidity of those who expect that their first sight of Saint Mark's in Venice will afford them no surprise, because they have seen the shape of its domes in photographs, I made no further attempt to listen to it); but, more important, even after I had listened to the whole sonata from beginning to end, it was still almost entirely invisible to me, like those indistinct fragments of a building that are all one can make out in the misty distance. Therein lies the source of the melancholy that accompanies our discovery of such works, as of all things which can come to fruition only through time. When I came eventually to have access to the most secret parts of Vinteuil's sonata, everything in it that I had noticed and preferred at first was already beginning to be lost to me, carried away by habit out of the reach of my sensibility. Because it was only in successive stages that I could love what the sonata brought to me, I was never able to possess it in its entirety—it was an image of life. But the great works of art are also less of a disappointment than life, in that their best parts do not come first. In the Vinteuil sonata, the beauties one discovers soonest are also those which pall soonest, a double effect with a single cause: they are the parts that most resemble other works, with which one is already familiar. But when those parts have receded, we can still be captivated by another phrase, which, because its shape was too novel to let our mind see anything there but confusion, had been made undetectable and kept intact; and the phrase we passed by every day unawares, the phrase which had withheld itself, which by the sheer power of its own beauty had become invisible and remained unknown to us, is the one that comes to us last of all. But it will also be the last one we leave. We shall love it longer than the others, because we took longer to love it. This length of time that it takes someone to penetrate a work of some depth, as it took me with the Vinteuil sonata, is only a foreshortening, and as it were a symbol, of all the years, or even centuries perhaps, which must pass before the public can come to love a masterpiece that is really new. This is why the man of genius, wishing to avoid the discontents of being unrecognized in his own day, may persuade himself that, since his contemporaries lack the necessary hindsight, works written for posterity should be read only by posterity, much as there are certain paintings that should not be looked at from too close up. However, any craven urge to avoid being misjudged is pointless, as misjudgment is unavoidable. What makes it difficult for a work of genius to be admired at once is the fact that its creator is out of the ordinary, that hardly anyone is like him. It is his work itself which, by fertilizing the rare spirits capable of appreciating it, will make them grow and multiply. It was the quartets of Beethoven (numbers 12, 13, 14, and 15) which, over fifty years, created and expanded the audience of listeners to the quartets of Beethoven, thus achieving, as all masterpieces do, progress if not in the quality of artists, at least in the company of minds, which is largely composed these days of what was missing when the work appeared: people capable of liking it. What is known as posterity is the work's own posterity. The creator of the work of genius must make no compromises with, must take no account of, other geniuses, who may at the same period be following their own course toward creating for the future a more aware public, which will reward other geniuses but not himself; the work has to create its own posterity. So, if this work were to be held back, in the hope of its being known only to posterity, it would be greeted not by posterity but by an assembly of its contemporaries who simply happened to be living fifty years later. Which is why the artist who wishes his work to find its own way must do what Vinteuil had done, and launch it as far as possible toward the unknown depths of the distant future. There lies the masterpiece's true element; and yet, though poor judges can make the mistake of taking no account of the time to come, better judges can at times be tempted by the perilous precaution of taking too much account of it. It is no doubt easy to suffer from an illusion analogous to the one that cancels the differences between all things when seen on a distant horizon, and to entertain the notion that all the revolutions which have ever taken place in painting or music actually had in common a respect for certain rules, and that whatever is right under our nose—Impressionism, dissonance for dissonance's sake, the exclusive use of the Chinese scale, Cubism, Futurism—shows a flagrant dissimilarity with everything that has gone before. However, when we look at what has gone before, we fail to reflect that a long-drawn-out process of assimilation has turned it all into a substance which, though it is varied, we see as homogeneous, in which Hugo rubs shoulders with Molière. Imagine a youth reading a horoscope forecasting his own middle age, with all the preposterous incongruities he would see in it, in his ignorance of the years to come and the changes they must bring about in him. However, not all horoscopes turn out to be true; and the obligation to take into account the factor of the future, when devising the sum of a work of art's beauties, must affect our judgment with something as unpredictable, and therefore as devoid of real interest, as any other prophecy that is never fulfilled, an outcome which implies no intellectual mediocrity in the prophet, since whatever it is that gives or denies existence to the possible may not necessarily lie within the scope of the genius. It is possible that even a genius may have disbelieved that railways or airplanes had a future, as it is possible to be an acute psychologist yet disbelieve in the infidelity of a mistress or the deceit of a friend, whose betrayals can be foreseen by someone much less gifted.

Though I did not understand the sonata, I was delighted to hear Mme Swann play. Her touch on the keyboard, like her tea gown, like her perfume drifting down the stairs, like her coats, like her chrysanthemums, seemed to me to belong to a mysterious and individual whole that existed in a world far above the one in which the mind can analyze talent. "That sonata of Vinteuil's is nice, isn't it?" Swann said to me. "That moment of nightfall under the trees, when the violin arpeggios make everything feel cool. You must admit, it's very pretty. It's captured the whole static quality of moonlight, which is moonlight's most basic quality. It's not surprising that a sunlight treatment such as my wife is taking at the moment should act on the muscles, given that moonlight prevents leaves from moving. That's what's so neatly caught by that little phrase—the Bois de Boulogne in a catatonic trance. It's even more striking by the seaside, because then you've got the muted responses of the waves, and they can be heard quite distinctly, of course, since nothing else can move. In Paris it's just the opposite: merely a strange glow, barely noticeable, on the fronts of the great buildings, and that faint glare in the sky, like the reflection from a house on fire, colorless and dangerless, that hint of some immense but banal happening somewhere . . . I must say, though, that the little phrase, the whole sonata, for that matter, does take place in the Bois de Boulogne—I mean, in the *gruppetto* you can clearly hear someone's voice saying, 'There's almost enough light to read the paper by!' " Swann's words might have had the result of distorting my eventual understanding of the sonata, as music is so versatile, too prone to suggestion to exclude entirely whatever somebody hints we might hear in it. But I realized, from other things he said, that the leaves at night in their dense stillness were none other than the ones under which, on many an evening, dining in restaurants on the outskirts of Paris, he had sat listening to the little phrase. Instead of the depth of meaning which he had so often sought in it, what it now brought back to him was all that serried foliage, leafy motifs winding and painted all about it, leaves that the phrase made him yearn to go and see, because it seemed to live on inside them like a soul; it brought back the whole springtime of that past year, which, in a fever of sorrow, he had been too hapless to savor, and which it had kept for him, as one keeps for an invalid the nice things he has been too unwell to eat. The Vinteuil sonata could tell Swann of the charm of certain nights in the Bois de Boulogne, about which it would have been pointless to ask Odette, although she had been no less with him on those nights than the little phrase. But she had only been sitting beside him (whereas the theme by Vinteuil was inside him); and even if she had been gifted with vastly greater understanding, she would have been unable to see what cannot be externalized for anyone (at least, I believed for a long time that this was a rule to which there were no exceptions). "But I mean, it *is* rather a neat touch, isn't it," Swann said, "that there can be reflections from sound as there are from water or from a mirror? Mind you, the only things that phrase of Vinteuil's shows me now are all the things I didn't pay attention to at the time. It's swapped them for my worries and my love affairs, which it has completely forgotten." "Charles! If you ask me, it sounds as though what you're saying is not very complimentary to me!" "Not complimentary! Aren't women wonderful! I'm merely trying to point out to this young fellow here that what music shows, to me at any rate, is nothing like 'The Will-in-Itself' or 'The Synthesis of the Infinite,' but something like the palm house at the Zoo in the Bois de Boulogne, with old Verdurin in his frock coat. I'll have you know, that little phrase has come and taken me out to dine dozens of times at Armenonville. God knows it's far nicer than going out there to dine with Mme de Cambremer." "That's a lady who was said to have lost her heart to Charles," said Mme Swann, laughing, and in the same tone of voice in which she had just said of Vermeer of Delft, whom I was surprised to see she knew of, "Well, you see, that gentleman over there was greatly interested in that painter at the time when he was courting me. Isn't that so, Charles my love?" "Please do not take the name of Mme de Cambremer in vain," said Swann, who was really quite flattered. "I'm only repeating what I've heard said. Actually, she's supposed to be very clever, though I've never met her. I believe she's very *pushing*"—here Mme Swann lapsed again into English—"which really surprises me in a woman who's clever. Anyway, everyone says she was head over heels in love with you—there's nothing in that to take offense at." Swann turned a very obvious deaf ear, which served both to confirm the suggestion and to show his smugness. "Well," said Mme Swann, with mock peevishness, "since my playing reminds you of the Zoo, perhaps we could go there this afternoon, if this young man feels like an outing? It's a nice day, and you, my love, could relive your memories! Speaking of the Zoo, do you know that this young fellow was under the apprehension that we were very fond of someone that I cut dead as often as I can—Mme Blatin, can you imagine! I think it's degrading for people to think she's a friend of ours. Even nice Dr. Cottard, who wouldn't speak evil of a soul, says the woman's a pest." "Isn't she ghastly! Her sole redeeming feature is that she's the image of Savonarola. She's exactly the portrait of Savonarola by Fra Bartolommeo." There was nothing implausible in this quirk of Swann's, of seeing likenesses of real people in paintings: even what we call an individual expression in something general (as we discover to our chagrin when we are in love, and wish to believe in the unique reality of the individual), something that may well have manifested itself at different periods. If Swann was to be believed, the *Journey of the Magi*, anachronistic enough when Benozzo Gozzoli painted the faces of the Medici brothers into it, was even more in advance of its time, as it contained, he said, the portraits of a host of people, contemporaries not of Gozzoli but of Swann, dating not just from fifteen centuries later than the Nativity, but from four centuries after the time of the painter himself. According to Swann, not one notable Parisian was missing from the retinue of the

Magi, as in that scene from a play by Sardou in which, for the sake of their friendship with the playwright and the leading lady, so as to be in fashion, but also for fun, all the men about town, the most famous doctors, politicians, and lawyers, took turns in playing a tiny nonspeaking part, each of them being onstage at a different performance.[41] "But I don't see Mme Blatin's connection with the Zoo." "Oh, it's obvious!" "You mean she's got a sky-blue backside like a monkey?" "Charles, you're being indecent! No, I was remembering what that Singhalese chap said to her that time. Tell him—it's really such a *lovely* little story." "It's too stupid. You see, Mme Blatin likes to address people in a way that she thinks is friendly, but which gives the impression that she's talking down to them." "What our neighbors across the Channel call *patronizing*," Odette interrupted. "So recently she went to the Zoo, where there was this exhibition being given by black fellows, from Ceylon, I think, or so I'm told by my wife, who's much better at ethnography than I am." "Charles, do stop being facetious." "I'm not being facetious in the slightest. So there she is, saying to this black fellow, 'Good morning, blackie!' " "Isn't it just ducky?" "Well, this form of speech was not to the black fellow's liking—'Me blackie,' he bellowed at Mme Blatin, 'you camel!' " "I think that's a very funny story! I just love that story! Isn't it *lovely*? Can't you just see Mme Blatin's face: 'Me blackie, you camel!' " I expressed a strong desire to go and see the Singhalese, one of whom had called Mme Blatin a camel. Not that I had the slightest interest in them. But I knew that, in going to and from the Zoo in the Bois de Boulogne, we would cross the Allée des Acacias, where I had once distantly doted on Mme Swann; and I hoped that Coquelin's[42] half-caste friend, to whom I had always hoped in vain to show off by bowing to Odette as she passed, would see me now sitting by her side in the victoria.

While Gilberte had gone off to get ready to go out, M. and Mme Swann would sit with me in the drawing room and enjoy telling me about the rare virtues of their daughter. Everything I could see of her for myself seemed to prove they spoke nothing but the truth. I noticed little acts of thoughtful kindness, which confirmed what her mother had said about how she treated not only her friends but the servants and the poor, and a desire to please, premeditated considerateness, a reluctance to give offense, all of which meant she often put herself out to do inconspicuous favors. She had done some embroidery for our barley-sugar woman at the Champs-Élysées, and made a point of taking it to her, though it was snowing, wanting to deliver it in person and without a day's delay. Her father said, "I can tell you, that girl has a heart of gold, but she keeps it well hidden." Young as she was, she seemed much more sensible than her parents. When Swann spoke about his wife's grand acquaintances, Gilberte would turn away and say nothing. But she did this without appearing to disapprove, as she felt it would be impossible to criticize her father in any way. Once, when I mentioned Mlle Vinteuil, Gilberte said:

"She's a person I'll never have anything to do with. Because she wasn't nice to her father—I've heard she made him unhappy. You do agree, don't you? You'd be just as incapable as I am of wanting to outlive your father by a single day, wouldn't you? It's quite natural—I mean, how could anyone ever forget someone they've always loved?"

And on another occasion, when she had been more than usually loving with Swann, and I had referred to this after he had left us alone together, she replied:

"Yes, poor Papa. It will soon be the anniversary of the death of his father. So you can appreciate what he must be feeling. You understand what it's like. We feel the same about things like that, you and I, don't we? I'm just trying to be less of a bother to him than usual." "But he doesn't think you're a bother! He thinks you're perfect!" "Dear Papa, it's just because he's so kindhearted."

Her parents did not sing the virtues only of Gilberte, the girl who, in my imagination, long before I had even set eyes on her, used to appear standing in front of a church, in a landscape somewhere in the Île-de-France,[43] until the day when my dreams were replaced by memories, and I saw her always in front of a hedge of pink hawthorn, beside the steep little lane that led up to the Méséglise way. There came a day when I asked Mme Swann, taking great care to speak in the casual tone of a family friend asking about a child's likes and dislikes, whether Gilberte had a particular favorite among her friends; to which her mother replied:

"Well, I'm sure you must be more privy to these secrets than I am! Aren't you the great confidant, after all? Aren't you the great 'crack,' as our English friends say?"

When reality coincides at last with something we have longed for, fitting perfectly with our dreams, it can cover them up entirely and become indistinguishable from them, as two symmetrical figures placed against one another seem to become one; whereas, so as to give our joy its full intensity of meaning, we would actually prefer every detail of our desires, even at the instant of their fulfillment, to retain the prestige of still being immaterial, so as to be more certain that this really is what we desired. The mind is not even at liberty to remake its own earlier state, so as to compare it with the present one: the new acquaintance we have just made, the memory of those first, unexpected moments, the words we have heard spoken, blocking the entrance to our consciousness, and commanding the exits from memory much more than those from imagination, act backward against our past, which we can no longer see without their presence in it, rather than acting forward on the still-unoccupied shape of our future. For years I had been convinced that to go to the house of Mme Swann was a vague pipe-dream that would never come to pass; a quarter-hour after I first stepped into her drawing room, it was all the former amount of time I had spent not knowing her that had become the pipe-dream, as insubstantial as a mere possibility which has been abolished by the fulfillment of a different possibility. How could I have gone on dreaming of her dining room as an inconceivable place when I could not make the slightest movement in my mind without seeing it shot through by the unbreakable beams of light, radiating to infinity, illuminating the farthest nooks and crannies of my past life, given off by the lobster *à l'américaine* which I had just eaten? Something similar must have happened to Swann's way of seeing things too: these rooms in which he sat as my host could be seen as the place where two fancied dwellings had come together and become one, not just the ideal place my imagination had created, but another one, which his jealous love, as inventive as my dreams, had so often pictured: the home which he and Odette might one day share, but which, on nights such as the one when she had invited him to her house with Forcheville to have orangeade, he had despaired of ever being able to inhabit. For Swann, what had become amalgamated into the design of the dining room where we lunched was that inaccessible paradise, which in former years he could never imagine without being beset by a thrilling qualm at the prospect of being able to say one day to *their* butler the very words I could hear him speak now, in a voice of slight impatience touched with a certain self-satisfaction: "Is Madame ready yet?" I could never grasp my happiness, any more than he could, no doubt; and when Gilberte herself exclaimed, "You could never have imagined, could you, that the little girl you used to watch playing prisoner's base, without being on speaking terms with her, would one day be a great friend, whose house you can visit any day you like?," she spoke of a change which I could not help registering from the outside, but on which I had no inner purchase, as it was composed of two states, which I could not focus on at the same time without their becoming a single one.

And yet my own experience told me that, because Swann had subjected that apartment to such an intensity of purposeful desire, he must surely have found in it something of its former charm, just as it had not lost all its mystery for me. By entering their house, I had not completely banished from it the strange, fascinating element in which I had for such a long time imagined the Swanns having their being; I had tamed it a little, I had made it retreat in the face of the outsider I had been, the outcast to whom Mlle Swann now graciously offered a delightful, hostile, and scandalized armchair; and that charm, through memory, I can still feel close to me. Is this perhaps because, while I sat waiting on those days when M. and Mme Swann invited me to have lunch and then share their afternoon outing with Gilberte, my eyes reproduced—all over the carpet, the armchairs, the sideboards, the screens, and the paintings—the idea which was deeply imprinted in me, that Mme Swann, or her husband, or Gilberte was just about to come into the room? Was it because these objects have gone on living beside the Swanns in my memory and have at length absorbed something of them? Was it because, knowing the Swanns spent their lives among them, I had come to see all these things as the emblems of their special existence and of their habits, from which I had been too long excluded for their furniture not to go on seeming alien to me, even after I had been granted the boon of using it? For whatever reason, nowadays when I remember that drawing room, which Swann, without his objection to it implying in any way an intention to go against the wishes of his wife, saw as such a jumble of styles (because, though its design was still based on the concept of the greenhouse-cum-workshop which had been the guiding principle of Odette's house when he had first known her, she had begun to weed out of this medley some of the Chinese items, which she thought now a little "sham," quite "stale," but was replacing them with a clutter of little pieces upholstered in old Louis XVI silks, to which of course were added the masterpieces brought by Swann himself from his old *hôtel* on the Quai d'Orléans), I see its disparities in retrospect as forming a homogeneous, unified whole, as giving it an individual charm; and these are features one can never see in even the most coherent and uniform compilations left to us from the past, or in those most vividly marked by the imprint of a single person, for it is only ever we ourselves, through our belief that things seen have an existence of their own, who can impart to some of them a soul which lives in them, and which they then develop in us. All the fancies I had formed about the hours spent by the Swanns, different from those which other people experience, in that house which, by being to the daily tissue of their existence in time what the body is to the soul, was bound to express the unique quality of their life, were shared by whatever I saw, absorbed into the positioning of the furniture, the thickness of the carpets, the outlook from the windows, the attentions of the servants, equally thrilling and indefinable in them all. After lunch, when we went through into the drawing room to have coffee, sitting in the broad and sunny bay window, and Mme Swann asked me how many lumps of sugar I took, it was not just the silk-covered footstool that she moved toward me which gave off both the painful charm I used to sense in the name of Gilberte (through the pink hawthorn, then near the clump of laurels) and also the suspicion with which her parents had viewed me, and which this little footstool had apparently known of and shared so vehemently that I now felt unworthy and a little cowardly in placing my feet on its defenseless upholstery; a personal soul made it secretly one with the light of two o'clock in the afternoon, light that was unique to this bay, as it dappled our feet with its golden waves and lapped about the enchanted islands of the bluish sofas and hazy tapestries; and even the Rubens hanging above the mantelpiece glowed with the same kind of charm, almost the same potency of charm, as M. Swann's lace-up boots and Inverness cape, the like of which I had longed to wear, and which Odette now asked him to go and change for another overcoat, so as to look more elegant when I did them the honor of going out with them. She too went to change, despite my protests that no walking dress could possibly become her as much as the superb crêpe-de-Chine or silk tea gown, in old rose or cherry, Tiepolo pink, white, mauve, green, red, or yellow, self-colored or patterned, in which she had sat with us while having lunch and was now about to remove. When I told her she should wear it for going out, she would laugh, either in mockery of my naïveté or in pleasure at my compliment. She apologized for having so many tea gowns, saying they were the only garments in which she felt comfortable, then went to put on one of those breathtaking outfits that made all heads turn, after having invited me at times to choose the one I preferred to see her wear.

Once we had left the carriage, how proud I was to walk through the Zoological Gardens beside Mme Swann! Her easy step gave a loose, lazy sway to her coat, and she rewarded my admiring glances with a slow, flirtatious smile. If we met any of Gilberte's friends, girls or boys, they would greet us as we passed; and now I was looked upon by them as one of those blessed beings whom I had envied so much, those friends who also knew her parents and who belonged to the other part of her life, the part that took place away from the Champs-Élysées.

Quite often as we walked along the paths of the Bois de Boulogne or the Zoological Gardens, some grand lady, one of Swann's friends, might greet us in passing; and if he had not noticed, his wife would draw his attention: "Charles, haven't you seen Mme de Montmorency?" Though his casual smile bespoke years of friendly familiarity, he would sweep off his hat with an elegant flourish that was all his own. Sometimes the grand lady would pause, glad of the chance to be inconsequentially polite to Mme Swann, who, she knew, was well enough schooled by Swann in such things not to try taking undue advantage of it in the future. For all that, Mme Swann had mastered the manners of the fashionable; and, however elegant and dignified the grand lady might be, Odette was always her equal in them. As she stood for that moment beside the friend of her husband's, introducing Gilberte and me with such a serene and nonchalant air, she had such affable, unaffected poise that it would have been difficult to tell whether it was Swann's wife or the aristocratic passerby who was the great lady. On the day when we had gone to view the Singhalese, we saw an old but still-beautiful lady coming toward us, followed by two others who seemed to be escorting her; she was wrapped in a dark overcoat and wearing a little bonnet with its strings tied under the chin. "Now, here's someone you'll find interesting," Swann told me. The old lady, now only a few feet away, was gazing at us with a smile that was all warmth and gentleness. Swann took off his hat to her, and Mme Swann, in a low curtsey, tried to kiss the hand of the lady, who, looking as though she had stepped out of a portrait by Winterhalter,[44] drew her up and kissed her. "Look, for goodness' sake, will you put that hat back on," she said to Swann in a deepish voice that was full of a gruff friendliness. "I'll present you in a moment to Her Imperial Highness," Mme Swann said to me. Swann took me briefly aside, while Mme Swann chatted with the Princesse about the fine weather and the animals newly arrived in the Gardens. "It's Princesse Mathilde," he said. "You know, the friend of Flaubert, Sainte-Beuve, and Dumas. Just think, a niece of Napoleon I! Both Napoleon III and the Tsar of Russia wanted to marry her. Isn't that interesting? Have a little talk with her. I do hope, though, that she's not going to keep us standing about here for an hour." "I met Taine[45] the other day," Swann said to her. "He tells me Princesse Mathilde is no longer his friend." "He behaved like a pig," she growled, pronouncing *cochon* as though it were the name of the bishop who tried Joan of Arc.[46] "After that article of his on the Emperor, I left my card at his house with 'PPC' on it."[47] I was as surprised as one might be on reading the correspondence of Charlotte-Elizabeth, the Princess Palatine. Princesse Mathilde, full of very French sentiments, was given to feeling them with a forthright bluntness reminiscent of Germany as it once was, a trait that may well have come to her from her mother, who was from Württemberg. She was outspoken in a rather uncouth or mannish way; but as soon as she smiled, this was softened by a languid Italian manner. These impressions were complemented by her costumes, which were so Second Empire in style that, though her reason for wearing them was no doubt only that she was attached to the fashions she had loved when young, she seemed to have made a point of wearing nothing that was historically discrepant, so as not to disappoint those who expected her to remind them of a bygone era. I prompted Swann to ask her whether she had ever known Alfred de Musset.[48] "Hardly at all, sir," she told him in a voice that feigned ill temper, the "sir" being her little joke with someone she knew very well. "I invited him once to dinner. Seven o'clock, the invitation said. At half past, he still not having turned up, we went in to dine. He presented himself at eight, gave me a bow, then sat there without uttering a word, and made himself scarce when dinner was done. I hadn't so much as heard the sound of the man's voice. Dead drunk. Not the sort of thing to make one want to have him again." Swann and I were standing a little to one side. "I do hope this isn't going to take too long," he said to me. "The soles of my feet are killing me. I can't understand why my wife is keeping the conversation going like that. She'll be the one to complain afterward of feeling tired; but I'm the one who can't take all this standing around." Mme Swann was in the process of telling Princesse Mathilde something she had learned from Mme Bontemps: that the government, having at last admitted how churlish its recent behavior toward the Princesse had been, had decided to send her a ticket admitting her to the stands for the visit of Tsar Nicholas to the Invalides two days later. But, appearances to the contrary notwithstanding, despite having surrounded herself with artists and men of letters, whenever action was called for the Princesse was still very much the niece of Napoleon. "Exactly, madame," she said. "I received their invitation this morning and sent it straight back to the minister, who must have received it by now. I have told him I have no need of any invitation to go to the Invalides. If the government wishes me to attend, I shall not be in any stands, but in our family vault, where the Emperor lies. And for that I need no ticket—I've got my keys. I come and go as I please. The government need only inform me whether it desires my presence or not. But if I do go, that's where I shall be, and nowhere else." At that moment Mme Swann and I were greeted by a young man who, having said his "Good afternoon," did not stop, and whom I did not know she knew: Bloch. When I asked her about him, she said he had been introduced to her by Mme Bontemps and that he was on the minister's staff, which was news to me. However, she must not have seen much of him, or else she had wanted to avoid pronouncing the name Bloch, perhaps thinking it not "chic" enough, as she said his name was M. Moreul. I assured her she was mixing him up with someone else and that his name was Bloch. The Princesse noticed Mme Swann's admiring glances at her coat and straightened the train of it, which was twisted. "This is actually made from a fur that the Tsar sent me," she said, "so, since I've just been to see him, I decided to wear it and let him see how it looks when it's made up into a coat." "I hear that Prince Louis[49] has taken a commission in the Russian army," said Mme Swann, not noticing her husband's signs of impatience. "Your Highness will be very sad at not having him here at home." "Much good it'll do him, I'm sure! As I said to him, 'You shouldn't feel obliged to, just because we've had a soldier in the family already!' " the Princesse replied, referring in her simple, blunt way to the Emperor Napoleon. Swann was more and more impatient. "Madame, I am afraid I must be the one to behave like a highness and request your permission for us to take our leave. My wife has been quite unwell, and I am reluctant for her to remain standing in one spot." Mme Swann curtseyed once more, and the Princesse gave us all the blessing of a beautiful smile which she seemed to summon out of the past, from the gracious days of her youth and the evenings at Compiègne,[50] and which all at once smoothed out and softened the brief grumpiness of the face. Then she walked away, followed by her two ladies-in-waiting, who, like interpreters, children's nannies, or nurses, had done no more than punctuate the conversation with insignificant verbiage and unnecessary explanations. "One day this week you should go and sign the book at her house," Mme Swann said to me. "It's not every *royal,* as the English say, on whom you can leave a card. But with this one, if you sign, you'll get an invitation."

On occasion, before our outing we would go and look at one or another of the small exhibitions that were opening during those late-winter days; and in the galleries where they were held, Swann, a noted collector, was always greeted with marked deference by the dealers. The weather being still cold, all my old desire to go to the South, to Venice, was reawakened by those rooms, in which spring was already well established, where hot sunlight slashed the pink Alpilles with glowing purples and deepened a dark transparency of emerald in the Grand Canal. If the weather was unpleasant, we went on to a concert or the theater; and we finished the afternoon in a tearoom. When Mme Swann had something to say to me that she wished to keep from people sitting at tables near ours, or even just from the waiters, she addressed me in English, as though we were the only ones who could speak the language. But of course everybody could speak English—except me, that is, as I had not yet learned the language; and this I had to point out to Mme Swann, to make her desist from passing remarks on those who were drinking the tea, and those who brought it to them, remarks that I could tell were insulting, even though every word of them was lost on me, if not on the people insulted.

Once, in connection with an outing to the theater, Gilberte gave me a great surprise. It was the day she had referred to before, the anniversary of her grandfather's death. She and I were supposed to be going with her governess to hear a program of operatic extracts; and Gilberte, who had already changed into the outfit she was to wear to the performance, was showing her usual expression of indifference toward the event of the afternoon, saying she did not mind what we did, as long as I wanted to do it and her parents agreed to it. Just before lunch, her mother took us aside to say that Gilberte's father was quite put out by our intention of going to a concert on such a day. To me, this seemed quite understandable. Gilberte's face was expressionless, though she turned pale with anger that she could not conceal; and she said not another word. When M. Swann came home, his wife took him down to the other end of the drawing room, where they stood murmuring to each other. He eventually asked Gilberte to come with him into the next room. We could hear voices raised. I could not believe that Gilberte, who was so dutiful, so loving, so biddable, would refuse a request of her father's on such a day, and for such an unimportant reason. Swann said, as he came back in:

"Well, you've heard what I had to say. Now you must do as you see fit."

Throughout lunch, Gilberte's face was pinched with irritation. We had no sooner gone to her room afterward than she exclaimed, as though nothing had been further from her mind than the notion of canceling our outing, "Look at the time, will you! Two o'clock! It starts at half past!" And she told her governess to hurry up.

"But isn't your father annoyed about this?" I said.

"Not in the least."

"But didn't he think it would appear odd for us to be going out, because of the anniversary?"

"Look, what do I care about what people think! I think it's preposterous to worry about other people when feelings are involved. You feel things for yourself, not for an audience. My governess, who hardly gets out at all, has been looking forward to this concert, and I'm not going to spoil her pleasure just to please the gallery!"

She started putting on her hat.

"But, Gilberte," I said, taking her arm, "it's not to please the gallery, it's to please your father."

"Don't *you* start!" she snapped, snatching her arm away.

An even greater boon than to be taken to the Zoo in the Bois, or to a concert, was to be included in the Swanns' friendship with Bergotte, the thing that had been one of the sources of their charm long before I came to know Gilberte, in the days when I had dreamed that to be friends with such a girl, who was a friend of the divine old man, would be a thrilling experience, if only the disdain she must feel for me had not made it forever futile for me to hope I might one day accompany them on their excursions to the towns he loved. Then, one day, Mme Swann sent me an invitation to a special luncheon. I did not know who the other guests were to be. And as I arrived, I was disconcerted and intimidated by a small incident that happened just inside the Swanns' front door. Mme Swann rarely failed to adopt any of the short-lived customs that are supposed to be smart, which last for a season, then disappear—for instance, many years before, she had had her *hansom cab,*[51] and had her dinner invitations printed with the English words *to meet* immediately preceding the name of some guest of any importance. Many of these customs were quite unmysterious, even to the uninitiated. One such at that time was a little fad imported from England, which led Odette to have her husband's visiting cards printed with the title of *Mr.* before the name Charles Swann. After my very first visit to their house, Mme Swann had called on me and left one of these "pasteboards," as she termed them. It was the first time in my life that anyone had ever left a card on me! I had been seized with such a fit of pride, excitement, and gratitude that I scraped together all the money I possessed in the world, ordered a magnificent basket of camellias, and had them sent to her. I also begged my father to go and leave a card on her, but to be sure first to get some with *Mr.* in front of his name. He did neither of these things, which first plunged me into despair for a few days, then made me wonder whether he had not been right. Futile though it was, this fad for *Mr.* was at least not misleading. However, the same could not be said for another one, which was revealed to me, without its meaning, on the day of Mme Swann's special luncheon. Just as I was about to step from the anteroom into the drawing room, the butler handed me a long, thin envelope on which my name was written. Such was my surprise that I thanked him, while I cast a glance at the envelope. I had no more notion of what I was supposed to do with it than a foreigner has of the purpose of the little implements given to guests at Chinese dinners. I could see it was sealed; so, rather than be thought indiscreet by opening it there and then, I slipped it into my pocket with a knowing air. The note Mme Swann had sent me a few days before had mentioned a lunch "for a select few." Despite which, it was a party of sixteen; and I had no idea that among us was Bergotte. Mme Swann, who had just "named" me, as she put it, to several of the guests, suddenly appended to my name, in exactly the same voice as she had used for pronouncing it, and as though he and I were merely two guests of hers who must be equally glad to make each other's acquaintance, the name of my soft-voiced bard with the white hair. The name "Bergotte" startled me as though it were a shot fired from a gun; but I was already bowing, going through the motions of polite behavior. There, in front of me, bowing back at me, like the magician in his tails emerging unscathed while a dove flies up from the smoke and dust of a detonation, I saw a stocky, coarse, thickset, shortsighted man, quite young, with a red bottle-nose and a black goatee. I was heartbroken: it was not only that my gentle old man had just crumbled to dust and disappeared, it was also that for those things of beauty, his wonderful works, which I had once contrived to fit into that infirm and sacred frame, that dwelling I had lovingly constructed like a temple expressly designed to hold them, there was now no room in this thick-bodied little man standing in front of me, with all his blood vessels, his bones, his glands, his snub nose, and his little black beard. The whole Bergotte I had slowly and painstakingly constructed for myself, a drop at a time, like a stalactite, out of the limpid beauty of his books, had suddenly been rendered useless by the need to include the bottle-nose and the black goatee, just as our perfect solution to a mathematical problem turns out to be useless because we have misread the terms of it and ignored the fact that the total should add up to a certain number. The presence of the nose and the beard loomed so large and were so bothersome that they not only forced me to rebuild from scratch the character of Bergotte, but also seemed to imply, to create, to be secreting nonstop a certain type of busy and self-satisfied mentality, all of which was quite unfair, as it was a mentality which had nothing in common with the type of mind that informed the books I knew so well, steeped in their mild and divine wisdom. Starting from the books, I could never have foreseen the bottle-nose; but starting from the nose—which looked quite unworried by all of this, and was rather full of itself, like a false nose—I was on a quite different course, which would never lead me to the works of Bergotte, it seemed, but toward the attitudes of some engineer who is always pressed for time, the kind of man who, when you greet him, thinks it is the thing to answer, "Fine, thanks, and yourself?" though you haven't asked him anything yet, who, when you say you are delighted to make his acquaintance, replies with an abbreviation he thinks is stylish, clever, and up-to-the-minute, because it avoids wasting time in empty chat: "Likewise." Names are of course fanciful designers; the sketches they draw of people and places are such poor likenesses that we are often struck dumb when, instead of the world as we have imagined it, we are suddenly confronted by the world as we see it (which is not the real world, of course, as the senses are not much better at likenesses than the imagination; so we end up with approximate drawings of reality, which are at least as different from the seen world as the seen world was different from the imagined world). But with Bergotte, the embarrassment of the name, laden with its disconcerting preconceptions, was insignificant compared with the chagrin I felt at the prospect of tying this man with his goatee to the work I knew, as though to a balloon, and wondering whether it might still have the power to become airborne. However, it did appear that he was the man who had written the books I was so fond of, for when Mme Swann made a point of mentioning my liking for one of them he did not appear taken aback that this had been said to him rather than to some other guest, and gave no hint of thinking there must be some misunderstanding: he just stood there, his body, which was looking forward to lunch, filling the frock coat he had put on in honor of all these guests, his attention taken up by other, important things, and gave a reminiscent smile, as though thinking back to some fleeting incident from former years, as though what had been mentioned was the hose and doublet of the Duc de Guise costume he had worn one year to a fancy-dress ball, rather than his books, which instantly collapsed (dragging down with themselves the whole point and glory of Beauty, of the universe, of life itself) and showed that they had never been anything but a trite pastime for a man with a little beard. It occurred to me that he must have put a great effort into this pastime, but also that, if he had lived on an island surrounded by oyster beds, he would have engaged just as successfully in the buying and selling of pearls. His work no longer seemed as inevitable as before. I began to wonder whether originality really shows that great writers are gods, each of them reigning over a kingdom which is his alone, whether misleading appearances might not play a role in this, and whether the differences between their books might not be the result of hard work, rather than the expression of a radical difference in essence between distinct personalities.

We went in to dinner. Lying beside my plate was a carnation, its stem wrapped in silver paper. It bothered me less than the envelope given to me in the anteroom, which I had completely forgotten. Though also new to me, the meaning of this custom soon became clearer, when I saw all the other men at the table pick up carnations lying beside their plates and slip them into the buttonholes of their frock coats. I did the same, with the casual air of the atheist in church, who, though knowing nothing about the service, stands up when the others stand, and kneels with only a moment's delay when everybody else kneels. Another custom, just as unfamiliar to me but more lasting, was less to my taste. Just to the right of my plate was a smaller dish, full of a blackish substance which, unknown to me, was caviar. I had no idea what one was supposed to do with it; but I was determined not to eat any of it.

As Bergotte's place at the table was not far from mine and I could hear everything he said, I soon realized why his way of speaking had struck M. de Norpois. He did have a most singular voice. It is the fact that they have to convey thought which, more than anything else, alters the physical properties of a voice: not only are the resonance of the diphthongs and the power of the labials affected by it, so is the delivery itself. To my ear, Bergotte's way of speaking was completely different from his way of writing; and even the things he said differed from the things that fill his books. A voice emerges from a mask; unaided, it is not up to showing us immediately a face we have glimpsed naked in a style. During conversation, at moments when Bergotte took to talking in a way that M. de Norpois was not the only one to find affected and obnoxious, it took me a long time to discover any close parallel with those parts of his books where his form became so poetic and musical. At such times, Bergotte could see in what he was saying a beauty of form unrelated to the meaning of his sentences; and as human speech is in communication with the soul, albeit not expressing it as style does, Bergotte sounded almost as though he were speaking without meaning, droning on certain words, and, if he was following through a single image under the words, running them together as though they were a single sound, in a way that was fatiguing in its monotony. The fact was that a toneless, turgid, and pretentious delivery was a sign of the aesthetic value of his words; it was the manifestation in his conversation of the power that gave to his books their harmonies and sequences of images. The reason why I had such difficulty in noticing this was that what he said at such moments, for the very reason that it was from Bergotte, did not seem to be by Bergotte. It was composed of a rich flow of exact ideas, quite foreign to the "Bergotte manner" as misappropriated by reviewers; and that dissimilarity was probably another reflection of the fact—glimpsed vaguely through the spoken word, like something seen through smoked glass—that, when one read a page of real Bergotte, it never resembled what would have been written by any of the insipid imitators who kept touching up their prose, in newspapers and books, with pseudo-Bergottisms in imagery and ideas. This difference in style came from the fact that the real thing was first and foremost some precious, genuine element lying concealed within each object, waiting to be drawn out by the great writer with his genius; and it was this drawing out that was the aim of the soft-voiced Bard, not to toss off a page or two in the manner of Bergotte. He did of course write in the manner of Bergotte, given that Bergotte was who he was; and also in the sense that each new touch of beauty in his work was the particle of Bergotte hidden inside a thing, which he had drawn out of it. However, though each of these beauties had something recognizable to it, something in common with the others, it kept its own special quality, like the discovery that had brought it to light; and because it was new, it remained different from the so-called Bergotte manner, that vague composite of earlier Bergottes already found, drawn out, and written up by the man himself, none of which enabled men unendowed with genius to guess at what he might go on to discover in other things. All the great writers are like that: the beauty of their sentences, like the beauty of a woman one has not yet met, is unforeseeable; it is a creation, since its object is an external thing rather than themselves, something in their minds but not yet put into words. A memoirist trying unobtrusively to write like Saint-

Simon nowadays might well hit on a line like the opening one in the portrait of the Duc de Villars: "Quite a tall man, dark of complexion, and with a physiognomy that was bright, open, outgoing"—but no determinism could possibly make him say in the next line, of this same physiognomy, "and in truth a trifle mad."[52] The real thing smacks of that fullness of genuine and unexpected ingredients, of the branch crammed with blue flowers dangling unexpectedly from the springtime hedge, which already looked unable to bear more blossom; whereas the purely formal replica of the real thing (one could say the same of every other feature of style) is full of vacancy and sameness, full, that is, of what least resembles the real thing and, in the hands of an imitator, can pass for the real thing only in the minds of those who have never seen it in the words of the master.

Hence, just as the spoken manner of Bergotte might well have been pleasing if he had been some mere admirer quoting pseudo-Bergotte (whereas it was inseparable from the active workings of his mind, organically linked to it in ways the ear did not pick up at once), so the reason why there was something too matter-of-fact and overrich in his speech was that he applied his mind with precision to any aspect of reality that pleased him, thereby disappointing those who expected him to speak only of "the headlong torrent of fair forms" and "Beauty's thrilling enigma." And then his constant originality when he wrote became, when he spoke, a way of approaching topics that was so subtle in its avoidance of anything already familiar in them that it always sounded as though he were trying to come at it from some petty angle, taking it the wrong way on purpose, or being smart for smartness's sake; and in this way, his ideas usually sounded confused, each of us having the habit of seeing clarity in ideas that show the same measure of confusion as our own. Besides, as anything new must first do away with the stereotype we are so used to that we have come to see it as reality itself, any new style of conversation, just like any originality in painting or music, will always seem convoluted and wearisome. We find its structuring figures so unwonted that the talker seems to be nothing more than a metaphor-monger, which fatigues the ear and hints at a lack of truthfulness. (Of course, the earlier speech forms themselves were once images, which a listener unfamiliar with the world they described had difficulty in grasping. But they have long since come to be taken as the real world, the reliable world.) So, when one heard Bergotte say of Cottard that he was "a Cartesian devil forever trying to remain in equipoise"—it seems such an unremarkable thing to say nowadays—or of Brichot that "He was even more concerned than Mme Swann with the care of his hair, because, in his dual preoccupation with his profile and his reputation, the lie of his locks had to give him the constant appearance of being both a lion and a philosopher," one soon tired of it and wished for the firmer footing of something more concrete, by which one meant something one was more used to. The unrecognizable words emitted by the mask in front of me had to be attributed to the writer whom I admired, yet could not have been fitted like spare pieces of a jigsaw puzzle into spaces in any of his books; they existed on a different plane, and required to be transposed, as I discovered one day when, having repeated aloud some phrases I had recently heard uttered by Bergotte, I recognized in them the whole structure of his written style, which in spoken form had sounded so different that I had been unable to see and identify its component parts.

A more superficial thing, the special, intense, and more than punctilious pronunciation he used with certain words, certain adjectives which often recurred in his conversation, and which he slightly overemphasized, bringing out every single syllable and making the stressed one ring (as in the word "visage," which he invariably used instead of "face," cramming it with extra *v*'s, *s*'s, and *g*'s, all of which seemed to burst out of his gesturing hand as he spoke them), was the exact correlative of those fine and special places in his prose where he would set such favored words, which were always preceded by a sort of margin, and so precisely designed within the sentence's intricate balance that, in order to avoid spoiling the rhythm of it, one was obliged to give each of them its full quantity. However, in Bergotte's spoken words there was no sign of that particular lighting which in his books, as in the books of some other writers, often alters the appearance of words in a written sentence. That form of light comes no doubt from great depths, and its rays cannot reach our words at those times when, by being open to others through conversation, we are partly closed to ourselves. In that sense, one could hear in his books more intonations and more accent than in his speech; for this is an accent which is unrelated to the beauty of a style, which a writer himself may not even have noticed, as it is inseparable from his most private self. This was the accent which always marked its rhythm in the words Bergotte wrote when he was being entirely natural, however insignificant in themselves such words might be. It is an accent marked by no sign on the page, indicated by nothing in the text; and yet it clings to the sentences, which cannot be spoken in any other way; it was the most ephemeral but the most profound thing in the writer, the thing which will bear definitive witness to his nature, which will enable one to tell whether, despite all the harsh things he uttered, he was a gentle man, whether, despite all the sensuality, he was a man of sentiment.

Certain idiosyncrasies of elocution that could be faintly detected in the speech of Bergotte were not peculiar to him; and when I later came to know his brothers and sisters, I noticed that their speech was much more marked by these than his was. It had something to do with a sharp, hoarse fall to the last words of a cheerful statement, or a faint and fading voice at the end of a sad one. Swann, who had known the Master as a child, once told me that in those days Bergotte's voice was as full as his brothers' and sisters' of these more or less family inflections, outbursts of violent glee alternating with slow, melancholy murmurs, and that, when they were all together in the playroom, the young Bergotte could be heard holding his own amid a chorus scored for the deafening and the forlorn. However personal they may be, all these human sounds are transitory, and do not outlive the beings who emit them. But that was not the case with the Bergotte family pronunciation. It may be difficult to understand, even in *Die Meistersinger*, how any artist can ever invent music by listening to birdsong; but Bergotte had transposed and set in prose those ways of drawing out words which ring repetitively with the sounds of joy, or keep dropping away to the saddest sigh. In some of his books, there are sentence endings in which the long-drawn-out chords resound like those dying notes of an operatic overture which, in its reluctance to close, keeps murmuring its final, sublime harmonies, until the conductor at last lays down his baton, which I came to see later as a musical equivalent of the Bergotte family's phonetic brasses. But Bergotte himself, as soon as he started to transpose them into his writing, unconsciously gave up using them in speech. His voice, from the day when he started to write (and all the more by the later time when I came to know him), had forever lost the power to orchestrate them.

In wit or delicacy of mind, these young Bergottes, the future writer and his brothers and sisters, were no doubt not the equals of other young people, who thought them very rowdy, and actually rather vulgar, with their irritating jokes, which were typical of the household's partly pretentious, partly puerile style. But genius, or even great talent, lies less in elements of mind and social refinement superior to those of others than in the ability to transform and transpose them. To heat a liquid with a flashlight, what is required is not the strongest possible torch, but one in which the current can be diverted from the production of light and adapted to the production of heat. To fly through the air, it is not necessary to have the most powerful motorcar, but a motor which, by turning its earthbound horizontal line into a vertical, can convert its speed along the ground into ascent. Likewise, those who produce works of genius are not those who spend their days in the most refined company, whose conversation is the most brilliant, or whose culture is the broadest; they are those who have the ability to stop living for themselves and make a mirror of their personality, so that their lives, however nondescript they may be socially, or even in a way intellectually, are reflected in it. For genius lies in reflective power, and not in the intrinsic quality of the scene reflected. It was when the young Bergotte became capable of showing to the world of his readers the tasteless drawing room where he had spent his childhood, and the rather unamusing exchanges it had witnessed between himself and his brothers, that he rose above his wittier and more distinguished family friends. They could be driven home in their fine Rolls-Royces, sneering a little at the Bergottes and their vulgarities. But he, with his much less impressive flying machine, had at last taken off and soared over their heads.

Other features of his diction he shared not with members of his family but with certain writers of his day. Certain younger writers who were beginning to outgrow him, and who claimed to have no intellectual affinity with him, showed their debt to him unawares in their use of certain adverbs or prepositions that he was always using, in the sentences they spoke modeled on his, in the same dawdling and almost toneless manner of speech, which had been his reaction against the facile grandiloquence of a previous generation. It may be that these young men had never known Bergotte (this was certainly the case, as will be seen, with some of them). But, having been inoculated with his way of thinking, they had developed those modifications of syntax and accent which bear a necessary relation to intellectual originality. This is a relation that requires some interpretation. The fact was that, though Bergotte's way of writing owed nothing to anyone, he was indebted for his speaking style to one of his old friends, a wonderful talker who had had a great influence on him, whom he imitated unintentionally in conversation, but who, being less gifted than Bergotte, had never written a book that was in any way out of the ordinary. Thus, if judged only on originality of spoken delivery, Bergotte would have been properly deemed to be a mere disciple, a purveyor of hand-me-downs; whereas, despite having been influenced in speech habits by his friend, he had still been original and creative as a writer. His impulse to set himself apart from that previous generation, which had been too fond of grand abstractions and commonplaces, could probably also be seen in the fact that when he wanted to praise a book the thing he would single out or quote was always a scene giving a graphic glimpse of something, a picture without thematic relevance. "Oh, yes," he would say. "That's pretty good. That little girl wearing the orange shawl. It's really nice." Or else, "Yes, that's right! That part where there's a regiment marching through a town! Yes, that's a good bit!" On matters of style, he was not quite of his own period (though very much of his own country, abhorring Tolstoy, George Eliot, Ibsen, and Dostoevsky); and the word one always heard from him whenever he praised a writer's style was "smooth": "Well, actually the Chateaubriand I prefer is the one in *Atala* rather than the one in *Rancé*—yes, he's smoother there." He used the word as a doctor might to soothe a patient complaining that milk was not good for his stomach: "Oh, but it's very smooth." And it is a fact that in his own style there was a type of harmony, the like of which made the ancients praise some of their orators in ways that seem all but inconceivable to us, accustomed as we are to our modern languages, in which no one would try for such effects.

If anyone praised a piece of his own, he would say of it with a shy smile, "I think it's all right, it's not bad, it's worth saying"; but this was mere modesty, after the manner of the woman who, on being told that her dress or her daughter is lovely, replies, "Well, it's nice and comfortable," or "Well, she's a good-natured girl." But the artisan's instinct ran too deep in Bergotte for him to be unaware that the sole proof of his having worked to good purpose, and in accord with truth, lay in the joy to be derived from his own work, by himself in the first place, and then by others. Unfortunately, many years later, when his talent had run out, whenever he wrote something that dissatisfied him, rather than scratching it out as he should have done, he talked himself into publishing it with the words he had once spoken to others: "Well, yes, it's all right, it says something that's worth saying, for the sake of my country. . . ." The phrases his feigned modesty had murmured for an admirer were later spoken, in the sincerity of his most secret self, to allay the misgivings of pride; the words that had been his unnecessary apology for the quality of his first works became his futile consolation for the mediocrity of his last.

In his urge never to write anything of which he could not say, "It's smooth," there was a kind of strictness of taste which, though it had caused him to be seen for so many years as an artist of sterile preciosity, a finicking minimalist, was actually the secret of his strength. For habit is style-forming as well as character-forming; and the writer who, in the expression of his thought, becomes used to aiming only at a certain facility, sets bounds beyond which his talent will never go, just as surely as, by repeated recourse to a pleasure, to idleness, or to the fear of suffering, we pencil in, on a character that it is eventually impossible to touch up, the contours of our vices and the limits of our virtue.

However, though I was later to note many things common both to the writer and to the man, perhaps my very first impression of Bergotte was not quite wrong, that day at Mme Swann's, when I doubted that the person standing in front of me could be the author of so many divine books, for he himself "disbelieved" it too, in the true meaning of the word. He disbelieved it each time he fawned on fashionable people (not that he was a snob), or toadied to other writers or journalists, all of whom were clearly inferior to him. By now of course he knew about his genius from the plaudits of other people; and that knowledge is something beside which social position and official recognition are negligible. He knew all about his genius; but he disbelieved in it, going on feigning deference to mediocre writers, in the hope of being elected before long to the Académie Française, although neither the Académie nor the Faubourg Saint-Germain has anything more to do with that share of the eternal Spirit which writes the books of a Bergotte than it has to do with the principle of causality or the idea of God. Bergotte was aware of that too, of course; but his awareness was as ineffectual as that of the kleptomaniac who knows that stealing is wrong. Like a lord who cannot help pocketing the cutlery, the man with the goatee and the bottle-nose had to creep up on the coveted seat in the Académie, by courting the duchess who commanded several votes in each of the elections, but in such a way as to prevent anyone who might think this aim unworthy of him from noticing what he was doing. In this, he was only partly successful; and when he spoke, one could always hear, in among the real Bergotte's words, other words spoken by the self-seeker, the man of ambition who was forever trying to impress people by dropping the names of the influential, the noble, or the rich, despite having depicted in the books he wrote when he was truly himself, as limpid as a spring, the charm of the poor.

As for the other vices mentioned by M. de Norpois, the semi-incestuous affair, allegedly further complicated by some indelicacy about money, though they did flagrantly contradict the tendency of his latest novels (which were marked by such a painfully scrupulous care for all that is good that their heroes' slightest joys were poisoned by it, and that even the reader got from it an anguished feeling which made the easiest life seem hard to bear), they did not prove, even if they could be said to be well founded, that his works were a tissue of falsehoods and his great sensitivity mere play-acting. In pathology, certain states of similar appearance may have different causes, some being due to high blood pressure and others to low, some to an excess of secretion, others to not enough; and in the same way, a single vice can derive either from hypersensitivity or from a deficient sensitivity. It may only be in a life deeply steeped in its vice that the moral question can arise with the full power of its anxiety. This question the artist answers not on the plane of his individual life, but in the mode of existence that represents his true life; and there the answer given is a literary one, of general application. Just as the Fathers of the Church, good as they were, first had to practice the sins of all men, through which they found their own sanctity, so great artists, immoral as they are, often derive from their own vices a definition of the moral rule that applies to us all. It is usually on paper that writers inveigh against the vices (or just the foibles and follies) of their own small world, the prattle or scandalous frivolity of their daughters, the treachery of their wives, or even their own failings, while doing nothing to reform these regrettable or unseemly features of their family life. This disparity used to be less noticeable than in Bergotte's day, partly because the drift of society toward its own corruption was matched by a growing refinement of moral ideas, and partly because the reading public had become better informed than before about the private lives of writers; and on certain evenings at the theater, people would point out the author whom I had so admired in Combray days, sitting back in a box with people whose company, in relation to the idea he had advocated in his latest book, was tantamount to a flippant disclaimer, a singularly derisive or abject disparagement. His goodness or wickedness was never much clarified for me by any of the informants who spoke to me of the man himself. Someone who knew him well would attest to how harsh he could be; someone else would give an instance (touching, because clearly designed to remain a secret) of his deeply sympathetic nature. He had treated his wife callously. But then, in a country inn where he was spending the night, he had stayed on so as to look after a poor woman who had tried to drown herself; and when he could stay no longer, he had left a large sum of money so that the landlord would not turn her out, but take care of her. The more the great writer grew in Bergotte at the expense of the man with the goatee, the more his individual life was taken over by all the other lives he imagined, which seemed to relieve him of the obligation of performing real duties, replacing it with the duty of imagining those other lives. But at the same time, because he imagined the feelings of others as vividly as if they had been his own, when circumstances brought him into at least temporary contact with someone much less fortunate than himself, rather than adopt his own point of view, he always put himself in the position of the person who was suffering; and this was a position in which he would have been horrified by the language of people who, when faced with the distress of others, go on being engrossed in their own petty concerns. In this way, he gave grounds for many a justified grudge and for enduring gratitude.

Most important, Bergotte was a man who took his greatest pleasure in certain images, in composing and painting them in words, like a miniature in the bottom of a casket. In response to some trifling gift, if it afforded him the opportunity of devising some of these images, he would be lavish in expressing his appreciation, though he might well have nothing to say in return for an expensive present. If he had ever been on trial in a court of law, despite himself he would have chosen his words not for the effect they might have on the judge, but for the sake of imagery that the judge would not even have noticed.

On that occasion when I first met Bergotte at the house of Gilberte's parents, I told him I had recently been to see La Berma in *Phèdre,* to which he replied that in the scene where she stood with one arm outstretched at shoulder height—one of the scenes the audience had acclaimed—the nobility of her acting had managed to call to mind masterpieces that she might actually never have seen, a Hesperid making that very gesture on a metope at Olympia and the beautiful maidens from the older Erechtheum.

"It may be a sort of second sight on her part. Though I suspect she frequents museums. That would be an interesting thing to educe, wouldn't it?" ("Educe" was one of those words Bergotte was always using; and it had been taken up by certain young men who, though they

had never met him, spoke like him as though under the influence of remote hypnotism.)

"Do you mean the Caryatids?" Swann asked.

"No, I don't mean that," Bergotte replied. "Or, rather, yes, but only
in the scene where she confesses her love to Oenone, gesturing with exactly the hand movement of Hegeso on the stele in the Ceramicus. No,
usually she brings back to life a form of art that's much more ancient. I
was referring to the korai from the old Erechtheum—and I fully accept
that it's a form of art which is the antithesis of Racine. But, then, there
are so many things in *Phèdre* that one extra . . . Even so, I must agree,
that pretty little Phèdre straight out of the sixth century B.C. is very
nice, the perpendicularity of the arm, the curl of hair looking like marble, there's no doubt about it, it all adds up to a real brainwave. There's
much more antiquity in it than in many of this year's books about so-
called antiquity."

As one of Bergotte's books contained a celebrated address to these
archaic statues, his words were full of interest for me, as well as giving
me a further reason for my interest in La Berma as an actress. I tried
hard to remember what she had looked like in that scene where she
raised her arm to shoulder height; and I assured myself, "It's the Hesperid from Olympia! It's the sister of one of those admirable praying
figures on the Acropolis! What a noble art form!" The trouble was,
though, that these assurances could have convinced me of the beauty
of La Berma's gesture only if Bergotte had primed me with them before
the performance. Then, while the actress's posture was in actual existence before my eyes, during that instant when a thing taking place is
still pregnant with reality, I could have attempted to draw a notion of
archaic sculpture from it. But the memory I had kept of La Berma in
that scene was by now indelible, an image as thin as any that lacks those
depths full of present time which one can plumb, in which something
genuinely new can be found, an image on which I could impose no
retrospective interpretation verifiable by comparison with its objective counterpart. Mme Swann, wishing to be part of the conversation,
asked me whether Gilberte had ever remembered to let me have Bergotte's piece on *Phèdre*, adding, "That daughter of mine, you know,

she's such a scatterbrain!" Bergotte gave his modest smile and said it
was just a little thing of no consequence. "No, no! It's such a delightful
little piece! Your little *screed*," Mme Swann insisted, to show she was the
perfect hostess, and hinting that she had read the little essay, so as to
enjoy not just complimenting Bergotte but discriminating among the
things he had written, and being an intellectual influence on him. The
fact is, she did inspire him, but not in the way she thought. Between
the elegance that was once the salon of Mme Swann and a whole aspect
of the work of Bergotte, there are connections that make it possible, for
men who are now grown old, to read each of them in terms of the
other.

I was glad to tell Bergotte of my impressions of La Berma. Though
he thought many of them were not quite sound, he let me speak. I told
him how much I had liked the greenish lighting effect at the moment
when Phèdre held out her arm. "Well, now! The designer, who is a great
artist in his own right, would be delighted to know that. I'll certainly
tell him, because he's very proud of that lighting effect. Mind you, I
must say I don't fancy it very much myself. It floods everything with a
sort of glaucous glow and makes poor little Phèdre look too much like a
bit of coral decorating an aquarium. I know what you're going to say—
that it brings out the cosmic aspect of the drama being played out—and
I agree, it does. But it would still be preferable in a play set in Neptune's
realm. Of course, *Phèdre* does have something to do with Neptune's
vengeance. Goodness knows, I'm not one to say that Port-Royal with its
Jansenism is the be-all and end-all of Racine. But I mean, Racine's play
isn't about the love of a couple of sea urchins, is it? However, that lighting effect was exactly what my friend was aiming at, it's really first-rate,
and one can't deny it's quite pretty. So, yes, you liked it, you saw the
point of it, and when all's said and done, we think alike, you and I. His
idea was just a little crazy, wouldn't you say? But really very clever."
When Bergotte's view on something differed in this way from my own,
it never reduced me to silence, or deprived me of a possible rejoinder,
as M. de Norpois's opinion would have done. Not that Bergotte's opinions were any less valid than the former ambassador's. The fact is that a
sound idea transmits some of its force even to its contradictor. With its

share of the universal value of all mind, it takes root among other adjacent ideas, growing like a graft even in the mind of someone whose own idea it rebuts; and this latter person, drawing some advantage from the new juxtaposition, may round the idea out or adapt it, so that the final judgment on a matter is in some measure the work of the two people who were in disagreement. But the ideas that leave no possibility of a rejoinder are those that are not properly speaking ideas, those that, by being supported by nothing, find nothing to attach to in the other's mind: on the one side, no brotherly branch is held out, and on the other, there is nothing but a vacuum. The arguments advanced by M. de Norpois (on questions of art) were indisputable because they were devoid of reality.

As Bergotte had not dismissed my objections, I went on to tell him of the disdain with which M. de Norpois had treated them. "Look, he's just an old parrot," Bergotte said. "He took a peck at you because he always thinks whatever's under his nose is birdseed or a cuttlebone." "What's that?" Swann asked me. "You know Norpois?" "Oh, isn't he a dreadful old bore!" Mme Swann said. She had great faith in Bergotte's judgment and was probably anxious in case M. de Norpois had said something to her detriment. "I tried to have a conversation with him after dinner, and, possibly because of his age, or perhaps poor digestion, I thought the man was quite, quite inane. One had the impression that he had been drugged to the eyeballs!" "True, true," Bergotte said, "he is obliged to observe frequent silences, so as to reach the end of the evening without using up the supply of starchy stupidities that keep his white waistcoat stiff." "I do think Bergotte and my dear wife are being rather hard on M. de Norpois," said Swann, whose job at home was to be the man of sound common sense. "I can appreciate that one may not think he's all that interesting, but from another point of view"– Swann being something of a "collector" of life's little curios–"he really is rather a noteworthy man. Noteworthy in his capacity as great lover, I mean." He added, with a glance to make sure that Gilberte could not hear him, "In the days when he was an attaché at the embassy in Rome, he had left behind in Paris a mistress whom he adored to distraction. So, twice a week, he would find a pretext to dash back and see her for a couple of hours. Mind you, she *was* a very clever and beautiful woman at that time. A dowager nowadays, of course. And he's had plenty more since then. I must say that if it had been me, obliged to live in Rome while the woman I loved had to stay in Paris, it would have driven me mad. High-strung people should always choose objects of their affections who are 'beneath them,' as the saying goes, so that the self-interest of the woman one loves ensures that she will always be available." At that moment, Swann realized the connection I might make between this verity and his own love for Odette. This gave him a great fit of pique against me, for even the high-minded, at moments when one seems to be sharing in their higher things, are still capable of the pettiness of self-esteem. This grudge of Swann's was apparent only in an uneasy look in his eye; and he said nothing about it at that moment. Not that there is anything very surprising in that—a story, which is apocryphal, but which is re-enacted every day of the week in Paris, has it that when Racine spoke the name of Scarron in the presence of Louis XIV, the most powerful monarch on earth said nothing about it to his poet at the time; and he did not fall from favor until the following day.[53]

However, any theory likes to be fully expounded; and so Swann, after his momentary irritation, wiped the lens of his monocle and rounded off his idea in words that I later came to remember as a prophecy, a warning I would be unable to heed: "But the danger of such liaisons is that, though the subjection of the woman may briefly allay the jealousy of the man, it eventually makes it even more demanding. He reaches the point of treating his mistress like one of those prisoners who are so closely guarded that the light in their cell is never turned off. The sort of thing that usually ends in alarums and excursions."

I reverted to M. de Norpois. "I wouldn't trust him—he's always saying things behind people's backs," Mme Swann said in a way which, partly because Swann gave her a quick glance of disapproval, as though to warn her against saying anything more, made me suspect that M. de Norpois must have had something to say behind hers.

Gilberte, who had already been asked twice to go and make her preparations for going out, was still standing there between her parents, listening to us, leaning her loving head on her father's shoulder. At first sight, there could have been no greater contrast than between Mme Swann, who was dark, and the golden-skinned girl with the fairish hair. Then one began to recognize in Gilberte many features, such as the nose, neatly shortened by a stroke from the sculptor whose unerring chisel models several generations, the expression of her mother, her ways of moving; or, to draw a comparison from another art, Gilberte resembled a portrait of her mother, verging on a good likeness, but done by a fanciful colorist who had made her pose in semi-disguise, dressed for a costume ball as a woman of Venice. It was not just the blond wig she was wearing, but the fact that every last atom of her dark complexion had faded, making it look more naked when stripped of its browner veils, covered only by the glow of an inner sun, as though the makeup were not just superficial but ingrained. Gilberte looked as though she represented some creature out of a fable, or as though she were costumed as a mythological character. Her fair complexion was so clearly her father's that Nature, in order to create Gilberte, seemed to have been faced with the problem of imitating Mme Swann while being able to use as its sole material the skin of M. Swann. Nature had solved the problem to perfection, as a master cabinetmaker tries to exploit the visible grain of wood, even turning to advantage the knots in it. In Gilberte's face, just to one side of its perfect reproduction of Odette's nose, the skin rose slightly to show the two moles of M. Swann. In her, as she stood there with her mother, a new variety of Mme Swann had been achieved, like a white lilac growing beside a purple one. The line separating Gilberte's twin likenesses was not hard and fast, though. Now and then, as she laughed, you suddenly glimpsed the oval of her father's cheek in her mother's face, as though they had been put together to see what such a mixture might look like; the oval took firmer shape, after the manner of an embryo forming, lengthened obliquely, swelled, then disappeared almost at once. In her eyes, one could see the frankness of her father's fine, open gaze on the world, the one I had seen there on the day when she gave me the agate marble and said, "This is for you, as a memento of our friendship." Then, if you inquired about what she had been doing, those same eyes filled with the devious, forlorn embarrassment and perplexity that used to cloud Odette's as, in answer to a question from Swann about where she had been, she told one of those lies which had once reduced her lover to despair, but which now made her husband, a prudently uninquiring man, quickly change the subject. In the days when we used to meet at the Champs-Élysées, this expression of Gilberte's had often worried me. Usually, however, I need not have worried, as that particular look in her eyes was a mere physical inheritance, and had nothing else of Odette left in it. It was when Gilberte had been to her class, or when she had to be back home in time for a lesson, that her eyes went through the motions Odette's had once gone through because she feared letting it slip that one of her lovers had visited her during the day, or because she was anxious to be on her way to meet another of them. In this way the two natures of Swann and Mme Swann, each of them predominating by turns, could be seen to ripple and flow across the features of this Mélusine.[54]

Children do take after their parents, of course. But the rearrangement of the inherited qualities and defects is done so strangely that only one of a pair of qualities which seemed inseparable in a parent may turn up in the child; and it may be blended with a defect of the other parent that had once seemed incompatible with it. One of the laws of filial resemblance is that a moral quality will often manifest itself even through a bodily defect that is quite out of keeping with it. One of two sisters will combine the petty-mindedness of her mother with the fine, upright stance of the father, while the other one will receive the father's intelligence but the mother's appearance; and so the latter's big nose, her graceless waistline, and even her voice turn into the outer semblance of gifts one used to meet in a much finer form. It can be rightly said that either of such daughters takes more after either of the parents. Gilberte was, of course, an only child; but there were at least two of her. Her father's nature and her mother's did not just mingle in her: it would be truer to say they were in rivalry within her, although even that is an inaccurate description, since it implies there might be a third Gilberte, who found it irksome to be the periodic victim of the other two. But Gilberte was alternately one of the two and then the other, and never more than that single self at any given moment: that is, when she was the less good of the two, she was unable to regret it, since the better of the two Gilbertes, being momentarily absent, could have no knowledge of the lapse. Thus the less worthy Gilberte was free to enjoy unworthy pleasures. When it was the better one speaking from her father's heart, her views were broad, inspiring one to engage with her in some fine, uplifting enterprise; but when you had told her this, and it was time to launch into it, you found that her mother's heart had taken her over and was speaking through her; and a petty remark or a sly little snigger, in which she took pleasure as an expression of who she was at that moment, would disappoint you, irritate you, almost fascinate you, as though you were faced with an impostor. The disparity between these two Gilbertes could be so great that one would wonder, quite fruitlessly, what one had done to her that might explain the change. Not only did she not keep the appointment that she herself had suggested, not only did she not apologize for this, but, whatever the reason for her change of heart, her later behavior was so different that you could almost have believed it was a case of mistaken identity, like the one which shapes the plot of the *Menaechmi*,[55] and that you were no longer dealing with the person who had so demurely asked to see you, were it not that her present bad mood showed that she knew she was at fault, but wanted to avoid having to talk about it.

"Come on, please," her mother said to her. "You'll just make us all have to wait for you."

"But I'm so happy here with my nice old papa. I just want to stay here for a bit longer," Gilberte replied, nestling her head into her father's shoulder as he combed his fingers through her long fair hair.

Swann was one of those men whose lives have been spent in the illusions of love, who, having afforded comforts and, through them, greater happiness to many women, have not been repaid by gratitude or tenderness toward themselves; but in their child they believe they can sense an affection which, by being materialized in the name they bear, will outlive them. A time would come when Charles Swann would have ceased to exist, but there would still be a Mlle Swann or a Mme X, née Swann, who would go on loving her dead father. Swann may even have thought Gilberte would love him too much, for he said to her now, in that emotional voice full of misgiving about the future of someone whose love for us is too passionate, and who is bound to live on after our death, "What a good girl you are." To conceal the fact that he was moved, he joined in the conversation about La Berma, pointing out to me, albeit in a detached, bored tone that sounded as though he was trying to remain at a distance from what he was saying, the actress's percipience, the unexpected aptness of the way she had spoken to Oenone the words: "You knew about it!" He was right: that intonation at any rate did convey a genuine and manifest effect, and should therefore have satisfied my desire to find irrefutable reasons for admiring La Berma. But it did not satisfy it, because of its very transparency. Her intonation had been so perceptive, so clear in its meaning and intent, that it seemed to exist in its own right, and any clever actress should have been able to think of it. It certainly was an inspired piece of acting; but anybody capable of grasping it so clearly would also have been capable of producing it. The fact remained that it was La Berma who had thought of it—but could she really be said to have "invented" it, when the thing supposedly invented would have been no different if she had merely acquired it, a thing bearing no essential relation to herself, since it could be reproduced by someone else?

"Goodness me!" Swann said to me. "Doesn't your presence among us 'raise the tone' of the conversation?" It sounded like a discreet apology to Bergotte from the man who had borrowed from the Guermantes' circle their simple ways of befriending and entertaining great artists, inviting them to dinner, serving them their favorite dish, playing parlor games to please them, or, in the country, arranging for them to practice the sport of their choice. "We do seem to be talking about 'Art,' don't we?" Swann added. "I should think so too! I think it's very nice," Mme Swann said, thanking me with a glance in which I read kindness toward myself and a reminder of her former hankerings after more intellectual conversation. Bergotte turned to talk with some of the others, in particular Gilberte. I was surprised to realize how freely I had spoken to him of my thoughts and feelings. But over so many years, for so many private hours of reading and solitude, during which he had been simply the best part of myself, I had been so accustomed to relating to him in total sincerity, frankness, and trust that I was less shy with him than if I had been talking with someone else for the first time. And yet, for that very reason, I was full of qualms about the impression I must have made on him, as my expectation that he would scorn my ideas was no recent thing, but dated from the time long ago when I had first read him, sitting out in the garden at Combray. Perhaps it should have occurred to me that, since both my great attraction to the works of Bergotte and the unaccountable disappointment I had experienced at the theater were sincere, spontaneous reactions of my own mind, these two instinctive and irresistible responses could not be very different from each other, but must be governed by the same laws; and that therefore the spirit of Bergotte, which I had admired so much in his books, was very likely not so utterly alien and hostile to my disappointment, or to my inability to articulate it. For, after all, my mind had to be a single thing; or perhaps there is only a single mind, in which everybody has a share, a mind to which all of us look, isolated though each of us is within a private body, just as at the theater, where, though every spectator sits in a separate place, there is only one stage. No doubt the ideas Bergotte was in the habit of investigating in his books were not those I enjoyed trying to disentangle; but if it was true that he and I were bound to have recourse to the same mind, then it followed that, hearing me try to expound those ideas, he must recall them, like them, and smile on them, while probably keeping his inner eye, despite whatever else I thought he might be doing, fixed on an area of mind remote from the one which had left a remnant of itself in his books, and which had been the origin of all I had imagined about his mental universe. Just as the priests with the broadest knowledge of the heart are those who can best forgive the sins they themselves never commit, so the genius with the broadest acquaintance with the mind can best understand ideas most foreign to those that fill his own works. I should have thought of all this, unpleasant though its implications are: for the benevolence one encounters in the person of broad vision has its sorry counterpart in the obtuse and churlish ways of the petty; and the happiness one may derive from the kindly encounter with a writer through his books counts for much less than the unhappiness caused by the animosity of a woman whom one has not chosen for her qualities of mind, but whom one cannot help loving. I should have thought of all this; but it did not occur to me, and I was convinced that Bergotte thought I was stupid. Then Gilberte whispered to me:

"I'm so happy! You've really bowled over my great friend Bergotte! He's just told my mother that he thought you were highly intelligent."

"Where are we going?" I asked her.

"Well, you know me, I don't really mind where we go. . . ."[56]

But ever since what had happened on the anniversary of her grand-father's death, I had been wondering whether Gilberte's character was not different from what I had believed, whether her equable indiffer-ence to our outings, her pleasing, mild manner, her unfailing biddable-ness, might not actually conceal intense desires, which pride made her disguise, and which she did not reveal until some chance event thwarted them and brought out a sudden obstinacy in her.

As Bergotte lived not far from my parents' house, he and I shared a carriage. On the way, he spoke about my health: "The Swanns tell me you're not in the best of health. I am sorry to hear it. Although I must say I am not *too* sorry for you, as I can see you must enjoy the pleasures of the intellectual life. I daresay that's what really counts for you, as it does for anybody who's familiar with such pleasures."

Bergotte could not know how untrue this was, how indifferent I was to discussion, however elevated it might be, how happy I became with mere mental idleness, with simple contentment; but I was uneasily aware of how material were the things I looked for in life, of how un-necessary the intellectual life seemed to me. In my inability to distin-guish between the disparate origins of certain pleasures, some of them deeper and more durable than others, it occurred to me, as I answered him, that the life I would enjoy would be one in which I could be on friendly terms with the Duchesse de Guermantes and have frequent op-portunities of being reminded of Combray, as in the disused tollbooth at the Champs-Élysées, by a cool smell. And in that ideal way of life which I did not dare to speak of, intellectual pleasures had no part.

"Well, actually, no, sir. Intellectual pleasures don't mean very much to me. I'm not at all fond of them. I'm not even sure I know what they are."

"Really, is that so?" he replied. "No, look, honestly, you *must* be fond of them! Bound to be! I suspect you really are."

I remained unpersuaded; but I did feel happier, less cramped. M. de Norpois's words had made me see my moments of idle reflection, enthusiasm, and self-confidence as being purely subjective, devoid of reality. Yet Bergotte, who seemed quite familiar with the situation I found myself in, seemed to be implying that the symptoms to ignore were actually my self-disgust and doubts about my abilities. What he had said about M. de Norpois in particular had already done much to lessen the force of what had appeared to be a categorical judgment.

"Tell me, have you got sound medical advice?" Bergotte asked. "Who's looking after you?" I told him I had been seeing Dr. Cottard and would probably go on seeing him. "But, look here," he said, "I'm sure he's not at all the right man. I must say I don't know the fellow as a doctor. But I have seen him at Mme Swann's—and he's a prize idiot! Even if we accept that a man can be an idiot *and* a good doctor— which I do find hard to swallow—no one can be an idiot and a proper doctor for intelligent people, artistically inclined people. People like you need appropriate doctors and, I might even add, individually designed regimens and medications. Cottard will bore you, and boredom alone will prevent his treatment from working. In any case, such treatment can't possibly be the same for you as for any average individual. With intelligent people, three-quarters of the things they suffer from come from their intelligence. The thing they can't do without is a doctor who's aware of that form of illness. How on earth could Cottard cure you? He can foresee the ill effects of sauces on the digestion, he can predict the bilious attack, but he can't conceive of the effect of reading Shakespeare! And so all his calculations are thrown out, the little Cartesian devil can't remain stationary, and up he pops to the surface again. He'll say what you've got is distension of the stomach! He doesn't even need to examine you for that, because it's already in his eye. You'll see it if you look—it's reflected from his monocle." I was bewildered by this manner of speaking; and I thought, with the ineptitude of common sense: "But there's no more distension of the stomach reflected from Cottard's monocle than there are stupidities inside M. de Norpois's white waistcoat!" "If I were you," Bergotte went on, "I'd go and see Dr. du Boulbon. He's a very clever man." "He's a great admirer of your books," I said. I could see this was not news to Bergotte and decided that like minds seek each other out, that one has few "unknown" admirers. What he said about Dr. Cottard struck me, though it contradicted everything I believed. That my doctor might be a crashing bore did not bother me; all I required of him was that his art, the laws of which were beyond me, should enable him to examine my entrails and utter an infallible oracle on my health. My own intelligence was good enough for both of us, and I saw no need for him to understand it, as I saw it only as a possible means, of no great significance in itself, to the attainment of truth about the world. I was acutely skeptical of the notion that clever people have sanitary requirements that differ from those of fools, and I did not mind having to make do with theirs. "I'll tell you someone who needs a good doctor," said Bergotte. "Our friend Swann." I asked him whether Swann was ill. "No, but here we have the man who married a trollop, who accepts being snubbed every day of the week by women who choose not to know his wife, or looked down on by men who have slept with her. You can see it in that twisted smile of his. Have a look, one evening when he comes back to the house, at the way he raises his eyebrows as he wonders who's with his wife." The malice with which Bergotte spoke to a stranger about friends of long standing was as remarkable to me as the honeying manner he adopted with the Swanns when at their house. A person like my great-aunt, for instance, would have been incapable of treating any of us with the fulsome amiability of Bergotte toward the Swanns; and she could take pleasure in saying unpleasant things even to people she liked. But when they were absent, she would never have spoken a word about them that they would have been hurt to hear. Our little world of Combray was as remote as possible from smart society. The world of the Swanns was a first step closer to it, toward its untrustworthy waves. Though not quite the open sea, it was just inside the harbor bar. "This is just between you and me, of course," murmured Bergotte as he left me outside my par-

ents' house. A few years later, I would have said, "Of course, I never repeat anything I hear." This is the ritual statement of people in society,
serving as a false reassurance for the scandalmonger. I might even have
said it to Bergotte on that occasion, since one does not invent everything one says, especially when one is acting a social role; but I had not
yet come across it. In similar circumstances, my great-aunt's reply would
have been: "Well, if you don't want me to repeat it, why are you saying
it?" That is the reply of the unsociable, of those who do not mind being
thought "awkward." Not being one of those, I quietly acquiesced.

Literary people who to me were personages of note had to scheme
for years before succeeding in establishing a relationship with Bergotte;
and even then their contracts were restricted to vaguely literary things,
and never went beyond the walls of his study. Whereas, without ado, I
had quietly stepped into the circle of the great writer's friends, like a
spectator who, instead of having to line up with everyone else to get
one of the worst seats in the house, is ushered into one of the very best,
having been let in by a side door which is generally closed to the public.
It had been opened for me by Swann, after the manner of a king who
will naturally offer his children's friends a seat in the royal box, or take
them for a cruise on the royal yacht; so Gilberte's parents admitted
their daughter's friends among the precious things they owned, letting them share in the even more precious moments of the private life
which took place in that setting. But at that time I suspected, possibly
rightly, that Swann's kindness to me was indirectly aimed at my parents.
Long before, in Combray, I had formed the impression that, because of
my admiration for Bergotte, Swann had suggested to my parents that I
should meet the writer over dinner at his house; this invitation my parents had declined, saying I was too young and too high-strung to attend
such a function. The impression some people had of my parents, in particular those on whom I looked with great awe, was no doubt very different from my own impression of them; which was why, as on the
occasion when the lady in pink had sung such praises of my father, who
had then shown himself unworthy of them, I now wished my parents
could appreciate the priceless compliment I had received, and longed
for them to show proper gratitude to Swann, who in his kind, courteous

way had done this for me—or, rather, for them!—without seeming to have any more sense of how great a gift he was bestowing than the charming King in Bernardino Luini's[57] fresco *The Three Kings*, the fair-haired one with the aquiline nose, who I believe had once been said to look exactly like Swann.

Unfortunately, this great boon of Swann's, which I announced as soon as I stepped inside, before I had even taken off my overcoat, in the hope that it would warm my parents' hearts as it had warmed mine, and inspire them to some grand and decisive overture toward Swann and his family, did not appear to enthrall them. "So Swann has introduced you to Bergotte, has he?" my father said in an ironic tone. "Well, that's a fine thing, I must say! Nice company you keep! What next?" Then, when I told him Bergotte had nothing good to say about M. de Norpois, he added:

"Well, of course! Which just goes to show what a nasty and bogus mind the man has! My dear boy, we already knew you weren't gifted with a great deal of common sense. But it's a shame to see you fall among people who can only make things much worse in that department."

My parents were already irked that I was on visiting terms with the Swanns. They now saw my introduction to Bergotte as an understandably adverse consequence of an initial fault, their own weakness, what my grandfather would have called their "unheedfulness." I sensed that, to complete their ill humor, all I had to say was that the immoral man who had such a low opinion of M. de Norpois had also concluded that I was highly intelligent. The fact was that, whenever my father was convinced that someone—for instance, one of my school friends, or myself in this case—was not only risking perdition but also enjoyed the good esteem of a third person whom he did not respect, he took that esteem as mere confirmation of his own adverse diagnosis. The danger he foresaw was only aggravated by it. I knew perfectly well what he would exclaim: "But what do you expect? It's all of a piece!" This was a statement which, by the imprecision and immensity of the changes it suggested were about to be visited on my quiet little life, could strike terror into my heart. However, since not telling them of what Bergotte had said about me could in no way alter the poor impression my parents already had, it did not matter much if they ended up with a poorer one. I was also so sure that they were being unfair, so convinced they were mistaken, that I had not only no hope of making them take a more balanced view, but almost no desire to. So, though sensing even as I spoke the words how alarmed my parents would be to learn that I had earned the approval of a man who said intelligent men were stupid, who was roundly despised by all solid citizens, and whose praise was likely to lead me astray in the hope of receiving more of the same, I finished my account by delivering this last straw in a rather shamefaced mutter: "And then he told the Swanns he thought I was highly intelligent." As a poisoned dog in a field bites, without knowing why, at the herb which is the very antidote it requires to the toxin in its system, I had just uttered unawares the only possible statement that could counter my parents' prejudice against Bergotte, when nothing else I could have said, no argument in his favor, however admirable, no praise of him, however lavish, would have prevailed against it. At once the situation changed:

"Really?" my mother said. "He said you were intelligent? Well, that's good to hear, from such a talented man."

"Did he really say that?" my father asked. "Well, I've got nothing to say against him at all on literary things—nobody has. It's just a pity about those dubious goings-on of his that old Norpois hinted at." My father did not notice that, against the power of the magic words I had just spoken, Bergotte's moral depravity could not hold out much longer than his nasty and bogus mind had.

"But, my dear," my mother said, "nothing proves there's any truth in any of that. People say all sorts of things. And of course, although M. de Norpois is extremely nice, he's not always full of goodwill, particularly toward people who are not quite his cup of tea."

"True, true," said my father. "I've noticed that about him too."

"Anyway," my mother said, stroking my hair and gazing dreamily at me, "if Bergotte likes my little boy, we won't judge him too harshly."

Without knowing Bergotte's opinion of me, she had already told me that, the next time I had friends to tea, I could invite Gilberte. There were two reasons why I did not dare do this. One was that, at the Swanns', the only thing to drink was tea; whereas my mother insisted that, in addition to tea, we should have hot chocolate. I dreaded the thought that Gilberte would think this was common of us, and despise us for it. The other reason was a difficulty of protocol that I was never able to resolve. Each time I arrived at Mme Swann's, my hostess would ask:

"And how is your dear mother?"

To me, whether Mama would agree to follow suit when Gilberte came to tea was a more serious matter than Louis XIV's insistence that at Versailles only the Dauphin should be addressed as Monseigneur; and so I had broached it with her. She would hear nothing of it.

"Well, no," she said, "because I don't know Mme Swann."

"Yes, but she doesn't know you either."

"That may be. But we're not obliged to be exactly the same as each other. I can be nice to Gilberte in ways that are different from the ways her mother is nice to you."

But I was unconvinced, and preferred not to invite Gilberte to tea.

Having gone to my room, I was changing my clothes when I suddenly discovered in my pocket the envelope that the Swanns' butler had handed me just before showing me into the drawing room. Being no longer under the butler's eye, I opened it—inside was a card on which was written the name of the lady whom I was expected to take in to lunch.

It was about this time that Bloch disturbed my conception of the world and opened before me new vistas of possible happiness (which were later to turn into possibilities of great unhappiness): contradicting what I had believed about women in the days when I used to go for walks along the Méséglise way, he assured me that they were always on the lookout for opportunities to make love. This good turn he complemented with another, which I did not fully appreciate till much later: he it was who took me for the first time to a brothel. He had of course told me there were many pretty women in the world to be slept with. But the faces I had imagined for them were devoid of detail; and these brothels were to enable me to see that each of them had an individual

face. So it was that, on the one hand, because of Bloch's "good news"—
that happiness and the possession of beauty are not unattainable, and
that we are misguided if we despair of ever enjoying them—I was as indebted to him as one is to the optimistic doctor or philosopher who
gives one grounds for expecting a long life in this world, or a continued
contact with it even after one has passed into another world; and on
the other hand, the brothels I frequented some years later (by giving
me samples of happiness, and enabling me to enhance the beauty of
women with that element we can never invent, which is not just an
amalgam of types of beauty familiar to us, but the truly divine gift, the
only one we cannot receive from ourselves, the one beside which all the
logical figments of our mind fade away, and which can be acquired only
from reality: the charm of the individual) deserve to stand beside those
other benefactors, more recent in origin but equal in utility, thanks to
whom we can now revel in the full glory of Mantegna, Wagner, and
Siena, without having to invent pale, imagined versions of them based
on other painters, other composers, and other towns: the publishers of
illustrated volumes on the history of painting, producers of symphony
concerts, and the compilers of those series on "Cities of the Arts." But
the first hotel Bloch took me to, which he himself had not frequented
for some time, was of a rather inferior sort; its women were too nondescript, and they were not renewed often enough, for me to gratify familiar urges or contract unfamiliar ones. The madam did not know any of
the women one asked her for, and kept suggesting others that one had
no desire for. There was one woman in particular whom she praised to
the skies, saying with a suggestive smile, as though talking about a treat
or a rarity, "She's a Jewess! Eh? Couldn't you fancy that?" (That was
presumably why she called the girl Rachel.) And she added, filling her
voice with a vacuous, affected rapturousness, which she hoped would
be infectious, and dropping it almost to a moan of sensuous delight,
"Just think, dearie! A Jewess! I mean! That must really be something,
wouldn't you say? Yes, sir!" I was able to look at Rachel without her seeing me: she was dark, not pretty, but with an intelligent look, and as she
licked her lips with the tip of her tongue, she smiled pertly at the different customers who were being introduced to her, and whom I could

hear striking up conversation with her. Her face was thin and narrow, framed by curly black hair that looked so irregular as to have been crosshatched in an India-ink wash drawing. At each visit I assured the madam, who kept urging me to have the girl, stressing her high intelligence and level of education, that I would be sure to come back one day for the express purpose of meeting Rachel, for whom my private nickname was "Rachel, when of the Lord."[58] But the fact was that, on the very first evening, I had overheard the girl say to the madam as she was leaving:

"So that's agreed, all right? I'm available tomorrow, and if you've got somebody you'll be sure to send for me?"

These words had instantly prevented me from seeing her as a person, by making her indistinguishable from the ordinary run of those women whose common practice was to turn up there in the evening in the hope of earning a few francs. This statement of Rachel's rarely varied: sometimes she said "if you need me"; and sometimes it was "if you need anyone."

The madam, being unfamiliar with Halévy's opera, had no idea why I had taken to calling the girl "Rachel, when of the Lord." But an inability to understand a joke has never been an impediment to being amused by it, and she always greeted me with a great laugh and the words:

"So is tonight the night when I can fix you up with 'Rachel, when of the Lord'? Let's hear the way you say it, now: 'Rachel, when of the Lord'! It's very funny, you know! I'm going to betroth you to her. You won't be sorry, you'll see!"

On one occasion I had almost decided to accept the offer; but the girl was "on the job." Then, another time, she was with the "hairdresser" (this was an old gentleman whose hairdressing consisted solely of oiling the women's hair, once they had let it down, and then combing it for them). I tired of waiting for her, although several denizens of the establishment, of very humble charms, allegedly working-class women but always out of work, came up to make me a cup of *tisane* and engage me in a lengthy conversation, to which, despite the seriousness of the subjects we talked about, their partial or total nakedness gave a piquant simplicity. However, I gave up going to that house because, in my desire to do the madam a good turn, she being rather short of furniture, I made her a present of some pieces, notably a large couch, that had been left to me by my aunt Léonie. I rarely saw these things, since my parents, having no room to accommodate them, had put them into storage. But as soon as I set eyes on them again in that brothel, put to use by those women, I was assailed by all the virtues that had perfumed the air in my aunt's bedroom at Combray, now defiled by the brutal dealings to which I had condemned the dear, defenseless things. I could not have suffered more if it had been the dead woman herself being violated. So I stopped going to that procuress's establishment, as they seemed to be living creatures, crying out silently to me, like those apparently inanimate objects inside which, as a Persian tale has it, souls are imprisoned, subjected to constant torture, and begging forever to be freed. Moreover, given that memory does not usually produce recollections in chronological order, but acts more like a reflection inverting the sequence of parts, it was not until much later that I remembered this was the couch on which, many years before, I had been initiated into the pleasures of love by one of my cousins, a girl whose presence embarrassed and excited me to distraction, and who had urged me to take perilous advantage of an hour when our aunt Léonie was out of the room.

Another large lot of Aunt Léonie's furniture, including especially a magnificent set of old silverware, I sold, against the express wishes of my parents, so as to have more money with which to send more flowers to Mme Swann. When she received my huge baskets of orchids, she would say, "Young man, if I was your father, I'd have your allowance stopped!" But could I imagine that a day would come when I would regret having parted with that silver, a day when the greatest pleasure in my life, paying respects to Gilberte's parents, would have become absolutely worthless? Similarly, it was because of Gilberte, so as not to part from her, that I had decided not to undertake a career as a diplomat. Our furthest-reaching resolutions are always made in a short-lived state of mind. I could barely conceive that the strange substance inhering in Gilberte, and radiating from her parents and the house where she lived, making me feel indifferent to everything else, could detach itself from her person and migrate into another. The very same substance, yet destined to have completely different effects on me. The same illness can evolve; and a sweet poison comes to be less tolerated when, with the years, the heart's resistance has weakened.

Meanwhile, my parents would have preferred it if the intelligence that had so impressed Bergotte could have been made manifest in some achievement. As long as I had been excluded from the Swanns' acquaintance, I was convinced that my inability to get down to work was caused by the state of emotional disturbance to which I was reduced by the impossibility of seeing Gilberte as and when I wished to. But then, once I had free access to their house, I could hardly sit down at my desk before I had to jump up again and be off there to visit them. And when I had left the Swanns' and gone back home, it was only in appearance that I sat alone; my own thoughts could not withstand the torrent of words on which for hours past I had let myself be carried along: I went on turning out words and sentences that might have impressed the Swanns; to make the game more enjoyable, I even played the parts of the absent others, asking myself fictitious questions so designed that, in answering them, I could show off the brilliance of my banter. Silent as it was, this exercise was a real conversation and not a form of reflection; my solitude was a mental drawing-room scene, in which imaginary interlocutors and not myself were in charge of my speech, in which, by producing not ideas that I believed to be true, but ideas that came to me without trouble, without any action of the outer world on the inner, I enjoyed the same sort of pleasure as is enjoyed, in utter passivity, by the person who has nothing better to do after dinner but sit quietly, lulled into a dull somnolence by poor digestion.

If I had not been so determined to set seriously to work, I might have made an effort to start at once. But given that my resolve was unbreakable, given that within twenty-four hours, inside the empty frame of tomorrow, where everything fitted so perfectly because it was not today, my best intentions would easily take material shape, it was really preferable not to think of beginning things on an evening when I was not quite ready—and of course the following days were to be no better suited to beginning things. However, I was a reasonable person. When one has waited for years, it would be childish not to tolerate a delay of a couple of days. In the knowledge that by the day after tomorrow I would have several pages written, I said no more about my decision to the family: much better to wait for a few hours; then, once I had a piece of work in progress to show, my grandmother would be consoled and convinced. Unfortunately, tomorrow turned out not to be that broad, bright, outward-looking day that I had feverishly looked forward to. When it had ended, my idleness and hard struggle against my inner obstacles had just lasted for another twenty-four hours. After a few days, when my projects had still not come to anything, when some of my hope that they would very soon come to something had faded, and with it some of the courage I required in order to subordinate everything to my coming achievement, I went back to staying up late, as I now also lacked my incentive (the certain knowledge that the great work would be begun by the following morning) to go to bed early on any given evening. Before regaining my impetus, I was in need of a respite of several days; and on the only occasion when my grandmother hazarded a reproach in a tone of mild disenchantment—"So is anything happening about this writing?"—I was aggrieved at her, and I concluded that, by her inability to see the staunchness of my purpose, by the anguish her gross unfairness caused me, an utterly unsuitable state of mind in which to undertake such a work as mine, she had just succeeded in putting off once again (and possibly for a long time!) the moment when its accomplishing would be begun. She sensed that her skeptical air had offended an unsuspected but genuine resolve. She apologized with a kiss: "I'm sorry. I won't say another word about it." So that I would not lose heart, she added her assurance that a day would come when I would feel well again, and that, of its own accord, my work would then start to flow smoothly.

Anyway, I thought, what if I do spend a lot of time at the Swanns'? So does Bergotte! My family's view on this might almost have been that, though I was lazy, the life I was leading was actually the best suited to a developing talent, since I was frequenting the same drawing room as a great writer. Yet to acquire talent from someone else, to bypass the need to create it out of oneself, is as impossible as it would be to lead a healthy life by dining out frequently with a doctor, while flouting all the rules of hygiene and indulging in every sort of excess. The person who was most taken in by this illusion, shared by myself and my family, was Mme Swann. If I told her I could not accept one of her invitations, that I had to stay at home and work, she looked at me as though I were making difficulties for the sake of it, as though I had said something rather silly and pretentious:

"But, look here, Bergotte keeps coming, doesn't he? And you don't think *his* stuff isn't well written—surely, now—do you? You'll see, he'll be even better soon—since he's taken up journalism, he's actually sharper, and there's more to him than in his books, where he tends to be a bit thinnish. I've managed to get him into *Le Figaro*, he's going to do their *leader article*." She used the English expression, to which she added another:

"You'll see, it'll be a perfect case of *the right man in the right place*. So do come! Just think of the tips you can pick up from him about writing!"

It sounded as though she were inviting a private to meet his colonel: it was in order to further my career, as though knowing "the right people" could help produce a masterpiece, that she urged me not to miss dinner with Bergotte at her house the following evening.

So it was that my new sweet life with Gilberte was now untroubled both by the Swanns and by my family, the two sources that at different times had appeared likely to make a difficulty; and I could go on seeing her at will, with delight though not with peace of mind. Peace of mind is foreign to love, since each new fulfillment one attains is never anything but a new starting point for the desire to go beyond it. As long as I had been prevented from going to her house, my gaze had been riveted to that unattainable happiness, and it had been impossible for me even to imagine the new sources of emotional disturbance that awaited me in it. Once her parents' resistance had been overcome, the problem that had thus been solved was to go on being reformulated, but each time in different terms. In that sense, it really was a new relationship that began with Gilberte each day. Back at home each evening, I realized there were things of paramount importance that I had to say to her, things on which the future of our friendship depended; and yet, from one day to the next, they were never the same things. Still, I was happy and there was no sign of any threat to my continuing happiness. A threat was to materialize, however, coming from a source I had never seen as a potential danger—that is, from Gilberte and myself. I should really have been disturbed by what reassured me, by what I took for happiness. In love, happiness is an abnormal state, capable of instantly conferring on the pettiest-seeming incident, which can occur at any moment, a degree of gravity that in other circumstances it would never have. What makes one so happy is the presence of something unstable in the heart, something one contrives constantly to keep in a state of stability, and which one is hardly even aware of as long as it remains like that. In fact, though, love secretes a permanent pain, which joy neutralizes in us, makes virtual, and holds in abeyance; but at any moment, it can turn into torture, which is what would have happened long since if one had not obtained what one desired.

Now and then I had the feeling that Gilberte would have been glad to see me less often. The fact was that, when the desire to see her got the better of me, all I had to do was get myself invited to the house by her parents, who were more and more convinced I was an improving influence on her. Because of them, I thought, my love is in no danger: as long as they are for me, I needn't worry about anything, since Gilberte is in their hands. Unfortunately, occasional signs of impatience from her, at times when her father had me to the house more or less without her agreement, made me wonder whether the thing I had seen as a protection for my happiness might not be the secret reason why it could not last.

The last time I went to see her, it was raining and she had been invited to a dancing class at the house of some people who were not close enough friends for her to be able to take me with her. Because it was wet, I had taken more caffeine than usual. As Gilberte was about to leave, Mme Swann, perhaps because of the bad weather, perhaps because of some slight ill will she may have harbored toward the people in whose house the lesson was to take place, called out "Gilberte!" in a very sharp voice, and made a gesture in my direction, meaning that I was there to see her and that she should stay at home. It was for my sake that she had snapped "Gilberte!" or, rather, shouted the name; but from the shrug of the shoulders with which Gilberte took off her outdoor things, I realized that, without intending to, her mother had hastened the process—which until then it might still have been possible to arrest—whereby my sweetheart was gradually being separated from me. "One doesn't have to go dancing every day," Odette said to her daughter, possibly passing along a lesson in self-discipline once taught to her by Swann. Then, becoming Odette again, she broke into English; and it was instantly as though part of Gilberte's life was hidden behind a wall, as though some evil genie had kidnapped her. In a language we understand, we have replaced opacity of sound by transparency of idea. But a language we do not speak is a palace closed against us, inside which our beloved may deceive us, while we, left outside to the impotent devices of our own desperation, can see nothing and prevent nothing. A month earlier, this conversation would have made me smile; but now, with the few French proper names I could hear among the English words, it increased my disquiet, gave focus to suspicion, and, though conducted by two motionless people standing beside me, left me as cruelly isolated and abandoned as if Gilberte had been abducted. At length, Mme Swann left us alone together. That day, perhaps from a sense of grievance against me for having been the unwitting cause of her being deprived of an amusement, perhaps also because, sensing and hoping to avoid her ill humor, I myself may have been stiffer than usual, Gilberte's face was devoid of all joy, laid waste, a blank, melancholy mask, which for the rest of the afternoon seemed to grieve privately for those foursome reels being danced without her, because of my presence here, and to defy all beings, especially me, to comprehend the subtle reasons that had produced in her a sentimental inclination to do the Boston dip. She did no more than contribute occasional comments— on the weather, the fact that the rain was coming on again, or that the clock was a little fast—to a conversation of silences and monosyllables, during which I too, in a sort of rage of despair, outdid her in trying to destroy the moments in which we could have been close and happy. All the words we exchanged were stamped with a sort of stark hardness, by the crushing paradox of their crassness, an effect in which there was nevertheless something consoling, since it meant that Gilberte could not possibly be deceived by the banality of what I was saying and the indifference in my voice. Even though I said, "And yet the other day I had the impression the clock was actually a little slow," she translated this directly as, "How nasty you're being!" Even though I persisted throughout the rainy afternoon with my succession of pointless words without sunny intervals, I knew that my cold manner was not as steadfast as I pretended, and that Gilberte must be well aware that, if I had dared to repeat for the fourth time what I had already said three times—that the evenings were drawing in now—I would have had difficulty in not bursting into tears. When she was like that, when a smile was not filling her eyes and revealing her face, how inexpressibly desolate and monotonous were the sadness in her eyes and the gloom of her sulky features. At such moments, her face would turn almost ugly and resembled those bare, boring stretches of beach which, when the tide has receded almost out of sight, tire the eye with their unchanging glare bounded by the fixed and inhibiting horizon. Eventually, not having seen in Gilberte the comforting change of mood I had been hoping to see for hours past, I told her she was not nice. "You're the one who's not nice!" she said. "Me? I *am* nice!" I wondered what I had done and, being unable to think of anything, I asked her what I had done. "Naturally, you think you're so nice!" she replied with a long laugh. I was struck at that moment by what was so painful to me in being unable to have access to that other, more elusive reach of her mind described by her laughter. The laugh seemed to mean: "I'm not taken in by a single thing you say, you know! I know perfectly well you're madly in love with me, but it makes no difference, because I don't care for you at all!" But I reminded myself that laughter is not so determinate a form of speech that I could definitely assume I knew what Gilberte's meant. And her words had been spoken with a tone of affection. "Well, how am I not nice?" I asked. "Tell me. I'll do anything you ask me to." "No, that would be useless. I can't explain. . . ." For a moment I was afraid she believed I did not love her; and this was a new pain, no less sharp, but requiring to be reasoned with in a different way. "You would tell me if you knew how unhappy you make me." But the unhappiness I spoke of, which if she had doubted my love for her should have overjoyed her, only irritated her. So, realizing my mistake, determined to ignore whatever she might say, and even disbelieving her when she asserted, "I did love you, really I did. You'll find that out one day" (that day when, according to the guilty, their innocence will be established, which is never, for some mysterious reason, the day when they are being asked about it), I found the courage to make the sudden resolution never to see her again, and to do this without letting her know about it yet, because she would not have believed me.

A sadness caused by somebody one loves may be bitter, even when it happens amid a round of pastimes, joys, and preoccupations which are extraneous to that person and which, except for brief moments, divert our mind from it. But when such a sadness comes right at the moment when we are basking in the full delight of being with that person, as was my case with Gilberte, the sudden depression which replaces the broad, tranquil sunlight of our inner summer sets off within us a storm so wild that we may doubt our ability to weather it. As I went home that evening, my heart was buffeted and bruised with such violence that I felt I could only get my breath back by retracing my steps, by making up some excuse to return to Gilberte. But she would only have thought: "Him again! Obviously I can treat him like dirt! The more unhappy I make him, the easier he'll be to manage!" In my mind, however, I was irresistibly drawn back to her; and these alternating urges, the crazy fluctuations of my inner compass, persisted after I reached home, where they turned into the drafts of incoherent letters I wrote to her.

I was on the threshold of one of those difficult junctures which most of us encounter several times in our lives; and on each of those different occasions, we do not meet them in the same way, although in the meantime, despite having grown older, we have not altered our character, our nature (which of itself creates not only the loves we experience but almost the women we love, and even their defects). At such moments, our life is divided, as though apportioned in its entirety between the two sides of a pair of scales. On one of the scales lies our wish not to give offense, by appearing too docile, to the woman we love, albeit without completely understanding her; but this wish we think it advisable to leave to one side, to prevent her from feeling she is indispensable to us, and thus wearying of our devotion. But on the other lies pain—though not a localized and separate pain—which could be abated only if we were to ignore our desire to be liked, put aside our pretense of being able to live without her, and seek her out. If we lighten the scale containing our pride, by removing from it a little of the willpower we have been remiss enough to wear away with age, and if we add to the scale containing our unhappiness an acquired physical pain that we have allowed to become worse, it is not the courageous side that outweighs the other, as would have happened at twenty; it is the craven side which, having become too ponderous and lacking a counterweight, unbalances us at fifty. Also, since situations can change as well as repeat themselves, there is the possibility that, by the middle of life or toward the end of it, one's self-indulgence may have had the unfortunate effect of complicating love with an element of habit, which adolescence, preoccupied by too many other obligations and lacking personal freedom, has not yet acquired.

I had just dashed off a furious letter to Gilberte, being sure to place in it the life buoy of a few apparently casual words to which she could cling if she wanted us to make up; but then, in a quite different mood, I dashed off another, full of loving words, in which I savored the touching sweetness of certain forlorn expressions such as *Never again,* so moving for the one who writes, yet so boring for the one who reads, either because she suspects them of being false and translates *Never again* as *This very evening, please,* or because she thinks they are true and sees in them the promise of the sort of lifelong separation that we accept with utter indifference when dealing with people we do not love. But since we are unable, while we love, to act as the worthy predecessor to the next person we are going to be, the one who will no longer be in love, how could we accurately imagine the state of mind of a woman who, even though we knew we meant nothing to her, has always figured in our sweetest daydreams, a figment of our illusive wish to fancy a future with her, or of our need to heal the heart she has broken, whispering to us things she would have said only if she had been in love with us?

Faced with the thoughts or actions of a woman we love, we are as inca-
pacitated as the very first physicians when faced with natural phe-
nomena (in the time before science had come into being and shed a
little light into the unknown); or, even worse, we are like a being for
whom the principle of causality hardly exists, who is incapable of perceiving a connection between one phenomenon and another, for
whom the spectacle of the world is as unreliable as a dream. Of course I
tried to escape from such chaos and find causes. I even tried to be "objective," to remain aware of the disparity between the importance of
Gilberte to me and not only my importance to her, but hers to all people other than myself, since otherwise I might have seen what was a
mere civility on her part as a declaration of ungovernable passion, and
an unseemly and degrading act on my own part as the pleasing spontaneity that impels a man toward a pretty face. But I was also wary of
going to the other extreme, of reading a mere moment's unpunctuality
or bad temper as meaning that Gilberte had an implacable hostility
toward me. Somewhere between these two points of view, each of them
making for distortion, I tried to find a way of seeing things that was
more accurate; the mental efforts this required distracted me a little
from my pain; and whether from trust in the answers I arrived at, or
whether I had biased these answers toward what I wanted, I decided
the following day to go back to the Swanns', a resolution that left me
happy, but happy after the manner of the man who, having worried for
a long time about a journey he wishes he did not have to take, goes
only as far as the station before returning home to unpack his trunk.
And since, during the period one has spent in hesitations, the merest
glimpse of a possible determination to end them (unless one has pre-
cluded such a thought by resolving not to make such a determination)
is like a sturdy seed out of which grow first the broad lines, then all the
details of the feelings one could have once the act is accomplished, I reproached myself for having been so absurd, for having allowed my own
notion of never seeing Gilberte again to make me suffer as much as if I
had really been going to carry it out, telling myself that, since the long
and the short of it was that I was going back to see her, I might as well
have saved myself so many agonizing changes of heart and dispiriting

resolves. This renewal of my relationship with Gilberte lasted as long as it took me to reach her house. It ended, not because the butler, who liked me, said she was out (which was true, as I learned that evening from people who had met her), but because of the way he said it: "Mademoiselle is out, monsieur. I swear to Monsieur I am telling the truth. If Monsieur would like to check what I am saying, I can fetch the maid. As Monsieur well knows, I would do anything for him, and if Mademoiselle was in, I would take Monsieur straight to her." These words of the butler's, as important as only spontaneous words can be, because they give us at least a summary X-ray of an inscrutable reality that a rehearsed speech would conceal, proved that the household suspected my attentions were irksome to Gilberte; and as soon as he had finished speaking them, they aroused in me a gust of hatred, which I preferred to direct against him rather than against her; they focused on him whatever feelings of anger I had harbored against her; they cleansed my love of these feelings, and it lived on without them; but they also taught me that for some time I should not try to see Gilberte again. She would be writing to me, no doubt, to apologize. Even so, I would make a point of not going around to see her straight away, just to show her I could live without her. And of course, once I had received her letter, to see her again would be something I could more easily postpone for a time, since I would be certain of being able to be with her whenever I wanted to. To be able to bear that self-imposed separation from her without too much sorrow, all I needed was to feel that my heart had been freed from the dreadful uncertainty of not knowing whether we had fallen out forever, whether she might not be engaged to be married, or have left Paris, or eloped with somebody. The following days were somewhat like the New Year holiday I had once had to spend without a sight of Gilberte. But in those earlier days, I had been sure that, once the week was over, she would come back to the Champs-Élysées, and that I could see her as usual; and equally sure that there was no point in going to the Champs-Élysées until the New Year holiday had ended. Which was why, for the whole of that sad week, long past, it was with an untroubled mind that I had borne my sorrow, because it had neither fear nor hope in it. But this time my pain was unbearable, because I was tormented by a hope that was almost as strong as my fear. Not having received a letter from her by the afternoon mail, I reminded myself of how remiss she could be in such things, of how busy she was, and I had no doubt there would be one by the morning. I awaited the postman each morning with a beating heart, a state that turned into dejection each time I found the mail to consist either of letters from people who were not Gilberte or of no letters at all, an eventuality that was not harder to bear, since a token of friendship from someone else only made the evidence of her indifference to me the more wounding. Then, each day, I would start looking forward again to the afternoon mail. Even between the delivery times I did not dare leave the house, since she might be sending the letter by hand. Each evening the moment eventually came when neither the postman nor the Swanns' footman could be expected, and I had to postpone the hope of possible consolation till the following morning; in this way, because I believed my pain could not last, I was obliged to keep on renewing it, so to speak. The sorrow I felt may have been the same sorrow all the time; but, unlike my earlier sadness, it was not just a uniform continuation of an initial emotion; it started up several times each day, being at first an emotion which was so often renewed that, though it was a wholly physical state and quite momentary, it ended up at a stable level; and as the disturbance provoked by expectation barely had time to settle before a new reason for expectation arose, there was no moment of the day when I was not in the grip of that form of anguish which it is so difficult to bear even for an hour. So it was that my suffering was much crueler than it had been on that previous New Year's Day, because this time I was full not of a simple acceptance of it but of the hope, recurring at every instant, that it would end. I did eventually reach that state of acceptance. I reached too the realization that it was to be definitive, and so I gave up Gilberte forever, in the interest of my love itself, but also because I hoped more than anything that she might remember me without contempt. In the future, if she ever sent me an invitation or a suggestion that we meet, I even made a point of accepting some of these, so as to prevent her from suspecting I was acting on anything like lover's pique, and then, at the last moment, I wrote to cry off, with the sort of great protestations of disappointment that you send to someone you have no real desire to see. It seemed to me that these expressions of regret, usually reserved for people to whom one is indifferent, would be more successful in convincing Gilberte of my indifference toward her than the tone of feigned indifference that one uses with somebody one loves. Once I had proved to her, not just with words, but more effectively with reiterated actions, that I could see nothing pleasing in her company, perhaps she would come to realize there was something pleasing in my mine. Unfortunately, this was not to be: trying to make her discover something pleasing in my company by not seeing her was the surest way to lose her forever. For one thing, if she ever did come to this discovery, I would want its effects to last, and so I would have to be careful not to enjoy them too soon; besides, the worst of my torment would be over by then; it was *now* that she was necessary to me; I wished I could warn her that, before long, the only purpose of her seeing me again would be to soothe a pain that would have faded so much as no longer to be, as it still was at this moment, a reason for her to allay it by giving in, and for both of us to make up and see each other again. And in the future, when Gilberte's liking for me had once again become so strong that I could at last safely confess mine for her, I foresaw that mine would not have survived such a long absence, and that I would have come to feel indifferent to her. All this I knew; but if I had said so, she would just have assumed that, in saying I would stop loving her if I had to live without her for too long, my real purpose was to make her ask me to come back to her at once. Meanwhile, a thing that made it easier for me to condemn myself to this separation was that (with the purpose of making Gilberte clearly aware that, for all my statements to the contrary, it really was by choice, and not because of ill health, or some such thing beyond my control, that I was staying away from her), if I knew in advance that she was not going to be at home, was going out with a friend, and would not be back for dinner, I took to visiting Mme Swann, who thus once more became the person she had been in the days when it had been so hard to see her daughter, when if Gilberte did not turn up at the Champs-Élysées I would take a walk along the Avenue des Acacias. In this way, not only could I hear about

Gilberte, but I was sure she would hear about me too, and in a way that would make it plain I had lost interest in her. Also, like all those in pain, I had the feeling that my sorry situation could have been worse. Since I had open access to her house, I lived with the knowledge (even though I was resolved never to avail myself of the possibility) that, if ever my suffering became too much for me, I could always bring it to an end. So I was only unhappy for one day at a time. And even that is an overstatement. How many times per hour (but now free of the fever of expectation that had so anguished me in the first weeks after we had fallen out, before I started going back to the Swanns' house) did I read to myself the letter that Gilberte would definitely send me one day—which she might even bring to me herself! The constant vision of this imaginary happiness helped me to bear the ruining of my real happiness. With a woman who does not love us, as with someone who has died, the knowledge that there is nothing left to hope for does not prevent us from going on waiting. One lives in a state of alertness, eyes and ears open; a mother whose son has gone on a dangerous sea voyage always has the feeling, even when she has long known for certain that he has perished, that he is just about to come through the door, saved by a miracle, unscathed. This waiting, depending on the strength of her memory and her bodily resistance, may enable her to last out the years that will eventually bring her to an acceptance of the death of her son, so that she gradually forgets and goes on living—or it may kill her. Also, my sorrow drew some slight comfort from the knowledge that it benefited my love. Every visit I made to Mme Swann without seeing Gilberte was hurtful to me; but I sensed that it served me by bettering Gilberte's image of me.

In always making sure, before I went to Mme Swann's, that Gilberte would be away, I may have been responding not just to my determination to have fallen out with her, but as much to that hope for a reconciliation which overlaid my wish to forgo happiness (few of such wishes are absolute, at least not continuously so, one of the laws of human makeup being intermittence, which is further affected by the unpredictable recurrence of different memories) and masked from me some of its worst pain. I knew perfectly well how illusive that hope was. I was like a poor man who will wet his dry crusts with fewer tears if he imagines that a stranger is about to leave him a fortune. If we are to make reality endurable, we must all nourish a fantasy or two. My hope was more unqualified, while at the same time my severance from Gilberte was more effectively achieved, if we did not meet. If I had happened to see her while visiting her mother, we might have said something irreparable, which would have made our estrangement definitive and annihilated all hope, while setting off new anguish in me, reawakening my love, and making my resignation harder to bear.

Mme Swann had been saying to me for ages, since long before this falling out with Gilberte, "It's very nice of you to come to see her, you know. But I'd love it if you would come to see me for a change. I don't mean at my afternoon jamborees—there's always too much of a multitude, and you wouldn't like it one bit—but on any other day. I'm always here, you know, toward the end of the day." So, when I went to her house, it appeared as though I was just belatedly complying with a request of long standing. It was in the late afternoon, sometimes after dark, at a time when my parents would soon be dining, that I set off for the Swanns' house, where I was sure of never seeing Gilberte, but where I would think of nothing but her. In those days, in that part of Paris, which was seen as rather remote (indeed, the whole city was darker then than nowadays, none of the streets, even in the center of town, being lit by electricity, and very few of the houses), lamps glowing inside a drawing room on a ground floor or a mezzanine, which was where Mme Swann's receiving rooms were, could light up the street and draw the glance of passersby, who saw in these illuminations a manifest but veiled relation to the handsome horses and carriages waiting outside the front doors. The passerby, seeing one of these carriages move off, might think, not without a certain thrill, that there had been a change in this mysterious relation; but it would only be because a coachman, fearing his horses might catch a chill, was taking them for a turn around the block, their hooves striking sharp and clear against the background of silence laid down by the rubber-rimmed wheels.

The "winter garden," which the passerby would also generally glimpse, whichever street the house was on, and as long as the rooms were not situated too high above the pavement, can be seen now only in the photogravure illustrations of P.-J. Stahl's giftbooks; because of the profusion of indoor plants that people had then, and the total lack of stylishness in their arrangement, such a winter garden gives the impression, in contrast to the sparse floral ornamentation of today's Louis XVI drawing rooms (a single rose or Japanese iris in a long-necked crystal vase that could not contain one more flower), of having been the expression of some headlong and delectable passion among ladies for botany, rather than a frigid fixation with still life. In the large houses of that time, it brought to mind, on a much larger scale, the tiny portable greenhouses sitting in the lamplight on the morning of January 1 (the children having been too impatient to wait for daybreak) among the other New Year's Day presents, the loveliest of them all because the thought of the plants you were going to be able to grow in them consoled you for the bareness of the wintertime; or, rather, instead of resembling these actual diminutive greenhouses, the winter garden looked more like the one you could see right beside them in a lovely book, another of the New Year's Day presents, and which, despite being not for the children but for Mlle Lili, the heroine of the story,[59] delighted them so much that, though they are now almost in their old age, they wonder whether in those dear days winter was not the best of seasons. The passerby who stood on tiptoe might well see in the depths of this winter garden, through the branching foliage of the various species, which made the lamplit windows look like the panes of children's glass-houses, real or drawn, a gentleman in a frock coat, with a gardenia or a carnation in his buttonhole, standing in front of a lady who was sitting, neither of them very clear, as though intaglioed in topaz, amid the drawing-room atmosphere hazily ambered by the fumes from the samovar, a recent importation of that period, fumes which may still be given off nowadays but which, because of habit, nobody ever sees. Mme Swann was very attached to this teatime of hers; she thought she was showing originality and charm when she said to a man, "I'm always in toward the end of the day. Do come and take tea with me," words to which she gave a gentle, subtle smile and a brief touch of English accent, and which her listener duly noted as he gave her his most sober bow, as though they were an important and sin-gular message, demanding deference and attentiveness. In addition to those mentioned above, there was another reason why flowers were not mere ornaments in Mme Swann's drawing room, a reason that had nothing to do with the period but in part with the life which, as Odette de Crécy, she had once lived. The life of a high-class courtesan, such as she had been, being much taken up by her lovers, is largely spent at home; and this can lead such a woman to live for herself. Things one may see on or about a faithful wife, which may well have some impor-tance for the faithful wife, are the very things that have the most im-portance for the courtesan. The climax of her day is not the moment when she dresses for society, but when she undresses for a man. She has to be as elegant in a housecoat or a nightgown as in a walking-out dress. Other women show off their jewels; she shares her private life with her pearls. It is a type of life that demands, and eventually gives a taste for, the enjoyment of secret luxury—that is, a life which is almost one of dis-interest. This taste Mme Swann extended to flowers. Near her armchair there always stood an immense crystal bowl filled to the brim with Parma violets or the plucked petals of marguerites in water, which to the eyes of someone arriving in the room made it seem as though she had been disturbed in a favorite pastime, such as quietly enjoying the pri-vate pleasure of a cup of tea; but the spread flowers made it seem a more private pastime even than that, a mysterious one, and seemed to hint that one should apologize for an indiscretion, as one might on in-advertently glimpsing the title of a book lying open and divulging the secret of what she had just read, or perhaps even the thought in her mind at that very moment. But the flowers were more alive than a book: so notable and enigmatic was their presence that one felt embar-rassed, if one came to visit Mme Swann, to find she was not alone, or, if one came home with her, to find the drawing room already occupied. They suggested long hours of her life that one knew nothing of, not seeming to have been set out in expectation of visitors, but looking as though just left there by her, after sharing intimate moments with her which would come again soon, secret moments which one was loath to disturb, but which one yearned to be privy to, as one gazed at the wanton mauves, moist and faded, of her Parma violets. By the end of October, Odette would come home as regularly as possible to take tea—a ceremony that was still known in those days by the English expression "five o'clock tea"—because she had once heard it said, and enjoyed repeating, that the real origin of Mme Verdurin's salon had been the knowledge in people's minds that their hostess could always be found at home at the same time each day. She now prided herself on having built up a salon of her own, similar in design but freer in spirit, or, as she liked to put it, *senza rigore*. She saw herself as a latter-day Julie de Lespinasse,[60] whose rival salon had succeeded in attracting away from the little set's Mme du Deffand her most desirable men, especially Swann, who, according to a legend that Odette had understandably sown as truth in the minds of newcomers who knew nothing of her past, but not quite in her own mind, had supported her secession and been a companion to her in her retreat. But we play certain favorite parts so often for the eyes of others, and we rehearse them so much in our hearts, that we come to rely more readily on the fictions of their evidence than on a reality we have all but forgotten. On days when she had not been out, one found oneself in the presence of a Mme Swann sitting in a tea gown of crêpe de Chine, as white as newly fallen snow, with which she sometimes wore one of those long garments in fluted chiffon, which made her look as though she were wearing nothing but a sprinkle of pink or white petals, and which people nowadays would think, wrongly, was quite inappropriate for the winter. In the drawing rooms of that period, draped with door curtains and overheated, for which the fashionable novelists of the time could find no smarter epithet than "cozily upholstered," these flimsy clothes in their soft shades made women look as though they must feel as cold as the roses that stood beside them, braving the winter in their flesh-tinted nakedness, as though it were already spring. As the carpets muffled all sounds, and as she often sat secluded in an alcove, one's hostess, not having been told of one's arrival as she would be these days, might still be deep in her book as one stood before her; and this enhanced the impression of a romantic moment, the charm of having uncovered a secret, brought back to us nowadays by the memory of those dresses, which, though already out of date then, were still worn by Mme Swann alone, perhaps, and which to our minds suggest that their wearer must be the heroine of a novel, since most of us have only ever glimpsed them in the romances of Henry Gréville.[61] In those days, in the early winter, Odette's drawing room would harbor chrysanthemums, which were enormous and in a range of colors that Swann could never have seen in earlier times. No doubt my liking for them—during those sad visits I made to her, when my sorrow had given her back all the mysterious poetry of being the mother of Gilberte, to whom she would say after I had left, "Your young man's been to see me"—came from the fact that their pale pink matched the Louis XV silk of her armchairs, their snowy white her crêpe-de-Chine tea gown, their burnished red her samovar, and that the decoration of the drawing room was enhanced by this extra color scheme, which was quite as rich in its range, just as refined, gifted with life, though lasting only a few days. But, short-lived as they were, I was touched by something more durable in these shades than their pinkish and coppery counterparts, which the afterglow of the sunset spreads so gorgeously across misty late afternoons in November, when I arrived at Mme Swann's, and which, as they faded from the sky, were taken up again and transposed into the blushing palette of the blooms. As though a master of color had snatched their fleeting incandescence from the sunlit evening air so as to brighten a human place, these chrys-anthemums at teatime invited me, despite all my woe, to savor the short joys of November, which glowed beside me in their strange, secret splendor. Such splendor, however, was sadly lacking in the conversa-tions going on about me. Even with Mme Cottard, and though time was getting on, Mme Swann would put on her most cajoling voice: "No, no, it's not late! You mustn't pay any attention to that clock, that's not the right time, it's stopped. You can't be in that much of a hurry, surely?" And she urged the professor's wife, who still held her card case in her hand, to have another little tart.

"Really," Mme Bontemps would say to Mme Swann, "this is a *very* difficult house to get out of!" at which Mme Cottard exclaimed, in her surprise at hearing someone else say exactly what she was thinking, "Yes! That's exactly what *I* always say to myself! Me with my little brain! In my own mind, you know . . ." And all the gentlemen of the Jockey Club nodded their approval of her, much as their eager bowing and scraping had earlier given the impression that Mme Swann had done them a signal honor by introducing them to this charmless woman of no social distinction, who when faced with Odette's fine friends was always reserved, or, as she put it herself, being inclined to use inflated language to speak of the simplest things, "adopted a defensive posture." "Well, it certainly doesn't look like it," Mme Swann said in answer to Mme Cottard. "This is the first Wednesday for three weeks that you've actually come to see me!" "Oh, I know, Odette, I do know! I haven't seen you for ages—centuries, in fact! I plead guilty to the charge, but I must tell you"—and here Mme Cottard's manner became vague and prudish, for, though a doctor's wife, she could not have brought herself to speak bluntly about rheumatism or renal colic—"I've had quite a lot of little *distempers.* We each have our own, don't we? And also, I've had a crisis in my male household staff. I'm no more of a martinet than the next woman, but I've just had to make an example and let the butler go. I do believe he was actually looking elsewhere for a more lucrative situation. But his departure very nearly precipitated the resignation *en masse* of the whole Cabinet! My maid was all set to leave too! We've had *titanic* struggles. However, I stood alone on the burning deck, and, believe you me, it has taught me a thing or two that I won't forget in a hurry! I'm sorry to go on like this about *below-stairs business,* but you know how provoking it is to be obliged to undertake a thoroughgoing recasting of one's dramatis personae. So—are we not to see that delightful daughter of yours?" "No, the delightful daughter is dining at a friend's house tonight," Mme Swann said; then she added, as she turned toward me, "I understand she has written asking you to come and see her tomorrow." Then "And how are your babies?" she asked of Mme Cottard. I breathed deeply. Mme Swann's words, proving that I could see Gilberte whenever I felt like it, were exactly the soothing balm that I had hoped to receive from her, and which made it necessary for me to keep on visiting her at that time. "Well, no, actually," I said. "I'm going to write her a note this evening. In any case, Gilberte and I can't see each other anymore." I said this in a tone that suggested an air of mystery in our estrangement; and this in turn fostered in me an illusory feeling of love, which was further abetted by the affectionate manner in which Gilberte and I went on referring to each other. "You know she's very fond of you," Mme Swann said. "Are you sure tomorrow's not possible?" A sudden surge of joy went through me, and I thought: "Well, why not? I mean, it's her *mother* who's asking me!" But my dejection returned at once. I was afraid Gilberte might deduce from my presence that my recent indifference toward her had been only for show, and I decided that the separation should continue. During this exchange, Mme Bontemps was lamenting the fact that she was afflicted by the wives of so many politicians, for she professed to think that everybody was insufferably absurd, and that her husband's job made life very difficult for her. "So you don't actually *mind* being exposed to fifty doctors' wives one after another?" she said to Mme Cottard, who was full of goodwill toward all and respect for the notion of duty. "Well, I must say that is *heroic* of you! Of course, at the Ministry, as you can appreciate, one does have certain duties. But you know, after a time, mixing with all those wives of *civil servants*, I can't help it, I feel like sticking out my tongue at them! My niece Albertine is just the same! You've no idea how cheeky she is! Just last week the wife of the undersecretary of state at the Treasury was at my at-home, and she was saying how useless she was at anything to do with cooking. Well, my niece gave her the sweetest smile and said, 'But surely, madame, with a father who was a scullery boy, you if anyone should know all about it.'" "Now, isn't that a *lovely* story?" Mme Swann exclaimed. "I just love that story! But surely, Mme Cottard, on your husband's consulting days you should make sure of having a little den of your own, with your flowers and your books and all the things you like." "Ho-ho! Albertine doesn't mince words, I can tell you! Straight out! Just like that! And not a word to me beforehand! She's as artful as a bunch of monkeys. You're lucky, you know how to restrain yourself. I do envy people who can hide their thoughts." "Yes, but I don't need to, you see," Mme Cottard replied in her mild way. "I'm not hard to please. Unlike you, my position doesn't require it," she added in the more emphatic voice she used for stressing the clever little compliments she liked to slip into the conversation, the sprinkling of flattery which her husband admired so much, and which contributed to the advancement of his career. "And also I enjoy doing anything that may be of use to the professor."

"No doubt. But I mean, not everyone is capable of it, you know. You're probably not the high-strung type. As soon as I see that wife of the minister of war contorting her face the way she does, I can't help imitating her. You've no idea what it's like to have a passionate nature like mine!"

"Yes, you're right," Mme Cottard said. "I've heard she's got a twitch. You see, Dr. Cottard knows someone who moves in those exalted circles, and so when they meet they will talk. . . ."

"Or take the head of protocol at the Foreign Office—the man's a hunchback. Well, would you believe, he's only got to be in my house for five minutes and I can't keep my hands off his hump! My husband says I'll get him sacked one day. Well, what I say is, the Ministry be damned! Yes, the Ministry be damned! I really feel sometimes like having it printed on my letterhead. I'm sure you'll think me very shocking, because you're so well meaning. But I must say I do enjoy getting a good *dig* at people from time to time! Life would be so dull otherwise."

She went on talking about the Ministry as though it were Olympus. Changing the subject, Mme Swann said to Mme Cottard:

"Aren't you beautiful today! Is this one of Redfern's creations?"

"No, no, as you know, I'm a disciple of Raudnitz. In any case, it's just something I've had remodeled."

"Well, I never! It's so smart!"

"How much would you say it cost? . . . No, no, only three figures."

"Three! But that's *giving* it away! I was told the figure was three times as high."

"Well, that's how history's written, isn't it?"[62] said Mme Cottard. Then she drew Mme Swann's attention to a necklet she was wearing, a present from Odette herself:

"Do you recognize this, Odette?"

A face might then appear around the edge of the door curtain, its features set in a mime of polite and playful reluctance to interrupt: it was Swann: "Odette, I've got the Prince d'Agrigente with me in my study, and he wishes to know whether he may come and pay his respects. What am I to say?" "Tell him I'll be delighted, of course!" Odette would say, full of gratification, and quite unperturbed by the prospect of being visited by such a fashionable gentleman, something she had always been accustomed to, even as a courtesan. Swann went off to deliver the message; and he would soon come back with the Prince, unless in the meantime Mme Verdurin had made her entrance. On marrying Odette, Swann had asked her to resign from "the little set." For this he had many reasons; but even if he had had none, he would still have done so, by reason of a law of ingratitude which, quite without exception, demonstrates the improvidence of all go-betweens, or perhaps their disinterest. He had permitted Odette to exchange only two visits a year with Mme Verdurin, a number that seemed excessive to certain of the "regulars" who were offended at the insult done to "the Patronne," given that for so many years she had treated Odette and even Swann himself as her special favorites. Although the membership of the little clan included certain faithless souls who were capable of "welshing" on certain evenings, so as to slip off and surreptitiously attend some function of Odette's, and who if they were found out gave as an excuse their eagerness to meet Bergotte (the Patronne's view being that he never went to the Swanns', and was devoid of talent anyway, despite which she made constant attempts to, as she liked to put it, "bring him in"), it did also contain its extremists. They, in their disregard for the particular proprieties which can often dissuade others from whatever extreme course one may be urging upon them in one's desire to do a disservice to someone else, had pressed Mme Verdurin, but to no avail, to sever all contact with Odette, and thus deprive her of the pleasure of saying with a laugh: "We don't see much of the Patronne now, you know, not since the Schism. While my husband was still a bachelor, of course, there was no difficulty. But for a married couple, it's not always easy. . . . To be quite honest, M. Swann is not overfond of old Mother Verdurin, and he would not take kindly to my being among her boon companions. And I'm a very dutiful wife, you know." Swann would accompany Odette to a soirée of Mme Verdurin's; but he made a

point of not being at home for the latter's return visit. So it was that if
Mme Verdurin was present in the drawing room the Prince d'Agrigente
was sure to come in alone. He was also the only man whom Odette ever
introduced to Mme Verdurin; for her idea was that if "the Patronne"
was surrounded by faces unfamiliar to her, and if she heard the names
of no obscurities being uttered, she might believe these people were all
aristocrats of note, an idea which worked so well that Mme Verdurin
would sneer that evening to her husband, "Charming people! She's got
all the reactionary bigwigs!" As for Odette's illusion about Mme Verdurin, it was the opposite one. Not that the latter's salon at that time
had even begun to aspire to the status it will later be seen to have. Mme
Verdurin had not even reached the stage of incubation, when one post-
pones one's most lavish galas lest one's few recently acquired celebrities
should be swamped by the hoi polloi, and when one prefers to await
the moment when the generative power of the ten good men and true
whom one has managed to "bring in" shall bring forth a hundredfold.
As Odette's was soon to be, Mme Verdurin's aim was "Society"; but
the zones in which she launched her offensives were still so restricted, as
well as being remote from those in which Odette might hope to emu-
late her and begin to make a name for herself, that Odette lived in a
state of utter ignorance of the strategic plans drawn up by the Patronne.
So, when anyone spoke of Mme Verdurin as a snob, it was with the simplest sincerity that Odette would laugh and say, "No, no, she's the exact
opposite! I mean, she just hasn't got the basic requirement—she doesn't
know anybody! And to be fair, you must admit that's how she likes to
be. You see, what she really likes is those little Wednesday gatherings of
hers, with those inoffensive people who drop in for a chat." However,
Odette did nurse a surreptitious envy of Mme Verdurin's mastery of
those arts (though she rather prided herself too on having picked up the
rudiments of them from such an Oracle) to which the Patronne attached so much importance, though all they ever do is refine the nicer
quibbles of nonexistence, give vacancy its shape, being in the strictest
sense those Arts of Naught practiced by hostesses: the ability to "bring
people together," to "bring people out," to "match guests with one another," to "be present but invisible," to be "a good go-between."

The other ladies who visited Mme Swann were certainly impressed to see her drawing room graced by a woman whom they generally pictured in her own salon, set within the perpetual frame of her *habitués*, her little group, which seemed startlingly present, suggested, epitomized, and condensed in the single person sitting in her armchair, the Patronne herself turned into someone else's guest, cozily wrapped in her great grebe-lined coat, as downy as the white fur rugs strewn in this salon, where Mme Verdurin was herself a salon. The shiest women, deciding it would now be discreet for them to withdraw, said to their hostess, with that plural used by people trying to hint to an invalid's other visitors that it would be best not to tire her too much on her first day out of bed, "We must be off now, Odette." Mme Cottard was envied when the Patronne used her first name. "Shall I whisk you away home, then?" Mme Verdurin said, irked by the thought that one of her regulars might stay there rather than leave with her. "Well, actually, this dear lady has very kindly offered to give me a lift," Mme Cottard replied, loath to let it appear that she might give precedence to a more famous person over Mme Bontemps, whose offer of a lift in the carriage with its ministerial insignia she had already accepted.

"I must confess I am particularly grateful to dear friends who are kind enough to make room for me in their carriages. Having no jehu myself, I must say it's too good an offer to decline." "Yes, of course," replied the Patronne, choosing her words with care, as she was slightly acquainted with Mme Bontemps and had just invited her to one of her Wednesdays. "Especially since you're so far out of your way here at Mme de Crécy's— oh, goodness me, what have I said? I'll never get into the habit of saying 'Mme Swann'!" Among those of Mme Verdurin's regulars who had little wit of their own, it was a standing joke to pretend that you could not get used to speaking of Odette as "Mme Swann": "I tell you, I got so accustomed to referring to Mme de Crécy that I nearly went and said it again by mistake!" Mme Verdurin, the only one not to nearly say it by mistake, said it on purpose. "Odette, aren't you rather frightened by living in such a godforsaken part of town? I'm sure if I lived hereabouts I'd quake in my shoes at having to come all this way after dark. And it's so damp! I shouldn't think it can be very good for your husband's eczema. You haven't got rats, I trust?" "Heavens above! The very idea!" "Well, that's all right at least. Only, someone said you did. I'm glad to hear it's not true, because I have an utter phobia of rats, and I should never have set foot here again. So— goodbye, my dear sweet Odette. I do hope to see you soon. You know how pleased I am to see you. You're not very good at arranging chrysanthemums, are you?" she added on the way out, as Mme Swann was moving toward the door with her. "These are Japanese flowers, you know. They should be arranged as the Japanese do them." "I don't agree with Mme Verdurin, although I must say her word is gospel for me. But really, Odette, no one has such beautiful chrysanthemums as you—or, rather, chrysanthema, as I believe we're supposed to say nowadays," said Mme Cottard after the door had closed on the Patronne. "Dear, sweet Mme Verdurin is not always very kind to other people's flowers," Mme Swann replied gently. "So—who's your flower man?" asked Mme Cottard, cutting short such criticism of the Patronne.

"Is it Lemaître? I must admit there was a great big pink shrub outside Lemaître's the other day, and I threw economy to the winds!" Her sense of decency prevented her from going into the details of the price she had paid for the shrub; she said no more than that the professor, "who was after all the soul of mildness," had nearly had a fit, and told her she spent money like water! "No, actually, my only florist 'by appointment' is Debac." "Yes, he's mine too," said Mme Cottard. "But I confess to having been occasionally unfaithful to him and frequenting Lachaume." "Ooh! Infidelities with Lachaume! I'll tell on you!" exclaimed Odette, always trying to be the witty hostess who keeps the conversation going, which she felt she managed better at home than at the Verdurins'. "Actually, Lachaume charges too much now. His prices are quite exorbitant." Then, with a laugh, she added, "His prices are quite indecent!"

Mme Bontemps, who had declared a hundred times that she had no desire to go to the Verdurins', was overjoyed to be invited and was wondering how she could make sure of attending as many of the Wednesdays as possible. She was unaware that Mme Verdurin's wish was that her guests should attend every single week. Also, she was one of those people whose company is not much sought after and who, having been invited to a "run" of functions by the same hostess, instead of responding like those who know they will always be welcome, and who go to her house whenever they have the opportunity and the desire to go out, decide to abstain from the first and third occasions in the belief that they will be missed, but make a point of attending the second and the fourth; or else, having been assured that the third one will be a particularly brilliant soirée, they arrange their absences in a different sequence, and then apologize by saying "what a pity they weren't free last time." So Mme Bontemps calculated how many Wednesdays there were between now and Easter, and how she could manage to get herself invited to an extra one without seeming too forward. She was relying on Mme Cottard to give her some hints about this during the drive home. "Oh, Mme Bontemps!" exclaimed Mme Swann. "I see you're getting to your feet! I'll have you know it's very naughty of you to be giving the signal for a general withdrawal. You've got to make amends, don't you know, for last Thursday, when you didn't come. So—just sit down again for a minute. I mean, you're not going to fit in another visit between now and dinnertime, are you? No? Are you quite sure?" she added, proffering a plate of cakes. "Do have one of these little fellows. They may not look like very much, but if you just try one, you'll be very glad you did." "Mmm, they do look delicious," Mme Cottard said. "One is never short of a bite to eat at your house, Odette. I don't need to ask where these came from. I know you have your standing order at Rebattet's. I must say I'm not as single-minded as you—for little cakes and all delicacies, I often order from Bourbonneux. But I admit they don't really know about ices. Whereas Rebattet's are artists when it comes to ice cream or mousses or sherbets. As my husband says, they're just the *ne plus ultra*." "Well, actually, these are homemade. Are you quite sure you won't?" "No, really," said Mme Bontemps. "I'll have no appetite left for dinner. But I will sit down for a moment. I do so enjoy conversing with a woman as intelligent as yourself. Odette, you may think I'm a great gossip, but I'd love to know what you think of that hat Mme Trombert was wearing. I know that large hats are very fashionable at the moment. But doesn't that one go a bit far? Although, mind you, it's minute compared to the one she had on the other day, when she came to me." "I'm not intelligent," Odette replied, thinking this a becoming thing to say. "Really, I'm quite gullible. I'm just a woman who believes whatever she's told and who breaks her heart over a trifle." She insinuated that, in the early days of marriage, she had suffered much from life with a man like Swann, who had a life of his own and was unfaithful to her. The Prince d'Agrigente, who had caught the words "I'm not intelligent" and thought it behooved him to protest, was not quick-witted enough to interject. "Oh, come now!" exclaimed Mme Bontemps. "Not intelligent? You?" "My sentiments exactly!" the Prince said, grateful for this assistance. "I was just about to say, 'What's that I hear?' I must be hearing things." "No, no, I assure you," said Odette. "At heart I'm really just a little middle-class housewife, easily shocked, full of prejudices, living in her small corner, and very ignorant about everything." Then, taking care to use the English word, she asked the Prince for news of the Baron de Charlus: "What news of the dear *Baronet?*" "Ignorant? You?" exclaimed Mme Bontemps. "Well, I never! If you're ignorant, what about the world of officialdom, what about all those ministers' wives who have nothing better to talk about than clothes! Let me tell you, Mme Swann, no more than a week ago I decided to try a mention of *Lohengrin* on the wife of the minister of education. Do you know what she said? '*Lohengrin?*' she said. 'Isn't that the new revue at the Folies-Bergère? I'm told it's hilarious.' Believe you me, when you hear that sort of thing, it makes your blood boil! I felt like slapping her face. I don't mind saying I've got a bit of a temper. Would you not agree, monsieur?" she added, turning toward me. "Was I not right to feel like that?" "Well, actually," said Mme Cottard, "I do think one is quite within one's rights to answer back if one is bombarded with a question like that, point-blank and without warning. I know what it feels like—it's exactly the sort of thing Mme Verdurin likes doing." "Oh, speaking of Mme Verdurin," Mme Bontemps said to her, "do you know who she's likely to be having at her Wednesday this week? Oh dear, I've just remembered—M. Bontemps and I have been invited somewhere else this Wednesday! What would you say to dining with us the following Wednesday? You and I could then go on together to Mme Verdurin's.

I'm rather apprehensive about turning up there all by myself. She's such a great personage, as you know, and for some reason I've always been intimidated by her." "I know why that is," said Mme Cottard. "It's because of her imposing voice. I mean, we can't expect everybody to have the mellifluous tones of our Mme Swann, can we? But you'll see, after the first moment spent sizing each other up, as the Patronne says, the ice will soon be broken. She's really a most welcoming person. But I can understand the feeling. It's never very nice to venture into new territory like that." "You could join us for dinner too," Mme Bontemps said to Mme Swann. "Then, after dinner, all three of us could go and Verdurinate together, I mean Verdurinize. And if it turns out that the Patronne just glares at me and decides not to invite me again, the three of us can sit there and keep each other company. I'm sure that would be rather nice." Then, casting some doubt on the veracity of this, Mme Bontemps asked: "Who do you think she'll be having the following Wednesday? What will she have on the program, do you think? She wouldn't have too many people there, would she?" "Well, I for one won't be going," said Odette. "We'll just look in briefly at the last Wednesday of the run. If you don't mind waiting till then . . ." Mme Bontemps did not seem enraptured by this suggested adjournment.

Although the wittiness of any salon and its degree of fashionableness usually stand in inverse rather than direct relation to each other, it must be assumed, given that Swann thought Mme Bontemps was a pleasant person, that any acceptance of one's lowered status has its corollary in a relaxing of the standards one applies to the people whose company one is resigned to enjoy, whose wit one is prepared to find amusing. If that is so, then, once the independence of individuals is threatened, their culture and even their language, like those of nations, must also stand in jeopardy. Beyond a certain age, one of the effects of this indulgence is to exacerbate our tendency to take pleasure in hearing praise of our own ways of thinking and preferences, which we see as an invitation to air them again; it is the age at which a great painter may find that the company of his creative peers begins to pall, when he prefers to mix with his pupils, whose only common point with him is their respect for the letter of his tenets, but who listen to him, who extol him; it is the age when, at a party, an outstanding man or woman, living only for some beloved, will be convinced, on hearing some possibly mediocre individual say something which, by suggesting a sympathetic understanding of the life devoted to amorous things, flatters their fond obsession, that they are listening to the only real mind among those present; it was the age at which Swann, in his capacity as husband of Odette, liked both to hear Mme Bontemps say how stupid it is to frequent only duchesses (from which he concluded she was a sensible woman, full of wit, and without a touch of snobbery, the opposite of what he would have thought in earlier times at the Verdurins') and to share jokes with her that "tickled her fancy," because, though she had never heard any of them, she always "got" them, being eager to please and ever ready to enjoy a good laugh. "So," Mme Swann said to Mme Cottard, "you tell me the doctor isn't a great flower-fancier like yourself?" "Well, as you know, my husband is the soul of good sense—moderation in all things. Still, I must say, he does have one great passion." "And what's that, dear lady?" implored Mme Bontemps, her eyes gleaming with spite, glee, and inquisitiveness. "Reading," Mme Cottard replied in her artless way. "Oh, well! That's a reassuring passion for a husband to have!" Mme Bontemps exclaimed, stifling fiendish mirth. "Yes, just give him a good book!" "Well, dear lady, there's nothing much to be alarmed about in that." "Oh, but there is! His eyesight! Which reminds me, Odette, I really must be off now. But I'll be back, knocking on your door, at the earliest opportunity. Speaking of eyesight, have you heard the house that Mme Verdurin has just bought is going to have the electric light in it? It wasn't my little private police who told me, you know. It was Mildé the electrician himself! I like quoting my sources, as you can see. And even the bedrooms will have electric lamps, with shades on, to soften the light. Very nice, very luxurious! We belong to a generation of ladies for whom everything must be up-to-the-minute, the very latest thing. The sister-in-law of a friend of mine has actually got a telephone installed in her house! She can order something from a shopkeeper without stepping out of her own front door! I must admit I've been shamelessly currying favor, so that I'll be allowed to go and speak into the machine one day. The idea fascinates me—but only in someone else's house, not in my own. I don't think I'd like having a telephone about the house. Once the novelty of it wears off, it must be a definite nuisance. Now, Odette, I'm off! And you must also release Mme Bontemps, since she's looking after me. I really must go! You'll get me into hot water—Dr. Cottard will be home before me!"

I had to go home too, though I had not savored those promised winter pleasures that had seemed to lie concealed within the brilliant surface of the chrysanthemums. The pleasures had not materialized; yet Mme Swann seemed to be expecting nothing further. She let the servants carry away the tea things, as she might have announced, "Time, please!" She even said to me, "Really, must you go?" Then she added in English, "Well, *goodbye!*" I sensed that, even if I were to stay on, I would never find those secret pleasures, and that it was not only my sorrow that had withheld them from me. Was it possible they did not lie somewhere along the well-frequented path of those hours that always lead so soon to going-home time, but by some side path, branching off somewhere else unknown to me, which I should have taken? At least I had achieved the aim of my visit: Gilberte would know I had been to her house during her absence, where, as Mme Cottard kept saying, I had "straight off, from the word 'go,' completely won over Mme Verdurin!," whom she had never seen "go to so much trouble." She had added, "I expect it's a case of like attracting like." Gilberte would be told I had spoken about her affectionately, as I could not help doing; and she would know I did not suffer from the inability to live without her, which I felt was the source of her recent discontents with me. I had told Mme Swann I could no longer see Gilberte. I had made it sound as though my decision to sever contact with her was irrevocable. The letter I was going to send Gilberte would also be couched in those terms. But to keep my courage up, I told myself I would make the heroic but brief effort of staying away from her for only a few days longer: "This will be the very last invitation of hers that I decline! I'll accept the next one!" So as to make my separation from her easier to achieve, I tried to see it as not being definitive. I sensed, however, that it was going to be.

That New Year's Day was especially painful. When one is unhappy, anything that serves as a reminder or an anniversary can cause this pain.

If it is a reminder, say, of the death of a loved one, the grief comes from the sharpened contrast between present and past. In my position, however, it was aggravated by the unacknowledged hope that Gilberte might have been expecting me to make the first step toward a reconciliation, and that, now it was clear I had not made it, she might have decided to take the opportunity of the New Year, with its exchanges of greetings, to send me a note: "Look, what's the matter? I'm madly in love with you, I can't live without you, let's meet and sort it all out." By the last days of December, it had come to seem likely that I would receive such a letter. Whether it was really likely or not, our desire for such a letter, our need for it, is enough to make us believe it will probably come. The soldier is convinced that an indefinitely extendable period must elapse before he will be killed, the thief before he will be arrested, all of us before we must die. This is the amulet that protects individuals, and sometimes nations, not from danger, but from the fear of danger, or, rather, from belief in danger, which can lead to the braving of real dangers by those who are not brave. Such unfounded confidence sustains the lover who looks forward to a reconciliation or a letter. For me to stop expecting one from Gilberte, I would have had to stop wishing for it. Despite knowing one is an object of indifference to a woman one still loves, one fills her mind with imaginary thoughts (though they may amount only to indifference) and an urge to express them, one sees oneself as the focus of her complicated emotional life, albeit possibly only as a source of dislike, but by the same token as an object of her permanent attention. For me to have an inkling of what was in Gilberte's real mind on that New Year's Day, I would have had to be able to feel in advance what I would feel on some future New Year's Day, by which time I would have ignored entirely any notice or lack of notice Gilberte might take of me, any affection or lack of it that she might feel for me, just as I would have become incapable of having the slightest urge to seek solutions to such problems, for they would have long since ceased to be mine. When we are in love, our love is too vast to be wholly contained within ourselves; it radiates outward, reaches the resistant surface of the loved one, which reflects it back to its starting point; and this return of our own tenderness is what we see as the other's feelings, working their

new, enhanced charm on us, because we do not recognize them as having originated in ourselves. New Year's Day chimed its hours one after
another without Gilberte's letter being delivered. By January 3, then
the 4th, having just received some well-wishers' cards and letters that
had been mailed late, or held up in the great rush of New Year mail, I
had not given up my hope, although it had begun to fade. On the following days, I was often in tears. This meant, of course, that I had held
on to the hope of having a New Year letter from Gilberte because, in
giving her up, I had not been as sincere as I had thought. That hope
having now died, before I had been able to fortify myself with a replacement, I was as distressed as an invalid who has finished his vial of
morphine without having another one available. But it may also have
meant—the two explanations need not rule each other out; and a single
feeling may be made of opposites—that my hope of at last receiving a
letter had brought the image of Gilberte closer, re-creating in me the
feelings I had once had from looking forward to being with her, from
the sight of her and her ways with me. The immediate possibility of
being reconciled with her had abolished in me the thing of which
we never realize the full enormity: resignation. Neurotics never believe
people who assure them that, if they just stay in bed, read no letters,
and open no newspapers, they will gradually calm down. They foresee
that such a regimen can only worsen the state of their nerves. Those in
love see renunciation in the same light: they imagine it while living in a
state that is its opposite; and, never having so much as begun to try it,
they cannot believe in its power of healing.

My heart palpitations had become so violent that I was ordered to
reduce my consumption of caffeine. This having put a stop to them, I
began to wonder whether the caffeine might not be partly responsible
for the anguish I had felt when I more or less chose to fall out with
Gilberte, and which I had attributed, each time it recurred, to the grief
of separation from her, or the likelihood of being with her only when
she was still in the same bad mood. But if this medication was really the
source of a suffering that had then been misinterpreted by my imagination (which would not be unheard of, as the most acute emotional pain
suffered by a lover often comes from his sheer physical habituation to

the woman he loves), then its action was like that of the love potion which, long after Tristan and Yseult have drunk it, continues to bind them. For the physical improvement brought about almost at once by the reduction in caffeine did not inhibit the evolution of the sorrow which the toxic dose had possibly created, or which it had at least contrived to make more acute.

Then, about the middle of January, once my frustrated hopes for a New Year letter had faded, and the extra pain caused by their unfulfillment had settled too, I was assailed once more by the sorrow that had beset me before the holiday period. The cruelest thing in it was still that it was my own handiwork: that, actively and consciously, patiently and ruthlessly, I had brought it upon myself. The only thing I cared for, my relationship with Gilberte, was the very thing I was trying to sabotage, through my prolonging of our separation, through my gradual fostering not of her indifference toward me, but—which would come to the same thing in the end—of mine toward her. My unremitting effort was directed to bringing about the slow, agonizing suicide of the self that loved Gilberte; and this I did with a clear awareness both of my actions in the present and of the consequences of them for the future: I could tell not only that within a certain time I would have stopped loving her, but that she herself would be unhappy about this, that her attempts to see me then would be as pointless as any she might make today, not because I would love her, as now, too much, but because without a doubt I would be in love with some other woman, and all my hours would be spent in the desire for her, in the expectation of a moment with her, and not even a second would I dare subtract from them to spend with a girl I no longer cared for. In this present moment, when Gilberte was already lost to me (since I was determined not to see her again, unless she made an unambiguous request for us to clarify our relationship, accompanied by a full declaration of her love for me, both of which I knew were impossible), and when I loved her more than ever (I knew she meant more to me now than she had the previous year, when I could spend as many afternoons with her as I wished, when I believed nothing could come between us), I detested the thought that one day I might have these same feelings for someone else, as this deprived me not only of Gilberte, but also of my love and my pain, the very love and pain through which, as I wept, I tried to grasp the real Gilberte, though I was obliged to admit they did not belong to her in particular, but would sooner or later devolve to some other woman. For we are always (or so I thought then) detached from the other person: while we love, we are aware that our love does not bear her name, that we may feel it again in the future—or might even have felt it in the past—for someone other than her; and at times when we are not in love, it is precisely because our feelings are unaffected by it that we find it easy to be philosophical toward the contradictoriness of love, that we can speak such untroubled words about it, because we have no consciousness of it at that moment, knowledge in this being intermittent and not outliving the effective presence of the emotion. There would of course have been time to warn Gilberte that the future in which I would no longer love her, a future my pain could foresee, but which my imagination could not distinguish in detail, was bound to take shape piece by piece, that its arrival was, if not imminent, at least inexorable, unless she came to my assistance and nipped my coming indifference in the bud. How often I came close to writing to her or going to say to her: "I warn you, my mind is made up! This is my very last offer! I'm seeing you for the last time! Soon I'll have stopped loving you!" But what good would it have done? What right had I to reproach her for treating me with the very indifference which, without thinking it blameworthy, I showed for everything except her? The last time! The words appalled me, because I loved her. But they would have made no more impression on her than the sort of letter a friend who is going abroad sends us to suggest a meeting, and which we ignore, as we ignore, say, the importunities of a woman who loves us, because we are looking forward to some enjoyment or other. The time we have to spend each day is elastic: it is stretched by the passions we feel; it is shrunk by those we inspire; and all of it is filled by habit.

Even if I had spoken to Gilberte, she would not have heard me. We always fancy, when we speak, that it is our ears and our minds that listen. If any words of mine had reached Gilberte, they would have been distorted, as though by passing through the mobile curtain of a waterfall, and would have been unintelligible to her, full of ludicrous sounds, and devoid of meaning. Whatever truth one puts into words does not make its way unaided; it is not endowed with irresistible self-evidence. For a truth of the same order to take form within them, a certain time must elapse. When it has elapsed, the proponent of a political idea who, in the teeth of all counterarguments and proofs, once said the proponent of the opposite idea was a blackguard, comes at length to share the abhorrent belief, which has been abandoned in the meantime by the man who once wasted his breath on spreading it. The master-piece which, to the ears of the admirers who read it aloud, sounded pregnant with the proofs of inherent excellence, while to those of lis-teners it was inept or nondescript, comes eventually to be pronounced a masterpiece indeed by the latter, but too late for its creator to know of it. So it is with the barriers of love, which the efforts, however despair-ing, of the one who is excluded by them can do nothing to force; then a day comes when, as a result of quite extraneous influences at work in-side the feelings of the once-unloving woman, and though he no longer cares about them, the barriers give way suddenly, but to no purpose. So, even if I had gone to warn Gilberte about my future indifference to her, if I had told her how she might obviate it, she would just have deduced from this that my love for her, my need for her, were even greater than she had thought; and she would have been more irked than ever by the sight of me. It is also a fact that it was this love for her which, because of the sequence of discordant states of mind it created in me, helped me to foresee better than she how it would end. Nevertheless, I might still have sent or spoken such a warning to her after enough time had passed, which, though it would of course have meant she was by then not quite as necessary to me, would also have enabled me to demon-strate to her how unnecessary she was. But then, unfortunately, some well-meaning or ill-intentioned people would speak to her about me in ways which could only give her the impression that I had asked them to do so. Whenever I heard that Dr. Cottard, my own mother, even M. de Norpois had with a few ill-advised words undone the sacrifice I had so laboriously achieved, spoiling the whole effect of my silence toward Gilberte, by making it appear as though I had decided to end it, I was faced with a double difficulty. For one thing, my painful and profitable self-denial, which these meddlers had, unbeknown to me, just inter-rupted, and thus nullified, would have to be seen now as counting only from the day when they had spoken to her. What was worse was that I myself would have taken less pleasure in seeing her again, since she would have believed, not that I was living in a state of dignified resigna-tion, but that I was intriguing behind her back to bring about a meeting she had declined. I cursed the idle talk of people who, for no particular reason, not even trying to hurt or please, often just for the sake of some-thing to say, or because we have actually indulged in similar idle talk with them, turn out to be as indiscreet as we were, and harm us with a word out of place. However, in the sorry work done to cause the down-fall of our love, the contribution of these people is not nearly as impor-tant as that of two others, who are in the habit of spoiling it at the very moment when its course promised to run smooth, one of them by be-ing too kind, the other too unkind. Even so, we do not resent this pair as we do the meddling Cottards, as the second of them is the person we love and the first is ourself.

In fact, since Mme Swann, almost every time I went to visit her, would invite me to come to tea with her and her daughter, and told me to send my reply direct to Gilberte, I often had occasion to write to her, sending her notes that I filled not with words that might have won her over, but with words chosen for the sole purpose of letting my sorrow flow free and sweet. Regret, like desire, seeks satisfaction and not self-analysis: in the beginning of love, our time is spent not in finding out what love is made of, but in trying to make sure we can see each other tomorrow; and at the end of love, we do not try to ascertain the nature of our sorrow, but only to voice it in what we hope is its tenderest form to her who is the cause of it. We say things that we feel the need to say, and which she will not understand; we talk only for our own benefit. So I wrote to Gilberte: *I used to believe it couldn't be possible. But I can see now, alas, it's not that difficult. . . .* Though I added, *I expect I'll never see you again*, I was still careful not to adopt a distant tone, which might have made her suspect it was feigned; and as I wrote these words, I was in tears, because I felt they expressed, not what I would have liked to believe, but what was in fact going to happen. I knew that when her next invitation came I would once again be brave enough not to give in, and that each successive invitation declined would bring me gradually to a time when, having gone without seeing her for so long, I would have no further wish to see her at all. So, with tears, courage, and consolation, I sacrificed the happiness of being with her to the possibility of one day seeming lovable in her eyes, though knowing it would be a day when the prospect of seeming lovable in her eyes would leave me cold. Even the albeit highly unlikely hypothesis that at this very instant she still loved me, as she had claimed during my last visit to her, that what I saw as the annoyance of having to be with someone whose company is irksome was really only an expression of touchy possessiveness, an affectation of indifference no more genuine in her than mine was in me, served only to make my determination less cruel. And I felt as though, at a time several years hence, when we had completely forgotten one another, when I could look back on this letter I was writing and tell her there had been not one word of sincerity in it, she would say, "What? You mean you *did* love me? Oh, if you only knew how I had been looking forward to getting that letter! How I longed for us to meet! How I cried when I read it!" As I sat writing to her, having just come home from visiting her mother, the thought that I was possibly there and then in the act of consummating that very misunderstanding, the sadness of it all, the joy of believing Gilberte loved me, made me go on with my letter.

My thoughts, as I left Mme Swann's at the end of her teatime, were all for what I was going to say in my letter to her daughter; but Mme Cottard's thoughts were full of something very different. As she carried out her little "tour of inspection," she had made a point of congratulating Mme Swann on any new piece of furniture or any recent "acquisition" she had noticed in the drawing room. Among them she might also have noticed a meager remnant of the things Odette had once surrounded herself with in the rue La Pérouse house, especially the animals in precious stones and metals, her fetishes.

However, to Mme Swann, the word "sham," picked up from a friend whom she admired, had opened new horizons by its applicability to things which, years ago, she had called "chic"; and one after another, most of those things had followed into oblivion the gold-painted garden trellis against which her chrysanthemums had stood, many a bonbonnière from Giroux's, and the notepaper embossed with a coronet (to say nothing of the *louis* coins in golden cardboard adorning her mantelpieces, which a man of taste had once hinted, long before she met Swann, that she might dispense with). As well, in the artistic disarray, the bohemian jumble, of her rooms, with their walls still painted dark, making them as different as possible from the white drawing rooms she was to have a little later, the Far East was giving ground under the increasing onslaughts of the eighteenth century; and the cushions which Mme Swann plumped up and heaped behind me to make me (as she said in English) *comfortable* were decorated now with Louis XV posies, rather than Chinese dragons. In the room where one usually came upon her, of which she liked to say, "Yes, I'm quite fond of it, I'm in here a lot. I couldn't live among unfriendly things, you see, ugly-pretentious things. This is where I work"—though she never specified what it was she was working at, a picture, a book perhaps, those being the days when the idea of writing was occurring to the kind of women who like to have something to do, rather than sit idly about—she sat amid Dresden china, of which she would speak with an English accent, and which she liked so much that she was forever saying, about anything that took her eye, "Isn't it pretty? It's just like Dresden flowers!"; and as she feared for these pieces even more than she had once feared for her Chinese grotesques and vases, any clumsy servant who alarmed her by handling them the wrong way would be roundly abused in terms that Swann, the mildest and most urbane of masters, would hear but not be shocked by. Affection is undiminished by the clear sight of certain defects; it is what makes them appear charming. Nowadays, to receive guests, Odette less frequently wore a Japanese kimono, preferring the pale, foamy silks of her Watteau tea gowns, floating in them, seeming to caress their flowery froth against her breasts, basking, frolicking, and with such an air of health and well-being, of refreshment of the skin and deep breathing, that they looked as though their function was not just the decorative one of being a setting for her, but one as necessary as her daily "tub" or her "constitutional," satisfying both the demands of her looks and the finer requirements of the healthful life. She was in the habit of maintaining that she would go without bread sooner than be deprived of art and cleanliness, and that she would have been more upset by the burning of the *Mona Lisa* than by the annihilation of "swarms" of people of her acquaintance. These conceptions appeared paradoxical to her lady friends, giving her among them the renown of a high-minded woman, and brought the Belgian ambassador to visit her once a week; and in the little world that revolved about her sun, everybody would have been astounded to learn that elsewhere—at the Verdurins', for example—she was seen as stupid. It was this spirit of spontaneous repartee in Mme Swann that made her prefer men's company to women's. And when she had something to say against certain women, it was always the former courtesan who drew attention to defects that might tell against them with men, thick wrists and ankles, a stale complexion, bad spelling, hairy legs, a dreadful smell, false eyebrows. She could, however, be kinder in speaking of any woman who had been friendly or indulgent toward her, especially if it was someone who had known happier days. Odette would be shrewd in defense of the woman: "Oh, they say awful things about her. But she's really a nice person, I can assure you."

It was not only the interior decoration of Odette's drawing room that Mme Cottard and all who had known Mme de Crécy would have had difficulty in recognizing if they had not seen her for a long time, it was Odette herself. She seemed to have grown so many years younger! This was in part no doubt because she had filled out, enjoyed better health, looked calmer, cooler, more relaxed; and in part because the new, sleeker hairstyles gave more room to her face, which was enlivened by a little pink powder, and in which the former flagrancy of her eyes and profile seemed to have been toned down. But another reason for this change was that Odette had now reached the middle years of life, where she found in herself, or invented for herself, a personal style of face, full of a fixed character, a recognized pattern of beauty; and on her formerly undesigned features (which for so many years had been left to the random whims of the responsive flesh, briefly aging by years at the slightest indisposition, managing somehow to collaborate with her moods and daily demeanors in the composition of her variable face, unfocused, unshaped, and charming) she now wore this immutable model of eternal youth.

In Swann's own bedroom, instead of the grand photographs taken nowadays of his wife, in which, however unlike her different hats and dresses were, the same enigmatically imperious expression identified her triumphant figure and features, he kept a modest little old daguerreotype dating from the days before this unvarying model of Odette's, in which she seemed devoid of her new youth and beauty, as yet undiscovered by her. In this no doubt he clung, or had reverted, to a different conception of her, doting forever on the Botticellian graces of a slender young woman with pensive eyes and a forlorn look, caught in a posture between stride and stillness. The fact was, he could still see her as a Botticelli. Odette herself, who always tried to conceal things she did not like about her own person, or at least to compensate for them rather than bring them out, things that a painter might have seen as her "type," but which as a woman she saw as defects, had no time for Botticelli. Swann owned a wonderful Oriental stole, in blue and pink, which he had bought because it was exactly the one worn by the Virgin in the *Magnificat.* Mme Swann would not wear it. Once only, she relented and let him give her an outfit based on La Primavera's garlands of daisies, bellworts, cornflowers, and forget-me-nots. In the evenings, Swann would sometimes murmur to me to look at her pensive hands as she gave to them unawares the graceful, rather agitated movement of the Virgin dipping her quill in the angel's inkwell, before writing in the holy book where the word *Magnificat* is already inscribed. Then he would add, "Be sure not to mention it to her! One word—and she'd make sure it wouldn't happen again!"

Except at such yielding moments of un-self-conscious languor, when Swann could hope to catch a glimpse of Botticelli's melancholy attitudes, Odette's body was now blocked out as a single profile, a unitary shape that took its outline from the woman within and ignored the former fashions, with their fussy broken lines, the artificiality of their protrusions and indentations, their jutting angles and crisscrossings, their composite effect of disparate complexity, but which could also, if that anatomy within erred and made unwanted departures from the ideal design, correct these mistakes of nature with a firm stroke, redrawing whole sections of the contour so as to make good any deficiencies, whether of flesh or cloth. All the padding, the appalling "dress-improvers" and bustles, had gone; as had the long vest bodices that for so many years, overlapping the skirt and rigid with whalebone, had added a false abdomen to Odette and made her look like a creature of separate parts unlinked by any individuality. The vertical fringes of jet and the stiff curves of the ruches had been replaced by the suppleness of a body which, having freed itself like an independent and organized life-form from the long opacity and chrysaloid chaos of the outworn modes, now rippled silk as a mermaid ripples water and gave a human look to the gloss of percaline. Mme Swann had managed to retain a vestige of some of these modes, amid the others that had replaced them. Some evenings, when I was unable to work, and when I was quite sure that Gilberte had gone to the theater with a party of friends, I would call unannounced at her parents' house, where I was often greeted by Mme Swann in one of her handsome housedresses, the skirt of which, in one of those magnificent dark shades, a deep red or orange, which seemed to have a special meaning because they were no longer fashionable, showed through a broad diagonal panel of black lace reminiscent of an outmoded flounce. Before Gilberte and I had fallen out, on one of those wintry spring days when Mme Swann had taken me to the Zoo in the Bois de Boulogne, the indented edging of her blouse, under the jacket which she would unbutton a little as the walk warmed her up, had looked just like the absent lapel of the vest bodices she had once worn, and which she always preferred with such a slight zigzag edge; and she had been wearing a necklet (in a tartan pattern, which she had never abandoned, though she had by now so toned down its colors, the red having shaded into pink and the blue into lilac, that it could almost have been taken for one of those dove-colored taffetas which had just come in) knotted in a bow under the chin in a way that, because one could not see how it was fastened, instantly reminded one of those hats with long bands tied round the throat which nobody now wore. Before very long, young men, trying to define her ways of dressing, would be saying to each other, "Mme Swann is a real period piece, you know!" In her ways of dressing, as in a fine written style that embraces different forms of expression and is enriched by a concealed tradition, these semi-reminiscences of bodices and bows, an occasional instantly repressed hint of the "monkey jacket," and even a faint whisper of an allusion to long "follow-me-lads" hat ribbons, filled the actual forms of what she did wear with a constant unformed suggestion of older ones, which no real seamstress or milliner could have contrived, but which hung about her all the time, surrounding her with something noble— possibly because the very uselessness of these trappings made them appear designed for a more-than-utilitarian purpose, perhaps because of the remnant they preserved of former times, or even because of a kind of individuality in dress, peculiar to herself, which gave to what she wore, however dissimilar her ensembles, a sort of family resemblance. One could sense that, for her, dressing was not just a matter of comfort or adornment of the body: whatever she wore encompassed her like the delicate and etherealized epitome of a civilization.

Though Gilberte usually held her tea parties on her mother's at-home days, she sometimes went out instead; and when that happened I could go to one of Mme Swann's "afternoon jamborees." I would find her wearing a magnificent dress, sometimes of taffeta, sometimes of faille, or else of velvet, crêpe de Chine, satin, or silk, not a loose garment like the housedresses she usually wore at home, but with something of the walking dress in it, which somehow gave to her afternoon idleness indoors a quality of readiness and activity. The dashing simplicity of their cut suited her figure and her movements, which seemed to color her sleeves variously each day: on blue-velvet days, the material was full of sudden decisiveness, which became simple good nature when it was the turn of white taffeta; and, in order to become visible, a sort of supreme and distinguished reserve in her way of holding out her arm had taken on the glowing smile of self-sacrifice that shines in black crêpe de Chine. But at the same time, her complicated "accessories," which had no visible purpose or practical usefulness, added something to these brilliant dresses, something disinterested, thoughtful, and secret, matching the melancholy still to be seen around her eyes and in the delicate joints of her hands. Under the dangle of sapphire-studded lucky charms, enameled four-leaf clovers, silver medals, gold medallions, turquoise amulets, fine ruby chains, chestnut-sized topazes, there would be a colored pattern patched onto the dress itself, a borrowed panel enjoying a new lease on life, a row of little satin buttons that could neither button anything nor ever be unbuttoned, a length of matching braid trying to please with the unobtrusive aptness of a subtle reminder; and all of them, like the jewels, seemed to be there—for otherwise they had no conceivable function—to hint at a purpose, to be a token of tenderness, to keep a secret, exercise a superstition, commemorate a cure, a vow, a lover, or a philippine. Sometimes a hint of a Plantagenet slash in the blue velvet of a bodice, or a slight bulge in a black satin dress—either high on the sleeve, suggesting the 1830s and their leg-of-mutton, or under the skirt, suggesting Louis XV hoop petticoats—would almost make it look as though she were in fancy dress; and by slipping this sort of barely recognizable allusion to the past into the life of the present, they added to the person of Mme Swann the charm of certain historical or fictional heroines. If I said this to her, she replied, "Unlike some of my friends, I do not play golf. Unlike me, they have an excuse for being swaddled in sweaters."

Amid the jostle of people in her drawing room, as she came back in from seeing someone out or handed round a plate of cakes, Mme Swann would take me aside for a moment: "Gilberte has most particularly urged me to invite you to lunch the day after tomorrow. I didn't know whether I would see you or not, so I was going to drop you a note about it if you didn't come today." I persisted in my resistance to Gilberte's invitations. This resistance was now costing me less and less: however much one may savor one's poison, when one has been forcibly deprived of it for any length of time, one is bound to be struck by how restful it can be to do without it, by the absence of excitements and sorrows. We may be not entirely sincere in hoping never again to see the woman we love; but the same may well be true when we say we do hope to see her again. Of course, any absence from her can only be bearable if we mean it to be brief, if we keep thinking of being together again with her one day; but against that, we are aware of how much less disturbing these daily dreams of prompt but ever-deferred reunion are than a real encounter with her would be, with its likely resurgence of jealousy; and so the knowledge that one *is* going to see her again could cause a recurrence of upsetting emotions. And what we keep postponing now, day after day, is no longer an end to the unbearable anguish of separation, but the dreaded renewal of futile feelings. How preferable the malleable memory of her seems: instead of the real meeting with her, in your solitude you can dramatize a dream in which the girl who is not in love with you assures you that she is! This memory, which can become as sweet as possible, by being gradually flavored with what you most desire, is far better than the future encounter with a person whose words will be put into her mouth not by you, but by her foreseeable indifference and even her unforeseeable animosity. To be no longer in love is to know that forgetting—or even a fading memory—causes much less pain than the unhappiness of loving. What I preferred, without admitting it to myself, was the reposeful promise of that foreshadowed forgetting.

There is another reason why the pains of this treatment by isolation and emotional withdrawal may be gradually lessened, which is that, as a preliminary to curing us of the obsessive preoccupation of our love, it weakens the force of it. My own love was still strong enough for me to want Gilberte to look at me again with the eyes of admiration. So, with every day that passed, it seemed to me that my prestige, because of my self-imposed separation from her, must be slowly growing in her eyes; and that each of these days of calm sadness when I saw nothing of her, in their gradual accumulation, with neither interruption nor expected expiry time (unless some ill-advised person interfered with my arrangements), was a day gained, and not lost, to my love. A day pointlessly gained, perhaps, as I might soon be pronounced cured. Resignation, which is one of the modes of habit, favors the indefinite growth of some of our resources. By now, the puny forces which, on the evening of my first breach with Gilberte, were all I had at my command to help me bear my heartbreak, had been raised to an incalculable power. However, the tendency of all existing things to go on existing is sometimes interrupted by sudden impulses, which we obey without great qualms at breaking our own rule, since we know, from all those days and months when we have already managed to abstain, for how many more of them we would be able to make our abstention last. It is often when the purse in which we have been setting aside our savings is nearly full that we suddenly decide to spend them all; it is when we have become used to a course of treatment, rather than when it has had its full effect, that we abandon it. One day, as Mme Swann spoke the usual words about how pleased Gilberte would be to see me, setting within my reach the happiness I had deprived myself of for so long, all at once I was overwhelmed by the knowledge that it was still possible to have it. I could hardly wait for the next day—I had just decided to surprise Gilberte by turning up at her house the following afternoon, before dinnertime.

What helped me to bear the thought of waiting for a whole day was a plan I had. Now that the entire thing was forgotten and we were coming back together, it was inconceivable to me that I could go to her in any capacity other than as a lover. Not a day must pass without her being sent the loveliest flowers I could find! If her mother should happen to rule against daily deliveries of flowers (not that she was entitled to severity in such things), I could think of more valuable but less frequent presents to send. My pocket money from my parents did not allow me to buy expensive things. But I remembered a large vase in old Chinese porcelain that Aunt Léonie had left to me. My mother was forever predicting the day when Françoise would come and report, "It's gone and got broken!" and it would be irreparable. In that case, was it not wiser to sell it, so as to lavish every pleasure on Gilberte? I thought it might fetch a thousand francs. One good thing about getting rid of it was that it afforded me the opportunity to get to know it: as it was being wrapped up, I noticed how habit had prevented me from ever seeing it. I took it with me on my way out and told the coachman to drive to the Swanns' via the Champs-Élysées: on a nearby corner, I knew there was a large shop dealing in Oriental articles owned by a friend of my father's. To my amazement, he offered me on the spot not one thousand francs but ten thousand! I handled the banknotes with delight: a year's worth of daily roses and lilacs for Gilberte! From the shop, the coach set off again for the Swanns'; and as they lived not far from the Bois de Boulogne, instead of taking the usual route, the coachman naturally headed up the Avenue des Champs-Élysées itself. We had passed the corner of the rue de Berri and were very close to the Swanns' when I thought I saw Gilberte with a young man in the twilight: they were going in the opposite direction to myself, away from her house; she was walking slowly, but with a purposeful step, and talking to this young man, whose face I could not make out. I sat up, intending to tell the driver to stop; but then I hesitated. The pair were already at quite a distance, their two faint, close silhouettes fading slowly into the gathering Elysian gloom. Soon we drew up outside Gilberte's house. "Oh dear!" Mme Swann said. "She *will* be sorry! I can't imagine why she's not here. She came home from a class complaining of being too hot and said she felt like taking a little walk in the open air with one of her girlfriends." "I think I may have just glimpsed her along the Avenue des Champs-Élysées." "Oh, no, I don't think so. But, whatever you do, don't mention it to her father. He doesn't like her to be out and about at this hour of the day." She added in English *"Good evening!"* and I left. I told the cabman to go back the way we had come; but there was no sign of the pair. Where had they been? What manner of things had they been saying to each other in the gloaming, walking together in that intimate way?

I went home in despair, clutching my windfall of ten thousand francs, which was to have enabled me to give Gilberte so many little pleasures, and realizing that I was now determined never to see her again. The visit to the shop with the Chinese vase had gladdened me with the prospect that, now and forever, my sweetheart's sole feelings for me would be happiness and gratitude. Yet, if I had not made that detour to the shop, if the coach had not driven up the Avenue des Champs-Élysées, I would never have seen Gilberte with the young man. For the stem of a single event may bear counterbalancing branches, the unhappiness it brings canceling the happiness it caused. What had happened to me was the opposite of what is more usual: one yearns for a fulfillment that remains unattainable because one lacks the wherewithal required for it. As La Bruyère says, "It is sad to be a lover without wealth."[63] One's only resource is the relentless endeavor to stifle one's yearning. The wherewithal was not what I lacked; but at the very moment when it materialized, an adventitious if not logical consequence of its acquisition had deprived me of the expected joy. It would appear that this is the fate of all our joys. They do of course tend to last longer than the single evening on which we have acquired what makes them possible. More usually, our fever of expectation lasts longer. Even so, happiness can never happen. Once the external circumstances are overcome, if they can be, nature then transforms the struggle into an internal one, by bringing about a gradual change in our heart, so that the gratification it desires is different from the one it is about to receive. And if the change in circumstances has come about so quickly that our heart has not had time to change with it, nature, nothing daunted, taking its own time, sets about defeating us in a way which, though more devious, is no less effective. Fulfillment is snatched from our grasp at the last moment; or, rather, it is fulfillment itself which nature, the malicious trickster, uses to destroy happiness. Having failed with everything belonging to the world of fact and external life, nature creates its ultimate impediment to happiness by making it a psychological impossibility. The phenomenon of happiness does not come to pass; or else it leads to utter bitterness.

I locked away my ten thousand francs. They were of no use to me now; and they were to end up being spent even more quickly than if I had sent flowers to Gilberte every day, since as twilight came each evening I was so unhappy that, rather than stay at home, I went to lie weeping in the arms of other women, whom I did not love. As for trying to please Gilberte with presents, I had lost all desire to do so. To step inside her house now would have been to face the certainty of suffering. Just to see her—a thing that had seemed so exhilarating the previous evening—would have been of little help to me: every moment when I could not be with her would have revived my anxiety. This explains why every new pain that a woman inflicts on us (which she often does without meaning to) increases not only her power over us, but also the demands we make on her. By every use of her power to hurt, the woman constricts us more and more, shackling us with stronger chains;

but she also shows us the weakness of those that once seemed strong enough to bind her and thus to enable us to feel untroubled by her. Only the day before, had I not wanted to avoid upsetting Gilberte, I would have settled for infrequent meetings with her; but now these could no longer have satisfied me, and my conditions would have been very different. For in love, unlike war, the more one is defeated, the more one imposes harsh conditions; and one constantly tries to make them harsher—if one is actually in a position to impose any, that is. With Gilberte, I was not in this position. So, to begin with, I preferred not to go back to her mother's house. I also went on telling myself that Gilberte did not love me, that I had known this for ages, that I could see her whenever I liked, and that, if I preferred not to see her, I would eventually forget her. But these thoughts, like a medication that has no effect on certain disorders, were quite ineffectual against what came intermittently to my mind: those two close silhouettes of Gilberte and that young man, stepping slowly along the Avenue des Champs-Élysées. This was a new pain, but one that would eventually fade and disappear in its turn; it was an image which one day would come back to my mind with all its noxious power neutralized, like those deadly poisons that can be handled without danger, or the small piece of dynamite one can use to light a cigarette without fear of being blown up. For the time being, though, there was another force in me, fighting for all it was worth against the pernicious impulse that kept showing me, without the slightest alteration, Gilberte walking through the twilight: working against memory, trying to withstand its repeated onslaughts, there was the quiet and helpful endeavor of imagination. The force of memory went on showing the pair walking down the Avenue des Champs-Élysées, along with other irksome images from the past, such as Gilberte shrugging her shoulders when her mother asked her to stay in with me. But the second force, sketching freely on the canvas of my hopes, improvised a future that was much more lovingly detailed than the meager glimpses afforded by such a paltry past. To think that, against a single moment of the sullen Gilberte, I had a wealth of other moments, all devoted to her attempts to bring about our reconciliation—or even our engagement! This force, though directed toward the future by my imagination, did of course draw its sustenance from the past; and as my un-happiness at Gilberte's surly shrug of the shoulders gradually faded, so would my memory of her charm and the yearning for her that came with it. However, at the present moment, that death of the past was still remote. I still loved Gilberte, though I believed I hated her. Whenever somebody complimented me on the neatness of my hair, whenever anyone said I was looking well, I wished she could be there to hear it. Throughout that whole period, I was irritated by receiving so many invitations; and I turned them all down. On one occasion there was an unpleasant scene at home because I declined to accompany my father to an official function, at which M. and Mme Bontemps were to be present with their niece Albertine, who was then little more than a child. The different periods of our life overlap. Because you are now in love with someone who will one day mean nothing to you, you refuse out of hand to meet someone who means nothing to you now, but whom you will one day come to love, someone whom you might have loved sooner if you had agreed to an earlier meeting, who might have curtailed your present sufferings (before replacing them, of course, with others). My own sufferings were changing. I was surprised to notice certain feelings in myself, one day a particular emotion, the following day some quite different one, generally inspired by some hope or fear focused on Gilberte. The Gilberte of my private imaginings, I mean. But I ought to have borne in mind that the other Gilberte, the real one, was perhaps utterly different from this private one, that she probably lived in ignorance of all the regrets I invented for her to feel, and thought not only much less about me than I about her, but much less than I pretended she thought about me in my moments of private communion with the fictitious Gilberte, when I longed to know her real intentions toward me and pictured her as spending her days doting on me.

During these periods when sorrow, though already beginning to wane, still persists, there is a difference between the mode of sorrow caused by the obsessive thought of the loved one and the sorrow brought back to mind by certain memories: a nasty thing said, a verb once used in a letter. Let it be said here (all the diverse modes of sorrow will be described in connection with a later love affair) that the first of these modes is not nearly as cruel as the second. This is because our impression of the woman, living forever within us, is enhanced by the halo which our adoration constantly creates for her, and is tinged, if not by the glad promises of recurrent hope, at least by the peace of mind of lasting sadness. (It is noteworthy too that our image of a person who causes us pain takes up little space among the complications which exacerbate a heartbreak, which make it persist and prevent us from getting over it, just as in certain illnesses the cause is out of all proportion to the ensuing fever and the length of time required for a cure.) Though our image of the whole person we love is lit by the glow of a generally optimistic mind, this is not the case with the individual memory of the hurtful words spoken on a particular occasion or the unfriendly letter (I only ever had one like that from Gilberte): it feels as though these fragments, however minute they are, contain the whole person, amplified to a power well in excess of what she has in the usual imagined glimpses we have of her, entire though she is in them. Unlike the loved image of her, we have never gazed at the terrible letter with the untroubled eyes of melancholy and regret; the moment we spent reading it, devouring it, was fraught with the awful anguish of unexpected catastrophe. The difference in the making of these sorts of sorrows is that they come from the outside world and take the shortest and most painful route to the heart. The image of the woman we love, though we think it has a pristine authenticity, has actually been often made and remade by us. And the memory that wounds is not contemporaneous with the restored image; it dates from a very different time; it is one of the few witnesses to a monstrous past. Since this past goes on existing, though not inside us, where we have seen fit to replace it with a wondrous golden age, a paradise where we are to be reunited and reconciled, such memories and such letters are a reminder of reality; their sudden stab ought to make us realize how far we have strayed from that reality, and how foolish are the hopes with which we sustain our daily expectation. Not that this reality has to remain the same, although that can happen too. There have been many women in our lives with whom we have long since lost touch, and who have understandably matched our unpurposed silence with a similar lack of interest in ourselves. However, not being in love with them, we have never counted the years spent without them; and in our reasoning on the efficacy of separation, we disregard this counterexample, which should invalidate it, as those who believe in the possibility of foretelling the future overlook all the cases in which what they foresaw did not eventuate.

Even so, separation can be effective: the heart that at present ignores us may be visited by the wish to see us again, or by an expectation of pleasure in our company. It just takes time. And the demands we make on time are as inordinate as the requirements of a heart if it is to change. In the first place, time is the very thing we wish not to grant; for our pain is acute, and we are in haste to have it cease. As well, in the time it takes for the other's heart to change, our own heart will be changing too; and when the fulfillment desired comes within our reach, we will desire it no longer. Actually, the very notion that it *will* come within reach—that there is no fulfillment which will be forever denied us, as long as it has ceased to be a fulfillment we desire—is one which, though true, is only partly true. By the time it comes to us, we have become indifferent to it. And our very indifference has made us less critical of it, which enables us to believe in retrospect that it would have delighted us at a time when, in fact, it might well have seemed grossly deficient. One's standards are not high, and one is no great judge, in things one does not care about. The friendliness of a person whom we no longer care for, though it may seem too much to our indifference, might have been deemed too little by our love. The affectionate words, the suggestion of a meeting make us think of the joy they might have led to, but not of all the other joys by which we would have wanted them to be immediately followed, and which that very eagerness of ours might well have prevented from ever coming to pass. So it is not certain that the happiness that comes too late, at a time when one can no longer enjoy it, when one is no longer in love, is exactly the same happiness for which we once pined in vain. There is only one person—our former self—who could decide the issue; and that self is no longer with us. No doubt too, if the former self did come back, identical or not as it might be, that would be enough for the happiness in question to vanish.

The belated coming true of these dreams, at a time when I would have ceased to long for it, was still in the future; and because I went on inventing, as in the days when I hardly knew Gilberte, words for her to say to me, letters in which she begged for forgiveness, confessed to never having loved another, asked me to marry her, this sequence of sweet and constantly regenerated images came to occupy more space in my mind than the glimpse of her with the young man, which weakened for lack of nourishment. I might well have gone back to Mme Swann's, had it not been for a dream I had, in which a friend of mine, quite unknown to me in the waking world, behaved toward me with the most villainous duplicity, while believing I was the treacherous one. This caused me such pain that I woke with a start; and as my pain did not abate, I thought again of the dream, in an attempt to identify the friend who had visited my sleeping mind and whose name, a Spanish one, was now fading away. As both Joseph and the Pharaoh, I set about interpreting the dream.[64] I knew that in many dreams one must disregard the appearance of people, who may be disguised or may have exchanged faces with one another, like those mutilated saints on the fronts of cathedrals which have been repaired by ignorant archaeologists in a jumble of mismatched heads and bodies, attributes and names. Those we give to characters in our dreams can be misleading. The one we love can be recognized only by the quality of the pain we feel. It was this that identified for me the person who as I slept had turned into a young man, and whose recent treachery still ached within me—Gilberte. I remembered then that, on the last occasion when we had been together, the day when her mother had forbidden her to go to a dancing lesson, she had burst out with a strange laugh and refused, either sincerely or in pretense, to believe that my intentions toward her were quite proper. By association, this memory brought to mind another: long before that day, Swann himself had been the one to doubt my sincerity, to suspect that I was not a suitable friend for his daughter. I had written him my futile letter, which Gilberte had brought back and given to me with that same baffling laughter. She had not given it back immediately, of course; and I could remember the whole scene behind the clump of laurels. Unhappiness is a great promoter of morality. Gilberte's present unpleasantness toward me now seemed a punishment meted out by life because of my behavior that day. Because one can avoid dangers by watching out while crossing the street, one has the impression that one can also avoid punishment. But punishments can come from within; and the unexpected danger may arise from the heart. The words she had spoken, "If you like, we could wrestle a bit more," now horrified me. I imagined her behaving like that with the young man I had seen with her on the Avenue des Champs-Élysées, at home perhaps, up in the linen room. So, just as, some time ago, I had been ill advised enough to believe I had come to a state of tranquil, stable happiness, I had been rash enough, now that I had accepted that happiness was not for me, to believe I had achieved at least a haven of lasting calm. The fact is that, as long as our heart harbors the dear image of another person, it is not only our happiness that runs the constant risk of sudden destruction; even when happiness has gone and pain has come, even when we have contrived to lull our pain, the state of calm we reach is no less illusory and precarious than happiness once was. My own state of calm did eventually come back, as whatever enters our minds in the guise of a dream, affecting our desires and our inner being, sooner or later fades away like all other things, grief being no more capable than anything else of aspiring to permanence. Besides, those who suffer the torments of love are, as is said of people suffering from certain diseases, their own doctors. As the only consolation they can find must come from the person responsible for their pain, and as the giving of that pain is an attribute of that person, the remedy they eventually find for it lies within it. One day, their pain reveals their remedy—as they mull it over, the pain shows them a new aspect of the person whom they miss so terribly: sometimes she is so hateful that they lose all desire to see her again, and any pleasure they might take in her company demands that they first wound her in their turn; sometimes she is so loving that they turn this lovingness into an objective quality of the loved one, and see in it a reason to hope. In my own case, although this new phase of my suffering did gradually come to an end, I was left with a much-diminished desire to go back to see Mme Swann. In the hearts of those whose love is unrequited, the state of expectation in which they spend their days—

even though it may be an unrecognized expectation—turns very gradually into a second phase, which, though it seems identical to the first, is in fact its exact opposite. That first phase was the consequence, the reflection of the hurtful incidents that caused the initial sorrow. Our expectation of what might happen next is mixed with apprehension, especially since, if we hear nothing more from the beloved, we are full of the urge to do something, but are unsure of the likely outcomes of any step we might take, including the possibility that the one we do take may well rule out any further one. But soon, without our realizing it, our continuing expectation is determined, as we have seen, not by our memory of the past we have just been through, but by the imaginary future we look forward to. By then, our expectation is almost pleasant. After all, if the first phase has lasted for some time, we have already become used to living with an eye to tomorrow. The pain we felt during our final encounters with her still lives in us, albeit subdued. We are reluctant to have it revive, especially since we cannot see what further demands we could possibly make. To possess a little more of her would only increase our need for the part of her that we do not possess; and in any case, within that part, since our needs arise out of our satisfactions, something of her would still lie forever beyond our grasp.

When this reason was later reinforced by another one, I completely gave up my visits to Mme Swann's. This belated reason was not that I had already forgotten Gilberte: it was that I hoped in that way to forget her sooner. Of course, since the end of my acute unhappiness, my residual sorrow had once again drawn from my visits to Mme Swann the sedative and the diversion which I had found so comforting at an earlier stage. But the reason why the sedative was effective was also the reason why the diversion was a drawback: that the memory of Gilberte was inseparable from such visits. The diversion could have been beneficial only if it could have pitted thoughts, interests, or passions unrelated to Gilberte against a feeling that was no longer reinforced by her presence. Such states of mind, from which the loved one is entirely absent, serve to take up a space which, though minimal to begin with, leaves a little less room in the heart for the love that once occupied it entirely. They must be fostered, they must be fortified, in time with the waning of the emotion that is no more than a memory, so that the new elements provided to the mind can encroach on a larger and larger area of the self and finally take it over completely. I realized it was the only way to kill a feeling of love; and I was young enough and brave enough to undertake to do this, to inflict this wound on myself, the cruelest of all wounds, since it comes from one's knowledge that, however long it may take, one is bound to succeed. When I wrote to Gilberte now, the reason I alleged for my reluctance to see her was some mysterious misunderstanding, utterly untrue of course, which had come between us, and about which I had at first been hoping she would invite me to explain myself. But in fact no clarification, even in the most trivial relationships, is ever required by any correspondent who knows that a designedly obscure, untrue, or incriminating statement is included in a letter for the express purpose of provoking a protest, and who is satisfied to see in it a proof that he (or she) not only enjoys a commanding position and retains the initiative, but will continue to do so. In love relationships this is even more true, for love has so much eloquence, and indifference so little curiosity. As Gilberte had never expressed a doubt on this supposed misunderstanding, or tried to find out what it was, it had become a reality for me, and I alluded to it in each letter. There is, in such readiness to misinterpret, in the pretense of standoffishness, a dire charm that leads you further and further on. Having so often used the phrase "since we fell out," so as to make Gilberte reply, "But we haven't, let's talk about it," I had managed to persuade myself that we had. By so often writing statements like "Life may have parted us, but it can never alter the feeling we shared," in the hope of being told, "Nothing has parted us, our feeling is as strong as ever," I had become used to the idea that life *had* parted us, that our erstwhile feeling would live in our memories, as certain neurotics start by simulating an illness and end by really being ill. Whenever I had occasion to write to Gilberte now, I made a point of mentioning life's imagined parting of us. And, this role of life having been tacitly accepted by virtue of Gilberte's never referring to it in her replies, it would go on parting us. But then, eschewing mere reticence, she overtly adopted my point of view; and thenceforward, as a visiting head of state will incorporate into his speech of reply to an official welcome some of the words used by his host, each time I wrote, "Life may have come between us, but the memory of our time together will live on," she took to saying, "Life may have come between us, but it can never make us forget the dear days we shared" (why "life" should be said to have come between us or to have changed anything, we would have been hard put to say). By now my pain had much abated. But then, one day when I was telling her in a letter that I had just heard of the death of our old barley-sugar woman from the Champs-Élysées, as I wrote these words, "I'm sure you must have been sad to hear of it; it certainly brought back many memories to me," I collapsed in helpless tears, as I realized that, though I had gone on hoping against hope that our love was still a living emotion, or at least one that could revive, I was now speaking of it in the past, as though it too had died and was all but forgotten. How affectionate this correspondence was, between friends trying not to meet! Her letters were fully as considerate as any I wrote to people who meant nothing to me; and I was greatly comforted to receive from her the very same tokens of apparent affection that I sent to them.

Gradually, the more often I declined her suggestion that we meet, the less pain it caused me. As she became slowly less dear to me, my hurtful and incessantly recurring memories of her lost the power to prevent the thought of a visit to Florence or Venice from giving me pleasure. At such moments, I regretted that I had turned down the diplomatic career and tied myself to a life without travel, so as not to absent myself from a girl whom I would not now be seeing again, whom I had already more or less forgotten. We design our life for the sake of an individual who, by the time we are able to welcome her into it, has turned into a total stranger, and never comes to share that life with us; and so we live on, imprisoned in an arrangement made for someone else. Though my parents judged Venice to be too distant and fever-ridden for me, at least it was easy and untiring to go for a time to Balbec. But that would have entailed leaving Paris and giving up my visits, infrequent though they were, to Mme Swann's, where I could hear her speak about her daughter, and where I was even beginning to discover other pleasures, which had nothing to do with Gilberte.

As spring advanced, as the Ice Saints[65] and Eastertime with its squalls of hail brought back the cold, Mme Swann was convinced that the house was freezing, and I often had occasion to see my hostess wearing furs: her shivery hands and shoulders disappeared under the dazzling white of a great flat muff and tippet, both of ermine, which she had been wearing outside, and which looked like winter's last and most persistent patches of snow, unthawed by the warmth of her fireside or the change of season. The composite truth of those icy but already flowering weeks was brought into that drawing room, which I was soon to cease visiting, by whiteness of a more affecting sort, such as the snowballs of the Guelder roses, each of their tall stems, as bare as the Pre-Raphaelites' linear flora, topped by its single clustered globe, as white as a herald angel and surrounded by the scent of lemon. For Odette, as befitted the lady of Tansonville, knew that even the iciest April is never without its flowers, and that winter, springtime, and summer are not as hermetically partitioned from one another as may be supposed by the man about town who, until the first warm weather arrives, cannot imagine the world containing anything other than bare housefronts dripping rain. No doubt Mme Swann did not rely solely on what her gardener regularly sent up from Combray, and she did not decline to palliate, with the assistance of her "florist by appointment," the insufficiencies of her artificial springtime by drawing on the resources afforded by Mediterranean precocity. Not that this mattered to me. Apart from the snows of Mme Swann's muff, all that was required to set me yearning for the countryside was that the snowballs of the Guelder roses (which may have had no other purpose than to join with my hostess's furniture and her own outfit in making the "Symphony in White major" that Bergotte liked to talk of) should remind me that the Good Friday Spell[66] represents a natural miracle, which we could witness every year, had we but the good sense to do so, and that these white flowers, along with the heady, acid perfume of blooms of other species, the names of which were unknown to me, but which had often made me pause on my walks about Combray, should give to Mme Swann's drawing room an air that was as virginal, as candid, as blossomy without leaves, as thick with genuine smells as the steep little path leading up to Tansonville.

But even the memory of the little path was almost too much. The danger of it was that it might keep alive in me the remaining vestige of my love for Gilberte. So, despite the fact that my visits to Mme Swann now caused me no grief at all, I made them even more infrequent, trying to see her as little as possible. I did allow myself, since I persisted in not leaving Paris, to walk with her a few times. Fine, warm weather had at last arrived. Knowing that Mme Swann went out each day before lunch and took a short walk in the Avenue du Bois-de-Boulogne, not far from the Arc de Triomphe, quite close to the spot that was known in those days, in honor of the citizenry who went there to see all the rich people they had heard of, as the "Hard-Up Club," I had asked my parents' permission to go out for a walk late on Sunday mornings (not being free on weekdays at that time) and not to come back to lunch till a quarter past one, which was much later than their own lunchtime. During that month of May, I did not miss a single Sunday, Gilberte having gone off to spend some time in the country with friends. I would arrive at the Arc de Triomphe about midday and stand at the end of the Avenue du Bois-de-Boulogne, from where I could watch the corner of the side street from which Mme Swann would emerge, coming from her house, which was only a few steps away. It was the hour at which many of those who had been out for a walk were going home to lunch; of the few remaining, most belonged to fashionable society. Then it was, stepping onto the fine gravel of the avenue, that Mme Swann would make her entrance, as late, languid, and luxuriant as the most beautiful flower, which never opened until noon, in outfits that gave her a bloom of radiance, and which, though they were always different, I remember as mainly mauve. The bright moment of her flowering was complete when, on an elongated stretch of stem, she unfurled the silky vexillum of a broad sunshade blending with the full-blown shimmer of her frock. She was accompanied by a whole retinue: Swann was there, as were four or five other clubmen who had either dropped in to see her that morning or whom she had just encountered. And as the blacks and grays of this disciplined formation executed their almost mechanical movements, lending an inert frame to Odette, they made the woman, the only one with any intensity in her gaze, appear to be staring past them all, looking straight ahead as though leaning out of a window, and made her stand out, fragile and fearless, in the nudity of her gentle colors, as though she were a creature of a different species or of some mysterious descent, with a suggestion of something warlike about her, all of which enabled her single person to counterbalance her numerous escort. Beaming with smiles, contented with the lovely day and the sunshine, which was not yet too warm, with all the poise and confidence of a creator who beholds every thing that he has made and sees it is very good, and knowing (though vulgar passersby might not appreciate this) that her outfit was more elegant than anyone else's, she wore it for herself but also for her friends, naturally, without show but also without complete indifference, not objecting if the light bows on her bodice and skirt drifted slightly in front of her, like pets whose presence she was aware of but whose caprices she indulged, leaving them to their own devices as long as they stayed close to her; and as though her purple parasol, often furled when she first emerged into the avenue, was a posy of Parma violets, it too at times received from her happy eyes a glance which, though directed not at her friends but at an inanimate object, brimmed with so much gentle goodwill that it still seemed to be a smile. A margin of elegance, which Mme Swann's choice of outfit made all her own, was accepted as her essential and exclusive prerogative by the gentlemen whom she addressed most familiarly; and in this they deferred to her with the air of ignorant outsiders who do not mind recognizing themselves as such, conceding the aptness of her authority, as they might with an invalid on the matter of the special care he must take, or with a mother on how best to bring up her children. It was not just this suite of retainers, surrounding her and seeming not to notice passersby, that suggested Mme Swann's indoor life: by reason of the lateness of her advent on the avenue, she brought to mind the house in which she had spent long morning hours, where she would soon have to return for lunch; the proximity of it was in the calm and leisured simplicity of her manner, as though she were strolling down her own garden path; the cool, subdued light of its interior seemed to hang about her as she passed. But this vision of her only gave me a heightened sense of the fresh air and the warmth of the day, especially since (in my conviction that, in accordance with her pious expertise in the rites and liturgy of such things, Mme Swann's ways of dressing were linked to the season and the time of day by a bond that was necessary and unique) the flowers on her soft straw hat and the little bows on her frock seemed a more natural product of May than any flowers cultivated in beds or growing wild in the woods; and to witness the thrilling onset of the new season, I needed to lift my eyes no higher than Mme Swann's sunshade, opened now and stretched above me like a nearer, more temperate sky, full of its constantly changing blue. Though subordinate to none, these rites were honor-bound, as was consequently Mme Swann herself, to defer to the morning, the springtime, and the sunshine, none of which I ever thought seemed flattered enough that such an elegant woman should make a point of respecting them, of choosing for their pleasure a frock in a brighter or lighter material, its lower neckline and looser sleeves suggesting the moist warmth of the throat and the wrists, that she should treat them as a great lady treats the common people whose invitation to visit them in the country she has cheerfully condescended to accept, and for whose special occasion, though they are nobodies, she makes a point of giving her dress a bucolic touch. As soon as she appeared, I made my bow to Mme Swann; she paused with me and gave me her smiling English *"Good morning!"* As we strolled, I realized that it was for her own sake that she observed these standards in dress, as though they were the tenets of a superior form of worship, which she merely served as a high priestess; for, if she felt too warm, if she unbuttoned or even took off and asked me to carry the jacket that she had originally meant to keep buttoned, I discovered in the blouse she wore under it a host of details of handiwork which might well never have been noticed, after the manner of those orchestral parts that the composer has worked with exquisite care although no ears among the audience will ever hear them; or else in the sleeves folded over my arm I picked out and studied, for the pleasure of looking at them or for the pleasure of being pleasant, this or that tiny detail, a strip of cloth of a delightful shade, or a mauve satinet normally unseen by any eye, but just as delicately finished as any of the outer parts of the garment, like the fine Gothic stonework hidden eighty feet up a cathedral, on the inner face of a balustrade, just as perfectly executed as the bas-relief statues in the main doorway, but which no one had ever set eyes on until an artist on a chance visit to the city asked to be allowed to climb up there, walk about at sky level, and survey a whole townscape from between the twin steeples.

For those who were ignorant of Mme Swann's practice of taking a "constitutional," the impression she gave of walking along the Avenue du Bois-de-Boulogne as though it were a pathway in her back garden was enhanced by the fact that she was on foot, that no carriage followed her, even though by the month of May she could usually be seen sitting behind the neatest pair of high-steppers in Paris, attended by grooms in the smartest livery, as relaxed and serene as a goddess, basking in the clement open air of a vast C-springed victoria. By walking, especially with her leisurely warm-weather gait, Mme Swann appeared to have acted on a whim, to be committing a graceful little breach of protocol, like a queen at a gala performance who, without telling anyone, and, as her household looks on in a slightly shocked wonderment, none of them daring to protest, leaves the royal box during an intermission, so as to spend a few moments mingling with ordinary members of the audience. Watching Mme Swann as she walked, people sensed between her and themselves the barriers of a certain form of wealth, which always seem to the crowd to be the most impassable barriers of all. But the Faubourg Saint-Germain has its barriers too, albeit less striking to the eye and the imagination of members of the "Hard-Up Club." When the latter see a great lady who is unaffected in manner, whom, because she has never lost the common touch, they can almost take for someone as lowly as themselves, they will never have the feeling of inequality, one might say the feeling of their own unworthiness, that they have when faced with the likes of Mme Swann. Unlike them, a woman of her sort is no doubt unimpressed by the sumptuous world in which she moves; she ignores it, for the very reason that she has become accustomed to it; that is, she has come to see it as all the more natural and necessary to herself, she has come to judge other people according to their greater or lesser familiarity with these standards of luxury; and so, the grand manner (which she enjoys showing off and recognizes in others) being entirely material, flagrantly noticeable, long to acquire, and hardly replaceable by anything, when such a woman deems a passerby to be someone of no consequence, it is in the same way as he has seen her to be someone of the greatest consequence—without hesitation, at first sight, and once for all. It may be that this particular class of women no longer exists, or at least not with the same character and the same charm. It was a social class which at that time included women like Lady Israels, who was on terms with women of the aristocracy, and Mme Swann, who was one day to be on terms with them, a class that was intermediate, lower than the Faubourg Saint-Germain, since they courted it, but higher than others who were not part of the Faubourg Saint-Germain; and it was peculiar in that, though existing apart from the society of the rich, it was of course a moneyed class, but one in which money had become tractable and had taken to responding to artistic ideas and purposes—it was malleable money, poetically refined money, money with a smile. In any case, the women who belonged to it then would have by now lost the quality that was their greatest claim to ascendancy: having aged, almost all of them have lost their beauty. For the stately, smiling, gentle Mme Swann who sauntered along the Avenue du Bois-de-Boulogne was not only in the prime of her noble wealth, she was also at the glorious height of her own mellow and still-delectable summertime, from which, like Hypatia, she could watch the turning of worlds beneath her measured tread.[67] Young men, seeing her pass, glanced anxiously at her, unsure whether their tenuous acquaintance with her (and apprehensive too about whether Swann, whom they had hardly met on more than a single occasion, would recognize them) could justify their daring to greet her. When they plucked up the resolve to do so, they were full of trepidation, in case such a foolhardy and provocative act of sacrilege, slighting the inviolable supremacy of a caste, might set off a catastrophe or bring down upon their heads the thunderbolt of divine retribution. All it did set off, however, in a sort of clockwork reaction, was the gesticulation of many little characters, who suddenly started to bow—Odette's courtiers, following the example of Swann, who, with the gracious smile once learned in the Faubourg Saint-Germain, but without the indifference that would once have accompanied it, was raising his topper lined with green leather. As though he had been infected by the prejudices of Odette, his former indifference had become both the annoyance of having to acknowledge somebody so badly dressed and the satisfaction of having a wife who knew so many people, mixed feelings which he expressed to the retinue of their fashionable friends: "Another one! I must say, I do wonder where Odette *gets* these people!" "So it's really all over between you?" Mme Swann said to me, having nodded at the alarmed passerby, who was now out of sight but whose heart was still palpitating. "You're never going to come and see Gilberte again? I'm certainly glad you've made an exception for *me* and that I'm not to be completely jilted. I do like it when you come. But I also liked your influence on my daughter. I'm sure she's sorry about it all too. Still, I'm not going to bully you—you might decide you'd had enough of me too!" "Odette, there's Sagan[68] saying good morning to you," Swann murmured. And there was the Prince, like a knight in an old painting, or as though taking part in a grandiose finale on a theater stage or in a circus ring, making his horse wheel around, and greeting Odette with a grand dramatic gesture that was almost allegorical in its evocation of politeness and chivalry, of the nobleman's homage to Woman, even though she was embodied in a woman whom his mother or sister would never stoop to frequent. From all sides now, through the liquid transparency and glossy luminosity of the shadow cast on her by the sunshade, Mme Swann was being recognized and greeted by the last of the late riders, who looked as though filmed at a canter against the white midday shimmer of the avenue, members of fashionable clubs, whose names—Antoine de Castellane, Adalbert de Montmorency,[69] and many more—famous to the public mind, were to Mme Swann the familiar names of her friends. So it is that the average life expectancy, the relative longevity, of memories being much greater for those that commemorate poetic sensation than for those left by the pains of love, the heartbreak I suffered at that time because of Gilberte has faded forever, and has been outlived by the pleasure I derive, whenever I want to read off from a sundial of remembrance the minutes between a quarter past twelve and one o'clock on a fine day in May, from a glimpse of myself chatting with Mme Swann, sharing her sunshade as though standing with her in the pale glow of an arbor of wisteria.

PART II

Place-Names: The Place

B Y THE TIME my grandmother and I left for Balbec, two years later, I had reached a state of almost complete indifference toward Gilberte. At times, as when I was under the spell of a new face, or if the companion with whom I imagined discovering the great Gothic cathedrals, the palaces and gardens of Italy was some other girl, I would reflect sadly that the love one feels, insofar as it is love for a particular person, may not be a very real thing, since, although an association of pleasant or painful fancies may fix it for a time on a woman, and even convince us that she was its necessary cause, the fact is that if we consciously or unconsciously outgrow those associations, our love, as though it was a spontaneous growth, a thing of our own making, revives and offers itself to another woman. However, when I set off for Balbec, and during the first part of my stay there, my indifference was still only intermittent. Often I found (life being so unchronological, so anachronistic in its disordering of our days) that I was living farther back in time than I had been on the day or two before, back in the much earlier time when I had been in love with Gilberte. Suddenly it was as painful to be living apart from her as it would have been in that earlier time. The self of mine that had once loved her, though now almost entirely supplanted in me by another self, would revisit me; and when it did, it was brought back much more often by some trifling thing than by something important. For instance (if I may step forward for a moment to the actual visit to Normandy), one day in Balbec I was to overhear a stranger mention, as I walked past him on the esplanade, "The family of the chief undersecretary at the Postmaster General's." At the time, given that I had no idea then of the influence that family would have on my life, this mention should have passed me idly by. But it gave me a sharp stab of pain, the pain felt by a self that had long since mostly ceased to exist but which could still mourn the absence of Gilberte. For a conversation about the family of the "chief undersecretary at the Postmaster General's," which Gilberte and her father had once had in my presence, had gone completely from my mind. Memories of love are, in fact, no exception to the general laws of remembering, which are themselves subject to the more general laws of habit. Habit weakens all things; but the things that are best at reminding us of a person are those which, because they were insignificant, we have forgotten, and which have therefore lost none of their power. Which is why the greater part of our memory exists outside us, in a dampish breeze, in the musty air of a bedroom or the smell of autumn's first fires, things through which we can retrieve any part of us that the reasoning mind, having no use for it, disdained, the last vestige of the past, the best of it, the part which, after all our tears seem to have dried, can make us weep again. Outside us? Inside us, more like, but stored away from our mind's eye, in that abeyance of memory which may last forever. It is only because we have forgotten that we can now and then return to the person we once were, envisage things as that person did, be hurt again, because we are not ourselves anymore, but someone else, who once loved something that we no longer care about. The broad daylight of habitual memory gradually fades our images of the past, wears them away until nothing is left of them and the past becomes irrecoverable. Or, rather, it would be irrecoverable, were it not that a few words (such as "chief undersecretary at the Postmaster General's") had been carefully put away and forgotten, much as a copy of a book is deposited in the Bibliothèque Nationale against the day when it may become unobtainable.

However, this recurrence of pain and the renewal of my love for Gilberte did not last longer than they would have in a dream of her, for the very reason that my life at Balbec was free of the habits that in usual circumstances would have helped it to prevail. Such effects of Habit may seem contradictory; but the laws which govern it are many and varied. In Paris, it was because of Habit that I had become more and more indifferent to Gilberte. The change in my habits—that is, the momentary suspension of Habit—put its finishing touch to that process when I set off for Balbec. Habit may weaken all things, but it also stabilizes them; it brings about a dislocation, but then makes it last indefinitely. For years past, I had been roughly modeling my state of mind each day on my state of mind the day before. At Balbec, breakfast in bed—a different bed, a different breakfast—was to be incapable of nourishing the ideas on which my love for Gilberte had fed in Paris. There are instances, albeit infrequent, in which, the passing days having been immobilized by a sedentary way of life, the best way to gain time is to change place. My journey to Balbec was like the first outing of a convalescent who has not noticed until that moment that he is completely cured.

Nowadays people would likely make the journey to Balbec by motorcar, in the belief that it would be pleasanter. As we shall see, it would certainly be a truer way to travel, in a sense, given that one's relationship to the various changes in the surface of the earth would be closer, more immediate. But the specific pleasure of traveling is not that it enables one to stop when tired or to stay somewhere along the way; it is that it can make the difference between departure and arrival not as unnoticeable as possible, but as profound as possible; it is that one can experience that difference in its entirety, as intact as it was in our mind when imagination transported us immediately from where we were living to where we yearned to be, in a leap that seemed miraculous less because it made us cover such a distance than because it linked two distinct personalities of place, taking us from one name to another name, a leap that is epitomized (more acutely than by a run in a motorcar, which allows you to get out where you like and thereby all but abolishes arrival) by the mysterious performance that used to be enacted in those special places, railway stations, which, though they are almost separate from the city, contain the essence of its individuality, as they bear its name on a signboard.

But, then, in all sorts of ways, our age is plagued by the notion that objects should be shown only with things which accompany them in reality, thus depriving them of the essential, the act of mind that isolated them from reality in the first place. So a painting is "featured" amid furniture, knickknacks, or hangings from the same period, the sort of insipid interior decoration which yesterday's ignoramus among hostesses, who now spends her idle hours in the archives and the libraries, is today adept at composing, and among which the masterpiece that we glance at as we dine does not give us the intensity of pleasure we more rightly expect from it in an art gallery, where the bareness of walls unadorned by any distracting detail symbolizes much more aptly the inner spaces into which the artist withdrew to create it.

Sad to say, those wonderful places, railway stations, our starting point for a distant destination, are also tragic places, for, though they are the setting for the miracle that will turn a land hitherto nonexistent except in the mind into one we are going to live in, for that very reason, as soon as we venture outside the waiting room, we must abandon all hope of returning to the familiar bedroom, which we left only a moment before. We have to give up all prospect of sleeping at home tonight, as soon as we have decided to venture into the reeking cavern that is the necessary anteroom to mystery, one of those huge glass-roofed machine shops, such as the Gare Saint-Lazare, which was where I had to seek out the train for Balbec, and which, above the great chasm slitting the city, had spread out one of those vast bleak skies, dense with portents of pent-up tragedy, resembling certain skies of Mantegna's and Veronese's, fraught with their quasi-Parisian modernity, an apt backdrop to the most awesome or hideous of acts, such as the Crucifixion or a departure by train.

As long as I had been content to lie in my snug bed in Paris and see Balbec's Persian church buffeted by blizzard and storm, my body had raised no objection to this journey. Objections only began once my body realized it was to be included, and that on the evening of our arrival I would be shown to "my" room, which would be completely unfamiliar to it. Its disagreement with this was especially acute since I had learned only on the eve of our departure that my mother was not to accompany us; my father, who was unable to get away from the Ministry until the date set for his visit to Spain with M. de Norpois, had decided to rent a house at Saint-Cloud, on the outskirts of Paris. Not that to be able to gaze upon Balbec seemed less desirable because it could only be enjoyed at the cost of pain to myself. On the contrary, this pain seemed to embody and guarantee the reality of the impression I sought; and that impression could never have been replaced by some other, supposedly equivalent sight, such as a "fine view" that I might have been able to go and see without its preventing me from going home at bedtime. Not for the first time, I sensed that those who know love and those who enjoy life are not the same people. I was sure my desire to go to Balbec was as strong as my doctor's when he said, on the very morning of our departure, surprised as he was by my unhappy expression, "Believe you me, if I could just take a single week off, to enjoy the sea air, you wouldn't have to ask me twice! Just think: there'll be the races and the regattas—it will be lovely!" Long before going to see La Berma, however, I had learned that whatever I longed for would be mine only at the end of a painful pursuit; and that this supreme goal could be achieved only on condition that I sacrifice to it the pleasure I had hoped to find in it.

My grandmother, of course, saw our impending departure in a rather different light. She was still as convinced as she had ever been that any present given to me should have an artistic element to it; and so she had at one point decided, in order to give me a sort of old "print" representing our journey, that we should retrace, partly by train, partly by carriage, the route taken by Mme de Sévigné in 1689, when she had gone from Paris to "L'Orient," as she called it, via Chaulnes and "the Pont-Audemer."[1] My grandmother had eventually had to abandon this plan, faced with my father's refusal to countenance such an itinerary—he foresaw that her idea of a tour designed for intellectual benefit would turn into a series of missed trains, lost luggage, sore throats, and disregard of doctors' orders. However, she took heart from the thought that at least, when we were due to go down to the beach, we would never run the risk of being prevented from doing this by the arrival of what her dear Mme de Sévigné calls "a carriage load of plaguey visitors," given that we would know no one in Balbec, Legrandin having offered us no letter of introduction to his sister. (His remissness in this regard was not seen in the same light by my great-aunts Céline and Victoire:[2] having long been in the habit of referring to this sister, whom they had known before her marriage as "Renée de Cambremer," who had given them the sort of presents which may figure in bedrooms or in reminiscences but which now denote no more than a former closeness, they felt it incumbent upon themselves, when visiting old Mme Legrandin, never to name the daughter, and even to congratulate each other later with statements such as, "I never so much as mentioned you-know-who" and "I think we can say the point was taken," in the belief that they were thereby avenging this snub to our family.)

So our departure from Paris was to be quite simple, by that 1:22 train on which, perusing the railway timetables, drawing from it each time the excitement and almost blissful illusion of setting off, I had doted so often that I fancied I had already taken it. As our imagination, in fixing the definitive features of a future happiness, is more influenced by the unchangingness of our desire for that fulfillment than by any accuracy in the information we may have about it, I was sure I had a close acquaintance with this one; and I had no doubt that I would feel a special pleasure in our compartment as the warmth of the day began to wane, that as we drew into this or that station I would recognize a particular feature; for this train, having always given me glimpses of the same towns, which I saw tinged by the light of the afternoon hours through which it runs, seemed different from all other trains; and, as we often do with somebody we have never seen but whose friendship we like to fancy we already enjoy, I had come to picture it as a fair artistic wayfarer, to whom I had even given a particular and constant expression, who let me accompany him on his journey, and whom, having bade him farewell outside the cathedral of Saint-Lô, I would then watch as he disappeared toward the setting sun.

As my grandmother could not resign herself to "just" going to Balbec, she had decided to spend a day along the way visiting a friend; but I was to travel on alone that same evening, so as "not to be a nuisance" and so as to be able to make a visit the following day to the Balbec church, which we had recently learned was some distance away from Balbec-Plage,[3] a fact that might make it difficult for me to go and see it once my course of sea-bathing had begun. It was perhaps less painful for me to know that the grand object of my journey was now to precede the unhappy first night to be spent in the strange room which I was going to have to accept as my new home. But first it had been necessary to leave the old one. My mother had arranged to move into the house at Saint-Cloud that very day; and she had made, or had pretended to make, all necessary preparations that would enable her to go straight there after seeing us off at the Gare Saint-Lazare, without having to go back to our own house, in case I should take it into my head to go home with her rather than set off for Balbec. She had even decided, alleging that there was too much to do in too short a time at the newly rented house, but really so as to spare me the sorrow of a last-minute leave-taking, not to stay with us until the departure of the train, that moment when the coming separation, which has lain concealed and possibly not inevitable among the preliminary bustle and haste, suddenly becomes unbearable and looms before us, impossible to elude now, concentrated into a stark and flagrant instant of impotent awareness.

I was beginning to realize for the first time that it was possible for my mother to live without me, to live for reasons unrelated to me, to lead a life of her own. She was going to live for herself, with my father, who she may have thought deserved a simpler and more enjoyable life than my ill health and nervous disposition allowed him. This separation from her saddened me even more, as I told myself that she very likely saw it as a welcome pause in the succession of disappointments I had brought upon her, which she had never spoken of, but which must have made her see the prospect of spending the holidays with me as irksome; very likely she even saw it as a first experimental step toward the future life to which she would have to resign herself, as she and my father advanced in years, in which I would see less of her, in which—and this I had never glimpsed in my worst nightmares—she would become something of a stranger to me, a lady to be seen going home alone to a house where I did not live, and where she would ask the concierge whether there was not a letter from me.

I was barely able to speak to the porter who offered to carry my suitcase. My mother tried to comfort me in ways that seemed appropriate to her. Instead of pretending not to see how unhappy I was, which she knew was pointless, she bantered:

"Dear me, whatever would the church of Balbec say if it knew we were getting ready to come and see it with such a long face? Can this be the delighted traveler that Mr. Ruskin writes about? Anyway, I'll know whether you've managed to keep a stiff upper lip. Even though I'll be miles and miles away, I'll still be with my little fellow—and he'll have a letter from his loving mama tomorrow."

"My dear," said my grandmother, "I can see you'll be just like Mme de Sévigné, following our every movement on the map!"

My mother then tried to distract me by asking what I was going to order for dinner, admiring Françoise, complimenting her on her hat and coat, which she had not recognized as ones which, when new and worn by my great-aunt, had once filled her with dismay, the hat because it had a huge bird perched on top of it and the coat because it was over-loaded with jet and ghastly designs. But, my great-aunt having cast off the coat, Françoise had had it turned and its inside now showed as a fine cloth in a handsome self-color. The bird had long since been broken and thrown out. And, just as it is sometimes strange to notice refinements that the most deliberate artist might have to strive for, in a popular song or in a single white or yellow rose blooming at exactly the right spot on a peasant's house, so with her sound and simple taste Françoise had placed on the hat, which was now a pleasure to behold, the velvet bow and the cluster of ribbon that would have delighted one in a portrait by Chardin or Whistler.

Or, to go further back in time, the nobility often given to the face of our old servant by modesty and honesty had spread to the clothes which, like the retiring person she was, a woman quite devoid of base instincts but "knowing her place," she had chosen for this journey, so as to be worthy of being seen with us while not appearing to be attracting attention to herself; and Françoise, in the faded cerise material of her overcoat and the uniform pile of her fur collar, called to mind one of those depictions of Anne of Brittany painted by an old master in a book of hours,[4] in which everything is so aptly matched, the feeling of the whole so evenly shared among all the parts, that the rich quaintness of the costume expresses the same pious solemnity as the eyes, the lips, and the hands.

To speak of thought in connection with Françoise would have been inappropriate. She knew nothing, in the most complete meaning of "knowing nothing," which is understanding nothing except those rare truths to which the heart has direct access. The vast world of ideas had no existence for her. But to see the clear look from her eyes, the fine lines of her nose and lips, all those indications so often lacking in the faces of cultured people, in whom they would have denoted the supreme distinction or high-minded disinterest of a superlative soul, was to be touched as though by the intelligent and kind eyes of a dog, though one well knows all human conceptions are foreign to it; and one might wonder whether, among our humbler brethren the peasants, there might not be individuals who are as it were the outstanding men and women of the simple-minded world, or, rather who, though condemned by an unjust fate to dwell forever in the outer darkness of the simple-minded, though more naturally and more essentially related to higher natures than most educated people, resemble the dispersed members of the holy family, lost and mindless, close relations of the finest minds, who have never grown up, who, as one can see in the unmistakable light shining from their eyes onto nothing, would have required only one thing to be talented, and that single thing was knowledge.

My mother, seeing I was on the verge of tears, said, "Regulus was accustomed, at moments of great consequence . . .⁵ And it's not very nice for his dear mama either. We'd better take a leaf out of your grandma's book and quote from Mme de Sévigné: 'I'll have to draw on all the courage that you lack.' "⁶ Then, knowing that affection for others can divert one from grief for self, she tried to amuse me by saying that she thought her trip out to Saint-Cloud would be enjoyable, that she was very pleased with the hansom she had booked, that the driver was polite and his cab comfortable. Nodding with apparent acquiescence and satisfaction, I did my best to smile at these details. But all they did was help me to imagine more graphically Mama's departure; and I stared at her, sick at heart, as though she were already separated from me, in her round straw hat, bought for the stay in the country, and the light frock, put on because of the long trip by cab on such a hot day, which changed her into someone else, made her belong already to the Villa de Montretout, where I would never see her.

To avoid the fits of breathlessness that the journey might bring on, the doctor had suggested that, just before the train left, I should drink a little too much beer or brandy, so as to be in the state he called "euphoria," in which the nervous system is briefly less susceptible. I was still not sure whether I was going to comply; but I did want my grandmother to admit that, should I decide to do so, it would be in accordance with both authority and good sense. So, when I mentioned it, I made it sound as though my only hesitation concerned the place where this alcohol would be drunk, the station buffet or the dining car. But my grandmother's face showed an expression of such disapproval, as though she was dismissing the idea out of hand, that I instantly resolved to have a drink, an act that had become necessary to demonstrate my freedom, since the merest hinting at it had been met with protest, and exclaimed, "What? You know how unwell I am! You know what the doctor's orders are! And yet this is how you behave!"

Once I had explained how unwell I felt, my grandmother said, "Well, go on, then, quickly! Go and get a beer or a liqueur, if it's supposed to be good for you," with an expression of such sorrowing kindness that I fell into her arms and kissed her again and again. The only reason why I then drank too much in the bar on the train was that I felt I might have a very severe attack, which would be even more upsetting for her. When I got back into our compartment at the first stop, I told her how happy I was to be going to Balbec, that I was sure everything would come out right in the end, that I would pretty soon get used to living apart from my mother, that this was a pretty nice train, that the barman and the other railway people were such good fellows that I would not mind traveling this way often, so as to be able to enjoy their company again. All this good news did not appear to give my grandmother the same joy as it gave me. Not looking at me, she said, "I think it might be a good idea for you to take a little nap," then sat looking out of the window. Though we had lowered the curtain, it did not make an exact fit with the whole of the window frame; and so, as a slant of sunshine slid over the polished oak of the door and the cloth of the seat (like a much more evocative advertisement for a life amid nature than those the company had affixed to the walls of the compartment, too high up for me to read the names of the landscapes they showed), it brought in the same warm, soothing glow that drowsed outside among the quiet clearings.

Now and then, when my grandmother thought my eyes were closed, I could see her glance toward me, through her veil with its large spots, then look away, only to glance at me again in the same way, like someone attempting to practice a slight movement despite the pain it causes.

I spoke to her; but she did not appear to enjoy this. To me, however, there was a pleasure in the sound of my voice, as there was in the imperceptible internal motions made by my body. So I tried to draw them out, letting each inflection of my voice dwell at length on each word, enjoying my eyes' way of resting on whatever it was they were looking at and gazing at it for longer than usual. "Look, I do think you should have a little rest," my grandmother said. "If you can't sleep, at least read a book or something." She handed me a volume of Mme de Sévigné's letters, which I opened; and then she settled down to her own book, the *Mémoires* of Mme de Beausergent.[7] These two ladies were her favorite writers; and a volume of each of them would invariably accompany her whenever she traveled. I sat facing the blue blind drawn down on the window, holding the volume of Mme de Sévigné but not looking at it, as I was full of reluctance to move my head at such a moment, and full of a vivid pleasure at remaining in any position my body happened to have adopted. To sit gazing at the blue Holland seemed to me a wonderful experience; and if anyone had tried to divert my attention from it, I would not have bothered answering. In the color of the cloth, it was not so much its beauty as the sheer intensity of its blueness that seemed to outshine all other colors which had ever met my eye between my birth and the moment when my drink had begun to have its effect, leaving them as drab and dull as they would have been for someone, once blind from birth, who remembers the darkness in which his days were spent before the operation that at last enabled him late in life to see color. An old ticket-collector came along to check our tickets. I was fascinated by the silvery sheen of the metal buttons on his tunic. I was about to ask him to take a seat beside us, but he went on to the next carriage, leaving me full of a yearning wonder about the life of the rail-waymen who, by spending their whole time on the trains, must have daily opportunities to see the old ticket-collector. The pleasure I felt in gazing at the blue blind and in being aware that my mouth was hanging open began to lessen. I felt more mobile and made a couple of movements; I leafed through the book my grandmother had passed me and was able to attend to a page or two here and there. As I read, I could feel my admiration for Mme de Sévigné grow.

It is easy to be misled by purely formal features of Mme de Sévigné's style, which, though only the mark of her period or of life in its *salons*, are taken to be the real Sévigné voice by some who write things like "I await these news, my good woman," or "The said Count seemed to me to have much wit," or "Hay-making is quite the jolliest thing to do." Even Mme de Simiane imagines she takes after her grandmother.[8] When she writes, "Monsieur, I shall have you know that M. de la Boulie excels in health and that he is quite ready to hear tell of his own decease," or "Oh, my dear Marquis, your letter affords such pleasure! One cannot desist from answering it!" or "It appears to me, monsieur, that you owe me a reply and that I owe you some bergamot-peel snuffboxes. Here are eight of them; there will be more; never has there been such a crop! It is evidently for your pleasure," or when she writes in similar tone her letter about being bled, or the one about the lemons, she clearly believes these are Mme de Sévigné–like letters. But my grandmother, having come to Mme de Sévigné from the inside, as it were, through her love for her own family and her love of nature, had taught me to see the true beauty of her manner, which lies in very different things. This was soon to be brought home to me even more, as Mme de Sévigné is a great artist of the same family as a painter I was to meet at Balbec, Elstir, who was to have a profound influence on my way of seeing things. I realized at Balbec that her way of depicting things is the same as his—that is, she presents them in the order in which we perceive them, instead of explaining them by their causes. But even on that first afternoon, in the train, rereading her letter about the moonlight—"I could not resist the temptation, so I put on all my cloaks and coifs, which were unnecessary, and went out to the mall, where the air was as fine as that in my bedroom, and where I came upon figments and fantasms, *black-and-white monks, several gray-and-white nuns, raiment tossed hither and thither, men buried upright against trees,* etc."—I was delighted by what I would have called not much later the Dostoevsky side (for does she not sketch background as he does character?) of the *Letters* of Mme de Sévigné.⁹

That evening, having seen my grandmother to her friend's house, where I stopped for a few hours, I once more took the train, alone this time, but at least not looking forward to an unpleasant night. For I was not going to have to spend it imprisoned in a bedroom in which I would be kept awake by the sleeping of all things around me; I was surrounded by the reposeful activity of all the train's various movements, which kept me company, engaged me in a dialogue if I could not manage to sleep, soothed me with their noises, which, as I used to do with the church bells of Combray, I linked together sometimes in one particular rhythm, sometimes in another (fancying first that I could hear four equal semiquavers, then a single semiquaver banging violently against a quarter note); and these noises neutralized the centrifugal force of my insomnia by pitting against it counterpressures that kept me in a state of equilibrium, and on which my motionless and soon unconscious form felt itself supported with the same impression of release and relief as I would have drawn from sleep entrusted to the wild and wakeful forces of living nature, if I could have briefly turned into a fish asleep in the ocean swell, steered by the unknowing tides, or an eagle hanging on the wings of a high wind.

Sunrises are a feature of long train journeys, like hard-boiled eggs, illustrated papers, packs of cards, rivers with boats straining forward but making no progress. As I sifted the thoughts that had been in my mind just a minute before, to see whether or not I had slept (my uncertainty about the matter already inclining me to the affirmative), I glimpsed in the windowpane, above a little black copse, serrated clouds of downy softness in a shade of immutable pink, dead and as seemingly indelible now as the pink inseparable from feathers in a wing, or a pastel dyed by the fancy of the painter. But in this shade I sensed neither inertia nor fancy, only necessity and life. Soon great reserves of light built up behind it. They brightened further, spreading a blush across the sky; and I stared at it through the glass, straining to see it better, as the color of it seemed to be privy to the profoundest secrets of nature. Then the train turned away from it, the railway line having changed direction, the dawn scene framed in the window turned into a village by night, its roofs blue with moonlight, the washhouse smeared with the opal glow of darkness, under a sky still bristling with stars, and I was saddened by the loss of my strip of pink sky, till I caught sight of it again, now reddening, in the window on the other side, from which it disappeared at another bend in the line. And I dodged from one window to the other, trying to reassemble the offset intermittent fragments of my lovely, changeable red morning, so as to see it for once as a single lasting picture.

The landscape became hilly and steep, and the train came to a halt at a little station between two mountains. Through the gorge, beside the swift stream, all one could see was the house of a grade-crossing keeper up to its windowsills in the flowing water. If a person can be the epitome of a place, conveying the charm and tang of its special savor, then this was demonstrated, more so than by the peasant girl I had longed for in the days of my lonely rambles along the Méséglise way, through the Roussainville woods, by the tall girl whom I saw come out of the keeper's house and start walking toward the station, along a footpath lit by the slanting rays of the sunrise, carrying a crock of milk. In that valley, hidden from the rest of the world by the surrounding heights, the only times she ever saw people would be when a train made its brief halt there. She walked along beside the train cars, pouring out coffee with milk for a few of the passengers who were up and about. Glowing in the glory of the morning, her face was pinker than the sky. Looking at her, I was filled with that renewed longing for life which any fresh glimpse of beauty and happiness can bring. Forgetting that beauty and happiness are only ever incarnated in an individual person, we replace them in our minds by a conventional pattern, a sort of average of all the different faces we have ever admired, all the different pleasures we have ever enjoyed, and thus carry about with us abstract images, which are lifeless and uninspiring because they lack the very quality that something new, something different from what is familiar, always possesses, and which is the quality inseparable from real beauty and happiness. So we make our pessimistic pronouncements on life, which we think are valid, in the belief that we have taken account of beauty and happiness, whereas we have actually omitted them from consideration, substituting for them synthetic compounds that contain nothing of them. Likewise, a well-read man, hearing of the latest "great book," can give a jaded yawn, assuming the work to be a sort of composite derived from all the fine works he has ever read. But the fact is that a great book is not just the sum of existing masterpieces; it is particular and unforeseeable, being made out of something which, because it lies somewhere beyond that existing sum, cannot be deduced simply from acquaintance with it, however close. No sooner has the well-read man discovered the new work than he forgets his earlier indifference and takes an interest in the reality it sets before him. In the same way, this lovely girl, utterly different from the patterns of beauty devised by my mind in isolation, gave me an instantaneous taste for a particular form of happiness (the only form in which we can have the taste of happiness) that I might experience if I came to live here and shared her life. Of course, for this too the momentary intermission of Habit was largely responsible. I invested the milkmaid with advantages which came from the fact that it was my entire self, ready to gorge on life's sweetest delights, that confronted her. We commonly live with a self reduced to its bare minimum; most of our faculties lie dormant, relying on habit; and habit knows how to manage without them. But on that morning, their presence had once more become essential, so that I could cope with travel, departure from life's daily round, a change of place, the unwonted time of day. My habit, which was sedentary and unused to morning hours, was found wanting; and all my faculties had come flooding back to stand in for it, outdoing themselves, vying with each other, rising to the same unusual occasion, the basest of them and the noblest, from mere breathing and appetite, even the circulation of the blood, to sensitivity and imagination. I could not say whether the wild beauty of that place increased the beauty of the girl and made me see her as superior to other women; but she certainly beautified all things around her. How delightful life would have been if only I could have spent it with her, hour after hour, walking beside her to the river, to her cow, then out to meet the trains, being in her company at all times, feeling that she knew me, having a place reserved for me in her thoughts! She would have initiated me into the charms of rural life and the pleasures of early rising. I beckoned to her to bring me the coffee and milk. I needed her to notice me. She did not notice me, so I hailed her. Her tall person was topped by a face with a complexion so golden-pink that I seemed to be seeing her through the radiance of a stained-glass window. She turned and walked back toward me: I could not look away from her face, which, as it neared and grew larger, was like a sun that did not dazzle the stare, no matter how close it came, which you could look straight at as it deluged you with its blaze of glorious golds and reds. Her eye, which had a piercing gaze, met mine; but just then, as the guard and stationmaster were shutting the doors, the train started to move. In broad daylight now, I watched as she walked away from the station and along her footpath: I was traveling away from the dawn. Whether my excitement had been caused by the girl, or whether it had been the cause of much of the enjoyment afforded me by the nearness of her, she was so much a part of my feeling that my desire to see her again was above all the longing to retain something of that excitement, not to let it die, not to be severed forever from the one who, though she was unaware of this, had been part of it. It was not just that this feeling was pleasant. It was especially because (as the tightening of a string or the more rapid vibration of a nerve produces a different note or color) it gave a sharper tone to what I saw, gave me a part to act in an unknown and infinitely more interesting world; and for as long as the gathering speed of the train allowed me to see the beautiful milkmaid, she was like a part of some other life, separated from the one I knew by a narrow borderline, another life, in which the feelings transmitted to me by things were not the usual ones, and the leaving of which felt like a sort of inner death. To have the comfort of feeling that I was at least not cast out of her life, I would have been glad to live near enough to the little railway station to be able to come down every morning and have this country girl pour out coffee and milk for me. But, unfortunately, she would be forever absent from the life toward which I was now heading faster and faster, a prospect I could accept only by imagining a plan to take this same train on some other day, and thus be able to stop again at the same station, a scheme that had the added advantage of fueling the mind's selfish, active, practical, mechanical, lazy, and centrifugal predisposition to shirk the effort required to analyze in an abstract and disinterested way any pleasant impression we have experienced. And since we also want to dwell on such an impression, the mind prefers to imagine a future recurrence of it, to design clever circumstances that could bring it about, none of which teaches us anything about the essence of it; it just relieves us of the bother of trying to replicate it within ourselves and enables us to hope that the outside world will bring it back to us.

The principal church of certain towns, Vézelay or Chartres, Bourges or Beauvais, is sometimes called, for short, by the name of the town itself. This habit of synecdochism has the result, if it concerns towns where we have never been, of sculpting the broader meaning of the name, which, when we attempt to fit the image of the whole unknown town back into it, will shape it like a mold, stamping on it the same toolings, in the same style, and turning it into a sort of great cathedral. It was, however, on a sign in a railway station, hanging above a refreshment stand, in white lettering against a blue background, that I was to read the name of Balbec, of almost Persian style. I strode out through the station and across the boulevard that led to it, where I asked for directions to the beach, so as to set eyes on this church by the sea. People stared at me as though not understanding what I meant: Balbec-le-Vieux, Balbec-en-Terre, where I had arrived, was neither a seaside resort nor a port. Had not fishermen brought back from the sea, or so said the legend, the miraculous Christ, whose coming to that spot was depicted in a stained-glass window of the church standing only a few yards from where I was? Had not the stone for its nave and its steeples been hewn from wave-washed cliffs? But the breakers, which for those reasons I had imagined splashing their spray about that very window, were nearly fifteen miles away, at Balbec-Plage; and the steeple by the dome, which, because I had read of it as a stark Norman cliff braving the worst of the sea weather, with birds wheeling in the squalls, I had always seen as being soaked by the spindrift blown from the tumultuous deep, now stood in a town square at the junction of two trolley lines, opposite a café with the word *Billiards* above it in gilt lettering, against a background of houses with no masts swaying above their roofs. The church impinged on my mind with the café, the passerby whom I had asked for directions, and the railway station to which I would soon return; it was just a part of its surroundings, with an accidental look to it, as though it were a detail of a late afternoon in which the dome against the sky had the mellow swell of a fruit ripening its golden melting pink in the same sunshine as touched the chimneys of the houses. But when I recognized the Apostles, whose statues I had seen as moldings in the Trocadéro Museum, and who now stood to the left and right of the Virgin, waiting by the deep recess of the porch as though to pay me homage, I tried to close my mind to everything but the eternal significance of the sculptures. Slightly stooping, with their kind faces, snub noses, and mild expressions, they looked like choristers come to fill the fine day with a welcoming hallelujah. Then one noticed that their expressions were as fixed as those of the dead, not changing unless one stepped over to see them from the other side. I stood there telling myself: "This is it! This is the church at Balbec! This town square, which looks as though it's aware of its claim to fame, is the only place in the world that possesses the church of Balbec. Until now, all I've ever seen of it was just photos of the church and moldings of the Apostles and the Virgin. But now this is the church itself, the statue in person, the real things! And the real things are unique—this is much more!"

It was also much less, perhaps. Just as a young man, having taken an examination or fought a duel, sees the answers he gave to the questions, or the bullet he fired, as paltry achievements compared with the great potential of learning or courage that he would have liked to display, so my mind, which had rescued the Virgin of the porch from the reproductions I had seen, protecting her forever from any vicissitudes which might jeopardize them, letting her stand unscathed amid their annihilation, ideal, full of her universal value, was now amazed to see that the statue it had so often sculpted was reduced to nothing but its own shape in stone, right next to an election notice, no less within arm's reach than it, no less touchable with the tip of my cane, rooted to the square, inseparable from the junction with the high street, incapable of hiding from any eyes looking out from the café or the horse-trolley depot, her face sharing half of the rays of the setting sun—and soon, in a few hours, half of those of the streetlamp—with the local branch of the Savings Bank, and assailed, also like it, by the smells from the pastry cook's kitchens, subjected so utterly to the tyranny of the Particular that, if I had felt like writing my name on the stone, it would have been this fabled Virgin, she whom until then I had endowed with a general existence and an inaccessible beauty, the unique (which meant, alas, the only) Virgin of Balbec, who would have been unable to avoid show-ing to all admirers who came to gaze upon her the mark of my piece of chalk and the letters of my name scrawled on her body, which was stained with the same soot as the neighboring houses, she whom, like the church itself, I now found transformed from the immortal work of art that I had longed to see into a little old woman in stone, whose height I could measure, and whose wrinkles I could count. Time was getting on; I had to make my way back to the station, from where, hav-ing met my grandmother and Françoise, I was to travel on to Balbec-Plage. I kept remembering everything I had ever read about Balbec and the words Swann had spoken: "It's a delight—every bit as fine as Siena." Blaming my disappointment on mere contingencies, my unready mood, the fact that I was tired, my inability to look at things properly, I tried to draw consolation from the knowledge that, intact and unvisited, other towns awaited me elsewhere, that I might soon be able to walk about Quimperlé, amid a shower of pearls and a cool murmuring of constant droplets, or step through the greenish-pink glow surrounding Pont-Aven. But with Balbec it felt as though, by going there, I had bro-ken open a name which should have been kept hermetically sealed, and into which—through the breach I had been ill advised enough to make, replacing all the images I had allowed to escape from it—a horse trolley, a café, people crossing the square, a branch of the Savings Bank, under the irresistible forces of external pressure and air suction, had rushed into the vacuum left in the syllables, which had now closed upon them, turning them into a frame for the porch of my Persian church, and would never again be rid of them.

I did meet my grandmother on the little local branch line that was to take us to Balbec-Plage; but she was unaccompanied. Intending to have everything arranged in advance for our arrival, she had sent Françoise on ahead of us; but by giving her misleading instructions, she had managed to send her off on the wrong train; so Françoise, all unknowing, was now traveling at full speed toward Nantes and might even not wake up until her train reached Bordeaux. I had barely sat down in the compartment, which was lit by the fading glow of sunset and still warm from the heat of the day (the former of these enabling me to see clearly on my grandmother's face the saddening evidence of how much the latter had exhausted her), when she said, "So? How was Balbec?," with a smile of such radiant expectation, full of the great pleasure I must have had, that I could not bear to blurt out my disappointment. Also, the closer we came to the place to which my body would have to become accustomed, the less I thought about the mental impression I had been looking forward to in visiting Balbec. Though we were still more than an hour away from the end of this journey, I was trying to imagine the manager of the hotel where we were to stay in Balbec, knowing that, for him, I was at that moment nonexistent, and wishing that I could have entered the field of his awareness in the company of someone more impressive than my grandmother, who would no doubt ask him to give us a reduction. I could picture him already, very imprecise in his bodily appearance, but stiff with arrogance.

Every now and then, when our little train stopped at one or another of the stations on the Balbec line, I was struck by the strangeness of their names—Incarville, Marcouville, Doville, Pont-à-Couleuvre, Arambouville, Saint-Mars-le-Vieux, Hermonville, Maineville—whereas, had I read them in a book, I would have been struck by their obvious points of similarity with the names of certain places in the neighborhood of Combray. To the ear of a musician, two phrases that have several notes in common may appear quite dissimilar, if they are colored by different harmonies or orchestrations. And in the dismal litany of these names, which were full of sand and salt and too much empty, breezy space, with the startling syllable *ville* shrilling about them like a seabird, there was nothing to call to mind names like Roussainville or Martinville, which, because I had heard them said so often by my great-aunt, over the dinner table or in the "parlor," had taken on a subdued patina of charm, an essence perhaps compounded of the taste of jam, the aroma of the wood fire, the smell of the paper in a book by Bergotte, and the color of the freestone house opposite, and which to this day, when they drift up like gas bubbles from the depths of memory, retain their full specific virtue, though they have to traverse one after another the many different layers of other mediums before reaching the surface.

These little places, perched high on their dune above a distant sea or already settling down for the night in the lee of flagrantly green hills, which were as ungainly as a hotel-room sofa when one sees it for the first time, were composed of a few villas, a tennis court, and sometimes a casino with its pennant flapping in the fretful, freshening, vacuous wind, and showed me now for the first time their habitual denizens, leading their outside lives—tennis players in white caps, a stationmaster living on the premises with his tamarisk and his roses, a lady in a boater calling her dawdling whippet, then walking back toward her holiday house, where the lamp was already lit, her steps revealing the daily shape of a life that I would never come to know—all of which, with the uncanny familiarity and disdainful everydayness of these glimpses, wounded my stranger's eyes and my homesick heart. However, this was nothing to the pain I was to suffer once we had come to rest in the vestibule of the Grand-Hôtel at Balbec and were faced with its monumental staircase in imitation marble and its manager, a dumpy little person whose face and voice were covered with scars left by the removal of many pimples and the addition of many accents betokening distant origins and a cosmopolitan upbringing, who was wearing tails like a fashionable gentleman, whose acute psychological glances at those who stepped off the "omnibus" usually enabled him to take a duke for a skinflint and a hotel thief for a duke, and with whom my grandmother, oblivious of the animosity and disdain she must be fostering in the strangers among whom we were to live, set about a discussion of terms. The manager, no doubt forgetting that his own salary did not amount to five hundred francs a month, had a withering scorn for anyone who thought five hundred francs, or, as he put it, "twenty-five *louis*," was a substantial sum, and he looked down on them as a breed of untouchables whose place was not at the Grand-Hôtel. There were, of course, even at the Grand-Hôtel, guests who could enjoy living quite cheaply without forfeiting the good opinion of the manager, as long as he was sure their penny-pinching was motivated not by poverty but by miserliness. For miserliness, being a vice and therefore at home in any social class, is in no way incompatible with prestige. Class was the only thing the manager paid attention to, or, rather, he was impressed by anything he believed showed high class, such as a man stepping into the vestibule without taking off his hat, or people who wore plus fours with a waisted coat and extracted purple-and-gold-banded cigars from cases of crushed morocco (none of which signs, alas, could I display). He sprinkled his commercial patter with choice expressions, which he misused.

As I sat there on an ottoman and heard my grandmother, who was unperturbed by the fact that he listened to her with his hat on and whistled a little tune to himself, inquire of him in an artificial tone of voice, "So what are your . . . charges? Goodness me, much too much for my slender means!," I tried to shrink as far as possible into myself, to flee on the wings of eternal verities, to leave nothing of myself, nothing live, on the surface of my body—desensitized like the body of an animal which by inhibition feigns death when wounded—so as not to suffer too much pain in a place where my total lack of habit was made all the more agonizing by the sight of people who seemed to be in their element, an elegant lady for whom the manager showed his respect by freely fondling the little dog that followed her about, a young dandy who came strolling in wearing a hat with a feather and asking whether there was "Any post?," people for whom climbing the imitation-marble stairs meant they were almost home. At the same time, the baleful glare of Minos, Aeacus, and Rhadamanthus,[10] in which I steeped my naked soul as though in some dread unknown where it had lost all protection, was turned upon me by three unreceptive individuals dignified by the title "Reception Service"; and a little farther along, behind a glass partition, people sat in a reading room to describe which, if I had borrowed colors from Dante, I would have had to use first those with which he depicts paradise, then those with which he depicts hell, as I imagined both the bliss of the chosen who had the right to sit in there quietly reading, and the torture my grandmother would visit upon me if, in her disregard for such emotions, she were to tell me to go in and join them.

My loneliness was further increased a moment later. I had told my grandmother I was not feeling very well and that I thought we might find ourselves obliged to go back to Paris; and without a word of protest she had said she was going out to buy a few things that would be of service to us whether we stayed in Balbec or went home (and which I later found out were all for me, Françoise having been in charge of the things I might have needed). During her absence, I also went out and, among hordes of people who made the streets feel as hot and stuffy as an overcrowded room, wandered up and down, past a barbershop that was still open, near a tearoom where customers were eating ices, around the statue of Duguay-Trouin.[11] The sight of this statue afforded me about as much enjoyment as it would to a patient coming on an illustration of it in a magazine lying in a surgeon's waiting room. I was amazed that the world contained people sufficiently different from myself for the manager of the hotel to have urged such a stroll upon me as a form of amusement, for there to be some to whom such a torture chamber of unfamiliar quarters could actually be an "abode of delight," as the hotel styled itself in its leaflet, possibly with some degree of license, although it was undeniably addressing a wide public whose views it shared. So, to attract such people to the Grand-Hôtel of Balbec, it expatiated not only on "the exquisite cuisine" and "the entrancing view from the gardens of the Casino" but on "the great god Fashion, whose decrees no man of good breeding will care to flout, unless he does not mind being thought a Philistine."

My need for my grandmother was sharpened by the fear of having been a great disappointment to her. She must be disheartened by the thought that, if I could not put up with this degree of fatigue, it was impossible ever to hope that any trip could be of benefit to me. I decided to go back and wait for her in the hotel. The manager himself came to push a button for me; and a personage hitherto unknown to me, called in a sort of English the "lift" (who, like a photographer behind his window or an organist in his loft, dwelt at the very top of the hotel, where the lantern in a Norman church would be), began to descend toward me with the agility of a captive, hardworking household squirrel. Then, with me on board, he slid up his pillar again toward the dome of the commercial nave. At each floor, fanning out from both sides of a short communication stairway, gloomy galleries opened, a chambermaid lugged a bolster about. To her face, which was unclear in the inner dusk, I held the mask of my most passionate fancies; but I could read in the glance she gave me my own appalling nullity. During the endless climb, to allay the dreadful anguish that clutched at me from the silence we traversed, with the mystery of its unpoetic dimness relieved only by a vertical succession of panes casting a little light from the single WC on each story, I spoke to the young organist, this functionary of my ascent and associate of my captivity, as he went on pushing and pulling the knobs and stops of his instrument. I apologized for taking up so much space and giving so much trouble; and I asked him whether I was not in his way as he exercised his art, in which, to flatter the virtuoso, I showed more than mere curiosity, professing to have a passion for it. He did not answer, whether because of surprise at my statement, attentiveness to his work, a sense of protocol, hardness of hearing, respect for place, fear of danger, laziness of mind, or the manager's instructions.

To give us an impression of the realness of people and things external to us, even if they are insignificant, there are few comparisons more instructive than the change their disposition toward ourselves undergoes between the time before we know them and the time after. I was the same person who had taken the late-afternoon train on the little branch line to Balbec; the self in me was the same. But now, inside that self, occupying the space that at six in the evening had been fraught with my inability to picture the manager, the Grand-Hôtel, and its employees, as well as with a vague, uneasy expectation of the moment of arrival, there were the erstwhile pimples on the face of the cosmopolitan manager (who was actually a naturalized Monégasque of, as he put it, "Romanian originality," being given to sprinkling his speech with malapropisms which he thought very distinguished), the gesture he had made to summon the "lift," not to mention the "lift" himself, and a whole frieze of puppetlike characters out of the opened Pandora's box of the Grand-Hôtel, undeniable, unremovable, and, like all things that have come to pass, sterilizing in their effect. But at least this change, which I had not brought about, proved that something external to myself had happened, however trite a thing it was in itself; and I was like a traveler who, having set out on his journey with the sun in front of him, realizes that hours must have passed, because it is now behind him. Feeling exhausted and with a touch of fever, I would have been glad to go to bed; but all my bedtime things were missing. I would have liked at least to lie down for a moment on the bed: but that would have done me no good, since I would have been incapable of granting any rest to that bundle of sensations that the waking body, even the material body, is for each of us, and also because the unknown objects that surrounded it, by forcing it to keep its perceptions in a permanent state of defensive alertness, would have held my eyes and ears, all my senses, in a posture as cramped and uncomfortable, even if I had stretched out my legs, as the one Louis XI inflicted on Cardinal La Balue[12] by having him locked in a cage that made it impossible either to sit or to stand. As our attentiveness furnishes a room, so habit unfurnishes it, making space in it for us. In that room of mine at Balbec, "mine" in name only, there was no space for me: it was crammed with things which did not know me, which glared my distrust of them back at me, noting my existence only to the extent of letting me know they resented me for disturbing theirs. Without letup, in some unfamiliar tongue, the clock, which at home I would never have heard for more than a few seconds a week, on surfacing from a long reverie, went on making comments about me, which must have sounded offensive to the tall violet curtains, for they stood there without a word in a listening posture, looking like the sort of people who will shrug their shoulders to show they are irked by the mere sight of someone. They gave to that bedroom with its high ceiling an almost historical air: it was the perfect sort of place for the Duc de Guise to have been assassinated in,[13] say, and for lines of tourists to file through led by a guide from Cook's—but not for me to get some sleep. I was tormented by the presence of low glass-fronted bookcases, which ran all round the walls, and especially by a tall cheval glass which stood athwart a corner of the room and which I knew would have to be taken away if I was ever to enjoy any possibility of calm. Constantly glancing or staring upward (activities which, in Paris, were as unhindered by the things in my room as by my eyes themselves, these things being nothing but accessories of my own organs, extensions of myself), I looked at the vast height of the ceiling in this belvedere stuck on the very top of the hotel, which my grandmother had selected for me; and in the part of me that is more private than those used for seeing and hearing, the part where one is aware of shades of smell, almost inside the self, an assault by vetiver threw me back on my deepest defenses as I tried to repel it, in my tiredness, with a pointless, repeated, and apprehensive sniffing. Deprived of my universe, evicted from my room, with my very tenancy of my body jeopardized by the enemies about me, infiltrated to the bone by fever, I was alone and wished I could die. It was then that my grandmother entered the room and, as my shriveled heart expanded, broad vistas of hope opened to me.

She was in a tea gown of cotton cambric which she always wore about the house if one of us was ill (because she felt more at home in it, or so she said, always alleging selfish motives for what she did), and which was her nun's habit, the handmaid's and night nurse's tunic in which she would care for us and watch over us. But, unlike the attentions of nuns, handmaids, and night nurses, the kindness they exercise, the excellence we admire in them, and the gratitude we owe them, which have the effect of increasing both our impression of being a stranger to them and the feeling of aloneness that makes us keep to ourselves the unshared burden of our thoughts and our desire to live, I knew with my grandmother that, however overpowering any cause of my sorrow might be, its expression would be met by a sympathy that was even greater, that whatever was in me, my cares, my wishes, would rouse within my grandmother a desire, even stronger than my own, for the protection and betterment of my life; and my thoughts became hers without alteration, passing from my mind to hers without changing medium or person. So—like a man in front of a mirror wrong-handedly try-ing to fasten his bow tie, without realizing that the end he can see must cross to the other side, or a dog snapping at the flittering shadow of an insect—misled by the appearance of the body, as we are in this world, where souls are not directly perceptible, I fell into my grandmother's arms and pressed my lips to her face as though that were how to take refuge in the greatness of heart she offered to me. Whenever my mouth was on her cheeks or her forehead, I drew from them something so nourishing, so beneficent, that I had all the immobility, gravity, and placid gluttony of an infant on the breast.

Nor could I ever tire of gazing at her large face, outlined like a beau-tiful cloud, calm and glowing, illuminated from within by its tender-ness. Anything that partook, however faintly, however remotely, of her sensations, anything that could be said to be still a part of her being, was thereby so spiritualized and sanctified that, in smoothing under my hands her lovely hair, which was hardly gray yet, my touch was as re-spectful, careful, and gentle as though it were her goodness itself I was handling. She took such pleasure in any trouble that spared me trouble, such delight in a moment of rest and peace for my weary limbs, that when I tried to prevent her helping me untie my laces and get ready for bed, making as though to undress myself, her pleading glance halted my hands, which were already on my boots and the first buttons of my jacket.

"Please! Let me!" she said. "Your old grandma loves to do it. And you must be sure to knock on the wall if you need anything during the night. My bed's back to back with yours, you know, and it's just a parti-tion. In a moment, once you've hopped into bed, you try knocking, and we'll see how easy it is to communicate."

So, that evening, I did give three knocks; and a week later, when I felt unwell for a few days, I did the same thing each morning, because she wanted me to have an early glass of milk. As soon as I thought I could hear she was awake, so as not to make her wait, to let her go back to sleep as soon as possible, I would try giving my three little knocks, gently and tentatively, but quite clearly, since, though I was reluctant to interrupt her sleep when it was possible I might have been mistaken and she was not awake, I would not have wanted her to lie there expecting a renewal of a summons that it was possible she might not have heard distinctly, but which I did not dare repeat. No sooner had I tapped on the wall than I heard her three answering knocks, quite different in their intonation from my own, full of a tone of serene control, repeated twice so that there should be no mistake, and clearly stating: "Not to worry—I heard; and I'll be with you in a moment or two." And, sure enough, she soon appeared. I said I had been anxious in case she might not have heard me or in case she thought it was someone else knocking on a wall close by. She would say with a laugh:

"What! How could I mistake my dear little fellow's knocking for someone else's? I'd know it a mile away. Do you really think there's anyone else in the whole world who's as silly and anxious and torn between the fear of waking me up and not being heard? Even a tiny little scratching on the wall would be enough for me to recognize a mouse like you, especially when you're such a dear and doleful little mouse. I was lying there listening to my mouse rummaging about in its nest, getting ready to knock, working up to it. . . ."

When she parted the blinds, the sun would already be up, on the roofs of the protruding annex of the hotel, like a slater on the early shift, working in silence so as not to wake the sleeping town, which in its inactivity makes him appear all the more nimble. She would tell me what time it was, what the weather would be like that day, that I need not get up and go to the window, that there was a drift of mist on the sea, whether the baker's was open yet, whose carriage it was that we could hear passing, commenting on the daily insignificant curtain-raiser, the banal *introit* that no one ever attends, a scrap of life shared only by us, to which I would smugly refer later, in Françoise's presence, or when talking with other people, informing them of the pea-souper there had been at 6 A.M., showing off not because I had been gifted with special knowledge, but because I had been singled out for affectionate attention by this quiet and gentle morning moment, opening like a symphony with the rhythmic dialogue between my three knocks and the answering three, ardently desired and twice repeated, given back by the partition full of love and joy, its solid substance turned into happy harmonies and singing like an angels' chorus, filled by the whole soul of my grandmother and the promise of her coming, sounding its glad annunciation with the fidelity of music. But on the night of our arrival, after my grandmother had left my room, I started feeling miserable again, as I had in Paris when it was time to leave for the station. The trepidation that overwhelmed me at the prospect of sleeping in an unfamiliar bedroom—which is felt by many—may be nothing more than the lowliest, most obscure, organic, and all-but-unconscious mode of the supreme and desperate refusal, by the things that make up the best of our present life, to countenance even our theoretical acceptance of a possible future without them: a refusal which was the core of the horror I had so often felt at the thought that my parents would one day be dead, that the requirements of life might force me to live apart from Gilberte or just make me settle for good in a country where I would never see my friends again; a refusal which lurked beneath the difficulty I found in trying to think about my own death or even the kind of afterlife promised by Bergotte in his books, in which there would be no place for my memories, my defects, my very character, all of which found unconscionable the idea of their own nonexistence and hoped on my behalf that I was fated neither to unbeing nor to an everlasting life that would abolish them.

One day in Paris, when I had been feeling particularly unwell, Swann had said, "What you should do is be off to the South Seas, the islands. . . . You'd very likely never come back." I almost answered, "But that would mean I'd never see your daughter again—I would live among things and people she would never have set eyes on!" But at the same moment, reason was murmuring: "Well, what difference will that make, since I won't be upset about it? When M. Swann says I very likely won't ever come back, what he means is I won't *want* to come back, and if I don't want to come back, that will be because I'll be perfectly happy to stay there." Reason was aware that habit (which was going to set about making me like these unknown quarters, change the position of the cheval glass, tone down the curtains, silence the clock) also undertakes to endear to us people whom we disliked to begin with, alters the shape of their faces, improves their tone of voice, makes hearts grow fonder. This liking for new places and people is of course worked into our forgetting of older ones; but reason suspected I could foresee without qualms a life without certain people, who would even fade forever from my memory, and so the promise of forgetting which it held out, though intended as a consolation, was heartbreaking. Not that the heart does not also benefit, once such a divorce is consummated, from the analgesia of habit; but until that time comes, it goes on suffering without letup. The fear of a future deprived of the faces and voices of those we love, those who today give us our dearest happiness, rather than diminishing, may in fact be made worse by the thought that the pain of this deprivation is to be compounded by something which at the moment seems even more unbearable—our no longer being affected by it as a pain, but being indifferent to it—for that would mean our actual self had changed, and not just that we had lost the delight in our parents' presence, the charm of a mistress, the warmth of a friend; it would mean that our affection for them had been so utterly obliterated from our heart, of which it is an integral part today, that we would be able to take pleasure in a life spent without them, horrible though that seems at present; it would amount to a death of our self, albeit followed by a resurrection, but a resurrection in the form of a different self, whose love will remain forever beyond the reach of those parts of the former self that have gone down to death. It is those parts of us, even the most insubstantial and obscure of them, such as our attachment to the dimensions or the atmosphere of a particular room, which take fright, withhold consent, and engage in rebellions that must be seen as a covert and partial yet tangible and true mode of resistance to death, that lengthy, desperate, daily resistance to the sporadic but nonstop dying which attends us throughout our lives, stripping off bits of us at every moment, which have no sooner mortified than new cells begin to grow. For a nervous disposition such as mine (that is, one in which the functioning of the intermediaries, the nerves, is impaired, so that they fail to stifle the voice of the lowliest elements of self doomed to decease, and their harrowing many-headed lament, in all its sorrow, rises unmuted to the wearied ears of consciousness), the anguish and alarm I felt when lying beneath a ceiling that was unknown and too high was nothing but the protest of my surviving attachment to a ceiling that was known and lower. No doubt that attachment would end and be replaced by another: first death, then a new life would have done their dual work at the behest of Habit. But until that end, this attachment would suffer every evening; and on that first evening especially, in revolt at being confronted with a future which had already taken shape, in which there was no role for it, it tortured me with the din of its wailing every time my eyes, unable to look away from what affronted them, tried to reach that inaccessible ceiling.

But what delight there was the following morning! After a servant had come to waken me and bring hot water, and while I washed and vainly rummaged in my trunk for necessary things, pulling out a jumble of unnecessary ones, how exhilarating it was, amid pleasant prospects of breakfast and a walk, to see not only the window but all the glass doors of the bookcases, as though they were the portholes of a ship's cabin, filled by the open sea, which showed no dark designs toward me (though half of its expanse was actually darkened by a shadow, marked off from the rest of it by a thin, shifting frontier), and to gaze at the long rollers that came plunging in, one after another, like divers from a board! Holding the stiff, starched towel inscribed with the name of the hotel, with which I was making unavailing efforts to dry myself, I kept going back to the window to look again at the huge, dazzling amphitheater, mountainous with the snowy peaks of its breakers of emerald, here and there polished and translucent, which with placid violence let their beetling, lionlike crags and towering slopes topple into avalanches and collapse upon themselves under the faceless smile of the sun. Every morning from then on, that window was where I posted myself, as though leaning out at the door of an overnight coach to see whether a range of hills that one longs to reach has come closer or receded during the hours of darkness—for the hills of the sea, before they come dancing back toward us, can retreat so far that often it was only at a distance, beyond a great stretch of sandy plain, that I caught sight of their closest undulations, in a transparent, vaporous, bluish remoteness calling to mind those glaciers one sees in the backgrounds of paintings by Tuscan primitives. On other days, the waves would be very near; and the sunlight laughed on a green that was as soft as the green brought out in Alpine meadows (among mountains where the sun sprawls about like a reckless giant blithely tumbling downhill) not so much by the moistness of the ground as by the liquid mobility of the light. Moreover, in the breach that a beach and its waves make in the rest of the world, so as to let the light flood in, it is especially the light, according to the direction it shines from and the point of view it thereby gives to the eye, that makes for the placement and displacement of a seascape's hills and dales. Variations in lighting can alter the outlook of a place, can bring before us new goals and give us the desire to attain them, no less effectively than can the laborious making of a long journey. In the mornings, when the sunlight came from behind the hotel, baring the illuminated sands for me all the way to the sea's first foothills, it appeared to be showing me a concealed slope of them and to be urging me to undertake a varied though stationary tour, by way of the turning road of its rays, through the most impressive sites of the hours' changing landscape. On the very first morning, the sun kept smiling and pointing out to me the sea's distant blue summits, named on no map, until its sublime transit of the resounding chaos of their cliffs and avalanches brought it dazzled into my room, out of the wind, to lie about on the unmade bed and strew its wealth on the wet washstand, in my opened trunk, its very splendor and incongruous extravagance increasing the effect of untidiness. Unfortunately, my grandmother's opinion of the sea breeze, an hour later, as we had lunch in the large dining room—sprinkling from a lemon's leather gourd a few golden drops on a brace of sole, which soon left on our plates the plumes of their skeletons, as fragile as feathers and as resonant as zithers—was that it was a shame not to feel its bracing effects, of which we were deprived by a screen which, transparent but closed, made the beach look like an exhibit behind plate glass, exposing it completely to our view but separating us from it, while the sky seemed so much a part of the room that its blue appeared to be the color of the panes, and the white of the clouds looked like flaws in the glass. Fancying that Baudelaire's lines about "lounging on the esplanade" or "in the boudoir" applied to me, I was wondering whether his "sunbeams gleaming on the sea"—unlike the evening sun-

beam, simple and shallow, a tremulous golden shaft—might not be
those I could see at that very moment burnishing the surface of the
waves to topaz, fermenting it to a pale milky beer, frothing it like
milk, while every now and then great blue shadows passed over parts
of it, as though high above us a god were having fun moving a mirror about. Compared with the "parlor" at Combray, looking out on
the houses opposite, its aspect was not, alas, the only way in which this
dining room in Balbec differed, with its great bare emptiness filled
to the brim by sunshine as green as water in a swimming pool, and
with the high tide and broad daylight only a few feet away, as though
guarding the celestial city with their indestructible moving barrier of
emerald and gold. In Combray, where we were known by everybody, I
paid attention to no one. But on holiday at the seaside, one is surrounded by strangers. I was not yet old enough, and had remained too
sensitive, to have given up the wish to please others and to possess
them. I had none of the dignified indifference that a man of the
world would have felt toward the people lunching in that dining
room or the young men and girls walking past on the esplanade: it
was galling to think I could go on none of their outings—though less
galling than if my grandmother, in her disdain for polite convention and her concern for my well-being, had humiliated me by asking
them whether I might not join them! Whether they were wandering
back to some vacation house unknown to me, strolling out to tennis
carrying racquets, or riding past on horses whose hooves trampled
my heart, I sat gazing at them with passionate curiosity, as they dawdled
in that seaside dazzle that alters social dimensions, watching their every
move through the transparency of the grand glassed-in bay that let in
so much light. However, it also kept the breeze out; and that was a
shortcoming in my grandmother's estimation, she finding it intolerable that I should lose the benefit of a single hour of fresh air. So
she surreptitiously opened one of the windows, which had the effect
of blowing away the menus, newspapers, veils, and caps of the other
people having lunch, while she herself, invigorated by the bracing
breath from heaven, was as unruffled and full of smiles as Saint Blandine,[14] braving the abuse that increased my feelings of aloneness and

dejection and united the other guests against us in contempt, outrage, and dishevelment.

Some of these people (and this was a feature which, at the Balbec hotel, gave quite a marked regional character to the guests, those who frequent such grand establishments being usually unremarkable in their common wealth and cosmopolitanism) were eminent personalities in the principal *départements* of those parts, one of Caen's First Presidents, a *bâtonnier*[15] from Cherbourg, a notary of note in Le Mans, who at each holiday season, leaving the far-flung points where they spent their workaday lives as disbanded free spirits, or pawns on the chessboard of western France, foregathered in this hotel. They always reserved the same rooms; and with their wives, who had pretensions to aristocratic connection, they formed a small group that also included a celebrated lawyer and a famous doctor, both from Paris, who would say on the last day of vacation:

"Ah, yes, of course, we're not taking the same train, are we? How fortunate you are—home by lunchtime!"

"What do you mean, 'fortunate'? You're from the capital, Paris, the hub of the nation. Whereas our humble abode is a mere country town of a hundred thousand souls—I tell a lie: a hundred and two thousand at the last census! But what's that to you Parisians, with your two and a half million, your asphalted pavements, your metropolitan glamour?"

This would be spoken with a peasantlike rolling of the *r* and without provincial rancor, for these were men of some consequence in their part of the country, men who could have gone up to Paris like many another—the First President from Caen had several times been offered a seat on the bench of the Cour de Cassation[16]—but who had chosen to stay put, because of their fondness for their native town or a preference for obscurity or for basking in local glory, because they were reactionary or else enjoyed being on friendly terms with the owners of local châteaux. Not all of them went straight back to their county towns either.

The fact was that—since the Bay of Balbec was a little universe all to itself set amid the wider one, a posy of seasons composed of different sorts of days and many months, this meant that not only on days when one could see Rivebelle clearly (the sun shining on houses over there while the sky darkened over Balbec was a thunderstorm warning), but also when the colder weather had come to Balbec, one was always sure of two or three months more of warm days on that distant shore—each year, when rains and fogs promised the coming of autumn, those regulars at the Grand-Hôtel whose vacations started late or lasted a long time had their luggage hoisted onto a boat and sailed across to continue their summer at Rivebelle or Costedor. This little group at the Balbec hotel would look askance at any newcomers and, though seeming to take no interest in them, would interrogate their friend the headwaiter about them. Aimé by name, this headwaiter was there for the season every year and made sure they all had the tables they preferred. Each of their good ladies, knowing that Aimé's wife was expecting a baby, would work after mealtimes at making baby clothes, now and again glaring through their lorgnettes at my grandmother and me because we liked to have hard-boiled eggs in our salad, a taste known to be "common," quite unheard of among the best families of Alençon. They and their husbands affected a posture of ironic disdain toward a Frenchman whom everyone called "Your Majesty" and who had actually proclaimed himself king of the few savage tenants of a tiny islet in the South Seas. He was living at the hotel with his pretty mistress; and whenever she tripped out toward her bathing cabin, little boys would shout, "Hurrah for the Queen!," she being in the habit of tossing handfuls of half-franc pieces in their direction. The *bâtonnier* from Cherbourg and the First President from Caen did their best to appear not to see her; and if anyone in their acquaintance looked at her, they felt duty-bound to point out that she was a mere mill-girl.

"What? I was told they use the royal bathing machine at Ostend!"

"Well, of course! Anyone can rent it for twenty francs, you know. You could have it if you felt like it. I also have it on very good authority that he tried to get an audience with the King, who let him know it was out of the question for a real king to have anything to do with the likes of him!"

"Well, I never! The things you hear ... The people one meets nowadays!"

No doubt all this was true; but it was also because they were miffed by the knowledge that, for much of the world, they themselves were mere provincials unacquainted with this open-handed royal couple, that the notable notary, the First President, and the *bâtonnier* were so upset by witnessing what they called "a circus" and voiced aloud their indignation, which was no secret to their friend the headwaiter, who, though obliged to smile upon the more generous than genuine royals, made a point, as he took their order, of addressing a distant but meaning wink at his regular customers. There may also have been something of the same chagrin at being mistakenly thought less "smart" and being unable to explain that they were *more* "smart," in the "Pretty fellow!" with which they greeted the appearance of the young "masher," the consumptive prodigal son of a great industrialist, who drank champagne every day with his lunch, wearing a new jacket with an orchid in its buttonhole, then took his impassive pallor and smile of indifference off to the baccarat tables at the Casino, where he squandered a fortune— "Which he can ill afford to lose, believe you me," as the notary, with a knowing air, vouchsafed to the First President, whose wife had it "on the *very* best authority" that this deplorably *fin-de-siècle* young man would be the death of his long-suffering parents.

The *bâtonnier* and his friends also lavished sarcasm on the person of one old lady, rich and titled, because she would never travel without her entire household. Whenever the notary's wife and the good lady of the First President saw her at mealtimes in the dining room, they would hold up their eyeglasses and give her a good, long, insolent stare, with such an air of punctilious distaste and misgiving that she might have been a dish of pompous name and dubious appearance which, after subjecting it to a rigorous inspection, one waves away with a distant gesture and a grimace of disgust.

Presumably all they wished to show was that, though there might be some things they lacked, such as certain of the old lady's prerogatives and the fact of being acquainted with her, this was not because they could not aspire to them, but because they would not. But they had eventually come to convince themselves of the truth of this; and all desire for or curiosity about modes of life unknown to oneself, all hope of ever striking up new friendships, had been negated in these women and supplanted by a feigned disdain, a simulacrum of enjoyment of life, with the untoward effect that they called their displeasure satisfaction and had to lie to themselves all the time, two things that made for their constant unhappiness. But, then, no doubt everyone in that hotel behaved in the same way, albeit in different forms, sacrificing, if not to self-esteem at least to certain principles of breeding or habits of mind, the disquieting delights of mixing with unknown company. I have no doubt the little world to which the old lady restricted herself was free of the virulent embitterments and warped mockeries poisoning the lives of the wives of the notary and the First President. But her world, though it was fragrant with a fine old-fashioned perfume, was no less factitious than theirs. And if she had tried to please, if she had set out to win the mysterious regard of new people, which would have required her to renew herself too, she would most likely have experienced a charm that is absent from the twin pleasures of mixing only with one's own sort and reminding oneself that, one's own sort being the best sort, one can treat the ignorant disdain of others with the contempt it deserves. But perhaps she had sensed that, by arriving incognito at the Grand-Hôtel of Balbec, wearing her black woolen dress and her old-fashioned bonnet, she might startle a smile out of some roisterer recuperating in his rocking chair ("Ye gods! What a miserable old duck!") or more likely that some worthy with the open face and witty sparkle to the eye that she liked in a man, such as the First President's between his pepper-and-salt whiskers, would have instantly drawn the attention of the conjugal lorgnette's magnifying lens to the manifestation of this bizarre phenomenon; and so it may have been the old lady's unconscious apprehension of that moment of first encounter, which one knows is brief but dreads all the same, like the first time one dives into deep water, that made her send ahead a servant to inform the hotel of her character and her customs, then brusquely turn a deaf ear to the manager's speech of welcome, so as to move speedily, albeit more from shyness than pride, to her room, where curtains of her own instead of the hotel's hung at the windows, and where, what with her private screens and family photographs, instead of adapting to the outside world, she could erect between it and herself a bulkhead of habit so deftly constructed that it was her own home, with her inside it, that had done the traveling, and not her.

Then, having placed between herself and tradesmen not only the employees of the hotel but also her own servants, who took it upon themselves to deal with this new race of people and maintained the accustomed atmosphere about their mistress, having placed her prejudices between herself and the bathers, unperturbed at any offense she might give to people whom her friends would never have received, she continued to dwell in her own world, through exchanges of correspondence with these friends, through memory, through the private conviction she had of her own situation, of the quality of her own manners and the adequacy of her politeness. Every day, when she walked downstairs to take her carriage exercise, the footman who preceded her and the maidservant carrying her things who brought up the rear were like the guards who stand at the entrance of an embassy in the shade of the flag of the country it represents, and are the guarantors, in an alien land, of its privilege of extraterritoriality. On the day of our arrival, she did not leave her room until the middle of the afternoon; and we did not see her in the dining room, to which, in our capacity as newcomers, the manager himself condescended to conduct us, as a noncommissioned officer marches a pair of recruits to the quartermaster sergeant's to have them kitted out. However, we did see, after a moment, a squireen with his daughter, M. and Mlle de Stermaria, of an obscure but very old Breton family, at whose table, in the belief that they would not be back till that evening, we had been put. The sole purpose of their stay in Balbec being to meet certain landed families they knew in that district, the time they spent in the dining room of the hotel, what with the invitations they accepted and the return visits they received, was the shortest possible. Their arrogance protected them against any liking for their fellow man, against the slightest interest in the strangers sitting all about them, amid whom M. de Stermaria adopted the manner one has in the buffet car of a train, grim, hurried, standoffish, brusque, fastidious, and spiteful, surrounded by other passengers whom one has never seen before, whom one will never see again, and toward whom the only conceivable way of behaving is to make sure they keep away from one's cold chicken and stay out of one's chosen corner seat. My grandmother and I had barely started lunch when we were asked to change tables, on the order of M. de Stermaria, who had just arrived, and who, in a loud voice and without the slightest token of apology toward us, required the headwaiter to be sure not to let any such contretemps happen again, as he did not like the idea of his table being taken by "persons unknown to him."

There were other people (a certain actress, really better known for her elegance, her wit, and her collection of fine Dresden than for the few parts she had had at the Odéon; her lover, a very wealthy young man, for whose sake she had acquired her cultured tastes; and a pair of very visible aristocrats) whose preference for no company other than their own—they only ever traveled as a group, while at Balbec lunched very late, long after everyone else, then spent their days over cards in their private drawing room—was motivated not by ill will toward others but only by the requirements of the pleasure they took in a certain conversational bantering and in particular refined tastes in food and wines, which meant they could only enjoy things together, even mealtimes, and would have found it unbearable to spend their time with other people uninitiated into their preferences. Even when sitting at a dinner table or a gambling table, each of them needed to be sure that, in their fellow guest or partner at cards, there reposed in a suspended and latent form a certain shared knowledge enabling one to detect the fake furniture that in so many Parisian households passes for genuine medieval or Renaissance, and, in general, a common set of criteria for discriminating between the good and the bad. At such moments, the special element in which they wished to have their being could show only in an occasional witticism proffered amid the silence of the dinner party or the game, or in a charming new dress that the young actress had put on specially for lunchtime, or because they were going to play poker. But this element, by enveloping them in habits that were second nature to them, was enough to keep at bay the mysteries of life about them. Throughout the long afternoons, the sea hung before their eyes like a mere canvas of a pleasing shade on the wall of a well-to-do bachelor's sitting room; and it was only between hands that one of the players, for lack of anything better to do, would glance out at it for a glimpse of a fine day or a clue to what time it might be, then remind the others that it was nearly teatime. In the evenings, they never dined in the hotel, where the electric fountains gushed their light into the spacious dining room, turning it into an immense and wonderful aquarium, while, invisible in the outer shadows beyond the glass wall, the working classes of Balbec, the fishermen, and even middle-class families pressed against the windows, in an attempt to see the luxurious life of these denizens, glowing amid the golden sway of the eddies, all of it as weird and fascinating for the poor as the existence of strange fish and mollusks (but whether the glass barrier will go on protecting forever the feeding of the marvelous creatures, or whether the obscure onlookers gloating toward them from the outer dark will break into their aquarium and hook them for the pot, therein lies a great social question). In the meantime, perhaps among the nameless clusters in the night there may have been a writer, a fancier of human ichthyology who, at the spectacle of the closing jaws of old female monsters gulping down a bite of food, could enjoy classifying them by species, by innate characteristics, but also by acquired characteristics, which may mean that an old Serbian lady with a great ocean fish's mouth parts eats her lettuce—because since childhood she has swum in the fresh waters of the Faubourg Saint-Germain—like a La Rochefoucauld.

At that hour, one could see the three men in dinner suits waiting for the woman: she was late but, having rung the "lift" from her floor, wearing a new dress almost every night, with a scarf or a stole dictated by a taste peculiar to her lover, she would soon step out of the elevator as from a toybox. Then all four of them, who thought that the sprouting of this palatial international establishment at Balbec had fostered mere luxury rather than fine cuisine, clambered into a carriage and were driven off to dine a couple of miles away, at a small but highly regarded restaurant, where they would have interminable consultations with the chef on the composition of the evening's menu and the preparation of the different dishes. And as they drove, the road from Balbec, lined by apple trees, was mere mileage—not very different in the dark from the distance separating their houses in Paris from the Café Anglais or the Tour d'Argent—which they had to cover in order to reach the smart little restaurant, where they would sit among friends who envied the wealthy young man his possession of such a well-dressed mistress, and where her scarves drew a sort of sleek perfumed veil over the little group, while secluding it from the rest of the world.

Unfortunately for my peace of mind, I was quite unlike all these people: I was greatly concerned about many of them. I wished not to be so ignored by a man with a low forehead and a pair of shifty eyes flitting between the blinkers of his prejudices and breeding, who was the first gentleman of those parts, none other than Legrandin's brother-in-law, who occasionally came into Balbec, and whose wife's weekly garden party deprived the hotel of a contingent of its inhabitants each Sunday, one or two of them because they were invited to these functions, and many others who, so as not to appear to have been excluded from them, chose that day to go on a lengthy outing. The first day he turned up at the hotel he had had a very poor reception, as the staff had only recently arrived from the Riviera and had no idea who he was. Not only was he not wearing white flannel but, unused to the ways of such grandiose establishments, he had removed his hat, in his old-fashioned French manner, as soon as he stepped into a vestibule with women in it, which was why the manager had not so much as tipped his to him as they spoke, in the belief that this must be someone of no social importance, what he called "a man of no extraction." The only person who had viewed him with some favor was the wife of the notable notary, who, sensing in him the stilted vulgarity of the prim and proper, had declared, with all the infallible and authoritative insight of one whose acuity had been acquired through long contact with the very best circles of Le Mans society, that one could see at a glance that here was a man of great distinction and impeccable breeding, a man who was a cut above everybody else one might meet at Balbec (all of whom she deemed it impossible to be seen with, until she started to be seen with them). This favorable judgment of hers on the brother-in-law of Legrandin was perhaps inspired by the drab demeanor of a man who was anything but imposing, or perhaps by the fact that in this gentleman farmer with the look of a sexton her clericalism had read the secret signs that showed he was a kindred spirit.

Even though I soon learned that the young horsemen who rode past the hotel every day were the sons of a dishonest tradesman—he owned a drapery-and-fancy-goods business—whom my father would never have condescended to know, the fact of being "on vacation at the seaside" made them equestrian statues of demigods in my eyes; and the best I could hope for was that they would never deign to notice my own paltry person, who had nothing to do other than exchange a seat in the hotel dining room for a seat on the sands. I wanted to be liked, even by the adventurer who had been king of a desert island in the South Seas, even by the consumptive young "masher," who I imagined was really hiding a diffident and loving nature behind a standoffish appearance, and would have been capable of lavishing on me alone all the unspent treasures of his friendship. Moreover—and it is usually the opposite of this that one hears in accounts of holiday relationships—since being seen about with certain people, at a resort that one revisits from time to time, may give one a certain cachet that has no equivalent in real society, the social world of Paris, rather than discouraging relationships struck up at the seaside, in fact cultivates nothing more sedulously. I was anxious about the esteem in which I was held by all these personages of temporary or local importance; and, in my habit of putting myself in others' shoes and viewing the world as they must view it, I saw them not as occupying their proper rank, the one they would have had in Paris, say, which would have been a very lowly one, but the one they must believe was theirs by rights, and which actually *was* theirs in Balbec, where the lack of a common yardstick endowed them with a mode of relative superiority and a pregnant interest. Sad to say, the contempt of none of these people wounded me so deeply as that of M. de Stermaria.

I had noticed his daughter as soon as she came in, the bluish pallor of her pretty face, her height and distinctive way of carrying herself, her gait, all of which brought accurately to mind her lineage and aristocratic upbringing, all the more acutely because I knew her name—like those evocative themes invented by gifted composers which, for any listeners who have already glanced at the score and set their imagination on the right track, bring vividly to the mind's eye the shimmer of a flame, the rippling murmur of a stream, the calm of the countryside. "Breeding" enhanced the charms of Mlle de Stermaria, added to them the knowledge of their cause, made them more intelligible and more complete. It also made them more desirable, with its hint that they were possibly out of my reach, as a high price adds to the value of an object we find attractive. The hereditary strain imbued her complexion with choice savors, the tang of an exotic fruit, the bouquet of a fine vintage.

It was chance that afforded my grandmother and myself a way of endowing ourselves, in the eyes of all the hotel's inhabitants, with instantaneous prestige. On our very first day there, as the old lady came down from her apartments, radiating an influence, through the footman before her and the maidservant scurrying after with a forgotten book and blanket, which affected every mind, inspiring curiosity and respect in all, visibly more so in M. de Stermaria than in anyone else, the manager leaned toward my grandmother and in a kindly way, as one points out the Shah of Persia or Queen Ranavalona of Madagascar to some obscure bystander, who cannot possibly have the slightest link with the potentate but may be intrigued to realize who it is passing by, murmured to her, "The Marquise de Villeparisis," and at that very moment the old lady, catching sight of my grandmother, gave a start of joy and surprise.

The sudden appearance, in the guise of a little old lady, of the most influential of fairy godmothers could not have caused me greater pleasure, devoid as I was of any device to bring myself closer to Mlle de Stermaria in a place where I knew no one. No one, I mean, of any practical assistance. The aesthetic range available to the human countenance being so narrow, one frequently has the pleasure, wherever one may be, of meeting faces known to one, without needing to seek them out, as Swann did, in the paintings of old masters. So it was that, in the very first days of our stay at Balbec, I had happened upon first Legrandin, then Swann's concierge, and finally Mme Swann herself, turned into a waiter in a café, a visiting foreigner whom I never set eyes on again, and a bathing monitor. There is a sort of magnetism that brings together, and keeps together, certain features of physiognomy and mentality, so that when Nature fits such a person into a different body, it does so without much mutilation. Though transformed into a waiter, Legrandin had kept his stature, the line of his nose, and a part of his chin; Mme Swann, though she had undergone a sex change and was a bathing monitor, had retained her usual facial features and even something of her own ways of speaking. However, even with her red belt and waving her flag to warn swimmers out of the water at the slightest swell (bathing monitors being cautious creatures, so few of them being themselves swimmers), she was of no more help to me in the present circumstances than she would have been in the *Life of Moses* fresco, where Swann had once noticed her disguised as Jethro's daughter. Mme de Villeparisis, however, was there in person; not only had no spell stripped her of her power, but she could actually cast a spell on my power, greatly increasing it and enabling me in an instant, as though on the wings of some fabled bird, to sweep over the infinite social distance—infinite in Balbec, at least—separating me from Mlle de Stermaria.

Unfortunately, it would have been impossible to find a person who lived more enclosed within her own little world than my grandmother. It was not that she would have despised me, she would not even have understood me, if she had realized that the good opinion of, and personal acquaintance with, people whose very existence she had not even noticed, whose names she would never have found out by the time she left Balbec, were for me matters of consuming interest; I did not dare tell her that, if only these people could see her chatting with Mme de Villeparisis, I would be overcome with pleasure, because I sensed that being friends with the Marquise, who had such prestige within the hotel, would have greatly enhanced our own in the eyes of Mlle de Stermaria. Not that I thought of my grandmother's old friend as someone belonging to the aristocracy: I was too used to hearing her name spoken at home during my childhood, at a time long before I had given any conscious thought to it; and the title she bore was only an added strangeness, rather like that conferred by an unusual first name or one of those noble names given to Paris streets, like the rue Lord-Byron, the rue de Gramont, or the rue de Rochechouart, which has come down in the world, none of them any nobler than the names of ordinary streets, such as the rue Léonce-Reynaud or the rue Hippolyte-Lebas. The name of Mme de Villeparisis conjured up no special world for me, any more than did the name of her cousin Mac-Mahon, someone no different from M. Carnot, who like him had been a president of the Republic, or from Raspail, whose photograph Françoise had bought along with that of Pius IX. For my grandmother, however, it was a matter of principle that when you go on vacation, you sever relations with people; you do not go to the seaside to meet people, there is plenty of time for that in Paris; they just make you squander in trite civilities the invaluable time you should be spending exclusively in the open air, communing with the waves. So, finding it convenient to believe that her view on this was shared by everyone else, that it allowed old friends whose paths happened to cross in a hotel lobby to maintain the polite fiction of a reciprocal incognito, when the manager murmured the name of Mme de Villeparisis, my grandmother saw fit to glance away and appear not to see her old friend, whereupon the latter, sensing that my grandmother was not in the mood for a reunion, also averted her eyes. As she walked away, I stood there as forlorn as a shipwrecked mariner who has watched the approach of a vessel, which then sails on its way without rescuing him.

Mme de Villeparisis also took her meals in the dining room, but she sat right at the other end. She was unacquainted with anyone who was staying in the hotel or who occasionally visited it, even with M. de Cambremer: I noticed that he did not greet her, one day when he and his wife came to lunch at the invitation of the *bâtonnier* from Cherbourg, who, intoxicated by the heady honor of having this noble at his table with him, made sure to keep away from his everyday acquaintances, at whom he just winked from a distance, to mark the historic occasion, but discreetly enough for them not to take this as permission to come over.

"So we're hobnobbing now, are we?" the wife of the First President from Caen said to him that evening. "Mixing with the upper crust, is that it?"

"Upper crust? Why on earth?" the *bâtonnier* asked, masking his delight with a show of astonishment. "What—oh, you mean my guests?" he added, unable to keep up the pretense. "But what's 'hobnobbing' in having some friends to lunch? They've got to have their lunch somewhere!"

"Of course it's the upper crust! They're the *de* Cambremers, aren't they?[17] I knew it was them. The wife's a marquise. In her own right. Not from the distaff side."

"She's a very unspoiled lady, you know, quite charming. A less stuck-up person would be hard to find. I thought you might come over. I tried to tip you the wink. I could have introduced you!" said the *bâtonnier*, moderating with a slight irony the enormity of the suggestion, like Aha-suerus saying to Esther, "So now must I give you half of my Estate?"[18]

"No, no! We're shy, retiring little violets!"

"Well, take it from me, you should really have come over," said the *bâtonnier* from Cherbourg, full of boldness now that the danger was past. "They wouldn't have eaten you. So—is it time for our little hand at bézique?"

"But of course! We were reluctant to suggest it, now that you're rubbing shoulders with marquises!"

"Oh, come now! I do assure you, there's nothing very special about them! Look, I'm supposed to go there to dinner tomorrow night. Would you like to go instead of me? I mean it sincerely, I really do! Honestly, I wouldn't at all mind just staying here."

"Out of the question! I'd be turned off the bench as a reactionary!" exclaimed the First President, guffawing at his own joke; then he added, to the notary, "But of course you're on visiting terms up at Féterne."

"Well, yes, I do go up there on Sundays. It's in one door and out the other, actually. But they don't come and have lunch with me, unlike our *bâtonnier* here."

M. de Stermaria was away from Balbec that day, to the great chagrin of the *bâtonnier*. However, he had a quiet word with the headwaiter: "Aimé, would you mind dropping the hint to M. de Stermaria that he's not the only noble who has graced this dining room? You saw that gentleman lunching with me this forenoon? Toothbrush mustache, military bearing? The Marquis de Cambremer no less!"

"Is that so? Well, I'm not surprised!"

"That would let him know he's not the only one with a title. Take that, eh? Do these nobilities good to be taken down a peg or two from time to time! Actually, Aimé, if you'd rather not say anything, then don't bother. I wasn't speaking my own views there, you understand. And, anyway, he knows the man quite well."

The following day, M. de Stermaria, who knew that the *bâtonnier* had on one occasion represented a friend of his in court, introduced himself.

"Our mutual friends the de Cambremers had been trying to bring us together, but it was never the right day for both of us, or something of that kind," said the *bâtonnier*, who was like many another liar in imagining that no one will bother to check such an insignificant detail; yet, if chance puts anyone in possession of the humble fact that contradicts the detail, it can be enough to damn a character and spoil trust forever.

As usual, though more easily now that her father's conversation with the *bâtonnier* had left her to her own devices, I sat and watched Mlle de Stermaria. One was struck not only by the eye-catching singularity and beauty of her every posture, as when she set both elbows on the table, her raised glass poised above her forearms, but also by the curt glance from an eye that let itself be only briefly caught, by a voice in which one sensed an underlying inbred hardness, barely masked by her individual inflections, which had irked my grandmother, as though Mlle de Stermaria had inherited some sort of preset ancestral mechanism which after any expression of a private view, in a look or an intonation, automatically brought her back to neutral; and the observer's mind was forever drawn to the lineage that had handed down to her such a dearth of simple humanity, such deficiency in sensitivity, such meanness of spirit just below the surface. Yet, from certain soft gleams that flitted across her eye only to be quickly dulled, in which one could sense the almost humble docility that a penchant for the pleasures of the flesh gives to the haughtiest woman, who soon values only one thing in the world, and that thing is any man who affords her those pleasures, possibly just an actor or some paltry entertainer for whose sake one day she may even be prepared to leave her husband; and from a certain shade of sensual pink that bloomed on her pale cheeks, reminiscent of the blushes that glowed in the heart of the water lilies on the Vivonne, I suspected she might not mind letting me be the one to taste on her person the poetic flavor of the life she led in Brittany, a life which, whether through a surfeit of habit, an innate distinction, or her displeasure at the poverty or avarice of her family, she seemed to find uninspiring, but which even so she contained within her body. From the meager reserve of willpower which she had inherited, and which gave something craven to her expression, she might not have been able to summon up very vigorous resistance. The gray felt hat she invariably wore at mealtimes, with its pretentious and rather out-of-fashion plume, endeared her to me a little, not because it suited her complexion of pink and silver, but because, by letting me see her as impoverished, it brought her closer to my own level. It was just possible that, though constrained in the presence of her father to follow convention in the attitudes she adopted, but with principles different from his for the perceiving and classifying of other people, she saw in me not lowly rank but sex and youth. If only M. de Stermaria would go on an outing one day without her, and especially if Mme de Villeparisis had chosen that day to come and sit at our table and thus given Mlle de Stermaria an opinion of me that might make me bold enough to approach her, perhaps we might have been able to exchange a few words, arrange to meet, strike up an acquaintance. If her parents had left her to herself for a month in her romantic Breton château, we might have been able to wander alone in the gloaming, by the darkening waters, where the pinkish heather would have a softer glow under the oaks lashed by the leaping waves. Together we could ramble about her island fastness, which was steeped in so much charm for me because it had bounded the banal days of Mlle de Stermaria, and because the memory of it would haunt her eyes forever. It felt as though I could never properly possess her anywhere else, as though I would have to trespass on the places that surrounded her with so many memories, as though these memories were a veil that my desire for her would have to strip away, one of those that are drawn between a woman and certain men by Nature (with the same purpose that makes it interpose the act of reproduction between all its creatures and their keenest pleasure, setting between the insect and the nectar it desires the pollen it must carry away) so that, misled by the illusion of possessing her more completely in that way, they feel compelled first to take possession of the landscapes among which she lives and which, though much more fruitful for the imagination than the sensual pleasure, would not have sufficed without it to attract them.

I had to look away from Mlle de Stermaria, whose father—presumably believing that making a person's acquaintance was a peculiar, perfunctory act, accomplished in a single movement, lending itself to no development worthy of a man's interest, beyond a mere handshake and a sharp glance, neither requiring conversation on the spot nor leading to any later intercourse—had now taken his leave of the *bâtonnier* and was on his way back to sit across from his daughter, rubbing his hands together like a man who has just had a windfall. As for the *bâtonnier,* once the initial excitement of the encounter had subsided, he was to be heard, as on other days, saying to the headwaiter:

"I'm not a king, you know, Aimé—go away and serve the King! I say, Your Worship, just look at those little trout—why don't we ask Aimé for some of them! Aimé, I must say, those little fish of yours look very irresistible! Why don't you bring us some of them, Aimé? We'll help ourselves!"

He kept repeating the name Aimé; and whenever he had a guest to dinner, the latter would say, "Well, I can see you're highly regarded hereabouts," and would take to dropping the name of Aimé too, in accordance with that propensity certain people have, part shyness, part vulgarity, part foolishness, to believe it is smart and amusing to behave exactly like someone they happen to be with. The *bâtonnier*'s incessant repetitions of Aimé's name were always accompanied by a smile, as he was pleased to show not only that he was in the headwaiter's good graces but also that the latter was beneath him. At every mention of his name, the headwaiter also showed in a smile how touched and proud he was, how much he appreciated the honor and shared in the joke.

Daunting as mealtimes always were for me in the Grand-Hôtel's immense dining room, which was usually full, they turned into an even greater ordeal with the arrival for a stay of a few days of the owner (or possibly just a managing director elected by a body of shareholders) not just of this palace but also of seven or eight others established in widely separated parts of the country, who would turn up from time to time at one or another of them and spend a week there. Every evening, shortly after the beginning of dinner, through the entrance to the dining room would come a small man with white hair and a red nose, strikingly proper and impersonal, known, it was said, from London to Monte Carlo as one of Europe's premier hotel proprietors. On one occasion, having slipped out just as dinner was beginning, I found he was there when I came back in: he gave me a little bow, presumably to acknowledge that I was under his roof, but the stiffness of his manner made me wonder whether it expressed the reserve of the man who knows his own importance or the disdain deserved by the insignificant customer. With customers who were themselves people of importance, the managing director's bow was just as stiff, but much deeper, and he lowered his eyelids with an appearance of muted respect, as he might have done at a funeral service when condoling with the father of the deceased or contemplating Holy Communion. Apart from these cold and infrequent bows, he made no movement whatsoever, as though to show that his eyes, which were very bright and seemed to protrude, could be aware of all things, dominate all things, and make sure that all things, from the tiniest finishing touch to the broad effect of the whole, combined to make a perfect "Dinner at the Grand-Hôtel." It was clear that he saw himself as no mere stage manager or orchestral conductor, but as a commander-in-chief. In the belief that he needed nothing but a gaze of the greatest intensity to know that everything was in order, that, whoever might blunder, defeat could not ensue, and so as to shoulder every single one of his responsibilities, not only did he make no gestures, he even kept his eyes quite still, fixed in a stare of concentration, encompassing and directing the entire theater of operations. I suspected that the very movements of my soupspoon did not escape his notice; and even if he went away soon after the soup, the result of his tour of inspection was that he took away with him my appetite for the rest of dinner. His own appetite was excellent, as could be seen at lunch, when he sat in the dining room at the same time as all the other guests, as though he were no one special. The table at which he sat was distinguished by a single peculiarity: as he ate, the other manager, the ordinary one, stood by his side making conversation. Being the managing director's subordinate, he sought to flatter him and went in great fear of him. My own fear of him was less acute at lunchtimes, because when he sat like that among all his customers he had the discreet air of a general who happens to be sitting in a restaurant where some of his troops are eating, but pretends not to notice them. All the same, I breathed more freely when the commissionaire, surrounded by his pages and porters, announced: "He's off again tomorrow morning. First to Dinard, then on to Biarritz, and over to Cannes."

My life in the hotel was now not only sad, because I knew so few people, but also inconvenient, because Françoise knew so many. Her contacts should perhaps have made many things easier for us. In fact, they did the opposite. Although members of the working classes had great difficulty in being treated as acquaintances by Françoise, and could manage to achieve this only at the cost of extreme politeness toward her, once they had been accepted by her, they became the only people to whom she accorded the slightest importance. Her time-honored code held that she owed no deference to any of the friends of her employers and that, if she was pressed for time, she could refuse to bandy words with a lady inquiring about my grandmother. However, her ways of dealing with her own acquaintances—that is, with the few lower-class persons who were the beneficiaries of her infrequent friendships—were governed by the most delicate and inflexible protocol. For example, having struck up relationships with the hotel's coffee waiter and with a young chambermaid who did some sewing for a Belgian lady, Françoise gave up her practice of going back upstairs to attend to my grandmother as soon as lunch was over, delaying her return by a full hour, because the coffee waiter wanted to make her a cup of coffee or *tisane* down in the pantry, or the chambermaid had suggested she come and watch her sew, and to decline such offers was out of the question, was quite simply not done. The young chambermaid was particularly deserving of this sort of propriety, as she was an orphan who had been brought up by people not of her family, and she occasionally went to spend some days with them. This circumstance brought out all of Françoise's pity and benevolent disdain. She, who had a family to belong to, a little farmhouse handed down by her parents where a brother of hers kept a few cows, could never have considered such a person, quite without roots, to be her equal. As the girl was looking forward to the mid-August holiday and the chance to go and stay with her foster family, Françoise could not contain herself: "She makes me laugh, really. 'I'll be home,' she says, 'for the fifteenth of August,' she says— *home*! And it's not even hers! It's just some folks that took her in, and there she is, going on about 'home' as if it was a real one! The poor girl! Imagine being so badly off that you haven't even got a home to call your own!" But if Françoise's new friends had been only chambermaids in the employ of guests at the hotel, who ate with her in the guests' servants' quarters, and assumed from her lovely lace cap and her fine profile that she must be a real lady, possibly of noble birth but now living in reduced circumstances, or else choosing from affection to live as lady's companion to my grandmother; if Françoise had limited her acquaintance, that is, to people who did not belong to the hotel, the inconvenience would not have been very great, as she could not then have prevented them from being of service to us, for the simple reason that there were no conceivable circumstances in which, whether acquainted or unacquainted with her, they might have been of any service to us at all. However, she had also got to know one of the wine stewards, a kitchen assistant, and a housekeeper from one of the floors. The result of this for our daily arrangements was that, whereas at the very beginning of her stay Françoise, knowing no one, had kept ringing for the most trivial of reasons, at times when my grandmother and I would never have dared to ring—and if we raised some mild objection to this, she replied, "Well, we're paying them enough!," as though she herself were footing the bills—now that she was on friendly terms with one of the personalities from below stairs, a thing that had initially seemed to augur well for our comfort if either of us happened to have cold feet in bed, she would not countenance the idea of ringing, even at times that were in no way inappropriate; she said it would "put them out," it would mean the furnaces would have to be relit or the servants' dinner hour would be disturbed, and they would not like that. She would enforce her pronouncements with a form of words which, despite her unsure way of delivering it, was abundantly clear in the way it put us in the wrong: "The fact is . . ." Whereupon we would desist, so as not to make her come out with another one of far greater severity for us: "It's the limit!" The long and the short of it was that we had to make do without proper hot water because Françoise was a friend of the man whose job it was to heat it.

We too, eventually, found a friend, despite and because of my grandmother. She and Mme de Villeparisis, finding themselves face-to-face one morning in a doorway, were at last obliged to exchange greetings, but only after exchanging gestures of surprise and hesitation, going through a pantomime of standing back and doubting, then at length coming together with glad cries and polite exclamations, like a pair of actors in a scene by Molière who have been standing apart from one another, each delivering a soliloquy and supposedly not seeing the other, though there is no more than a few feet between them, and who suddenly catch sight of each other, cannot believe their eyes, start speaking at the same time, interrupting each other, all this under the eyes of the chorus, before at last falling into each other's arms. After a moment's conversation, Mme de Villeparisis tried tactfully to pass by; but my grandmother suggested they sit together until lunchtime, with the aim of discovering how she managed to have her mail delivered earlier than we did and be treated to such excellent grills (as a connoisseur of fine cuisine, Mme de Villeparisis was unimpressed by the fare offered by the hotel, where we were served meals that my grandmother would describe, with one of her quotations from Mme de Sévigné, as "so sumptuous that you starve").[19] Every day from then on, the Marquise took to spending a moment with us in the dining room, sitting at our table until her own meal was served, insisting that we not stand at her approach, that we should not put ourselves out in any way on her account. Sometimes, after we had finished eating, we sat on with her, chatting, at the squalid moment when knives and crumpled napkins lie about on the tablecloth. I sat there trying to look far beyond this scene, casting my eyes seaward in an attempt to preserve my attachment to Balbec and the idea that I was now on the farthest extremity of the land, scanning the waves for Baudelaire's words, and paying no attention to the table, unless it was one of those days when we were served a giant fish, a sea monster, which, unlike the knives and forks, came to us straight from the primitive ages when wildlife first began to teem in the Ocean, in the days of the Cimmerians,[20] where its body, with its countless vertebrae, its pink-and-blue nerves, though put together by Nature, had been built to an architectural design, like a polychromatic cathedral of the deep.

Just as a barber, seeing that an officer to whose hair he gives special attention has recognized another customer who has just come in and stands chatting with him, cannot help smiling as he goes to fetch the soap bowl, because he is pleased to realize they belong to the same circles, and pleased too that his establishment is not a mere barbershop but a place where the most down-to-earth needs are compatible with the most refined pleasures of sociability, so Aimé, seeing that Mme de Villeparisis was treating us like old friends, went to fetch our *rince-bouches* with the tactfully knowing smile, full of subdued pride, of the hostess who knows when her guests can do without her. His expression, happy and touched, was that of a father doting on the joy of a young couple whose futures have been plighted at his dinner table. To bring this look of happiness to Aimé's face, one needed only to speak the name of a titled person; and in this he was the opposite of Françoise, in whose hearing one could not mention "Count This" or "Viscount That" without her expression's turning dark and her voice's sounding curt and sour, which actually meant she cherished the nobility not less than Aimé but more. Also, Françoise had the quality which, in other people, she always found so unforgivable: she was proud. She was not of Aimé's breed, amiable and full of good cheer. If you tell them about some intriguing circumstance which is new to them, which they have never read about in the newspaper, say, the pleasure they feel and show is wholehearted. But Françoise preferred never to appear surprised. If one said in her presence that the Archduke Rudolf, of whom she had never even heard, was not really dead, as was universally assumed to be the case, but still alive,[21] she would have replied, "True," as though she had known about it for ages. Moreover, if Françoise was able to resist an impulse to anger on hearing the name of a noble spoken even by us (whom she humbly called her "masters," to whom she was, in most things, entirely subservient), it was very likely because the lineage from which she sprang had enjoyed a comfortable, independent position in her village, rivaled for good esteem only by the sort of noble family in whose household the likes of Aimé would have been employed since childhood as a servant, or who might even have taken him in as an act of charity. So, in the eyes of Françoise, Mme de Villeparisis might well have been expected to apologize for being of noble birth. However, at least in France, being forgiven their nobility is not only the talent of lords and ladies, it is their sole occupation. Françoise, after the manner of servants, who are constantly accumulating fragmentary observations about the relations between their masters and other people, from which they draw sometimes faulty deductions—as humans do about the lives of animals—was forever jumping to the conclusion that we had been "slighted," a notion inspired as much by her exaggerated love for us as by her delight in being unpleasant to us. But once she had unmistakably registered Mme de Villeparisis's countless little acts of considerateness toward us, and even toward herself, Françoise forgave her for being a marquise; and since she had never ceased being grateful to her for being a marquise, Mme de Villeparisis was her favorite of all the people we knew. The fact was that none of these people took such constant trouble to be pleasant. If my grandmother merely remarked on a book that Mme de Villeparisis was reading, or exclaimed at a gift of fine fruit sent to her by a friend, an hour later a footman came upstairs with the book or the fruit. Then, the next time we saw her, she would receive our thanks as though trying to excuse her kind gift on the grounds of some special usefulness it might have, saying only, "It's no masterpiece, but with the newspapers arriving here so late, one must have something to read," or "At the seaside it's always best to have fruit one can be sure of."

"You know, I have the impression that you never eat oysters," Mme de Villeparisis said to us one day, increasing the distaste I felt at that time, as I was more disgusted by the thought of the living flesh of oysters than I was by the sticky remains of jellyfish littering the beach at Balbec. "You really should–they're magnificent on this stretch of the coast! And I must tell my maid to fetch your letters when she goes down for mine. You mean to tell me your daughter writes to you *every* day! What on earth can you find to say to each other?" To this my grandmother said nothing, perhaps because she could not bring herself to speak of it to someone incapable of sympathizing with Mme de Sévigné, whose words she would quote to my mother: "Each time I receive your letter, I wish straight away I could receive another one. They are the breath of life to me. Few people are worthy of understanding what I feel."[22] I was afraid she might even apply to Mme de Villeparisis the conclusion: "Of these happy few I seek the company, avoiding all others." My grandmother chose instead to praise the fruit sent up to us by Mme de Villeparisis the day before. It was so good that even the manager, mastering the discomfiture caused by our disdain for his fruit dishes, had said to me, "I'm just like you–I regale in fruit more than any other dessert." My grandmother told her friend that she had savored it even more because of the generally inferior quality of the fruit served in the hotel: "So I can't honestly say, like Mme de Sévigné, that if we were perverse enough to want bad fruit we should have to send to Paris." "Yes, of course, you're reading Mme de Sévigné. I've seen you carrying her *Letters* about with you ever since you've been here." (She was forgetting that she had never set eyes on my grandmother until their meeting in the doorway.) "So you don't think all that concern for the daughter is just a bit overdone? If you ask me, she talks about it too much for it to be quite sincere. There's a lack of naturalness in her." My grandmother, feeling that it was futile to disagree, and so as not to have to speak of things she loved to someone whose mind was closed to them, concealed her copy of Mme de Beausergent's *Mémoires* by laying her handbag on top of the book.

If Mme de Villeparisis happened to meet Françoise when the latter was going down (at "twelve o'clock time," in Françoise's parlance), wearing her neat cap and amid universal esteem, to lunch in the guests' servants' quarters, she would pause with her on the stairs and ask after us. When Françoise told us about it later, she would say, with an attempt to imitate Mme de Villeparisis's voice, "And she said to me, 'And be sure to not forget to tell them I was asking after them,' she said." Françoise was clearly convinced that she was faithfully reproducing the very words uttered by Mme de Villeparisis, though she distorted them no less than Plato distorted those of Socrates, or Saint John those of Christ. She was naturally very impressed by the interest that Mme de Villeparisis took in her. Not that she believed my grandmother, who she knew was lying out of class solidarity (these rich, always sticking together!), when she said Mme de Villeparisis had once been a great beauty. It was true there were very few vestiges left of this beauty; and to reconstruct from them the glory that was gone, Françoise would have had to be more of an artist than she was. To see how pretty an old woman once was, it is not enough just to look at each feature; they must be translated.

"I must remember to ask her one day whether I'm wrong in thinking she'd got some family connection with the Guermantes," my grandmother said, to my indignation. What possible common origin could there be in two names that had entered my experience in such dissimilar ways, one of them via the low, undignified door of the everyday, the other through the golden portals of the imagination?

For some days past, a tall and beautiful woman with red hair and a rather prominent nose had been seen about in a very grand carriage: the Princess of Luxembourg, who had come down from town to spend a few weeks in the vicinity. Her barouche had drawn up outside the hotel, a footman had come in to talk to the manager, had gone back to the carriage, and had then carried in a magnificent basket of fruit which, like the Bay of Balbec itself, combined a range of seasons, as well as a card bearing the legend *The Princess of Luxembourg* and a few words added in pencil. Which princely traveler, living incognito in our hotel, was being sent such glaucous plums, their glowing roundness swelling to match the sea at that very moment, such translucent grapes hanging like a bright autumn day on their dried-up twig, pears of such celestial ultramarine? It was not possible that the person whom the Princess had been intending to visit was the old friend of my grandmother. And yet, the following evening, Mme de Villeparisis sent us the bunch of cool golden grapes, with some plums and pears that we also recognized, although the plums, like the sea about dinnertime, had started to shade toward mauve, and the bluish surface of the pears now reflected patches of pink cloud. A few days later, we met Mme de Villeparisis at the end of the symphony concert given each morning down at the beach. I was convinced that the music I heard there (the prelude to *Lohengrin*, the overture to *Tannhäuser*, etc.) expressed the most exalted truths; and in my efforts to comprehend them I strove upward, I yearned toward them, I drew the best out of my deepest self to offer up to them.

We were coming up from the concert and turning our steps toward the hotel, pausing for a moment on the esplanade with Mme de Villeparisis, who told us she had ordered "rarebits" and creamed eggs for our lunch, when I caught sight of the Princess of Luxembourg, still quite a way off, but coming in our direction. As she walked, she was almost leaning on a sunshade, in a way that gave to her tall and wonderful body a slight inclination, a long undulation, so much a part of women who were beautiful during the Second Empire, whose drooping shoulders and raised back, gaunt hips and slow, fluid stride swayed a silky ripple through their whole person, as though an invisible, inflexible rod slanted through their bodies and they were trying at each step to drape themselves about it. When she went out for her morning stroll along the esplanade, it was always about the time when everyone else who had been down for a swim was coming back up for lunch; and, her own lunchtime being half past one, she never got back to her villa until long after the bathers had abandoned the esplanade, which stretched empty before her in the full glare of the sun. Mme de Villeparisis introduced my grandmother to her; but when it was my turn to be introduced, unable to remember my surname, she had to ask me what it was. She may actually never have known, or, if she had, she had forgotten years before the name of the man to whom my grandmother had married her daughter. On hearing it now, Mme de Villeparisis seemed much struck by it. The Princess of Luxembourg, having shaken hands, stood chatting with the Marquise, glancing tenderly now and then at my grandmother and me with an expression full of the incipient kiss that rises to lips which smile at a baby with his nanny. Despite her wish not to appear to dwell in spheres far above ours, she must have misjudged the distance between us; and her eyes, not properly adjusted, overflowed with such loving sweetness that I would not have been surprised if she had reached out a hand and patted us, as though we were a brace of docile animals, poking our heads through the railings at the Zoo in the Bois de Boulogne. This idea of being animals in the Zoo was instantly underlined for me. It was the hour when hawkers of sweets, cakes, and other delicacies haunt the esplanade, barking their wares in strident tones. At a loss to show her goodwill toward us in a fitting manner, the Princess stopped the next one who came along. All he had left was a little loaf of rye bread, the sort you feed to the ducks. The Princess took it, saying to me, "This is for your grandmother." But she then handed it to me, with a smile full of feeling: "You be the one to give it to her," meaning no doubt that my enjoyment would be greater if nobody came between me and the animals. Other hawkers having gathered around us, she filled my pockets with all sorts of things, little surprise packages tied with string, rolled wafers, babas, barley sugars: "These are for you to eat. But you must let your grandmother have some too." The hawkers were paid, at the Princess's behest, by the little black boy in a red satin suit who always walked behind her, to the amazement of the whole seafront. Taking leave of Mme de Villeparisis, she proffered us a hand once again, trying to show that she treated her friends and the friends of her friends exactly alike, and that she had not lost the common touch. This time, however, her expression was aimed at not quite so lowly a level in the hierarchy of creatures; and the equality she shared with us was signified to my grandmother in the doting, motherly smile with which one takes leave of a small boy when pretending he is a grown-up. My grandmother, by a vast stride of evolution, had stopped being a duck or an antelope and had turned into what Mme Swann would have termed, in her best English, a *baby*. Having taken her leave of us, the Princess of Luxembourg, with the slow undulations of her magnificent figure, took up again her interrupted stroll along the sun-drenched esplanade, her whole person winding itself around the rolled-up blue-and-white sunshade she held in her hand, as a snake coils about a wand. She was my very first highness, not counting Princess Mathilde, who in any case had nothing high and mighty about her. My second one, as will be seen, was to astonish me just as much by her graciousness. I was to become acquainted with one mode of the civility of the great the very next day, when Mme de Villeparisis gave us this report: "She thought you were both just charming. She's a woman of great discernment, and her heart's in the right place. She's quite unlike your ordinary highness or royal—she's a woman of genuine qualities." To which she added, with an expression of conviction, very pleased at being able to say so: "I expect she would be delighted to meet you again."

I was even more struck by something else Mme de Villeparisis said that very forenoon, shortly after the Princess of Luxembourg had left us, and which had nothing to do with civility.

"Aren't you the son of the department head at the Ministry? Well, I must say I hear your father is a charming man. And he's off on a nice trip at present."

A few days before, a letter from my mother had told us that my father and his traveling companion M. de Norpois had lost all their luggage.

"It has turned up, or, rather, it was never lost in the first place. You'll never guess what happened," Mme de Villeparisis said, seeming inexplicably better informed than either of us about the details of my father's journey. "I think your father will return home early, next week, since he will probably decide not to go on to Algeciras. However, he does want to have one day longer in Toledo, being a great admirer of one of Titian's pupils—the name escapes me, but if you want to see his best things, you've got to go there."

I was left wondering by what strange chance Mme de Villeparisis was able, given the dark and distant glass through which she looked at the rudimentary, insignificant, and uncertain doings of the host of people known to her, to focus on my father through a tiny area of lens of such prodigious magnification that she could gaze in close-up and with so much detail at what was charming about him, the unforeseen circumstances obliging him to change his plans, his difficulties with the Spanish Customs, his liking for El Greco, and, with the scale of her vision thus increased, see a single man so huge among so many tiny ones, like

Gustave Moreau's Jupiter painted with his superhuman stature because he is with a mere female mortal.[23]

My grandmother took leave of Mme de Villeparisis outside the hotel so that we could enjoy a little more of the sea air before lunchtime, of which we would be informed by beckonings through the glass screens. We heard a chorus of shouts: the young mistress of the King of the South Seas, having just been down for a swim, was coming back up for lunch.

"Is that not an outrage!" exclaimed the *bâtonnier* from Cherbourg, who happened to be passing. "It's enough to make a man want to shake the dust of France off his feet for good!"

The wife of the notary from Le Mans was gazing spellbound at the alleged queen.

"I wish I could tell you how it irritates me when Mme Blandais stares at those people like that," the *bâtonnier* said to the First President. "I feel like giving her a good slap across the face. It's people like her that make people take an interest in riffraff like that. And of course riffraff love it when people take an interest in them. Tell her husband, would you, to tell her it's ridiculous. I for one will certainly not be going out with them again if they look as though they're fascinated by a couple in fancy dress!"

The advent of the Princess of Luxembourg, on the day when her barouche had stood outside the hotel while the fruit was being delivered, had not been overlooked by the wives of the notary, the *bâtonnier,* and the First President, who for some time had been much exercised on the question of whether that old Mme de Villeparisis, whom everyone treated with such consideration, was a genuine marquise, rather than just an adventuress quite undeserving, as the ladies would have loved to learn, of all the bowing and scraping. Each time Mme de Villeparisis walked through the vestibule, the wife of the First President, always on the lookout for loose women, set aside her embroidery and inspected her in a way that moved her two friends to irresistible laughter.

"I make no apology," she said with pride, "for believing the worst of people! I'm never convinced anyone's an honest woman until I've set

eyes on her birth certificate and her marriage lines. So I've got a few little inquiries to make—you mark my words."

Every day, the ladies gathered in their mirthful group.

"What have you learned?"

On the evening of the Princess of Luxembourg's arrival, the wife of
the First President put a finger to her lips.

"I've got something for you."

"Isn't our Mme Poncin wonderful! I've never seen anyone as— What
have you got?"

"What have I got? Just a female with dyed hair, if you don't mind,
made up to the eyeballs, and with a carriage that smacked of 'immoral
earnings' a mile away, the kind that sort of woman always has, and who
turned up a while ago asking to see our alleged marquise!"

"Goodness me! Oh dear, oh dear! Would you believe it! It must
be that woman we saw, *bâtonnier*, don't you remember? We certainly
thought she looked pretty fishy, but we didn't know she was looking for
the Marquise. A woman with a Negro, wasn't it?"

"Precisely."

"Well, is that so? And do you happen to know her name?"

"Oh, yes. I picked up her card, pretending to think it was someone
else's. She purports to be called the 'Princess of Luxembourg'! Didn't I
tell you I could smell a rat? Isn't it charming to have to rub shoulders
with the likes of the Baronne d'Ange!"[24] The *bâtonnier* quoted Mathurin
Régnier and *Macette*[25] in the ear of the First President.

It should not be thought this was a misunderstanding of short duration, like those that arise in the second act of a musical comedy and are
resolved in the final scene. Whenever the Princess of Luxembourg, who
was a niece of the King of England and the Emperor of Austria, came
to fetch Mme de Villeparisis so that they could take carriage exercise
together, they could not help looking like a pair of retired demireps,
of the sort whom it is difficult to avoid in fashionable resorts. Three-
quarters of the gentlemen who belong to the Faubourg Saint-Germain
are looked down on by many middle-class people as impecunious de-
bauchees and wastrels (which of course some of them may well be)
whom no honest man could mix with. In this, the middle class is too

moral, as the defects of these gentlemen would never prevent them from being welcomed with open arms in places where the middle class will never be. The gentlemen in turn are so convinced that the middle class is aware of this that they affect a straightforward attitude toward their own doings, even going so far as to disapprove of those of their associates who are most hard up; and this only reinforces the misunderstanding. If by some chance a gentleman from the Faubourg, whose great wealth happens to qualify him to be a director of the leading banking houses, has to mix with members of the lower-middle classes, the latter, seeing for once a noble they think worthy of being one of themselves, are convinced that he would have nothing to do with a gambling bankrupt of a marquis, who they think, especially because he is such a likable man, must be quite out of favor with his class. They are taken aback when the duke who is the managing director of the enormous enterprise marries his son to the daughter of the gambling marquis, who happens to bear a name which is that of the oldest family in France, just as a sovereign will prefer to be father-in-law to the daughter of an erstwhile king rather than to the daughter of a present president of the Republic. This means that the view which the two worlds have of each other is as imaginary as the view that one seaside town has of another when they stand at opposite ends of the Bay of Balbec: from Rivebelle, it is just possible to see a little of Marcouville-l'Orgueilleuse; but that misleads Rivebelle into thinking its delights are visible from Marcouville, when they are more or less invisible.

The Balbec doctor, summoned to my bedside because of a bout of fever, having ruled that, while the very hot weather lasted, I ought not to sit about on the shore in the sun, wrote out some prescriptions, which my grandmother received from his hand with an appearance of respect in which I recognized at once her firm resolve to have none of them made up for me. She did, however, heed his advice about leading a healthier life, and accepted Mme de Villeparisis's offer to take us out and about in her carriage. Before lunchtime, I kept toing and froing between my room and my grandmother's. Unlike mine, hers did not directly overlook the sea, although it had three different aspects: on a short stretch of the esplanade, a courtyard, and the countryside. Its furnishings were also very different, including armchairs embroidered in filigree and embossed with pink flowers, which seemed to be the source of the fresh and pleasant smell one encountered on entering. At that late-morning moment, when rays of sunlight came in from more than one aspect and seemingly from other times of day, breaking the angles of the walls, setting side by side on the chest of drawers a reflection from the beach and a wayside altar of colors as variegated as flowers along a lane, alighting brightly on the wainscot with the warm tremble of folded wings ready to fly away, warming like bathwater a country mat by the little courtyard window, which the sunshine festooned like a vine, adding to the charm and the decorative complexity of the furnishings by seeming to peel away the flowered silk of the armchairs and unpick their braidings, that room where I loitered for a moment before dressing for our outing was a prism in which the colors of the light from outside were dispersed, a hive in which all the heady nectars of the day awaiting me were still separate and ungathered but already visible, a garden of hopes shimmering with shafts of silver and rose petals. My very first act had been to open my curtains, in my impatience to see which sea was playing by the shore each morning like a Nereid. Whichever one it was, it was never there for more than a day. The following day, it would be replaced by another one, which at times resembled it; but I never saw the same one twice.

Some of them were full of such rare beauty that my delight in seeing them was increased by surprise. When I opened my window, why did my marveling eyes have the mysterious privilege, on one morning rather than on another, of seeing the nymph Glauconome,[26] whose lazy, soft-breathing loveliness had all the glow of a cloudy emerald, through which I could see the swell of the elements that gave her body and color? She flirted with the sunshine, her melting smile veiled by an invisible mist that was only a vacant space about her translucent surface, making it more succinct and striking, like the goddess shaped by a sculptor on a block, the rest of which he leaves rough-hewn. With her unique color, she whetted the appetite for an outing; and all day long, as we rode in Mme de Villeparisis's carriage along rough, land-bound roads, we would look at the cool, smooth-swelling, unattainable sea.

Mme de Villeparisis had her horses harnessed at an early hour, so that we could have time to go as far as Saint-Mars-le-Vêtu, the rocks at Quetteholme, or some other destination, which at a pace as sedate as ours lay rather far away and would require the whole day to go there and back. Looking forward to the lengthy excursion, I walked up and down, humming a tune recently heard as I waited for Mme de Villeparisis to come down. If it was a Sunday morning, there would be other carriages besides hers standing outside the hotel: several hired cabs would have come for the people who had been invited by Mme de Cambremer to her château at Féterne, and also for those who, rather than sit about moping like children deprived of a treat, announced that a Sunday in Balbec was unbearable, then set off as soon as breakfast was over to take refuge in a nearby resort or visit one of the local beauty spots. If anyone asked Mme Blandais whether she had been to the Cambremers', she would bark, "Of course not! We went to the waterfalls at Le Bec," as though that was the sole reason why she had not spent the day at Féterne. The *bâtonnier* would say in a sympathetic voice:

"I must say I do envy you. I wish we could have changed places. They're so much more interesting."

Like a rare species of shrub in a tub, near the carriages, in front of the porch where I was waiting, stood a young page who amazed the eye as much by the remarkable harmonies of his colored hair as by his plantlike skin. Inside the hotel, in the vestibule, which could be entered by people not staying at the hotel, and which corresponded to the narthex or church of the catechumens in Romanesque church buildings, the outside page's fellows, though just as inactive as he was, were at least in motion. Very likely they helped with the cleaning in the mornings. But in the afternoons, they stood about like members of the chorus who, even when serving no musical purpose, remain onstage to fill out crowd scenes. The managing director, he whom I found so awesome, was considering increasing their numbers the following summer, for he was a "man of vision." This was a decision that upset the manager of the hotel, who was convinced that all these lads were just "obstruberant," by which he meant they got in everybody's way and served no useful purpose. However, they did at least fill up that slack time, punctuated only by the comings and goings of guests, between lunch and dinner, as

Mme de Maintenon's charges used to walk on, in the guise of young Is-
raelites, at each exit of Esther or Joad.²⁷ But the outside page, with his
remarkable hues and his tall, willowy figure, near whom I stood waiting
for the Marquise to appear, was a model of immobility, with something
weepy in his posture as well, as his brothers had left this hotel behind
them on their rise to higher destinies, and he felt lonely planted in
this foreign field. Mme de Villeparisis came down eventually. To busy
himself about her carriage, to hand her into it, might have seemed to be
part of the outside page's duties. But he was well aware that those who
travel accompanied by servants not only expect them to serve but also
hand out a few tips to employees of hotels, and that the nobles of the
erstwhile Faubourg Saint-Germain behave in the same way. Mme de
Villeparisis belonged to both of these groups. The arborescent page, deciding that he could expect nothing from the Marquise, and leaving it
to the headwaiter and her own maidservant to settle her in with all her
things, went on sadly envying his roaming brothers' freer fates and
maintaining his vegetable stillness.

We would set off. Some time after having driven past the railway station, we would come to a rural road that was soon to become as familiar to me as any in Combray, from the sharp turn off the main road,
between pleasant little orchards, as far as the bend where we branched
off, with plowed fields on either side. Dotted here and there in the
fields could be seen single apple trees, minus their blossoms, of course,
and showing only bunches of pistils; but this was enough to delight me,
as I recognized the broad spread of those inimitable leaves which, like a
carpet in church once a wedding ceremony is over, had been visited not
long since by a white satin train of blushing blossoms.

Back in Paris, in May of the following year, how often I was to buy
a sprig of apple from a flower shop, then spend the night hours in the
presence of its blossoms, which were steeped in the same creamy essence as the frothy dust on the unopened leaf buds, and which looked
as though the florist himself, as a special favor to me, in a moment of
creativity and with an ingenious matching touch, had set off the white
of the full-blown corollas by flanking each of them with extra little buds
of pink. I would sit and gaze at them, posing them under my lamp,

spending so long with them that I was often still there when dawn tinged them with the same red with which it must have been tingeing Balbec, striving to see them with the eyes of imagination as they might have been along that road, multiplying them, setting them within the prepared frame and on the waiting canvas of those little orchards and fields, which were familiar to me as a mere drawing, but which I longed to see again, which one day I was actually to see again, when springtime, with the rapture of genius, had colored in this bare sketch.

Before getting into the carriage, I had composed the seascape that I was looking forward to seeing, full of Baudelaire's "sunbeams gleaming on the sea," which down in Balbec itself I only ever saw in patches among a vulgar clutter of bathers, their bathing machines, and their yachts, from which my fancy averted its disgruntled eye. Each time Mme de Villeparisis's carriage came to the brow of a hill, I caught sight of the sea through the branches of trees; and the distance separating me from it canceled out the contemporary features which had as it were removed it from the world of nature and history, so that as I gazed down on the waves I could try to tell myself they were the ones Leconte de Lisle had described in his version of the *Oresteia*, when he shows the shaggy warriors of heroic Hellas coming down "like a flight of raptors in the dawn" and "flailing the sounding flood with their hundred thousand oars."[28] But now I was too far away from it; it no longer seemed to be a living thing, but more like a still life; and I could sense no power behind its spread of colors, which looked painted between the leaves and as insubstantial as the sky, differing from it only in that it was a deeper blue.

Mme de Villeparisis, who had noted my liking for churches, told me we would go one day to see this one, another day to see that one, and stressed especially the church at Carqueville. Saying it was "cozily clad in its old ivy," she gestured in a way that seemed to enfold the absent façade in a delicate drapery of invisible foliage. This little descriptive hand movement would often accompany some striking thing she said as she defined the charm and character of a building; and though she always eschewed technical terms, she could not conceal the fact that she was an expert on the things she spoke of. It was as though she felt she must apologize for this expertise, putting it down to the fact that one of the châteaux belonging to her father, where she had spent her childhood, stood in a part of the country where there were churches of the same style as those in the vicinity of Balbec, and that it would thus have been inexcusable for her not to have taken an interest in architecture, if only because the château itself was the finest example of the architecture of the Renaissance. But since it was also a veritable museum, where Chopin and Liszt had played, and Lamartine had recited poetry, where every celebrated artist for a century had left a thought, a tune, or a sketch in the visitors' book, Mme de Villeparisis preferred, whether because of good breeding, graciousness, genuine modesty, or even an unphilosophical cast of mind, to explain her familiarity with all the arts by that purely material circumstance, managing to let it appear that she looked upon painting, music, literature, and philosophy as merely the unavoidable accomplishments of any young girl given an aristocratic upbringing and happening to live in a building famous enough to figure on the list of national monuments. She gave the impression of believing that the only paintings worth anything are the ones you inherit. It was a pleasure to her one day when my grandmother admired a necklace she was wearing, which showed above the neckline of her dress. It was to be seen in a portrait of one of her forebears, by Titian, which had been in the family ever since. This was how the painting was known to be genuine. She had no interest in hearing about pictures bought up by some immensely wealthy man, being quite convinced they would be forgeries and that it would not be worth the trouble to look at them. We were aware that she did watercolors of flowers; and my grandmother, who had heard praise of them, mentioned them to her. Mme de Villeparisis's modesty made her change the subject, but with no greater show of surprise, or even of pleasure, than if she had been an established artist whose head is not to be turned by compliments. All she said was that it was a pleasant hobby, since, though painted flowers might not be as good as the real thing, at least one had to live in the company of natural blooms in order to paint them; and when one was obliged to examine them closely for the purpose of imitation, there was an inexhaustible delight in their beauty. However, in Balbec, Mme de Villeparisis intended to do none of this, as she needed to rest her eyes.

My grandmother and I were astonished to discover how left-of-center her views were, much more so than those of most middle-class people. She in her turn was astonished that anyone could be shocked by the expulsions of the Jesuits, saying that there was nothing new in it, that it had been done in the time of the monarchy, and even in Spain. She was in favor of the Republic; and her only objection against its anticlericalism she expressed as follows: "I should be as much against being prevented from going to Mass if I wanted to go as I should be against being made to go to Mass if I *didn't* want to go!" She even said things like, "The nobility nowadays, I ask you, what are they worth?" and "If you ask me, a man who doesn't work is beyond the pale!" Of course, her reason for speaking like this may only have been that she sensed how strikingly paradoxical and provocative it would sound, coming from her.

The overt and frequent advocacy of such advanced opinions—they fell short of socialism, however, which was Mme de Villeparisis's pet aversion—by the very sort of person whose fine mind one esteems to the point of being reluctant, in one's sedulously diffident impartiality, to condemn the ideas of conservatives, brought my grandmother and me close to believing that in our pleasant companion were to be found the measure and model of truth in all things. When she was pronouncing upon her Titians, the colonnade at her château, or Louis-Philippe's caliber as a conversationalist, we took her word for it. But—like those scholars who can astound listeners when they hold forth on Egyptian painting or Etruscan inscriptions, while having nothing but shallow platitudes to deliver on literary works from nearer our own time, making us wonder whether we have not been mistaken in thinking their academic specialty interesting, since we have noticed in it none of the mediocrity of mind that they must have brought to it, just as they brought it to their vapid studies of Baudelaire—Mme de Villeparisis, when I asked her about Chateaubriand, Balzac, or Victor Hugo, all of whom had been guests in her parents' house and whom she herself had even glimpsed, found my admiration of them laughable, told me anecdotes about them that were just as mordant as any she had recounted about great nobles or statesmen, and frowned on them as writers, because they had been immoderate, full of themselves, deficient in that sobriety of manner which achieves its art in a single true stroke, without ever overdoing anything, which shuns especially the tomfooleries of grandiloquence, because they had lacked the deftness of touch and certain qualities of measured judgment and simplicity in which she had been taught to see the mark of genuine worth; and it was clear she had no hesitation in seeing them as inferior to men who, by virtue of those very qualities, might well have outshone the Balzacs, Hugos, and Vignys, in a salon, an Academy, or a cabinet, men like Molé, Fontanes, Vitrolles, Bersot, Pasquier, Lebrun, Salvandy, Daru.[29]

"I mean, take the novels of Stendhal, whom you seem to think so highly of. He would have been excessively surprised to be told of any such thing. My father, who used to see him at the house of M. Mérimée—now, *there* was a man of talent, I can assure you!—my father often told me that Beyle (his real name) was a man of the most frightful vulgarity. But he *was* a witty fellow to have at a dinner, and he never went in for bragging about his books. You've presumably read for yourself the piece with which he shrugged off the inordinate praise heaped on him by M. de Balzac. So at least in that respect he knew how to behave." She possessed pieces in the handwriting of every one of these great men; and she appeared to believe, on the strength of the personal acquaintance her family had enjoyed with them, that her judgment of their value was more accurate than that of people who, like myself, were too young to have known them.

"You can take it from me. Because the fact is they were in and out of my father's house. As M. Sainte-Beuve used to say, and he was a fine judge of wit, one should take the word of people who knew them at first hand and could size them up properly."[30]

At times, as we climbed a rise with plowed land on either side, hesitant cornflowers, reminiscent of those in Combray, came straggling after the carriage, making the fields more real, adding a touch of genuineness, like the precious little flower used by certain old masters as a signature on their canvases. The horses soon outdistanced them; but a few paces farther on, there would be another one waiting for us, twinkling its blue star in the grass. Some even dared to stand right beside the roadway; and these tame flowers clustered together with my remote memories into a nebula.

As we drove down the other side of the rise, we would come upon some other lovely creature who was walking up the hill, climbing it on her bicycle, sitting on a cart or in a carriage, one of those flowers of the bright and beautiful day, but unlike the wildflowers sprinkled about the fields in that each of them showed some feature which none of the others had, and which would create a desire for her that it would be forever impossible to satisfy with any of them except herself, whether she was a farm girl leading a cow or sprawled on a wagon, a shop girl out for a walk, or some smart young lady perched opposite her parents in their barouche. Bloch had, of course, opened a whole new era for me and had given a new point of life by informing me that the solitary dreams I had once dramatized during my walks along the Méséglise way, starring a peasant girl who would fall into my arms, were not just idle fancies unrelated to the world outside me, but that every single one of these girls, from the village girl to the smart young lady, was ready and willing to oblige me. Though I was now in ill health and did not go out alone, and though I might never aspire to making love with them, it still gladdened me to know this, as though I were a child who, having been born in prison or a hospital, and having come to believe that the human organism can digest nothing but dry bread and medicines, suddenly learns that peaches, apricots, and grapes are not just pretty things that grow in the countryside, but mouth-watering delicacies on which one may feed. Even though the jailer or the nurse may prevent him from picking such fine fruit, the world seems a better place, and life itself more worth living. Any desire we may feel seems to us a finer thing, and we have an impression of it as a more reliable thing, when we know that external reality is in conformity with it, even if its fulfillment remains out of our personal reach. So, on condition that we avert our mind's eye for a moment from the small accidental impediment standing between such a desire and ourselves, the thought of living gives us greater joy now that we can imagine the enjoyment of it. As soon as I knew that each beautiful girl I happened to see would welcome my kiss on her cheek, I became curious about her soul; and the whole universe had begun to seem more interesting.

Mme de Villeparisis's carriage went too quickly for me to do more than glimpse the girl coming up toward us; and yet, since beauty in a human being is different from the beauty of a thing, since we feel it belongs to a unique person with an awareness of the world and a will, no sooner had the girl's individuality, a vague hint of soul, a will unknown to me, taken shape in a microscopic image, minute but complete, caught from her passing glance, than I could feel quickening within myself, like a mysterious replica of pollens ready for the pistils, the equally vague and minute embryo of the desire not to let this girl go on her way without having her consciousness register my presence, without my intervening between her and her desire for somebody else, without my being able to intrude upon her idle mood and take possession of her heart. The carriage passed the beautiful girl, leaving her behind us; and since her eyes, which had barely glimpsed me, had gathered nothing of the person in me, she had forgotten me already. Had I thought her so lovely only because I had caught a mere glimpse of her? Perhaps. For one thing, the impossibility of stopping and accosting a woman, the likelihood of not being able to find her again some other day, gives her the same sudden charm as is acquired by a place when illness or poverty prevents one from visiting it, or by the succession of drab days of one's unlived future when it is forfeit to death in battle. Were it not for habit, life would seem delightful to beings constantly under threat of dying, in other words to all humankind. And for another thing, though the imagination is easily teased by the desire for something we cannot possess, its wings are never clipped as they would be by a closer glimpse of reality, in these encounters where the charm of the passing beauty is generally in direct relation to their brevity. Nightfall and a coach traveling fast, in the country or in town, are all that any female torso requires, mutilated like an ancient marble by our speeding departure and the concealing dusk, standing at a streetcorner and in every lighted shop, shooting the arrows of Beauty at our heart, and making us wonder at times whether Beauty in this world is ever anything other than the makeweight that our imagination, overwrought by regret, adds to a fragmentary and fleeting passerby.

If I had been able to get out and speak to one of these girls we passed, I might well have been disillusioned by some flaw in her complexion that I had been unaware of from the carriage. (In that case, it would suddenly have felt impossible for me to make any effort to become part of her life. For beauty is a succession of hypotheses, and ugliness restricts these by blocking the way that seemed to be already leading us into the heart of the unknown.) A single word from her, a smile might have given me an unsuspected key or clue, enabling me to read the expression on her face or the way she walked, and I might then have recognized these as nondescript. That would have been possible, for I have never met in real life any girls as desirable as the ones I saw when in the company of some important personage who baffled all my ingenious attempts to get rid of him. One evening in Paris, some years after this first visit to Balbec, I was on an errand with a friend of my father's when from the carriage I caught sight of a woman walking away into the dark: the thought struck me that it was absurd to forfeit, for a reason of mere propriety, a share of happiness in this life, it being no doubt the only one we are to have, and so I jumped out without so much as a by-your-leave, ran after the intriguing creature, lost her at a crossing of two streets, saw her again on another street, and eventually ran her to ground under a lamppost, where I found I was out of breath and face-to-face with the aging Mme Verdurin, whom I usually avoided like the plague, and who now cried in delight and surprise, "Oh, how nice of you to chase after me just to say good evening!"

That year in Balbec, when we passed these girls on the road, I told my grandmother and Mme de Villeparisis that I had a bad headache, but that I would feel much better if I could get out of the carriage and walk home unaccompanied. They never agreed to my suggestion. So the lovely girl, like a famous building (though much more difficult to see again than any building, being nameless and of no fixed location), was added to the collection of all those I had been promising myself to have a closer look at. There was one, however, whom I did catch sight of a second time, in circumstances that made me think it might be possible to get to know her properly. She was a milkmaid; and she came down one day from her farm to deliver an extra supply of cream to the hotel. The way she looked at me made me think she had recognized me too, though her interest may only have been caused by her surprise at the way I was looking at her. The following day, when Françoise came to open my bedroom curtains about midday, I having spent the whole morning resting, she brought me a letter that had been left for me by hand. Knowing no one in Balbec, I was sure it must be from the milkmaid! But, sad to say, it was only from Bergotte: he had been passing through and had called at the hotel to see me; but when they told him I was still asleep, he had left a charming note, which the "lift" had slipped into an envelope and addressed in a hand that I had taken for the milkmaid's. I was dreadfully disappointed; and the idea that it was much more difficult, as well as more flattering, to have a letter from Bergotte than from a milkmaid was no consolation. And I was to see no more of the girl than of the others, only glimpsed from Mme de Villeparisis's carriage. These glimpses, and the loss of every girl glimpsed, aggravated the state of agitation in which I spent my days; and I wished for the wisdom of the philosophers who counsel the curbing of desires (assuming they mean one's desire for another person, as that is the only mode of desire which can lead to anxiety, focusing as it does on a world beyond our ken but within our awareness—to assume they mean desire for wealth would be too absurd). At the same time, I was inclined to find something lacking in this wisdom, sensing well enough that these glimpsed encounters made for greater beauty in a world which sows such flowers, rare though common, along every country roadside, a new spice being added to life by the untried treasures of each day, by every outing with its unkept promises, my enjoyment of which had hitherto been prevented only by contingent circumstances that might not always be present.

Of course, it may be that, in looking forward to a freer day when I might meet similar girls along different roads, I had already begun to adulterate the exclusive desire to share one's life with an individual woman whom one has seen as pretty; and the mere act of entertaining the possibility of artificially fostering it was an implicit acknowledgment that it was an illusion.

On the day Mme de Villeparisis took us to Carqueville, to see the church she had described as "clad in old ivy," which stands on a knoll above the village with its river still running under the little bridge from the Middle Ages, my grandmother, so that I could enjoy the pleasure of going on alone to view the building, suggested to her friend that they stay in the village square, which stood out clearly under an old-gold patina making it look like just one part among others of a single object of great antiquity, to sample the pastry cook's tea and cakes. We agreed that I would come back down to meet them. To make out the shape of a church in the lump of greenery in front of which I stood required an effort that made me re-examine the very notion of a church: as can happen to a schoolboy who, by being made to translate a sentence into another language, divests it of shapes with which he is familiar and comes to grasp its meaning more clearly, the concept of a church, which I hardly ever needed when faced with most of the steeples I looked at, was now indispensable to me; and so as not to overlook the fact that an arch shaped from growing ivy was actually the top of an ogival stained-glass window, and that a projection of leaves was really the contour of a cornice, I had to keep it constantly in mind. When a breeze sprang up, it sent a thrill through the movable porch, eddying and rippling all over it like light, turning it into a tremulous cascade of leaves; and as the façade of vegetation swayed and shivered under the caress, it warped its shimmering pillars.

As I left the church, I noticed a few village girls in their garish Sunday finery, standing about down by the old bridge and bantering with the local boys. One of the taller of the girls, less showily dressed than the others, but apparently superior to them in some way (she paid little attention to what they said to her), with a more solemn and bolder look to her, was half sitting on the parapet of the bridge, dangling her legs, beside a little jar full of fish that she had presumably just caught. Her face was tanned; her eyes, though gentle, were full of disdain for her surroundings; and the line of her neat little nose was delicate and charming. My eyes rested on her skin, and my lips could almost believe they had done likewise. It was not only her body I was after, it was the person living inside it, with whom there can be only one mode of touching, which is to attract her attention, and one mode of penetration, which is to put an idea into her mind.

But the inner self of the beautiful fishergirl seemed to remain closed against me; and I doubted that I had managed to gain entry to her, even after I had seen my own image furtively reflected by the mirror of a look she gave me, which was affected by a refractive index as unfamiliar to me as though I stood within the field of vision of a deer. But just as it would not have been enough for me, in kissing her, to take pleasure from her lips without giving her any in return, so I wished that the idea of me, in entering her, in becoming part of her, might attract not only her attention, but her admiration, her desire, and might force it to keep a memory of me against the day when I might be able to benefit from it. Not far away I could see the little square where I was supposed to rejoin Mme de Villeparisis's carriage. There was not a moment to waste; I could already sense that these girls were on the point of starting to giggle at seeing me stand there. I had a five-franc piece in my pocket, which I took out; and before explaining to the lovely girl what it was I wanted her to do, I held up the coin so that she could see it, and in the hope that it would make her listen to me:

"You appear to belong here," I said. "Would you please do me a small favor? There's a carriage waiting for me somewhere around here—I'm not quite sure where, actually, outside some cake shop in a square, I believe—and if you could just find it for me ... Now, before you go, just to be sure it's the right one, do make sure you inquire whether it's the carriage of the Marquise de Villeparisis. But you can't really mistake it—it's got two horses."

That was what I wanted her to know about me, so that she could be impressed. No sooner had I spoken the words "Marquise" and "two horses" than I felt a sudden great calm spread through me: knowing that the fishergirl would remember me, I was simultaneously aware that I had lost not only my anxiety at perhaps not being able to see her again, but with it part of my desire to do so. It felt as though I had touched her person with invisible lips and that she had liked it. As happens with physical possession, this forcible insertion of myself into her mind, this disembodied possession of her, had taken away some of her mystery.

We drove down toward Hudimesnil, and suddenly I was filled with a feeling of profound bliss, which I associated with Combray but had seldom felt since those days, rather like the feeling I had once had from things such as the steeples of Martinville. This time, however, nothing came of it. It was just three trees that I had noticed, set back a little from the steeply cambered road we were on, looking as though they stood at the entrance to a covered drive, and making a pattern that I knew I had seen somewhere before. I could not manage to recognize the place they had, as it were, been separated from; but I sensed that it must have been somewhere familiar to me, long ago; and as my mind stumbled about between a former year and the present moment, the countryside around Balbec shifted and faltered, and I had to ask myself whether this whole outing was not just some figment, Balbec merely a place where I might once have been in my imagination, Mme de Villeparisis someone out of a novel, and the three old trees nothing but the solid reality that meets the eye of a reader who glances up from a book, his mind still held by the spell of a fictional setting.

I gazed at the three trees, which I could see quite clearly; but my mind suspected they hid something on which it could have no purchase, as our fingertips at the full stretch of our arm may from time to time barely touch but not quite grasp objects that lie just out of reach. So one rests for a moment before trying harder, with the arm outstretched, in the hope of catching hold at last. However, for my mind to be able to pause and summon up the effort required, I would have had to be unaccompanied. How I wished I could leave the others behind, as I used to along the Guermantes way, wandering away from my parents! I even had the feeling that I *ought* to do so now. I could sense in this moment the presence of one of those pleasures which, though they require the mind to work upon itself, reduce to insipidity the sweets of the mental idleness that makes one prefer to abandon the effort. It was a pleasure that came to me seldom, and its object always lay beyond my mental scope, requiring me to create it myself; but on each occasion when it did come, I would have the feeling that all the things which had happened to me since the last time were more or less devoid of significance, and that, for my real life to begin at last, I must now attend to nothing but this unique reality. I put my hand briefly over my eyes, so as to be able to close them without Mme de Villeparisis's noticing. I sat there for a moment thinking of nothing; then, with the fresher impetus of pent-up consciousness, I managed to leap farther in the direction of the trees, or, rather, toward the inner part of me where I could see them. Once again I could detect, just behind them, the same familiar but imprecise object, which I could not quite take hold of. Meanwhile, as the carriage rolled on, I could see them coming nearer. Where had I set eyes on them before? In the countryside near Combray, there was no such place with an opening to a drive. Nor did the place they reminded me of fit anywhere into the countryside around a German spa where I had gone one year with my grandmother. Did this mean they belonged to years of my past life which were so distant that the landscape surrounding them had been utterly wiped out, and that, like those passages one recognizes with sudden excitement in a text one fancied one had never read, they were the only scrap left from the forgotten storybook of my early childhood? Or did they belong to one of those places one glimpses in dreams, always the same places, or so they were in my dreams, where their strange aspect was only sleep's translation of the efforts I kept making while awake, either to see through the appearance of a place to a mystery which I sensed lay beyond it (which had so often happened along the Guermantes way), or to restore mystery to a place that I had longed to see and which, once I had been there, had turned into something quite superficial, as Balbec had? Were they perhaps a very recent image, a small fragment from a dream of only the night before, but already so faded that it seemed to derive from much longer ago? Or perhaps I had never seen them anywhere; and though I thought they were a memory to be recalled, were they in fact only an invitation to comprehend an idea, concealing behind themselves, like certain trees or clumps of grass glimpsed along the Guermantes way, a meaning that was every bit as obscure and ungraspable as a distant past? Or else might it actually be that they concealed no idea at all, and that it was only an impairment of my eyesight, making me see double in time as one can see double in space? I could not tell. Still coming toward me, they might have been some mythological apparition, a coven of witches, a group of Norns propounding oracles. But I saw them as ghosts from my past, beloved companions from childhood, sometime friends reminding me of shared moments. Like risen shades, they seemed to be asking me to take them with me, to bring them back to the realm of the living. In their naïve and passionate gesticulations, I read the impotent regret of a loved one who, having lost the power of speech, knows that he will never be able to let us know what he wants, and that we can never deduce his meaning. Soon, at a crossroads, the carriage left them behind. Like my life itself, it was carrying me away from what seemed the only truth, from what would have made me truly happy.

I watched the trees as they disappeared, waving at me in despair and seeming to say, "Whatever you fail to learn from us today you will never learn. If you let us fall by this wayside where we stood striving to reach you, a whole part of your self that we brought for you will return forever to nothing." And it is true that, though the same mode of pleasure and disquiet that I had just experienced once more was to come back to me in later years, though I did attend to it at last one evening—too late, but forever—I never did find out what it was these particular trees had attempted to convey to me, or where it was that I had once seen them. When the carriage went around a corner, I lost sight of them somewhere behind me; and when Mme de Villeparisis asked me why I looked so forlorn, I was as sad as though I had just lost a friend or felt something die in myself, as though I had broken a promise to a dead man or failed to recognize a god.

It was time to think of turning for home. Mme de Villeparisis, who had a certain feeling for nature, albeit less warm than my grandmother's, and whose capacity for the appreciation of simple grandiose beauty in certain ancient things was not limited to the contents of museums and the houses of the aristocracy, told the coachman to return to Balbec by the back road, which was lined with old elm trees that we thought very fine, and where one rarely saw anyone.

For the sake of variety, once we had become used to this old back road, we would make a point of driving home by another route (unless we had taken it on our way out), which took us through the woods of

Chantereine and Canteloup. The invisibility of the countless birds very close at hand calling to each other among the trees gave the same restful impression as one can have by closing one's eyes. Bound to my little folding seat, like Prometheus to his rock, I listened to my Oceanids. And if I chanced to see one of these birds, slipping from one leaf to the shelter of another, there was so little apparent link between it and the songs that I could barely believe they were produced by that restless little body, full of surprise and lack of expression.

This road was similar to many another French road of the same kind, first a steep climb, then a long gentle downward slope. At the time, it did not impress me as having any great charm; I was just glad to be on the way home. But in later years, it did come to be a source of other joys, by staying in my memory as a starting point giving immediate access to all similar roads which I would travel in the future, on a short outing or a longer journey, and which because of it were able to take a shortcut to my heart. For, as soon as the later carriage or motor turned into one of those roads that resembled a stretch of the one I had driven along in Mme de Villeparisis's carriage, what adjoined my then consciousness, as contiguously as though it were my most recent past, abolishing all the intervening years, was the impressions in my mind on those late afternoons, after the horses' heads had been set toward Balbec, when we drove through the lovely smell of leaves into the rising mists and could see the sunset, beyond the next village, through the trees, looking just like one of the next wooded localities along that road, but rather too distant for us to reach before nightfall. These impressions, mingling with the ones I would be experiencing in that other place, on that similar road, and surrounded by all the accessory feelings common to both states, and only by them—the sensation of breathing freely, curiosity, the enjoyment of being lazy, a good appetite, cheerfulness—would grow in volume, take on the consistency of a particular type of pleasure, almost of a way of existence, one that I seldom had occasion to revisit but within which reawakened memories blended a physically perceived reality with enough remembered, fancied, ungraspable reality for these places I was passing through to give me, not just an aesthetic experience, but a heady desire, however fleeting, to live there forever. How often the mere breath of trees in full leaf has made me see the act of sitting on a folding seat opposite Mme de Villeparisis, as she acknowledges the greeting of the Princess of Luxembourg passing by in her carriage, then driving home to dinner at the Grand-Hôtel, as among those inexpressible joys of life which neither the present nor the future can ever bring back, which can be tasted once and once only!

Daylight had often completely faded by the time we reached Balbec. I would venture to quote to Mme de Villeparisis, indicating the risen moon, a fine line from Chateaubriand, Vigny, or Victor Hugo: "The moon revealing her old secret of melancholy" or "Weeping like Diana by her fountains" or "The shades were nuptial, august, and solemn."[31]

"You like that, do you?" she would say. "You think it's 'brilliant,' as you say. Let me tell you, I am forever being surprised to see that people nowadays treat very seriously things which the friends of these writing gentlemen, whose merits they were well aware of, took plenty of pleasure in bantering them for. Words like 'brilliant' and 'genius' were not bandied about then, as they are these days—credit a writer with mere 'talent' and he thinks you're insulting him! I can assure you, I have good reason to resist the blandishments of your M. de Chateaubriand—and his moonshine. He was a gentleman who was often in my father's house. Very pleasant to be with when there was no other company, quite unaffected, an amusing man. But no sooner would other guests come on the scene than he started his ridiculous posturing and showing off—he actually stated that he had tossed his resignation in the King's face and directed the whole Conclave of Cardinals, forgetting that in fact he had got my father to beg the King to take him back, and that my father had overheard him make the most wildly inaccurate forecasts about the election of the Pope! No, the man to hear on the subject of that Conclave was M. de Blacas, who was more than a cut above your M. de Chateaubriand. And as for his fine phrases on the moonlight, they were one of our family jokes. Why, on nights when there was a full moon, we would take the newest guest aside and suggest he take a turn in the park after dinner with M. de Chateaubriand. Then, when they came back in, my father would make a point of murmuring to the new fellow, 'And was M. de Chateaubriand in fine voice tonight?' 'Ah, yes!'

'And did he allude to the moonlight?' 'Indeed he did, but how did you know?' 'And did he not say the moon was revealing her old secret of melancholy?' 'Yes, he did! But how on earth—?' 'And did he not also refer to the moonlight in the Roman countryside?' 'You've got second sight!' Now, of course, my father did not have any such thing, but M. de Chateaubriand was always happy to trot out the same well-rehearsed speech."

At the mention of Vigny, she burst out laughing.

"He was the fellow who used to say, 'I am the Comte Alfred de Vigny.' There are plenty of people who are counts, and plenty who aren't—as if it mattered, for goodness' sake!"

However, she may have thought it did matter a little, for she added:

"For one thing, I'm not sure he *was* a count. And even if he was, he was of pretty low extraction. Just think—mentioning his 'escutcheons of a noble' in his poetry! How tasteful! How intriguing for the reader! Musset was another one: a mere Parisian, if you please, yet he went on about 'The golden hawk I bear upon my helmet'—no genuine noble would ever say any such thing. Mind you, at least Musset had some talent as a poet. But anything by your M. de Vigny, apart from *Cinq-Mars*, bores me to death—the man's unreadable. M. Molé, who had so much of the wit and tact that M. de Vigny had so little of, gave him what he deserved, in his speech of welcome at the Académie Française. D'you mean you haven't *read* it? It is a masterpiece of mischievous impertinence!"

In her astonishment at seeing Balzac revered by her nephews and nieces, Mme de Villeparisis complained that he had professed to describe a stratum of society about which, "since it was not open to him," he had written a tissue of implausibilities. As for Victor Hugo, she said that her father, M. de Bouillon, had friends among the young Romantics, who had managed to get him into the opening night of *Hernani*,[32] but that he could not bear to stay till the end of the play, with its ridiculous lines turned out by a writer who was gifted but given to bombast, and who came to be deemed a great poet only as the result of a deal, as a reward for the sedulous self-interest with which he promoted the dangerous ravings of the socialists.

The hotel was now within sight, its lights, which had been so un-friendly on the evening of our arrival, now glowing with the gentle re-assurance and promise of a homecoming. As our carriage neared the door, the doorman, the pageboys, and the "lift," standing in a body on the front steps, looking out for us, eager and ingenuous, slightly worried by our lateness, now that they too had become familiar to us, were ex-amples of those in whom, though they change so often during our life-time, as we ourselves change, we are soothed to see, for as long as they serve as our temporary mirrors, the faithful and friendly reflection of our habits. We prefer them to friends whom we have not set eyes on for ages, for they contain more of what we are at the moment. So as to be spared the rigors of the evening air, the outside page, having been ex-posed to the sunlight all day long, had been taken inside and wrapped in woolens, which, among all the glass of the vestibule, along with the forlorn orangy foliage of his hair and the peculiar rose-pink of his cheeks, made one think of a hothouse plant being protected from the cold. We would get out of the carriage, assisted by many more retainers than necessary; but they had sensed the significance of the scene, and felt it incumbent upon them to play a part in it. As I was usually fam-ished, rather than postpone the start of dinner, I chose not to go up to my room (which had so genuinely become mine that to stand among its long violet curtains and low bookcases was to be alone with the self that saw its own image in furnishings, as in people); and so all three of us stayed in the vestibule, waiting for the headwaiter to come and tell us that dinner was served. This gave us another opportunity to attend to Mme de Villeparisis.

"We're imposing on you," my grandmother said.

"Not at all, I'm delighted. I find it quite charming," her old friend replied, with a winning smile, and descanting on a mellifluous note that contrasted with her customary plainness of speech.

The fact was that, at such moments, her manner was not natural; it was her unforgotten upbringing that spoke, with its aristocratic ways, which a great lady must display so as to impress upon commoners that she is happy to be among them, that she does not look down on them. The only deficiency in Mme de Villeparisis's politeness was the excess

of it, for it could be seen as the professional mannerism of a lady of the
Faubourg Saint-Germain who, accustomed as she is to seeing in certain
middle-class people the malcontents whom she is bound to make of
them sooner or later, takes full advantage while she can of any opportunities to have the account books of her friendly relations with them
record in advance a credit balance, so that, when she is debited with not
inviting them to her next dinner party or reception, it shall be without
qualm. So, with a keen and irresistible earnestness, and as though there
were little time left for her to show how considerate she was, the spirit
of the caste to which Mme de Villeparisis belonged, having long since
indelibly affected her, and in its ignorance of the fact that the circumstances were now different, the people not the same, and that, once
back in Paris, she would be glad of our frequent presence in her house,
kept prompting her into lavishing upon us, for as long as our stay in
Balbec lasted, bouquets of roses, melons, loans of books, outings in her
carriage, and many honeyed words. In this way, not only the dazzling
beauty of the beach, the bedrooms with their many-hued radiance and
suboceanic glints, and the riding lessons that turned the sons of shop-
keepers into godlike Alexanders of Macedonia, but also each day's
friendly overtures from Mme de Villeparisis, and even the brief, sum-
mery ease with which my grandmother accepted them, all these survive
in my memory as the typical redolences of a vacation by the sea.

"Hand over your coats, so that they can be taken up for you."

My grandmother handed them to the manager; and because he was
in the habit of being pleasant to me, I was dismayed by this inconsider-
ateness, which seemed to be hurtful to him.

"I do believe that gentleman is annoyed," Mme de Villeparisis said.
"He probably thinks he's too grand to be laden with people's things. I
remember the Duc de Nemours,[33] when I was just a slip of a girl, coming to see my father—he lived on the top floor of the Hôtel Bouillon—
with a big bundle of newspapers and letters under his arm. I can see the
Prince as though it were yesterday, in his blue tailcoat, standing under
the lintel of our front door, which had such pretty workings in the
wood—by Bagard,[34] I think—you know those delicate beadings, so soft
that the woodworker could shape them into little bows and flowers, like

ribbons tied around a posy. 'Here you are, Cyrus,' he said, 'here's what your concierge gave me to bring up to you. "If you're going up," he said, "there's no point in my climbing the stairs too—but mind you don't spoil my string." ' Well, now that you've got rid of your things, do sit down—look, have this one," she said, taking my grandmother by the hand, to usher her toward an armchair.

"Oh, really, if you don't mind, not that one! It's rather small for two people, but far too big for me. It would make me feel uneasy."

"That reminds me of an armchair, exactly like this one, that I had for a long time, but which I eventually had to get rid of, because it had been given to my mother by the ill-fated Duchesse de Praslin.³⁵ You see, my mother, though she was quite the most unpretentious person imaginable, had retained certain ways of seeing things which belonged to another period, and which even then I was beginning to find rather difficult to understand, and to begin with she had declined to be presented to Mme de Praslin, who was only Mlle Sébastiani–that-was, whereas Mme de Praslin, who *was* a duchess, took the view that it was not for *her* to be presented. And of course," added Mme de Villeparisis, forgetting that she found such social niceties rather difficult to understand, "had she been Mme de Choiseul proper, rather than just Mme de Choiseul-Praslin, her view might well have been able to prevail, since than the Choiseuls there are none greater—being descended from a sister of King Louis the Large, they were once true sovereigns in their ancient fiefdom of Bassigny. I must confess that we Bouillons take precedence, through our marriages and illustrious achievements, but in point of ancientness there is little difference in rank. So—that matter of protocol had given rise to certain comical incidents, such as a luncheon that was an hour late in starting because one of these two ladies required to be persuaded that she should agree to be the one presented to the other. Despite all that, they had become firm friends, and she gave my mother an armchair of this very sort, in which, just like you, everyone was reluctant to sit. One day my mother heard a carriage arriving in the courtyard and asked of a servant lad who it was. 'It's Her Ladyship the Duchesse de La Rochefoucauld, Your Ladyship.' 'Fine, show her in.' A quarter of an hour later, there was still no sign of her. 'So where's Her

Ladyship the Duchesse de La Rochefoucauld?' 'She's comin' upstairs, Your Ladyship. Stopped for a breather, see,' replied the servant lad, who had only recently come up from the country, it being my mother's sound practice to acquire them there. Many a time she had known them from birth. That's how one gets good people. And good people are the first luxury in life. So—there was the Duchesse de La Rochefoucauld painfully ascending, she being gigantic, so gigantic indeed that when she came in my mother had a moment's bother as she wondered where she might seat her. That was when the armchair from Mme de Praslin caught her eye; so she moved it forward and said, 'Do be so kind as to take a seat.' The Duchesse de La Rochefoucauld filled it to overflowing. Despite being, shall I say, so imposing, she was still a perfectly agreeable person. One of our family friends used to say of her, 'She still makes quite an effect when she arrives,' to which my mother would reply, 'She makes an even greater one when she leaves.' My mother was freer in speech than would be thought proper nowadays. But even at her own house, no one felt inhibited about chaffing Mme de La Rochefoucauld on her inordinate proportions, and she laughed as readily as anyone. Once, when my mother went to visit her, having been welcomed at the door by the husband, she said to him, not having seen the Duchesse, who was sitting in an alcove toward the back of the room, 'Oh, are you all alone? Isn't Mme de La Rochefoucauld at home? I don't see her.' 'How kind you are!' the Duc replied, he being the man with the faultiest judgment I have ever known, but one who could rise to wit on occasion."

After dinner, when my grandmother and I had gone upstairs, I said that the qualities in Mme de Villeparisis which we found charming—tactfulness, delicacy, discretion, unselfishness—were perhaps not worth all that much, since the people who were best known for embodying them were relatively uneminent men, like Molé or Loménie, and that, though the absence of such qualities may make for some unpleasantness in everyday relations, the lack of them had been no drawback for the Chateaubriands, the Balzacs, the Vignys, and the Hugos of the world, men full of vanity and lacking in judgment, men whom the likes of Bloch could scoff at. . . . My grandmother protested at the mention of Bloch, preferring to sing the praises of Mme de Villeparisis. Just as it is supposed to be a concern for the species that influences choices in love, steering fat men toward thin women and thin men toward fat women, so that the makeup of the future child may be as well balanced as possible, so it was my grandmother's inkling of the requirements of my happiness, under constant threat from my inclination to nerves and my unwholesome tendency toward melancholy and solitude, that made her stress qualities such as steadiness and judgment, peculiar not only to Mme de Villeparisis but to a social milieu that might afford me distraction and solace, a milieu reminiscent of those which, in earlier days, fostered the flowering of a spirit shared by people like Doudan or M. de Rémusat, to say nothing of a Mme de Beausergent, a Joubert,[36] or a Mme de Sévigné, a spirit bringing more happiness and dignity to life than were ever afforded by cultivation of the opposite tastes, which led the Baudelaires, the Edgar Allan Poes, the Verlaines, and the Rimbauds into sufferings and low esteem, the likes of which my grandmother wished to spare me. I interrupted her with a kiss and asked whether she had noticed something said by Mme de Villeparisis that was the mark of the woman who set more store by birth than she liked to admit. In these evening conversations, I compared impressions with my grandmother, never knowing how much I should admire any person until she pronounced. I submitted to her the sketches I had done during the day of all these other people who, because they were not her, were nonexistent for me. On one of these occasions I said, "I couldn't live without you." "That's not the way to be, you know," she said in an unsteady voice. "We've got to toughen up a bit. I mean, what would you do if I went away on a journey? I would hope you'd be a good boy and have a happy time." "Well, I might be if you went away for a few days. But I'd be counting the hours till you came back." "But what if I was away for months"—the thought of it chilled my heart—"for years perhaps . . . or even . . ."

A silence lengthened between us; we dared not catch each other's eye. I was affected more by her distress than by my own. I stepped over to the window and, looking away from her, said quite clearly:

"You know I'm a creature of habit. When I'm away from the people I'm fond of, I'm unhappy for the first few days. But then, though I still go on being fond of them, I get used to it, life goes on, undisturbed, and I could put up with being parted from them for months, or years, or . . ."

I had to stop talking and gaze right out of the window. My grandmother left the room for a moment. Then, the following evening, I launched into philosophy, speaking in a detached voice but making sure that she was paying attention to my words: it was remarkable, I said, that the latest advances in science seemed to have made materialism untenable, and that the most likely outcome was still the eternal life of the soul and reunion beyond the grave.

Mme de Villeparisis informed us that she would soon not be able to see so much of us: a young nephew of hers who was preparing for entry to the cavalry school at Saumur, and who was garrisoned nearby at Doncières,[37] was coming to spend a few weeks' holiday with her, and she would have to devote much of her time to him. On some of our drives together, she had spoken very warmly of his high intelligence and especially his kind heart, and I had been imagining how he would take a liking to me, how I would become his favorite friend; then, when his aunt hinted to my grandmother, before his arrival, that he had had the misfortune to fall madly in love with some impossible woman who now had him in her clutches and would not let him go, as I was convinced that love affairs of that sort could only lead to mental derangement, crime, and suicide, the thought of how little time was left for our friendship, which was already so strong in my heart although I had not set eyes on him, moved me to tears for the misfortunes that must attend it, as though it were some beloved companion who one learns is seriously ill and not expected to live long.

One very hot afternoon, from inside the dining room, which was in half-darkness, sheltering from the sun behind drawn curtains, which were a yellow glow edged by the blue dazzle of the sea, I saw, traversing the hotel's central bay, which extended from the beach to the road, a tall, slim young man with piercing eyes, a proud head held high on a fine uncovered neck, and with hair so golden and skin so fair that they seemed to have soaked up the bright sunshine of the day. In a loose off-white garment, the like of which I would never have believed a man would dare to wear, and which in its lightness was as suggestive of the heat and brilliance of outdoors as was the cool dimness of the dining room, he was advancing at a quick march. His eyes, from which a monocle kept dropping, were the color of the sea. We all sat there intrigued, watching him as he passed, knowing that we beheld the young Marquis de Saint-Loup-en-Bray, famous in the fashionable world. The newspapers had recently been full of descriptions of the suit he had worn when attending at a duel, as a second for the young Duc d'Uzès. It seemed as though the very special quality of his hair and eyes, his skin and bearing, which would have distinguished him in a crowd, as a pale, precious vein of luminous opal stands out among crude earth, must be the mark of a life quite unlike those lived by ordinary men. In the days before the beginning of the liaison lamented by Mme de Villeparisis, when the prettiest women of the Faubourg Saint-Germain had vied for his attentions, his presence at a seaside resort, for example, with whichever celebrated beauty he was courting at the time, not only thrust the lady into the limelight, but also turned all heads toward him. Because of his general "stylishness" as a young "lion," his cavalier manner, and above all his own remarkable beauty, some thought there was something effeminate about him, though no one ever said such a thing against him, as his virility and passionate liking for women were well known. This was the nephew of whom Mme de Villeparisis had spoken. I was warmed by the thought that, for these few weeks, I would have the opportunity to know him, and by the certainty that he would give me his affection. He strode right through the hotel, seeming to be in pursuit of his monocle, which fluttered in front of him like a butterfly. He had come up from the beach; and the sea, which filled the lower half of the plate glass in the lobby, was a background against which his whole figure stood out, as in those portraits in which the painter, without departing from the strictest observation of present-day life, chooses to put his model in an apt setting—a polo ground, a golf course, a racetrack, the deck of a yacht—making a modern equivalent of the old masters' canvases in which a human figure stands in the foreground of a landscape. A carriage and pair awaited him at the door; and with his monocle now flitting about against the background of the sunny roadway, the nephew of Mme de Villeparisis, with all the grace and command that a virtuoso pianist is somehow able to show even in the simplest passage, where it would have seemed barely possible for him to display any superiority over a lesser performer, climbed up beside his coachman, accepted the reins from the latter, and, opening the while an envelope that the manager of the hotel had handed to him, set the horses off.

What a disappointment it was for me, on each of the days following, whenever our paths crossed outside or inside the hotel, he with his high collar, and keeping his limbs in perpetual equilibrium about the dancing flight of his monocle, which seemed to be their center of gravity, to realize that it was not his intention to make our acquaintance, that he never once greeted us, although he could not be unaware we were friends with his aunt! When I remembered how polite Mme de Villeparisis, and before her M. de Norpois, had been toward me, I wondered whether they might not be mere mock nobility, whether there might not be some secret provision in the code of laws governing the aristocracy that perhaps, for some reason unknown to me, permitted women or the odd diplomat who might have dealings with commoners not to treat them with the sweeping disdain a merciless young marquis must show. Reason could have contradicted this. But the salient feature of the absurd age I was at—an age which for all its alleged awkwardness, is prodigiously rich—is that reason is not its guide, and the most insignificant attributes of other people always appear to be consubstantial with their personality. One lives among monsters and gods, a stranger to peace of mind. There is scarcely a single one of our acts from that time which we would not prefer to abolish later on. But all we should lament is the loss of the spontaneity that urged them upon us. In later life, we see things with a more practical eye, one we share with the rest of society; but adolescence was the only time when we ever learned anything.

The insolence I sensed in M. de Saint-Loup, and the ingrained callousness to be inferred from it, were to be confirmed by his demeanor each time he passed through our vicinity, lean and straight as a ramrod, his head always held high, his eye quite blank, or, rather, quite implacable, devoid even of that hint of latent considerateness toward other persons (even though they may not know your aunt) which meant that my own attitude, for instance, toward an old lady was not the same as it was toward a lamppost. The distance between his standoffish ways and the fulsome letters into which, only the other day, I had imagined him pouring his affection for me, was as great as the gulf between the obscurity of the daydreamer and the orator he fancies himself to be, swaying his fellow citizens with an unforgettable speech, filling his solitude with the sound of his own voice, carried away by the "hear-hears" of the House and the acclaim of the country, but then, once the fictitious hubbub has died down, finding he is still the same mute, inglorious nobody as before. When Mme de Villeparisis, no doubt hoping to correct the bad impression left on us by such appearances, with their suggestion of a haughty and bilious nature, rehearsed the inexhaustible goodness of her grand-nephew (he was the son of one of her nieces and not much older than I was), I marveled at the ways of the fashionable, whose total disregard for truth enables them to praise the kind hearts of people whose hearts are hard, however cordial they may be with the brilliant members of their own set. Mme de Villeparisis, albeit indirectly, soon afforded me a confirmation of what I now knew were the essential features of her grand-nephew's nature, when I encountered them one day in a lane that was so narrow as to leave her no choice but to introduce me to him. He gave no sign that someone's name had just been uttered in his presence; not a muscle moved in his face; and had it not been for the fact that his eyes, in which there glowed not the slightest spark of humane feeling, showed a mere exaggeration of their insensitivity and emptiness of all expression, nothing would have distinguished them from lifeless mirrors. Then, staring at me with his hard eyes, as though he wished to be informed about me before acknowledging my greeting, suddenly set in motion as though by a muscular reflex rather than by an act of will, and putting between himself and me the greatest distance possible, he thrust out his arm as far as it would go and, from a great distance, gave me his hand. When he sent up his card the following day, I thought it must be at least a challenge to a duel. But his talk was of literature; and after a long conversation with me, he announced that he was very much looking forward to spending several hours in my company every day. Throughout that first visit of his, not only did he show a keen preference for intellectual things, but he showed a liking for me that was quite out of keeping with the handshake of the previous day. It was not until I had seen him repeat it with several other people that I realized it was nothing more than a habit, part of the manners common to some of his family, passed down to him by his mother, who had trained his body to show the excellence of his breeding; and he always shook hands like that, giving it no more thought than he gave to his fine clothes or his handsome hair; it was something that had none of the inner meaning I had seen in it, something he had merely acquired, just as he had come to have another habit, that of making sure of being introduced immediately to the relatives of his friends, which had become so irresistible to him that, when he saw me with my grandmother on the day after our first meeting, he walked straight up to me and, without even saying good morning, asked me to introduce him to her, with such feverish haste that his request might have been prompted by some impulse of self-defense, such as ducking to avoid a punch or closing the eyes against a spray of boiling water, as though he were faced by a danger demanding immediate evasive action.

These first rites of exorcism having been enacted, as a malevolent fairy divests itself of its first appearance and takes on the most captivating grace and beauty, I saw the man of disdain turn into the most likable and considerate fellow I had ever met. "Well," I thought, "I've already misread the man once, I've been fooled by a mirage; but now that I've seen through it, here I am being taken in by another one, because he's clearly just one of the high and mighty, full of his own nobility, while pretending he's not." In fact, before very long, all the charming manners and agreeableness of Saint-Loup were indeed to reveal another person in him, but a very different one from the person I now suspected him of being.

The only things valued by this young man, who looked like an aristocrat and a supercilious sportsman, the only things that aroused his interest, were intellectual things, and especially the most modernistic examples of literature and art, which his aunt thought so ludicrous. In addition, he was imbued with what she called the "ravings of the socialists," spoke of his own class with heartfelt contempt, and spent hours deep in Nietzsche and Proudhon.[38] He was one of those "intellectuals"[39] whose ready admiration keeps them immersed in books, satisfying a hunger for ideas. Actually, the manifestation of this very abstract tendency in Saint-Loup, which was at such a remove from my own usual mental activity, though it struck me as touching, also annoyed me somewhat. For instance, after I realized who his father was, if I happened to have been reading somebody's memoirs full of anecdotes figuring the doings of the famous Comte de Marsantes, whom I saw as the epitome of the special elegance of a period already long past, in the mood of vague yearning aroused in me by the book I found it galling that my appetite for information on the life that M. de Marsantes had led must remain unsatisfied, because Robert de Saint-Loup, rather than being content to be a chip off the old block, rather than being able to lead me through the chapters of the outmoded romance of his father's life, had aspired to familiarity with Nietzsche and Proudhon. Not that his father would have shared my regret. For he too had been an intelligent man, whose embrace of the world reached well beyond the fashionable Faubourg. He had had little time in which to become acquainted with his son, but had hoped the son would turn out to be a better man than he was himself. I suspect that, unlike the rest of the family, he would have admired his son, would have rejoiced to see his own trivial pastimes exchanged for serious pursuits, and that, without a word to anyone, like the witty but modest nobleman he was, he would have dipped privately into his son's favorite authors, so as to ascertain by how far Robert had outdistanced him.

It was of course rather sad that, whereas the Comte de Marsantes was open-minded enough to appreciate a son so different from himself, Robert de Saint-Loup had kept a memory of his father which, though affectionate, was rather scornful, because he was one of those for whom merit is inseparable from certain forms of art and ways of life, and all he could remember was a man who had devoted his whole life to hunting

and racing, who had yawned through Wagner and delighted in Offenbach. Saint-Loup was not intelligent enough to realize that intellectual
worth is unrelated to belief in any particular aesthetic doctrine; and
the disdain in which he held the intellectual life of M. de Marsantes
was akin to what one might have expected in a son of Boieldieu or
Labiche,[40] if either of them had had a son who was a lover of the most
advanced symbolist writing or the most abstruse music. "I hardly knew
my father," Robert said. "By all accounts, he was a delightful man. His
trouble was just the awful period in which he lived. I mean, being born
into the Faubourg Saint-Germain and being alive in the period of *La
Belle Hélène*[41] is enough to ruin anyone's existence. If he had been, say, a
petit bourgeois with a passion for Wagner's *Ring*, it's conceivable that
he might just have made some sort of a mark. They actually say he had
a liking for literature, but it's not really possible to tell, because what he
thought was literature was made up of works that are all dead and forgotten." Though I thought Saint-Loup was rather serious, he found it
strange that I was not serious enough. Judging all things by their intellectual content, and being unaware of the delights that my imagination
took in what he dismissed as frivolous, he was amazed that I, whom he
thought of as far superior to himself, could take any interest in such
things.

From the very first days of our acquaintance, Saint-Loup completely
won over my grandmother, partly by the unfailing kindness with which
he contrived to treat us, partly by the naturalness of the way he went
about it, which was his way of going about everything. Naturalness,
no doubt because it gives a glimpse, through human artistry, into nature itself, was the one quality my grandmother preferred to all others,
whether in gardens, which she disliked if, like the garden at Combray,
their plots and flower beds were too regular; in cookery, in which she
abhorred fancy contraptions like wedding cakes, with their barely recognizable ingredients; or in piano-playing, which displeased her if it was
too polished, too immaculate, a style to which she even preferred Ru-
binstein's slight mistakes of fingering or wrong notes. She also found
naturalness to enjoy in Saint-Loup's clothes, which showed a soft elegance, as far from the "flashy" as from the "prim and proper," without

stiffness or starch. Even more to her taste were the casual, easy ways of this rich young man, who managed to live amid luxury without "smacking of money," without giving himself airs; and the charm of his naturalness she saw too in something that Saint-Loup had never outgrown, though it generally disappears with the loss of childhood, along with some of childhood's physiological characteristics: his inability to master his face, which revealed his every emotion. Taken by surprise, for example, by something he had wished for but not expected to receive, even just a compliment, he would be overcome by such a sudden gust of pleasure, so burning, so volatile, so expansive, that it was impossible for him to contain and conceal it; his features would set in an irresistible grimace of gratification; through the skin of his cheeks, of excessive fineness, there glowed a bright flush, and his eyes reflected embarrassment and joy; and my grandmother was greatly touched by this gracious show of candor and guilelessness, in which, at least in the days when I first came to know Saint-Loup, there was nothing misleading. I must say, though, that I have known another person—indeed, there are many—in whom the physiological sincerity of the passing blush was entirely compatible with moral duplicity; in many such people, all it proves is that, for those who are capable of the direst treachery, there can be an intensity of enjoyment so disarming as to require immediate disclosure. But in nothing was the naturalness of Saint-Loup so endearing to my grandmother as in the open way he expressed his liking for me, in words that she herself, as she said, could never have bettered for their aptness and true devotion, words worthy of Mmes de Sévigné and de Beausergent; he made no bones about bantering me for my defects—the perspicacity with which he had surmised them had delighted her—but he did it in a way that was her own, with affection, and with a compensatory admiration for my qualities that was full of the warm spontaneity that eschews reserve and avoids disdain, the ways in which the self-importance of young men of his age usually likes to express itself. In his anticipating my slightest indisposition, tucking my blankets around my legs at moments when I had not noticed the weather was turning cool, secretly arranging things so that he could stay late with me on evenings when he thought I was feeling doleful or not quite well,

the care he took of my health, which might have required sterner measures, seemed all but excessive to my grandmother, though she was very
touched by it as a token of his attachment to me.

It was very soon agreed between us that we had become firm
friends forever, and each time he said "our friendship" it was as though
he spoke of some important and delightful entity existing outside
ourselves—before long he even came to say that, apart from his love for
his mistress, it was the greatest joy in his life. Such talk saddened me in
a way, and I never knew how to respond to it: for, in spending my time
chatting with him, I felt none of the happiness I was capable of deriving
from being without company; and in this, I suspect it would have been
the same for me with any other person. It was only when I was alone
that I would be swept on occasion by one of those impressions that
brought with them such deeply satisfying feelings. But I only had to be
in the presence of someone else—talking with a friend, for instance—for
my mind to face the wrong way, occupying itself with thoughts directed
toward the other person rather than toward myself; and thoughts going
in that other direction never afforded me any enjoyment. No sooner
had I left the company of Saint-Loup than I sought words with which
to tidy up the disordered minutes I had just spent with him: I assured
myself that I had a close friend and that a close friend is a rarity; yet, in
knowing I was the recipient of things difficult to come by, what I felt
was the exact opposite of the mode of enjoyment natural to me, the opposite of the pleasure that could come from finding something lying
deep within myself, from bringing it out of its inner darkness and into
the light of day. Whenever I spent two or three hours talking with
Robert de Saint-Loup, and if he was impressed by what I had been saying, I was overcome by something like remorse, regret, or weariness,
vexed at not having spent the time alone, at not having got down once
and for all to the work that awaited me. Then I would assure myself that
there is no law against others' appreciation of one's cleverest ideas, that
even the greatest minds may be excused for being admired, that it was
not right to see a waste of time in hours which had led my friend to
form a high opinion of me; I had no difficulty in convincing myself
that I should really be happy about all this, and my hope that such hap-

piness would never leave me was as strong as my knowledge that I had never in fact felt it. The joys we most dread losing are those that have remained outside us, beyond the reach of our heart. Although I felt I was better able than most to practice the virtues of friendship (in that I would always see the interests of my friends as counting for more than the sort of selfish advantage that motivates others, but which I ignored), I was aware of my own inability to find joy in a feeling which, rather than enhancing the differences between my mind and the minds of others—differences that exist among all minds—would abolish them. However, there were also moments when my mind could detect in Saint-Loup a creature of wider generality than himself, the "nobleman," a being which, like some inner daemon, moved his limbs, directed his gestures and his actions; and at such times, though sitting beside him, I was as alone as I would have been gazing at a landscape and appreciating its harmonies. He had become an object for my thoughts to toy with in an idle moment. To glimpse through him the earlier, immemorial, aristocratic self that Robert sought to avoid being was to experience a keen joy, but it was a joy generated by the mind, not by friendship. In the moral and physical agility that gave him such grace in friendliness, in his easy manner as he offered my grandmother a lift in his carriage and handed her in, then in the nimble way he jumped down from the box when he feared I might be feeling the cold, so as to drape his own overcoat about my shoulders, I sensed not only the hereditary deftness of generations of great hunters, the ancestors of this young man who prized nothing so much as things of the mind, not only their disdain for wealth, which, though he also enjoyed being wealthy for the sole reason that he could afford to make much of his friends, had come down to him in a casual habit of lavishing luxury on them, but also, especially, the knowledge (or possibly the illusion) these grand personages had entertained of being "above other people," which had prevented them from handing on to Saint-Loup any wish to show he was "no better than other people," any reluctance to appear overfriendly, of which he was genuinely devoid, but which can spoil even the sincerest affections of the less-than-noble with much stiff and awkward posturing. Occasionally I would feel a little guilty at delighting in this view of my friend as a work of art, at seeing the smooth interplay of his component parts as being regulated by a general idea which underlay their structure and function, but which, because he was unaware of it, added nothing to his inherent qualities as an individual, or to those personal values of mind and morality that he saw as paramount.

Yet that same general idea was, in some measure, the condition of the existence of such qualities and values. It was because he was a noble that his passion for ideas and his attraction to socialism, which made him seek the company of young, pretentious, and badly dressed students, attested to something genuinely pure and disinterested in him, though the same could not be said about them. In his belief that he was the heir to an ignorant and selfish class, he endeavored in all earnestness to have them forgive his aristocratic origins; yet it was these very origins that fascinated them and made them seek him out, though they made a show of coolness and even insolence toward him. So he would find himself making overtures to people the likes of whom my astounded family, imbued as they were with the sociology of Combray, would have expected him to shun. One day, as I sat with him on the sands, we overheard a voice from a nearby tent bemoaning the dense infestations of Jews that one had to put up with in Balbec: "You can't walk ten yards without stepping on one! Not that I'm a dyed-in-the-wool enemy of the chosen people, but hereabouts there's a glut of them. One's surrounded by people saying, 'I say, Apraham, I've chust seen Chacob.' One might as well be on the rue d'Aboukir."[42] Eventually, the man who found Jews so distasteful stepped out of the tent, and we glanced up to look at the anti-Semite: it was my old school friend Bloch. Saint-Loup immediately asked me to remind Bloch that they had met before: once when they both sat for the Concours Général, at which Bloch had won the top prize, and on a later occasion, in one of the *universités populaires*.[43]

I sometimes permitted myself a smile when I noticed in Robert the lessons once taught to him by the Jesuits, evident in the embarrassment that overcame him each time he risked hurting someone's feelings, as when one of his intellectual friends committed a social solecism or did something outlandish, the sort of thing which Saint-Loup saw as quite insignificant but which, if it had come to the attention of others, he sensed the person in question would have blushed for. So it was always Robert who blushed, as though he were the culprit—for instance, on the day when Bloch said he would call at the hotel to see him, then added:

"Since the idea of kicking my heels among all the bogus gimcrackery of these palatial caravanserais is intolerable to me, and since Gypsy orchestras make me feel ill, just tell the 'lyfte' to make them be quiet and inform you without further ado of my presence."[44]

I was none too pleased at the thought that Bloch might turn up at the hotel. The trouble was that he was not alone: he had come to Balbec with his sisters, who had many relatives and friends there. This Jewish colony was more picturesque than pleasant. Balbec, in this respect, was rather like certain countries—Russia or Romania, for example—where, as geography classes inform us, the Jewish population does not enjoy the same favor, and has not attained the same degree of assimilation, as in Paris, say. Eternally together, quite without admixture of any extraneous element, whenever Bloch's uncles or female cousins, or any of their coreligionists of either sex, went to the Casino, some of them heading for the "ball," others turning toward the baccarat rooms, they formed a homogeneous procession, quite distinct from the people who watched them pass and who recognized them from previous years without ever exchanging a greeting with them, whether it was the Cambremers' set, the little clan of the First President from Caen, people of exalted social position or of the mere middle classes, even simple grain merchants down from Paris, none of whose daughters, beautiful, proud, and scornful, as French as the statues of Rheims Cathedral, would have dreamed of mixing with a rabble of ill-bred hussies who thought "seaside" modishness so important that they always looked as though they had just been shrimping or were dancing the tango. As for the men, despite their glossy dinner jackets and patent-leather shoes, they were so unmistakable in their physical characteristics that they brought to mind those allegedly "clever" likenesses contrived by painters who, in illustrating the Gospels or the *Arabian Nights*, remember the country where the story unfolds and give to Saint Peter or Ali Baba the features of the most self-important "punter" in Balbec. Bloch introduced his sisters to me, girls at whom he would suddenly snap to make them shut up, but who hailed with gales of mirth the slightest joke of this brother of theirs, their admiration and their idol. It is quite likely that this Jewish community, like any other, perhaps more than any other, could boast of many charms, qualities, and virtues. The enjoyment of these, however, was restricted to its members. The fact was they were disliked; and this, once they became aware of it, became a proof in their eyes of anti-Semitism, against which they ranged themselves in a dense phalanx, closing ranks in the face of a world that was, in any case, of no mind to join their group.

The reference to the "lyfte" had come as no surprise to me: a few days earlier, Bloch having asked me what I was doing in Balbec (he seemed to take it for granted that his own presence there was self-explanatory) and whether I was hoping to "pick up a few useful connections," and as I had replied that my visit there was the fulfillment of one of my oldest dreams, not quite as strong, however, as my longing to see Venice, he said, "Ah, yes, sitting about with the lovely ladies, sipping sherbet, pretending to read *The Stones of Venyce* of Lord John Ruskin—a moping monomaniac, by the way, and one of the crashingest bores ever invented." Bloch clearly thought that in England not only all individuals of the masculine gender were lords, but that the letter *i* was always pronounced like a *y*. My new friend Saint-Loup looked on this mispronunciation as nugatory, tending to see it as indicating the mere absence of certain attributes of an elegant class, attributes which he dismissed with a scorn that was as profound as was his own mastery of them. However, his apprehension that one day Bloch would learn not only the proper pronunciation of "Venice" but that Ruskin was no lord, and that with hindsight he might suspect Robert of having thought him ridiculous, made Robert feel as guilty as though he had shown a lack of the considerateness he actually had in abundance; and so, with foresight and his capacity for seeing himself as others might, he felt his own face color with the blush that would darken Bloch's face on the day when he discovered his mistake. He was pretty sure, of course, that Bloch would see it as much more important than he did. Bloch himself proved this some time later, when he overheard me speak of the "lift" and interrupted me with, "I see—so it's 'lift.' " To which, in a sharp and supercilious tone, he added, "Anyway—doesn't matter." One may hear this statement, which is analogous to a reflex, spoken by all who have a touch of self-esteem, in circumstances which can vary from the trivial to the tragic, and which reveals, as it did on the present occasion, how much the thing that is said not to matter does matter to the speaker; and in the tragic vein, the first thing to come to the lips of any man who takes a certain pride in himself, if his last hope has just been dashed by someone's refusal to help him out, may well be the brave, forlorn words, "Oh well, it doesn't matter, not to worry—I'll think of something else," the something else that is the alternative to what "doesn't matter" being sometimes the last resort of suicide.

Bloch's next words to me were very kind. There can be no doubt that he was trying to be as pleasant as possible. But then he asked, "Tell me, are you hobnobbing with de Saint-Loup-en-Bray because you imagine rising to the level of the nobility? Of course, his branch of the nobility is small beer—but you always *were* naïve. You must be going through a fine fit of snobbery, eh? *Are* you a snob, do you think? You are, aren't you?" It was not that he had suddenly taken leave of his intention to be pleasant. But, his defect being what is known as "bad manners," it was the one defect he never noticed in himself, the one he thought nobody could be offended by. Taking humankind as a whole, the incidence of the virtues shared by all is no more remarkable than the multiplicity of the defects peculiar to each. It is probably true to say that it is not "common sense that is the commonest thing in the world,"[45] but common kindness. In the remotest regions, one can be amazed by seeing it suddenly and unexpectedly flower, as one can come upon a single poppy standing all by itself in a little valley, identical to every other poppy in the world, though it has never seen any of them, and has never known anything other than the wind that from time to time ruffles the silk of its lonely scarlet standard. Even if this kindness is so paralyzed by self-interest as to be in abeyance, it still exists; and whenever its functioning is not thwarted by some selfish urge— for example, during the reading of a novel or a newspaper—it opens like a spreading bloom and, even in the heart of someone who, though a murderer in real life, is still easily moved by tribulations in fiction, becomes the wish to succor the weak, the just, and the persecuted. But that variety in faults is no less striking than the similarity in virtues. The most perfect of persons has a particular fault, which gives rise to rage or shock. A man may have an admirable mind, may see all things with the loftiest disinterest and never speak ill of a soul, but he forgets he still has in his pocket the urgent letter he himself offered to mail for you, thus making you miss an appointment of the utmost importance; yet, instead of apologizing, he will smile, because he takes pride in never letting his own life be ruled by the clock. Another one is so considerate, so thoughtful, so mild-mannered, that in conversing with you he only ever speaks of you in ways calculated to cheer you; but you have reason to suspect there are other reflections that he never voices, quite different things about you that he keeps to himself, things that fester in the heart; yet the pleasure he takes in being with you is so great that he will wear you out with kindness rather than leave you alone. Or there is the one whose sincerity is greater, but who takes it so far as to inform you, after you have pleaded ill health as a reason for not visiting him, that you were seen going to the theater, in what appeared to be a state of robust health, or that, since the good turn you tried to do him was only partially successful, and since in any case three other people have already offered to do it, he now feels little sense of obligation toward you. In both of these circumstances, the second friend would have feigned ignorance of your outing to the theater and of the fact that the same good turn could have been done for him by several others. The third friend, having also felt the need to repeat or divulge to someone else something that you have said that can only embarrass you, basks in his own frankness and boasts, "That's how I am!" And of course there are those who irritate you by their inquisitiveness, or even by their lack of curiosity, which can be so great that, even though you tell them of the most amazing events, they have not the slightest notion of what you are talking about; and there are others who will put off answering your letter for months, as long as it deals with something of concern to you but not to them; or who will let you know they are coming to see you about some matter, which makes you stay at home so as not to miss them, and then do not come, so for weeks you hear nothing more from them, because, not having received from you an answer their letter did not seem to require, they assumed they had offended you in some way. There are people who, heeding their own wishes rather than yours, keep talking without letting you get a word in, if it happens they are in good spirits and are pleased to see you; but the same people, if they, or the weather, are out of sorts, will be struck dumb, meeting your best efforts with languid inertia, no more eager to utter so much as a monosyllable in reply than if they had not heard you speak. Each of our friends is so inseparable from his faults that, if we are to go on liking him, we must leaven them with reminders of his talent, his kind heart, his affectionate ways, or, rather, we must try, by exercising all our goodwill, to overlook them. Unfortunately, this stubborn willingness on our part to over-look the fault in our friend is outweighed by his own dogged persistence in it, he being either blind to himself or convinced that others are blind to him. Either he does not see it or he believes we do not. As the danger of giving offense lies mainly in the difficulty of gauging what will and what will not pass unnoticed, we should make a rule of never speaking of ourselves, given that it is a subject on which we may be sure our own view and that of others will never coincide. On seeing into the real life of another person, learning the truth of an existence that is overlaid by an appearance of truth, we can expect as many surprises as though we were exploring a house of ordinary demeanor that turns out to be full of ill-gotten gains, cat burglar's jimmies, and corpses; and the opposite surprise can result if, instead of the image of ourselves we have formed from the things others say of us to our face, we discover from what they say in our absence the utterly dissimilar image they have of us and our life. Each time we have spoken of ourselves, we may be sure that our harmless, cautious words, received with ostensible politeness and a pre-tense of approval, have later inspired a diatribe of unfavorable judg-ment on us, full of exasperation or hilarity at our expense. If nothing else, we run the risk of being thought irritating, because of the disparity between our idea of ourselves and our words, which is what usually makes the things people say about themselves as laughable as the ap-proximate hummings of would-be music-lovers who, when they feel the need to tra-la-la their favorite piece, have to make up for the meagerness of their inarticulate rendition of it by an energetic pantomime and an air of admiration that is quite out of keeping with the impression they make on their listeners. The bad habit of speaking of oneself and one's faults should not go without mention of its corollary, the habit of criticizing in others faults closely analogous to our own. These are always the ones we choose to speak of, as though this were an unobtrusive way of speaking of ourselves, one that adds to the pleasure of self-forgiveness the pleasure of confession. It seems too that our attention, constantly attracted to whatever distinguishes us, notices this in others more than anything else. "He can hardly see his hand in front of his face," says one shortsighted person of another; a consumptive will voice a misgiving about the state of the healthiest man's lungs; someone who never washes keeps talking about the baths that others never take; the man who stinks says people stink; the deceived husband seeks cuckoldry everywhere; the flighty woman speaks of flighty women; the snob's talk is of snobs. And of course each vice, like each of the professions, requires and acquires a special knowledge that we are not displeased at being able to display. It takes a homosexual to detect a homosexual; a dressmaker at a fashionable party has not so much as chatted with you, yet he already appreciates the fabric of the clothes you are wearing, and his fingertips itch with the desire to feel it; and if after several moments' conversation with an odontologist you were to ask him for his true opinion of yourself, he would tell you the number of your bad teeth. To him, there is nothing more important; to you, who have noticed his own bad teeth, there is nothing more ridiculous. It is not only when we speak of ourselves that we think others are blind: we act as though they were. Each of us is watched over by a special god, who hides our fault, or promises us it shall be invisible, just as he masks the eyes and blocks the nostrils of those who never wash, persuading them that they can blithely ignore the tidemark near their ears and the smell of sweat hanging about their armpits, as these will remain imperceptible to the world in which they move. Those who wear or give fake pearls as presents always assume that others will think they are genuine. Bloch was a bad-mannered, neurotic snob; and since he belonged to a family of no note,

he suffered, as though at the bottom of the ocean, from the incalculable pressures bearing upon him from not just the Gentiles on the surface, but the superimposed layers of Jewish society, all more estimable
than the one he belonged to, and each of them pouring scorn on the
one immediately below itself. To rise to the fresh air, through each level
of Jewish families, would have taken Bloch several thousand years. A
much better solution was to find a way out in some other direction.

When Bloch spoke of the fit of snobbery I must be having and invited me to own up to being a snob, I could have answered, "If I were a
snob, I wouldn't be mixing with you." But all I said was that it was not
a very nice thing to say. He made an attempt at an apology; but it was
of the sort often favored by the ill-mannered man, who is glad to revisit
words of his that have given offense, as it gives him the chance to com-
pound the latter. "Do forgive me," he would say thereafter. "I was a
brute, I was horrible to you, I took pleasure in being nasty to you. And
yet, mankind in general and your good friend in particular being such a
singular animal, you have no idea of the depth of affection for you harbored in this heart of mine. Though I tease you unmercifully, it has
been known to move me to tears." These words he accompanied with a
little sob.

There was one thing about Bloch that surprised me more than his
tactlessness, and that was how uneven his conversation was. This fellow,
who could dismiss the most up-to-the-minute writer with, "The man's a
dismal imbecile, an out-and-out idiot!," was capable of reveling in un-
funny anecdotes and judging a complete mediocrity to be "somebody
really interesting." This dual standard of judgment, applied to the mind,
the merit, and the interestingness of people, was something of a mystery to me until the day I met M. Bloch senior.

I had assumed we might never have the privilege of being introduced to him, Bloch the younger having spoken ill of me to Saint-Loup
and of Saint-Loup to me. In particular, he had told Saint-Loup that I
was (still) a dreadful snob. "Yes, he is, he is, I tell you! He's beside himself at being acquainted with M. LLLLegrandin." This habit of Bloch's,
of stressing a certain word, was a marker of both irony and literature. Saint-Loup, who had never heard of Legrandin, said in surprise,

"Really? Who's he?" "Oh, he's really someone!" said Bloch with a laugh, slipping his hands, as though for warmth, into his jacket pockets, and convinced that what he was witnessing was the quainter side of a petty provincial gentleman more preposterous than any in the pages of Barbey d'Aurevilly.[46] In his inability to describe M. Legrandin, he contented himself with multiplying his initial consonant and savoring the flavor of the name, like a connoisseur with a mouthful of a fine old vintage. This, however, was a private pleasure, to which others had no access. Having spoken ill of me to Saint-Loup, Bloch then did the same about Saint-Loup to me. It was no later than the following day that each of us learned all about what had been said—not that either of us had repeated Bloch's statements to the other (that would have seemed too reprehensible to both of us), but Bloch himself thought it would be only natural and inevitable for us to do that; so, in his uneasiness, and in the conviction that he was telling us something we were bound to find out anyway, he chose to take the initiative. Taking Saint-Loup aside, he told him he had spoken ill of him on purpose, but only so that it would get back to him; and he swore, "by the Kroniôn Zeus, keeper of oaths,"[47] that he was much attached to him, that he would willingly die for him, then wiped away a little tear. That same day, he made a point of seeing me alone, owned up to what he had said about me, insisting that he had acted only for my benefit, because he was firmly of the belief that, for me, there were certain social relations from which nothing good could ever come, and that I "deserved better." He took my hand, as maudlin as a drunkard, though his intoxication was purely nervous: "Do believe me! May the black Ker carry me off this instant and bear me beyond the gates of Hades, detestable to men, if I did not spend last night weeping for you, in memory of Combray, my inexhaustible affection for you, and certain afternoons at school that *you* won't even remember. Yes, there I was, crying all night long! I swear it— but, alas, I speak as one who knows what men are like, and I know you won't believe me." I did not believe him, of course; and no great weight was added to words that I knew had been invented on the spot by his invocation of "the black Ker," as Bloch's Hellenic cult was a purely literary thing. Besides, every time he felt a touch of maudlin coming over him and wanted you to share a moment's bogus emotion, he always said, "I swear it!"—not so much with the aim of having you believe he was telling the truth, but, rather, for the hysterical delight he took in telling a lie. So I did not believe him; but I bore him no ill will, as my mother and grandmother had handed down to me not only their inability to bear a grudge, even against those who deserved it more than he did, but their reluctance to condemn anybody.

Not that Bloch was irredeemably flawed; he was in fact capable of acts of great kindness. Now that the Combray breed, the strain from which there once sprang people of utter integrity, like my grandmother and mother, seems all but extinct, and if one's choice among men is more or less reduced, on the one hand, to uncomplicated troglodytes, unfeeling, straightforward creatures the mere sound of whose voice tells you they have not the slightest interest in any of your concerns, and, on the other, a race of men who, while they are in your company, can sympathize with you, cherish you, be moved to tears by you, and then, a few hours later, contradict all this by making a cruel joke about you, but who can go on being charming toward you, full of understanding, still on the same footing of momentary closeness, then I am inclined to think that, of the two, I prefer men of the latter breed, if not for their human value, at least for their company.

"You've no idea," Bloch would say, "how sad it makes me to think of you. There really is a Jewish streak in me somewhere," he added with an ironic narrowing of the eyes, as though trying to measure by microscope a minute drop of "Jewish blood," as might be said (but most certainly never would be) by a great French aristocrat whose exclusively Christian ancestors might just have included a Samuel Bernard,[48] or, even more remotely, the Virgin Mary herself, from whom all people called Lévy descend, it is said. "Yes, just my Jewish streak coming out. Among my various emotions, I do quite like to be aware of the feeble few that may just derive from my Jewish origins." He made this statement because it seemed to him both witty and bold to speak the truth about his racial origins, while making sure to mitigate them somewhat, like a miser who, having decided to pay his accumulated debts, can pluck up the courage to settle only half of them. The type of fraudulence that consists of being bold enough to utter a difficult truth while diluting it with enough untruths to falsify it, is more widespread than one might think; and even those who do not make a habit of this may now and then have recourse to it, if some critical episode in life, particularly one involving a love affair, gives them the opportunity.

The outcome of all these confidential diatribes of Bloch's to Saint-Loup against me, and to me against Saint-Loup, was an invitation to dinner. I think he may even have made a preliminary attempt to invite only Saint-Loup. Everything I know about him makes for the plausibility of this hypothesis; but it was unsuccessful, and it was in the presence of both Saint-Loup and myself that Bloch said one day, "Good my lord, and you, knight favored of Ares, de Saint-Loup-en-Bray, subduer of steeds, since I have met you on this surf-resounding strand of Amphitrite, close by the tents of Menier of the swift ships,[49] would you both please come to dinner one evening during the week, at the table of my illustrious father of irreproachable heart?" Bloch issued this invitation because of his desire for closer relations with Saint-Loup, who he hoped would give him access to aristocratic circles. If I had been the one to have such a desire, with such an intent, Bloch would have seen it as a mark of the most detestable snobbery, in keeping with the view he had formed of an aspect of my character (an aspect which, at least for the moment, he did not consider to be my most important feature); but the same desire on his part struck him as proof of his own mind's commendable curiosity about social explorations of a kind that might afford him some literary material. When he informed his father that he was bringing a friend of his to dinner, a friend whose name and title he announced in a tone charged with sarcastic satisfaction, "the Marquis de Saint-Loup-en-Bray," M. Bloch senior had been seized by a fit of vehement emotion. "The Marquis de Saint-Loup-en-Bray!" he gasped. "Egad!" This was the exclamation which, for him, best expressed deference toward one's social superiors. The gaze he turned upon this son of his, who was capable of having such friends, was full of admiration and clearly meant: "What an amazing boy! Can such a prodigy really be a son of mine?" The younger Bloch basked in this glory, and looked as though his monthly allowance had just been increased by fifty francs.

Within the family, he lived usually in a state of some unease, feeling that his father believed he had gone to the dogs, with his admiration of poets like Leconte de Lisle, Heredia,[50] and other such "bohemians." But to be friendly with Saint-Loup-en-Bray, whose father had been the president of the Suez Canal Company (egad!), was an "incontrovertible" advantage. What a pity that the stereoscope, which might have suffered some damage in transit, had been left in Paris! M. Bloch senior was the only one with the skill, or, rather, the right, to make use of the stereoscope. This he did only on rare, judiciously selected occasions, on special gala evenings when they had taken on extra menservants. These stereoscope sessions conferred upon those who attended them a sort of distinction, a feeling of being singled out and privileged, and there devolved upon the host who was responsible for them a form of prestige akin to that accorded to talent, which could not have been greater if the images projected had been taken by M. Bloch himself, or if the instrument had been of his own invention. "You didn't have an invitation to Salomon's yesterday?" one member of the family would ask another. "No, I wasn't one of the chosen few—what was going on?" "Oh, a great bean-feast, with the stereoscope and everything!" "Well, if it was a stereoscope occasion, then I'm sorry to have missed it. I'm told Salomon is just brilliant with it." "But look here," M. Bloch senior said to his son, "it will be better not to give him everything all at once. Then he'll still have something to look forward to." M. Bloch, like a good father who wishes to do right by his son, had certainly considered sending for the apparatus. However, time was "of the essence," or so they thought; but then the dinner had to be postponed, as Saint-Loup could not get away, one of his uncles being expected in Balbec to spend forty-eight hours with Mme de Villeparisis. This uncle was very fond of physical exercise, especially in the form of long walks; and so, as he was coming on foot from the château where he was at present a guest, sleeping overnight at farmhouses along the way, the timing of his arrival at Balbec was rather uncertain. Saint-Loup, who did not wish to risk missing him, even asked me to go to Incarville, where there was a telegraph office, and send the dispatch he was in the habit of cabling every day to his mistress. The expected uncle was called Palamède, a name handed down from the princes of Sicily, his ancestors. In later life, whenever I read historical texts that contained this name, a fine medallion of the Renaissance—some said a genuine antique—a name borne by some *podestà* or prince of the Church, which had always remained in the family, being handed on from descendant to descendant, from the chancellery of the Vatican right down to my friend's uncle, I would experience the special pleasure savored by those who, in their inability to afford a collection of medals or to constitute a private gallery of artworks, cultivate instead a passion for old names (place-names, as documentary and picturesque as an out-of-date map or isometric projection, a tradesman's sign, or a customary; and baptismal names, with their fine French final syllables, in which one still hears the ring of the long-standing mutilations that our ancestors, by speech defects, the intonation of some ethnic vulgarity, or mispronunciation, inflicted on Latin and Saxon words, in a way that later elevated them into the grammarians' noble statutes), repertoires of antique sonorities that enable them to enjoy private concerts, like those people who acquire a viola da gamba or viola d'amore so as to play ancient music on period instruments. Saint-Loup told me that, even within the most exclusive aristocratic circles, his uncle Palamède was distinguished by being even more exclusive, peculiarly difficult to get to know, disdainful, infatuated with his own nobility, and at the center of a group that included his brother's wife and a few other hand-picked associates, known as the Circle of the Phoenixes. Even within that inner circle, he was so dreaded for his insolent words that in the past, when fashionable people seeking an introduction had on occasion approached his brother, the latter had been known to refuse out of hand. "No, please don't ask me for an introduction to Palamède. Even if my wife were to try on your behalf, even if any or all of us were to try, it would be pointless. Or else there would be the danger of his being less than friendly, and I would prefer to avoid that." At the Jockey Club, with a few friends, the uncle had drawn up a list of two hundred members whom he would never permit to be introduced to him. In the household of the Comte de Paris, he was dubbed "the Prince," in virtue of his elegance and his haughtiness.

Saint-Loup told me something of his uncle's younger days, long past. He had shared an apartment with two friends who were as hand-some as he was, which was why they were known as "the Three Graces"; and every day he would bring women to it.

"One day, a fellow who has nowadays become what Balzac would have called "one of the most prominent members of the Faubourg Saint-Germain," but who in those early days went through an unfortunate period when he showed rather untoward tendencies, made an appointment with my uncle at the apartment. When he got there, the fellow made his intentions quite clear—but toward my uncle Palamède, not toward the women! My uncle pretended not to understand, then on some pretext or other sent for his two friends. They turned up, took the miscreant, stripped the clothes off him, beat him till his blood ran red, then kicked him out—it was ten below zero, and when he was found he was lucky to be alive. The police started an investigation, and the fellow had great difficulty in getting them to drop it. These days, my uncle would never have anything to do with such a cruel punishment—despite his unapproachability with people of his own station, you've no idea of the number of working-class men whom he takes a liking to, whom he takes under his wing, though he may well get no thanks for it in the end. A footman who attends him in a hotel somewhere and whom he'll set up in Paris; a peasant lad whom he gets apprenticed to a trade—that sort of thing. It's just this rather nice side of his nature, as opposed to his society side." Saint-Loup was one of those young men of fashion who live at an altitude where certain expressions can take root and grow—for instance, "the rather nice side of his nature" or "there's rather a nice thing about him," somewhat precious blooms, which soon turn into a way of seeing things that reduces oneself to nothing, while exalting "the proletariat"; quite the opposite, in fact, of the plebeian's pride in his origins. "It seems we have no idea of the way he used to set the trends as a young man, the standards he set for the whole of society. At all times, he only ever did what was convenient, what struck him as enjoyable, but whatever it was, it was instantly imitated by all the snobs. If he felt thirsty at the theater, say, and sent out for a drink to be brought to him in his box, the following week all the little sitting rooms behind the boxes were full of refreshments. Or one rather wet summer, when he'd had a touch of rheumatism, he wanted a vicuña overcoat—it's a cloth that is soft but warm, normally used only for traveling rugs—and the one he got still had the blue-and-orange stripes on it. All the best tailors were immediately inundated with orders for shaggy blue overcoats with a fringe. On another occasion, if he was spending a day or two at a château, he might turn up without his tails, because for some reason he felt like dining without any great ceremony; and so he would go in to dinner wearing his town clothes, and in country houses it became the fashion not to change for dinner. If he took to eating his cake not with a spoon but with a fork, or some other instrument of his own design, specially made for him by a goldsmith, or even with his fingers, then it was soon inconceivable not to do likewise. Once, when he wanted to be reminded of some of the quartets of Beethoven (despite his preposterous ideas, he's no fool, he's a gifted man), he just got a group of musicians to come to his house each week, and they played them for him and a few of his friends.[51] So the really elegant thing that year was to hold very select little gatherings with chamber music. I'm pretty sure he's had a fair amount of pleasure in life. A man as handsome as he was—think of the number of women he must have had! I've no idea who they were, as he's a very discreet man. But I do know he was very unfaithful to my late aunt. Mind you, he was also very attentive and charming toward her, and she adored him, and after her death he was inconsolable for a long time. Even now, when he's in Paris, he still visits the cemetery nearly every day."

On the morning after Robert told me these things about this expected uncle, who had eventually failed to materialize, I was walking back to the hotel when, right in front of the Casino, I had a sudden feeling of being looked at by someone at quite close quarters. I glanced around and saw a very tall, rather stout man of about forty, with a jet-black mustache, who stood there nervously flicking a cane against the leg of his trousers and staring at me with eyes dilated by the strain of attention. At times, they seemed shot through with intense, darting glances of a sort which, when directed toward a total stranger, can only ever be seen from a man whose mind is visited by thoughts that would never occur to anyone else, a madman, say, or a spy. He flashed a final look at me, like the parting shot from one who turns to run, daring, cautious, swift, and searching; then, having gazed all about, with a sudden air of idle haughtiness, his whole body made a quick side-turn and he began a close study of a poster, humming the while and rearranging the moss rose in his buttonhole. From his pocket he produced a little notebook, and appeared to write down the title of the performance advertised; he looked a couple of times at his fob watch; he pulled his black straw hat lower on his brow and held his hand to the rim of it like a visor, as though looking out for someone he was expecting; he made the gesture of irritation that is meant to suggest one has had enough of waiting, but which one never makes when one has really been waiting; then, pushing back his hat to reveal close-cropped hair with rather long, waved side-wings, he breathed out noisily, as people do, not when they are too hot, but when they wish it to be thought they are too hot. It crossed my mind that he might be a hotel thief who, having perhaps noticed me and my grandmother over the last few days, and having some dishonest intent, had just realized I had noticed him while he was watching my movements; and, so as to put me off the scent, he may only have been trying to express absentmindedness and nonchalance, but he did it with such marked exaggeration that his purpose appeared to be not just to disarm suspicion, but also to avenge some humiliation I had inflicted upon him unawares, to make me think not so much that he had not seen me, but that I was so insignificant an object that he could not be bothered to pay the slightest attention to me. He had drawn himself up with a challenging air, setting his lips in a sneer, twirling his mustache, and charging his eye with something hard and indifferent, something close to insulting. It was the strangeness of his expression that made me think he must be a thief, if not a madman. Yet his way of dressing, which was the acme of good taste, was both much more serious and much more simple than that of any of the bathers I saw at Balbec, as well as being something of a comfort to me in my suit, which had so often been humiliated by the bright and banal whiteness of their beach outfits. My grandmother now appeared, and we went for a little walk. An hour later, she having gone back in for a moment, I was waiting for her outside the hotel when I saw Mme de

Villeparisis come out in the company of Robert de Saint-Loup and the stranger who had stared at me near the Casino. His glance flashed rapidly through me just as before; then, as though he had not seen me, it lowered, seemed to settle somewhere outside his eyes, dull and neutral, like a look that feigns to see nothing outside itself, and is incapable of seeing anything inside, the look expressing nothing but the satisfaction of knowing it is edged by eyelashes, among which it merely sits, roundly pleased with its own crass candor, the smug and sanctimonious look of certain hypocrites, the conceited look of certain fools. I saw that he had changed his clothes: the suit he now wore was even darker than the other one—no doubt true elegance is closer to simplicity than is false elegance, but there was something else about him: at close range, one sensed that the almost complete absence of color from his clothes came not from any indifference to color, but because, for some reason, he deprived himself of it. The sobriety apparent in his clothing gave the impression of deriving from a self-imposed diet, rather than from any lack of appetite. In the fabric of his trousers, a fine stripe of dark green harmonized with a line visible in his socks, the refinement of this touch revealing the intensity of a preference which, though suppressed everywhere else, had been tolerated in that one form as a special concession, whereas a red design in the cravat remained as imperceptible as a liberty not quite taken, a temptation not quite succumbed to.

"How are you? Allow me to introduce my nephew, the Baron de Guermantes," said Mme de Villeparisis. The gentleman so named, without looking at me, mumbled a vague "How d'you do?" which he followed with "Hmmm, hmmm," as though to mark the fact that this politeness had been forced upon him; then, withholding his thumb, his little finger, and his index finger, he proffered the other two, neither of which bore a ring, and which I shook through his suede glove. Then, still without having given me a glance, he turned his eyes to Mme de Villeparisis.

"Good heavens!" she exclaimed. "What am I saying? Baron de Guermantes indeed! Allow me to introduce my nephew, the Baron de Charlus! Not that it's a very heinous error—you are, after all, a Guermantes."

My grandmother appeared, and we all walked along the road to-gether. Saint-Loup's uncle neither spoke a single word to me nor gave me so much as a glance. Though he glared at strangers (two or three times during our brief stroll, he flashed his awesome and searching eye deep into the heart of nondescript passersby of the most humble extrac-tion), he was in the habit, if his attitude toward me was any guide to his behavior, of avoiding at all moments the eye of people he knew, like a police officer on a secret mission who excludes his friends from the scope of his professional observations. I fell back a little with Saint-Loup, letting the uncle walk on with my grandmother and Mme de Villeparisis:

"Tell me—did I hear right? Madame de Villeparisis said to your uncle that he was a Guermantes."

"But of course—he's Palamède de Guermantes."

"Do you mean the same Guermantes family who have a château near Combray and who claim descent from Geneviève de Brabant?"

"Absolutely. My uncle, who's terribly heraldic, would soon let you know that our 'cry,' our war cry, which later became *Passavant*, was origi-nally *Combraysis*,"[52] Saint-Loup said with a laugh, which was meant to forestall any suspicion that he might take pride in sharing in the preroga-tive of the "cry," enjoyed only by houses of nearly royal status, by the greatest warlords. "He is the brother of the present owner of the château."

Mme de Villeparisis was therefore related, and very closely at that, to the Guermantes, though she had for such a long time been only the lady who, when I was little, had given me a duck holding a box of chocolate, more remote in those days from the Guermantes way than if she had been enclosed in the Méséglise way, less splendid, less highly valued by me than the optician of Combray, but now suddenly experi-encing one of those fantastic elevations, the corollary of equally unex-pected devaluations of other objects in our possession, which, whether rising or falling, fill our adolescence and the parts of our lives in which a little of our adolescence lives on with metamorphoses as numerous as those Ovid speaks of.

"And doesn't the château contain busts of all the former lords of Guermantes?"

"Yes, it's a grand spectacle!" Saint-Loup said ironically. "Between ourselves, I think all that sort of thing is just a little quaint. But one thing there is at Guermantes that's really interesting is a very touching portrait of my aunt by Carrière.[53] It's every bit as good as anything by Whistler or Velázquez," he added, the tyro's enthusiasm getting the better, as it sometimes did, of his sense of proportion. "And there are other canvases, very stirring ones, by Gustave Moreau.[54] My aunt is the niece of your friend Mme de Villeparisis, who brought her up, and she then married her cousin, the present Duc de Guermantes, who is also a nephew of my aunt de Villeparisis."

"So what's your uncle?"

"He bears the title of Baron de Charlus. Strictly speaking, at the death of my great-uncle, my uncle Palamède should have taken the title of Prince des Laumes, which was his brother's before he in his turn became the Duc de Guermantes—the people in my family change their titles the way other people change their shirts. However, my uncle has his own way of thinking on such things: he takes the view that there are rather too many Italian duchies and Spanish grandees and the like, and so, though he could have chosen any one of four or five titles that would have made him Prince of This or That, he remained plain Baron de Charlus, as a sort of protest, but with a lot of pride concealed under the apparent simplicity of it. 'Nowadays,' he says, 'when every Tom, Dick, or Harry is a prince, one requires something else with which to differentiate oneself. I'll keep my "Prince" for when I'm traveling incognito.' According to him, there's no title as ancient as Baron de Charlus: if he undertakes to prove to you that it's older than the titles of the Montmorency family, who falsely claim to be the first Barons of France, when all they were was Barons of Île-de-France,[55] because that's where their feudal lands were, he'll take a delight in inundating you, submerging you with facts and figures about it. It must be said that, although he's very clever, very gifted, he thinks that's a brilliant topic of conversation," Saint-Loup said with a smile. "But I'm not like him, and you're not going to get me to talk for hours about genealogies—life is too short to spend it prattling about boring, out-of-date nonsense like that."

I now realized that the fierce stare that had attracted my attention earlier that afternoon outside the Casino was the one I had seen at Tansonville, when Mme Swann had called out the name of Gilberte.

"Did Mme Swann ever happen to be one of the many mistresses you say your uncle, M. de Charlus, used to have?"

"Oh, no, absolutely not! He's a great friend of Swann's, that is, and has always stood by him, but no one has ever suggested he might have been the wife's lover. You would create consternation in the ranks of society if it was thought you believed that."

I did not dare reply that I would have created greater consternation in Combray if it was thought I did not believe it.

My grandmother was delighted with M. de Charlus. There was no doubt that he did attach extreme importance to all matters of birth and social status; but her awareness of this was uncolored by any of the severe disapproval that is the mark of a secret envy and the vexation of seeing someone else enjoying advantages one would like to enjoy, but which are out of reach. My grandmother, quite content with her lot in life, untroubled by any wish to live in grander society, exercised on M. de Charlus only her mind, which enabled her to observe his foibles and to speak of this uncle of Saint-Loup with the benevolent, smiling detachment that is close to affection, and is our way of rewarding the object of our disinterested observation for the pleasures we find in it, in this case especially because the object was a personage full of pretensions which, though possibly misplaced, she found at least picturesque, and which sharply differentiated him from all the other people with whom she usually had occasion to mix. But there were things in M. de Charlus, such as intelligence and sensibility, which one sensed were of acute potency, distinguishing him from the many society people whom Saint-Loup found painfully amusing; and it was especially these things that made my grandmother so indulgent toward his aristocratic bias. Unlike the nephew, the uncle had not sacrificed this preference to values seen as higher: he had reconciled it with them. In his capacity as descendant of the Ducs de Nemours and the Princes de Lamballe, he owned archives, furniture, tapestries, portraits painted for his ancestors by Raphael, Velázquez, or Boucher, and could quite properly have said, when merely glancing over a few family souvenirs, that he was visiting a museum or some grand library; and it was this rich heritage of the aristocracy that he valued so highly and his nephew so little. In addition, there being less of the ideologue in him than in Saint-Loup, less readiness to take fine words at face value, more realism in his judgment of men, he may have been loath to neglect something that they see as essential to prestige, something that, as well as affording its disinterested delights to his imagination, could also be powerfully effective as an aid to his practical purposes. There is no common ground between men of his sort and those who aspire to an inner ideal that urges them to divest themselves of such advantages and to devote themselves solely to it, who thereby show a similarity with painters or writers who renounce their virtuosity, artistic peoples who embrace modernization, warlike peoples who opt for total disarmament, dictatorial governments that turn democratic and repeal harsh laws, though often the world will not reward them for this noble effort: some lose their talent, some their hereditary predominance; pacifism can lead to war, and indulgence can foster crime. However noble and sincere the impulse of Saint-Loup toward emancipation, when one saw the result, one was convinced that it was just as well it was not shared by M. de Charlus, who had had most of the admirable wood paneling transferred from the Guermantes family *hôtel* to his own house, rather than replace it, as his nephew had done, with an Art Nouveau décor and paintings by Lebourg and Guillaumin.[56] Even so, M. de Charlus's ideal was factitious in the extreme, and—if one may say such a thing of an ideal—it was one that aspired toward the fashionable world as much as to the world of art. In certain women who were exceptionally beautiful and extraordinarily cultivated, whose great-great-grandmothers, two centuries before, had been part of the full glory and elegance of the *ancien régime,* he perceived a form of distinction that made them the only women whose company he found at all pleasant; and though no doubt this admiration was sincere, it was colored by the reminders of history and art that rang for him in their names, just as reminders of antiquity may explain the pleasure a cultured man enjoys in an ode of Horace, though it may be inferior to poems of our own day that leave him indifferent. In the view of M. de

Charlus, a pretty woman of the middle classes, in relation to any of these women, was like a contemporary painting of a road or a wedding party in relation to an old master, the history of which we know, from the pope or the king who commissioned it to the various personages in whose company it has lived, as a result of donation, purchase, legacy, or looting, and because of which it can recall an event or at least a union of two houses, some historical interest, some element of learning, all of which adds to it an extra dimension of usefulness, and increases our appreciation of the richness of what we can possess through memory or erudition. M. de Charlus drew comfort too from the fact that a similar bias to his own prevented these few great ladies from frequenting other women of lesser breeding, thus enabling him to worship them in their unimpaired nobility, as intact as an eighteenth-century façade still supported by its shallow columns of pink marble, unchanged in any particular by modern times.

In celebrating the true *nobility* of mind and heart of these women, M. de Charlus was playing on a double meaning of the word, which deceived him, and in which there lay not only the falseness of such a misbegotten notion, this medley of aristocracy, magnanimity, and art, but also its dangerous attractiveness for people such as my grandmother, in whose eyes the flagrant but harmless prejudice of the noble who attends to the number of quarterings in another man's escutcheon, and for whom nothing else counts, would have seemed too ridiculous; but she was susceptible to something masquerading as a spiritual superiority, which was why she thought princes were the most blessed of men, in that they could have as their tutor a La Bruyère or a Fénelon.[57]

The three Guermantes took their leave of us in front of the Grand-Hôtel; they were going to lunch with the Princess of Luxembourg. While my grandmother, Saint-Loup, and Mme de Villeparisis were saying their farewells, M. de Charlus, who had still not spoken a syllable to me, dropped back a few steps and said, "This evening, after dinner, in the rooms of my aunt de Villeparisis, I shall take tea. I hope you will do me the pleasure of attending, in the company of your grandmother." He then rejoined the Marquise.

Though it was a Sunday, there were no more cabs in front of the hotel than at the beginning of the season. The wife of the notary from Le Mans, in particular, was of the opinion that it was rather expensive to hire a carriage once a week so as not to go to the Cambremers', and she preferred to stay in her room all day instead.

"Is Mme Blandais not well, then?" people asked the notary. "We haven't seen her all day."

"She has a slight headache. . . . The heat, you know, this stormy weather. The slightest thing . . . But I expect you'll see her tonight. I've suggested she should come down. I'm sure it would do her good."

I imagined that M. de Charlus, by inviting us to the suite of his aunt, whom he had no doubt consulted on the matter, intended to make amends for his discourtesy toward me during our walk that morning. Yet, when I arrived in Mme de Villeparisis's sitting room and attempted to greet her nephew, however hard I tried to catch his eye, I found it impossible: he just went on recounting in a shrill voice a rather disobliging story about one of his relatives. I decided to bid him good evening in a loud voice, so that he could be aware of my presence, but I soon saw that he had noticed me: just as I was about to bow, and before a word had passed my lips, I saw his two fingers extended for me to grasp, although he had not even glanced toward me or stopped talking. He had obviously seen me, but had given no hint of it, which was what made me realize that his eyes, which never met those of the person with whom he was speaking, were in constant motion in all directions, like the eyes of some animals when frightened, or those of peddlers who, while they recite their patter and display their illicit wares, manage to study all the points of the compass without so much as looking around, in case the police are about. I was also rather surprised to see that Mme de Villeparisis, though pleased to see us come in, had seemed not to have been expecting us; and then I was even more surprised to hear M. de Charlus say to my grandmother, "Well, how nice of you to think of dropping in like this! Isn't it charming of them, Aunt?" He must have noticed Mme de Villeparisis's expression of surprise at our arrival and thought, as a man accustomed to setting the tone, that to turn her surprise into pleasure all he had to do was make it plain that he himself took pleasure in the present circumstance, and that pleasure was an appropriate response. In this he was a good judge, for Mme de Villeparisis, who greatly esteemed her nephew and knew how hard to please he was, instantly appeared to discover new qualities in my grandmother and welcomed her with open arms. It was difficult to accept that, in the few hours which had passed since the morning, M. de Charlus could have forgotten an invitation which, though curtly delivered, had had all the appearances of being intentional and premeditated, and that he should now say my grandmother was just "dropping in," when it was he who had asked us to come! With a respect for the facts, which I retained until the day when I realized that the truth about a man's motive is not to be got from him by direct questioning, and that the damage likely to be done by a misunderstanding that could pass unnoticed may well be less than that done by naïve persistence, I said to him, "Surely you must remember, sir, that it was you who asked us to come this evening?" He gave no hint, either by word or movement, of having heard me. So I repeated my question, like a diplomat or a youngster who, after a falling out, tries and tries again, with indefatigable but futile goodwill, to reason with someone who is determined not to be reasoned with. M. de Charlus persisted in not replying. I thought I could see a smile flicker about his lips: the smile of the man who looks down from a great height on the characters and manners of lesser men.

In the face of M. de Charlus's refusal to explain himself, I was reduced to conjecture, though I knew that none of the possible explanations which came to mind might be the right one. Perhaps he did not remember; perhaps I had misheard what he had said that morning. . . . It appeared more likely that it was his pride making him wish to avoid appearing to seek out people whom he despised, and that he therefore shrugged off onto them the idea that they should come to visit. But if he despised us, why had he wanted us to come—or, rather, since he addressed not a syllable to me all evening and spoke only to my grandmother, why had he wanted her to come? Sitting almost behind her and Mme de Villeparisis, and all but hidden by them, as though in a theater box, he contented himself from time to time with glancing away from them and letting his penetrating eye rest on my face, which it investigated with an air of gravity and preoccupation, as though I were a manuscript full of indecipherable things.

If it had not been for his eyes, M. de Charlus's face would have been similar to those of many handsome men. When, at a later date, Saint-Loup said, of other men of the Guermantes family, "I tell you, there's not one of them who has my uncle Palamède's air of breeding, that look of being every inch a peer," confirming for me that there was nothing mysterious or new in a thoroughbred air and aristocratic bearing, that these consisted of elements I had already recognized without difficulty, without experiencing any special emotion, I was to sense the fading of one of my illusions. However, although M. de Charlus was careful to keep a hermetic seal on the expression of his face, to which a faint dusting of powder gave something theatrical, his eyes were like a crack in a wall, or a loophole in a fortification, which he had been unable to close up, and through which, depending on one's position with regard to him, one felt oneself to be suddenly in the line of fire of some inner device that seemed potentially perilous, even for the person who, without having it completely under his control, carried it about with him in a state of permanent instability and readiness to explode; and the expression in his eyes, circumspect and incessantly uneasy, left on his face, whatever its fineness of design and construction, deep marks of fatigue, including dark circles hanging low under them, and made one think of an incognito, a disguise adopted by a powerful man threatened by some danger, or at times just of an individual who was dangerous but tragic. I wished I could guess what this secret was that other men did not have to bear, which had made such an enigma of the very first look he had shot at me near the Casino. Now that I knew something of his family history, I could no longer entertain the notion that it was the glance of a thief; and, having listened to his conversation, I was sure he was no madman. That he should be so cold to me, while being so amiable with my grandmother, might have nothing to do with any personal antipathy, for generally speaking he was as well disposed toward women (whose faults he could speak of without in any way departing from his habitual indulgence in their favor) as he was disgusted by men, and especially young men, his violent criticisms of whom were of the sort that some misogynists reserve for the opposite sex. When Saint-Loup happened to mention the names of two or three gigolos who were relations or friends of his, M. de Charlus said, with an expression close to ferocity, which was markedly different from his customary lack of warmth, "They are nasty little beasts!" I gathered that the thing he disliked most about young men of today was their effeminacy. "They are just women," he said scornfully. But the life led by any man would have seemed effeminate compared with the kind of life he would have preferred to see men lead, ever more energetic and virile. (During the long walks he enjoyed, after hiking for hours, his body burning, he would throw himself into icy streams.) He even disliked it if a man wore a ring on his finger. Not that this bias in favor of virility prevented him from having some of the finest qualities of sensibility. Mme de Villeparisis asked him to describe for my grandmother a château where Mme de Sévigné had stayed, adding that she detected a fair amount of writer's posturing in the despair the letter-writer expresses at being separated from that tedious Mme de Grignan.[58]

"There I must disagree," M. de Charlus said. "It seems to me to be completely genuine. Also, it was a time when such sentiments were better appreciated. You might well think, my dear aunt, that in La Fontaine, the inhabitant of Monomotapa hurrying to see his friend because of a dream in which he had seemed a little sad, or the pigeon who thinks the greatest of misfortunes is the absence of the other pigeon,[59] are as exaggerated as Mme de Sévigné in her impatience for the moment when she can be alone with her daughter. Think of what she says on leaving her: 'This separation pains me to the soul, and I feel it like an ache in the body. In absence, we make free with the hours: we live already in the time we long for.'[60] Is it not beautiful?" My grandmother was delighted to hear Mme de Sévigné's *Letters* spoken of exactly as she would have spoken of them herself. She was amazed that a man could appreciate them so well; and she detected in M. de Charlus feminine sensitivity and intuitions. Later, when she and I were alone together, we agreed that he must have been profoundly influenced by a wife, his mother, or perhaps a daughter, if he had had any. "A mistress," was what I thought, remembering the influence I believed Saint-Loup's mistress must have had on him, which enabled me to have an idea of what power for the refinement of men is given to the women they lived with.

"Oh, once she was back together with her daughter," said Mme de Villeparisis, "she probably had nothing to say to her."

"Nothing of the kind," said M. de Charlus. "She would have said the sort of things she says are 'so slight that none, save you and I, ever notices them.'[61] And in any case, she was *with* her, which, as La Bruyère says, is the most essential thing in life: 'To be with those one loves is enough: to talk with them or not to talk with them is all the same.'[62] He's right—it is the only happiness," he added in a melancholy tone. "Life is, alas, so badly arranged that we rarely enjoy that happiness. Mme de Sévigné was actually better off than most: she spent much of her life with a loved one."

"You're forgetting that it wasn't love, though—it was just her daughter."

"But the important thing in life is not *whom* one loves," he exclaimed, in a voice that was authoritative, peremptory, almost cutting. "The important thing is to love. The feelings of Mme de Sévigné for her daughter can more properly deserve the name of the passion depicted by Racine in *Andromaque* or *Phèdre* than the paltry goings-on between the young Sévigné and his mistresses. The same goes for the love of a mystic for his God. The limits we set to love are too restrictive and derive solely from our great ignorance of life."

"Do you really like *Andromaque* and *Phèdre*, then?" Saint-Loup asked his uncle in a tone of slight disdain.

"There is more truth in a single tragedy by Racine than in all the melodramas of M. Victor Hugo put together," M. de Charlus replied.

"Aren't fashionable people the limit?" Saint-Loup murmured to me. "Preferring Racine to Victor! I ask you!" He was sincerely dejected by what his uncle had said, but the pleasure of saying "the limit" and especially "I ask you" was of some consolation to him.

In expressing these views on the sadness of the life lived without the loved one (views which led my grandmother to say to me later that the nephew of Mme de Villeparisis was in some ways a better judge of books than his aunt, and in particular that there was something in him

that made him far superior to the majority of clubmen), M. de Charlus not only showed a delicacy of sentiment that is indeed rarely to
be found in a man; but his very voice, like certain contralto voices in
which the middle register has been insufficiently trained and which, in
song, sounds rather like an antiphonal duet between a young man and a
woman, rose as he expressed these subtle insights to higher notes, took
on an unexpected gentleness, and seemed to echo choirs of brides and
loving sisters. This bevy of girls which M. de Charlus, with his horror of
effeminacy, would have been dismayed to know took over his voice,
played a part not only in his interpretation and modulation of the passages full of sentiment. While he spoke, one could often hear their light
laughter, the giggling of coquettes or schoolgirls full of pranks, mischief,
and teasing talk.

He spoke of an estate that had once belonged to his family, with a
house in which Marie-Antoinette had slept and a park designed by Le
Nôtre,[63] now in the possession of the Israels, the wealthy financiers who
had bought it. "Israel, at least that's the name borne by the persons in
question, although it does seem to me to be not a proper name, but a
generic or ethnic term. Who knows, it may be that such people do not
have names. Perhaps they are identified only insofar as they belong to a
particular grouping? However!" he shrieked. "Just think—to have been
the dwelling of the Guermantes and to be owned by the *Israels*! It puts
one in mind of the room in the château at Blois where the guide showing you around says, 'And now this here is where your Mary Queen of
Scots used to say her prayers, and now it's where I keeps me brooms.'
Naturally, I now have not the slightest wish to have any knowledge of
that house, which has disgraced itself, just as I have no desire for contact with my cousin Clara de Chimay, who has left her husband.[64]
However, I do keep a photograph of the house as it was when unsullied,
just as I have one of the Princesse de Chimay taken at a time when her
great eyes were full of no one but the cousin of mine who married her.
Photography acquires a certain dignity, which it does not normally
have, when it is not just a reproduction of reality but can show us
things that no longer exist. I could give you a copy," he added to my
grandmother, "since you have an interest in that manner of architec-

ture." At that moment, noticing that his embroidered handkerchief was revealing part of its colored edging, he thrust it back into his pocket with a startled glance, like a prudish but not innocent woman concealing bodily charms that in her excessive modesty she sees as wanton. "Can you believe," he said, "that the first thing those Israel persons did was lay waste Le Nôtre's park? Why, it's like defacing a canvas by Poussin! The place for such people is behind bars. Although, of course," he added with a smile after a moment of silence, "there are probably plenty of other reasons why they should be behind bars! However! I leave to your imagination the effect produced by an English-style garden in front of the architecture of such a house!"

"Well, actually," said Mme de Villeparisis, "the architecture of the house is the same as that of the Petit Trianon at Versailles. That didn't stop Marie-Antoinette from having her English garden in front of it."[65]

"Yes," said M. de Charlus. "And it completely spoils the façade, which is by Gabriel. Obviously it would be an act of barbarism if anyone were nowadays to raze Marie-Antoinette's English cottages. But whichever fad each day may bring, I do find it difficult to believe that a passing fancy of a Mme Israel could have the same value as a memento of the Queen."

My grandmother had signaled to me that it was time for bed, despite the protests of Saint-Loup, who, to my great shame, had been referring in his uncle's hearing to the feelings of evening sorrow that often afflicted me around bedtime; and I was sure that M. de Charlus would think this was very unmanly of me. I delayed for a few minutes, then went off to bed. Not long afterward, having heard a knock at my bedroom door and having asked who was there, I was surprised to hear the voice of M. de Charlus say in a sharp tone:

"Charlus here. May I come in, monsieur?" Then, having stepped in and closed the door, he said in the same tone, "Monsieur, my nephew said you might be rather unsettled before getting to sleep. He also tells me you are a great admirer of the books of Bergotte, and since I happened to have in my trunk a Bergotte that is very likely unfamiliar to you, I have brought it for you, in the hope that it may help you feel better at a time you find distressful."

I thanked M. de Charlus with all the effusion at my command and told him that my fear had been that Saint-Loup's words about my disquiet at nightfall might have made him think me more of a fool than I was.

"Not at all," he replied in a gentler voice. "You may well be devoid of personal worth, but in that case you're like nearly everyone else! However, at least for a time you have youth, and youth is always irresistible. Moreover, young man, it is the height of stupidity to think there is something ridiculous or reprehensible in feelings one does not share. I love the night and you say you dread it. I love the scent of roses, yet I have a friend in whom it sets off a fever. Do you suppose that, for me, that makes him a lesser man than I am? I strive to understand everything and do not allow myself to condemn anything. However! Do not feel too sorry for yourself. Not that I would ever maintain that such dejection as yours is not hard to bear—I know how much one can suffer for things others could never understand. But at least you have your grandmother to whom to entrust your affection. You can see her all the time. And it is a permissible mode of affection, I mean a requited love. There are so many other modes of affection of which one cannot say the same!"

He was striding about the room, lifting or staring at an object here or there. I felt he had something he wanted to say to me but that he could not find the right words.

"I have another volume of Bergotte with me," he said as he rang the bell. "I'll just get it for you." A page appeared, to whom M. de Charlus said haughtily, "Fetch me the butler, boy. He's the only one around here who's clever enough to run an errand." "Do you mean M. Aimé, monsieur?" asked the page. "I do not know the fellow's name! But, now you mention it, yes, I seem to remember he's called Aimé. Look sharp—it's urgent!" "He'll be here straight away, monsieur. I saw him downstairs just now," said the page, wishing to appear efficient. After a moment, he came back: "M. Aimé is in bed, monsieur. But I could do the errand instead." "No, you must get him out of bed." "Monsieur, I can't. He doesn't sleep at the hotel." "In that case, leave us." "Monsieur," I said when the page had left, "you are too kind—a single volume of Bergotte will suffice." "Yes, I agree, actually." M. de Charlus was still striding up and down. Several minutes went by; then, after hesitating for a few moments and making as though to leave several times, he swung round and made his exit, calling out in his former scathing voice, "I bid you good evening, monsieur!" After all the elevated sentiments I had heard him express that evening, he amazed me on the beach the following morning: just before he was to leave Balbec, and as I was about to go in for a swim, he came down to tell me my grandmother would like to see me as soon as I came out of the water, and as he spoke he pinched me on the neck, with a most vulgar laugh and air of familiarity:

"Who's the naughty little rascal, then, who couldn't care less about what his old granny wants?"

"I adore her, monsieur!"

"Monsieur," he said icily, stepping back, "you are young! But you should take advantage of your youth to learn two things: The first is that you should abstain from expressing sentiments that are too natural not to be taken for granted. And the second is that it is a mistake to get on one's high horse and take offense at things said to one before one has properly understood their meaning. Had you taken that precaution just now, you might have contrived not to appear to be giving voice at random, speaking without rhyme or reason, and thereby compounding the ludicrousness of wearing that bathing suit with anchors embroidered upon it! I lent you a volume of Bergotte which I need to have back. Send it to me within the hour by the butler with the hilarious and undeserved Christian name,[66] who, one assumes, is not in bed at this time of day. You have made me aware that, in speaking as I did last evening of the irresistibleness of youth, I spoke too soon—I should have done you a greater service had I pointed out youth's foolishness, its inconsistencies, and its wrongheadedness! I trust, monsieur, that this little dressing down will prove as beneficial to you as your dip in the sea. However! You must not stand about like that—you might catch cold. I bid you good day, sir!"

M. de Charlus must have regretted his words, for some time later I received another copy—morocco-bound and with a panel of incised leather on its front cover showing a sprig of forget-me-not in half-relief—of the book that he had lent me and which, it being Aimé's day off, I had asked the "lift" to take back to him.

M. de Charlus having departed, Robert and I were at last able to go to dinner at Bloch's. I realized that evening that the anecdotes at which Bloch was inclined to laugh too heartily were stories he had heard from M. Bloch senior, and that the "somebody really interesting" who figured in them was always one of the latter's friends, whom he described in those words. We can all recall certain people we admired as children, a father who was wittier than the rest of the family, a teacher whose mind we saw as better than it was because he revealed philosophy to us, a fellow pupil more advanced than ourselves (as Bloch had been in relation to me), who despises the Musset of "L'Espoir en Dieu" at a time when we still admire him, but who, by the time we have moved on to old Leconte de Lisle or Claudel, will still be full of enthusiasm for the Musset of:

> À Saint-Blaise, à la Zuecca,
> Vous étiez, vous étiez bien aise . . .

without forgetting:

> Padoue est un fort bel endroit
> Où de très grands docteurs en droit . . .
> Mais j'aime mieux la polenta . . .
> . . . Passe dans son domino noir
> La Toppatelle

and who rejects all of the "Nuits" except:

> Au Havre, devant l'Atlantique,
> À Venise, à l'affreux Lido,
> Où vient sur l'herbe d'un tombeau
> Mourir la pâle Adriatique.[67]

When we are impressed by someone, we remember and quote with admiration things that are markedly inferior to other things we would not even consider saying if left to the resources of our own invention, just as in a novel a writer will include real characters and their sayings because they are true, notwithstanding the fact that they represent a mediocre element, a dead weight in the living whole. The portraits of Saint-Simon are admirable, though presumably he did not admire himself as he wrote them; and the words he quotes as charming, spoken by wits of the time, have remained mediocre or become incomprehensible. He would have scorned to invent what he quotes as so acute or so vivid from Mme Cornuel[68] or Louis XIV, a feature which can be remarked in many others, and which lends itself to various interpretations, the only one of which relevant here is the following: that, in the state of mind in which one "observes," one is well below the level at which one creates.

So, set within my old school friend Bloch was Bloch senior, forty years behind the times of his son, who recounted stupid stories and laughed at them in the son's voice, as much as the real Bloch senior laughed at them in his own voice, since whenever he bayed with laughter and repeated the funny part several times, so that his audience would properly savor the point of each anecdote, the gales of the son's faithful guffaws would never fail to celebrate in unison with the father the latter's table talk. The younger Bloch was capable of saying things that were strikingly clever, which he would follow immediately by showing what he owed to his family, telling for the thirtieth time some jokes of his father's that the latter trotted out, along with his frock coat, only on those ceremonial occasions when Bloch the younger brought home somebody it was worth going to some trouble to impress: one of his former teachers, a "chum" who was a great prize-winner, or, as on this occasion, Saint-Loup and myself. So we were treated to this: "A military commentator of genius, who had proved without the shadow of a doubt why, in the Russo-Japanese War, the Japanese would be beaten and the Russians could not fail to win . . ."; and then to this: "He's an eminent man who's seen as a great financier in political circles and a great politician in financial circles." These statements were interchangeable with others concerning the Baron de Rothschild and Sir Rufus Israels, two characters who were introduced ambiguously, in a way that could make a listener infer that M. Bloch senior had known them personally.

I was caught out by this habit of M. Bloch's: his way of referring to Bergotte gave me to understand that he too was one of his old friends. But the fact was that the only famous people whom M. Bloch knew were those he knew *of,* people whom, "without being acquainted with them," he had seen in the distance at the theater or about town. He was pretty sure his own person, his name, his identity as a personality were not unknown to these people, who, when they caught sight of him, probably had to resist a frequent furtive urge to greet him. Though people in high society may well be acquainted at first hand with people of talent, may have them to dinner, this does not mean they understand them any better. But when one has a certain familiarity with society, the vacuity of those who compose it makes one overwilling to frequent obscure people, who know the famous "without being acquainted with them," and overready to expect them to be intelligent. I was to discover this when speaking of Bergotte. M. Bloch senior was not the only one to be a success in his own house: my old school friend was even more celebrated among his sisters, at whom he kept grumbling, with his face almost in his plate. At this, they laughed till they cried. They had also adopted their brother's lingo: they spoke it fluently, as though it were compulsory, as though it were the only language that intelligent people could use. On our arrival, the eldest daughter said to one of the younger ones, "Go and tell our wise father and our venerable mother." "Minxes and hussies," said Bloch, "I bring you my lord Saint-Loup of the swift javelins, who is come for some days from Doncières of the smooth-stoned dwellings, Doncières the dam of horses." Bloch being as vulgar as he was cultured, his speech usually ended with a less Homeric pleasantry: "Look here, close up your peplos of the beautiful clasps a bit! What sort of goings-on are these? I mean, he's not my father,[69] is he?" Whereupon Mlles Bloch collapsed in a maelstrom of merriment. I told their brother how much pleasure he had given me by recommending to me to read Bergotte, whose books I loved.

M. Bloch senior, who had no acquaintance with Bergotte but had heard something of his life by lending an ear to gossip in theaters, had an equally indirect way of being familiar with his books, relying on judgments of apparent literary relevance. His world was that of approximations, where greetings are half exchanged, where half-truths usurp the place of judgment. Inaccuracies and incompetence in no way reduce self-assurance. The opposite is more usual: self-esteem works its beneficent miracle and, since few of us can enjoy intimacy with the great or familiarity with higher learning, those who are excluded from these can still see their own position as the most enviable; the point of view we have from the social tier we occupy makes each of us believe it is the best, for we can see not only many who are worse off than ourselves and to be pitied, but also the great, whom we can name and condemn without knowing them, misjudge and disdain without understanding them. Those who believe they deserve a share of happiness greater than that accorded to others, who find deficient the degree of it afforded them even by self-esteem's magnification of their meager personal advantages, can call upon envy to make up the deficit. Envy may well express itself, of course, in the accents of disdain; and "I have no wish to know him" must be translated as "I have no possibility of knowing him." The latter is the literal translation; but the passionate meaning remains: "I have no wish to know him." We know it is untrue; yet it is not simple dishonesty that makes us say it: we say it because that is how we feel, and that is enough to abolish the difference between truth and untruth, enough for our happiness.

Self-centeredness thus making each man a king, enabling him to see the ordered ranks of the universe beneath him, M. Bloch enjoyed the luxury of absolute monarchy every morning as he leafed through the paper, over his bowl of chocolate, whenever he caught sight of the name of Bergotte at the foot of an article: he granted him a haughty and cursory audience, handed down his judgment, and, between sips at his scalding beverage, savored the joy of sneering: "Really, that Bergotte fellow has become unreadable. What an old bore! Makes you feel like stopping your subscription. What a piece of convoluted nonsense! What a rigmarole!" And he helped himself to some more bread and butter.

M. Bloch senior's illusion of importance reached a little beyond the confines of his own range of vision. For one thing, his children saw him as an outstanding man. All children tend either to underrate or to overrate their parents; but a good son always sees his father as the best of all possible fathers, without reference to any objective grounds for admiration. Such grounds, in the case of M. Bloch senior, were not completely absent: he was educated, percipient, affectionate toward his relations. Those relations who were closest to him were particularly attached to him, especially since in middle-class life, with its multiplicity of smaller worlds (unlike in "society," where people are judged by a single standard which is fixed, however absurd and false it may be, and which is, for purposes of comparison, an aggregate derived from the sum total of all elegant people), there will always be supper parties and family celebrations that have as their life and soul somebody who is deemed to be amusing and agreeable, yet who in society proper would be given short shrift. Also, in those smaller worlds, where the aristocracy's factitious scale of grandeurs does not exist, it is replaced by distinctions that are even sillier. So it was that, within the family, even well beyond the closest circles, because of a supposed likeness in the cut of his mustache and the bridge of the nose, M. Bloch was known as "the Duc d'Aumale's double."[70] (Among clubmen who hunt and shoot, the one who wears his cap at a jaunty angle and buttons his tunic very tight, so as to give himself what he thinks is the look of an officer from a foreign army, will always be seen as something of a character by the others.)

This resemblance was remote; yet it seemed to be viewed as a sort of title. People said, "Which Bloch do you mean—the Duc d'Aumale?" as they might say, "Which Princesse Murat do you mean—the Queen of Naples?" One or two other minute features were enough to make all the kith and kin exclaim about how distinguished he looked. Though his style of life did not run to a carriage, on certain days M. Bloch would hire an open victoria and pair, and have himself driven through the Bois de Boulogne, nonchalantly sprawling, with two fingers at his temple and two under his chin; and though passersby who did not know him may have thought he was "just a joker," the whole family knew that, when it came to "the high life," Uncle Salomon could show a thing or two to Gramont-Caderousse himself.[71] He was one of those men who, when they die, are described in the social column of *Le Radical*, because they used to eat in a restaurant on the boulevards at the same table as the editor of that little newspaper, as "a personality well known to Parisians." M. Bloch said to Saint-Loup and me that Bergotte was well aware why he, M. Bloch, never greeted him, that Bergotte averted his eyes as soon as he caught sight of him at the theater or at the club. Saint-Loup started to blush at the thought that such a club could not possibly be the Jockey Club, of which his father had been the chairman. Yet it had to be quite an exclusive one, as M. Bloch had just said that nowadays Bergotte would not be elected to it. So, with some apprehension, in case he was "underestimating the opponent," Saint-Loup asked whether the club in question was not the Cercle de la Rue Royale, which was a club deemed to be "beyond the pale" by his family, to which he knew certain Jews had been elected. "No," replied M. Bloch with an air of negligence, pride, and shame, "it's a small club, but much more enjoyable than that one: the Old Duffers' Club. We're very select, you know." "Isn't Sir Rufus Israels the chairman?" the younger Bloch asked, to give his father the opportunity to tell a lie that would put him in a good light, and quite without realizing that the financier's name did not have the same prestige for Saint-Loup as it had for him. In point of fact, the Old Duffers' Club counted among its members not Sir Rufus Israels but one of his employees. This man, being on good terms with his employer, carried about a supply of cards bearing the financier's name, one of which he would give to M. Bloch whenever the latter was about to travel with a railway company of which Sir Rufus was a director. M. Bloch would say, "I must look in at the club and get a recommendation from Sir Rufus." Once he was on the train, the card enabled him to impress the guard. Mlles Bloch being more interested in Bergotte than in pursuing the subject of the Old Duffers, the youngest of them asked her brother in a voice that was completely serious (for she was under the impression that the only way to speak of talented men was to use her brother's repertoire of expressions), "Is this Bergotte customer really an outstanding sort of a fellow? I mean, is he one of your Villiers or your Catulles,[72] really big customers like that?" "I've met him at a few opening nights," said M. Nissim Bernard. "He's awkward, a sort of Peter Schlemihl."[73] M. Bloch had nothing against this reference to the Count von Chamisso; but the mention of a word like "Schlemihl," though it belonged to the sort of semi-German, semi-Jewish dialect which delighted him within the family circle, he thought was vulgar and out of place when spoken in front of strangers. He shot a dark look at his uncle. "He does have some talent," Bloch said. "Oh, I see," the sister replied, in a very sober voice, as though meaning that in that case I was to be excused. "All writers have some talent," M. Bloch senior said scornfully. "It's even being said," said the son, brandishing his fork and screwing his eyes into a diabolically ironic expression, "that he's going to present himself for election to the Académie Française!" "Oh, for goodness' sake! The man's a lightweight!" replied M. Bloch senior, who seemed not to hold the Académie in such low esteem as his son and daughters. "He doesn't have the necessary caliber." "In any case, the Académie is a salon and Bergotte enjoys too little credit," pronounced Mme Bloch's uncle, a harmless and gentle individual with money to leave, whose surname, Bernard, might have been enough to stimulate my grandfather's diagnostic gift, though it might also have seemed insufficiently in harmony with a face that could have been brought back from the palace of Darius and recomposed by Mme Dieulafoy,[74] had it not been preceded by the name of Nissim, chosen by some expert wishing to crown this visage from Susa in an aptly Oriental way, by spreading above it the wingspan of some androcephalous bull from Khorsabad. M. Bloch senior would often insult this uncle, either because he was stimulated to pick on him by the man's simple but vulnerable good nature, or because, the villa being rented in the name of M. Nissim Bernard, he wanted to show that, though his beneficiary, he was not beholden to him in any way, and especially that he was not trying to ingratiate himself with the aim of inheriting all that money when the time came. M. Nissim Bernard was upset mainly at being treated rudely in the presence of the butler. He murmured something unintelligible, in which all one could make out was, "When the Meschores are here." In the Bible, "Meschores" means the "servant of God." Among themselves, the Blochs used the word with the meaning of "the servants" and they had great fun in using it: their belief that neither Gentiles nor indeed their servants understood the allusion quickened for both M. Nissim Bernard and M. Bloch senior the gratification they derived from their double status of "masters" and "Jews." However, the latter satisfaction turned into dissatisfaction when guests were present. When M. Bloch heard his uncle say "Meschores," he felt he was drawing too much attention to his Easternness, as a courtesan entertaining some of her kind along with more respectable people will be annoyed if the loose women raise the subject of their profession or use objectionable language. So, rather than mollifying M. Bloch, his uncle's murmur of complaint irritated him beyond measure; and he lost no opportunity to berate the poor man. "Naturally, when there's some pompous stupidity to utter, one may be sure you will do it. You would be the first to lick Bergotte's boots if he was here!" M. Bloch exclaimed, while M. Nissim Bernard lowered the dense locks of the beard of King Sargon toward his plate. Young Bloch too now wore a beard, which was also frizzed and blue-black, bringing out in him a close resemblance to his great-uncle. "What, do you mean you are the son of the Marquis de Marsantes?" M. Nissim Bernard said to Saint-Loup. "I knew him well." I thought he must mean "knew" in the way M. Bloch senior said he "knew" Bergotte, by sight. But M. Nissim Bernard then added, "Your father was a good friend of mine." Young Bloch had turned extremely red, his father looked profoundly upset, Mlles Bloch were stifling laughter. In M. Nissim Bernard, the art of showing off, which was curbed in M. Bloch senior and his offspring, had led to a habit of perpetual mendacity. If staying at a hotel when traveling, M. Nissim Bernard, as M. Bloch senior might have done, always had his manservant bring all the newspapers to him in the dining room, in the middle of lunch, so that the other guests could see he was a man who traveled with a manservant. But if he struck up an acquaintance with any of these guests, M. Nissim Bernard would be sure to say he was a senator, which his nephew would never have done. Although he knew perfectly well that it would come out one day that he had no right to this title, at the moment of speaking of it, he could not resist the temptation to acquire it. These lies told by his uncle, and the difficulties they could create, were a trial to M. Bloch. "Pay no attention," he murmured to Saint-

Loup. "It's just his way of making a little joke." Saint-Loup, who had a strong interest in the psychology of liars, was very interested in all of this. "A bigger liar than Odysseus of Ithaca," said Bloch, "despite the fact that Athena said of the latter that he was the greatest liar among men." "Well, I must say," exclaimed M. Nissim Bernard, "I did not expect to find myself dining with the son of my friend! I have in Paris a photograph of your father and any number of letters from him. He always called me 'Uncle,' for some reason. A charming man, of sparkling wit. I remember a dinner I once gave in Nice, for Sardou, Labiche, Augier ..."[75] "Molière, Racine, Corneille," M. Bloch senior continued ironically, his list being completed by his son: "Plautus, Menander, Kalidasa."[76] M. Nissim Bernard, with hurt feelings, abandoned his story, ascetically forgoing a great pleasure, and said not another word throughout the rest of dinner.

"O bronze-helmeted Saint-Loup," said Bloch, "do have some more of this duck with thighs thick with fat, whereon the illustrious sacrificer of poultry has poured copious libations of the red wine."

Usually, once M. Bloch senior, in order to impress one of his son's important friends, had brought out his choicest stories about Sir Rufus Israels, he would withdraw, feeling that he had already touched a chord of deepest gratitude in his son, and not wanting to "go too far" in front of "the lad." But if there was some quite exceptional reason, such as the time when "the lad" passed the *agrégation*,[77] then M. Bloch would augment the normal series of anecdotes by bringing out an ironic remark that he generally preferred to keep for his select group of friends, and which, now that it was offered to friends of the younger Bloch, filled the latter with an excess of pride: "The government's behavior is an outrage! They have not sought the view of M. Coquelin! M. Coquelin has let it be known he is extremely upset." (M. Bloch took pride in being reactionary and scornful toward theater people.) ·

Mlles Bloch and their brother blushed to the roots of their hair, a sign of how impressed they were, when their parent, to show that he knew how to behave like a king when occasion demanded it, gave the order to serve champagne, then let drop the news that, as a "treat" for his son's "faithful friends," he had booked three seats for the performance to be given at the Casino that very night by a touring comic-opera company. He was sorry he could not get a box, but they were all taken; however, he had often tried every one of them, and you were far better off in the front stalls. Whereas the son's failing—that is, a way of behaving he thought was invisible to others—was bad manners, the father's fault was avarice. So he had the "champagne," really a mediocre sparkling wine, poured from a carafe, and he treated us to "front stalls" that turned out to be seats in the back stalls, half the price of the others, under the miraculous persuasion of his failing that no one would notice the difference, whether at dinner or in the theater (where all the boxes were in fact unoccupied). M. Bloch having let us wet our lips in shallow champagne glasses, which his son described as "craters with deep-swept flanks," he invited us to admire a painting he liked so much that it had accompanied him to Balbec. It was a Rubens, he told us. Saint-Loup was naïve enough to ask whether it was signed. M. Bloch replied with a blush that he had had the signature cut off because of the frame, but this was of no importance, as he had no intention of selling it. Then he bundled us out, so as to catch up on his reading of the *Journal officiel*,[78] piles of which were to be seen about the house, and which he said he could not avoid reading, because of his "parliamentary situation," on which he did not enlighten us further. "I'll just get a scarf," said Bloch, "as Zephyrus and Boreas are abroad on the fish-teeming seas, and if we delay even a little after the performance, our homecoming will be lit by the first glimmerings of rosy-fingered Eos. By the way," he said to Saint-Loup once we had left the house (and I had my heart in my mouth, having immediately realized that Bloch's irony was now being exercised at the expense of M. de Charlus), "who's the priceless clown in the dark suit that you were parading on the beach the other day?" "That was my uncle," Saint-Loup answered curtly. Such a blunder was not the sort of thing to give Bloch pause. He spluttered with laughter: "Congratulations! I ought to have realized—he's very neatly turned out, and he's got a physiog that stamps him as a codger of the first water." "You are utterly and completely mistaken," Saint-Loup snapped. "He is a man of high intelligence." "Well, that's a pity," Bloch said, "because it makes him less than perfect. I wouldn't mind getting to know him, though, as

I'm sure I could write something pretty good on customers like him. When you see him walk past, it's just huge! Mind you, I would have to underplay the face, with its burlesque aspect, caricature being beneath any artist who's really interested in the plastic beauty of his sentences—though, mind you, it did give me a good laugh! And I'd bring out your uncle's aristocratic side, which really makes a splendiferous effect, and once you get over the first fit of the giggles it really does strike you with its grand manner. Tell me," Bloch said to me, "just to change the subject for a moment, there's one thing I keep meaning to ask you; then, every time we meet, some divinity, some blessed denizen of Olympus, makes me completely forget to find out from you something that could come in handy someday—that might *already* have come in handy! Who is that beautiful creature I saw you with once at the Zoo? She was with a gent that I know by sight and a damsel with long hair." I had of course noticed at the time that the name of Bloch was unfamiliar to Mme Swann, who had called him by some other name and said he was attached to a ministry, a statement I had never thought to ask him to verify. I could not understand how Bloch, who, according to what she had said, had sought an introduction to her, could remain in ignorance of her name. This so surprised me that I was speechless for a moment. "Well, anyway," he said, "you deserve to be congratulated—she must have given you a nice time. I had just met her a few days before, you see, riding on the suburban line. She had no objection to yours truly, and so a nice ride was had by one and all, and we were just on the point of arranging to do it again, on a future occasion, when someone she knew had the bad form to get on, just one stop before the terminus." I said nothing, which did not appear much to his liking. "So," he said, "I was sort of hoping you could let me have her address, and then I could pop round there a few times a week and share with her the joys of Eros, favorite of the gods. But look, if you're reluctant to let *me* into the secrets of a professional who, between central Paris and the Point-du-Jour, had no reluctance about letting me into *her*, three times in a row and with refinements, then so be it, I won't insist. I'm bound to come across her again, one of these evenings."

I went to see Bloch shortly after this dinner, and when he came to the hotel to return my visit, I was out. As he was asking for me, he was noticed by Françoise, who, as it happened, though he had once come to Combray, had never set eyes on him before. All she knew was that "one of my gents" had called to see me, but she "didn't know for why"; all she could say was that it was a man dressed in no particular style who had made no great impression on her. Though I knew that some of Françoise's notions about social things would remain forever impenetrable to me, that they derived from misheard words, names once mistaken and never thereafter put right, and though I had long since taken the view that any investigation into this was pointless, I could not help wondering, to no avail, of course, what there could possibly be in the name "Bloch" that she found so stupendous. For I had no sooner told her that the young man she had seen was M. Bloch, than she stepped back, dumbfounded and disappointed. "What! You mean *that's* M. Bloch?" she gasped, quite staggered, as though such a prestigious personage should have had an appearance that would make manifest to all and sundry that they were in the presence of a prodigy of nature; and, like someone finding out that a historical figure does not live up to his reputation, she repeated in an awestruck voice which suggested that in future she would be a sadder but wiser, if more skeptical, woman, "So *that* was M. Bloch! Well, all I can say is, you wouldn't think so to see him!" She seemed to bear me a grudge, as though I had misled her about him, or exaggerated his importance. She did, however, have the considerateness to add, "Well, if that's your M. Bloch, sir, then all I can say is you're every bit as good as he is!"

Françoise soon had to endure, with regard to Saint-Loup, whom she adored, a disillusionment of a different order, but more short-lived: she learned that he was a Republican. Despite the fact that, when she spoke, say, of the Queen of Portugal, she could say, with that homely disrespect which is the expression of supreme respect among the lower classes, "Amélie, that sister of Philippe's," Françoise was a royalist. But that someone who was not only a marquis, but a marquis who had dazzled her, could be a supporter of the Republic, seemed beyond the bounds of the possible. She was as peeved at me as though I had given her a box that she had believed to be of solid gold, for which she had thanked me from the bottom of her heart, only to be told by a jeweler that it was just gold-plated. She instantly lost her admiration for Saint-Loup—which she soon gave back to him, however, it having occurred to her that, since he was the Marquis de Saint-Loup, he could not possibly be a Republican and was therefore only pretending, out of self-interest, since, with "a government like that, he stood to make a bit out of it." From then on, her coolness toward him and her spite toward me disappeared; and when she spoke of Saint-Loup, she would say, "He's just a hypocrite," her broad, kindly smile showing that she thought as well of him as before and that she had forgiven him.

Saint-Loup's sincerity and disinterest were—*pace* Françoise—absolute. In fact, it was this complete integrity of his which, in its inability to find entire fulfillment in a self-regarding emotion such as love, and since he was, unlike myself, free of the impossibility of finding spiritual sustenance anywhere but within the self, made him as capable as I was incapable of friendship.

Françoise was equally mistaken when she said of Saint-Loup that he "just *looked* as though he didn't look down on people beneath him," but that this was really untrue: you only had to see the way he got angry with his coachman. Robert, it was true, had more than once had occasion to speak rather severely to the man; but that, rather than a proof of any consciousness of class distinction, was a proof of his belief in equality between the classes. "But look here," he said, when I reproached him for having treated his coachman harshly, "why should I affect to speak politely to the fellow? Are we not equals? Is he not as close to me as my uncles and my cousins? You seem to suggest that I should handle him with care, like an inferior!" And he added disdainfully, "You're speaking like an aristocrat."

If anything, Saint-Loup's class-consciousness, expressed as a bias or a prejudice, went against the aristocracy, to the extent that he was as ready to disbelieve in the moral superiority of a man of fashion as he was ready to believe in that of a man of the people. When I mentioned the Princess of Luxembourg and her encounter with me and my grandmother, he said:

"She's just a silly old bore, like all her kind. A sort of cousin of mine, actually."

Robert rarely went into society, with his prejudice against the people who made it up; and when he did, the attitude of disgust and coldness he took with him increased all his close relatives' distress about his liaison with a woman "of the theater," which they believed was doing him great harm, in particular because it had fostered his tendency toward willful and systematic disparagement, because it had "led him astray" and "addled his mind," and could be expected to lead him to complete abandonment of his social position. This explained why many of the most frivolous men of the Faubourg Saint-Germain said the most cutting things about Robert's mistress: "Harlots have their job to do, they're a necessary evil, but she is quite unforgivable! She has done too much harm to someone we are very fond of." Not that Robert was the first man ever to fall victim to a loose woman; but the others saw their women as a mere pastime for men of the world, and went on thinking as men of the world in all things, politics included. Robert's family thought he was "embittered." They did not understand that, for many young men in fashionable society, who might otherwise never acquire a certain cultivation of mind or a measure of mildness in friendship, who might never be exposed to good taste or gentler ways of doing things, it is often in a mistress that they find their best teacher, and in relationships with such women that they make their only acquaintance with morality, serve an apprenticeship in higher culture, and learn to see the value of knowledge for its own sake. Even among the lowest classes, who can often vie in uncouthness with the highest, it is the woman, with her greater sensitivity and delicacy and her idle mind, who inquires further into certain refinements, aspires to modes of beauty or art which, even though she may not fully grasp them, she still sees as more important than the things, like money or position, that to the eyes of the man would have seemed more desirable. The lover, whether a young clubman like Saint-Loup or a young workingman (nowadays electricians, for example, have a rightful place in the ranks of the true nobility), has so much admiration and respect for his mistress that he will naturally extend these sentiments to what she respects and admires, and this leads to a complete reversal of his scale of values. By virtue of her sex, she is weak and prone to inexplicable nervous troubles, which, if he encountered them in a man, or in some other woman—an aunt or a cousin of his, for instance—the sturdy youngster would dismiss with a smile. But the woman he loves he cannot bear to see in pain. When a young aristocrat like Saint-Loup takes his mistress to dinner at an exclusive little restaurant, he soon acquires habits, such as making sure he has in his pocket the valerianate that she may need during the evening, or telling the waiter, forcefully and without irony, not to let the doors bang, and not to include damp moss among the table decoration, so as to prevent her from feeling ill, a reaction that he himself has never had to it, but which is part of an occult world which she has taught him to see as real, which despite his lack of personal experience now arouses his sympathy and will continue to arouse it in the future at the sight of somebody else suffering in the same way. Because she was fond of animals (her dog, her canaries, and her parrots went everywhere with her), Saint-Loup's mistress had taught him—as the earliest monks in the Middle Ages had taught Christendom—not to inflict suffering on dumb creatures; and he now took great care of all her pets and spoke of people who were cruel to animals as brutes. In addition, an actress, whether real or, like the one who lived with Saint-Loup, so called, whether she was intelligent or unintelligent (and her intelligence was something I knew nothing about), by making him see the company of fashionable ladies as insipid and the requirement to attend their functions as intolerable, had saved him from snobbery and cured him of frivolity. Although his mistress had helped reduce the importance of society and its relations in his life, she had had the converse effect of making him invest with real nobility and refinement his relations with friends, which, if he had been merely a frequenter of fashionable salons, would have been governed by vanity or self-interest and dominated by grossness. With her woman's instinct, better able to appreciate in men certain qualities of sensitivity that her lover might otherwise have overlooked or mocked, she had the gift of immediately identifying among his friends the ones whose affection for him was genuine, and also the habit of preferring them to the others. She knew how to make him feel real gratitude to these friends, to make him show it and pay attention to the things they enjoyed and the things they disliked. Before long, he came to have no need of her reminders and attended to all this himself; and so, in her absence, at Balbec, though she had never set eyes on me, though he had perhaps never even mentioned me in the letters he wrote to her, he took care to close the windows of carriages for me, took away flowers that might make me have an attack, and when he was taking his leave of several people at once, made sure to say his farewells in such an order as to be able to have a few final minutes alone with me, marking a difference between them and me, treating me in a way that contrasted with the way he treated other people. The mistress had opened his mind to things invisible; she had brought serious considerations into his life; she had changed his heart for the better. But none of this was apparent to the family, who went on lamenting, "That whore will be the death of him! She has already led him into a life of dishonor!" By this time, to be sure, Robert had derived from her all the benefit she had to give; and now she could do nothing but hurt him, as her feelings for him had turned to disgust and she tortured him. It had started one day when she had thought for the first time that he was stupid and ridiculous, some friends of hers, writers and actors, having assured her this was the case; and she had taken to repeating what they had said of him, with all the passion and lack of moderation that one puts into the expression of opinions and the display of attitudes of which one has just discovered the existence. She maintained, like her theatrical friends, that there was now an unbridgeable gulf between her and Saint-Loup, because their worlds were too dissimilar, she being an intellectual and he, whatever he might say, being a born enemy of the intellectual life. This way of seeing herself and Saint-Loup struck her as acute, and she enjoyed looking for proof of it in his most insignificant statements and his slightest actions. Then, once these same friends had convinced her that she was squandering on someone unworthy of her the great promise she had already shown, that her lover was bound to have a bad effect on her, that by living with him she was throwing away her chance to become a great actress, the scorn she had for him was combined with a hatred that could not have been more virulent if he had been trying to infect her with a fatal disease. She saw him as infrequently as possible, while still putting off the moment of a definitive break with him, an eventuality that seemed remote to me. The sacrifices Saint-Loup made for her were so great that, unless she was strikingly lovely (he had always declined to show me a photograph of her, saying, "For one thing, she's no great beauty; and for another, she doesn't photograph well. They're just snaps I took myself with my Kodak, and they'd give you a misleading impression of her"), I thought she would have trouble finding another man who would be prepared to do so much for her. It did not occur to me that, even for an obscure little tart, the passing fancy of being famous, though one may have no talent to speak of, or just the good opinion of a few people who matter to her, may be (though, of course, that might not be the case for Saint-Loup's mistress) much more powerful motives than the satisfaction of making money. Although Saint-Loup, without clearly understanding what was in her mind, did not believe she was entirely sincere, either in her unfair criticisms of him or in her promises of undying love, he did now and then suspect she would break with him when it suited her; and so, no doubt acting on his love's instinct for self-preservation, which may have been more perceptive than he was, and exercising a practical side of his nature which could function in tandem with the most passionate and spontaneous urgings of his heart, he had refused to advance her any sizable capital, while borrowing a huge sum so that she should lack for nothing, but making sure it was paid to her in the form of a daily allowance. If she really did intend to leave him, no doubt she would wait quietly until she had "made her pile," which, in view of the sums doled out by Saint-Loup, looked as though it might take a very short time, although any time, however short, would afford my new friend a little extra happiness—or unhappiness.

This dramatic period of their liaison (now reaching not only its climax but its cruelest phase for Saint-Loup, since in her exasperation with him she had forbidden him to remain in Paris and had obliged him to spend his leave at Balbec, not far from where he was garrisoned) had begun one evening at the house of one of his aunts, Saint-Loup having prevailed upon this lady to put on a performance by his mistress, in which she recited, before the aunt's many guests, excerpts from a symbolist play in which she had once acted on an avant-garde stage, and which she admired so much that she had communicated her liking for it to him.

However, when she made her entrance in front of the gathering of clubmen and duchesses, with a tall lily in her hand and wearing a costume copied from the *Ancilla Domini*,[79] which she had assured Robert was a true "vision of art," her appearance had been greeted by smiles, which the singsong monotony of her delivery, the outlandishness of certain words, and the frequent repetitions of them had changed into tittering, quickly stifled at first, but then becoming so irrepressible that the poor artiste had had to abandon the performance. The following day, Saint-Loup's aunt had been unanimously condemned for having presented such a bizarre performer. A prominent duke made no secret of the fact that, if people were criticizing her, she had only herself to blame: "Well, for goodness' sake, what do you expect, if you will expose people to that sort of nonsense? If the woman actually had a bit of talent—but she hasn't, nor will she ever! And, heavens above, Paris isn't as stupid as it's said to be. Society isn't entirely composed of idiots. It's obvious that your little lady thought she could show Paris a thing or two. But it takes a bit more than that to show Paris anything, and there are some things that just won't wash!"

The artiste herself said to Saint-Loup as she was leaving, "God, what a gang! Brainless hussies, ill-mannered bitches, and rotten pigs, all of them! I don't mind telling you that those dirty old men spent the evening making eyes at me, every single one of them, and trying to play footy-footy with me, and it was because I refused to have anything to do with them that they decided to get back at me!"

These words had changed Robert's antipathy toward society into a much deeper and more painful abhorrence, which he felt especially in the presence of some toward whom it was least justified, those devoted relatives who, at the family's behest, had attempted to persuade his mistress to give him up, and who she told Robert were motivated solely by their own desire for her. Though he had immediately broken off all contact with these men, Robert sometimes thought, especially when he was away from her, as he was at Balbec, that they or others would take advantage of his absence to make further advances to her, and that she had perhaps given in to them. When he spoke of the sort of rake who could deceive a friend, attempt to seduce women, lure them into bawdy houses, his face contorted with pain and hatred.

"I could kill them with less compunction than if they were dogs—a dog is at least a loving, loyal, and faithful animal. People like that deserve the guillotine, more so than the poor devil who has been pushed into crime by poverty and the ruthlessness of the rich."

At Balbec, he spent most of his time writing letters to his mistress and sending off telegrams to her. Every time she managed not just to prevent him from returning to Paris, but to provoke a squabble with him, even at such a distance, I had only to glance at his wretched expression to know what had happened. She would never say outright what her grievance against him was; and Robert, with the idea that her silence on this matter meant she had no particular grievance but just a general feeling of having had enough of him, kept asking by letter for the frank discussion he would have preferred: "Please tell me what I have done wrong. I'm quite willing to admit I've behaved badly." His sorrow had the effect of convincing him that he was the one at fault.

She always kept him waiting for her answers, which, when they came at last, made no sense. I usually saw him coming back empty-handed and with furrowed brow from the post office, the only person in the hotel, apart from Françoise, who fetched and carried his own letters, he being impelled to do this by lover's haste, she by servant's distrust. (To send his telegrams, he was obliged to go much farther afield.)

A few days after the dinner party at the Blochs', my grandmother told me, with an overjoyed air, that Saint-Loup had just asked her whether she would not like him to take a photograph of her before he left Balbec; and when I saw that, in view of this, she had put on her best clothes and was trying to decide which hat to wear, I felt a touch of irritation that she should make such a fuss over something so trivial, which struck me as surprising in her. I even wondered whether I was not mistaken in my estimate of my grandmother, whether I had not put her on too high a pedestal, whether concern for self was as genuinely foreign to her as I had always thought, whether she did not have some slight measure of what I believed her completely free of: affectation.

I was ill advised enough, in Françoise's presence, to show something of my disgruntlement at the intended photography session, and at the gratification that my grandmother seemed to derive from it; and Françoise, having noticed this, unintentionally aggravated my mood by making a sentimental and lachrymose remark, which I greeted with an expression calculated to dissociate myself from it.

"Oh, master, your dear grandmother will love having her photo took—and she's even going to wear the hat that her dear old Françoise has done up for her. We mustn't stand in her way, sir."

I told myself it was not unkind to scorn Françoise's mode of sensibility, with the reminder that my mother and grandmother, my models in all things, often did so. But my grandmother, noticing that I looked put out, said that, if the taking of the photograph was bothersome to me, she would not go ahead with it. I did not want her to abandon the idea, told her I had no objection, and let her titivate herself. But I thought it was pretty clever and superior of me to say a few hurtful and sarcastic words to her, so as to neutralize the pleasure she seemed to look forward to from being photographed; and though I was obliged to see her magnificent hat, at least I managed to banish from her face the signs of a joy that I ought to have been happy to share with her, but which, as so often happens while those whom we love best are still alive, can strike us as a mere irritant, a mark of something silly and small-minded, rather than the precious revelation of the happiness we long to give to them. My bad mood was mainly the result of the fact that, throughout that week, my grandmother had appeared to be avoiding me, and that I had been unable to have a moment with her, either during the day or in the evening. When I went back to the hotel in the afternoons, to have a little time with her, I was told she was not in; or else she was closeted with Françoise, having long confabulations that I was not supposed to interrupt. Or if I had been out all evening with Saint-Loup, and came back to the hotel savoring the prospect of being with her again and giving her a kiss, I would wait in vain for her little knocks on the wall, which were her invitation to me to go in and kiss her good night; I would get into bed, a little resentful of this unfamiliar indifference in her, of her way of depriving me of a pleasure that I had been much looking forward to; and with my heart throbbing as much as it had ever done when I was a child, I would lie there listening to the silence of the wall, until sleep came to dry my tears.

That day, as on the preceding days, Saint-Loup had had to go to Doncières, where his presence was required until late each afternoon, and where he would soon have to return full-time. I missed him in Balbec. I could see young women alighting from carriages, some of them going into the ballroom at the Casino, some into the ice-cream parlor, and from a distance they seemed lovely. I was at one of those times of youth when the idle heart, unoccupied by love for a particular person, lies in wait for Beauty, seeking it everywhere, as the man in love sees and desires in all things the woman he cherishes. We need only to see in passing a single real feature of a woman, a glimpse of her at a distance or from behind, which can be enough for us to project Beauty onto her, and we imagine we have found it at last: the heart beats faster, we lengthen our stride, and, on condition that she disappears, we may be left with the certainty of having set eyes upon it—it is only if we succeed in catching up with her that we discover our mistake.

Also, my health was going from bad to worse, and I was inclined to magnify the simplest of pleasures because of the obstacles that lay between me and the possibility of enjoying them. Beautifully dressed women seemed to be everywhere, because I was unable to approach them, being either too weary if I saw them on the beach, or too diffident if I saw them in the Casino or in a cake shop. If I was fated to die young, I wished I could first find out for myself what real life had to offer in the persons of the prettiest girls, even if someone other than me, or possibly no one, was ultimately to enjoy them (I did not recognize that, underlying my curiosity about them, there was a desire for possession). I would have been brave enough to walk into the ballroom if only Saint-Loup had been with me. By myself, I was standing about outside the Grand-Hôtel, waiting for the moment when I would go into sit with my grandmother; and there, still far away along the esplanade, where they made a strange mass of moving colors, I saw five or six young girls, as different in their appearance and ways from all the other people one was used to seeing in Balbec as the odd gaggle of seagulls that turns up out of the blue to strut along the beach, the stragglers flapping their wings to catch up with the leaders, in a procession that seems as obscure in its purpose to the bathers, whom they seem not to see, as it is clear to their bird-minds.

One of these girls was walking along pushing her bicycle; two others carried golf clubs; and their accoutrements made a flagrant contrast with the appearance of other young girls in Balbec, for even those who practiced certain sports did not walk about dressed in a particular way.

It was the hour for ladies and gentlemen to take their daily walk along the esplanade, directly into the merciless line of fire of the lorgnette held by the wife of the First President from Caen, who scrutinized each and every one of them as though they might be tainted with some blemish which she felt bound to inspect in its minutest details, as she sat in her proud posture in front of the bandstand, midway along the redoubtable row of chairs in which the subjects of her scrutiny would themselves soon come to sit, actors turned critics, and set themselves to the task of examining all the other people strolling past. All these esplanade walkers were pitching about as though stepping along the deck of a ship (for they could not take a stride without also swinging an arm, shifting their glance, setting their shoulders straight, counterbalancing on one side of their body the movement they had just made on the other, and becoming flushed about the face), and though they pretended not to see the other strollers walking beside them or coming in the other direction, so as to let it be thought they had no interest in them, while actually glancing at them surreptitiously so as to avoid colliding with them, they collided with them nonetheless, or jostled them, because all of them had been furtively looking at each other, their attention concealed behind the same apparent disdain for everyone else; for love, hence fear, of the crowd is one of the most powerful motives in all individuals, whether they wish to please others, astonish them, or show that they despise them. In a recluse, the most irrevocable, lifelong rejection of the world often has as its basis an uncontrolled passion for the crowd, of such force that, finding when he does go out that he cannot win the admiration of a concierge, passersby, or even the coachman halted at the corner, he prefers to spend his life out of their sight, and gives up all activities that would make it necessary for him to leave the house.

Amid all these people, some of whom were following a train of thought but revealed its mobility through restless gesturing or wandering looks, all of which made them look just as uncoordinated as the others with their circumspect lurchings, the girls I had seen, with the confidence of gesture that comes from the perfect mastery of a supple body and sincere contempt for the rest of humanity, strode straight on, without hesitation or stiffness, making exactly the movements they wished to make, each of their limbs in complete independence from all the others, while most of the body retained the poise that is so remarkable in good waltzers. They were now not far from me. Though each of them was of a type quite different from the others, all of them were beautiful; but I had been looking at them for so few moments, and was so far from daring to stare at them, that I had not yet been able to individualize any of them. With the exception of one, whose straight nose and darker complexion marked her out among the rest, as a king of Arabian looks may stand out in a Renaissance painting of the Magi, they were knowable only as a pair of hard, stubborn, laughing eyes in one of the faces; as two cheeks of that pink touched by coppery tones suggesting geraniums in another; and none of even these features had I yet inseparably attached to any particular girl rather than to some other; and when (given the order in which I saw their complex whole unfold before me, wonderful because the most dissimilar aspects were mixed into it and all shades of color were juxtaposed, but also as confused as a piece of music in which one cannot isolate and identify the phrases as they form, which once heard are as soon forgotten) I noticed the emergence of a pale oval, of two green eyes, or black ones, I had no idea whether they were those whose charm had struck me a moment before, in my inability to single out and recognize one or another of these girls and allot them to her. The fact that my view of them was devoid of demarcations, which I was soon to draw among them, sent a ripple of harmonious imprecision through their group, the uninterrupted flow of a shared, unstable, and elusive beauty.

It may not have been mere fortuitousness that, in bringing all these girls together, had managed to choose only beautiful ones; the girls themselves (whose attitudes sufficed to show their tough, daring, and frivolous nature), by their excessive sensitivity to anything ridiculous or ugly, their inability to feel an attraction of an intellectual or moral sort, may have naturally coincided in feeling repelled by any of their coevals whose pensive or sensitive dispositions were revealed by shyness, embarrassment, or awkwardness, by girls whom they probably saw as "horrid" and whom they had ruled out as possible friends; and they may have taken up with others to whom they felt drawn by a blend of gracefulness, ease, and bodily elegance, the only appearance through which they could conceive of candor and attractiveness in a character, offering a promise of good times together. It may also have been that the social class to which they belonged, which I could not define with any degree of precision, had reached a stage in its evolution where—by reason of growing prosperity and leisure, or because of the new interest in sports, spreading now even among the working classes, and in physical training without any concomitant training of the mind—a social environment similar to that of certain schools of sculpture, in which harmony of line and prolific creativity aspire as yet to no overelaboration or distortions, produces naturally an abundance of beautiful bodies with lovely limbs and handsome hips, with lusty, unperturbed faces and an air of sprightly cunning. For surely these were noble and tranquil models of human beauty that met my eye, against the sea, like statues in the sun along a shore in Greece.

As though with a single mind, this gang of girls, making its way along the esplanade like a shining comet, seemed to think the crowd of people all about them was composed of beings of another species which, even if it was capable of suffering, could not move them to sympathy, as they advanced seemingly oblivious to it, forcing everyone who stood in their way to move aside, to give way as though to a locomotive bearing down upon them without the slightest likelihood that it would avoid pedestrians; and their only reaction, if some fearful or furious old gentleman, of manifestly negligible existence, whom they swept aside as they passed, hobbled urgently or ludicrously out of their path, was to exchange a look among themselves and burst out laughing. For anyone or anything outside their group they affected no scorn; their sincere scorn was enough. They could not see an obstacle without taking pleasure in jumping over it, either by running at it or from the standing position, because they were full to overflowing with youthfulness, which must expend itself, which even when one is sad or unwell makes one obey the needs of age rather than the mood of the day, so that one can never come upon the possibility of leaping or sliding without making a point of leaping or sliding, and deliberately punctuating one's slow progress, as Chopin does with even the most melancholy of his phrases, with serial detours full of grace, impulsiveness, and virtuosity. The wife of an old banker, after having indecisively tried several different places for her husband to sit, had eventually settled him in his deck chair facing the esplanade, where he was sheltered from the wind and the sun by the bandstand. Once he was comfortable, she went off to buy a newspaper, so as to read to him and keep him amused, never being away for more than five minutes at a time, while he sat by himself during her brief absences, which he found long but which she repeated, in the hope that her aged husband, the beneficiary of her close but unobtrusive care, could have the feeling that he was still capable of living a normal life and did not require help and support from anybody. The floor of the bandstand jutted out above the old man's head, forming a natural springboard so tempting that the eldest of the little gang[80] of girls, without the slightest hesitation, dashed across and jumped off the edge, sailing right over him; he was terrified by a pair of nimble feet grazing his nautical cap, to the great amusement of the other girls, and especially of a pair of green eyes in a chubby face full of admiration, merriment, and possibly also some slight shyness, or, rather, a sort of bare-faced bashfulness, which was not apparent in the others' expressions. "Oh, what a poor old guy! He'd break your heart, he really would—he's got one foot in the grave!" said one of them in a broad, husky accent that was half ironic. They all walked on a few paces, then halted for a moment right in the middle of the promenade, unconcerned about holding up the procession of strollers, forming a dense, shapeless, untoward mass, loud with squawking, like a prattle of birds that gather just before flying off; and then they took up again their own slow stroll along the esplanade, above the sea.

By now, their charm was not blended into undifferentiated features. I could separate these from one another and apportion them to individual girls (in lieu of their names, which I had no knowledge of), such as the tall one who had jumped over the old banker; the small one who set off her plump pink cheeks and her green eyes against the horizon of the sea; the one whose darker coloring and straight nose made her look so different from the others; another one with a face as white as an egg, on which a little nose, like a chick's beak, drew an arc of a circle, a face reminiscent of some very young men's; the other one who was tall and wearing a hooded cape, which made her look so poor, and was in such contrast with the rest of her elegant outfit that my idea of her was that she must have parents whose brilliance and self-esteem, drawn from things well above the heads of Balbec and its bathers, things utterly divorced from considerations of the elegance or otherwise of their own offspring, enabled them to be totally indifferent to the fact that this daughter of theirs went walking along the esplanade wearing something that people of the lower classes would have deemed too unprepossessing; a girl with shining, laughing eyes and full, matte-complexioned cheeks, a little black toque pulled right down, who was pushing a bicycle along and swinging her hips so freely, while using slang words that were so strong, and which she shouted out so loud as I passed close by (among which I distinctly heard the unladylike expression "She's no better than she should be"), that I had to replace the hypothesis I had built on the hood and cape of her friend by another more plausible one: every one of these girls belonged to the crowds who frequent velodromes, and must be the extremely youthful girlfriends of racing cyclists. Certainly, in none of my conjectures did I entertain the possibility that they might be chaste. I had known as much at a glance: I saw it in the way they kept exchanging looks and laughs, and in the insistent stare of the one with the cheeks and the matte complexion. Moreover, my grandmother's concern for me had always been so overscrupulous that I had come to believe that the things one must not do are a single indivisible set, and that young girls who are prepared to be rude to old age might well have few qualms about infringing other prohibitions, in which the pleasures to be enjoyed are more tempting than just jumping over an octogenarian.

Though the girls were now individualized, the connivance in the glowing glances they kept exchanging, bright with conceit and their joy in being the little clique they were, flashing with self-interest or insolent indifference, depending on whether they were looking at each other or at people passing, as well as their sense of knowing one another closely enough to be always out together, to be "as thick as thieves," linked their separate and independent bodies into an invisible harmony, as though they shared the same warm shade, walked within a separate atmosphere, which made of them an entity as alike in its parts as it was unlike the throng through which their closed little company wended its slow way.

For an instant, as I passed close to the brunette with the full cheeks and the bicycle, I glimpsed her oblique, laughing glance, looking out from the inhumane world that circumscribed the life of their little tribe, an inaccessible *terra incognita,* obviously incapable of harboring or offering a home to any notion of who or what I was. With her toque pulled down low on her brow, entirely engrossed in what her companions were saying, did she see me at the moment when the black ray from her eyes encountered me? If so, what must I have seemed like to her? What sort of world was the one from which she was looking at me? I could not tell, any more than one can tell from the few details that a telescope enables us to descry on a neighboring planet whether it is inhabited by human beings, whether or not they can see us, or whether their view of us has inspired any reflections in them.

If we believed that the eyes of such a girl were nothing but shiny little disks of mica, we would not be eager to enter her life and link it to our own. But we are well aware that whatever it is that shines in those reflective discs is not reducible to their material composition; that flitting about behind them are the black incognizable shadows of the ideas she forms about the people and places she knows—the paddocks at racecourses, the sandy paths along which she might have pedaled, drawing me after her, over hill and meadow, like a little Peri[81] more seductive than the sprite from the Persian paradise—the dimness of the house into which she will disappear, her own impenetrable projects, and the designs of others upon her; and what we are most aware of is that she herself lies behind them, with her desires, her likes and dislikes, the power of her inscrutable and inexhaustible will. I knew I could never possess the young cyclist, unless I could also possess what lay behind her eyes. My desire for her was desire for her whole life: a desire that was full of pain, because I sensed it was unattainable, but also full of heady excitement, because what had been my life up to that moment had suddenly ceased to be all of life, had turned into a small corner of a great space opening up for me, which I longed to explore, and which was composed of the lives led by these young girls, because what was laid out now before my eyes was that extension and potential multiplication of self that we know as happiness. The fact that they and I shared nothing, no habit, no idea, was surely bound to make it more difficult for me to make their acquaintance and meet with their approval. But perhaps it was my very awareness of these differences between us, my knowledge that, in the nature of the girls as in their every action, there was not one iota of an element that was known to me or that I could have access to, which had replaced my satiety of life by a thirst, akin to that of a drought-stricken land, for a life which my soul, having gone forever without a single drop of it, would now absorb in great greedy drafts, letting it soak me to the roots.

I had been staring so much at the bright-eyed cyclist that she seemed to notice it: she said something to the tallest girl, which I did not catch but which made her laugh. This bicycling brunette was not in fact the one I liked best, for the very reason that she was a brunette: for me, the unattainable ideal, ever since the day I had caught sight of Gilberte from the steep little lane by Tansonville, had been a golden-skinned girl with fairish ginger hair. But, then, had I not also fallen in love with Gilberte because she had appeared to me surrounded by the halo of glory conferred upon her by being the friend of Bergotte, by going with him to look at cathedrals? In the same way, was it not promising that I had seen the brunette look at me (which made me hope it might prove easier to get to know her first), since she would be able to introduce me to the others, to the ruthless one who had jumped over the old man's head, to the heartless one who had said, "Oh, what a poor old guy!," and then all of them, one after another, in her capacity, and her prestige, as their inseparable companion? And yet, in the assumption that I might one day be a friend of one or another of those girls, that the eyes which passed their unknown glances over me, as unaware of me as a touch of sun on a wall, might ever undergo the miraculous alchemy that would enable a notion of my existence, or friendship for my person, to merge with the inexpressible minutiae of their minds, that I myself might one day be a member of their bevy as it roamed along the seafront, there was a contradiction as insoluble as though I had thought it possible not just to stand and admire the parading figures in an ancient frieze or fresco, but to be admired in return and step up to join in their divine progress.

Was the happiness of knowing these young girls really unattainable? It would certainly not have been the first happiness of that sort that I had abandoned all hope of ever enjoying. I needed only to think of all the unknown girls, even on the roads around Balbec, whom I had had to give up as the speeding carriage parted me from them forever. Even the joy I derived from this little group, as noble as though composed of Hellenic virgins, had something in it akin to the feeling I got from those fleeting passersby on the road. The transience of brief strangers who enter our life and force us out of the normality in which all the women we are used to will eventually reveal their blemishes, puts us into a state of readiness to pursue them, in which nothing inhibits the imagination. For a pleasure divested of imagination is a pleasure reduced to itself, to nothing. If they had been offered to me by a madam—in the sort of house that, as has been seen, I did not disdain—divorced from the element that lent them so many colors and such attractive imprecision, they would have been less enchanting. The imagination, aroused by the possibility that it will not achieve its aim, is obliged to mask it with another, and, by replacing sensual pleasure with the idea of penetrating someone's life, makes sure we neither recognize that pleasure, experience its true flavor, nor restrict it to its dimension of mere pleasure. If we were to set eyes on a fish for the first time as it might be served on a dinner table, it would hardly appear to be worth the countless ruses and devious tricks required to land it, unless between us and it there were afternoons spent fishing, eddies through which glimpses barely caught of fleshy gleams and an imprecise shape ruffle the surface of our indecision about what to do with them, in the blue fluidity of a transparent and mobile medium.

The girls benefited also from the alteration in social proportions that is characteristic of holiday life at the seaside. All the ways in which our usual environment confers advantages on us, extending and inflating our importance, become invisible there, indeed are abolished, while other people in whom we imagine such advantages, which may be nonexistent, move in a world enriched for us by this same fictitious density. It was this that made it easy for unknown women, as on that day this group of girls, to assume enormous significance in my eyes, while making it impossible for me to give them any indication of my own significance.

Though this little sauntering gang of girls was an example of the countless occasions when young passersby had escaped my grasp, a failure that had always irked me, this time the escapers had slowed their pace almost to the point of immobility. That faces, instead of dashing past, should make a slow enough disappearance for their features to be set and distinct, yet still appear beautiful, prevented me from believing, as I had so often believed when Mme de Villeparisis's carriage was whisking me farther and farther away from a young woman, that at close range, if I had been able to pause for a moment, certain details of her face or body—a pock-marked complexion, an imperfection in the nostrils, a dull look, a crude smile, a graceless waist—would have supplanted those my imagination had seen in her; for often I had needed no more than a pretty contour of a body, a glimpse of a cool complexion, to create in all good faith a lovely shoulder to go with it, or a look from delightful eyes, memories or preconceptions that I carried about with me at all times; and such cursory decipherings of a creature seen in a fleeting glimpse expose us to the same misconceptions as hasty readings of a text, whereby, on the faith of a single syllable, and without pausing to identify the others, we replace the word printed by another quite different word proffered by memory. But this occasion had to be different: I had been able to have a close look at each of their faces; and though I had been unable to see any of them from both sides, and few of them in full face, I had still managed to sketch two or three aspects of them that were sufficiently different from one another for me to be able to make either the necessary adjustments to their different hypothetical contours and colors, as jotted down by my first glance, or the verification and proof of them, and to see through their few overlaid expressions to something immutably material. So I knew I could say with certainty that, whether in Paris or in Balbec, assuming the most favorable possible outcomes with any of the young women who had ever caught my eye in passing, if I had been able to pause for a while and chat, there had never been any whose appearance, then disappearance without anything's coming of it, would have left me with such regrets as would these, or who could have made me believe there would be such excitement in being their friend. No actress, no peasant girl, no boarder at a convent school had ever been so beautiful to me, so fascinating in a suggestion of the unknown, so invaluably precious, so probably unattainable. The exemplar these girls offered of life's potential for bringing unsuspected happiness was so full of charm, in a state of such perfection, that it was almost for intellectual reasons that I despaired of ever being able to experience, in unique conditions that would allow no room for possible error, the profound mystery to be found in the beauty one has longed for, the beauty one replaces, because one knows it is forever beyond one's reach, by seeking mere pleasure from women one has not desired—which Swann had always refused to do, before meeting Odette—with the result that one dies without ever having enjoyed that other form of fulfillment. It was of course possible that there would have been no revelation in such a fulfillment, that the mystery would have been nothing but a projection or mirage of desire, to be dispelled by proximity. If so, I would have to blame an inescapable law of nature (which, if it was applicable to these girls, would be applicable to all girls), and not any defectiveness in the present object. For this present object was the one I would have preferred above all, as I knew perfectly well, having botanized so much among such young blossoms, that it would be impossible to come upon a bouquet of rarer varieties than these buds, which, as I looked at them now, decorated the line of the water with their gentle stems, like a gardenful of Carolina roses edging a cliff top, where a whole stretch of ocean can fit between adjacent flowers, and a steamer is so slow to cover the flat blue line separating two stalks that an idling butterfly can loiter on a bloom that the ship's hull has long since passed, and is so sure of being first to reach the next flower that it can delay its departure until the moment when, between the vessel's bow and the nearest petal of the one toward which it is sailing, nothing remains but a tiny glowing gap of blue.

I had to go back to the hotel, as Robert and I were going out to dinner at Rivebelle and my grandmother insisted that on such occasions I take an hour's rest on my bed, a siesta that the Balbec doctor soon ordered me to extend to all other evenings as well.

To go back into the hotel, there was now no need to leave the esplanade, walk around the back, and enter by the main lobby: by a change of timetable analogous to Combray's Saturday, when lunch was one hour early, the midsummer days had become so long that, when the tables were being set for dinner at the Grand-Hôtel of Balbec, the sun was still high in the sky, making it feel like afternoon teatime. And as the tall sliding glass doors, which opened right onto the esplanade, stayed wide open, all I had to do was step over a low wooden frame, straight into the dining room, then walk directly to the elevator.

As I passed the office, I gave the manager a smile and received one in return, signaled by his face, which, since the beginning of our stay at Balbec, my studious attentiveness had been injecting and gradually transforming as though it were a specimen in natural history. The features of his face had become nondescript, expressive of a meaning which, though mediocre, was as intelligible as handwriting one can read; they no longer resembled the outlandish and unbearable characters printed on this face as I had seen it on our first day, when I had been confronted by a personage now forgotten—or at least, if I ever contrived to remember him, now unrecognizable—and difficult to identify in this polite and insignificant person, of whom the other had been only a caricature, hideous and summary. Freed of the shyness and distress of the evening of my arrival, I rang for the "lift," who did not now observe unbroken silence as we ascended together, as though inside a mobile rib cage gliding upward along the vertical column, but kept saying, "Not as many people around now as a month ago. Days getting shorter. They'll all start leaving soon." He said this not because it was true, but because he had another job waiting for him on a warmer stretch of the coast and wished we would all go away as soon as possible, so that the hotel would close and he might have a few days to himself before "recommencing" his "new situation." "Recommencing" and "new" were in no way contradictions for him, "to recommence" being for him the normal form of the verb "to start." The only thing that surprised me in what he said was the word "situation," for he belonged to the working classes of modern times, who try to remove from their speech all reminder of the system of domestic service to which they belong. He also told me that in this "situation" where he was about to "recommence," he would have a handsomer "tunic" and higher "remunerations," the words "uniform" and "wages" seeming antiquated and unseemly to him. Vocabulary having, by an absurd contradiction, outlived the idea of inequality in the minds of the "bosses," I always had trouble in understanding what the "lift" said. For instance, if what I really wanted to know was whether my grandmother was in or out, the "lift" would anticipate my questions and say, "The lady has just left your rooms." This caught me out every time without fail: I always thought he meant my grandmother. "No, I mean that lady that's an employee of yours, I think." A cook, at least in middle-class terminology of former times, soon no doubt to be abolished, never having been "an employee," I would think for a moment: "He's mistaken: we're not factory-owners—we don't have employees." Then I remembered that the word "employee" is as essential to the self-esteem of servants as wearing a mustache is to waiters in cafés, and realized that the "lady" who had just left our rooms was Françoise (probably off to visit the pantry or to watch the young chambermaid sewing for the Belgian lady); though even this degree of self-esteem was insufficient for the "lift," who, as he bemoaned the lot of his own class, also liked to say not "workers" but "the worker," not "commoners" but "the commoner," using the sort of singular with which Racine, meaning "poor men," refers to "the poor man." Usually, however, since I had lost all my early eagerness and timidity, I no longer spoke to the "lift." He was the one who spoke, without receiving an answer, as he put his little craft to full speed ahead and, with his hand on the tiller, piloted us up through the hotel, which was like a hollow toy, and which, as story replaced story, deployed all about us its branching corridors, where distant light faded away into soft shadows, thinning down communicating doors and the faint steps of stairways, converting them into that golden amber, as insubstantial and mysterious as twilight, from which Rembrandt models a window ledge or the handle of a well. And at each of these stories, a golden glow on the carpet showed it was now sunset beyond the lavatory windows.

I wondered whether the girls I had seen lived in Balbec and who they might be. When the focus of our desire singles out a tiny human tribe, whatever may bear upon them in any way sets off an emotion in us, which then becomes a wondering daydream. On the esplanade I had overheard a lady say, "Yes, she's one of the friends of the Simonet girl," with the smug, superior knowledge of the person in the know who says, "Yes, he's very tight with the young Duc de La Rochefoucauld." I was instantly aware of a look of curiosity on the face of the person being told this, a quickened interest in somebody who was so favored as to be "one of the friends of the Simonet girl." It was clear this was a privilege not open to all and sundry. Aristocracy is relative: there are all sorts of inexpensive little resorts where the son of a furniture salesman may be the arbiter of all things elegant, holding court like a young Prince of Wales. Since that moment when I first heard the name "Simonet," I have often tried over the years to remember how it must have sounded there on the esplanade, in my uncertainty about its shape, which I had not quite noticed, about its meaning and the identity of this or that person to whom it might belong: full of the imprecision and foreignness we later find so moving, when our unremitting attention to this name, with its letters more deeply imprinted in us with each passing second, has turned it (as the name of "the Simonet girl" was to be turned for me, but not until several years later) into the first word to

come to consciousness, whether on waking each morning or after faint-
ing, even before any inkling of the time of day or where we are, almost
before the word "I" itself, as though the one it names were more us than
we are ourselves, as though the first respite, always to end after a few
moments' oblivion, was the respite of not thinking of it. Why I decided, there and then, that the name "Simonet" must belong to one of
the gang of girls, I have no idea: how to get to know the Simonet family
became my constant preoccupation, and especially how to be introduced to them by people they would see as above themselves—which
should not prove difficult, if the girls were just vacuous and immoral
specimens from the working classes—so that they could not look down
on me: perfect knowledge of those who disdain you, like complete absorption of any such person, is impossible unless you have overcome
that disdain. Every time we are assailed by images of women very different from ourselves, unless these images are eliminated by being forgotten or overlaid by others, we can have no peace of mind until we have
converted these strangers into something more like us, the self in that
respect being similar in its action and reactions to the physical organism, which is incapable of accepting a foreign body within itself without
immediately setting to work to digest and assimilate the intruder. The
Simonet girl must be the prettiest of them, and also, it seemed to me,
the one who might be able to become my mistress, since she was the
only one who, by turning slightly away two or three times, had appeared aware of my staring eyes. So I asked the "lift" whether he knew
of anyone in Balbec called Simonet. Being reluctant to admit to ignorance of anything, he replied that he thought he had "heard tell of
some such a name." When we reached the top floor, I asked him to
have them send up the latest list of newcomers.

On leaving the elevator, instead of going directly to my room, I
walked farther along the corridor, as at that time of day the servant on
duty, despite his aversion to drafts, had opened the window at the far
end of it, and this window, though it overlooked the hillside and the
valley instead of the sea, never let one see them, since its panes were of
opaque glass and it was usually kept shut. I stood for a moment in front
of it, long enough to make my devotions to the view it had for once dis-

closed: this went beyond the hill against which the hotel backed, and contained a single house, set some distance away, but with its bulk preserved by the perspective and the evening light, which had worked delicately on it, embossing it and setting it within a velvet-lined casket, as though it were an example of miniaturized architecture, a tiny temple or chapel worked in gold and enamel, used as a reliquary, and exposed only on rare occasions to the veneration of the faithful. But my moment of worship had gone on too long, and the servant on duty, holding a bunch of keys in one hand and touching the other to his sexton's cap, rather than exposing himself to the cool evening air by raising it to me, came along to close the windows, like the little double doors of a monstrance, thus putting an end to my adoration of the golden relic of the miniature church. I went to my room, where the painting on show in the window frame kept changing as the season advanced. At the beginning of my stay, it was broad daylight, its tones sometimes dulled by bad weather: the sea, through the glaucous glass bulging with its round waves, held between the iron uprights of the frame as though set in the lead of a latticed window, teased out along the deep, rocky fringe of the bay triangles plumed with spray which hung motionless, touched in with the delicacy of down or a feather penciled by Pisanello, and fixed by the creamy white never-fading enamel used for a fall of snow in glassworks by Gallé.[82]

Then the days grew shorter; and when I went to my room, the violet sky, which seemed to have been branded by the rigid, geometrical, fleeting, flashing iron of the sun (as though in representation of some miraculous sign or mystical apparition), hung down over the sea at the juncture of the horizon like a religious canvas above a high altar, while the different parts of the sunset, exhibited in the glass doors of the low mahogany bookcases running around the walls, and which I mentally compared to the marvelous painting from which they had been detached, were like the different scenes with which an old master once decorated a shrine for a religious house, now divided into separate panels, for display in a museum, where only the imagination of a visitor to the exhibition can reassemble them on the predellas of the altarpiece. Some weeks later, when I went up, the sun would have already set. Lying above the sea, there would be a band of red, as dense and fine-edged as a slab of aspic, similar to the red that striped the sky at Combray, above the wayside cross, on evenings when I was nearing home after a walk and intended to go down to the kitchen before dinner; and before long, right on top of the water, which had the coldness and the color of the fish known as gray mullet, there would be another sky, of the same pink as one of the salmon we would soon order at Rivebelle; and these shades whetted my expectation of the pleasure of changing into evening clothes to go out to dine. Very close to the shore, trying to rise over the sea, in tiers that spread ever wider, its layers superimposed upon one another, there was a haze as black as soot, but also with the smooth sheen and consistency of agate, its highest parts, visibly top-heavy, beginning to tilt above their deformed support, leaning away from the center of gravity of those that had hitherto underpinned them, and seeming about to crumble and collapse into the sea, dragging down with them from halfway up the sky the whole precarious edifice. The sight of a ship leaving, like a night traveler, gave me the impression I had once had in the train, of being freed of the restrictions of sleeping and staying closed up in a room. Not that I felt hemmed in by this room, since within the hour I was going to walk out of it and go off in a carriage. I lay down on the bed; and, as though I were on a bunk aboard one of the boats I could see not far away, which after nightfall people might be surprised to see moving slowly through the darkness, like dim, silent swans that never sleep, I was surrounded on all sides by images of the sea.

However, quite often they were nothing but images: I would forget that, beneath the color of them, there was the forlorn, empty shoreline, with the uneasy evening wind, which had so upset me on my arrival in Balbec. Also, even in my room, my thoughts were full of the girls I had seen walking along the esplanade, and my state of mind was neither calm enough nor disinterested enough for me to be able to attend properly to vivid impressions of beauty. Because I was looking forward to the dinner at Rivebelle, my state of expectancy made me feel even more frivolous; and my mind, occupying at such moments the surface of my body, which I was about to clothe in such a way as to appear as attractive as possible to the eyes of women staring at me under the bright lights of the restaurant, was unable to see through the colors of things to anything deeper. Had it not been for the tireless and restful aerobatics of the swifts and swallows outside my window, their sudden vertical spurts like water jets, fireworks of vitality, filling the intervals between their vertiginous rocketlike ascents with the straight white wake of a long unwavering glide, making a delightful miracle of a natural and local phenomenon, linking the landscapes before my eyes to reality, I could have seen these landscapes as a mere selection of paintings, changed every day, arbitrarily exhibited at the spot where I happened to be, but having no necessary relation to it. One evening it would be an exhibition of Japanese prints: beside the flimsy cutout of the sun, red and as round as the moon, a yellow cloud was a lake against which black blades, and the trees on its bank, were silhouetted; a bar of soft pink, in a shade I had not set eyes on since my very first paintbox, swelled like a river, with boats seemingly beached on both sides of it, looking as though waiting there to be refloated. With the bored, disdainful superficiality of the sated expert, or the elegant lady glancing in at an exhibition during her crowded day of visits to fashionable friends, I dismissed it with the thought: "Quite an interesting sunset, rather different, but I've seen plenty of others that are just as delicately done and every bit as striking." On other evenings, there was greater enjoyment to be had: from a ship which had been absorbed and liquefied by the horizon, and which had such an appearance of being of the same color as it, as though in an Impressionist painting, that it also seemed to be made of the same material, as though, once the hull and rigging had been cut out of it, it had faded away into the hazy blue of the sky. Or it was the sea itself that took up almost the whole height of the window, having been extended upward by a broad band of sky topped by a strip of the same blue as the sea, which I thought was the sea, the difference in shade being due to an effect of the light. Or else the sea was painted only in the lower part of the window, all the rest being filled by clouds in horizontal stripes piled on top of one another, so numerous that it looked as though the artist might have intended the panes to contain one of his specialties, a *Study in Clouds*, while the different glass-fronted doors of the bookcases, showing clouds that were similar but reflected from other points of the horizon, and variously colored by the light, seemed to be, as one sees in the works of certain contemporary masters, endless repetitions of a single effect, none of them noted at the same time of day, but all of them, through the immobility of art, now available to be viewed together in one room, executed in pastel, and displayed under glass. Sometimes, with exquisite delicacy, a touch of pink was added to the uniform gray of sea and sky; and at the very bottom of this *Harmony in Grey and Pink* after Whistler,[83] a tiny moth asleep on the windowpane seemed to lend its wings to the favorite signature of the master from Chelsea. Then even the pink disappeared, and there was nothing else to look at. I got up to close the tall curtains, then lay down again. From my bed, I could see the fading line of daylight that lingered above the curtains, growing dimmer and fainter; but I had no qualms or regrets about letting the last daylight hour die behind the curtains at a time when I was usually in the dining room, for I knew this day was of a different kind from the rest, lasting longer, like those polar days that turn into a night of a few minutes' duration; I knew that a brilliant metamorphosis was at work within the chrysalis of this twilight, and that from it there would soon emerge the dazzling illuminations of the restaurant at Rivebelle. I thought, "It's time"; I stretched, still lying on the bed, then arose and finished getting ready to go; and I found a great charm in these slack moments unburdened by any material concern, which everyone else spent sitting downstairs at the dinner table, as I used the energy stored during the inactive evening, drying my body, putting on a dinner jacket, tying my bow tie, going through all these motions that were already informed by the expected pleasure of being once again in the presence of a particular woman whom I had noticed the last time we had gone to Rivebelle, who had appeared to look at me, who had even left the room for a moment, conceivably for the sole purpose of giving me the chance to follow her out; it was a joy to put on this finery, so that I could be ready to devote myself wholly to my new life of freedom and lack of care, when my hesitations could rest on Saint-Loup's untroubled certainties, and I could choose, from all the species of natural history and products from all countries, those that

would challenge my appetite or my imagination to make the most unusual dishes, which my friend would order for me forthwith.

Then, right at the end, there came days when it was no longer possible to step straight from the esplanade into the dining room, because it
was already dark outside and the glass doors were not open, and the
swarms of the poor and the curious, chilled to the marrow by the north
wind, drawn toward the blazing, unreachable illuminations, were cling-
ing in thick black clusters to the glowing sliding panels of our hive of
glass.

There was a knock at the door: it was Aimé, making a point of being
the one to bring me the latest list of newcomers.

Before he left the room, Aimé felt the need to inform me that there
could be no doubt that Dreyfus was guilty, totally and utterly.[84] "The
whole truth," he said, "will come out, not this year, but next. It was this
gent that's very close to the General Staff that told me." I asked him
whether it would not be decided to divulge everything all at once, before the end of the year. "Look, he put down his cigarette," Aimé said,
acting the scene for me, shaking his head and his forefinger at me, as
the hotel guest had done, meaning: Don't be so demanding. " 'Not this
year, Aimé,' he says, giving me a tap on the shoulder. 'Out of the question. But just you wait and see what Easter brings!' " Aimé gave me a
tap on the shoulder, then said, "There, that's exactly what he did," either because he was flattered at having been treated so familiarly by a
great man, or so that I could better appreciate the force of the argument
and the validity of the reasons why we must live in hope.

It was not without a little palpitation that I read, on the first page of
the list of newcomers: *The Simonet family*. There was in me a residue of
old dreams of love, dating from my childhood, full of all the tenderness
my heart was capable of, all the love it had ever felt, and which was now
indistinguishable from it, which could be suddenly brought back to me
by someone as different as possible from me. This someone I now once
more invented, this time using the name "Simonet" and the memory of
the harmony shared by the group of young bodies I had seen making
their way along the seafront in an athletic procession worthy of ancient
Greece or Giotto. I had no idea which of these girls—or, indeed, whether

any of them—might be Mlle Simonet; but I knew that Mlle Simonet loved me and that, because of Saint-Loup's presence, I was going to try to make her acquaintance. Unfortunately, he was obliged to return to Doncières every day, that being the condition on which he had managed to have an extension of his leave approved. Despite this, in the hope of having him disregard his orders, I had thought I might be able to play, if not on his friendship for me, at least on the same sort of naturalist's curiosity about human beings that in my own case (on hearing a mere mention of a pretty cashier working in a fruit market, and without even having set eyes on the person spoken of) had so often led me to an observation of a new variety of feminine beauty. However, I had been mistaken in thinking that, by telling Saint-Loup about my gang of girls, I might stimulate this curiosity in him. It had been paralyzed by his liaison with the actress whose lover he was. And even if he had been tempted to feel it, he would have repressed it, under the influence of a sort of superstitious belief: that the fidelity of his mistress to him might depend on his to her. So he gave me no promise to further my cause with the girls, and we set off to dine at Rivebelle.

The first few times we went there, the sun had just set when we arrived, but there was still light: in the garden of the restaurant, they had not yet lit the lamps, and the heat of the day was dropping, subsiding, as though into a vase, lining the inner surface of it with the dim, crystalline transparency of the air, which seemed so firm that a tall rosebush, veining with pink the darkened wall against which it stood, resembled the arborization to be seen inside an onyx. Before long, it was dark by the time we stepped out of the carriage, or even by the time we left Balbec, if the weather was bad and we had delayed the moment of harnessing up in the hope of an improvement. Even on those days, I was not upset by the bluster of the wind; I knew it would not frustrate plans for the evening or result in my having to stay indoors; I knew that, as we walked into the large dining room of the restaurant, to the music of the Gypsy band, the countless lamps would easily cure the dark and the cold, by applying to them their broad golden cauteries; and I happily took my place alongside Saint-Loup in the brougham that stood waiting in the rain. For some time, the conviction expressed by Bergotte that, despite what I said, I was made for the pleasures of the intellectual life, had made me think again about what I might do with my life, reviving hopes that were, however, doomed to frustration every time I sat down to a desk to sketch the draft of a critical study or a novel. "Well," I thought, "it may be that the pleasure to be taken in writing it is not an infallible criterion of the value of a fine page. Perhaps it's only an accessory state, often present, but not necessarily invalidating the writing by its absence. Perhaps it's possible to yawn all the way through the composition of a masterpiece." My self-doubt was assuaged by my grandmother, who assured me that if I were in good health I would work well and with enjoyment. Our doctor having thought it wiser to add the view that my state of health could expose me to serious risks, setting forth all the precautions I must take so as to avoid having an attack, I now subordinated all pleasures to the aim, which seemed infinitely more important than they were, of becoming well enough to accomplish the work I might have it in me to produce; and since coming to Balbec I had been paying constant and close attention to my health. No one could have made me drink a cup of coffee, and jeopardize thereby the night's sleep I needed if I were not to suffer from fatigue the following day. But as soon as we arrived at Rivebelle—because of the excitement generated in me by a new pleasure, and having crossed the line that anything exceptional makes us cross after it has severed the thread, patiently woven over so many days, that was leading us toward a more sensible way of living—as though no tomorrow would ever come, as though the worthier achievements were of no importance, the whole careful arrangement of wiser precautions, the whole point of which was to make those achievements possible, would disappear. While a servant helped to relieve me of my overcoat, Saint-Loup would say:

"Won't you feel the cold? It might be better to keep it on, it's not very warm here."

To which I replied, "No matter." Perhaps I did not even feel the cold, but certainly I had lost all fear of being ill; and the need to protect myself against the possibility of dying, like the importance of getting down to work, had likewise vanished from my mind. I handed over the coat, we stepped into the dining room to the strains of a swashbuckling march played by the Gypsies and walked between the rows of set tables as though we were conquering heroes; and though we could feel in our bodies the thrill of exuberance communicated by the rhythms of the band, as it accorded us these military honors and an undeserved triumph, we hid it behind an appearance of glacial gravity and a world-weary gait, avoiding any suggestion of the type of swaggering songstress who performs in cabarets, strutting onto her little stage with the martial air of a victorious general, and launching into a bawdy adaptation of a marching song.

From that moment on, I was a different person, no longer the grandson of my grandmother, to whom I would not give another thought until after having left the restaurant, but briefly the brother of the waiters who were about to serve us.

An amount of beer, let alone of champagne, that I would not have wanted to drink in a week at Balbec, even though my mind, when unclouded and sober, was capable of having a clear appreciation of the taste of these drinks as a pleasure, albeit one that could easily be forgone, now passed my lips in the space of an hour, interspersed with a little port, which I was too preoccupied even to taste; and to the violinist, who had just played for us, I gave the two golden *louis,* saved over the previous month to enable me to buy something that had now completely gone from my head. Some of the waiters rushed along the aisles between the rows of tables, on outstretched hand bearing a dish that it was the seeming purpose of this type of race not to drop. Sure enough, the chocolate soufflés reached their destination without spilling, the potatoes *à l'anglaise,* despite the canter and the apparent shaking about, always arrived as they had set out, neatly ranged about the Pauillac lamb.[85] I noticed one of these servers, very tall, with a superb plume of black hair, and wearing makeup of a color more suggestive of certain species of rare birds than of a human face, who ran to and fro, without letup and, it seemed, without purpose, from one end of the room to the other, and brought to mind the macaws that fill the large aviaries in zoos with their gorgeous coloring and incomprehensible agitation. Soon the spectacle became more ordered, at least to my eyes, turning into something nobler and calmer. All the giddy activity slowed down and settled into a soothing harmony. I could see the round tables, a countless constellation of them filling the restaurant like so many planets, as depicted in allegorical paintings from earlier times. These different heavenly bodies also exercised irresistible attractions on one another, and at every table the diners kept looking at the other tables, except for a rich man entertaining guests, including a famous writer whom he had managed to attract, whom he was now plying with questions, in the hope that the virtues of the turning table would induce him to utter inanities, which the ladies would marvel at. The harmony of these astral tables did not impede the incessant revolutions of the innumerable servers who, being on foot, unlike the seated diners, moved in a higher realm. Of course, one or another of them dashed in with the hors d'œuvres, changed the wine, brought extra glasses. But despite these particular reasons, their perpetual hurrying about among the round tables eventually clarified the law of its own restlessness, dizzying but regulated. Like a pair of witches, sitting behind a great floral decoration, two ghastly cashiers, endlessly busy with their arithmetic, seemed engaged in astrological calculations of the upheavals that might on occasion disrupt life in this planetary system, designed in accordance with the science of the Middle Ages.

I felt rather sorry for the diners, because I sensed that for them the round tables were not planets, and that they were unpracticed in the art of cross-sectioning things so as to rid them of their customary appearance and enable us to see analogies. Their heads were full of the knowledge that they were dining with such-and-such a person, that the meal would cost this or that much, that they would probably eat another dinner the following day. They seemed absolutely impervious to the appearance of a procession of young assistant waiters who, probably having no urgent business to attend to, were processionally bringing in bread in baskets. Some of them, too young, and victimized by the senior waiters, who cuffed them about the head in passing, had their hangdog eyes on a distant daydream, and cheered up only if a guest staying at the Balbec hotel, where they had been formerly employed, recognized them, spoke to them, and asked them in person to take away the champagne, which was undrinkable, an event that filled them with pride.

I could hear the muffled protests of my nerves, in which there was actually a feeling of well-being, unconnected with the external objects which can supply it, but which the slightest movement I made with my body or my mind sufficed to give to me, as a gentle pressure on a closed eye can create an impression of color. I had already drunk a great deal of port; and when I asked for more, it was less because I was hoping the next glasses would give a feeling of well-being than because the previous ones had already given it. I let the music conduct my pleasure to each note, and it rested on them docilely. While the restaurant at Rivebelle, like the chemical industries that produce great quantities of substances which, in nature, occur only by chance and are very rare, brought to-gether more women and their prospects of happiness for me than a year of chance encounters during journeys or outings in the country could have brought me, the music we could hear (arrangements of waltzes, German operettas, and cabaret songs, all of it new to me) was itself like an airy place of pleasure, superimposed on the real one and more excit-ing than it: each musical phrase, though as individual as a particular woman, limited the secret of its sensual thrills not to a single privileged person, as she would have done—it offered them to me, it ogled me, it accosted me, it toyed with me in seductively whimsical or vulgar ways, it caressed me, as though I had suddenly become more attractive, pow-erful, or wealthy; and in the tunes I detected something cruel: the fact that the slightest disinterested sense of beauty or vestige of intelligence was foreign to them—for them, there is nothing beyond physical plea-sure. They are the most merciless form of hell, the hell with no way out, for any poor victim of jealousy who hears that pleasure in them—the pleasure the woman he loves enjoys with someone else—and who hears it as the only thing desired in the whole world by the woman who is the whole world to him. To me, as I hummed over the tune and returned its kiss, the special sensual pleasure it gave enchanted me so much that I would have left my parents to follow the echoes of the phrase through the singular world it created in its invisible element, its outlines at times languishing, at times sprightly. At such moments, despite the fact that this secret joy is not of a sort that increases the attractiveness of the person who has acquired it, since no one else can perceive it, and though any failure to impress a woman who may have dismissed us at a single glance cannot possibly be imputed to our having or not having this inner and subjective bliss, since, in her unawareness of its presence or absence in us, her view of us is bound to be unaffected by it, I felt endowed with a power that seemed to make me almost irresistible. It felt as though my love was no longer something irksome, something to be dismissed with a smile, but that it had exactly the touching beauty, the wistful charm of this music, which itself now gave the impression of being a favorable place and time that had brought me and the woman I loved together, to meet and become close.

Women of easy virtue were not the only people to frequent this restaurant; there were also people from the most fashionable society, who would go to it for afternoon tea or else held lavish dinner parties there. Afternoon tea was served in a long, narrow gallery, like a corridor walled with glass, leading from the entrance hall to the dining room and forming one side of the garden, from which it was separated only by its few pillars of stone and the large windows, many of which were often open. The result of this arrangement was not only that it was very drafty, but that one was exposed to sudden and intermittent sunlight, a dazzling and unreliable form of illumination that made it all but impossible to make out the women having tea; and when they sat there, crammed at pairs of tables along both sides of the narrow passageway, shimmering at every movement they made as they sipped their tea or greeted each other, the place looked like a tank or a creel that a fisherman has filled with his shiny catch, some of the fish being half out of the water, their sheen glistening and changing under glossy lights.

Some hours later, during dinner, which was served of course in the dining room, the lamps would be lit though it was still daylight outside, and in the garden one could see, alongside outlying pavilions still lit by the dusk, and looking like pallid evening ghosts of themselves, arbors of green gloom shot through by the last rays of sunlight, and resembling, out there beyond the glass of the lamplit room where we sat dining— and unlike the late-afternoon ladies at tea, enmeshed in the sparkling moisture of their bluish-gold passage—plants in a giant aquarium bathed in a faint, supernaturally green light. As dinner finished and the room began to empty, the diners who, though they had spent their time during the meal looking at, recognizing, or asking to be informed of the names of other diners nearby, held together in complete cohesion around their own tables, now began to be freed of the gravitational force which had kept them close to their host of the evening, which lost its power over them at the moment when they drifted out to take coffee in the corridor where afternoon tea had been served; and a dinner party on the move would often shed one or more of its corpuscles, which had been too strongly affected by the attractive power of a competing dinner party, and was briefly replaced by a lady or gentleman who stepped across to greet a friend, before going back to his or her own group, saying, "Must go—I'm with M. X's party tonight." One had a momentary impression of two separate bouquets exchanging a few of their flowers. Then even the corridor was deserted. Some nights this long corridor was left unlit, as there was still a little daylight even after dinner, and with the trees hanging down nearby, just outside the glass, it had the look of a path through a shadowy, overgrown garden. On occasion a lady, detached from a dinner party, lingered in the half-dark. One evening, as I crossed the corridor on my way out, I noticed, sitting among a group of people unknown to me, the beautiful Princess of Luxembourg. I raised my hat to her but did not stop. She recognized me and inclined her head, smiling: from far above this movement of her head, and emitted by it, a few melodious words for me rose into the air, probably an elongated "good evening" intended not to delay me, but just to round off the nod of the head, to make it a spoken nod. Her words were so indistinct to me, and the sound of them, which was all I heard, lasted so long and was so musical, that it was as though a nightingale amid the close, leafy twilight had burst into song. If, as sometimes happened, Saint-Loup decided to finish the night with a group of his friends whom we had met, and with whom he went on to the Casino of one of the neighboring seaside towns, he would put me into a carriage by myself: I told the cabman to set the horse at a gallop, so as to abridge as much as possible the interval during which I could rely on no one but myself to provide my sensitivity—by engaging its reverse gear, and switching off the mechanism of passivity in which I had been held— with the stimuli which, ever since arriving at Rivebelle, I had been receiving from other people. Nothing, not even the possibility of colliding with a carriage coming in the other direction, along these paths that were pitch-dark and wide enough for only a single vehicle at a time, the uneven ground often littered with earthfalls from the cliff above, or the nearby precipice on the other side dropping straight to the sea, could bring me to make the small effort required for the idea of danger, and the fear of it, to rise to my reasoning mind. Just as it is not the wish to be famous, but a habit of hard work, that may make a creative artist of us, so it is not the joy we take in the present, but sober reflection on the past, that may enable us to safeguard the future. In my own case, not only had I begun the evening at Rivebelle by throwing away my crutches of rationality and self-discipline, which help us in our infirmity to walk a straight path, and had been afflicted thereby by a sort of moral ataxia, but then the alcohol, with its heightened effect on the nerves, had filled the present minutes with a quality and a charm whose effect had not been to make me more able, or even more willing, to defend myself against them: my state of light-headedness segregated them from the rest of my life and made me see them as vastly preferable to it; I was trapped in the present, as heroes are, or drunkards; in brief eclipse, my past had ceased to project in front of me that shadow of itself which we call our future; seeing the purpose of my life not in any past dreams coming true but in the simple bliss of the passing moment, I could see no further than that moment. So, by the working of a contradiction that was one only in appearance, it was at the very moment when I experienced an exceptional pleasure, when I sensed that my life could be one of fulfillment, and should therefore have seen it as having increased in value, that I felt liberated from the anxieties it had hitherto inspired in me, and was prepared to commit it without hesitation to the unsure hands of chance. In fact, what I was doing was condensing into one evening the unconcern that others dilute in their whole existence: every day they take the needless risk of a sea voyage, a ride in an airplane, a drive in a motorcar, when the person who would be stricken by grief if they were to die sits waiting for them at home, when the book, as yet unrevealed to the world, in which they see the point of their whole life, still lives only within their fragile brain. If somebody had turned up at the Rivebelle restaurant with the intention of killing me on one of the evenings when we stayed on there, when my grandmother, my life to come, and my unwritten books had all shrunk to a remote unreality, when I had no mind to give to anything but the fragrance of the woman at the next table, the courtesies of the headwaiter, the outlines of the waltz tune being played, when I was glutted with the present sensation and had no existence beyond it, no wish except to be never separated from it, I would have died in its embrace, I would have let myself be torn limb from limb, without raising a hand to defend myself, like a bee so bemused by tobacco smoke that it has lost its intent to garner away the supplies its efforts have gathered, and all hope of ever reaching the hive.

It must be added that the insignificance that all serious things acquired in the face of my intense exhilaration eventually touched even Mlle Simonet and her friends. The enterprise of getting to know them now seemed easy, but a matter of indifference, since nothing but my present sensation, because of the extraordinary power of it, the euphoria afforded by its slightest variations, and even by the mere continuity of it, had any importance; everything else, my parents, my work, my pleasures, my gang of girls at Balbec, was reduced to the insubstantiality of a fleck of spray in the high wind that prevents it from coming to earth, and had no existence except insofar as it related to my sensation of power: drunkenness brings about, for the space of a few hours, subjective idealism, pure phenomenalism; all things become mere appearances, and exist only as a function of our sublime selves. This does not mean that genuine love, if we happen to have such a feeling, cannot survive in these conditions. But we are well aware, as though we had moved into a new element, that unknown pressures have altered the dimension of our feeling, and we can no longer consider it as we did before. We know it is still there somewhere, but it has shifted, it no longer weighs on us, it is satisfied with the sensation afforded it by the present, a sensation that satisfies us too, for we have no interest in anything that is not the present. Unfortunately, the coefficient that alters values in this way works only during the hour of drunkenness. Tomorrow the individuals who had become insignificant, whom we blew away like soap bubbles, will again take on their full density; and the work left undone, which had lost all meaning, will have to be faced once more. Even more seriously, these morning-after mathematics, which are no different from day-before mathematics, are not only the making of the unavoidable problems which we must still contend with, they are also the mathematics which, unknown to ourselves, have in fact been governing our life during the drunken hours. If at those moments we are with a woman whose virtue or unfriendliness made her inaccessible, what was implausible the day before (that she should be attracted to us) now seems a million times easier, although it has not become any easier in fact, it being only in our eyes, our inner view of ourself, that we have changed. At the moment when we take a little liberty with her, she is as displeased as we will be the morning after, when we remember having tipped the porter a hundred francs, and for the same reason, which for us has simply been delayed: the fact of not being drunk.

I knew none of the women who were at Rivebelle and who, because they were part of my drunkenness, as reflections are part of a mirror, seemed infinitely more desirable than the more and more nonexistent Mlle Simonet. A young blonde with a forlorn air, sitting alone, wearing her straw hat with wildflowers about its brim, gave me a brief wistful glance and seemed attractive to me. I noticed another one, then a third; she was replaced by a brunette with a magnificent complexion. Almost all of them were known, if not to me, to Saint-Loup.

Before meeting his present mistress, he had in fact been so familiar with the small world of debauchery that, of all the women who dined on those evenings at Rivebelle, many of whom were there quite by chance, some having come to the coast at the behest of their present lovers, others in the hope of finding a new lover, there were very few whom he did not know, either he or one or another of his friends having spent at least a night with most of them. If a woman was in the company of a man, he did not greet her; and though the women glanced at him more than at other men, since the indifference they knew he felt toward any woman who was not his actress gave him a strange prestige in the eyes of the others, they too gave the appearance of not knowing him. One of them would murmur, "There's young Saint-Loup. It seems he still loves his little trollop. It's the great love of his life! What a handsome fellow, though! I think he's just lovely. And what style! Some women have *all* the luck. He's a good sort in all other ways too. I knew him well when I was with d'Orléans–they were inseparable. Mind you, he burned the candle at both ends in those days! He's stopped all that now, though: he's only got eyes for her. I wonder if she knows how lucky she is. And I wonder what he sees in her. He must be a bit of a fool, though: she's got feet like barges and a walrus mustache–and her undies are just filthy! Even a factory girl wouldn't have drawers like hers! Take a look at those eyes–a girl could really go for a man like him. Not a word, now, he's recognized me, he's laughing–he knew a thing or two about me! Just ask him about me!" I caught knowing glances passing between him and them. I wished he would introduce me to these women, so that I could ask them for an appointment and they agree to me, even though I might not be able to keep it. Otherwise, in my memory, a particular part would be forever missing from the face of each of them–as though she had been wearing a veil–a part that varies from woman to woman, which we cannot imagine on an individual face when we have never seen it there, as it appears only in eyes looking at ours, accepting our desire, and promising that it will be satisfied. However, even in this unfinished form, the faces of these women meant much more to me than those of women I suspected of being virtuous, having none of the flatness and emptiness of theirs, which were made out of a single piece and without depth. For me, of course, these faces were not what they must have been for Saint-Loup: in his memory, through the transparent indifference of impassive features that feigned not to know him, under the ordinariness of a greeting that could have been exchanged with anyone else, he could see the tumbled hair, the gasping mouth, the half-closed eyes, all the detail of a silent scene which a painter, wishing not to offend visitors to his studio, conceals behind a more seemly canvas. For me, aware as I was that nothing of my life had penetrated these women's, and that, whichever roads they might take in the future, nothing of me would go with them, their faces remained closed. But the simple knowledge that they could open was enough to make me see them as prizes worth winning, which they would not have seemed if they had been mere medals, however fine, rather than lockets with mementos of love hidden inside. As for Robert, who became restless as soon as he had to sit for a while, concealing behind the smile of the courtier the warrior's zest for action, I only had to look at him closely to realize how similar the emphatic bone structure of his triangular face must be to that of his ancestors, more that of the ardent archer than of the sensitive bookman. Through the fine skin, the strong shapes of feudal architecture were visible. His head reminded one of an ancient castle keep, with its unmanned battlements still preserved but its interior transformed into a library.

All the way back to Balbec, if it happened that Robert had introduced me to one or another of these unfamiliar women, I kept repeating to myself, as though singing over a remembered refrain, without a second's pause, but almost without noticing what I was doing, "What a delightful woman!" The words, rather than expressing a lasting judgment, were prompted by a state of nervous excitement. Nevertheless, if I had had a thousand francs on me, and if any jewelers had been open at that hour, I would have bought a ring for her. When the compartments in which we live parts of our lives are too different from one another, we can expend ourselves on a person who, by the following day, may come to seem uninteresting. But we feel responsible for what we may have said the night before, and wish to honor it.

As I was back late to the hotel on those nights, it was a pleasure to walk into the bedroom, which had stopped being hostile, and find the bed, in which I had been sure on first arriving that I could never go to sleep, and which was now a comfort to my weary limbs; and one after the other, my thighs, my hips, my shoulders tried to imprint their every feature in the sheets enveloping the mattress, as though my fatigue were a sculptor molding a cast of the whole human body. However, sleep evaded me: I was aware of the imminence of the morning; peace of mind and well-being of body were no longer in me. In my distress, I felt I had lost them forever. To enjoy them again, I would have needed to sleep for a long time. But even if I had fallen asleep, I would still have been wakened a couple of hours later by the symphony concert. Then, suddenly, I was unconscious, submerged in the dense sleep that reveals to us mysteries such as youth regained, the rediscovery of years past, and emotions once felt, disincarnation, the transmigration of souls, the summoning up of the dead, the illusions of the mad, travel in time back to the most primitive stages of nature (for it is said we often see animals in our dreams, forgetting that, almost always when we dream, we ourselves are animals deprived of the clarity of certainty shed on all things by our faculty of reason; instead of it, all we can turn on the spectacle of life is an infirm gaze, which is abolished by oblivion at every successive moment, each reality no sooner glimpsed than vanishing in the face of the next one, as the slides projected by a magic lantern succeed one another), mysteries which we think are closed to us, yet which we are admitted to almost every night, just as we are to the other great mystery of annihilation and resurrection. The difficulty of digesting the Rivebelle dinner meant that it was in a more fitful light that I visited, in incoherent succession, the darkened zones of my past life, and that I became a creature for whom supreme happiness would have been to meet Legrandin, with whom I had just had a dream conversation.

In addition, even my own daily life would be completely hidden from me by new scenery, like the décor set out near the edge of the stage, in front of which, while the scene-changing is going on behind it, actors present a divertissement. The one in which I was cast to play a part was after the manner of Oriental tales: I had no knowledge of my past life or of myself, because of the extreme nearness of the intervening scenery; I was just a character getting a good flogging, being punished in various ways for an unexplained misdemeanor, which was that I had drunk too much port. Suddenly awake, I would realize that a long sleep had prevented me from hearing the symphony concert. It was already the afternoon, as I would see from my watch, after attempts to sit up, unsuccessful at first and interrupted by collapses onto the pillow, brief collapses of the sort that follow sleep, the drunkenness caused by wine, or that other intoxication one experiences in convalescence; but in any case, before I had looked at the time, I knew for certain it was after midday. The night before, I had been a creature without substance, weightless, and unable to stop moving or talking (as, in order to sit up, it is necessary to have been lying down, and in order to stop talking, it is necessary to have been asleep); I had had neither consistency nor center of gravity, I was unstoppable, I felt my monotonous trajectory could have taken me as far as the moon. But in sleeping, though my eyes had been incapable of telling the time, my body had known how to, measuring it not according to the surface markings of a clockface, but by its continuous hefting of all my refreshed energies, which, cog by cog, like the mechanism of a powerful timepiece, it had gradually lowered, moving them from my brain down into the rest of my body, where they were now stocked, the unused abundance of their supply reaching already above my knees. If it is true that the sea was once our life-giving environment, in which we must reimmerse our blood so as to restore our strength, the same can be said of forgetting, of mental oblivion: for some hours, we seem to live outside time; but the energy accumulated unspent during that period measures it by itself, as accurately as the weights of a clock or the trickling little sandhill in an hourglass. Such a sleep is no easier to leave than a period of prolonged wakefulness, all things tending to endure; and if it is true that some narcotics make one sleep, sleep itself, if long, is a more powerful narcotic, from which we have great difficulty waking. Like a sailor who can see the pier where he must moor but whose boat is still rocked by the waves, I had a clear impression of looking at the time and getting up; but my body was tossed back again and again into sleep; my landing was a difficult one, and before I could stand up and reach for my watch, to compare its time with the time indicated by the wealth of materials stored in my once-weary legs, I fell back two or three more times on the pillow.

Able at last to make out the time—"Two o'clock in the afternoon!"—I rang; but then I immediately fell into another sleep, which, to judge by the feeling I had on waking from it, of being fully rested, and the vision I had of having slept through an immense length of night, must have been infinitely longer than the previous one. Yet, since what woke me was Françoise coming in, in answer to my ring, this sleep that had seemed so much longer than the earlier one, and had afforded me such a depth of beneficent relief from consciousness, had lasted no more than half a minute.

My grandmother was opening my bedroom door; I asked her some questions about the Legrandins.

I had done more than just return to mental repose and well-being: between them and me, the night before, there had been more than a slight distance, and I had had to struggle all night long against a strong current; yet now here they were, not only back within my reach, but inside me. My ideas had taken up their former places in precise and as yet rather painful corners of my empty head, which would one day be split open, scattering them to the winds and ending an existence they had so far put, alas, to little profit.

Once more I had escaped the impossibility of sleeping, and the ravages and the havoc of nervous disorder it brought. Things that had been a menace to me the night before, when I was without rest, were now incapable of alarming me. A new life stretched before me: without making a single movement, since I still felt crippled though already alert, I reveled in my exhaustion; it had dismembered me and broken the bones in my arms and legs, which I could feel lying there nearby, ready to be reassembled, and which I was going to bring together again, with a mere song, like the builder in the fable.[86]

I suddenly remembered the young blonde with the wistful look who had glanced at me at Rivebelle. During the evening at the restaurant, many other women had seemed just as nice, yet she was the one who now stood alone in my memory. I had the feeling that she must have noticed me: one of the waiters from Rivebelle might even now be bringing me a note from her! She was not known to Saint-Loup, who had thought she was respectable. It would be difficult to see her, and to go on seeing her. But I was prepared to do anything that would make it possible; I could think of nothing but her. Philosophy talks of free acts and necessary acts. Perhaps none is so completely inescapable as the one which, on the release of a hitherto compressed elevating force, brings up to the surface of the idling mind a memory that was weighted down at the same level as others by the ballast of activity and preoccupation, and makes it spring to the mind's eye because, unknown to us, it contains a charm that the others lack, and which we notice only twenty-four hours later. But perhaps none is so completely free either, since such an act is still unaffected by habit, that type of mental obsessiveness which, under the aggravation of love, becomes the exclusive rehearsal of the memory of a certain person.

It was the day after I had seen my group of girls profiled in beautiful procession against the sea. I asked several of the hotel guests about them, people who often spent their summers at Balbec, but they could tell me nothing. Some time later, a photograph was to explain why: in the group as it was now, in these girls who had barely, but definitively, left behind the age at which we change forever, could anyone have recognized the delightful, amorphous mass of little girls, still children, who only a few years before were to be seen sitting in a circle on the sand, by a tent, a white blur of a constellation, in which a pair of eyes finer than any other pair, a mischievous face, a head of fair hair, once noticed, would soon have gone unnoticed, blended back into the milky, indistinct nebula?

No doubt, at that time, so few years before, it was not the vision of the group that lacked clarity, as it had been the day before, when they first appeared to me, but the group itself. In those days, the girls were too young to have gone beyond the elementary degree of formation of self, when personality has not yet stamped its seal on each face. Like primitive organisms in which the individual hardly exists, or, rather, in which it is constituted more by the polypary than by each of its component polyps, they lived in a close conglomerate, huddled together. One of them would suddenly push another one over, and a fit of the giggles, which seemed to be the only manifestation in them of personal life, convulsed them all at once, masking and unifying the undefined, grimacing faces in the sparkle and translucency of a single, quivering cluster. In an old photograph they subsequently gave me, which I have kept, their pack of children numbers no fewer of them than were to figure later in their feminine company; it suggests that even then the blur of color they made on the beach was remarkable enough to make eyes turn toward them, but in order to recognize any of them individually, one must resort to deduction, try to imagine the whole range of their possible transformations during later childhood, up to the point at which their remodeled forms started to coincide with another individual set of features, which one must attempt to identify also in the beautiful face (now accompanied by full height and hair that is waved) that might once have belonged to the photo's wizened and grimacing gnome; and the distance covered in so short a time by the physical characteristics of each of the girls was such an unreliable criterion—in addition to which, their collectiveness, so to speak, and the things they had in common, were already so marked—that even their best friends could look at that photograph and mistake them for one another; with the result that the uncertainty could be dispelled only by the presence of some article of clothing that one of them knew without a doubt she, and not one of the others, had worn. Different though those earlier days were from the day when I had seen them on the esplanade—different, yet so close to it—the girls still enjoyed laughing with gusto, as I had noticed the day before; but this laughter was not the intermittent and almost automatic sort indulged in by children, the spasmodic release that had once made the whole group of heads duck down as one, as a block of minnows in the Vivonne used to dive and disintegrate, before re-forming a moment later; their individual faces had now become capable of self-mastery, their eyes remaining fixed throughout on the aim they pursued; and the day before, it had been only my indecision and the vacillation of my initial perception which, like their former hilarity and the old photo, had fused into an indistinct whole the now individualized and separated sister stars of the pale madrepore.

Of course, when I saw pretty girls pass by, I often promised myself I would make a point of seeing them again. Usually, such girls make no reappearance in one's life; and memory, quickly mislaying their existence, would be hard put to remember their features; perhaps our eyes would not even recognize them again, and before long we see others passing by, whom we shall not see again either. However, on other occasions—and this was what was to happen with this little gang of impudent girls—further chance encounters bring them back into our field of vision. In such chance there is seeming beauty, for we see in it an incipient intent or effort to organize our life, to give it shape; and it is this same chance that can make it easy, inevitable, and sometimes even cruel—after intermissions that may have made us hope for a cessation of such memories—for us to acquire a sort of fidelity to mental images that we may come to believe we were predestined to acquire, yet which, had it not been for that chance, we could have forgotten at the very beginning, like so many others, so easily.

Saint-Loup's stay at Balbec was soon to come to an end. I had not seen any of the girls on the beach again. He could spend too few afternoons at Balbec to be able to busy himself with getting to know them on my behalf. In the evenings, he had more time and often took me out to Rivebelle. In those sorts of restaurants, as in public parks and trains, one comes across people enclosed in an ordinary appearance, whose names astonish us if, having asked by chance what they are called, we discover them to be, not the nondescript nobodies we had supposed, but none other than the minister or the duke whom we have so often heard of. In the Rivebelle restaurant, Saint-Loup and I had several times noticed a tall man, very well built, with regular features and a beard turning gray, who, having arrived when most other diners were leaving, would sit at a table resolutely staring at nothing with pensive, unfocused eyes. When we asked the owner one night who this unknown, solitary, belated diner was, he replied, "What? Don't you know the famous painter Elstir?" Swann had once spoken the name of Elstir in my presence, though I had completely forgotten in what connection; but the loss of a memory, like the omission of a phrase during reading, rather than making for uncertainty, can lead to a premature certainty. "He's a friend of Swann's, a very well-known artist, among the best," I said to Saint-Loup. The immediate thought that thrilled through the mind of each of us was that Elstir was a great artist, a famous man; and the next was that he must look on us as he looked on the other diners, and be quite unaware of the excitement that filled us at the knowledge of his brilliance. Had we not been at the seaside, we would not have been irked to realize he knew nothing of our admiration for him or our acquaintance with Swann. But we were still at an age when enthusiasm cries out to be known of; and with a sudden conviction that our incognito was intolerable, we wrote a letter, which we both signed, telling Elstir that the two diners sitting not far away were ardent admirers of his ability and friends of his great friend Swann, and asking his permission to present our compliments. We got a waiter to take our message to the famous man.

To tell the truth, Elstir may not have been quite as famous at that time as the owner of the restaurant claimed, or as he became not many years later. He had been one of the first to live in the restaurant, at a time when it was still little more than a farmhouse, to which he had brought a colony of artists (all of whom had later migrated elsewhere, once the farmhouse, where they had eaten out of doors under a simple canopy, had become a fashionable rendezvous; the only reason Elstir himself had come back to eat at that time at Rivebelle was that his wife, with whom he lived not far from there, was briefly away from home). But a great talent, even when it goes largely unrecognized, is bound to give rise to certain manifestations of admiration, such as those the owner of the farmhouse had seen in the questions of more than one visiting Englishwoman, eager for information on the life led by Elstir, and in the number of letters the artist received from abroad. The owner had also noticed that Elstir disliked being interrupted while he was working, that when the moonlight was good he got up in the middle of the night, so as to take a young model down to pose in the nude by the sea; and on recognizing in one of Elstir's paintings a wooden cross that stood just outside Rivebelle, he had decided that such self-imposed discipline was not wasted, and the admiration of the tourists not unjustified. "It's the very same cross, I tell you!" he would say in amazement. "You can see the four bits of it! Mind you, he really goes at it."

And he wondered whether a little *Sunrise on the Sea*, given to him by Elstir, might not be worth a fortune.

We saw Elstir read our letter, slip it into his pocket, go on with his dinner, then ask for his things and leave the table. By now we were so sure that by writing to him we had given offense that we would have preferred (as much as before we would have been reluctant) to leave the restaurant without being noticed by him. We gave not the slightest thought to a thing that should have seemed the most important of all:

that our enthusiasm for Elstir, the sincerity of which we would not have allowed anyone to doubt (and in its support we could, of course, have alleged our bated breath and our wish to do anything for the great man, as long as it was difficult or heroic), was not, as we believed it was, admiration, since we had never seen any of his canvases; it was possible for such a feeling to be inspired by the empty idea of "a great artist," but not by work that was completely unknown to us. At best, it was theoretical admiration, the nervous framework and emotional skeleton of an admiration without object—that is to say, something as inseparably linked to childhood as certain organs that no longer exist in the body of a grown man: we were still boys. Elstir had almost reached the door when he turned and came toward us. I felt myself flooded with a feeling of delicious terror, the likes of which I would have been incapable of experiencing a few years later, for not only does age diminish the ability, but habituation to society takes away all impulse, to bring about such strange occasions and the sort of feelings that accompany them.

Elstir sat with us at our table and spoke a few words; but he did not pursue any of the allusions I made to Swann. I could easily have believed he did not know him. He did, however, invite me to go and see him at his studio in Balbec, an invitation that did not include Saint-Loup, and which I owed to the fact that I had said a few things which made him think I had an interest in the arts (an invitation, be it said, that might never have been issued in response to a recommendation from Swann, if Elstir had been a close friend of his, as the influence of disinterest on the feelings of men is greater than is commonly believed). He treated me in a markedly friendly manner, which outdid Saint-Loup's as much as Saint-Loup's outdid the affability of a person from the lower-middle classes. However charming the kindness of a lord may be compared with the kindness of a great artist, it always suggests play-acting, pretense. Saint-Loup's aim was to please; Elstir's was to give, and to give himself: he would have gladly given whatever he possessed—ideas, works, and all the rest, which he valued much less highly—to anyone who understood him. But he found something lacking in the company of most people, and lived in a state of isolation and unsociability that fashionable people saw as ill mannered and affected, the powers-that-be as wrongheaded, his neighbors as mad, and his family as arrogant and inconsiderate.

To begin with, even in his solitude, he must have taken pleasure in the thought that, through his works, he was addressing, albeit at a re-move, those who had misunderstood or offended him, and giving them a better opinion of himself. Perhaps his choice of the solitary life was motivated not by indifference toward others, but by love for them; and, much as I had given up Gilberte in the hope of being able to appear to her in the future in a more lovable guise, perhaps he painted with cer-tain people in mind, in a sort of gesture of reconciliation toward them, so that, without ever meeting again, they would love him, admire him, speak about him; renunciation is not always total from the very first moment—the self that commits us to it is a former self, one that has not yet been acted upon by the fact of renunciation itself, whether it be the renunciation of the invalid, the monk, the artist, or the hero. However, even if Elstir's intention had been to work with a view to impressing certain people, in working he had lived only for himself, turning his back on the society to which he had become indifferent: the practice of solitude had given him a love for it, which is what happens with any important thing that we have ever begun by fearing, because we knew it was incompatible with pettier things to which we were attached, and from which it must sever us forever, rather than just distract us from them. Before we have committed ourselves to it, our whole concern is to know how we may be able to reconcile it with certain pleasures, which will cease being pleasures as soon as we have experience of it.

Elstir did not sit talking with us for very long. I told myself I would go to his studio at some time over the next two or three days; but then, the very next afternoon, my grandmother and I having been for a walk to the cliffs of Canapville, right at the far end of the esplanade, we were on our way back when we passed a young girl, at the corner of one of the side streets that run perpendicular to the beach: hanging her head, like an animal being forced back to the stable, and carrying golf clubs, she was walking in front of an authoritative-looking personage, pre-sumably her English governess, or the English governess of one of her friends, who looked like John Jeffreys in the portrait by Hogarth, with a complexion so red as to make one think she drank gin rather than tea, and a black trace of tobacco adding its curl to a gray mustache, which was quite pronounced. The girl walking in front of her bore some resemblance to the one in the group whose chubby, motionless face, with its laughing eyes, had been topped by a black toque; this girl also wore a black toque, but she seemed much prettier than the other one, the line of her nose being straighter and the wings of her nostrils wider and more fleshy. The first one had looked like a pale and proud young lady; this one was more like a pink-faced child, grudgingly submissive. However, as she was pushing a similar bicycle along, and wearing the same reindeer-skin gloves, I deduced that the differences might have to do with my angle of vision and the circumstances, since it was unlikely there would be a second young girl in Balbec whose face looked so much like hers, and with so many other similarities in articles of dress and equipment. She sidled a quick glance toward me; and over the following days, each time I caught sight of the little gang of girls on the beach, and even later, after I had come to know all of them, I could never be absolutely sure whether any of them, including the first one with the bicycle, who looked more like her than any of the others, was in fact this one I had seen that evening, at the far end of the beach, by the streetcorner, this one who was hardly any different, but who was actually a little bit different, from the one I had noticed in their procession.

From that moment on, although until then I had been thinking mostly about the tall one, it was once more the girl with the golf clubs, whom I assumed to be Mlle Simonet, who preoccupied me. Walking along with the others, she would often stop, making her friends, who seemed to respect her greatly, also come to a standstill. That is how I see her to this day: standing there, her eyes shining under her toque, silhouetted against the backdrop of the sea, and separated from me by the transparent sky-blue stretch of time elapsed since that moment, the first glimpse of her in my memory, a very slight image of a face first desired and pursued, then forgotten, then found again, a face that since then I have often projected into the past, so as to say to myself, of a girl with me in my bedroom, "That was her!"

But I was not really sure whether the girl I would have preferred to know was not perhaps the one with the green eyes and the cheeks suggesting geraniums. And whichever one of them I chose to look out for on different days, the presence of the others, even without her, was enough to fill me with excitement: though my desire bore on one of them some of the time and on another at other times, it went on seeing them all, as on the first day of my indistinct vision of them, as one, as a little world apart, living a single life, which was probably how they liked to see themselves; and if I could have become friends with only one of them, I would have gained access—like a refined pagan, or a Christian full of scruples, fallen among barbarians—to a whole society with powers of rejuvenation, a society based on rude health, recklessness, bodily pleasure, cruelty, nonintellectuality, and joy.

My grandmother, whom I had told of my encounter with Elstir, and who was pleased to think of all the intellectual advantage there could be for me in the friendship of such a man, thought I was absurd and impolite not to have gone and visited him before this. But I could think of nothing other than the little band of girls; and unsure as I was of when they might appear, I did not dare to leave the esplanade. My grandmother was also surprised at how elegantly I dressed, as I had suddenly remembered suits which till then had remained in my trunk. Now I wore a different one every day and had even written to Paris to ask that new hats and ties be sent down.

The life we lead in a seaside resort such as Balbec can acquire much charm if the sight of a pretty face, a seller of seashells, a florist, a girl in a cake shop, painted in its vivid colors in our morning memory, becomes the aim of each of the sunlit days we idle away on the sands. It is this aim that makes them, though holidays, as busy as workdays, marked by directions and destinations, tending always toward the coming moment, when in buying our fossil shells, our shortbread, or our roses, we can delight in the colors of a feminine face, as pure and clear as those of a flower. But with shopgirls, at least one can chat, which avoids the necessity of filling in by imagination all the aspects of them not directly perceptible to the eye, of inventing a life for them and exaggerating the charm of it, as though extrapolating from a mere portrait;

and for another thing, for the very reason that they can be chatted with, one can learn where and when to meet them. This, of course, was nothing like the position I was in with the girls of the little gang. On days when I did not see them, as their habits were unknown to me, I was in total ignorance of the possible cause of their nonappearance: did they only come every second day, or in certain weather, or were there days when they were never to be seen? I imagined being their future friend and being able to say, "But you didn't come on such-and-such a day?" "True, because it was a Saturday, and we never come on Saturdays because . . ." Not that it was as simple as just knowing that on sad Saturdays it was futile to hope against hope, and that I could walk up and down the beach, sit in the window seat of the cake shop, pretend to eat an éclair, wander into the curiosity shop, moon around waiting for it to be time to go for a swim, listen to the concert, watch the fishing boats come in, see the sunset, then nightfall, and still not have seen the little group I longed for. It was possible the dreaded day did not come round once a week. Nor might it be a Saturday. Certain atmospheric conditions might have an influence on it—or, conversely, might have nothing at all to do with it. How many patient, but not dispassionate, observations must be recorded about the apparently erratic movements of these unknown worlds, before one can be sure of having ruled out misleading coincidences, of having confirmed one's predictions, and being able to draw up the infallible laws, arrived at through cruel experience, of this passionate astronomy! I would remember that I had not seen them on this day last week and conclude that they would not appear, that it was pointless to stay down on the beach. And then I would see them! But there would come another day, which, insofar as I could detect the functioning of laws in the recurrences of their constellation, I had calculated must be an auspicious one, yet they did not appear. Then my initial uncertainty about whether I would see them or not on a particular day was aggravated by another, much more serious one, whether I would see them ever again—for all I knew, they might be leaving for America or returning to Paris. This was enough to make me begin to fall in love with them. Having a liking for someone is one thing; but to be afflicted with the sadness, the feeling of something irreparable having happened, the anguish that all accompany the onset of love, what is necessary is the risk—which may even be the object to which passion in its fretfulness tries to cling, rather than to a person—of an impossibility. These forces were already working within me, and they revive each time one falls in love (they can in fact attach themselves, though usually this only happens in town life, to working-class girls, if one is unaware of their day off and fails to see them leaving the factory at the end of the day's work), or at least that is what happened with my successive love affairs. Perhaps such forces are inseparable from all love: it may be that whatever particularities were present in our first experience of it become incorporated into the following ones, by the workings of memory, suggestion, or habit, and that, throughout the consecutive periods of our existence, they give a common character to its different phases.

On all possible pretexts, I went down to the beach at any hour when I hoped they might be expected. Having seen them once while we were having lunch, I became very unpunctual at that mealtime, waiting about on the esplanade in case they came along; for the short time I sat in the dining room, my stare questioned the blue of the glass doors; I went without dessert so as not to miss them if they had been out for their walk at some different hour; and I was annoyed at my grandmother's unintentional unkindness when she made me sit there with her after the time I thought the most propitious. I tried to lengthen the horizon by setting my chair at an angle to the table; and if by some chance I caught sight of any one of the girls, it suddenly felt, since all of them had a share in the same special essence, as though a fickle and diabolical hallucination had projected before my eyes a scene from the latent dream, baleful yet ardently desired, that a moment before had existed only in my mind, where it always lay in readiness.

Loving them all, I was in love with none of them; and yet the possibility of meeting them was the only element of delight in my days, the only source of those hopes which make one feel capable of overcoming all obstacles, and which for me, if I did not see them, were often dashed and turned to rage. The girls eclipsed my grandmother: I would gladly have left for a long journey if it had promised to lead me to where they were. They were what was always hovering agreeably in my thoughts, whenever I thought I was thinking of something else, or of nothing. And even when I was unaware of thinking about them, at a deeper level of unconsciousness they were the towering blue waves or the shapes of a parade passing in front of the sea. If I went to another town where I might meet them, it was the sea I looked forward to seeing. The most exclusive love for any person is always love for something else.

My grandmother, because I had now developed an acute interest in golf and tennis, which was preventing me from seizing the opportunity of going to watch an artist at work—an artist she knew to be among the greatest—and listen to his talk, now treated me with scorn, which seemed to me very narrow-minded of her. At the Champs-Élysées I had had an inkling, which since those days had become clearer to me, that when we are in love with a woman all we are doing is projecting onto her a state of our own self; that, consequently, what is important is not the merit of the woman, but the intensity of that state; and that the emotions a mediocre young girl can give us may enable us to bring up to consciousness elements of ourself that are more private and personal, more remote and essential than anything we may acquire from the conversation of an extraordinary man, or even the admiration with which we gaze at his works.

I eventually had to comply with my grandmother's urgings, though I did so with a bad grace, which was aggravated by the fact that Elstir lived nowhere near the esplanade, but in one of the newest avenues of Balbec. The heat of the day made me take the trolley along the rue de la Plage; and I sat there trying to imagine I was in the ancient realm of the Cimmerians, in the land of King Mark, or perhaps on the very spot where the Forest of Broceliande had been,[87] so as to avoid looking at the sham luxury of the buildings all around me, among which Elstir's villa was perhaps the most sumptuous in its ugliness, despite which he had rented it because it was the only one of all Balbec's villas that afforded him the use of a spacious studio.

As I walked through the garden, I kept my eyes averted also from the lawn—smaller than, but reminiscent of, that of any middle-class philistine in the suburbs of Paris—the statuette of a lovelorn gardener, glass balls for looking at one's reflection, borders of begonias, and a little arbor with rocking chairs set out around a metal table. After all these approaches full of citified ugliness, once in the studio itself I paid no attention to the chocolate-colored moldings on its baseboards: I was perfectly happy among all the studies ranged about, for I glimpsed in them the possibility that I might rise to a poetic awareness, rich in fulfilling insights for me, of many forms that I had hitherto never distinguished in reality's composite spectacle. Elstir's studio seemed like the laboratory out of which would come a kind of new creation of the world: from the chaos made of all things we see, he had abstracted, by painting them on various rectangles of canvas now standing about on all sides, glimpses of things, like a wave in the sea crashing its angry lilac-shaded foam down on the sand, or a young man in white twill leaning on a ship's rail. The young man's jacket and the splash of the wave had taken on a new dignity, in virtue of the fact that they continued to exist, though now deprived of what they were believed to consist in, the wave being now unable to wet anyone, and the jacket unable to be worn.

As I came in, the creator, paintbrush in hand, was just putting the last touch to the shape of the sun as it set.

The blinds being down on most sides, the studio was rather cool; and, except for one part where daylight's fleeting decoration dazzled the wall, it was dim; the only window open was a small rectangle framed in honeysuckle, looking out on a strip of garden, then a road; so most of the studio was in half-darkness, transparent and compact in its mass, but moist and glistening at the angles where the light edged it, like a block of rock crystal with one of its sides already cut and polished in patches, so that it shines like a mirror and gives off an iridescent glow. While Elstir, at my request, went on with his painting, I wandered through this chiaroscuro, stopping here and there in front of a picture.

Most of those in the studio were not what I would have preferred to see: the paintings from his first and second periods, so called by an English art magazine I had found lying on the table in the salon at the Grand-Hôtel—that is, his mythological manner and the paintings in which a Japanese influence had become evident, both of which were admirably represented, the article said, in the collection of Mme de Guermantes. Almost all of the works I could see around me in the studio were, of course, seascapes done recently here in Balbec. But I could see that their charm lay in a kind of metamorphosis of the things depicted, analogous to the poetical device known as metaphor, and that, if God the Father had created things by naming them, Elstir re-created them by removing their names, or by giving them other names. The names of things always express a view of the mind, which is foreign to our genuine impressions of them, and which forces us to eliminate from them whatever does not correspond to that view.

At the hotel in Balbec, there had been mornings when Françoise unpinned the blankets keeping out the light, or evenings when I was waiting for it to be time to go out with Saint-Loup, when an effect of sunlight at my bedroom window had made me see a darker area of the sea as a distant coastline, or filled me with joy at the sight of a zone of liquid blue that it was impossible to say was either sea or sky. The mind quickly redistributed the elements into the categories the impression had abolished. Similarly, in my room in Paris, I had heard sounds of squabbling, almost rioting in the streets, until I had linked them to their cause—for instance, the rumbling approach of a dray, the sound of which, once identified, made me eliminate from it the high-pitched, discordant shouting which my ear had really heard, but which my mind knew is not made by wheels. Those infrequent moments when we perceive nature as it is, poetically, were what Elstir's work was made of. One of the metaphors that recurred most often in the sea pictures surrounding him then was one that compares the land to the sea, blurring all distinction between them. And it was this comparison, tacitly, tirelessly repeated in a single canvas, imbuing it with its powerful and multifarious unity, that was the source of the enthusiasm felt, though sometimes they were not quite aware of this, by many lovers of Elstir's painting.

It was to a metaphor of this sort—in a painting showing the harbor of Carquethuit, which he had finished only a few days before, and which I looked at for a long time—that Elstir had alerted the mind of the spectator, by using marine terminology to show the little town, and urban terms for the sea. Whether because the houses hid part of the harbor and the caulking basin, say, or perhaps because inlets of sea indented the land, as is very frequent in the country around Balbec, beyond the extreme promontory on which the town stood, masts rose above roofs, like chimneys or steeples, as though making citified things of the ships to which they belonged, things built on land, an illusion enhanced by the presence of other boats lying alongside the pier, in ranks so serried that men conversed from one deck to another without there being any visible separation between them, any interstice of water, giving the impression that the fishing fleet was more out of place on the sea than, for instance, the churches of Criquebec, which seemed to be standing in the water, surrounded by it on all sides, so distant as to be seen without their town, amid a sparkling haze of sunlight and spindrift, blown out of alabaster or foam, and making, when bounded by the versicolored sash of a rainbow, an unreal and mystic picture. On the beach in the foreground, the painter had accustomed the eye to distinguish no clear frontier, no line of demarcation, between the land and the ocean. Men pushing boats out moved in the tide as on the sand, which, being wet, reflected the hulls as though it were water. The sea did not invade evenly, but followed the irregularities of the shoreline, which the perspective made more jagged, and a ship out to sea, half hidden by the outworks of the arsenal, seemed to be sailing in the thick of the buildings; women shrimping among rocks looked, because they were surrounded by water, and because, beyond the circular barrier of rocks, the beach dipped down to the level of the sea at the two points closest to the land, as though they were in an undersea grotto, with waves and boats above, open yet miraculously protected from the inrush of waters. Though the whole painting gave the impression of seaports where the waves advance into the land, where the land almost belongs to the sea, and the population is amphibious, the power of the marine element was everywhere manifest; and out by the rocks or at the end of the pier, where the sea was rough, the efforts of the sailors, and the slanting of the boats, lying at an acute angle near the upright stability of the wharf, the church, and the houses of the town, with some people coming in and others setting out to fish, made one sense the urgency in their step as they scurried over the heaving water, as though it were a swift and spirited animal which, had it not been for their nimbleness, might throw them to the ground. A group of holiday-makers were setting out gaily in a yawl, which was shaken about like a farm cart; a sailor, cheerful but also careful, controlled it as though with reins, driving the spirited sail, all sitting in their proper places so as not to overload the equipage at one side and capsize it, and she cantered across sunlit fields and through shaded places, prancing down the slopes. The morning was radiant, despite a recent thunderstorm. One could even sense the powerful activity that the motionless boats had had to contend with, as they lazed now in their fine equilibrium in the sun and the cool, on parts of the sea which were so calm that the reflections were almost more solid and real than the hulls, which were turned to vapor by an effect of the light and run into one another by the perspective. Or, rather, they did not look like other parts of the sea: there was as great a difference between these areas of sea as between any one of them and the church rising out of the waters, or the ships behind the town. It was the mind which, on second thoughts, came to see as one and the same element what was stormy black at one point, at another indistinguishable from the sky in color and sheen, and elsewhere so blanched by sunlight, mist, and spray, so compact, so landlike, so hedged about by houses, that one was reminded of a causeway of stone or a snowfield, on which it was alarming to see a ship steeply climbing the dry slope, like a carriage shaking water as it rattles up from a river ford, but which one realized before long, as one saw other ships lurching about on the high, uneven expanse of its solid plateau, was identical in all its differences, and nothing other than the single sea.

Although it is said, and rightly so, that it is only in the sciences, and not in art, that there can be progress or discovery, and that no artist who launches into his own endeavor can ever be helped or hindered by the endeavors of any others, it must be recognized that, insofar as art establishes certain laws, and once an industry has vulgarized them, the art of earlier times loses in retrospect something of its originality. Since the earliest period of Elstir, we have seen supposedly "admirable" photographs of landscapes and cities. If one tries to define what it is that art-lovers mean by that adjective, it can generally be seen to apply to some unfamiliar image of a familiar thing, an image that is different from the ones we are in the habit of noticing, unusual yet true, which for that reason seems doubly striking, since it surprises us and shakes us out of our habits, while at the same time it turns us in on ourselves by recalling an impression. For instance, one of these "magnificent" photographs will illustrate a law of perspective by showing a cathedral we are accustomed to seeing in the center of the city, but taken from a point of view chosen to make it appear thirty times higher than the houses and jutting out beside the river, whereas it is nowhere near it. The fact was that Elstir's intent, not to show things as he knew them to be, but in accordance with the optical illusions that our first sight of things is made of, had led him to isolate some of these laws of perspective, which were more striking in his day, art having been first to uncover them. A bend in the course of a river, or the apparent contiguity of the cliffs bounding a bay, seemed to make a lake, completely enclosed, in the middle of the plain or the mountains. In a painting done at Balbec on a stiflingly hot summer's day, a recess of the coastline, held between walls of pink granite, appeared not to be the sea, which could be seen farther off: the unbrokenness of the ocean was suggested only by seagulls wheeling above what looked like solid stone, but which for them was wind and wave. The same canvas defined other laws, such as the Lilliputian grace of white sails at the foot of the immense cliffs, set on the blue mirror like sleeping butterflies, and certain contrasts between the depth of the shadows and the pallor of the light. This play of shadows, which photography has also spread far and wide, had fascinated Elstir so much that at one point he had enjoyed painting veritable mirages, in which a château topped by a tower looked like a completely circular château with a tower growing out of the roof, and another one, inverted, beneath it, either because the extraordinary purity of a fine day gave the shadow reflected in the water the hardness and glitter of stone, or because morning mists made the stone as insubstantial as shadow. Similarly, beyond the sea, behind a stretch of woodland, the sea began again, turned pink by the setting sun, but it was the sky. The sunlight, as though inventing new solids, struck the hull of a boat and pushed it back beyond another one lying in the shade; it laid the steps of a crystal staircase across the surface of the morning sea, which, though in fact smooth, was broken by the angle of illumination. A river flowing under the bridges of a city was shown from a point of view that split it, spread it into a lake, narrowed it to a trickle, or blocked it by planting a hill in it, covered with woods, where the city-dwellers like to go for a breath of evening air; and the rhythm of the disrupted city was marked only by the inflexible verticality of the steeples, which did not climb skyward but seemed, rather, like gravity's plumb line marking the beat in a triumphal march, to have the whole vague mass of houses hanging beneath them, ranged in misty tiers along the crushed and dismembered river. Even that semihuman part of nature, a footpath along a clifftop or on a mountainside (Elstir's earliest works dating from the period when landscapes had to feature the presence of a character), was affected, like rivers or the ocean, by the eclipses of perspective. And whether a mountain ridge, a haze of spume rising from a waterfall, or the sea prevented one from seeing the road in its entirety, visible to the character but not to us, the little human figure in outdated clothes, lost among this wilderness, often seemed to have stopped in front of an abyss, the route he was following having come to an end; and then, three hundred yards higher up, among the pine woods, we would be touched and reassured to see the reappearance of the thin white line of sandy path, friendly to the wanderer's tread, the intervening turns and twists of which, disappearing around the gulf or the waterfall, had been hidden from us by a mountainside.

The effort made by Elstir, when seeing reality, to rid himself of all the ideas the mind contains, to make himself ignorant in order to paint, to forget everything for the sake of his own integrity (since the things one knows are not one's own), was especially admirable in a man whose own mind was exceptionally cultivated. When I told him of my disappointment on seeing the church of Balbec, he said, "What's that? Disappointed by that porch! Why, it's the finest collection of Bible stories that the faithful could ever have had. That Virgin, and all those bas-reliefs telling her life story, make up the most tender and inspired expression of the long poem of adoration and praise that the Middle Ages dedicated to the glory of the Madonna. If you only realized, not just the closeness and fidelity to the sacred text, but the old sculptor's touches of genius, the profundity of some of his ideas, the delicacy and poetry of the thing! The idea of the great veil in which the angels bear away the body of the Virgin, which is too holy for them to dare to touch it"—I told him the same subject was to be seen in the church at Saint-André-des-Champs; he said he had seen photographs of the porch, but observed that the scurrying of all those little peasants around the Virgin was not quite the same thing as the gravity of Balbec's two great angels, almost Italian in their tall, gentle slenderness—"the angel taking away the soul of the Virgin to reunite it with her body; then, in the meeting between the Virgin and Elizabeth, the gesture of the latter when she touches the breast of Mary and expresses her surprise at finding it already swollen; or the bandaged arm of the midwife who had been reluctant to believe, without touching for herself, in the Immaculate Conception; or the sash that the Virgin tosses to Saint Thomas to prove her resurrection; and the veil that the Virgin tears from her own breast to cover the nakedness of her son, from whose pierced side the Church gathers His blood, the liquor of the Eucharist, while on His other side the Synagogue, its reign over, blindfolded, and holding a half-broken scepter, drops its crown and the tablets of the old Law; and what about the husband, at the hour of the Last Judgment, helping his young wife to step out of the tomb, and holding her hand against his heart to reassure her and prove to her that it's really beating—isn't that a neat little touch? Then there's the angel taking away the sun and the moon, because they're useless now, since it's written that the Light of the Cross will be seven times brighter than that of the heavenly bodies; or the one dipping his hand in Jesus' bathwater to make sure it's warm enough; or the other one coming down from the clouds to set his crown on the brow of the Virgin; and all the rest of them looking down from on high, peeping through the banisters of the heavenly Jerusalem, throwing up their hands in horror and joy at the sight of the evil ones in torment and the bliss of the chosen! It's all the circles of heaven you've got there, you see, a huge theological and symbolic poem. It's crazy, it's divine, it's far superior to anything you'll ever see in Italy—and the Italians, by the way, literally copied the tympanum of Balbec, but they were sculptors with much less genius. For, you see, it all comes down to genius. There's never been a period when everyone was a genius—that's just nonsense, as much of a joke as the golden age. The fellow that did that porch at Balbec, you can be sure, was every bit as good, with ideas every bit as sharp, as the people nowadays that you admire the most. If we go there one day, I can show you all that. There's a phrase from the liturgy for the Assumption that is illustrated with a subtlety your Redon[88] can't match."

Though Elstir spoke of a grand vision of heaven and gave me the idea of a gigantic theological poem written on the face of the church, the eyes full of desires with which I had looked at it had seen nothing of them. I mentioned the large statues of saints on their stilts, forming a sort of avenue.

"It's an avenue that begins at the dawn of time," Elstir said, "and leads to Jesus Christ. On one side, you've got His spiritual ancestors, and on the other, the Kings of Judah, His ancestors in the flesh. All the centuries are there. And if you had taken a closer look at what you call 'stilts,' you'd have been able to put names to the ones standing up high—under the feet of Moses, there's the Golden Calf; under the feet of Abraham, the ram; and under the feet of Joseph, the devil advising Potiphar's wife."

I told him the church I had been looking forward to seeing was almost Persian in character, and that this was no doubt one of the reasons why I had felt so disappointed. "Well," he said, "there's a lot of truth in that Persian idea. Some parts of it *are* completely Eastern. And on one of the columns, there's a capital which reproduces so accurately a Persian subject that it can't be explained just by the survival of Eastern traditions. The sculptor must have copied a casket brought back by navigators." In this connection, he was later to show me a photograph of a capital with very Chinese-looking dragons devouring each other, a little detail of sculpture which, as I stood before the church, I had failed to notice in the overall effect of a building that had not corresponded to the image created in my mind by the words "almost Persian."

The intellectual pleasures I enjoyed by being in the studio did not prevent me from taking pleasure in other things, though they surrounded us in an incidental way: the room, with the tepid scumbles of its walls, its glowing penumbra; and beyond the little window set among honeysuckle, along the rural-looking road, the rough, desiccated surface of the sunburnt earth, which distance and the shadows of trees did no more than hazily veil. Perhaps the unconscious well-being drawn from the summer's day helped to swell, like a tributary, the joy I had taken in seeing *Harbor at Carquethuit*.

I had assumed that Elstir was modest; but I realized I was mistaken in this when, in thanking him, I spoke the word "fame," then saw a faint sadness in his expression. Those who think their works will last, and he did, come to see them as belonging to a time when they themselves will have become mere dust. By making them think of their own annihilation, any idea of fame saddens them, because it is inseparable from the idea of death. To disperse the cloud of arrogant melancholy which I had unwittingly brought to his features, I changed the subject. "I was once told," I said, recalling the conversation with Legrandin at Combray, and thinking it would be interesting to know Elstir's view, "to stay away from Brittany. It was supposed to be bad for someone inclined to wistfulness." "Not at all," he replied. "When the soul of a man inclines to the wistful, he mustn't be kept away from it, he mustn't have it rationed. If you keep your mind off it, your mind will never know what's in it. And you'll be the plaything of all sorts of appearances, because you'll never have managed to understand the nature of them. If a little wistfulness is a dangerous thing, what cures a man of it is not less of it, it's *more* of it, it's all of it! Whatever dreams one may have, it is important to have a thorough acquaintance with them, so as to have done with suffering from them. A certain divorce between dreaming and daily life is so often useful to us that I wonder whether one should not take the precaution of practicing it preventively, so to speak, in the way some surgeons recommend appendectomy for all children, so as to avoid the possibility of future appendicitis."

Elstir and I were now right at the far end of his studio, by the window that looked out on the garden and a narrow side street beyond it, little more than a country lane. The late-afternoon air was cooling, and we were standing by the window to enjoy it. I felt I was far from my gang of girls; and the hope of seeing them I had for once, if belatedly, sacrificed to my grandmother's wish that I should be here with Elstir. We do not know where to find what we seek; and often we avoid for a long time the very place to which others, for other reasons, invite us, not knowing that it is the very spot where we could meet the one who is in our thoughts. I stood there, vaguely seeing the country lane that skirted the property where Elstir had his studio, but did not belong to it. Suddenly the young cyclist from the little group of girls came tripping along the lane, with her black hair, and her toque pulled down, her plump cheeks, and her cheerful, rather insistent eyes; and in that blessed place, pregnant with the miracle of sweet promises, under the trees, I saw her give Elstir a smile and greet him like a friend, making a rainbow for me between our terraqueous world and spheres that until then I had believed to be inaccessible. She even came over to shake hands with the painter, without stopping, and I could see she had a small beauty mark on her chin. "Do you know that young lady?" I asked him, realizing that he could introduce me to her, invite her to the house. The tranquil studio, with its rustic outlook, was now filled with a delicious awareness of something more to come, like a house in which a child is enjoying himself when he learns that, in addition to his present pleasures, in accordance with the generous propensity of beautiful things and nice people to go on being beautiful and nice, he is to be treated to a magnificent feast. Elstir told me her name—Albertine Simonet—and the names of her friends, whom I was able to describe accurately enough for him to have little hesitation in identifying them. It turned out that I had been mistaken about their social status, but in a way that was unlike my usual mistakes in Balbec, where I was in the habit of assuming that the merest son of a shopkeeper riding a horse must be a prince. My mistake this time had been to see the daughters of extremely wealthy lower-middle-class families, from the world of industry and business, as belonging to some unsavory milieu. Their world was one which, *prima facie,* had least interest for me, as it was devoid of the sense of mystery I perceived among both the working classes and the society frequented by the Guermantes. If the shallow and flashy nature of seaside life had not made me see them through the prestige of a preconception, giving them a dazzle and charm they would never lose in my eyes, I daresay I might not have been able to overcome the knowledge that they were the daughters of big wholesalers. I could only stand amazed at the range of different sculptures produced, as in a wonderful workshop, by the French middle classes—so many unexpected patterns, so much inventiveness in the characters of faces, such decisive lines, such freshness and simplicity in the features! The miserly old burghers who had engendered such Dianas and nymphs I now saw as masters in statuary. Before I had time to notice the social metamorphosis of the girls—this type of discovery of a mistake, or a readjustment of one's idea of a certain person, happens with the instantaneousness of a chemical reaction—behind these faces, young female ruffians as they had appeared to me, the girlfriends of racing cyclists and champion pugilists, there had already appeared the idea that they could very well be related to the family of a notary known to my own parents. As for Albertine Simonet, I had no more idea about what she might represent than she had about the importance she would one day come to have for me. Even the name of Simonet, which I had already heard down on the esplanade, was unfamiliar to me: I would have spelled it, if asked to, "Simonnet," in my ignorance of the importance that her family attached to having only one *n*. The lower the level that people occupy in the social scale, the more snobbery they attach to insignificant things, which may be no more vacuous than the things valued by the aristocracy, but which, by being more obscure, more peculiar to individuals, are always more surprising. Perhaps at one time there had been Simonnets who had failed in business, or worse. Whatever the case, the Simonets had always been affronted, it seems, as though they had been defamed, whenever anyone doubled their *n*. The pride they took in being the only single-*n* Simonets was possibly comparable to that of the Montmorency family in being the first Barons of France. I asked Elstir whether the girls lived in Balbec: the answer was that some of them did. The villa of one of them happened to be situated right at the far end of the seafront, near the cliffs of Canapville. I saw the fact that this particular girl was a great friend of Albertine Simonet as a further reason to believe it was the latter I had seen on the day when I was out walking with my grandmother. Not that I could have clearly identified at which corner of which side street I had seen her, there being many of them running perpendicular to the beach and making a similar angle with it. We would like our memories to be clear; but at the time, our vision is unclear. It was almost certain that Albertine and the girl going to her friend's house were one and the same. And yet, although the innumerable images that the dark-haired golfing girl showed me at later times, however dissimilar they are, can be superimposed on one another, because I know she was the model of them all, and though, if I wind in the clew of my memories of her, I can follow the same identity from one to the other, find my way through the labyrinth, and come back always to the same person, on the other hand, if I try to find my way back to the girl I passed when I was with my grandmother, I lose my way. I am sure it must be Albertine, the same girl who used to come to a standstill among her friends as they walked, profiled against the horizon of sea. But all the other images remain separate from this one, because I cannot give it in retrospect an identity it did not have for me at the moment when it impinged on my sight. In the strictest sense of the term "to see again," whatever the theory of probabilities has to say on the matter, that particular girl with full cheeks, who looked at me so boldly at the junction of the side street with the seafront, and who I think could have fallen in love with me, I was never to see again.

Was it my initial hesitancy, my inability to choose among the different girls of the little gang, in each of whom was preserved something of the collective attractiveness that had first excited me, which added to the other causes and, at the time of my greater love for Albertine, my later, second love for her, gave me, albeit intermittently and very briefly, the freedom not to love her? Because it had wandered about among all her friends, before opting definitively for her, my love kept some "slack" between it and the image of Albertine, enabling it, like a badly adjusted beam of light, to settle briefly on others before returning to focus on her; the relation between the pain in my heart and the memory of Albertine did not seem a necessary one; I could perhaps have made it match the image of another person. And that enabled me, for a split second, to make reality vanish, not just external reality, as in my love for Gilberte (which I had recognized as an inner state, in which I was the source of the particular quality, the special character, of the girl I loved, and of everything that made her indispensable to my happiness), but also the inner, purely subjective reality.

"There's hardly a day," Elstir said, "when one or another of them doesn't come down that lane and drop in to pay me a little visit," a statement that reduced me to despair—if I had gone to see him as soon as my grandmother had suggested it, I might well have made the acquaintance of Albertine long since!

She had walked on and was now out of sight from the studio. I guessed she had gone down to the esplanade to meet her friends. If I could be down there with Elstir, I might make their acquaintance. I tried to think of pretexts to have him come for a walk with me. The peace of mind I had enjoyed before the appearance of the girl had gone, and the frame of the little window, which had been so charming draped in its honeysuckle, was now very empty. Elstir filled me with joy and torture by saying he would be glad to take a stroll with me, but that he must first finish the piece he had been working on. It was a group of flowers, though not any of those—hawthorns, white and pink, cornflowers, apple blossom—whose portrait I would have liked to commission from him, in preference to that of any person, in the hope of having his genius reveal what it was in them I had so often sought in vain as I stood before them. As he worked, he spoke of botany, but I barely listened: to me, he was no longer sufficient in himself, being only the necessary intermediary between the girls and myself; and the only value of the prestige that his talent had lent him, only a few moments before, in my eyes, was that, when he introduced me to the little gang, it might lend some of itself to me, in their eyes.

I walked up and down, impatient for him to finish; of the many studies stacked against one another, face to the wall, I took up some and looked at them. So it was that I came upon a watercolor that must have dated from a much earlier time in the life of Elstir, and which made me feel that particular enchantment one gets from works that are not only painted to perfection, but the subject of which is so singular and delightful that we see it as accounting for much of the charm of the thing, as though the painter only had to notice this charm, study it as it stood before him fully present in the material reality of the natural world, then reproduce it. That such objects can exist, beautiful in themselves and without any painter's interpretation of them, is something that satisfies an innate materialism in us, though resisted by reason, and serves as a counterbalance to the abstractions of aesthetics. The watercolor was the portrait of a young woman who, though not pretty, was of a curious type: she was wearing a close-fitting headdress, something like a bowler hat edged with a ribbon of cerise silk; in one of her hands, which wore lace mittens, there was a lighted cigarette; and the other held at knee height a sort of large garden hat, a mere screen of straw against the sunlight. On a table beside her, a little vase full of roses. Often, and it was the case here, the singularity of such works lies in the fact that they were executed in particular circumstances which we do not clearly appreciate at first—for instance, whether the odd getup of a female model is in fact a costume worn for a ball, or whether the red robe worn by an old man who looks as though he has just put it on at the passing whim of the painter might not be his professor's gown or his cardinal's cape. The ambiguous character of the person whose portrait I was looking at came from the fact, which I did not understand, that it was a young actress of an earlier period, partly cross-dressed. However, her bowler, set on hair that was puffed out but cut short, and her velvet jacket, without lapels and open on a white dickey, made me hesitate about the date of the fashion and the sex of the model, so that I could not tell what I was looking at, except that it was a brilliant piece of painting. My pleasure in it was mitigated only by the fear that Elstir might delay so long as to make me miss the gang of girls, for the sun was now angling very low through the little window. The watercolor contained nothing that served merely as a factitious accessory to the scene depicted (the costume, for instance, for no better reason than that the woman had to be wearing something, or the flower-holder because there were flowers): the glass of the receptacle, lovingly seen in its own right, seemed to surround the water in which the stems of the carnations stood with a substance that was no less limpid and almost as liquid; the garments worn by the women enclosed her in a material that had its own charm, independent, fraternal, and, if man-made things can equal the charm of nature's wonders, as delicate, as satisfyingly smooth to the eye's touch, and as neatly painted as the fur of a cat, the petals of a carnation, or the feathers of a dove. The shirtfront, its white as fine as hail and its frivolous pleating smocked with little bells like lily-of-the-valley, shone with bright reflections from the room, themselves sharply seen and as delicately shaded as though there were flower motifs brocaded on the linen. The velvet of the jacket, which had a pearly luster in its pile, was roughened in places, frayed and shaggy in a way that was like the ruffled carnations in their vase. One's main impression was that Elstir, not only unconcerned about what might appear immoral in this young actress dressed like a man, who was herself less interested in how well she would play her part in the performance than in the fascination and stimulation she was bound to offer to the sensuality, surfeited or depraved, of certain spectators, had actually focused on these points of ambiguity as an aesthetic element in his picture, which he had worked hard to bring out. In the lines of the face, the sex of the person seemed at times on the point of owning up to being that of a rather boyish girl, faded at others into the impression of an effeminate young man, perverted and pensive, then changed again, always elusive. In the look of the eyes, there was something wistful or forlorn which, in the contrast it made with the accessories from the worlds of the theater and debauchery, gave a strange thrill. But one also felt that this look was affected, and that the young person in the provocative costume, seemingly asking to be fondled, must have thought there would be something even more intriguing in an expression suggestive of romantic or secret feelings, a hint of unspoken heartbreak. At the bottom of the picture were the words *Miss Sacripant, October 1872*.[89] I could not contain my admiration. "Oh, that's nothing—just a thing done by a young man. A costume from a pantomime at the Théâtre des Variétés. It's all a very long time ago." "And what became of the model?" At my question, his face showed surprise, which he replaced a moment later by a look of inattentive indifference. "Quick, let me have that canvas," he said. "I can hear Mme Elstir coming. And though I can assure you the young creature in the bowler hat had no part to play in my life, it would be pointless to let my wife see this watercolor. I only kept it as an entertaining memento of the theater of that period." Before hiding the work behind him, Elstir, who had perhaps not seen it for a long time, stared at it and murmured, "The head's the only thing worth keeping. Those lower parts are dreadful. The hands are by a beginner." I was quite annoyed by the arrival of Mme Elstir, which was likely to make us delay even longer. The window ledge soon turned pink. It would be futile to go out now: there was no longer the slightest chance of seeing the girls, and so it did not really matter whether Mme Elstir went away or stayed. In fact, she left again after only a short time. I thought her a bore: at twenty, leading a bullock in the Roman countryside, she would have been beautiful; but her black hair was turning white; and she was common but not simple in her manner, since she believed that a certain dignity of bearing and majesty of attitude were required by her mode of statuesque beauty, which had lost, in aging, all its attractiveness. Her dress was striking in its utter simplicity. And it was touching and surprising to hear Elstir say, with great frequency and in a tone of caressing respect, as though by just speaking the words he was moved to tenderness and veneration, "My beautiful Gabrielle!" At a later time, when I had become acquainted with his mythological paintings, I too came to see beauty in Mme Elstir; and I realized that, in a certain ideal pattern, the few outlines and arabesques of which could be seen to recur in his work over and over again, in a certain model of beauty, he had once seen something almost divine, since all of his time, the whole intellectual effort of which he was capable, in short the whole of his life, was devoted to the task of seeing those outlines more clearly and reproducing them more accurately. This ideal had become a form of worship, of such solemnity, and so demanding, that he could never be content; it was the innermost part of his self, and so he had never been able either to view it with detachment or to transform it into feelings, until the day when he came upon it externally manifested in the body of a woman who later became Mme Elstir, in whom he had at last been able—as we only ever are able, with that which is not part of ourselves—to see it as meritorious, moving, and divine. What peace there was in placing his lips on Beauty, which until then he had had to drag out of himself, create in pain, but which now, in a mysterious incarnation, offered itself for a sequence of efficacious sacraments! By that time, Elstir had outgrown youth's first confidence in the unaided power of thought to achieve the ideal. He was reaching the age at which one looks to the body and its fulfillments to stimulate the energy of the mind, when we are inclined by its weariness to materialism, by the lessening of its activity to the possibility of passively receiving influences, when we begin to accept that there may be certain bodies, certain professions, certain privileged rhythms which achieve our ideal very naturally, and that even without genius one can produce a masterpiece merely by copying the movement of a shoulder or the taut lines of a neck; it is the age at which we enjoy letting the caress of our eye rest on Beauty outside ourselves, close to us, on a tapestry, on a beautiful sketch by Titian discovered in an antique shop, or on a mistress every bit as beautiful as the sketch by Titian. Once I had come to understand this, I could never see Mme Elstir without pleasure; and her body lost all its ungainliness, for I filled it with an idea: that she was a creature of immateriality, a portrait by Elstir. And for Elstir too, that is what she was. The bare materials of life do not count for the artist; they merely offer him the opportunity to show his genius. Set side by side ten portraits of different people, all by Elstir, and their most flagrant feature is that they are Elstirs. But then, after the high tide of genius which once swamped the whole of life, once the brain has started to tire, gradually the equilibrium is lost, and, like the flow of a great river beginning to prevail against the counterflow of an exceptional tide, life reasserts itself. During his first period, the artist has managed to define the law, the formula, of his unconscious gift. He knows the situations, if he is a novelist, and the landscapes, if he is a painter, that can best provide him with the material which, though inessential in itself, is as indispensable to his research as a laboratory or a workshop. He knows he has made his masterpieces out of effects of attenuated light, remorse that changes the view of a wrong once done, women posed under trees or half immersed in water like statues. A day will come when, with the onset of mental fatigue, he will face the materials that once served his genius, without finding in himself the intellectual vigor required for the creation of a work, yet will continue to seek them out and to enjoy their presence, because of the spiritual pleasure which, as the sometime spur of work, they still afford; and, viewing them with a sort of superstition, as though they were superior to everything else, or as though they already contained a good part of the work of art, latent and ready-made, he will do no more than frequent and adore his subjects. He will continue to seek out rehabilitated criminals, whose remorse and repentance used to be the subjects of his novels; he will buy a country house in a region where the light is attenuated by mists; he will spend hours watching women swimming; he will become a collector of fine fabrics. So it was that, even for Elstir, a day would eventually come when he regressed to the attitude toward beauty (which I had seen in Swann, and beyond which he had never gone) implicit in the expression "the beauty of life," a phrase almost devoid of meaning, suggesting beauty that never rises to art, a day when his creative genius would begin to dissipate, gradually giving way to idolatry, mere worship of the forms that had once nourished it, and to the beguiling temptations of inertia.

He had just put a final dab of paint on his flowers, and I wasted another moment in looking at them. This wasting of a moment did not redound at all to my credit, as I knew that by now the girls would have left the beach; but even if I had known for sure that they were still there and that this waste of minutes would make me miss them, I would still have looked at the painting, as I would have told myself that Elstir's flowers were more important to him than my meeting the girls. Though my grandmother's nature was the exact opposite of my complete egoism, it could be reflected in mine. In a situation where someone who inspired indifference in me, but for whom I had always feigned affection or respect, might be caused some bother and I might be exposed to a danger, I would have been incapable of not sympathizing with him and treating his nuisance as something important, and the threat to me as unimportant, because that would be how I would imagine our respective positions seemed to him. To be precise, it was more than that: not just ignoring the danger I was in, but willfully exposing myself to it, while trying to make sure, even if this increased my own chances of being harmed, that the other person would be able to avoid being disturbed. This can be explained by several reasons, none of which say much in my favor. One of them is that, though I have managed to reason myself, in theory, into the belief that I am attached to my own life, there have been times when, beset by emotional problems, or mere nervous anxieties, some of them so childish that I would not dare speak of them here, an unforeseen circumstance has arisen bringing with it a risk of death for me, and this new consideration has actually appeared of such slight consequence to me, compared with the others, that I have welcomed it with a feeling of relief approaching exhilaration. Though I am the least intrepid man in the world, I have in this way experienced something I had contrived to convince myself was so foreign to my nature as to be inconceivable: the intoxication of danger. But in the face of danger, mortal danger, even if I am going through a period of total calm and happiness, I would find it impossible not to shield someone else from it by putting myself in the dangerous position. Having learned from a significant number of experiences that I always acted in that way, and with pleasure, I discovered to my shame that, contrary to what I had always believed and affirmed, I was very sensitive to the opinions of others. Such unconfessed self-importance has no connection, however, with conceit or pride: the satisfactions afforded by either of these sentiments could never tempt me, and I have always abstained from them. But though I have always been able to conceal from certain people the petty advantages of my own that might have made them see me as slightly less paltry, I have never been able to resist the pleasure of letting them see that I am more concerned to avert death for them than for myself. My motive being self-esteem and not virtue, I see it as quite natural that their own behavior in every situation should be quite different. I do not in the slightest blame them for this, as I might do if I had been motivated by a conception of duty, which would then appear to me to be as binding on them as on myself. On the contrary, I think it is entirely sensible of them to look out for themselves, though I cannot help subordinating my own interest to theirs, and though I must say this does appear singularly absurd and blameworthy, when I consider that the lives of many of those whose bodies I shield with mine when a bomb drops are even less valuable than my own. Anyway, at the time of my visit to Elstir, the day of my discovery of that difference in value was still far in the future; and there was no danger, but only the importance I saw (a forewarning of the pernicious self-esteem) in not appearing to think the pleasure I was longing for was more important than his task of finishing his watercolor. He finished it at last. As soon as we went outside, I noticed it was not as late as I had thought, the days being long at that time of year; and we walked down to the esplanade. I racked my brains to think of ways of keeping him near the place where I thought there was still a chance that the girls might appear. I pointed to the cliffs nearby and kept asking him questions about them, in the hope of making him forget the time and keeping him there. I suspected we might have a better chance of catching up with the little gang if we went toward the far end of the beach. "Perhaps we could look at those cliffs from a little closer," I said, knowing that one of the girls often walked in that direction. "And as we walk, perhaps you could tell me about Carquethuit? How I would love to go to Carquethuit!" I added, without thinking that what was so novel and powerful in *Harbor at Carquethuit* probably came from the vision of the painter rather than from some special quality in the place itself. "Since seeing your painting, that's the place I would really like to see—as well as the Pointe du Raz, of course, but that would be quite a journey from here." "In any case," Elstir said, "even if it wasn't nearer to Balbec, I'd still be inclined to recommend Carquethuit. The Pointe du Raz *is* magnificent, but it's really just your typical tall cliffs on the coast of Normandy or Brittany, which you're quite familiar with. But Carquethuit is completely different, with its rocks and its low, sandy beach. I've never seen anywhere else like it in France—it looks more like somewhere in Florida. A most curious place, and very wild country too. In between Clitourps and Nehomme—you know what a wilderness that whole area is, with the lovely line of the beaches. Hereabouts the line of the beaches is nondescript. But in those parts, it's full of grace, very sweet."

Daylight was fading; it was time to go. I was walking back toward the villa with Elstir when, with the suddenness of Mephistopheles materializing before Faust, there appeared at the far end of the avenue— seemingly the simple objectification, unreal and diabolical, of the temperament opposite to my own, of the almost barbaric and cruel vitality which, in my feebleness, my excess of painful sensitivity and intellectuality, I lacked—a few spots of the essence it was impossible to mistake for any other, a few of the stars from the zoophytic cluster of young girls, who, although they looked as though they had not seen me, were without a doubt at that very moment making sarcastic remarks about me. Seeing that a meeting between them and us was inevitable, and knowing that Elstir would call me over, I turned my back, like a bather as a large wave comes in: I stopped, letting my illustrious companion walk on without me, and stood outside the antique shop we happened to be passing, stooping toward its window as though fascinated by something. I was not sorry to be able to appear to have something other than the girls to think about, and I could vaguely foresee already that, when Elstir called me over to introduce me, I would put on the interrogative look that reveals not so much surprise as the desire to appear surprised—each of us being as bad at acting as our witness is good at reading faces—that I would even go so far as to point at my own chest as though asking, "Who? Me?" and then walk quickly over to them, my head bent in docile obedience, and my expression a cold mask hiding annoyance at being dragged away from my study of old china merely to be introduced to people whom I had no desire to know. I went on gazing into the shopwindow, waiting for the moment when Elstir would shoot my name at me, like a harmless, expected bullet. The certainty of being introduced to the girls had made me not only feign indifference toward them, but feel it. The pleasure of their acquaintance, having become inevitable, was compressed and reduced; it now seemed a smaller thing than the pleasures of chatting with Saint-Loup, having dinner with my grandmother, going on outings in the surrounding country, which, because of this imminent connection with people who very likely had little interest in historical architecture, I would feel reluctantly obliged to forgo. Also, the joy awaiting me was diminished not only by the imminence, but by the incongruity, of its coming to pass. The order of the images we form in our minds, one above another, is maintained by the functioning of laws as precise as those of hydrostatics, but the proximity of an event can disturb it. Elstir was about to call my name—but this was nothing like the scene in which, down on the beach, up in my bedroom, I had so often pictured my first encounter with the little gang of girls! What was about to happen was a different event, one for which I was unprepared: in it, I could recognize neither my desire nor its object; I was almost sorry to have gone out for a walk with Elstir. But the main reason for the shrinking of the pleasure to which I had been so looking forward was the knowledge that nothing could now prevent me from enjoying it. It only went back to its previous dimensions, as though by the working of an elastic force, when that knowledge ceased to constrain it; and that occurred at the moment when, happening to glance around, I saw Elstir just a few feet away, taking his leave of the group of girls. Something in the face of the one standing closest to him, plump and illuminated by the bright look in her eyes, made me think of a cake with a bit of sky in it: her eyes, even when motionless, gave an impression of mobility, as happens on blowy days when the air, though invisible, shows the rate at which it is skimming over the sky-blue surface. For an instant her eyes passed across mine, like those flowing skies on stormy days when clouds moving at different speeds come close, touch, then part: they do not meet or ever become one. In a momentary intersection of eyes we stood there, each in ignorance of the promises or threats for the future that the other silent, passing continent might contain. Only at the instant when her glance lowered, without slowing in its movement, did it fade slightly, as, on a clear, windy night, the moon is swept behind a cloud, veiling its brightness, then immediately reappears. Elstir parted from the girls without calling me over. They turned up a side street and he came toward me. It was a fiasco.

I have said that, on that day, Albertine did not appear to be the same as on previous occasions, and that each time I saw her she was to seem different. But at that particular moment, I sensed also that certain changes in the appearance, the importance, or the size of a person can be explained by the variability of the factors that may interpose between us and the other. One of the most potent in that regard is a belief in our mind: on that evening, within a matter of seconds, my belief that I was going to meet Albertine, then the annihilation of that belief, had made her almost insignificant to me, then infinitely precious; and some years later, the belief that she was faithful to me, followed by disbelief, would have analogous results.

At Combray, depending on the time of day, and on whether I was entering one or the other of the two dominant modes of my sensitivity, I had already experienced the decrease or increase of my sorrow at being parted from my mother, which all afternoon could be as imperceptible as moonlight while the sun shines, but after nightfall, banishing recent memory, would cast its unhappy pallor into my sickly soul. But on that day, seeing Elstir bidding goodbye to the girls without calling me over, I realized that the variable measure we apply to joys and sadness may be affected not only by such fluctuation between two states of mind, but also by a transformation in invisible beliefs, which may, for instance, make death seem insignificant, because they shed a light of unreality on it, enabling us to see our attendance at a musical evening as imperative, though it would lose its charm for us if the belief coloring that evening with inevitability were suddenly to dissolve because we learned we were just about to be guillotined; it is true that something in me, the will, knew this about the importance of belief; but what is known to the will remains inefficacious if it is unknown to the mind and the sensitivity: they can believe in good faith that we wish to leave a woman, when only the will is privy to our attachment to her. They are fooled by the belief that we will see her again in a moment. But let that belief vanish, in the realization that she has just gone and will never come back, and the mind and sensitivity, having lost their bearings, are afflicted with a fit of madness, and the paltry pleasure of being with her expands to fill everything in life.

A variation in belief can also cause the death of love. Love, mobile and pre-existing, focuses on the image of a certain woman simply because she will be almost certainly unattainable. From then on, one thinks not so much about her, it being difficult to imagine her anyway, as about possible ways of getting to know her. A whole process of anxieties comes into play, which is enough to fixate our love on her, though she is the barely known object of it. Love having become immense, we never reflect on how small a part the woman herself plays in it. And if, as had happened to me when I saw Elstir stop beside the girls, we have sudden cause to lose our feeling of anxiety or uneasiness, since our love amounts to nothing more than that, our love too seems to have vanished at the very moment when we come into possession of a prize the value of which we have never really thought about. What did I know of Albertine? One or two profiles of her against the sea, definitely less lovely than those of women by Veronese, women whom, if my feelings were motivated by aesthetic considerations, I ought to have preferred to her. Could they be motivated by other considerations, since, once the anxiety abated, I was left possessing nothing but these mute profiles? Every day since I had first seen Albertine, I had entertained thousands of thoughts about her, I had carried on, with what I called "her," an extended interior conversation, in which I had questions put to her and had her answer them, think, and act; and in the endless series of imagined Albertines who occupied my head one after another, for hours on end, the real Albertine, the one glimpsed down at the esplanade, was merely the forerunner, like an actress, the star who, having created a part, hands it over after the very first performances to others. This real Albertine was little more than an outline: everything else that had been added to her was of my own making, for our own contribution to our love—even if judged solely from the point of view of quantity—is greater than that of the person we love. This is true of love even in its most effective forms. Often very little suffices for love not only to form but to subsist, even after it has attained its fulfillment through the flesh. A former drawing teacher of my grandmother's had had a daughter with an obscure mistress. The latter died soon after the birth of the child; and this was such a heartbreak to the drawing teacher that he did not long survive her. During the final months of his life, my grandmother and some ladies from Combray, who had never so much as wished to refer in his presence to the woman, with whom he had never officially lived and who had occupied little space in his life, decided to contribute to a fund that would give the little girl a life annuity. It was my grandmother's proposal; but some ladies proved reluctant: Was the child really worth it? Was she actually the daughter of the man who believed he was her father? One can never be sure, with women like her mother. . . . However, it was decided; and the child came to thank them: she was ugly and bore a marked resemblance to the old drawing teacher, thus dispelling all doubts. Her hair being her best feature, one of the ladies said to the father, who had brought the child, "What lovely hair!" My grandmother added, thinking that, the fallen woman being now dead and the drawing teacher almost dead, there could be no harm in alluding to past events of which everyone had feigned ignorance at the time, "It must run in the family. Did her mother have such lovely hair?" To which the father gave the guileless reply: "I don't know—I only ever saw her wearing a hat."

I had to rejoin Elstir. A mirror showed me my reflection: in addition to the disaster of not having been introduced, I noticed that my tie was crooked and that my hair, which was too long, was sticking out from under my hat. Still, it was a good thing that they had at least seen me with Elstir, even in such a state, and would not be able to forget me; and it was lucky that I had heeded my grandmother's suggestion that I put on my handsome waistcoat, when I had all but decided to wear an awful one instead, and that I carry my best cane: no event we look forward to ever turns out quite as we wish it to, but in the absence of the advantages we had hoped to be able to count on, others arise unexpectedly, and there are compensations; we so dreaded the worst that we are ultimately inclined, taking one thing with another, to think that chance was, on balance, on our side. "I would have been so happy to meet them," I said to Elstir as I came up with him. "Well, in that case, what did you stand miles away for?" Those were the words he spoke, not because they expressed his own mind, since if he had intended to grant my unspoken wish it would have been easy for him to call me over; but possibly because they were one of those phrases he had heard, used by vulgar people who think they are in the wrong, and because even great men are like vulgar people in some things, taking their everyday excuses from the same repertoire, as they buy their daily bread from the same baker; or possibly because such words, which must in a sense be read back to front, since the letter of them means the opposite of their truth, are the necessary effect, the negative graph, as it were, of a reflex. "Anyway, they were in a hurry." I was sure they must have prevented him from introducing someone they saw as dislikable: otherwise he would have been bound to call me over, after all the questions I had asked about them, and the interest he could see I took in them. "I was talking to you about Carquethuit," he said, before I left him at his front door. "I once did a little sketch which catches much better the neat loop of the shoreline. The painting's not bad, but it's not the same thing. If you like, I could give you the sketch, as a memento of our friendship," he added, for the people who decline to give you the things you desire give you other things.

"I would very much have liked to have a photo of your little portrait of Miss Sacripant,[90] if you have such a thing. Where does the name come from?" "It was the name of a character acted by the model in a stupid little operetta." "But you're aware that I've no idea who she is—though you seem to believe the opposite." Elstir said nothing. "You're not going to tell me it's Mme Swann before her marriage?" I said, leaping in a sudden fluke to the truth, one of those fortuitous discoveries which are really quite rare occurrences, but of which there are enough to give a sort of basis to the theory of presentiments—after the event, that is, and on condition that one also discounts all the errors that invalidate it. Elstir still said nothing. It was in fact a portrait of Odette de Crécy, which she had not wished to keep, for many reasons, some of which are perfectly obvious. There were others. The painting dated from before the time when Odette, taking to designing her own appearance, had made of her face and figure the creation from which, over the years, in its broad lines, for her dressmakers, her hairdressers, and for Odette herself, in her ways of standing, speaking, smiling, holding her hands, casting her glances, or even of thinking, there could now be no departure. It required the degeneration of taste in the sated lover for Swann to reject the numerous photographs of his beautiful wife in her *ne varietur* mode, in favor of the little photo of her that he kept in his bedroom, showing a thinnish young woman wearing a straw hat adorned with pansies, rather plain, with puffed-out hair and drawn features.

But even if the portrait had belonged, not to a time (like Swann's favorite photograph) before the definitive redesign of Odette's features into their new pattern, full of majesty and charm, but to a later period, Elstir's vision would have sufficed to disorganize that pattern too. An artist's genius functions like extremely high temperatures, which can dissociate combinations of atoms and reshape them into a totally opposite order, one that corresponds to a different pattern. The whole factitious harmony a woman imposes on her features, checking the continuity of it in her mirror each day before she goes out, making sure that it inheres in the angle of the hat, the smoothness of the hair, the vivacity of her expression, can be dismantled in a second by the eye of a great painter, who puts in its stead a rearrangement of her features more in accordance with a certain feminine and pictorial ideal of his own. Similarly, it often happens that, after a certain age, the eye of the great researcher, wherever it looks, notices elements essential to the establishing of the only relationships that interest him. Such men, like versatile workers or card-players who do not mind turning their hand to any job or game, could say of any material: This will do. In this connection, a cousin of the Princess of Luxembourg, a woman of great beauty and arrogance, having taken a fancy to a form of art that was new at the time, commissioned a portrait of herself from the most prominent of the painters of the naturalist school. The artist's eye had instantly detected what it sought everywhere: on the completed canvas, instead of the grand lady, there was a dressmaker's errand girl, against a broad inclined background of violet which called to mind the Place Pigalle. But even without going to those lengths, not only will the portrait of a woman by a great artist not try to satisfy any of its subject's requirements—such as those that make a woman who is beginning to age want to be photographed wearing things more suited to young girls, which flatter her with a youthful figure and make her look like the sister, or even the daughter, of her daughter, whom she may even have stand beside her in a suitably dowdy dress for the occasion—but it will underscore unfavorable features of her which she tries to conceal (such as a feverish, vaguely greenish flush to the face) and which the artist will find interesting because they have "character," but which will eventually disgust the vulgar viewer, as they reduce to nothing the feminine ideal of which her person was once the impressive embodiment, and which had seemed to place her, in her unique, irreducible form, beyond and far above the rest of humanity. Deposed, expelled from her own pattern, over which she had once reigned supreme, she has become a mere woman like any other, a sometime paragon in whom all faith has been lost. In our minds, the pattern constituted by an Odette de Crécy used to consist not just in her beauty, but also in her personality, her identity, so much so that, faced with the portrait which strips her of that pattern, we are tempted to exclaim not only, "How ugly he's made her!" but, "He can't even paint a likeness!" We have difficulty in believing it is the same woman; we cannot recognize her. Despite which, we sense perfectly well the presence of someone we have already seen, but it is someone who is not Odette. Yet the face, the body, the appearance are very familiar to us. They remind us, not of this woman, who has never stood like that, whose habitual posture never traces such a strange and provocative outline, but of other women, all those whom Elstir has painted, and whom, however different they may be from one another, he has always liked to pose in full face like that, one arched foot showing under the skirt, the large round hat hanging from one hand, a symmetrical reminder, at the level of the knee it conceals, of the other full round disk of the face. A brilliant portrait not only disassembles the pattern of the woman, as her pride in her appearance and her self-centered conception of beauty had defined it, but if it is an old portrait it also ages the original in the same way photographs do, by showing her in her old-fashioned finery. In a portrait, however, it is not just a woman's style of dress that dates, it is also the painter's style of painting. And Elstir's earliest style, from his first period, gave Odette her most merciless birth certificate, not just because, like photographs of her from that time, it made her a junior among well-known courtesans, but because it showed that the painting dated from the period of the many portraits by Manet or Whistler of sitters long vanished, consigned to history, gone to oblivion.

These thoughts, which I ruminated silently as we walked back toward the villa, were inspired by the discovery I had just made about the identity of Elstir's model for "Miss Sacripant"; and they were to lead me to a second discovery, even more thought-provoking for me, about the identity of Elstir himself. He had painted a portrait of Odette de Crécy—could such a brilliant man, a solitary, a philosopher, who had accumulated wisdom, who stood above all things, whose conversation was so enthralling, possibly be the painter, vacuous and devious, adopted long ago by the Verdurins? I asked him if he had known them, and whether they had not nicknamed him "M. Biche." He answered, in a very simple manner, that this was indeed the case, as though speaking of a part of his life that was rather remote, as though not realizing his answer caused me an acute disappointment. Then, glancing at my expression, he did realize it; and this brought an expression of displeasure to his own face. A lesser man, a man less proficient in things of the mind and heart, now that we were nearing the house, might have just taken his leave of me without ceremony, and avoided me thereafter. However, this was not Elstir's way: like the true master he was (and to be a master, at least in this sense of the word, may have been, from the point of view of pure creativeness, his sole defect, since an artist, if he is to live in tune with the truth of the spirit, must shun company, even that of disciples, and so avoid frittering himself away in such things), he endeavored to draw from every circumstance, whether relative to himself or to others, and for the benefit of those younger than himself, whatever element of truth it might contain. So, instead of venting hurt pride, he preferred to speak in a way that would be of some profit for me. "There is no such thing," he said, "as a man, however clever he may be, who has never at some time in his youth uttered words, or even led a life, that he would not prefer to see expunged from memory. He should not find this absolutely a matter for regret, as he cannot be sure he would ever have become as wise as he is, if indeed getting wisdom is a possibility for any of us, had he not traversed all the silly or detestable incarnations that are bound to precede that final one. I know there are young men, sons and grandsons of distinguished men, whose tutors, since their earliest high-school years, have taught them every nobility of soul and excellent precept of morality. The lives of such men may contain nothing they would wish to abolish; they may be happy to endorse every word they have ever uttered. But they are the poor in spirit, the effete descendants of doctrinarians, whose only wisdoms are negative and sterile. Wisdom cannot be inherited—one must discover it for one-self, but only after following a course that no one can follow in our stead; no one can spare us that experience, for wisdom is only a point of view on things. The lives of men you admire, attitudes you think are noble, haven't been laid down by their fathers or their tutors—they were preceded by very different beginnings, and were influenced by what-ever surrounded them, whether it was good, bad, or indifferent. Each of them is the outcome of a struggle, each of them is a victory. I can understand that the image of what we were in an earlier time might be unrecognizable and always irksome to behold. It should not be rejected for all that, as it is testimony to the fact that we have lived, that, in ac-cordance with the laws of life and the spirit, we have managed to derive, from the common constituents of life, from the life of the studio and artists' cliques, if we're talking of painters, something that surpasses them."[91] We had reached his door. I was disappointed not to have met the girls. But at least there was now a possible opening into their lives; the days when they did nothing but pass across a horizon, when I could believe they might never appear on it again, were over. They were no longer surrounded by the great turbid swirl which kept us apart, which was nothing but the translation of the desire—perpetually ablaze, mobile, urgent, constantly fueled by worry—ignited in me by their inac-cessibility, their possible disappearance from my life forever. This desire for them could now be turned down, kept in reserve, alongside so many others whose fulfillment, once I knew this was a possibility, I post-poned. I left Elstir and was alone. Despite my disappointment, I could see in my mind all the unforeseeable improbability of what had taken place: that he in particular should turn out to be known to the girls; that they, who had been, only that morning, figures in a picture against a background of the sea, had now set eyes on me; that they had seen me in the company of a great painter; that he now knew of my wish to know them, and would help to bring this about. All of this had given me pleasure, but it was a pleasure that had remained hidden from me: it was one of those visitors who do not approach us till all the others have gone and we can be alone together; that is when we notice them, when we can say, "I'm all yours," and give them our full attention. Sometimes, between the moment when such pleasures have entered our mind and the moment when we too can withdraw into it, so many hours have elapsed, and we have seen so many people in the meantime, that we fear they may not have waited. But they are patient, they do not weary, and when the last visitor has gone, there they are looking at us. And sometimes it is we who are so tired out that we feel we cannot find the strength in our weary mind to entertain these memories, these impressions for which our feeble self is the only habitable place, the sole medium of their realization. But this we would regret, for almost the only interest in existence lies in those days when a pinch of magic sand is mixed with the dust of reality, when a trite incident can become the spur of romance. An entire promontory of the inaccessible world takes sudden shape, lit by a dream, and becomes part of our life, that life in which, like a sleeper awakened, we can see the people of whom we had dreamed with such longing that we had become convinced that it was only ever in dreams that we would see them.

The relief brought by the likelihood that I could come to know the girls whenever I wanted to was precious to me, especially because I would have been unable to stay on the lookout for them over the next few days, which were taken up with the preparations for Saint-Loup's departure. My grandmother wished to show my friend how much she had appreciated his many kindnesses toward us. I told her he was a great admirer of Proudhon, and gave her the idea to send for a number of letters written by the thinker, which she had bought. When they arrived, the day before his departure, Saint-Loup came to the hotel to see them. He read them eagerly, handling each page with respect and trying to memorize phrases from them. When he stood up to go, excusing himself for having stayed so long, he heard my grandmother say:

"You must take them with you. They're for you—I sent for them so that you could have them."

Saint-Loup, overjoyed, was no more able to control his reaction than if it had been a bodily state produced without the intervention of the will. He turned scarlet, like a child who has been punished; and my grandmother was much more touched by the sight of all the efforts he made, unsuccessful as they were, to contain the joy that surged through him than by all the thanks he could have expressed. The following day, doubting whether he had shown enough gratitude, he was still asking me to excuse him as he leaned out of the window of the little local train that was to take him back to his garrison, which was not far away. He had originally thought he might drive over, as he often did when he had to return there in the evening, when he was to be away from Balbec for only a short time. But he had so much luggage this time that it would have had to go by train; so he had thought it more convenient to take the train himself, a view confirmed by the manager of the hotel, who, when asked about the respective merits of carriage or train, replied that either of these modes of travel would be "more or less equitable to the other." By which he meant "equivalent," roughly what Françoise would have expressed as "it's all the same as one or the other." "Right," Saint-Loup had said, "I'll take the little Slowcoach." I would have taken it too and accompanied my friend to Doncières if I had not been tired out; but during the time the little train spent in the station at Balbec— that is, the time the driver spent waiting for friends who were late and without whom he did want to start, and having a drink—I promised Saint-Loup I would visit him several times a week. Bloch had also come to see him off, to Saint-Loup's great displeasure; and, having noticed that Bloch had overheard him urging me to come to Doncières for lunch or dinner, or even to stay, he eventually said to him, in a tone of great coldness, intended to counter the forced politeness of the invitation, and to prevent Bloch from thinking he meant it: "If you should ever happen to be passing through Doncières some afternoon when I'm off duty, you could ask for me at the barracks, but I'm hardly ever off duty." Robert may also have feared that if left to myself I might not come; and in the belief that I was closer to Bloch than I had given him to understand, he may have thought the latter could be relied upon to make me bestir myself, to serve as a traveling companion.

I was afraid this tone, this way of inviting someone while implying that he should not come, would offend Bloch; and I thought Saint-Loup would have done better to say nothing. In this I was mistaken, for, after the train had left, and as Bloch and I were walking together as far as the crossroads where our paths diverged, one of them leading toward the hotel, the other toward his villa, he kept asking which day we would go to Doncières, since, in view of "all the overtures of Saint-Loup toward him," it would be "too ill mannered of him" not to accept the invitation. I was glad that he either had not noticed, or was unoffended enough to wish to appear not to have noticed, the less-than-eager tone, almost impolite, in which the invitation had been delivered. However, for his sake, I would have preferred him to avoid the ridicule of going over to Doncières straight away. I did not dare advise him on this, though, as I could only have done so in a way that would displease him, by revealing that Saint-Loup's eagerness to invite had been much less than his own to accept. He was in fact overeager; and though all his faults in that line were compensated by remarkable qualities, which someone less forward would not have had, he was so tactless that it was a constant annoyance. According to him, we must not let the week pass without visiting Doncières (he said "we" because, I think, he was half counting on my presence to excuse his). All the way along the road, in front of the gymnasium among its trees, by the tennis court, in front of the town hall, in front of the seashell vendor's, he kept making me stop, begging me to settle on a day; and as I declined, he walked off in a huff, saying, "As it please Your Lordship, then. But I at least am obliged to go, since he did invite me."

Saint-Loup was so uneasy at the thought of not having properly thanked my grandmother that he asked me again to be sure to pass on his gratitude to her, in a letter that I received two days later. It was from the town where he was garrisoned, the name of which postmarked on the envelope seemed to be bringing it to me, telling me that inside its walls, in the Louis XVI cavalry barracks, he was thinking of me. The notepaper bore the arms of Marsantes, in which I could make out a lion on a crown closed by the cap of a peer of France.

"After a successful journey," his letter said, "during which I read a book bought in the station, by Arvède Barine[92] (a Russian writer, I believe; it struck me as remarkably well written for a foreigner, but do give me your view, you who must know, as you've read everything and are a mine of knowledge), here I am once more back in this coarse life where I feel like an exile, where I have nothing of what I left in Balbec, a life without reminders of affection, devoid of the charm of intellectual things, a life lived in an atmosphere that you would no doubt despise, yet which is not without its own charm. Everything seems to have changed since I left, for in the meantime something has marked an era in my life: the beginning of our friendship. I hope it will never end. I have spoken of it, and of you, to a single person, my darling mistress, who gave me a pleasant surprise by coming down here to spend a moment with me. She would like to meet you; and I'm sure you would get along together, as she too is extremely literary. On the other hand, the better to remember the talks we had together, you and I, to recall times I'll never forget, I have also been keeping away from my fellow officers, who, though capital fellows, would be incapable of appreciating such things. For this first day, I could almost have preferred to keep the memory of our times together to myself, rather than write about it. But I was afraid that you, with your subtle mind and your ultrasensitive heart, might begin to worry if you received no letter—assuming, that is, that you have deigned to lower your thoughts to the rough trooper whom you will be hard put to refine, to make a little more subtle and worthy of you."

This letter, in its affectionateness, was really very reminiscent of those which, at a time when I did not know Saint-Loup, I had imagined him writing to me, in the daydreams eventually canceled by the icy reality of his initial greeting, which had proved not to be his definitive manner. After that first letter, each time the post was brought in, at lunchtime, I recognized instantly any letter from him, as they all showed the second face every person has, the one seen in his or her absence, and in the features of which (the letters of the script) there is no reason not to believe we can see the individual spirit so clearly perceptible in the line of their nose or the tones of their voice.

At the end of lunch, I was inclined now to stay on as the tables were being cleared; and if it was a moment at which the little gang of girls could not be expected to pass, my eyes looked on things other than the sea. Since seeing such things in the watercolors of Elstir, I enjoyed noticing them in reality, glimpses of poetry as they seemed: knives lying askew in halted gestures; the tent of a used napkin, within which the sun has secreted its yellow velvet; the half-emptied glass showing better the noble widening of its lines, the undrunk wine darkening it, but glinting with lights, inside the translucent glaze seemingly made from condensed daylight; volumes displaced, and liquids transmuted, by angles of illumination; the deterioration of the plums, green to blue, blue to gold, in the fruit dish already half plundered; the wandering of the old-fashioned chairs, which twice a day take their places again around the cloth draping the table as though it is an altar for the celebration of the sanctity of appetite, with a few drops of lustral water left in oyster shells like little stone fonts; I tried to find beauty where I had never thought it might be found, in the most ordinary things, in the profound life of "still life."

Some days after the departure of Saint-Loup, when I had managed to prompt Elstir to hold a little reception at which I would be able to meet Albertine, I was rather sorry that the charm and elegance, albeit momentary, on which I was complimented as I stepped out of the Grand-Hôtel, which were the result of a long rest and extra expenditure on appearance, could not be reserved, along with the prestige of Elstir, for my conquest of some other, more interesting person, rather than being lavished on Albertine and the pleasure of making her acquaintance. My mind saw this pleasure, now that it was assured, as being worth not very much. But the will in me did not share that illusion for an instant, being the persevering and unwavering servant of our successive personalities, hidden in the shadows, disdained, forever faithful, working unceasingly, and without heeding the variability of our self, making sure it shall never lack what it needs. When a journey we have longed to make begins to become a reality, and the mind and sensibility are starting to wonder whether it is really worth the effort, the will, which well knows that, if it turned out the journey could not be made, these feckless masters would immediately long for it to become possible again, lets them loiter in front of the station, having their say, hesitating until the last minute, while it makes sure of buying the tickets and getting us into the train before departure time. It is as invariable as the mind and sensibility are changeable; but because it is silent and never gives its reasons, it seems almost nonexistent; all the other parts of our self march to its tune unawares, though they can always see clearly their own uncertainties. So my mind and sensibility set up a debate on how much pleasure there might be in making the acquaintance of Albertine, while in front of the mirror I considered the vain and fragile charms that they would have preferred to preserve unused for some better occasion. But my will did not lose sight of the time at which I had to leave; and it was Elstir's address that it gave to the coachman. My mind and sensibility, now that the die was cast, indulged in the luxury of thinking it was a pity. If my will had given a different address, they would have been in a state of panic.

On arriving at Elstir's a little later, I thought at first that Mlle Simonet was not in the studio. There was only a young lady, sitting down, wearing a silk dress, bare-headed, but whose magnificent hair was unknown to me, as were her nose and complexion, in none of which could I recognize the being I had constructed out of a young girl walking along the esplanade, pushing a bicycle, and wearing a toque. Albertine it was, however. Yet, even after realizing this, I paid no attention to her. On going into a fashionable gathering as a young man, one takes leave of the person one was, one becomes a different man, each new salon being a new universe, in which, subject to the law of a new moral perspective, we focus acute attention on individuals, dances, games of cards, as though they were destined to be part of our life forever, though we will have forgotten them by the following morning. Being obliged, in order to come eventually to a chat with Mlle Simonet, to follow a route that was not of my own design, which reached a first destination in front of Elstir, before leading me on to other groups of guests, to whom I was introduced, then along the buffet, where I was handed, and where I ate, strawberry tarts, while pausing to listen to music that had just begun to be played, I found myself giving to these various episodes the same importance as to my introduction to Mlle Simonet, which was only one among their sequence, and which I had by now completely forgotten had been, a few minutes before, the sole object of my presence there. Does not the same happen, in busy everyday life, to our truest joys and greatest sorrows? We stand among other people, and the woman we adore gives us the answer, favorable or fatal, that we have been awaiting for a year: we must go on chatting; ideas lead to other ideas, making a surface beneath which, rising only from time to time, barely perceptible, lies the knowledge, very deep but acute, that calamity has struck. Or, if it is happiness rather than calamity, we may not remember until years later that the most momentous event of our emotional life happened in a way that gives us no time to pay close attention to it, or even to be aware of it almost, during a fashionable reception, say, despite the fact that it was in expectation of some such event that we had gone to it.

At the moment when Elstir suggested I go with him and be introduced to Albertine, who was sitting a little way away, I finished a coffee éclair and inquired with interest of an old gentleman, whom I had just met, and to whom I saw fit to offer the rose he had admired in my buttonhole, about certain agricultural shows in Normandy. This is not to say that the introduction that followed gave me no pleasure, or that it did not have a character of some gravity in my eyes. The pleasure, of course, I did not experience till a little later, back at the hotel, when, having been alone for a while, I was myself again. Pleasures are like photographs: in the presence of the person we love, we take only negatives, which we develop later, at home, when we have at our disposal once more our inner darkroom, the door of which it is strictly forbidden to open while others are present.

Unlike the awareness of my pleasure, delayed for some hours, the gravity of the introduction was perceptible to me at the time. At a moment of introduction, though we feel an immediate gratification, though we know we are now in possession of a voucher valid for future pleasures of the sort we have been seeking for weeks past, we also sense that its possession puts an end, not only to our wearisome searching, a reason for unmitigated joy, but also to the existence of a particular person, the figment created in our imagination and magnified by the fretful fear that we might never come to be acquainted with that person. At the moment when our name sounds in the voice of our introducer, and especially if the latter accompanies it, as Elstir did, with words of praise (a moment as sacramental as the one in pantomimes when the genie commands a person to turn all of a sudden into someone else), the girl we have been longing to approach vanishes—for one thing, how could she go on being the same, since, by the very attention she is obliged to give to our name and display to our person, the conscious gaze and unknowable mind that we had been vainly seeking in her eyes, which were infinitely distant from us yesterday, and which we thought our own eyes, wandering, unfocused, desperate, divergent, would never manage to meet, have just been miraculously and simply replaced by our own image, pictured as by a smiling mirror? If our own reincarnation as something that formerly seemed as distant as possible from ourselves is what most transforms the unknown girl to whom we have just been introduced, her own form is still rather vague; and we may wonder whether she will turn into a goddess, a table, or a bowl.[93] With the agility of a wax-modeler who, as we watch, can make a bust in five minutes, the few words she is about to speak will rough out her form and give it something definitive, eliminating every previous hypothesis elaborated by our desire and imagination. Before she attended Elstir's little party, Albertine was no doubt not quite the mere phantom that a passerby becomes, whom we have barely glimpsed, of whom we know nothing, and who may haunt our life thereafter. Her being related to Mme Bontemps had already restricted these marvelous hypotheses, by blocking off one of the channels via which they might have proliferated. As I came closer to the girl and gradually knew her better, my acquaintance with her proceeded by subtraction, as each part of her made out of imagination and desire was replaced by a perception worth much less, although to each of these perceptions was added a sort of equivalent in human relations of that "continuing dividend" which finance companies go on paying after the redeeming of the original share. Her name and her family connections had fixed a first limit to my suppositions. Another was set by the pleasantness of her manner as I stood beside her, noticing again the beauty mark on her cheek, just under the eye; and I was astonished to hear her use the adverb "perfectly" instead of "completely" when talking of two people, one of whom she said was "perfectly mad, but really quite nice," and the other a "perfectly common person, and perfectly boring." Inelegant as it was, this usage of "perfectly" suggested a level of cultivation far above what I would have imagined to be that of the bacchante with the bicycle, the orgiastic muse of the golf course. And after that initial metamorphosis, Albertine was of course to go through many other changes in my eyes. The qualities and faults of any person, as they appear in the foreground of the face, will be arranged in a different order if we come upon them from another angle, as the landmarks of a city, seen lying along a straight line in a random order, are shuffled into different dimensions of depth, and exchange among themselves their relative sizes, when glimpsed from another point of view. At the beginning, I thought Albertine looked somewhat intimidated, rather than ruthless; she seemed proper, and not ill mannered, judging by statements she made about every one of the girls I mentioned to her, such as "She's very 'fast,'" or "She's perfectly unladylike"; and the focal point of her face was one of her temples, flushed and unpleasant to look at, instead of the singular expression in her eyes, which until then had been the thing about her that had always been in my thoughts. But this was only my second sight of her, and there would undoubtedly be a sequence of other points of view from which I would have to see her. To achieve accurate knowledge of others, if such a thing were possible, we could only ever arrive at it through the slow and unsure recognition of our own initial optical inaccuracies. However, such knowledge is not possible: for, while our vision of others is being adjusted, they, who are not made of mere brute matter, are also changing; we think we have managed to see them more clearly, but they shift; and when we believe we have them fully in focus, it is merely our older images of them that we have clarified, but which are themselves already out of date.

Yet, whatever disappointments it is bound to bring, that way of approaching what one has glimpsed, what one has had the leisure to imagine, is the only wholesome one for the senses, the only one that keeps them in appetite. What monotony and boredom color the lives of those who, from laziness or timidity, drive directly to the houses of friends whom they have come to know, without first having imagined them, without ever daring to dally along the way with what they desire!

On my way home from Elstir's little reception, I thought about it, remembering the coffee éclair I had finished before letting him take

me to meet Albertine, the rose I had given to the old gentleman, all
these details which, selected without our knowledge by the circumstances, constitute in their special haphazard arrangement our picture
of a first meeting. It was this same picture that, some months later, I
had the impression of seeing from another point of view, one very remote from my own, and of realizing that it had not existed only for me:
one day, as I spoke to Albertine about our first meeting, to my amazement she reminded me of the éclair, the flower I had given away, everything that I believed, not to be of importance only to myself, but to
have been noticed only by me, and yet here they were, transcribed in a
version I had not suspected existed, in the mind of Albertine. Back at
the hotel on that first day, when I could focus on the memory I had
taken away with me, I saw the conjuring trick that had been done, and
how I had spent some time chatting with a person who, by the magician's sleight of hand, had been substituted for the girl I had watched so
often along the esplanade, and who had nothing in common with her.
This I could have suspected in advance, as the young girl on the esplanade had been my own creation. Even so, since I had identified her
with Albertine in my conversations with Elstir, I now felt a moral obligation toward the real Albertine to keep the promises of love made to
the imaginary one. Betrothed by proxy, we feel constrained to marry
the intermediary. Besides, though my life was now at least temporarily
free of an anguish any recurrence of which could have been quickly
canceled by the memory of her properness, the expression "perfectly
common," and the flushed temple, this memory now roused in me a
different sort of desire, which, though sweet and quite painless, rather
like a brotherly feeling, was capable of becoming in time just as dangerous, by giving me a constant need to kiss this new person, whose good
manners, shyness, and unexpected availability curbed the futile surges
of my imagination, but gave rise to a touching gratitude. Also, since
memory immediately begins to take snapshots that are quite independent of one another—abolishing all links and sequence among the
scenes they show—in the collection of them that it displays, the latest
does not necessarily obliterate the earlier ones. Beside the unremarkable and touching Albertine with whom I had chatted, I could see the

mysterious Albertine against the backdrop of the sea. Both were now memories, pictures—that is, neither seemed truer than the other. The final image of my introduction to her that afternoon was that, when I tried to remember the little beauty mark on her cheek, just below the eye, I realized that, after my first sight of her, when she had greeted Elstir in passing, I had seen it on her chin. Each time I saw Albertine, I noticed she had a beauty mark, and my misguided memory moved it about her face, sometimes putting it in one place, at other times in another.

Disappointed as I was with Mlle Simonet, a young girl not very different from others I knew, I consoled myself with the thought (just as my disappointment with the church of Balbec had not affected my desire to go to Quimperlé, Pont-Aven, and Venice) that, even though she had not lived up to my expectations, at least through her I would be able to meet her friends in the little gang.

I thought at first that I was going to fail in this aim. As she was going to be staying in Balbec for quite a while, as I was myself, I had decided that it would be better not to seek her out too directly, but to wait for an opportunity when circumstances would bring us together. However, if that were to happen every day, it was very likely that she would do no more than greet me without stopping, and by the end of the season I would be no further forward.

Not many days later, one morning when it had rained and was almost cold, I was accosted on the esplanade by a young girl with a little flat hat and a muff, so different from the person I had seen at Elstir's reception that it appeared to be a feat beyond the power of the human mind to recognize her. My mind, however, managed it, but only after a second's surprise, which I think did not escape Albertine's notice. Also, remembering the good manners which had so struck me, I was now surprised by their opposite, her coarse tone and her "little gang" manners. And then her temple was no longer the reassuring optical center of her face, either because I was now on her other side, or because her hat concealed it, or because its flush was not constant. "What weather!" she said. "Balbec's endless summer is just a great joke, of course. Don't you do anything here? You're never to be seen at the golf course or the dances in the Casino, and you're never out riding a horse either. You must find it all a great bore. You don't think that people who just stay on the beach are a bit silly? Oh, I see, you like just lazing about. Well, you've got plenty of time. I can see you're not like me—I love all sports! You weren't at the races at La Sogne? We went by trolley, and I can understand that you wouldn't want to set foot in a rattletrap like that. It took two hours! I could've gone there and back three times on my bike!" I had admired Saint-Loup for referring quite naturally to the little local train as the "Slowcoach" because of all the twists and turns of the line, but her fluency with words like "trolley" and "rattletrap" disconcerted me: I sensed in it a mastery of forms of speech in which I was afraid she must recognize my inferiority, and for which she would despise me. At that time, the wealth of synonyms current among the little gang for that little train had not yet been revealed to me. When she spoke, Albertine held her head still, keeping her nostrils tight and barely moving her lips. This gave her a nasal drawl, perhaps partly composed of the accents of provincial forebears, a youthful affectation of imperturbable Britishness, the coaching of a foreign governess, and a blocked nose. This pronunciation, which, once she got to know people better, disappeared and was replaced by a more naturally girlish manner, could have sounded quite unpleasant. But I found the peculiarity of it enchanting. When I had not seen her for a few days, I could excite myself by repeating, "You're never to be seen at the golf course," with the nasal twang she had used, speaking straight at me, without moving her head. And I thought there could be no one more desirable in the whole world.

That morning, we were one of the couples who here and there punctuate the esplanade with their momentary meetings, pausing long enough to exchange a few words before separating to take up again their two diverging trajectories. I took advantage of this brief immobility to make a thorough check of the place where the beauty mark was to be found. Just as a phrase of Vinteuil that had delighted me in the sonata, and which my memory kept moving from the andante to the finale, until the day when, with the score in hand, I was able to find it and localize it where it belonged, in the scherzo, so the beauty mark, which I had remembered on her cheek, then on her chin, came to rest forever on her upper lip, just under her nose. In the same way, we are astonished to come upon a stanza we know by heart, but in a poem where we did not realize it belonged.

At that moment, as though for the purpose of displaying, in the full variety of its forms, against the backdrop of the sea, all the fluent freedom of the rich decorative ensemble made by the procession of the virgins, both golden and pink, colored by the sun and the wind, the group of Albertine's friends, with their lovely legs and their lithe waists, but all different from one another, came toward us, nearer to the sea than we were, stretched out in a long line. I asked her if I might walk with her for a moment. Unfortunately, she did no more than wave to them. "But won't your friends feel you've abandoned them?" I asked, in the hope that we might all go for a walk together. A young man with regular features and tennis racquets approached us. It was the baccarat-player whose follies so scandalized the wife of the First President. With a manner that was cold and expressionless, that he clearly believed was one of supreme distinction, he said good morning to Albertine. "Have you been golfing, Octave?" she asked. "Did you have a good game? Were you in good form?" "Oh, I'm disgusted with myself. I'm just an also-ran." "And was Andrée there?" "Yes, she had a round of seventy-seven." "Goodness me! That's a record!" "I went around in eighty-two yesterday." He was the son of a very wealthy industrialist who was to play a rather important part in the organizing of the next International Exhibition. I was struck by how knowledgeable this young man and the other few male friends of the girls were in things like clothes, ways of wearing them, cigars, English drinks, horses—a form of erudition that in him was highly developed, which he wore with a proud infallibility, reminiscent of the scholar's modest reticence—an expertise that was quite self-sufficient, without the slightest need for any accompanying intellectual cultivation. He could not be faulted on the appropriate occasions for wearing dinner jacket or pajamas, but he had no idea of how to use certain words, or even of the most elementary rules of good grammar. That disparity between two cultures must have been shared by his father, who, in his capacity as president of the Association of Property Owners of Balbec, had written an open letter to his constituents, now to be seen as a placard on all the walls, in which he said, "I was desirous of talking to the Mayor about this matter, however, he was of a mind to not hear me out on my just demands." At the Casino, Octave won prizes in all the dancing competitions—the Boston dip, the tango, and so on—a qualification, if he should ever need one, for a good marriage, among seaside society, a milieu in which a young girl quite literally ends up married to her "partner." He lit a cigar and said to Albertine, "If you don't mind," as one excuses oneself for going on with an urgent piece of work in the presence of someone. For he always "had to be doing something," though in fact he never did anything. Just as a total lack of activity can eventually have the same effects as overwork, whether in the emotional domain or in the domain of the body and its muscles, the constant intellectual vacuum that resided behind the pensive forehead of Octave had had the result, despite his undisturbed air, of giving him ineffectual urges to think, which kept him awake at night, as though he were a metaphysician with too much on his mind.

Thinking that if I knew their friends I might have more opportunities to see the girls, I had been about to ask Albertine to introduce me to him. As soon as he had walked away, repeating, "I'm just an also-ran," I said so to her, with the idea that this might inspire her to introduce us on the next occasion. "Oh, goodness!" she said. "I couldn't introduce you to a lounge lizard! The place is crawling with them! But they'd be incapable of conversing with you. He's good at golf and that's all he's good at. Believe me, he wouldn't be your type at all." "Your friends will feel neglected if you stay away from them like this," I said, hoping she would suggest we go and meet them together. "Not at all, they don't need me." We soon came upon Bloch. He gave me a shrewd and meaning smile; then, in some perplexity toward Albertine, whom he did not know, or, rather, whom he did know but "without being acquainted with her," with a stiff, uncouth movement he gave a nod. "Who's that savage?" she asked. "I can't think why he's nodding at me—he doesn't know me. I'll ignore him." I had no time to reply, as Bloch came straight over and said to me, "Excuse me for interrupting, but I just wanted to let you know I'm going over to Doncières tomorrow. It would be impolite of me to leave it any longer, and I don't know what Saint-Loup-en-Bray must think of me. So I'm letting you know that I'll be taking the two o'clock. It's up to you." However, I had no thoughts for anything but Albertine and the need to meet her girlfriends. Hence, a visit to Doncières, where they never went, which would get me back to Balbec long after their time for appearing on the beach, seemed like a trip to the end of the earth. So I told Bloch I could not go. "In that case, I'll go by myself. And to charm Saint-Loup-en-Bray's clericalism, I shall speak to him of you with the ridiculous couplet of Master Arouet:

> My duty on his shall never depend;
> I must, unlike him, be true to my friend."[94]

"I can see he's really quite handsome," Albertine said. "But I must say I don't like him at all!"

It had never occurred to me that Bloch might be "quite handsome." But he was: with his slightly protruding forehead, his pronounced Roman nose, his look of being extremely astute (and of believing he was extremely astute), he had a very pleasant face. Even so, he was not to Albertine's liking. This may have been explainable by the dislikable sides of her own character, the toughness of the little gang, its insensitivity, its rudeness toward all things outside itself. Later, when I had introduced them, her dislike did not lessen. Bloch belonged to a world which, with its sneer at good society and yet the tolerance of good manners which a man must retain if he is not to be seen as untouchable, has reached a sort of special compromise by the use of manners which, though not quite those of fashionable society, manage to achieve a peculiar kind of detestable fashionableness. When you introduced him to someone, he would bow with a skeptical smile and an exaggerated show of respect, and if it was a man whose hand he was shaking, he would say, "Charmed to meet you, sir," in a voice which, though it mocked the words it spoke, knew it did not belong to a boor. Having occupied that second in simultaneously observing and scoffing at a custom (just as he would say, on New Year's Day, "I wish you a Happy New One"), he would then affect an acute and wily expression, and "let fall pearls of wisdom," which

I often found full of good sense, but which Albertine "could not abide."
On that first day, when I told her his name was Bloch, she exclaimed, "I
wouldn't have minded betting he was a Jew boy! They always know
how to get your back up!" At a later stage too, Bloch was to irritate Albertine in another way. Like many intellectuals, he could not say simple
things simply. He would describe them with precious epithets, then
generalize. Albertine, who disliked it when people paid attention to
what she was doing, was annoyed that, when she had sprained her ankle
and was resting, Bloch said, "She's lying on her chaise longue. But, being gifted with ubiquity, she continues simultaneously to haunt ghostly
golf courses and the tritest of tennis lawns." It was merely his "stylish"
banter; but to Albertine, who felt it might create difficulties for her with
people who had invited her out, and whom she had told she was incapable of moving, it was enough to make her loathe the sight and the
sound of the person who said such things. Having agreed to go out together soon, she and I parted. While talking to her, I had been as unaware of my words and where they went as though I had been throwing
pebbles into a bottomless well. That in general the people to whom we
speak draw from within themselves the meaning they give to our words,
and that this meaning is very different from the one we put into them,
is a truth constantly revealed to us by everyday life. But if in addition
the person to whom we are speaking is, as Albertine was for me, someone whose upbringing is inconceivable, whose inclinations and principles, even the books she reads, are a mystery to us, then we cannot tell
whether our words have any more semblance of meaning for her than
they would have if we tried to explain ourselves to an animal. Trying to
strike up a relationship with Albertine felt like relating to the unknown,
or even the impossible, an exercise as difficult as training a horse, as
restful[95] as keeping bees or growing roses.

Some hours before, I had believed Albertine would give me only a
distant nod. Now we had just agreed to an outing together. I resolved
that, the next time I met her, I would be more forward; and I drew up a
detailed scheme for what to say to her and even, since I had a strong impression that she was not overburdened by virtue, for all the pleasures
she would lend herself to at my suggestion. But the mind is as suscepti-

ble to influence as any plant, any cell, any chemical elements; and the milieu that modifies it is the changed circumstances by which it is surrounded, a new setting. The presence of Albertine was enough to make me different; and when I was next with her the things I said were also completely different from what I had planned. Then, remembering her flushed temple, I wondered whether she might not be more appreciative of a kindness on my part that she would know was not self-interested. I was also perplexed by some looks she gave me, a way she had of smiling. They might be taken to mean easy virtue; but they might also mean the guileless if silly gaiety of a girl who, though vivacious, is fundamentally virtuous. There being more than one connotation for a single expression, whether on her face or in her speech, I was as hesitant as a pupil faced with the difficulties of a Greek unseen.

On this occasion, almost without delay, we met the tall girl, Andrée, the one who had jumped over the First President;[96] and Albertine had to introduce me. Her friend's face was lighted by eyes that were extraordinarily limpid, as a dimly lit apartment is brightened through an open bedroom door by the sunshine and greenish glow reflected up from the sea.

Five gentlemen walked past; since the beginning of my stay at Balbec, I had come to know all of them well by sight, and had often wondered who they might be. "They're not very smart people," Albertine said, with a snigger of contempt. "Take a look at that little old fellow with the dyed hair and the yellow gloves! Isn't he the limit? Well, he's the local dentist, not a bad old fellow, actually. The fat one's the mayor. I don't mean the *little* fat one—you must have seen *him*, he's the dancing teacher; he's a bit of a brute too: he can't *stand* us, because we make too much noise at the Casino, we demolish his chairs, we want to dance with the carpet rolled up, so he's never given us the prize, though we're the only ones that can dance! The dentist's quite a nice fellow, and I wouldn't have minded saying hello to him just to annoy the dancing teacher, but I couldn't, because that's M. de Sainte-Croix with them, the member of the Conseil Général,[97] a gentleman of very good family who's gone over to the Republicans now, for money—all proper people ignore him totally. He knows my uncle, because of the government, but the rest of my family cut him dead. The thin one in the raincoat is the conductor of the orchestra. What? You don't know him? His playing's divine! You didn't go and hear *Cavalleria Rusticana*?[98] Oh, I think it's just lovely! He's giving a concert this evening, but we can't go because it's in Town Hall—the Casino's all right, but Town Hall's out of bounds: they've gone and taken down the crucifix,[99] and Andrée's mother would throw forty fits if we went! I know my aunt's husband's in the government, but I can't help that—my aunt may be my aunt, but that doesn't make me like her, you know! She has only ever wanted one thing—to get rid of me. The only person who was ever anything like a mother to me—and who really deserves double credit for it, as she's not even family—is a friend that I actually love like a mother. I'll show you a photo of her." We were briefly joined by the golf champion and baccarat-player, Octave. I thought I might have discovered a link between us, on learning from the conversation that he had some slight family relationship with the Verdurins, who were also rather fond of him. However, he disparaged the celebrated Wednesdays, and added that M. Verdurin was ignorant of the proper wearing of the dinner jacket, which made it pretty embarrassing to encounter him in certain music halls, where one would rather not be accosted by a gentleman wearing an ordinary suit and a black tie, looking like a village notary up in town and calling out, "Good evening, whippersnapper!" Octave walked on; and soon afterward Andrée also left us, as we had reached her chalet. She went in, having said not a single word to me throughout the whole walk. I was sorry to see her disappear, especially because, while I was remarking to Albertine how unfriendly her friend had been, and mentally comparing the difficulty Albertine appeared to have in letting me make the acquaintance of her girlfriends with the reluctance Elstir had also seemed to encounter on the very first day in trying to effect the same thing, two young girls passed, the d'Ambresac sisters, whom I greeted, and to whom Albertine also said good morning.

This made me think that my situation with Albertine might improve. The mother of these two girls was a relative of Mme de Villeparisis's, and she also knew the Princess of Luxembourg. M. and Mme d'Ambresac, who owned a small villa at Balbec, though exceedingly rich, lived very simply, the husband always wearing the same jacket, the wife forever a dark dress. They always made a great show of bowing to my grandmother, but went no further. The daughters, both very pretty, were more elegant dressers, but it was Paris elegance, not seaside elegance. In their long dresses, under their expansive hats, they seemed to be a very different breed from Albertine. She was quite aware of who they were. "Oh, so you know the d'Ambresac girls, do you? In that case, you know some pretty smart people. Actually, they're very simple people," she added, as though there were some contradiction in this. "They're very nice, but so well bred that they're not allowed to go to the Casino, especially because of us, because we're so unladylike. Do you like them? Well, they're not everyone's cup of tea. Little innocents, the pair of them. The sort of thing some people might find quite to their taste. If you fancy little innocents, there you are, plenty to choose from. And it seems there *are* people who like that sort of thing: one of them's already betrothed to the Marquis de Saint-Loup. And the younger one, who was in love with the gentleman herself, is breaking her heart. I must say I can't stand the way they speak, as though butter wouldn't melt in their mouths. And they wear such ludicrous things—imagine, playing golf in a silk gown! At their age, their getup is more pretentious than older women who have a sense of dress. I mean, Mme Elstir, for instance, there's a woman who dresses well." I said Mme Elstir's way of dressing had struck me as very simple. Albertine burst out laughing: "Of course she's simple in her way of dressing! But her way is so delightfully right! And to get the effect that you see as simplicity, she spends a fortune." To someone whose taste in things of dress was poor or deficient, there was nothing remarkable in Mme Elstir's dresses. Taste in these things, which I lacked, Elstir had in abundance, or so Albertine said. I had had no idea of this; nor had I noticed that the objects ranged about his studio were wonders of elegance, but also of simplicity, things he had yearned to possess for a long time, kept an eye on at every auction, things whose whole history he knew, until the day came when he had made enough money to acquire them. Albertine, who was as ignorant as I was on this aspect of Elstir, could tell me nothing about it. However, on women's dress, with her instinctive delight in attractive clothes, and perhaps also with something of the longing of the girl who, though poor, is disinterested and modest enough to enjoy the spectacle of rich people wearing what she will never be able to afford, she could tell me things about Elstir's standards of taste, so refined and exacting that in his view all women were badly dressed, and that, with his concern for every proportion and slightest nuance, he would spend huge sums having his wife's sunshades, hats, and cloaks made, explaining to Albertine the while the charm of such things, of which a person devoid of taste would have been as ignorant as I had been. Albertine had also dabbled in painting, though she had, as she said herself, no "bent" for it, and greatly admired Elstir; and, from what he had told her and shown her, she had acquired an appreciation of good painting that was in marked contrast to her liking for *Cavalleria Rusticana*. The fact was, invisible as this was to me at the time, she was highly intelligent; and though there was stupidity in things she said, it was not her own, but that of her peers. Elstir had influenced her for the better, but only partially. Not all modes of cultivation and sensibility were equally developed in her. Her appreciation of painting now almost equaled her liking for clothes and for all things fashionable, but it was unaccompanied by an appreciation of good music.

Despite her awareness of the significance of the d'Ambresac family, despite my having greeted their daughters, since ability in greater things may accompany inability in lesser, I did not find Albertine any more prepared to introduce me to her group of girlfriends. "It's very sweet of you to bother about them. But they're nobody, just pay no attention to them. I mean, a fellow as clever as you should have nothing to do with a group of silly girls like that. Actually, Andrée's very clever, and she's a very nice girl, although perfectly skittish. But, honestly, the others are just silly." As soon as Albertine had gone, I felt very sad to realize that Saint-Loup had concealed his engagement from me and that he should be contemplating such an immoral thing as to marry without first giving up his mistress. A few days later, I was introduced to Andrée, and after she chatted with me for quite a while, I took the opportunity to say that I would like to meet her the following day; but she replied that it would not be possible, as she thought her mother was unwell and did not wish to leave her alone. Two days later, I went to see Elstir, who told me how much Andrée had liked me; to which I replied, "Well, I liked her a lot too, from the very first! I asked her to meet me the next day, but she couldn't manage it." "Yes, I know," Elstir said. "She told me about it. She was rather sorry, but she had agreed to go on a picnic, an outing by wagonette to a place more than twenty miles away, and she couldn't get out of it." Even though the lie Andrée had told was negligible, she being such a new acquaintance, I ought not to have gone on seeing someone who was capable of it: what people have done once, they will go on doing forever. If we make a point of paying an annual visit to a friend who has broken several such engagements before, who has caught a cold, we shall find him with his cold on later occasions; he will fail to keep the other appointments—and the reason will be the same each time, although he will believe he has given a range of different reasons, each of them conditional on differing circumstances.

One morning, not long after the day when Andrée had told me she had to stay with her mother, I was walking along beside Albertine, whom I had chanced to meet, and who was holding up a strange device on a string which made her look rather like Giotto's *Infidelitas*: it was actually called a "diabolo," and it is now so out of date that, faced with a picture of a girl holding it, scholars may discourse in the future, as they do now on certain allegorical figures in the Arena Chapel, about what it is she is holding in her hand. After a moment, one of the group of girls, the one who looked rather poor and tough, who on the day when I first saw them had sneered in such a broad, unpleasant way, about the old gentleman whose head had been endangered by Andrée's flying feet, "He'd break your heart, that poor old guy!" came over and said to Albertine, "Morning! Not in the way, I hope!" Her hat had been a bother to her, so she had taken it off, and her hair, like some unfamiliar and beautiful botanical variety, lay on her forehead in all the delicate and minutely detailed luxuriance of its foliation. Albertine, who may have been annoyed with her for being bare-headed, gave no reply to her greeting and walked on, icily silent; despite which, the other girl did not move away, although Albertine kept her at a distance from me, at times moving closer to her than to me, at other times walking by my side and leaving the girl behind. In order to be introduced, I had to ask Albertine directly, in the other girl's hearing. As Albertine spoke my name, I saw a smile, open and affectionate and full of blue eyes, flash across the face of the girl who had seemed so cruel when she said, "What a poor old guy—he'd break your heart!" and who now stood there holding out her hand to me. Her hair was golden, as was everything else about her: for, though she had pink cheeks and eyes of blue, they too looked like the colors of the morning sky when everything is touched and tinted by the gold of summer sunlight.

She went straight to my head. I told myself she was just a shy girl in love, that she had stayed with us, despite being snubbed by Albertine, for my sake, for the love of me, and that she must have been happy to be able to tell me at last, with this softhearted smile, that she would be as tender toward me as she was cruel toward others. She must have noticed me down on the beach, at a time when I had no knowledge of her, and must have been thinking about me ever since—perhaps her reason for laughing at the old gentleman had been so that I should admire her; perhaps her reason for going about, the following days, with such an unhappy look, was her displeasure at not being able to get to know me! Sitting in the hotel, I had often noticed her taking an evening stroll down by the beach. She must have been hoping to meet me! And now, as embarrassed by the presence of Albertine as she would have been by the whole gang of her girlfriends, it was clear that her only reason for dogging our footsteps, in the face of her friend's increasing hostility toward her, was the hope of outstaying Albertine, of arranging a meeting with me for a moment when she would be able to slip away without the knowledge of her family or friends and come to me at some secluded spot, before Mass or after her game of golf. It would be very difficult to see her, especially as she was on bad terms with Andrée, who hated her. "I've put up with her awful dishonesty for ages," Andrée told me, "her nastiness, all the dirty tricks she's played on me! I've put up with it all for the sake of the others. But the latest bad turn she's done me is really the last straw." She told me something the girl had said against her, which could indeed have had serious consequences for Andrée.

The words Gisèle's eyes promised would be spoken to me as soon as Albertine left us alone together were not to be uttered, as Albertine went on obstinately keeping us apart, giving shorter and shorter answers to the girl, and eventually ignoring her altogether, so that she at length gave up and walked away. I reproached Albertine for having been so unpleasant. "Well, that'll learn her! I mean, why does she have to be so pushy? She's not a bad sort, but she's a pain in the neck. There's no need for her to come and stick her nose in everywhere. Why does she have to come and be a fifth wheel when she's not wanted? I'd a good mind to tell her to buzz off. Anyway, I can't stand it when she shows her hair like that, it's very unladylike." While Albertine was speaking, I watched her cheeks and wondered what flavor they might have, what fragrance: that day, she did not look cool, but all smooth, and with a uniformly purplish-pink blush, creamy, like certain roses with a waxy sheen. I had a passion for her cheeks, as one can have for a variety of flower. "I didn't notice," I said. "Well, you took a good look at her," she said, unmollified by the fact that she was the one I was now taking a good look at. "You looked as if you wanted to paint her portrait. Anyway, I don't think you'd like her: she's definitely not a flirt, and I suppose you probably prefer girls that are flirts. In any case, her time for being a little pest to be got rid of is nearly up, because she's going back to Paris this afternoon." "And are your other friends going back too?" "No, just her, her and her English governess, because she's got exams to retake—she's going to have to do some cramming, poor kid. And that's no joke, I can tell you. Still, you can always have the luck to get an easy theme—anything's possible. One of us got 'Describe an accident you have seen'—just a gift! But I know a girl that got 'Who would you prefer to have as a friend, Alceste or Philinte?'[100]—and in the written paper too! I wouldn't have had a clue! I mean, for one thing, it's not a question for girls! Girls are friends with other girls, and they're not supposed to *have* gentlemen friends." In this statement I heard an intimation that I had little chance of being accepted by the little gang, which struck fear into my heart. "But even if boys were asked a question like that, what sort of an answer could they possibly write? Several families have written to the editor of *Le Gaulois*[101] to complain about the difficulty of that sort of question. And the worst of it is that, in a collection of the best essays by prize-winning pupils, that subject has been treated twice, but in completely opposite ways! So it all depends on which examiner you get. One of them wanted them to say Philinte is a scheming flatterer, and the other one wanted them to say that you can't help admiring Alceste but that he's too peevish, and so for a friend you have to prefer Philinte. How are poor girl-pupils supposed to make sense of things if teachers can't agree among themselves? And in any case they're making it harder every year. Gisèle's only chance of passing is if she can get a string pulled for her."

When I got back to the hotel, my grandmother was not there; after waiting a long time for her to come back, I begged her to let me go off on an excursion, unexpected but not to be missed, which might last for up to forty-eight hours. I lunched with her, ordered a carriage, and was driven to the railway station. Gisèle would not be surprised to see me; and once we had changed trains at Doncières, we would have a corridor train to Paris: while the English governess dozed, I would have Gisèle all to myself, slipping off with her to dark corners and arranging times and places so that we could meet after my own return to Paris, which I would try to bring about as soon as possible. Depending on her attitude toward me, I would travel with her as far as Caen or Évreux, then double back to Balbec by the next train. But whatever would she have thought, if she had known how long I had hesitated in my choice between her and her friends, and that I had been prepared to fall in love with Albertine, or the girl with the limpid eyes, or with Rosemonde, rather than with her! This thought filled me with remorse, now that Gisèle and I were to be joined together in a requited love. In any case, I could have assured her with total veracity that I was no longer attracted to Albertine. That morning, as she walked over to speak to Gisèle, I had caught a glimpse of her from behind: her head was bowed, a posture that made her look moody, and the hair at the back was different, even blacker than it was at the front, and shining as though she had just come out of the water. It had made me think of a wet hen and see her as embodying a soul very unlike the one that filled the mauve of her complexion and the mystery in her eyes. For a moment, she had been reduced to the sheen of this hair on the back of her head; and it was still the only thing I could see in my mind's eye. Our memory is like one of those shopwindows where different photographs of a certain person are displayed on different days. Sometimes it is the most recent one that stays on show for a time, in isolation. While the coachman urged on his horse, I could hear Gisèle assuring me of her gratitude and tenderness, in words that were a direct translation of her lovely smile and ready handshake: for, at those moments in my life when I was not in love but wished I was, the ideal of physical beauty I carried about with me— which, as has been seen, I could recognize in a distant glimpse of any passing stranger who was far enough away for the imprecision of her features not to impede that recognition—was partnered by the emotional shadow, ever ready to be brought to real life, of the woman who was going to fall in love with me and step straight into the part already written for her in the comedy of fondness and passion that had been awaiting her since my childhood, and for which every young girl I met, as long as she had a pleasant disposition and some of the physical characteristics required by the role, appeared eager to be auditioned. In this play, whoever it was I cast as the new star or her understudy for this part of leading lady, the outline of the plot, the main scenes, and even the words to be spoken had long since taken the form of a definitive edition.

Within a few days, despite Albertine's reluctance to bring us together, I had made the acquaintance of the whole gang of girls I had seen on the first day, all of them having stayed on in Balbec (with the exception of Gisèle, whom I had been prevented from meeting at the station by a long delay at the barrier, whose train in any case had left five minutes early because the timetable had been changed, and who now could not have been further from my thoughts), plus two or three of their other friends whom I had asked to be introduced to. The hope of pleasure to be enjoyed with a new girl having been transmitted to her by the other girl who had introduced us, each of them came to seem like one of those new roses that can be developed from a rose of a different variety. Then, going back along my chain of flowers, from corolla to corolla, the joy of discovering each different specimen made me revert to the one who had led me to her, with as much desire in my gratitude to her as there was in my hope for the new one. Before long, I spent every day with the girls.

In the freshest bud, alas, one may read the all-but-imperceptible signs that tell the practiced eye what the future, through the desiccation or fecundation of the flesh in full blossom today, holds for the seed, immutably predestined in form and outcome. We delight in the line of a young nose, as beautiful as a delicate ripple ruffling the surface of the morning sea, seemingly motionless and sketchable, the water being so calm that the rise of the tide is invisible. When we look at faces, they do not appear to be changing, the revolution they are undergoing being so long drawn out as to escape our notice. But to see one of these young girls standing beside her mother or her aunt was to glimpse the remoter reaches of ugliness to which, in response to an inner attraction, the features of most of them would have come less than thirty years later, the time of waning glances, the time when such a face receives no more light and slips forever below the horizon. I knew that, under the present rosy blossoming of Albertine, Rosemonde, or Andrée, unknown to them, biding its time, as deep-rooted and inescapable as Jewish clannishness or Christian atavism in people who believe they have risen above their race, there lurked an outsized nose, a graceless mouth, a propensity to overweight which would surprise people but which had been standing by, awaiting only the favor of circumstance, as unforeseen, as fated as others' Dreyfusism, clericalism, national and feudal heroisms, which the fullness of time suddenly summons from a nature predating the individual himself, through which he thinks, lives, and evolves, from which he draws his sustenance, and in which he dies without ever being able to distinguish it from the particular motives he mistakes for it. Even mentally, we depend much more than we believe on natural laws; and our mind, like the humblest plant, the merest grass, contains particularities that we think we have chosen. All we can grasp, though, is the secondary ideas, while the first cause (Jewishness, French family, etc.), which gives rise to them, and which we respond to at a time of its choosing, remains beyond our ken. Though we think our thoughts are ours by choice, and our ills a mere consequence of our own recklessly unhealthy life, it may well be that, just as papilionaceous plants produce a seed of a certain shape, our family hands down to us the ideas that keep us alive, as well as the illness that will cause our death.

As though on a seedling whose blossoms ripen at different times, I had seen in old ladies, on that beach at Balbec, the dried-up seeds and sagging tubers that my girlfriends would become. But now that it was the time for buds to blossom, what did that matter? If Mme de Villeparisis invited me out for a carriage ride, I made up an excuse for not going. The only times I went to visit Elstir were when my new friends went with me. I could not even find a spare afternoon to keep my promise to go and see Saint-Loup in Doncières. If my outings with the girls had been replaced by gatherings of the fashionable, earnest conversations, or even just a chat with a friend, it would have felt like a lunchtime at which, instead of being fed, I had been expected to take an interest in somebody's picture book. The men and youths, the old or middle-aged women, in whose company we think we take pleasure, we conceive of as shallow beings, existing on a flat and insubstantial surface, because our only awareness of them is that of unaided visual perception; but when our eye ventures in the direction of a young girl, it is as though it acts on behalf of all our other senses: they seek out her various properties, the smell of her, the feel of her, the taste of her, which they enjoy without the collaboration of the hands or the lips; and because of desire's artful abilities in transposition, and its excellent spirit of synthesis, these senses can draw from the color of cheeks or breasts the sensations of touching, of savoring, of forbidden contact, and can rifle girls' sweet succulence, as they do in a rose garden when plundering the fragrances of the flowers, or in a vineyard when gloating with greedy eyes upon the grapes.

If it was raining—not that wet weather daunted Albertine, who could be seen in her raincoat dashing along on her bicycle, through the pelting rain—we would spend the day in the Casino. On such days it would have been inconceivable to me not to go there. I scorned the d'Ambresac girls, who had never set foot in it; and I was glad to be a party to the tricks played on the dancing teacher. We usually brought down on our heads the wrath of the proprietor or of any of his employees who saw themselves as acting in his stead, since my girlfriends (even Andrée, who on the very first day had made me think she was such a Dionysiac creature, yet who was actually not at all robust but intellectual, and, that year, quite unwell; despite which, unconcerned for the good of her health, she acted in conformity with the spirit of her time of life, an age that carries all before it, infecting with its gaiety not just the hale and the hearty but the lame and the halt as well) were incapable of walking from the entrance hall to the reception room without breaking into a run, hurdling the chairs, sliding back across the floor toward the others, keeping their balance with gracefully outstretched arms, singing, mingling all the arts, youth's first blush manifesting itself in them as it did in those poets of antiquity for whom the different genres had not yet diverged, and who would adorn an epic poem with agricultural advice and theological instruction.

The Andrée who had struck me to begin with as being the most unfriendly of them all was in fact much more sensitive, affectionate, and astute than Albertine, to whom she was all sweetness, as gentle and caressing as though she were her elder sister. At the Casino, she would come and sit by my side and, unlike Albertine, could even decline an invitation to waltz; or, if I was tired, she would come to see me at the hotel rather than go to the Casino. The words in which she expressed her liking for me, and for Albertine, were exquisitely well chosen, showing the subtlest insight into things of the heart, which may have come in part from her acquaintance with ill health. She always gave a bright smile, by way of excuse for the childish and vehement directness of Albertine's ways of expressing her irresistible fascination with outings and parties, which she could not bring herself to forgo, as Andrée did, so as to stay and chat with me. If we were all together when the hour set for a tea party at the golf club was approaching, Albertine would get ready to go, then say to Andrée, "So what are you waiting for? You know we're going to have tea at the golf club." "No, I'm going to stay here with him," Andrée replied, with a nod in my direction. "But as you know, Mme Durieux invited you," Albertine exclaimed, as though the real reason for Andrée's intention to stay with me must be that she did not know she had been invited. "Oh, look, do stop being silly," Andrée replied. And Albertine let the matter drop, in case she should be requested to stay with me too. She shook her head and, as though dealing with an invalid who takes a reckless delight in committing very slow suicide, said, "Well, on your own head be it. I'm off, though, because I think my watch is a bit slow." She dashed away. "She's just lovely, but quite preposterous," Andrée said, with an indulgent but critical smile for her friend. In this liking of Albertine's for amusement there was something of the Gilberte I had known in the earliest days, the explanation of which is that there is a degree of resemblance between the women we love at different times; and this resemblance, though it evolves, derives from the unchanging nature of our own temperament, which is what selects them, by ruling out all those who are not likely to be both opposite and complementary to us, who cannot be relied on, that is, to gratify our sensuality and wound our heart. Such women are a product of our temperament, an inverted image or projection, a negative, of our sensitivity. A novelist could shape the whole life of his hero by depicting his consecutive loves in more or less the same terms, giving thereby the impression, not of being self-repetitive, but of being creative, there being less power in an artificial innovation than in a reiteration designed to convey a hitherto unrevealed truth. However, the novelist should take care to note in the character of the lover a factor of variability, which becomes more marked as the lover moves into new regions and explores some of life's other latitudes. He might even speak a further truth if, in his apportionment of character to the other members of his cast, he made a point of giving none to the woman his hero loves. We are thoroughly acquainted with the characters of people who mean nothing to us; but how could we possibly grasp anything of a person who is intricately involved in our life, who soon becomes inseparable from our very self, whose motives are the subject of our anguished, incessant, and constantly revised hypotheses? Our curiosity about the woman we love, the roots of which lie far beyond our reasoning mind, reaches far beyond her character. Even if we were capable of pausing and focusing on it, we would probably not wish to. The object of our anxious investigations is her essence, not to be confused with peculiarities of character more akin to the minute diamond shapes on the surface of the skin, which in their varieties of combinations give rise to the rosy individuality of the person in the flesh. Our intuitive radiation sees through them, and the images it gives are not those of any particular face, but rather the lineaments of a skeleton, in all its dismal and dismaying universality.

Andrée, who was extremely wealthy, showed great generosity in sharing her luxury with Albertine, who was poor and an orphan. Toward Gisèle, however, Andrée's feelings were not quite those I had thought. News of the departed student soon came; and when Albertine showed the letter in which Gisèle, for the benefit of the whole group, recounted her journey and return to Paris, apologizing for being too lazy as yet to write to the others, I was surprised to hear Andrée, who I thought was at daggers drawn with her, saying, "I'll write to her tomorrow. If I wait till she writes to me, I might wait forever. She's so haphazard." She added, to me, "I expect you wouldn't think there was anything very outstanding about her. But she's such a nice girl, and I'm really very fond of her." I decided that when Andrée was on bad terms with someone it never lasted long.

Except on these rainy days, we usually went cycling along the cliffs or into the countryside behind Balbec; and an hour before it was time to go I would be fully occupied in titivating myself and nagging at Françoise if she had not laid out my things properly.

Even in Paris, at the slightest hint of a criticism, Françoise, who was so humble, capable of such charming modesty when her self-esteem was soothed by praise, would stiffen with offended pride, straightening her back, which was beginning to stoop with age. And as the pride she took in her work was what gave purpose to her whole life, her satisfaction and good humor were in direct proportion to the difficulty of the duties she was required to perform. At Balbec, her only tasks were so easy that she went about them with an air of discontent, which could be instantly intensified and aggravated into a grimace of ironic pride if I should complain, when I was about to set off to meet my girlfriends, that my hat was unbrushed or my ties in disarray. She did not mind putting herself to any amount of trouble; but if one so much as remarked that a jacket was not in the right place, not only did she take pleasure and pique in pointing out the care with which she had "put it away, so the dust wouldn't gather," but she would treat you to a diatribe on the subject of her tasks, the sad fact that this whole long time in Balbec was no vacation for her, and that you could never find another body to put up with it! "I can't understand how a body can be expected to just drop everything, and you mark my words, nobody else would be able to! A mess like this—it's more than flesh and bone should have to cope with!" Or else she would look regal, wither me with a glare, and say nothing—until, that is, she had left the room, closed the door, and was walking along the corridor, which then echoed with words which I could surmise were insulting, but which were as indistinct as those uttered by characters coming onstage and already speaking as they emerge from the wings. Moreover, at times when I was getting ready to go for an outing with the girls, even if everything was in order and Françoise was in a good mood, she could still show herself at her insufferable worst: she trotted out jokes which, in my need to speak of the girls, I had retailed to her, and seemed to think she was informing me of things which, if they had been true, I would have known more about than she did, but which were not true, because she had misunderstood something I had told her. Like everyone, Françoise had her own character: no one we know ever resembles a straight path; and we will always be astonished by every person's twists and turns, idiosyncratic, unavoidable, and irksome as they may be, which others may not even be aware of, but which we have to put up with. Whenever my speech with Françoise reached the "Hat not in the right place" stage or "Mention of the name of Andrée or Albertine," she obliged me to follow her ludicrous rigmaroles along the highways and byways of her thought processes, all of which greatly delayed my preparations. The same happened when I asked her to make up sandwiches of Cheshire cheese and lettuce, or to buy some tarts, which I intended for a picnic later that afternoon, up on the cliffs, "with those girls who," said Françoise, "could surely have been expected to buy their own once in a while, if they weren't just out for what they could get," all her atavistic avarice and provincial vulgarity coming out in such statements, which could have made one think the soul of Eulalie, dead, departed, and divided, had been reincarnated, more gracefully than in Saint Éloi, in the delightful persons of my little gang of girlfriends. I weathered these aspersions, galled to know that here I had reached one of the points where the familiar and rambling country lane of Françoise's character had just become impassable (though, fortunately, not for long). Then, the jacket having turned up, the sandwiches having been made, I would sally forth to meet Albertine, Andrée, and Rosemonde, and at times others of the group, and together, on foot or on bicycles, we would set off.

There was a time when I would have preferred such outings to take place in dreadful weather, when I looked forward to Balbec as "the land of the Cimmerians," a place where there could be no such thing as a sunny day, that anomalous intrusion of vulgar sea-bathers and their summer into my ancient land wreathed in its mists. Now, however, everything I had disdained, everything my eyes had shunned, not just the sparkle of the sunlight but even the regattas and the horseracing, I would have passionately participated in, and that for the same reason that once made me yearn only for raging seas, which was that all of these things, then as now, were linked to an aesthetic idea: the girls and I had been together to Elstir's, and on those days what the artist had shown us in particular was sketches he had penciled of pretty yachtswomen, or a drawing done at a racecourse not far from Balbec. With some diffidence, I had told Elstir of my reluctance to go to the events that took place there. "That's not the view to take," he said. "They're very pretty and full of interest. Take that particular figure, the jockey, the center of attraction: down in the paddock there, he looks so dull, so featureless in his glowing colors, at one with the horse, reining it in as it wheels about—yet wouldn't it be interesting to grasp his technical movements, to show the bright blob he makes, along with the glossy coats of the horses, out on the turf! Look at how all things are transformed in that vast and luminous space of the racecourse, full of so many surprising effects of light and shade that you can see nowhere else! Look at how pretty the women can be! The first race meeting I went to was especially magnificent, with women of exceptional elegance, amid a wash of moist light, a Dutch light, and you could sense the penetrating chill from the water reaching up into the sunlight. I'd never seen women arriving in carriages, and looking through their binoculars, bathed in that sort of light, which must be saturated by the air off the sea. How I wished I could capture it! I went home from that race meeting with my head reeling, bursting with the urge to paint!" Elstir spoke even more lyrically about yachting events than about horseracing, which made me realize that for a modern artist regattas and gatherings of sportsmen, where women are suffused by the glaucous glow of a seaside racecourse, could be a study fully as captivating as the ceremonial celebrations that Veronese and Carpaccio so liked to depict. "Your comparison is especially apt," Elstir said, "given that, in the city where they painted, those celebrations were partly nautical. Except that the beauty of the vessels of that period lay often in their cumbersomeness and intricacy. As is also done here at Balbec, they held jousting on the water, usually in honor of a visiting embassy, like the one Carpaccio shows in *The Legend of Saint Ursula.* The ships were massive, built like cathedrals, and they looked almost amphibious, like smaller Venices within the real one, when they were moored to landing stages, draped with crimson satins, and carpeted by Persian rugs, and carrying women in cherry-colored brocades or green damask, close to balconies inlaid with multicolored marble, where other women would lean out to get a good view, in gowns with black sleeves with white slashes in them thick with pearls or adorned with point lace. It was unclear where the land finished and the water began, what was still palace or possibly ship, a caravel, a galleass, the bucentaur." With passionate concentration, Albertine listened to these details of dress and adornment, and gloated upon Elstir's images of luxury: "Oh, I'd love to see point lace like that! Venice lace is so pretty! I'd really love to go to Venice." "Well," said Elstir, "before long you may be able to gaze on the wonderful fabrics they used to wear in Venice. It has been impossible to see them except in the canvases of Venetian masters, or sometimes among the relics and ornaments of a church, though now and again a garment would come up for auction. But I'm told that a Venetian artist, Fortuny by name,[102] has rediscovered the secret of their manufacture, and that within a few years women will be able to walk out, or sit at home more likely, wearing brocades as magnificent as any that Venice, to grace its great ladies, ever adorned with designs from the Orient. To tell you the truth, I'm not sure I would care for that, or whether it might not be too much your 'period costume' for women of today, even when they're on display at a regatta, because, after all, to revert to our modern pleasure craft, they're quite different from those of the time when Venice was 'Queen of the Adriatic.' The most charming thing about a yacht, about its fittings and the things people wear for yachting, is that they're so simple, it's their seafaring simplicity—and I do so love the sea! I don't mind saying I prefer today's styles to those of the time of Veronese and even Carpaccio. If there's one really pretty thing about yachts, medium-sized yachts, I mean, not your great enormous ones, which are more like ships—as with hats, there *is* a limit—then it's the plain and simple, the pale and the gray, which on hazy blue days takes on a creamy, blurred quality. The cabin where you sit should feel like a little café. And it's the same with women's clothes on board a yacht: the really graceful ones wear things that are light and white and plain, linen, lawn, duck, twill, which when you see them in the sunlight and against the blue of the sea are as white as the white of a sail. Actually, very few women dress well, although there are some who are quite exquisite: Mlle Léa at the races, for instance, with a little white hat and a little white sunshade—just delightful, I tell you. I would give a lot to have that little sunshade." I would have given a lot to understand what it was that made this little sunshade different from other sunshades; and for different reasons, related to feminine pleasure in appearance, Albertine would have given even more. But as Françoise used to say of her soufflés, "There's a knack to it," and the difference lay in the lines of the thing: "It was just small and round, like a Chinese parasol," Elstir said. I mentioned the sunshades of particular women, but, no, it was nothing like them. Elstir thought all these other sunshades were dreadful. He was a man of exact and exacting tastes, for whom a mere nothing, which was really everything, made the difference between what was worn by three-quarters of the women in the world, which he detested, and a single pretty thing which he thought charming, and which, unlike me (for I found luxury to have a numbing effect on the mind), filled him with the desire to paint and "try to make something as nice as that." "You see that girl there—she's someone who knows all about how that hat and sunshade looked," Elstir said, with a nod toward Albertine, who was gazing at him with a greedy gleam in her eye. "Oh, I'd love to be rich and have a yacht!" she said to the painter. "I'd ask your advice about fitting it out. Think of the lovely trips I could have in it! Wouldn't it be lovely to sail across to Cowes for the regatta! What about a car too? Do you think women's fashions for motoring are nice?" "No, I don't," Elstir said. "But that will come. There are so few dress-designers, you see, only one or two: Callot, for instance, though they go in rather too much for lacy things, Doucet, Cheruit, and from time to time Paquin.[103] But all the others are just rubbish." "So—is there such a huge difference between an outfit by Callot, say, and an average dressmaker?" I asked Albertine. " 'Huge' is the right word, young fellow!" she replied. "Oh, sorry! The only problem is, alas, that they charge you two thousand francs for what you can get for three hundred somewhere else! But, of course, it never looks the same—except to people who've got no idea, that is." "Precisely," Elstir said. "Though I wouldn't want to say the difference is as far-reaching as between a statue on the cathedral at Rheims and a statue in Saint-Augustin.[104] Speaking of cathedrals," he said to me, alluding to a conversation that the girls had taken no part in, and which would have been of no interest to them, "remember what I was saying the other day about the church of Balbec looking like a great cliff, a great outcrop of the stone of these parts? Well, have a look now at the opposite," he said, showing me a watercolor. "Look at those cliffs—it's a sketch done not far from here, at Les Creuniers[105]—see the power and delicacy in the way these rocks have been chiseled. Aren't they reminiscent of a cathedral?" They did resemble vast pink vaulted arches; but, having been painted on a very hot day, they appeared to have been turned to dust, pulverized by the heat, which, across the full breadth of the canvas, had also reduced the sea by half, diluting it to a haze. Illuminated in that way, reality had been almost destroyed by the light, but had been concentrated in dark, transparent creatures that by contrast gave a more vivid and faithful impression of being alive: the shadows. Gasping for coolness, most of them had abandoned the blaze of the open sea to cower under rocks, out of the sun's reach; others swam slowly on the surface like dolphins sidling along by moving boats, their sleek blue bodies broadening the hulls on the top of the pale water. It may have been their suggestion of a longing for coolness that gave the greatest impression of the heat of such a day, and made me exclaim with regret at not being familiar with Les Creuniers. Albertine and Andrée assured me that I must have been there dozens of times. In which case, it must have been without my knowledge, without my so much as suspecting that a day might come when the sight of them would give me such a yearning for beauty, not exactly the natural beauty I had hitherto sought in the cliffs about Balbec, but, rather, an architectural beauty. I could never have thought—having come there to set eyes on the realm of gales and tempests, having been on outings with Mme de Villeparisis when the ocean could only ever be seen in the distance, painted in the spaces between the trees, having never thought it real enough, liquid enough, alive enough, or giving a sufficient impression of the high seas tossing vast amounts of water about, having never wished to see it lie motionless except under a sheet of winter mist—that a day would come when the sea I would long for a glimpse of would be an expanse of whitish vapor, blanched of all consistency and color. It was the enchantment of this sea that Elstir, like the people who dozed in those boats held comatose by the heat, had experienced so profoundly that he had been able to capture and set down on his canvas the imperceptible ebbing of the tide, the throb and thrill of a minute of happiness; and to see it in this magic picture was to fall suddenly in love with it, to be filled with the resolve to seek out that vanished day, somewhere in the world, and savor it in all the dormant immediacy of its charm.

Whereas before my visits to Elstir's studio (before I had seen in one of his seascapes a young woman wearing a dress of *barège* or lawn, on the deck of a yacht flying the American flag, who imprinted the spiritual replica of a dress of white lawn and a flag in my imagination, giving it an instantaneous and insatiable desire to set eyes on dresses of white lawn and flags by the sea, as though I had never seen such a sight before) I had always striven, when looking at the sea, to exclude from my field of vision not only the bathers in the foreground but the yachts with their sails as excessively white as beach clothes—indeed, anything that prevented me from having the feeling I was gazing upon the timeless deep, whose mysterious existence had been rolling on unchanged since long before the first appearance of mankind, even the glorious weather that seemed to veil this foggy, gale-lashed coastline behind summer's trite and changeless aspect, filling it with an empty pause, the equivalent of what is called in music a rest—now, however, it was bad weather that seemed to have become the unfortunate accident and to have no place in the world of beauty; and so, burning with the desire to go and seek out from reality what had so stirred me, I hoped the day would be fine enough for me to see from the cliff top the same blue shadows as I had admired in Elstir's picture.

Nor could I continue, as we walked along, to blinker myself with my hands, as I had done in the days when I conceived of nature as being animated by a life of its own, dating from before the time of human beings and out of keeping with all these futile refinements of industry, which made me yawn with boredom at universal exhibitions or in dressmakers' displays, so as to see only the stretch of sea with no steamer on it, so as to go on imagining it as immemorial and still belonging, if not to that earliest era when it had been divided from the dry land, at least to the first centuries of ancient Greece, which enabled me to go on reciting to myself in all good faith the lines of "old Leconte" that Bloch was so fond of:

> Gone are the kings on their beakéd ships
> Bearing o'er the storm-tossed seas, alas,
> Those shaggy warriors of heroic Hellas.[106]

To despise dressmakers was no longer possible, since Elstir had said that the deft and gentle gesture with which they give a final ruffle, a last caress, to the bows and feathers of a just-completed hat was as much a challenge to his artistry as any movement by a jockey, a statement that had delighted Albertine. However, I could not hope to see a dressmaker till my return to Paris, or a horserace or a regatta till my return to Balbec, where no more were to be held until the following year. There was even a dearth of yachts with women on board wearing white lawn.

We would often encounter Bloch's sisters; and since I had dined at their father's table, I was obliged to greet them. My new friends did not know them. "I'm not allowed to be friends with children of Israel," Albertine said. Her way of pronouncing "Issrael" rather than "Izrael" would have been enough to let you know, even if you had not heard the beginning of her sentence, that the chosen people did not inspire warm feelings in the bosoms of these daughters of the middle class, who, with their good Catholic upbringing, probably believed that Jews fed on the flesh of infant Christians. "And anyway, there's something quite unseemly about your girlfriends," said Andrée, with a smile that meant she knew perfectly well they were not my friends. "As there is about the whole tribe," added Albertine, in the worldly-wise tone of the woman of experience. The fact was that Bloch's sisters, overdressed but half naked, managing to look both languid and brazen, resplendent and sluttish, did not create the best of impressions. And one of their cousins, a girl of no more than fifteen, shocked everyone at the Casino with her flagrant admiration for Mlle Léa, who, as an actress, was much to the taste of M. Bloch the elder, although her own tastes were reputed not to extend to gentlemen.

On some days, we would have tea in one of the neighborhood farm-house inns. These are the farms known as Les Écorres, the Marie-Thérèse, the Croix-d'Heuland, the Bagatelle, the Californie, and the Marie-Antoinette. It was the last of these that the little gang of girls had adopted.

Sometimes, though, instead of stopping at one of the farmhouses, we climbed to the top of the cliff; and, having reached our destination, we would sit on the grass and unwrap our sandwiches and cakes. The girls all preferred sandwiches and exclaimed at seeing me eat only a chocolate cake, with its Gothic architecture of icing, or an apricot tart. But sandwiches of Cheshire cheese and lettuce, untried and unknowing fare, had nothing to say for themselves. Whereas cakes were privy to much, and tarts were talkative. In cakes, there was a cloying creaminess, and in tarts, a refreshing fruitiness, which were aware of many things about Combray and about Gilberte, and not just the Gilberte of Combray days, but the Gilberte of Paris too, for I had renewed my acquaintance with them at her afternoon teas. They brought back the illustrated *Arabian Nights* side plates which had once afforded such a variety of entertainment to my aunt Léonie, depending on whether Françoise brought her one day *Aladdin and His Wonderful Lamp* or, on another day, *Ali Baba* or *The Sleeper Awakes* or *Sinbad the Sailor Taking Ship at Basra with All His Riches*. I wished I could see them again, but my grandmother did not know what had become of them; and in any case she believed they were just vulgar old plates, which had been bought locally. Even so, their multicolored vignettes glowed among the grayness of Combray-in-Champagne,[107] like the shimmer of the jeweled windows in the dark of its church, the illuminations from the magic lantern in the twilight of my bedroom, the buttercups from the Indies and the lilacs from Persia in the foreground of the view of the railway station and the little local line, or the collection of old Chinese porcelain at my great-aunt's, an old lady's gloomy house in a country town.

Lying there on the cliff top, I could see nothing but meadows; and above them stretched not the seven superimposed heavens of Christian physics, but only two, one of which was darker—the sea—and the other, on top of it, lighter. We would enjoy our picnic; and then, if I had brought with me a trinket of some sort that I thought one or another of the girls might like to have, their translucent faces would instantly turn red with such a vehement surge of joy that their mouths could not contain it, and they would burst into laughter. They were grouped about me; and between their faces, which were close together, the airy spaces were like azure paths, such as a gardener might make in order to move around in his rose garden.

Once we had eaten, we would play at games that would hitherto have seemed boring to me, some of them real children's games, such as "The King of the Barbarees" or "Who's Going to Laugh First?," which I would not have missed now for anything; the dawn flush of youth which still glowed in the faces of the girls, which had already faded from mine, shone on everything about them and, like the fluid painting of certain primitives, brought out against a background of gold the most insignificant details of their lives. The faces of most of them were indistinctly suffused by their daybreak's indiscriminate bloom, concealing the real features that would one day show through. All that was visible was an enchantment of coloring, behind which the profile of years to come was not yet distinguishable. The present profile was quite undefinitive; it might have been nothing more than a transient likeness to some long-dead relative, to whom nature accorded this commemorative acknowledgment. The moment comes so soon when there is nothing left to hope for, when the body is static, held in a state of immobility that promises no further surprises, when disappointment sets in at the sight of faces which, though still youthful, are framed by hair already thinning or fading, like leaves hanging dead on midsummer trees, when the brevity of their radiant early morning makes one able to love only very young girls, in whom the unleavened flesh, like a precious dough, has not yet risen. They are malleable, a soft flow of substance kneaded by every passing impression that possesses them. Each of them looks like a brief succession of little statuettes, representing gaiety, childish solemnity, fond coquettishness, amazement, every one of them modeled by an expression that is full and frank, but fleeting. This plasticity lends much variety and great charm to a girl who is trying her best to be nice to us. These qualities are of course indispensable in the grown woman too; and in our eyes, any woman who does not like us, or does not show that she likes us, takes on a depressing uniformity of manner. But after a certain age, even such graces are reflected only faintly in a face that the struggles of life have hardened into an immutable mask of righteousness or ecstasy. One face, through the relentless workings of the obedience that subjects helpmeet to husband, resembles a soldier's rather than a wife's; another, sculpted by the sacrifices a mother makes day in, day out, for the sake of her children, is an apostle's. A third, after years of hopes blighted and storms weathered, is the face of an old sea-dog, in a woman whose clothes alone reveal her sex. Of course, the loving attentions of a woman we love can still enchant the hours we spend with her. But she is not a series of different women to us. Her gaiety remains external to her unchanging face. Adolescence, however, comes before complete stabilization, and what is so refreshing in the presence of young girls is this spectacle of ceaselessly changing forms, reminiscent in its restless contrasts of the perpetual re-creation of nature's primordial elements that we witness by the sea.

Fashionable gatherings and Mme de Villeparisis's invitations to carriage outings were not the only pastimes I was willing to sacrifice to my games of ring-on-a-string and riddles with the girls. Robert de Saint-Loup had several times sent me word that, since I never went to visit him at Doncières, he had requested twenty-four hours' leave to come to Balbec. On each of these occasions I wrote to put him off, inventing the excuse of a family visit I said I was obliged to make that very day with my grandmother. He must have thought badly of me when he learned from his aunt the nature of this family visit and the identity of the people who were my grandmother for the occasion. Yet, in sacrificing not just the joys of foregathering with the fashionable, but the joys of friendship too, to the pleasure of dallying the whole day in this lovely garden, perhaps I was not ill advised. Those who have the opportunity to live for themselves—they are artists, of course, and I was long since convinced that I would never be one—also have the duty to do so; and for them, friendship is a dereliction of that duty, a form of self-abdication. Even conversation, which is friendship's mode of expression, is a superficial digression, through which we can make no acquisition. We may converse our whole life away without speaking anything other than the interminable repetitions that fill the vacant minute; but the steps of thought we take during the lonely work of artistic creation all lead us downward, deeper into ourselves, the only direction that is not closed to us, the only direction in which we can advance, albeit with much greater travail, toward an outcome of truth. Moreover, friendship is not just devoid of virtue, as conversation is, it is actively pernicious. Those of us whose law of growth is one of purely internal growth, and who cannot escape the impression of boredom inseparable from the presence of a friend, an impression that comes from having to stay at the surface of the self, instead of sounding our depths for the discoveries that await us, can only be tempted by friendship, once we are alone, to disbelieve this impression, to let ourselves be retrospectively moved by the words spoken by our friend, to see them as the sharing of something valuable; whereas we are not like a building to which a brick or a stone can be added on the outside, but, rather, like a tree, which distills from its own sap each new knot in its trunk and the next layer of its foliage. I lied to myself, I stunted my growth in the very direction that could lead me to genuine progress and happiness, each time I took pride in being liked and admired by a person as kind, as intelligent, as sought after as Saint-Loup, by adapting my mind not to my own confused impressions, which it should have been my duty to decipher, but to the words spoken by my friend, in which, as I repeated them to myself—or, rather, as I listened to them being repeated by that person other than ourself who lives in us, and by whom we are always glad to be freed from the onus of thinking—I sought to find a mode of beauty that was a far cry from the beauty I sought in the silence of my real solitude, but which I hoped might add merit to Robert, and to myself, while making my life more worthwhile. In the life his friendship made for me, I could see myself as cozily protected from solitude, and full of a noble aspiration to self-sacrifice for his benefit—in a word, deprived of the power of self-realization. When I was with the girls, however, though the pleasure I took in being there was selfish, at least it was not founded on a lie: the lie that tries to have us believe we are not inescapably alone in the world, and which, when we converse with someone, prevents us from admitting that it is not we who are speaking, that at such times we try to take on the semblance of other people, rather than be the self that differs from them. When we spoke, which was not often, the things said by me and the girls of the little gang were without interest; and on my part, they were interrupted by long silences. This did not prevent me from listening to what the girls said with as much pleasure as when just looking at them, discovering through the voice of each of them the vividly colored picture of her. It was a delight to listen to their piping chorus. Loving sharpens discernment and our power to make distinctions. In a wood, a bird-watcher's ear will instantly pick out the chirps and warbles peculiar to different species that the uninstructed cannot tell apart. The fancier of young girls knows that human voices are even more varied. Each of them has a wider range of notes than the most versatile instrument; and the combinations it can make of them are as inexhaustible as the infinite variety of personalities. When I chatted with one of the girls, I noticed that the outline of her individuality, original and unique, was ingeniously drawn and ruthlessly imposed upon me as much by the modulations of her voice as by the shifting expressions of her face, and that I was confronted by two performances, each of which rendered in its own mode the same singular reality. The lines of the voice, like those of the face, were not yet fixed once and for all: the former would deepen, the latter would develop. As infants possess a gland whose secretions help them digest milk, which grownups no longer have, the lilt of the girls' light voices struck notes that women's never reach. On their more adaptable instrument they played with their lips, with all Bellini's musical cherubs' diligence and ardor,[108] which also belong exclusively to youth. Later they would lose their accents of eager earnestness, which gave a charm to whatever they said, however simple it was, whether it was the authoritative voice used by Albertine for making puns, which the younger ones listened to admiringly until, with the irresistible violence of a sneeze, they suddenly burst into giggles, or the essentially childish solemnity with which Andrée spoke of their schoolwork, which was even more child's play than their play; and their words struck strangely different notes, like those strophes from ancient times in which poetry, still seen as not far removed from music, was chanted on a range of tones. In each of the voices there somehow managed to sound the viewpoint on life already adopted by these green girls, a bias with such an individuality to it that to define them by common terms such as "She takes everything with a laugh," or "She always lays down the law," or "She's forever in a state of cautious expectation," would be to use a statement far too broad in its application. The features of our face are little more than expressions ingrained by habit. Nature, like the catastrophe at Pompeii or the metamorphosis of a nymph, freezes us into an accustomed cast of countenance. In the same way, the intonations of our voice express our philosophy of life, what one says to oneself at each moment about things. The facial features of these girls did not, of course, belong just to them: they belonged to their parents. As individuals, each of us lives immersed in something more general than ourselves. Parents, for that

matter, do not hand on only the habitual act of a facial and vocal feature, but also turns of phrase, certain special sayings, which are almost
as deeply rooted and unconscious as an inflection, and imply as much
as it does a point of view on life. It is true that some of these set phrases
parents cannot hand on to young girls until they are of less tender
years, usually after they have married. Such expressions are held in reserve. If, for example, the talk turned to the paintings of a certain friend
of Elstir's, Andrée, with her girlish waist-length hair, was not at liberty
to say of him what her mother and married sister might have said: "I'm
told that, *as a man,* he is quite a charmer." But one day, like the permission to walk in the gardens of the Palais-Royal, that would come. Certainly Albertine had been saying since the time of her first communion,
copying one of her aunt's lady friends, "Well, I think that would be
pretty terrific." Another present she had received was her way of having
you repeat things you had just said, so as to appear interested in the
subject and give herself the air of wishing to form a personal view on it.
If someone said the work of this or that painter was good, or that he
had a nice house, she would say, "So his work's good, is it?" or "Is that
so, a nice house?" Also, more general features than these family heir-
looms were the body and redolence given to their whole speech by the
far-flung regions of France from which their voices came, and which flavored their intonations. Whenever Andrée gave a sharp twang to a deep
note, she could not prevent the Périgourdine string in her vocal instrument from singing its little provincial song, in harmony with the south-
western purity of her profile; and Rosemonde's perpetual pranking and
skittishness were a perfect match for her regional accent, which could
not help shaping the northern substance of which her face and her
voice were made. My ear enjoyed the bright dialogue between the province of origin and the temperament producing each girl's inflections, a
dialogue that never turned to discord. Nothing can come between a girl
and the part of the country from which she hails: she is it. Such reaction of local materials on the genius of the one who exploits them, and
whom it invigorates, does not make the outcome less individual; and
whether the work produced is that of an architect, a cabinetmaker, or
a composer, its minutely detailed reflection of the most distinctive

touches of the artist's personality is no less faithful because he had to work in the coarse buhrstone of Senlis or red sandstone from Strasbourg, because he put to good use the knots peculiar to ash, because his writing took account of possibilities and limitations in the sound range offered by the flute or the viola.

I was aware of all this, and yet we hardly ever had a conversation! With Mme de Villeparisis or Saint-Loup, my words would have made a show of much more enjoyment than I really felt, concealing the fact that they always wore me out; whereas, when I lay among those girls, the full cup of my joy, unaffected by the insignificance and sparseness of what we said, brimming in motionless silence, overflowed and let the murmuring wavelets of my happiness lap and ripple among these young roses.

No convalescent who rests all day long in a flower garden or an orchard is more aware of the scents of flowers and fruit, coloring the countless minutiae that sweeten his idle well-being, than I was of the tones and aromas that the presence of the girls fed to my feasting eyes, gradually permeating me with their deliciousness. Thus grapes mellow in the sunshine. The leisurely repetitiousness of the simple games we played had brought out in me, as in someone who just lies on a beach, relishing the salty air and the sun on the skin, a reveling in relaxation, a blissfully indulgent smile, an unfocused daze of the delighted eyes.

Now and then one or another of the girls would favor me in a way that sent a shock wave of pleasure through me and weakened my desire for any of the others. One day Albertine said, "Who's got a pencil, then?" Andrée supplied it, Rosemonde proffered some paper, and Albertine said, "All right, ladies, I forbid you to read what I'm writing." She took much trouble over shaping each letter, resting the paper on her knees; then she handed it to me, saying, "Make sure no one can read this." I unfolded it and read the words she had written: *I like you.*

"Look here!" she shouted to Andrée and Rosemonde, turning suddenly impetuous and serious. "Instead of sitting around writing silly things, why don't I show you this letter I got from Gisèle this morning? How stupid of me! It's been sitting in my pocket all this time, and it could be so useful to us!" Gisèle had had the idea of enclosing the composition she had written for her fourth-year examination, so that Albertine could show it to the others. The forebodings Albertine had expressed about the difficulty of the essays had been more than borne out by the two topics, of which Gisèle had had to choose one: "Writing to Racine from the Underworld, Sophocles commiserates with him over the failure of *Athalie*"; and "Imagine that Mme de Sévigné, having seen the first performance of Racine's *Esther*, writes a letter to Mme de Lafayette to say how much she wishes the latter could have been there too." Gisèle, whose willingness to please must have touched the examiners, had chosen the first and more difficult of the two subjects, in which she had acquitted herself so well that her essay had been marked at fourteen out of twenty; and she had even been specially commended by the examiners. Altogether, they would have awarded her a pass with distinction had she not "flopped" in her Spanish exam. Albertine now read aloud to us the copy of the essay Gisèle had sent; she was soon to sit the same examination herself and felt much in need of some advice from Andrée, who, being by far the cleverest of them all, might be able to give her some good tips. "She's as lucky as anything!" Albertine said. "She got to choose one of the subjects her French teacher made her bone up on when she was here!" Sophocles' letter to Racine, as drafted by Gisèle, began like this: "Dear Racine, Do forgive me for presuming to write like this without having the honor of being personally acquainted with you, but your new tragedy *Athalie* suggests that you yourself have a close acquaintance with my own modest productions. You have not only put verse into the mouths of the protagonists (the leading characters of the piece) but have also composed other lines—full of charm, if I may say so without incurring a suspicion of toadying—to be spoken by the chorus, which some have said was quite a good thing in Greek tragedy, but is a real novelty in France. Furthermore, your talent, which is such a graceful one, so delicate, so charming, so fine, so painstaking, has displayed itself so consummately that it deserves my congratulation. In Athalie and Joad, you have brought off a pair of characters whom your rival Corneille could not have developed better. You present personalities who are forceful, and a plot that is simple and solid. Here is a tragedy without love as its mainspring, on which I compliment you most sincerely. The most famous precepts are not always the truest ones. Let me quote as an example what Boileau says about love:

> 'Tis this passion that through the poet's art
> Best makes a pathway to the reader's heart.[109]

You show that religious feeling, as chanted by your chorus, is no less capable of touching the heart. The vulgar may be disaffected, but true connoisseurs salute you. Please accept the warmest admiration of one who begs to remain, my dear Racine, your most humble and obedient servant, etc."

As Albertine read, her eyes had been sparkling; and as soon as she had finished, she burst out: "I bet you she copied it! I wouldn't think Gisèle could write a thing like this all by herself. I mean, look at the poetry she quotes—where do you think she pinched it?" Her admiration, now shifting its focus to Andrée, continued to make her eyes "start out of her head," as did the close attention she paid to Andrée's words when the latter, in her capacity as the most senior and the best at French, commented on Gisèle's essay with a touch of irony at first, then redrafted the letter in her own way, with an air of lightheartedness that barely concealed true earnestness. "It's not bad," she said to Albertine. "But if I were you, having to write on that subject—and that's perfectly possible, you know, because it's one they set quite a lot—I wouldn't do it like that. Here's what I'd do: For one thing, if I'd been Gisèle, I wouldn't have plunged in straight away. I'd have started by writing out my plan on a separate page. On the first line, the statement of the question and the setting out of the subject. Next, the broad ideas to be brought into the discussion. And then, at the end, the appreciation, the style, and the conclusion. If you follow an outline like that, you always know where you're going. You see, Titine, right from the setting out of the subject, or, if you like, since it's a letter, right from the opening salutation, Gisèle went and muffed it. I mean, if he's writing to a man in the seventeenth century, Sophocles shouldn't say 'Dear Racine.'" "I know!" Albertine interjected, full of passion. "She should've made him

say 'My dear M. Racine.' That'd be much better." "Not at all," Andrée
replied in a slightly supercilious voice. "She should have put just 'Sir.'
And at the end she should have put something like 'While assuring you
of the high esteem in which I hold you, I remain, sir (or at the most
dear sir), yours etc.' Also, Gisèle says the chorus is a novelty in
Athalie, but she's forgetting *Esther*, as well as two other little-known
tragedies that the examiner himself has just written an analysis of this
year! So he's got a real bee in his bonnet about them, and all anyone
has to do to pass is mention them; they're called *Les Juives* by Robert
Garnier and *Aman* by Antoine de Montchrestien."[110] As she spoke these
names and titles, Andrée was unable to conceal a little smirk of indulgent self-satisfaction, which was not without charm. Albertine burst
out: "Andrée, you're a wonder! Write down those two titles for me. Just
think—if I got that subject, even just in the oral exam, I could quote
them straight away and really take his breath away!" (After that, every
time Albertine asked Andrée to say the names and titles again, so that
she could make a note of them, her well-read friend said she had forgotten them; and she never in fact repeated them.) "The next thing," Andrée said, in a tone of faint disdain for these more childish friends,
though glad of their admiration, and investing more self-esteem than
she meant to show in this matter of how she would have dealt with
the essay, "is that Sophocles in the Underworld is bound to be well
informed—he must know that *Athalie* wasn't performed for the vulgar,
but for the Sun King himself and a few privileged courtiers. Mind you,
what Gisèle says about true connoisseurs is really quite good, but it
doesn't go far enough. I mean, Sophocles is now immortal, so it would
be quite all right for him to have the gift of second sight, and be able to
predict that Voltaire will come along and say *Athalie* is 'not just the
masterpiece of Racine, but of the whole human spirit.' "[111] Albertine, her
eyes glowing with concentration, was not missing a single word of what
Andrée was saying: she declined indignantly Rosemonde's suggestion
that they should start a game. "And then," Andrée said, in the same detached, casual voice, with a tone of slight mockery and rather heartfelt
conviction, "if Gisèle had bothered to jot down the broad ideas she was
going to include in her discussion, she might have thought of doing

what I would have done: show the difference in religious inspiration between Sophocles' chorus and Racine's. I'd have made Sophocles point
out that, though Racine's chorus is as full of religious feeling as the
choruses in Greek tragedy, it's not for the same gods. The God of Joad
has got nothing to do with the god of Sophocles. And that would
lead naturally into the concluding question, after the end of the development. 'What does it matter that the beliefs are not the same?'
Sophocles would make a point of insisting on this, not wishing to hurt
Racine's feelings, and would then slip in a few words about the latter's
masters at Port-Royal, by way of congratulating his rival on his high-
minded poetic spirit."

Albertine, warmed by her efforts of admiration and attention, had
broken out in a sweat; whereas Andrée had the cool, self-possessed smile
of a female dandy. "It would be a good idea too to quote the views of a
few famous critics," she said, just before we started another game. "So
I've been told," Albertine said. "The best opinions to use are usually
Sainte-Beuve's and Merlet's, aren't they?" "You're not completely mistaken," said Andrée, still refusing to write down the other two names, despite Albertine's pleas. "Sainte-Beuve and Merlet are quite good. But the
ones you've *got* to quote are Deltour and Gasc-Desfossés."[112]

I had been thinking about Albertine's little slip of paper torn from
the notepad—*I like you*—and an hour later, climbing down the paths back
to Balbec, a little too steep for my liking, I was thinking she was the one
who would be the great love of my life.

No doubt my state of mind, marked by the presence of symptoms
that we usually interpret as meaning we are in love—such as the orders I
gave at the hotel that I was not to be disturbed for any visitor unless it
was one of the girls; the palpitations with which I waited for whichever
of them I was expecting to come; and my rage on those days if I had
been unable to find a barber to shave me and was obliged to appear
unkempt to the eyes of Albertine, Rosemonde, or Andrée—and which
shifted at will from one of them to another, was as different from what
we call love as human life differs from the life of zoophytes, in which
existence or individuality, so to speak, is divided among different organisms. Yet natural history teaches that such an animal, thus organized,

can be observed; and the life of any of us who have lived a little is no less instructive about the reality of states of mind of which we once lived in total ignorance, to which we are bound to come, though very likely also bound to grow out of at a later stage; and for me that was the loving state, simultaneously divided among several young girls, in which I lived. Divided, or, rather, undivided, for more often than not what I found delightful and different from everything else in the world, what had begun to endear itself to me so intensely that the sweetest joy in life was the hope of being with them again the next day, was really the whole group of girls, taken together, inseparable from those breezy afternoon hours up on the cliffs, on that stretch of grass where their faces lay, full of excitement for my imagination, Albertine, Rosemonde, Andrée, making it impossible for me to know which of them made this place so precious, which of them I most longed to love. At the very beginning of love, as at its end, we are not exclusively attached to a single beloved: it is the yearning to love, of which that person will be the loved outcome, and later the echo left in the memory, that wanders voluptuously in a place full of charms—sometimes deriving only from contingencies of nature, bodily pleasures, or habitation—interchangeable and interrelated enough for it to feel in harmony with any of them. Also, since my perceptions of the girls were at that time unsated by habit, whenever I was with them I was still able to see them—that is, to be profoundly surprised by setting eyes on them. This feeling of surprise can be explained in part no doubt by the fact that it is a new side that the person shows us each time; but there is such multiplicity in each woman, such richness in the lines of her face and body, so little of which is preserved during her absence by our high-handed and simple-minded memory, it having opted to single out one particular feature of her that has struck us, to isolate and exaggerate it, turning a woman who appeared to be tall into a study in elongated disproportion, or one who seemed pink and blond into a pure *Harmony in Pink and Gold*, that when we are once again in her presence we are beset by the complex confusion of all her other forgotten features, which balanced the one we have retained, and now reduce her height, dilute her pink, replacing the exclusive object of our anticipation with other particulars, which we now recall having noticed the last time and find it incomprehensible that we should not have looked forward to seeing again. Our recollection, our expectation, was of a peacock; the reality is a bullfinch. Nor is this inevitable surprise the only one that awaits us: there is another sort that comes not from the disparate stylizations of the remembered and the real, but from the difference between the person we saw on the previous occasion and the one we have before us today, seen from a new point of view and now showing a hitherto undisclosed aspect. The human face is truly like that of a god in some Oriental theogony, a whole cluster of faces side by side, but on different planes and never all visible at once.

But, then again, much of our surprise comes also from the very fact that the person does show the same aspect. It would take such a huge effort to re-create whatever we have derived from outside ourselves, even just the taste of a certain fruit, say, that as soon as we receive the slightest impression we slide gradually down memory's gentle slope; and before long, without realizing it, we have gone a long way from what we really felt. Each new encounter is a readjustment, bringing us back to what we in fact saw. Faithful recollection of it was already lost, since what is called remembering somebody is actually a process of forgetting. For as long as we are still capable of seeing, however, no sooner does the forgotten feature impinge on our sight than we recognize it, and are obliged to straighten the line that had deviated; and so the rich and ever-ready surprise that made my daily encounters with these lovely young girls by the sea so beneficial and refreshing was a thing not only of discovery but of retrieval. Add to that the commotion inspired in me by what they meant to me (a commotion that was never quite what I thought it would be; and what I looked forward to each time was not what I had looked forward to the previous time, that having been supplanted by the thrill of the memory of our last meeting) and it will be clear that each of our outings suddenly turned my thoughts in a wholly unexpected direction; and this direction was never the one which, in the seclusion of my room at the hotel, I had foreseen and calmly reconnoitered. It was now forgotten, abolished, each time I came back to my room, my head buzzing like a hive with words that had stirred me and went on reverberating for a long time in my mind. A person lost sight of is a person destroyed; a person who reappears is a new creation, different from the one before, and possibly from all previous incarnations. The minimum number of varieties that can exist in such creations is two. When what stays in our mind is the vivid flash of a bold glance, inevitably what will take us by surprise in our next glimpse, almost solely strike us, that is, will be a look close to languid, a gentle and pensive expression, overlooked in the former memory. It is this which, in our comparison of memory with the new reality, will color our disappointment or our surprise; and by its notifying us that our memory had been defective, it will seem to be reality itself that was in need of refocusing. Then the aspect of the face that was recently overlooked, having now become for that reason the most unforgettable, the most real, the most accurately corrective, will itself become an object for us to dream about and recall. What we long for now is a soft, languorous look, an expression full of gentle pensiveness. Then the same thing will happen the next time: it will be the strange determination in the piercing eyes, the pointed nose, and the tense lips that will cancel the disparity between our desire and the object it thought it had in mind. Of course, this fidelity to first impressions, the purely physical ones, which I re-encountered each time I saw the girls, was an effect not just of their facial features, since, as has been seen, I was also responsive to their voices (more responsive perhaps, for the voice not only offers the same singular and sensual surfaces as the facial features, it belongs to those unplumbable depths tempting us to the vertiginous peril of impossible kisses), in each of which sounded the unique note of a little instrument utterly expressive of its owner and playable by no one but her. A dark line in any of their voices, drawn by one of their intonations, surprised me each time I recognized it again, after having forgotten it. And the corrections I had to make, on each new occasion, so as to retrieve perfect accuracy, were as much those required of a tuner or a singing teacher as of a draftsman.

The various waves of feeling sent through me by the different girls, neutralized for a time by the resistance each of them set against the expansion of the others, were held in a harmony of cohesion which was to be disturbed in Albertine's favor one afternoon during a game of ring-on-a-string. We were playing in a little wood on the cliff top. My place was between two girls who did not belong to the little gang, who had been brought along just to make up the numbers needed for the game, and I kept gazing with envy at the person sitting beside Albertine, a young fellow, thinking that if only I had been her neighbor during these minutes, which might not come back, I could have known the fortuitous thrill of touching her hands, which might have led to all sorts of consequences. Even without such possibilities, the mere touch of her hands would have been a delight to me. Not that I had never seen hands more lovely than hers: without going beyond the little group itself, Andrée's hands were finer by far, slender and delicate, with a life all of their own, entirely docile and obedient, yet independent, often to be seen lying by her, like noble greyhounds, stretching lazily, idling in a dream, or suddenly flexing a knuckle, postures in which Elstir had made several studies of them. In one of these studies, in which Andrée could be seen warming them by the hearth, they glowed in the firelight with the golden transparency of two autumn leaves. Albertine's hands, however, which were fleshier, briefly gave, then tensed, under the pressure of any hand that held them, responding with an unmistakable sensation. A squeeze from the hand of Albertine had a sensual softness which seemed at one with the slightly mauve pink of her skin: it made you feel as though you were penetrating her, entering the privacy of her senses, an impression one had too from her resounding laugh, which was as suggestive of indecency as any throaty murmur of invitation, or as certain cries. She was one of those women whose hand it is such a pleasure to take and hold that one is grateful to civilized convention for having made the handshake a licit act between young men and girls when they meet. If the arbitrary habits of politeness had replaced shaking hands by some other mode of contact, my days would have been spent in gazing at the untouchable hands of Albertine, pining for the feel of them as acutely as I now yearned to be familiar with the taste of her cheeks. If I had been beside her in the game of ring-on-a-string, the joy of holding her hands between mine for a long time would not have been the only fulfillment I could foresee: what confessions, what declarations, unspoken by my shyness till now, I could put into this or that way of pressing her hand! How easy it would have been for her too, to hint in reply by other gentle pressings that she welcomed them! What complicity! What first steps toward sensuous delight! My love could make more progress in those few minutes sitting beside her than in all the time since I had known her. I could not bear it, just sitting there, knowing the brief time was running out, because this little game would very likely not last much longer, and once it was over it would be too late. So I made sure to get caught holding the ring and had to take my place in the middle: then, while pretending not to see the ring passing from hand to hand, I kept an eye on it, waiting for it to reach the hands of the fellow beside Albertine. She was laughing for all she was worth, pink and glowing with the joy and animation of the game. Andrée, with a nod toward the trees around us and an allusion to the words of the song, said, "We're *in* the pretty greenwood," and sent me a special smiling glance, as it were over the heads of the other players, as though she and I were the only ones clever enough to step outside ourselves for a moment and make a poetical reflection on the game we were playing. Though her voice sounded reluctant, her fine wit made her sing, "The ring in the wood, my ladies, the ring in the pretty greenwood," as though she were one of those people who cannot go to Trianon[113] without organizing a party in Louis XVI costumes, or who think it is jolly to hear a song sung in the setting for which it was written. I too would have been pleased to see the charm of this arrangement, had I had the mental leisure to think of it. But my mind was on other things. All the players, boys and girls alike, were beginning to exclaim in surprise at my stupidity in not snatching the ring. I was engrossed in watching Albertine, sitting there in all her beauty, her gaiety, and her indifference to me, unaware that she would soon have me beside her, as soon as I could catch the ring when it was in the right hands, having first made sure that she could not suspect me of having done it by design, for this ploy, I knew, would only annoy her. Some of her long tresses having come undone in the heat of the game, clusters of curls hung about her cheeks, the crisp dark brown setting off the perfect pink of her complexion. Getting closer to her, I murmured in her ear, "Your hair's like

Laura Dianti's and Eleanor of Aquitaine's, or her descendant who was Chateaubriand's sweetheart.[114] I wish you would always let your hair hang a little loose like that." The ring was suddenly in the hands of the person beside her: I grabbed at them, forced them open, and snatched it; he was the one who had to take my place in the middle, and I sat myself down beside Albertine. Only a few minutes before, I had been envying this fellow, who, each time I saw him slide his hands to and fro along the string, could touch hers. Now that I had the chance to do the same, I was too shy to seek her touch and too excited to enjoy it, conscious of nothing but the accelerated and painful thudding of my own heart. At one point, Albertine leaned toward me, a conspiratorial look on her plump pink face, pretending to have the ring, so as to trick the one in the middle into looking away from where it really was. I was perfectly aware that this feint was the purpose of her suggestive glances; yet there was a thrill in this glimpse into a secret shared between us, even one that was mere make-believe for the duration of a game, which, though nonexistent, instantly seemed a possibility, a delicious consummation to be wished for. In that moment of intoxication, I sensed a tiny squeeze of Albertine's hand on mine, a faint caress of her finger between my own, and I caught a wink from her that she meant to be barely perceptible. All at once a host of hopes, which had been invisible to me, took firm shape, and my joy sang within me: "She's taking advantage of the game to let me know how much she likes me!" My song was cut off by a furious stage-whisper from Albertine: "Take the thing, would you! I've been trying to pass it to you for about half an hour!" Abashed and deflated, I lost my grip on the string; the fellow in the middle saw the ring and dived on it; and I had to go back into the middle, where, as the shuffling hands did their frantic shuttle around me, I stood desperate and despised, the butt of all the girls' scorn, trying to laugh it off when I felt like crying, while Albertine kept saying, "People that don't want to play properly or just try to spoil it for the others shouldn't play. Next time we want to play this, Andrée, we'll just make sure he doesn't come. Or, if he does come, then I won't." Andrée, who found the game too easy and who was still singing her little "Greenwood" song, which Rosemonde had taken up too, in halfhearted imitation, said to me, trying to make up for Albertine's complaints, "You know Les Creuniers, which you said you wanted to see—they're not far from here, along a lovely little lane. If you like, I'll take you there, and these sillies can stay here and go on behaving like eight-year-olds." Andrée was always very nice to me, so as we walked I told her everything about Albertine that might endear me to the latter and make her love me. Andrée said she was also very fond of Albertine and thought she was a dear; but the complimentary things I said about her friend did not seem to please her much. Then, halfway down the little lane, I stood still, as the soft flutter of a childhood memory brushed my heart: I had just recognized, from the indentations of the shiny leaves overhanging the threshold, a hawthorn bush, which since the end of spring, alas, had been bare of all blossom. A fragrance of forgotten months of Mary and long-lost Sunday afternoons, beliefs, and fallacies surrounded me. I wished I could grasp it as it passed. Andrée, seeing me pause, showed her charming gift of insight by letting me commune for a moment with the leaves of the little tree: I asked after its blossom, hawthorn flowers like blithe young girls, a little silly, flirtatious, and faithful. "Those young ladies left long ago," said the leaves, possibly reflecting that, for someone who professed to be such a close friend, I was very uninformed about their habits. I *was* a close friend, though one who, despite his promises, had lost touch with them for many years. Yet, just as Gilberte had been my first sweetheart among the girls, they had been my first among the flowers. "Yes, I know," I replied, "they go away about the middle of June. But it's a pleasure to see the spot here where they lived. My mother brought them up to see me in my bedroom at Combray, when I was ill. And we used to meet in church on Saturday evenings during the month of Mary. Are they allowed to go here too?" "Of course! My young ladies are actually much in demand at the nearest parish church, Saint-Denis-du-Désert." "One can see them now, you mean?" "No, no, not till the month of May next year." "And can I be sure they'll be there?" "Every year, without fail." "I'm just not sure I can find my way back to this exact spot. . . ." "Of course you will! My young ladies are so gay, they never stop laughing, except to sing hymns—you can't mistake them, you'll recognize their perfume from the end of the lane."

I walked back toward Andrée and went on singing Albertine's praises. I spoke so emphatically that I had no doubt she was bound to repeat my words to Albertine. Despite this, I was never to learn whether Albertine heard a word of what I said about her. And yet Andrée was vastly more perceptive in things of the heart, more gifted with considerateness: to be nice to others with a carefully chosen word or a thoughtful glance, to keep to herself a remark that might hurt somebody's feelings, to sacrifice (while making it appear that it was no sacrifice) an hour of possible playtime, even an outing to a matinee or a garden party, for a friend who was feeling sad, so as to show him or her that she preferred such simple moments to indulging in frivolous pastimes, these were everyday acts of kindness for Andrée. Then, when you came to know her a little better, she put you in mind of those people whose poltroonery, through their reluctance to be afraid, can rise to heroism of a particularly meritorious kind: it seemed as though in her heart of hearts there was no trace of the constant kindness which, out of moral nobility, responsiveness to others, and a magnanimous desire to appear the devoted friend, so marked her conduct. From the charming things she said about the possibility of Albertine and me loving each other, one might have thought she would do everything conceivable to bring it about. Yet, perhaps unintentionally, despite all the tiny things it was within her power to do to bring us together, she never once did any of them; and though my own efforts to be loved by Albertine may not have made her friend resort to guile, with the aim of thwarting my desire, I wish I could swear they did not cause her anger; though, if they did, she hid it well, and her own sense of decency may have made her resist it. Andrée's behavior showed many touches of kindness that Albertine would have been incapable of; yet I had no conviction of Andrée's genuine goodness of heart, such as I later came to have of Albertine's. Andrée's softhearted indulgence of Albertine's exuberant frivolity expressed itself in words and smiles full of friendliness; and her actions too were those of a friend. I was to see her, day after day, trying to promote the happiness of this friend who was poorer than she was, by letting her share a little in the luxury she could afford; and without the slightest self-interest, she put herself to more trouble than a courtier seeking to ingratiate himself with a monarch. If anybody expressed sympathy with the plight of Albertine in her poverty, it was always Andrée, full of a plaintive gentleness, who found the words of sympathy and charm; and she put herself out for Albertine much more than she would ever have done for a friend who was rich. However, if anyone should hint that Albertine was perhaps not as poor as it might be thought, a faint cloud would veil Andrée's eyes and brow, and she seemed to be in a bad mood. If it was suggested that Albertine's marriage prospects might not be as bad as was supposed, Andrée scotched the notion and repeated in a furious tone, "Of *course* the girl's unmarriageable! I don't need to be told— I think it's terrible!" As for myself, she was the only one of the whole group of girls who would never have repeated to me some hurtful thing that had been said about me; nor was this all—if I myself told her of some such thing, she would pretend to disbelieve it, or else she ex- plained it away as meaning something quite innocuous. These qualities, taken together, are what is known as tact. It is to be found in the man who compliments you on having fought a duel, then adds that there was no need for you to take up the insult, thereby magnifying in your own eyes the courage you showed without being obliged to. Such a man is the opposite of those people who greet the same event with the words, "What a bore it must have been to fight a duel! Although of course you couldn't let him get away with such an insult—you really had no choice." However, there being pros and cons in all things, if the pleasure taken by friends in retailing to us something insulting said about us, or at least their indifference to its potential to hurt us, proves they are deficient in fellow-feeling, at least at the moment when they are speaking, sticking their pins into us, stabbing us with their knives as though we were some sort of stuffed dummy, then the contrary art of always hiding from us whatever nasty things they may have heard about our actions, or the private views they may have formed about these same actions, may prove that this other group of friends, the tactful ones, are experts in dissimulation. Not that there need be anything bad about that, if it means they are incapable of thinking evil, or if the evil spoken of us wounds them as they know it would wound us. I suspected this was the case with Andrée, though I could never be completely sure.

By now we were out of the little wood and into a network of rather deserted lanes, which Andrée followed without difficulty. "Well, here we are!" she said all at once. "Here are Les Creuniers for you! And you're in luck—the weather today and the light are just as in Elstir's watercolor." But the game of ring-on-a-string had knocked my high hopes from under me, and I was too sad to take the pleasure I might otherwise have enjoyed in suddenly coming upon the sea divinities whom Elstir had watched for and taken by surprise: there they were, directly beneath me, crouching among the rocks for protection against the rays of the sun, under the glow of a dark glaze as beautiful as any used by Leonardo, those wonderful, furtively sheltering Shadows, nimble and soundless, ready at the slightest feint of light to slip under their stones or hide in a hole, and just as ready, once the threat from the rays had passed, to slip out again and lie awake beside the rocks or the seaweed, watching over them as they drowse drenched in the light of the cliff-corroding sun and the faded ocean, unmoving, insubstantial guardians, showing on the surface of the water the viscid shimmer of their bodies and the vigilant dark of their eyes.

It was time to go home, and we walked back toward the other girls. I knew now that I loved Albertine, but I was in no hurry, alas, to tell her: the fact was that, since the time when I had played at the Champs-Élysées, my notion of love had undergone a change, while those to whom my love was addressed, though they were consecutive, remained unchanged. For one thing, the confession of love, the declaration of my tenderness to her whom I loved, no longer seemed to be one of love's classic and indispensable scenes; and for another, love itself, instead of appearing to be a reality external to me, now seemed a subjective pleasure. I sensed that the less Albertine knew about this pleasure of mine, the more she would be likely to let me go on enjoying it.

All the way back to Balbec, the image of Albertine, flooded by the glow from the other girls, was not the only one I could see. But just as the moon, after spending the daylight hours in the guise of a white cloudlet, more shaped and stable than others, begins to come into its own as soon as daylight fades, so, by the time I was back in the hotel, it was Albertine's image that rose to shine unrivaled above the horizon of my heart. My room suddenly seemed new to me. It had, of course, long since ceased to be the baleful bedroom it had been on my first night. We are tireless redesigners of the space we live in: gradually, as habit relieves us of the need to experience, we eliminate the pernicious elements of color, dimension, and smell which objectified our unease. By now, it was no longer even the room that retained power enough over my sensitivity, not to make me suffer, but to give me joy; it was not the reservoir of sunny days, like a swimming pool halfway up the sides of which they dappled their azure, watery with light briefly blanked out by the fleeting reflection of a sail, as white and impalpable as a flash of heat; nor was it the purely aesthetic bedroom of the evening picture-displays; it was merely the room I had lived in for so many days that I had stopped seeing it. But now my eyes had just begun to open to it again, seeing it from the selfish viewpoint which is that of love. I fancied that, if Albertine should ever visit me here, the fine slanting cheval glass and the handsome glass-fronted bookcases would give her a high opinion of me. Instead of being a mere place of transit, where I spent a moment or two before making my escape to the beach or over to Rive-belle, my room had once more become real and dear to me, had been renewed, because I could see and appreciate all its contents through the eyes of Albertine.

A few days after our game of ring-on-a-string, we went for such a long walk that, having reached Maineville, we counted ourselves fortunate to come upon a couple of little two-seater governess carts, which would enable us to get back in time for dinner. The effect of my love for Albertine, which was already acute, was to make me suggest, not to her, but first to Rosemonde, then to Andrée, that either of them should ride with me; and then, despite having expressed this preference for Andrée or Rosemonde, I raised certain secondary considerations related to the time of night, the road to be taken, and the coats being worn, thus convincing everybody that, though it was quite against my will, it would be preferable for Albertine to come with me; and I pretended to make the best of a bad situation by having to accept her as my passenger. The trouble was, though, as love tends always toward complete assimilation of the loved one, and as no one is eatable through mere conversation, Albertine's being as pleasant as possible during our drive homeward was of no avail: after I dropped her at her door, I was in a state of happiness, but also in a state of much greater hunger for her than before, and I saw the minutes we had just spent together as having no great importance in themselves, as being only a prelude to those that would follow. They did, however, have the charm there is in all beginnings, which never comes back. So far I had made no demands on Albertine. Perhaps she imagined what I wanted of her; but, in her ignorance of what it really was, she could suppose I had no particular end in view other than some undefined relationship, in which she must savor that sweet, indeterminate sense, rich in expected surprises, which is romantic readiness.

Throughout the following week, I made little attempt to see Albertine. I pretended to prefer Andrée. With the beginning of love, one would like to go on being, in the eyes of the woman one loves, the lovable stranger; but we need her; and what we need of her, rather than the touch of her body, is to catch her attention, to impinge upon her heart. We sprinkle a little spite into a letter, to move her from indifference to a request for a favor; and the infallible logic of love, with its alternating arguments, locks us into its vicious circle, making it as impossible for us not to love as it is inevitable that we remain unloved. If the other girls went off to a matinee, I would spend the time with Andrée, knowing she gave up such things willingly, and would even have done so unwillingly, from a spirit of moral distinction, so as to avoid letting others, or even herself, suspect that she could see any point in participating in anything that smacked, however slightly, of society. In this way, I managed to monopolize her each evening, with the aim not of making Albertine jealous but, rather, of rising in her estimation, or at least of not falling in it by letting her know it was herself I loved, and not Andrée. I said nothing of my love to Andrée either, in case she might repeat it to Albertine. When I spoke about her to Andrée, I feigned a cold demeanor, which may have fooled her less than her apparent credulity fooled me. She made a show of believing in my indifference toward Albertine; she made a show of wishing for the closest possible intimacy between Albertine and me. But it is much more likely that she doubted the indifference and had no desire for intimacy. While I was assuring her of how little her friend meant to me, my mind was full of a single purpose: how to effect my introduction to Mme Bontemps, who had come to stay near Balbec for a few days, three of which Albertine was soon to spend with her. Naturally, I gave Andrée no hint of this purpose; and whenever I made a mention of Albertine's relations, my manner was very absentminded. In the words that Andrée spoke in reply, there was no semblance of doubt about my sincerity. But if that was really the case, why did she happen to say one day, "I've actually just seen Albertine's aunt"? Now, she had not said, "I know what you're up to: you keep talking in that offhand way, but you're really thinking of getting in with Albertine's aunt." Yet her use of the word "actually" seemed to derive from some such idea, lurking in her mind, but suppressed by her as impolite. The word was of a piece with certain looks or gestures which, though they assume no logical or rational form designed to be communicable to the mind of the listener, contrive nonetheless to reach it with their true meaning, as human speech, having been converted into electricity by the telephone, turns back into speech for the purpose of being understood. From then on, so as to rid Andrée's mind of the idea that I was interested in Mme Bontemps, I made sure to speak of the lady not just absentmindedly but spitefully: claiming to have met her once, I said she was crazy and that I hoped never to have to renew the experience. Whereas I was really doing whatever I could to meet Mme Bontemps.

I tried to persuade Elstir to recommend me and bring about a meeting with her (without letting anyone know that I had asked him to). He undertook to do this, though he expressed surprise that I should want him to, Mme Bontemps being, in his view, a scheming female beneath contempt, as uninteresting as she was self-interested. Realizing that, if I did meet Mme Bontemps, Andrée would hear of it sooner or later, I thought it prudent to tell her myself. "The things you most want to escape are the ones you end up being unable to avoid," I said. "I can't imagine anything more irksome than meeting Mme Bontemps, but I'm going to have to—Elstir has invited us to the same occasion." "I knew it all along!" Andrée exclaimed bitterly, gazing away at some invisible point, her eyes enlarged and flawed by displeasure. Her words did not add up to the most coherent expression of the meaning, which can be stated as follows: "I am aware that you love Albertine and that you're moving heaven and earth to get in with her relatives." But they were the shapeless fragments that could be reassembled into that meaning, which, despite Andrée's best efforts, I had provoked into explosion. Just like her use of "actually," the level of meaning of these words was at one remove from them: they were of the kind which, though unrelated to a person's literal statements, may make us admire (or distrust) a person, or even bring about a falling out between us.

Since Andrée had disbelieved me when I said Albertine's relations were a matter of indifference to me, it meant that she believed I was in love with Albertine, and very likely that this made her unhappy.

She was usually present when Albertine and I were together. But there were other times when I was due to see Albertine without her, each of which I looked forward to in a fever of expectation, then looked back on with the knowledge that it had brought about nothing of significance, that it had not been the great day I had hoped for, a hope I immediately transferred to the next one, which would not live up to it either; and so, one after another, like waves, these pinnacles of promise rose, then broke, and were replaced by others.

About a month after the day when we played ring-on-a-string, I heard that Albertine was leaving the following morning to go and spend two days at Mme Bontemps's, and that, because she was taking an early train, she would be spending the night at the Grand-Hôtel, so as to be able to take the bus to the station and catch the first train without disturbing the friends with whom she was staying. I spoke to Andrée about it. "No, I don't think so," she said, looking discontented. "Anyway, it would get you nowhere, because I'm pretty sure Albertine won't want to see you if she's spending the night alone at the hotel. It wouldn't be protocol." (This was an expression Andrée had been using freely for some time, with the sense of "It's not done.") "I'm only telling you this because I know how Albertine's mind works. I mean, for all I care, you can see her as much as you like. It's nothing to me."

Octave the golfer soon came along and was glad to tell Andrée how many strokes he had gone around in the day before, then Albertine, who, as she walked, was as engrossed in playing with her diabolo as a nun might be in telling her beads. This game could keep her happily occupied for hours. No sooner had she joined us than the impertinent tip of her nose became apparent, having been omitted from my mental image of her over the previous few days; below the black hair, her forehead was vertical, as it had been more than once before, contradicting the indistinct shape of it left in my mind, while its whiteness was an eye-opener to me: Albertine, emerging from the dusty haze of memory, was once more taking shape. Golf encourages the development of solitary pleasures; and the pleasure of a diabolo is undoubtedly a solitary one. Yet, even though she was standing there chatting with us, Albertine went on playing with hers, after the manner of a lady who, despite the presence of visitors, does not lay aside her crochet work. "I'm told," she said to Octave, "Mme de Villeparisis has complained to your father." And behind her way of saying "I'm told" I could hear one of those tones peculiar to her: every time I noticed I had forgotten them, I simultaneously remembered having already glimpsed through them the set French face of Albertine. Even if I had been blind, they would have informed me, as accurately as did the tip of her nose, of some of her lively and slightly provincial qualities. In this, her nose and these tones were equal, interchangeable; and her voice was like the one that it is said will be part of the phototelephone of the future: the sound of it gave a vivid picture of her. "And she hasn't just written to your father, but to the mayor of Balbec too, to get diabolos prohibited on the esplanade, because she got hit in the face by a ball."

"Yes, I heard about that complaint. It's ridiculous, when you think of how little there is here in the way of entertainment."

Andrée took no part in this conversation, not being acquainted with Mme de Villeparisis, which was of course also the case with Albertine and Octave. However, she did say, "I can't see why she had to make such a fuss. I mean, old Mme de Cambremer got hit by a ball too and *she* didn't complain." "I'll tell you the difference," Octave said in a serious tone, as he struck a match. "If you ask me, Mme de Cambremer is a real lady and Mme de Villeparisis is just a vulgar upstart. You on for golf this afternoon, then?" And he went off, accompanied by Andrée, leaving me alone with Albertine. "As you can see," she said, "I'm doing my hair now the way you like it—look at this ringlet. Everybody makes fun of it, and nobody knows who it is I'm doing it for. My aunt'll probably laugh at it too. And I won't tell her the reason either." Her cheeks often looked pale; but, seen from the side, as I could see them now, they were suffused and brightened by blood, which gave them the glow of those brisk winter mornings when, out for a walk, we see stone touched and ruddied by the sun, looking like pink granite and filling us with joy. The joy that the sight of Albertine's cheeks gave me at that moment was just as keen, though the desire it induced was not for a walk, but for a kiss. I asked her whether what I had heard about her plans was true. "Yes," she said, "I'm to sleep tonight at your hotel—and actually I'll be going to bed before dinner, because I've got a bit of a cold. So you can come up and sit by my bedside while I'm having my dinner. Then we can play at something, whatever you like. I'd've liked you to come and see me off in the morning too, but it might look a bit funny—not to Andrée, mind you, she's too sensible, but to the others who'll be at the station. And if it got back to my aunt, there could be trouble. But at least we can have an evening together—and my aunt won't know a thing about *that*. I'm just off to say goodbye to Andrée. So I'll see you shortly. Come soon, so we can have a nice long time all to ourselves," she added with a smile. Her words carried me back further than the time when I had been in love with Gilberte, to the days when love had seemed to be a thing that was not only external to myself, but achievable. Whereas the Gilberte I had known at the Champs-Élysées was a very different girl from the one I knew so well in the privacy of my solitary heart, here, suddenly, the real Albertine, the one I saw every day, who I thought was hidebound in bourgeois prejudices and was so open with her aunt, had lent her form to the imaginary Albertine, the one who, at a time when I did not even know her, I had thought was taking furtive looks at me on the esplanade, the one who, when she saw me walking away, had seemed to be wending so reluctantly her own way home.

When I went in to dinner with my grandmother, I was full of the secret I carried within me, which she knew nothing about. Also, Albertine, the following morning, would be with her girlfriends, none of whom would know what was new between her and me; and when Mme Bontemps kissed her niece on the forehead, she would be unaware that I stood between them, and that I was in that hairstyle, the purpose of which, hidden to all eyes, was that I should be pleased, I who until then could only envy Mme Bontemps for being related to the same people as her niece, for having to wear mourning when she did and make the same round of family visits; yet here I was, meaning more now to Albertine than this same aunt. She would be with her aunt, but she would be thinking of me. As for what might take place between us later in the evening, I had no clear idea. But the Grand-Hôtel, and the evening before me, no longer seemed empty: they were the repository of my happiness. I rang the "lift," to go up to the room Albertine had taken, which overlooked the valley. The slightest motions, the mere act of sitting down on the little seat inside the elevator, were full of sweetness, because they were in direct touch with my heart; in the cables that hauled the lift upward, and in the few stairs still to be climbed, I saw nothing but the workings of my joy and the steps toward it, materialized. In the corridor, I was only a few paces away from the bedroom inside which lay the precious substance of her pink body—the room which, however delightful the acts to take place in it, would go on being its unchanging self, would continue to seem, for the eyes of any unsuspecting passerby, identical to all the other rooms, which is the way things have of becoming the stubbornly unconfessing witnesses, the conscientious confidants, the inviolable trustees of our pleasure. From the landing to Albertine's room it was a few steps, a few steps that no one could now prevent me from taking, and which, as though I were walking in a new element, as though what moved slowly aside to let me through were happiness itself, I took in a mood of utmost bliss and attentiveness, with an unfamiliar feeling of being all-powerful, of at last coming to claim an inheritance that had always been meant for me. Then it suddenly occurred to me that I was wrong to harbor any doubts: she had told me to come up after she had gone to bed. There could be no doubt! I could barely contain myself; I jostled past Françoise, who was in my way; I ran, with shining eyes, to the room where my sweetheart awaited me. I found Albertine in bed. Her white nightgown bared her throat and altered the proportions of her face, which seemed of a deeper pink, because of the warmth of the bed, or her cold, or her recent dinner; I thought of the colors I had seen close at hand a few hours before on the esplanade, which were now going to reveal their taste; her cheek was bisected from top to bottom by a lock of her long black wavy hair, which to please me she had completely undone. She smiled at me. Beside her, through the window, the valley was bright with moonlight. The sight of her naked throat and her excessively pink cheeks had so intoxicated me (that is, had so transferred reality from the world of nature into the deluge of my own sensations, which I could barely contain) as to have upset the balance between the tumultuous and indestructible immensity of the life surging through me and the paltry life of the universe. The sea, which through the window could be seen beside the valley, the swelling breasts of the closest of the Maineville cliffs, the sky where the moon had not yet reached the zenith, all of this seemed to lie as light as feathers between my eyelids, at rest upon eyeballs in which I felt the pupils had expanded and become strong enough, and ready, to hold much heavier burdens, all the mountains in the world, on their delicate surface. Even the whole sphere of the horizon did not suffice to fill their orbits. Any impingement of the natural world upon my consciousness, however mighty, would have seemed insubstantial to me; a gust of air off the sea would have seemed short-winded for the vast breaths filling my breast. I leaned over to kiss Albertine. Had death chosen that instant to strike me down, it would have been a matter of indifference to me, or, rather, it would have seemed impossible, for life did not reside somewhere outside me: all of life was contained within me. A pitying smile would have been my only response had a philosopher expressed the view that, however remote it might be now, a day was bound to come when I would die, that the everlasting forces of nature would outlive me, those forces with their divine tread grinding me like a grain of dust, that after my own extinction there would continue to be swelling-breasted cliffs, a sea, a sky, and moonlight! How could such a thing be possible? How could the world outlive me, given that I was not a mere speck lost in it—it was wholly contained within me, and it came nowhere near filling me, since, somewhere among so much unoccupied space, where other vast treasures could have been stored, I could casually toss the sky, the sea, and the cliffs! "If you don't stop that, I'll ring!" Albertine cried, realizing that I was attempting to kiss her. But I was convinced that any girl who entertains a young man in secret, after making sure that her aunt knows nothing of the assignation, must have an ulterior motive, and that in any case success lies in taking advantage of whatever opportunities are on offer; in my state of fevered excitement, Albertine's round face, glowing as though from an inner nightlight, had acquired such relief that, in imitation of a rotating fiery sphere, it appeared to be turning like those figures by Michelangelo being carried away by a motionless, vertiginous whirlwind.[115] I was about to find out the scent and the flavor of this unknown pink fruit. I heard a sudden noise, jarring and long drawn out—Albertine was pulling the bell for all she was worth.

I had thought the love I felt for Albertine did not depend on any hope of physical intimacy. However, once that evening's experience appeared to have ruled out all possibility of possessing her, once I had exchanged my initial certainty, acquired on the very first day down by the beach, that she was unchaste, and my various later notions of her, for the definitive conclusion that she was thoroughly virtuous, and when she said to me coldly a week later, having come back from her aunt's, "I forgive you, and I'm sorry if I was nasty to you, but you mustn't ever do that again," what followed was quite the opposite of what had happened when Bloch first informed me that women were there for the having: as though I had been in love not with a real girl but only a wax doll, it turned out that my desire to enter her life, to go with her to see the places where she had spent her childhood, to be initiated by her into the sporting life, gradually detached itself from her; my intellectual curiosity about what she might think on this or that subject did not outlast my belief that I might be able to kiss her. My dreams forsook her as soon as they ceased to be swayed by the hope of possessing her, which I had believed did not affect them. They were then free to recruit one or another of Albertine's friends, if her charm impressed me on a particular day, and especially if I could see a possibility of being loved by her; and so I turned first toward Andrée. Yet, had Albertine not existed, I might not have taken the pleasure I took, more and more over the following days, in being the beneficiary of Andrée's attentions. Albertine had told no one of my fiasco in her bedroom. She was one of those sorts of pretty girls who, from earliest youth, because of their beauty, or more usually a charm of manner or appearance, which remains something of a mystery and may lie in a fund of vitality in which those who are less favored by nature find something refreshing, have always been better liked–whether within the family, among their friends, or in the wider world–than others who are more richly endowed with beauty or fortune; she was one of those of whom, before attaining the age of love and even more so after, much more is demanded than they demand of themselves, much more too than they have it in them to give. Ever since childhood, Albertine had been surrounded by four or five admirers, little girls of her own age, one of whom, far superior to her and aware of it, was Andrée–it may even be that this attractiveness of Albertine's, exercised by her quite un-self-consciously, had been one of the founding principles of the little gang. The influence of her attractiveness had been known to be felt far and wide, and even among people who were, relatively speaking, more exalted than her family: if, for instance, a pavane was to be danced, it was Albertine who was chosen rather than a girl of better family. A consequence of this was that, with no prospect of a dowry, and dependent as she was on M. Bontemps– who begrudged what she cost him, was said to be corrupt, and would have been glad to have her off his hands–she was invited not only to dinner, but on weekend parties, by people who, though in Saint-Loup's eyes they might have been beyond the pale of fashion, represented unattainable heights for the mothers of Rosemonde or Andrée, women who, despite being very wealthy, could not aspire to the acquaintance of such people. So it was that, every year, Albertine would spend several weeks with the family of a man who was on the board of governors of the Bank of France, the managing director of one of the larger railway companies. This financier's wife was "at home" to important people, yet had never mentioned her "day" to Andrée's mother, who, though she thought this impolite of the lady, was still prodigiously interested in everything that went on at her house. She too made a point of urging Andrée to invite Albertine down to their villa every year: it was, she said, a good deed, to enable a girl like that to enjoy a stay at the seaside, a girl who could never afford such a holiday and whose aunt neglected her. In this, Andrée's mother was probably not motivated by the hope that the governor of the Bank of France and his wife, on learning that Albertine had been singled out by her and her daughter, would look kindly on them; nor could she have hoped that Albertine, for all her kind heart and astuteness, would be able to get an invitation, if not for herself, then at least for Andrée, to one of the financier's garden parties. However, each night at dinner, behind her pose of disdain and indifference, she was delighted to hear Albertine's tales of what had taken place at the château during her stay there, and of the people who had been invited, most of whom she knew either by sight or by repute. Even the thought that she knew these people only in that way—that is, knew them not at all (what she called having known people "forever")—veiled Andrée's mother's mind with a faint melancholy as she asked Albertine her stilted little questions about them in her haughty, offhand way; and it might also have sown in her mind some faint doubt or a misgiving about the eminence of her own position in society, had she not reassured herself and returned to "living in the real world" by saying to the butler, "Tell Chef his peas are too hard." She went back then to being imperturbable. She was determined that Andrée should marry not just a man of excellent family (that went without saying), but one who was rich enough to allow her also to have a chef and two coachmen. This was a plain matter of fact, it was the simple truth of having a position. Yet the other fact, that Albertine had dined at the château of the governor of the Bank of France with Mme This or Mme That, and that one of these ladies had even invited the girl to be a houseguest the following winter, made Andrée's mother see her as deserving of a certain esteem, which went quite well with the pity, not to say the contempt, inspired by her unfavorable circumstances, the contempt being sharpened by the knowledge that M. Bontemps had turned coat and become a supporter of the government—there was even a suggestion that he might have been slightly tainted by the Panama Affair.[116] Not that any of this prevented Andrée's mother, who was a lover of truth, from also turning the withering fire of her disdain on any who appeared to believe that Albertine was of lowly origin. "Why, they're top-drawer! They're Simonets—with one *n*!" It was true that, given the social stratum in which all this took place, where money plays such an important part, where position in the world may consist with issuing an invitation but not with a proposal of marriage, Albertine could not assume that a practical outcome of the esteem in which she was held by people of some distinction would ever be a fashionable marriage, since such people could never overlook her lack of means. Nevertheless, her successes, even devoid of any hope of a matrimonial consequence, still roused the envy and fury of the mothers of other, marriageable girls, who were exercised by the thought of Albertine's being treated "like a daughter" by the wife of the governor of the bank, and even by Andrée's mother, whom they hardly knew. So they took to telling mutual friends of theirs and these two ladies that the latter would be horrified if they only knew the truth: that, since they were ill advised enough to admit the girl to their family circle, she now regaled each of them with whatever she observed in the house of the other, retailing all sorts of tiny private matters that both of them would have been mightily distempered to have bruited abroad. In saying so, these envious ladies hoped it would eventually come to the ears of Albertine's two patronesses, and cause a falling out. However, as is often the case, these attempts failed in their object: the malice behind them was too undisguised; and the only result was that the ladies who had devised them attracted more dislike to themselves. The attitude of Andrée's mother toward Albertine was too entrenched for her to change her view: though "an unfortunate," the girl was gifted with great good nature and took pains to be nice to people.

Albertine's general popularity, though it seemed unlikely to lead to any advantageous consequence, had ingrained in her the distinguishing characteristic of those who, by being always sought after, never need to make overtures (a trait that can be found, for similar reasons, in another, remoter region of society, among the great ladies of the fashionable world), and who, rather than boasting of their successes, tend to conceal them. She would never have said of someone, "He's dying to see me"; and she spoke of everybody with great goodwill, giving the impression that she was the one seeking out others, trying to be liked by them. If one alluded to a young man who had just been cruelly berating her for not wishing to see him again, Albertine would sing his praises ("Such a *nice* fellow!") instead of priding herself publicly on a conquest, or bearing him a grudge. In fact, she was annoyed by being so well liked, because it meant that she sometimes had to be unpleasant to people; whereas her natural inclination was to be pleasant. This inclination had even led her to adopt a form of lying, which is peculiar to people who like to be useful, or the type of man who has come up in the world. This mode of insincerity, which exists in embryo in a great many people, consists in the inability to be satisfied with the pleasure that can be given to a single person by a single act. If, for example, Albertine's aunt required her attendance at a boring reception, she did not think that in the gratification she afforded her aunt by going to it there was enough moral benefit to herself. So her response to the kindly welcome of their hosts was to assure them that, having been looking forward to meeting them for a long time, she had begged her aunt to let her come on this occasion. Even this struck her as insufficient; and if she came across one of her friends at the reception, someone who had reason to be heartbroken, Albertine would say, "I didn't like to think of you being on your own, so I thought you might like me to keep you company. Perhaps you'd prefer us to leave and go somewhere else? I'll do whatever you like—I'd give anything for you not to be so sad" (which was, of course, quite true). However, there were times when the fictitious purpose destroyed the real purpose: on one occasion, she called on a particular lady with the intention of asking her to do a favor for a friend; but at the sight of this warmhearted lady, Albertine, responding all unawares to her own principle of the multifarious usefulness of the single act, thought it would be nicer if she could appear to have had no other reason for visiting the lady than the enjoyment she expected from her company. The lady was extremely touched to think that Albertine had come such a long way on an impulse of simple friendship. Albertine, seeing how affected the lady was, responded with an even stronger fondness for her. The trouble was, though, that she was so keenly affected by the friendliness she had falsely said was her reason for being there that she was reluctant to ask the favor for the friend, in case the lady should doubt the sincerity of her feelings (which were in fact quite sincere). The lady might believe that the favor was Albertine's real reason for coming, which was true; but then she would assume that Albertine had no real pleasure in seeing her, which was untrue. The upshot was that Albertine would return home without having asked the favor, after the manner of those men who, having done a good turn to a woman in the hope of having their way with her, then keep their desire for her to themselves, so as to preserve a semblance of selflessness. On other occasions, it could not be said that the true purpose was sacrificed to the subsidiary one invented on the spur of the moment; but the real one was at such variance with the ostensible one that, had the person who was so touched by hearing the latter learned the former, all pleasure would instantly have been turned into a shock of mortification. Such contradictions will be clarified, eventually, by the rest of my story. They are, however, very prevalent, in even the most diverse circumstances of life, as can be shown by an example deriving from a very different order of experience. A married man brings his mistress down to live in the town where he is garrisoned. His wife, who is still in Paris, half aware of how things stand, frets and broods, and pours her jealousy into letters to the husband. A moment comes when the mistress is obliged to go back to Paris for a day. Her lover finds her pleas that he should accompany her irresistible, and arranges to take twenty-four hours' leave. Then, because he is a goodhearted fellow and is sorry for the pain he causes his wife, he goes to see her and says, with the help of a few sincere tears, that her letters have so disturbed him that he managed to get away, so as to bring her consolation and a kiss. He has thus contrived, with a single journey, to prove his love both to the mistress and to the wife. But if the wife should find out the real reason why he came back to Paris, her joy would no doubt turn to pain, unless of course the pleasure of being with the miscreant should outweigh the sorrow of knowing him for a liar. One of the men who seemed to me to be most diligent in applying this principle of the plurality of purposes was M. de Norpois. He had been known to step in and act as an intermediary between two friends who had fallen out; and for this he was seen as the most obliging of men. But he was not satisfied just to seem to be helping out the one who had come to ask his advice: when speaking to the other party, he would present his intervention, not as resulting from a request by the first friend, but as being in the interest of the second; and this he had little difficulty in doing, faced with a man whose mind was already prepared to believe he was dealing with "the most helpful of men." In this way, by hedging his bets, operating "against" his client, as the parlance of the outside brokers has it, he never jeopardized his influence; the services he rendered never had the effect of compromising his credit, but always of partly enriching it. Also, each of these services, seemingly doubly rendered, enhanced in that same measure his reputation as a dependable friend, and an effectively dependable friend at that, one whose aim is true, whose every stroke counts, as was attested by the gratitude of the two assisted parties. Such duplicity in obligingness (not unbelied at times, as in all human creatures) made up a significant element of the character of M. de Norpois. At the Ministry, he often made use of my father, who was rather a guileless man, while letting him think he was being of use to him.

Being more popular than she would have liked, and having no need to trumpet her own triumphs, Albertine said nothing about our bedside scene, which a plainer girl might have wanted to share with the world. As for me, I could make no sense of the part she had played in it. My hypothesis about the thoroughness of her virtue (my initial explanation of the vehemence with which she refused to be kissed and possessed by me), though not indispensable to my conception of her fundamental goodness and integrity, had to be rethought and more than once reformulated. It was so diametrically opposite to the one I had formed on the day when I first set eyes on Albertine! Not only that, but the single act of brusque hostility, pulling the bell to thwart my designs, was set amid so many of her other acts, of a different sort, all of them well disposed toward me, whether affectionate or, as they sometimes were, anxious or alarmed, because of her jealousy at my preference for Andrée. So why had she invited me to spend the evening by her bedside? Why always speak the language of tenderness? What lies behind the desire to be with a friend, the fear that he might prefer one of your girlfriends, the intention to be nice to him, the romantic statement that none of the others will know he spent the evening with you, if you then refuse him such a straightforward pleasure, and if it is not in fact a pleasure for you? I could not accept that Albertine's virtue stretched quite that far; and I even began to wonder whether her violent reaction might not have been prompted by some other reason, such as squeamishness (if she had suddenly noticed a bad smell about her person, and thought it might offend me), or timidity (if she believed, in her ignorance of the realities of lovemaking, that my state of nervous debility might somehow be contagious, contractable from a kiss).

What was sure was that she was upset at not having been nice to me, and that she gave me a little golden pencil, acting on that virtuous perversity of people who are moved by the liking we inspire in them to do us a favor, not the one we would prefer, but some other: a critic, rather than writing a good review on a novelist, takes him out to dinner; a duchess, instead of including a social climber in her theater party, lends him her box for an evening when she stays at home. Thus conscience, in those who do little and who could do nothing, makes them do something more. I told Albertine that I was very pleased by her gift of a pencil, but that I would have been better pleased if she had let me kiss her on the evening when she stayed at the hotel: "It would have made me so happy! What difference could it have made to you? I'm surprised you didn't want to." "Well, *I'm* surprised you're surprised!" she replied. "What sort of girls must you be familiar with to be surprised at what I did?" "I'm sorry if I upset you, but I can't say, even now, that I think what I did was wrong. If you ask me, it's the sort of thing that's utterly unimportant, and I can't see why a girl who could so easily be nice to someone won't do it. Mind you," I added, the memory of the girl who was friendly with the actress Léa, and the odium heaped on her by Albertine and her group of friends, making me concede a sort of semi-agreement with her ideas of morality, "I don't mean girls can do just anything, or that there's no such thing as immorality. I mean, that Balbec girl you were all talking about the other day, who's supposed to be carrying on with that actress, well, I think that's just disgusting—so disgusting, actually, that I can only assume it's not true, but was invented by the girl's enemies. It just strikes me as improbable—impossible, in fact. But letting a fellow that you like kiss you, and go even further, since you say you like me . . ." "I do! But I've liked other fellows too. Believe you me, I've known other boys who were just as fond of me as you are. But there wasn't one of them who would've dared do any such thing! They knew perfectly well they'd have got a good slap in the face! Anyway, the thought never entered their heads—we just shook hands in the usual way, like ordinary good friends. No one would ever have thought of kissing, but that didn't stop us from being close friends. Look, if you really want us to be friends, then you can count yourself lucky—I must be pretty fond of you to forgive you like this. In any case, I'm sure you're just teasing me! Andrée's the one you really like—admit it! And I'm sure you're right—she's much nicer than me, and she's beautiful! Oh, you men!" That Albertine should speak so openly was balm to my recent hurt feelings; and this gave me a high opinion of her. The consolation I drew from her words may even have had, much later, far-reaching and grave consequences for me, because it contributed to the development of a sort of family feeling for her, a moral core that gathered in the center of my love for her, and was to be forever inseparable from it. Such a feeling can be the harbinger of acute suffering: if a woman is to cause us great pain, there has to have been a time when we trusted her implicitly. For the time being, this embryo of friendliness, of moral esteem, lay latent within me, a toothing stone for a future extension. Without that growth to come, if it had remained in the inert state in which it still was the following year, let alone during the last weeks of my first stay in Balbec, it would have been unavailing against my happiness. It lived in me like a quiescent parasite, which it would really be wiser to be rid of, but which one leaves to its own devices, undisturbed, harmless for the moment, weak and lost as it is in the further reaches of a foreign self.

My dreams were now free to recruit one or another of Albertine's friends, first and foremost Andrée, whose attentions to me might not have endeared her so much to me had I not known that Albertine would be bound to be told of it. My feigned fondness for Andrée had already given me, in the form of our cozy chats and murmured confidences, a sort of outer semblance of love for her, which lacked only the sincerity of a feeling that my heart, in its new state of availability, could now have afforded. However, it was impossible for any love of mine for Andrée to be true: she was too intellectual, too high-strung, too prone to ailment, too much like myself. Though Albertine now seemed empty, Andrée was full of something with which I was overfamiliar. At my first sight of her on the beach, I had supposed she was a racing cyclist's girl-friend, infatuated with the sporting life; yet Andrée now told me that, though she had taken an interest in sports, it was only on the advice of her doctor, who recommended it as a way of treating her neurasthenia and her eating difficulties, and that she was actually never happier than when translating into French a novel by George Eliot. This disappointment, the outcome of my own misconception about her, was actually of no consequence for me. But it was a misconception of the kind which, though they may foster the onset of love, and may not be recognized as misconceptions until love is beyond containment, can also foster sorrow. Such misconceptions (including some which differ from mine about Andrée, or which may even be the opposite of it) can be abetted by the fact—and this was exactly Andrée's case—that, in our desire to be seen as someone we are not, we take on enough of the appearance and the ways of that someone to create an illusion at first encounter. To that outward appearance, affectation, imitation, and the desire to be admired, either by the righteous or the unrighteous, add the misleading effects of words and gesture. Many a figment of cynicism or cruelty does not stand the test of closer acquaintance, any more than some acts of apparent goodness or generosity. A man renowned as a champion of charity can turn out to be a conceited skinflint; by showing off as though shameless, a simple girl full of the primmest prejudices can seem a Messalina. I had taken Andrée for a healthy, uncouth creature, whereas she was only a person seeking health, like many people in whom she herself may have seen evidence of rude health, but who came no closer to it than an overweight arthritic with a red face and a white flannel blazer comes to being a Hercules. In certain circumstances, our happiness may be compromised by the discovery that someone in whom we loved an appearance of good health is really an invalid, in whom the good health is as secondhand, as borrowed, as the light shed on us from the planets, or the electricity that certain inert bodies can conduct.

However, Andrée, like Rosemonde and Gisèle, and even more than they, was a friend of Albertine's, sharing her life, and imitating her ways so much that, at my first sight of them, I had been unable to tell which of them was which. My bevy of girls, like long-stemmed roses, whose main charm was that they stood against the blue background of the sea, was as indivisible now as in the days when its members were strangers to me, when any one of them only had to appear for me to be seized by the thrilling expectation that the whole group must soon come and join her. A moment with one of them could still give me a pleasure which was indefinably mingled with the joy of knowing that the others would be along soon; and even if they did not turn up that same day, I had the joy of talking with her about them, and of being sure they would be told I had been down to the beach.

My feeling was no longer the simple attraction of the first days: it was an incipient, tentative love for each or any of them, every single one of them being a natural substitute for any of the others. My greatest sorrow would not have been to be forsaken by the one I preferred: I would have instantly preferred the one who forsook me, since that would have focused on her the whole indeterminate mist of sadness and romance through which I saw them all. In that eventuality, it was all the others, in whose eyes I would soon come to lose all prestige, whom I would have unconsciously missed through my yearning for the forsaker, my collective love for them being of the sort felt by a politician or an actor who, having once basked in the approval of electors and audiences, cannot bear to fall from their favor. The sweets I had not managed to taste in Albertine's arms I went on expecting to enjoy with one or another of her friends, each of whom could suddenly attract my desire to herself, for a day at a time, merely by taking leave of me the evening before with a word or a glance into which I could read an ulterior meaning.

This desire of mine drifted from one to another, delighting especially in its awareness of a relative firming of the features on each of their unfinished faces, far enough advanced for a malleable and uncertain likeness to be already discernible through the promise of further change. What made the differences between these faces was not a set of corresponding disparities in the length or breadth of their features, which, however dissimilar the girls appeared to be, it might actually have been possible to superimpose on one another. The fact is, though, that our perception of faces is not mathematical in its functioning. For one thing, it does not set about it by measuring components; it starts from an expression, or an impression of the whole. In Andrée's face, for instance, the elegance of her gentle eyes seemed to belong with the thin stroke of her nose, which was as fine as a mere curve drawn so as to bring together into a single line the considerate intent expressed higher up via the divided smile in her twinned pupils. Another line, just as fine, was drawn in her hair, with all the fluency and depth of the lines swept in sand by the wind. This one must have been hereditary, for her mother's hair, though already quite white, had a similar sweep, like the swelling and falling lines of snowdrifts that flow over the rises and dips of the underlying terrain. Rosemonde's nose, to be sure, compared with the delicate lineaments of Andrée's, seemed to offer broad surfaces, suggesting a tall tower set on a solid base. But though a mere expression can mislead us into seeing vast disparities between things separated by minute distinctions—and though a minute distinction can be enough to create an absolutely singular expression, an individuality—in the case of all the girls' faces, it was not just a minute peculiarity of line or originality of expression that made them appear irreducible to one another. It was their coloring which set them so far apart; and that, not so much because of the range of beauty in the various hues it gave them—which were so dissimilar that the pleasure I derived from the sight of Rosemonde, with her skin suffused in pinkish gold still tinged by the greenish glow from her eyes, and the pleasure of looking upon Andrée, whose white cheeks took such austere distinction from her black hair, were the diverse pleasures I enjoyed in gazing at a geranium by the sun-drenched sea or a camellia by night—as because the unforeseen element of color, which acts not only as the dispenser of different shades but also as a great creator, or at least alterer, of dimensions, had changed everything, hugely magnifying the tiny differences in line and redesigning the relations between surfaces. So it was that different lighting effects—the pink glow shed by a shock of russet hair, the flat pallor cast by a colorless light—could stretch and thicken faces of largely similar design, turning them into other things, like those accessories of the Russian ballet, which when seen in the simple light of day may consist of a mere circular cutout of paper, but which the genius of Bakst, by flooding the stage set with a wash of flesh pink or a blank lunar tone, transforms into a sharp-faceted, hard turquoise, set into the façade of a palace, or a soft, full-blown Bengal rose growing in a flower garden. So our perception of faces does entail measuring; but our methods are those of painters, rather than of surveyors.

In such things, Albertine's face was no different from her girl-friends'. There were days when she was thin, with a dull complexion and a sullen look, with a dark-violet zone, oblique and transparent, somewhere in her eyes, such as can be seen at times in the sea, and seemingly oppressed by all the sorrows of an outcast. On other days, her face was smoother and it beguiled my desires, keeping them engrossed in its glossy surface, and preventing them from going beyond it, unless a quick sidelong glimpse of her, with an inner pink glowing through her cheeks, which were as matte white as wax on the surface, made me long to kiss them and get at that inaccessible inner tint of her. Or there were times when happiness rippled through her cheeks, so bright and mobile that their skin turned fluid and tenuous, as though traversed by underlying glances that gave it the appearance of being made from the same substance as her eyes, only of a different color; and sometimes, when one caught sight, unthinkingly, of her face with its punctuation of little brownish blotches, and its pair of bluer ones among them, one had the brief impression of having glanced at a gold-finch's egg, or an opalescent agate that had been worked and polished at only two spots, where, amid all the dusky stone, like the translucent wings of an azure butterfly, one caught the glow of the eyes, in which flesh becomes mirror and gives us the illusion that through them, more than through any other part of the body, we come closest to the soul. Mostly, however, she had more color, and was more animated; sometimes the single touch of pink, amid her whole white face, was the tip of her nose, as neat as the nose of a sly little kitten, made to be played with; sometimes the smoothness of her cheeks was so even that one's eye slid over their pink enamel as though it were the pink of a miniature, a semblance given more delicacy and intimacy by the black hair set above it like a locket lid half lifted; on occasion the shade of her cheeks was as deep as the purplish pink of cyclamens; and there were moments too, if she was feverish or flushed with warmth, when the midnight shades of certain roses, whose red is so dark as to be almost black, gave her complexion an unhealthy appearance, debasing my desire for her to something more sensual, filling her eyes with a look that was more perverse and unwholesome; and each of these Albertines was unlike the others, as the colors, the shape, the character of a ballerina may be transmuted, each time she comes on, by the constantly changing effects from a spotlight. It may be because the personalities I perceived in her at that time were so various that I later took to turning into a different person, depending on which Albertine was in my mind: I became a jealous man, an indifferent man, a voluptuary, a melancholic, a madman, these characters coming over me not just in response to the random recurrence of memories, but also under the variable influence of some intervening belief which affected this or that memory by making me see it differently. There was, there is, no getting away from these beliefs: most of the time, they fill our minds unawares; yet they are more important for our happiness than the very person standing there in front of us, since it is through these ideas that we see such a person, since it is they that endow the person seen with whatever importance he or she may have. In the interests of accuracy, I should really give a separate name to each of the selves in me that was to harbor a future thought of Albertine; and it would be even more appropriate if I had a different name for each of the Albertines who appeared in her single guise, none of whom was identical to any of the others, as variable as the seas I saw before me, which I simplified to the same word "sea," and which served as the backdrop to my inconstant nymph. But above all (analogously to, but more usefully than, the storyteller's mention of what the weather was like on a certain day), I should give her invariable name to whichever belief about her, when I saw her on different days, prevailed in my mind, constituting its atmosphere, as the appearance of each person seen, like that of each day's new sea, is modified by those barely visible clouds which, by their density and changeableness, their distribution across the sky and their impermanence, can alter the colors of all things, like the cloud that Elstir had banished on the evening when he failed to introduce me to the group of girls with whom he had paused to talk, and whose figures, as they started to move away from me, had immediately begun to seem more beautiful—a cloud that had re-formed a few days later, once I had met them, muting the glow of their loveliness, often passing between them and my eyes, which saw them now dimmed, as through a gentle haze, reminiscent of Virgil's Leucothea.[117]

The meaning to be read in their faces had of course changed, since their speech had revealed some of it; and the significance I saw in whatever they said was directly related to the fact that I could make them say it, in answer to my own questions, and that, like an experimental scientist who designs a control test to check an apparent finding, I could also make them say different things. One way of solving the problem of existence, after all, is to become so closely acquainted with things and individuals we once saw from farther away as being full of beauty and mystery, that we realize they are devoid of both: therein lies one of the modes of mental hygiene available to us, which, though it may not be the most recommendable, can certainly afford us a measure of equanimity for getting through life and—since it enables us to have no regrets, by assuring us we have had the best of things, and that the best of things was not up to much—in resigning us to death.

I had at last rooted out, from the minds of these girls, all aversion to chastity, any memory of their lives of casual fornications, and these I had replaced by staunch precepts which, though they might at times be severely tried, had managed to protect them against all misconduct and kept them in the paths of middle-class righteousness. However, when we have started out from a wrong assumption, even one affecting only minor things, when a faulty deduction or an unreliable memory, say, leads us away from the true originator of a piece of mischievous gossip, or the place where we have mislaid a possession, it is possible, once we have discovered our mistake, to replace it not with the truth but with another mistake. In assessing the girls' modes of life, in deciding how to behave toward them, I had inferred all the implications of the word "innocence," which I could now read, writ large on their faces, as I chatted with them. But my eye, baffled by its own haste, may have misread the word, and perhaps it was not to be seen there, any more than the name of Jules Ferry had figured on the program of the matinee at which I had had my first sight of La Berma—despite which, I had assured M. de Norpois that Jules Ferry, without the slightest doubt, was a writer of curtain-raisers.[118]

With any one member of my little gang of girls, was I not bound to recall only the most recently glimpsed of her possible faces, given that the mind eliminates from our memories of anyone whatever does not contribute in an immediately useful way to our daily dealings with the person, even if—especially if!—these dealings are colored by a tincture of love, which, by being perpetually unsatisfied, lives forever in the coming moment? The chain of past days runs through the memory, which only holds fast to the nearest end of it, and the metal of which this end is forged is often very different from the metal of the earlier links, which have already slipped away into the dark; in our journey through life, the only country the mind sees as real is the one in which we live during the present instant. My very first impressions, which were now at such a remove, could find no ally in my memory against their day-by-day deforming; throughout the long hours I spent among the girls, chatting, going on picnics, playing, I never once remembered that they were the same ruthless, sensual virgins whom I had once seen, like figures in a fresco, filing past against the sea.

Geographers or archaeologists may well take us to Calypso's island or unearth the true palace of King Minos. Unfortunately, though, Calypso then turns into a mere woman; and Minos is no more than a king, shorn of divinity. Even the qualities and defects that history can show to have been those of these very real people are often extremely unlike the ones we used to imagine in the creatures of fable who once bore their names. So it was that all my charming oceanic mythology, lovingly composed by me during the very first days, had faded away to nothing. However, time spent in close familiarity with those we once thought inaccessible, those we have longed for, is not, at least on occasion, time spent to no purpose. Even amid the factitious enjoyments we may eventually find in our later dealings with people whom we at first found unlikable, there always remains the sour aftertaste of the failings they have contrived to conceal; whereas, in relationships such as those I had with Albertine and her friends, the genuine delight in which they have originated always leaves a trace of the fragrance that no artifice can ever give to fruit that is forced, to grapes that have never ripened in the sunshine. The supernatural creatures they had briefly been for me could still, even without my knowing it, sprinkle a spice of wonder into the tritest things I did with them—or, rather, they forever banished the trite from the vicinity of such things. My desire had yearned so helplessly after the meaning in those eyes, which now knew me and smiled upon me, but which, at first sight, had met my own like light radiating from another universe, it had so broadly and so intricately distributed colors and scents on all the flesh-tinted surfaces of these girls who lay on the cliff top, handed me a simple sandwich, or played their guessing games, that often, as I sprawled there of an afternoon, I was like a painter who seeks the grandeur of antiquity in modern life, giving a woman cutting her toenail the nobility of the *Spinario*,[119] or like Rubens, using women of his acquaintance to figure as goddesses in a scene from mythology: I gazed on the loveliness of their bodies, the fair and the dark, so varied in their styles, as they lay about me in the grass, and I neither ignored all the mediocre contents with which daily life had filled them, nor recalled expressly their celestial origin, as though, like Hercules or Telemachus, I were disporting myself among the nymphs.

Then the concerts came to an end, the weather turned bad, and my girls left Balbec, not all at once, as the swallows leave, but within the same week. Albertine was the first to go, without warning, without any of the others' being able to understand, either then or later, why she had suddenly gone back to Paris, where her presence was required neither for business nor for pleasure. "Without even a with-your-leave or a by-your-leave," grumbled Françoise, "she just up and went." Françoise would have preferred us to do likewise. Her view was that we were behaving inconsiderately toward the employees of the hotel, of whom there were in fact few remaining to serve the needs of the by now sparse population of residents, and toward the manager, who was "wasting money like water." It was a fact that for a long time the hotel, which was soon to close, had been bidding farewell to almost all those who had spent the summer there—never had it been so pleasant to live in! Not that the manager shared this view: one came upon him in corridors and in lounges which were now freezing cold and had no pages standing by their doors, as he strode past wearing a new frock coat and so nattily barbered that his drab face seemed to be a blend of one part flesh and three parts cosmetics, forever changing his tie (these attentions to self cost less than making sure the heating works and retaining staff; like the man who, having decided he can no longer afford to donate ten thousand francs to a charity, finds it easy to appear generous by giving a princely five-franc piece to the telegram boy who brings him a cable). He looked as though he were conducting an inspection tour of nowhere, as though the purpose of his show of elegance were to give an air of temporariness to the dismal atmosphere of a hotel that had had a poor season; and he called to mind the ghost of a king haunting the ruins of what was once his palace. His displeasure was aggravated when a dearth of passengers made the local branch line close down until the following spring. "What's missing around here," he said, "is proper means of commotion." Despite his current deficit, he already had grandiose plans for future seasons. Being actually quite capable of using fine words properly, especially when they were suited to the hotel business and had the effect of aggrandizing it, he would say, "I was let down by my supporting troops, though I did have a fine squad in my dining room. Mind you, the pages left a little to be desired—but you'll see, next year I'll have a first-class phalanx of them!" Meanwhile, the suspension of services on the Balbec–Caen–Balbec line obliged him to send some-one out to fetch the mail, and even at times to have departing guests taken away by wagonette. I often asked the coachman to let me sit be-side him, and in this way I went out and about in all weathers, as I had done during the winter I once spent in Combray.

At times, however, the rain was too heavy and my grandmother and I had to stay indoors; the Casino having closed, we spent our days in sitting rooms that were almost completely deserted, like a ship's passen-gers keeping belowdecks out of the wind, where every day, as happens on a voyage, one or another of the people among whom we had spent three months without having made their acquaintance, the First Presi-dent from Rennes, the *bâtonnier* from Caen,[120] an American lady with her daughters, came to sit with us, struck up conversation, devised a way of making the hours seem less slow to pass, revealed a talent, taught us a game, invited us to tea, to make music with them, to foregather at a particular time of day, to collaborate with them in one of these diver-sions that have the happy knack of affording us true enjoyment, which consists not in being striven after, but in merely helping us to while away our boredom, and formed friendships with us right at the end of our stay that would be broken off the very next day by their successive departures. I even came to know the very wealthy young man, one of his two aristocratic friends, and the actress (who had come back down to spend a few days in Balbec); but their little closed group now con-tained only the three of them, as their other friend had returned to Paris. They asked me to go and have dinner with them at their special restaurant. I think they were quite relieved that I declined the invita-tion. Still, it had been issued in the nicest possible manner: though the inviter was really the wealthy young man, the other two being just his guests, when the actress asked me whether I would go with them, she automatically phrased it so as to flatter me: "Maurice would love you to come"—Maurice being the friend, the Marquis de Vaudémont, a man of exceptionally noble descent.

When I met all three of them in the lobby, it was M. de Vaudémont who said, as the wealthy young man hung back:

"So we're not to have us the pleasure of your company at dinner?"

Altogether, I had derived little benefit from being in Balbec, for which reason I was all the more determined to come back one day. I felt I had spent too short a time there. My friends took a different view, and had been writing to ask whether I intended to settle there for good. In the knowledge that the place-name they had to write on their envelopes was that of Balbec, and since the view from my window was not of the countryside or a streetscape but of the wide wilderness of the sea, since I could hear its restless echoes during the hours of darkness and entrusted my own rest to them each night as I fell asleep, as though venturing out in a boat, I harbored the illusion that this close relationship with the waves must imbue my mind unawares with the sense of their charm, as though it was one of those lessons you can learn in your sleep.

For next year, the manager promised me better rooms; but by now I was attached to mine: I could walk into it without noticing the slightest smell of vetiver; and my mind, which had once had such difficulty in occupying its upper reaches, had fitted itself so accurately into the room's dimensions that I had to train it to do the opposite, once I was back in Paris and getting ready for bed in my old room, which had a low ceiling.

For, eventually, we were obliged to leave Balbec, where the cold and the damp had become too penetrating for us to stay on in a hotel without fireplaces or heating system. Our final weeks there I forgot almost immediately. When I thought of Balbec, what came to mind almost invariably was the morning moments, at the height of summer, when, because I was going out with Albertine and the other girls in the afternoons, my grandmother made sure I obeyed the doctor's instructions that I should stay in bed and lie there in complete darkness. The manager ordered that no noise must be made on my floor and personally ensured that these instructions were obeyed. Because the daylight was so bright, I kept the curtains closed as long as possible, those tall violet curtains, which on the first evening had received me with such hostility. However, since Françoise never managed to close them completely and exclude every speck of light, despite the pins she stuck in them each evening, which no one else could get out again, despite the blankets, the red cretonne table-cover, the odds and ends of fabric she patched on, the darkness was in fact not complete, and they allowed a sprinkle of scarlet, as of a scatter of anemone petals, to dapple the carpet, in which I could not resist paddling for a moment with my bare feet. Opposite the window, on the wall that was partly illuminated, a golden cylinder stood upright, supported by thin air and slowly moving, like the pillar of fire that gave light to the Children of Israel as it led them through the way of the wilderness. Then I would go back to bed: obliged as I was to take all my pleasures simultaneously in imagination, without moving—playing, bathing, walking, whatever the morning sun advised—happiness made my heart beat louder, like a motor turning at full power but motionless and out of gear, so that it can only discharge its power into the empty air as it idles at full speed.

I knew that my gang of girls were already out there on the esplanade, but I could not see them as they walked past the uneven ranges of the sea, beyond which, perched amid its bluish peaks like an Italian hilltop village, the little town of Rivebelle appeared in an occasional sunny glimpse, vivid and detailed. I could not see the girls; but as the shouts of the newsboys—"Those journalists," as Françoise called them—floated up to my belvedere, along with the cries of bathers and children at their play, punctuating the quiet breaking of the waves along the shore like the calls of the seabirds, I could imagine their presence and hear their laughter, lapping like the laughter of Nereids among the gentle hush of tide-swell that rose to my ears. "We stopped to see whether you were going to come down," Albertine would say that evening, "but your shutters were still closed, even after the concert started." The concert always broke out at ten o'clock, under my windows. If the tide was in, one's ear caught the smooth legato of a wave sliding in among the instruments, blending the tones of the violin into its own ripples of crystal, and splashing its foam all over the broken echoes of underwater melodies. My things had not been set out, and the impossibility of getting up and dressing began to make me lose patience. Then the clock struck twelve, and at last Françoise came up. For months on end in Balbec, the place I had so yearned to visit because my imagination had lashed it with gales and shrouded it in fog, the summer weather had been so unvaryingly bright that whenever Françoise came in to open my window my expectation, never wavering and never disappointed, had been to see the same expanse of sunlight folded into the angle of the outside wall, so unchanging in its color that it was not so much a thrilling indicator of summer, as a drab enamel, inert and artificial. And as Françoise pulled her pins out of the transom and peeled off the extra layers of cloth, then drew back the curtains, the summer's day that she uncovered seemed as dead and immemorial as a mummy, magnificent and millennial, carefully divested by our old servant of all its wrappings and laid bare, embalmed in its vestments of gold.

Notes

Introduction

1. **"listless interlude . . ."**: letter to Gallimard, Dec. 1919, *Correspondance* (Paris: Plon, 1990), XVIII, pp. 490, 491.
2. **"a poor thing"**: ibid., p. 528.
3. **"utter nonchalance . . ."**: Michael Finn, *Proust, the Body and Literary Form* (Cambridge: Cambridge University Press, 1999), p. 177.
4. **". . . muddles the design"**: *Sur Proust* (Paris: Julliard, 1960), p. 25; my translation.
5. **"rid him of . . ."**: F. Lhomeau and A. Coelho, *Marcel Proust à la recherche d'un éditeur* (Paris: Olivier Orban, 1988), p. 130; my translation.
6. **"powers of observation . . ."**: Edmund White, *Marcel Proust* (London: Weidenfeld & Nicolson, 1999), pp. 7, 37, 83, 89.

PART I: *At Mme Swann's*

1. **Twickenham:** the place of residence of Louis-Philippe Albert d'Orléans, the exiled pretender to the French throne.
2. **"It is said . . ."**: Racine, *Phèdre*, V, 584: *"On dit qu'un prompt départ vous éloigne de nous, Seigneur."*
3. **three portentous strokes:** in the French theatrical tradition, the raising of the curtain is preceded by *les trois coups,* a loud hammering culminating in three strokes of the stage manager's *brigadier,* a staff.
4. **was to jeopardize his own interests:** if this comparison was suggested to Proust by the actions of Colonel Picquart, then this is the first reflection in the novel of the Dreyfus Affair.
5. **". . . Vatel . . ."**: François Vatel, the Prince de Condé's butler, has become a

byword for the perfectionist in cooking: in 1671, the fish having failed to arrive for a dinner prepared for Louis XIV, he committed suicide.

6. "... the Consulta ... Carracci gallery ...": the Consulta was the Italian Ministry of Foreign Affairs; the Farnese Palace was the French Embassy at Rome, containing a gallery of frescoes by Agostino and Annibale Carracci dating from about 1600.

7. "... Wilhelmstrasse ...": the German Ministry of Foreign Affairs in Berlin.

8. "At Pevchesky Bridge ... Ballhausplatz": Pevchesky Bridge, literally the Singers' (or the Choristers') Bridge, tsarist Russia's Ministry of Foreign Affairs in Saint Petersburg; Montecitorio, the lower house of the Italian Parliament; Ballhausplatz, the Austro-Hungarian Ministry of Foreign Affairs in Vienna.

9. "It was worse than a crime ...": Norpois's paradox was coined, it is said, by Talleyrand (or perhaps Fouché) describing Napoleon's execution of the Duc d'Enghien in 1804.

10. "... Admiral de Tourville": Anne de Cotentin, Comte de Tourville (1642–1701); his tomb can be seen, not in fictional Balbec, but in the church of Saint-Eustache in Paris.

11. "... Panurge's sheep ...": Rabelais tells, in chaps. 5–8 of the *Quart Livre*, his fourth book of the adventures of Pantagruel (1552), how Panurge avenges himself on an objectionable merchant by throwing one of the man's sheep into the sea; the whole flock jumps in after it.

12. "... Molière's word ...": the word *cocu* (= cuckold) figures in Molière's comedy *Sganarelle, ou le cocu imaginaire* (1660).

13. Comte de Paris: the title given to the pretender to the throne of France.

14. "... through their books ...": the "clever fellow" is Proust, who here refers to the theory of his essay *Contre Sainte-Beuve*.

15. "... Alfred de Vigny by Loménie ... Sainte-Beuve ...": Alfred de Vigny (1797–1863), historical novelist, Romantic poet, and dramatist; Louis-Léonard de Loménie (1815–78), a biographer and man of letters (who spoke of Vigny, but not in such terms); Charles-Augustin Sainte-Beuve (1804–69), the best-known literary critic of the nineteenth century. In *Contre Sainte-Beuve* and in parts of *In Search of Lost Time,* Proust taxes him with "blindness" toward the most important writers of his day, such as Stendhal and Baudelaire, a defect which, Proust says, derived from his focus on writers' lives instead of on the originality of their works.

16. Assurbanipal: also known as Sardanapalus, King of Assyria (669–640 B.C.). Proust, in saying "ten centuries before Christ," is misreading his source.

17. *L'Aventurière, Le Gendre de M. Poirier:* comedies by Émile Augier (1820–89).
18. ". . . Weber's . . .":* a restaurant once frequented by artists, men of letters, and politicians. Proust was a regular in the early 1900s.
19. **Café Anglais:** once the haunt of wealthy foreigners and crowned heads.
20. **Raspail:** François Raspail (1794–1878), a revolutionary, doctor, and journalist, has little in common with Pius IX (1792–1878), save the year of his death.
21. **"haunts the heart of the evening woods":** the allusion is to the opening and closing lines of Alfred de Vigny's poem "Cor" ("Horn").
22. **the palaces of Gabriel:** the two buildings by Gabriel, separated by the rue Royale, date from the 1760s.
23. **Palais de l'Industrie, Palais du Trocadéro:** both the Palais de l'Industrie, modeled on the Crystal Palace, and the Palais du Trocadéro, of Moorish design, were built for nineteenth-century exhibitions and later demolished.
24. *Orpheus in the Underworld:* Offenbach's comic opera *Orphée aux enfers* dates from 1858.
25. *lavabo:* the French word means a washbasin. The OED does not confirm that it has ever been used in English in the modern sense of "lavatory."
26. **Saint-Simon:** the *Mémoires* of Louis de Rouvroy, Duc de Saint-Simon (1675–1755), largely observe life at the Court of Louis XIV.
27. ". . . olé! au lait!":* a pun on the French *au lait* (– with milk).
28. **the Candlestick in Scripture:** in Exodus 25:31–40, Moses' candlestick has six branches (but seven lamps).
29. ". . . Berlier":* Jean-Baptiste Berlier (1843–1911), an engineer and inventor, one of whose ideas led to the construction of the Paris Métro.
30. **Renan's** *Life of Jesus:* Ernest Renan (1823–92) published his *Vie de Jésus* in 1863, a biography of "a peerless man" without supernatural dimension.
31. ". . . Gérôme's new painting":* Jean-Léon Gérôme (1824–1904), painter and sculptor, neo-Greek and academic in genre.
32. ". . . Colombin's . . .":* once a fashionable English-style tearoom and patisserie on the rue Cambon.
33. **Wolf:** Friedrich August Wolf (1759–1824) argued that the *Iliad* and the *Odyssey* were not by Homer, but were collections of short works by diverse anonymous authors.
34. ". . . Union Générale . . .":* a leading bank, of Roman Catholic inspiration, the collapse of which in 1882 ruined many small investors.
35. **"Strangers to Speak in Sparta":** the allusion is to the memorial to the 300 erected at Thermopylae, as recorded in Herodotus, bk. VII: "Stranger, go and speak in Sparta of us who lie here in obedience to her law."

36. an Opportunist: the "Opportunists," Republicans who practiced gradual-ism, belonged to governments, especially during the 1880s.

37. husband: Pléiade, I, 513, gives *ami* (= friend), presumably an error. Earlier editions give *mari* (= husband).

38. banging on the door: Proust says *à la porte* (= on the door). In the earlier scene (*Swann's Way*, pp. 287–88), Swann rings the doorbell and knocks on the window.

39. at six o'clock on that day: in the earlier scene, the time is both *à trois heures* (= at three o'clock) and *vers cinq heures* (= about five o'clock).

40. Klingsor's magic transmutations: Klingsor is the evil enchanter in Wagner's *Parsifal*.

41. a play by Sardou . . . different performance: the play was *Fédora* (1882), the leading lady Sarah Bernhardt. The "tiny nonspeaking part," that of a corpse lying on the stage, was "played" by, among others, the Prince of Wales, the future Edward VII.

42. Coquelin's: Constant Coquelin (1841–1909) was a celebrated actor, noted for his performances of Molière and in the title role of Rostand's *Cyrano de Bergerac*.

43. Île-de-France: the region around Paris that in medieval times was the ori-gin of the French monarchy, and the dialect of which eventually became the French language.

44. Winterhalter: Franz Xaver Winterhalter (1805–73), a German painter fa-vored in the courts of Europe.

45. ". . . Taine . . .": Hippolyte Taine (1828–93), a renowned historian and ideo-logue, was most influential in his determinist analyses of French (and English) society, literature, and psychology.

46. bishop who tried Joan of Arc: an untranslatable reference to the name of the bishop of Beauvais, Pierre Cauchon (1371–1442).

47. "After that article of his . . . 'PPC' . . .": Taine's article, published in 1887, spoke of Napoleon's mother's lack of cleanliness. PPC = *pour prendre congé* (to bid farewell).

48. Alfred de Musset: Louis-Charles-Alfred de Musset (1810–57), Romantic poet and dramatist.

49. ". . . Prince Louis . . .": Louis Napoléon (1864–1932), the nephew of Princesse Mathilde.

50. Compiègne: the château, fifty miles north of Paris, was a favorite resi-dence of Napoleon III.

51. *hansom cab:* in English in the text.

52. "Quite a tall man ...": Saint-Simon speaks of Villars, a military commander, in 1702. See note 26 to pt. I.

53. when Racine spoke ... the following day: Scarron was the former husband of the King's mistress, then secret wife, Mme de Maintenon. The story of Racine's disgrace in 1699 can be read in the *Mémoires* of Saint-Simon. See note 26 to pt. I.

54. Mélusine: a French water fairy, associated with elusiveness and transformations.

55. *Menaechmi*: Plautus' comedy turns on a pair of identical twins.

56. "Where are we going ... where we go": this exchange makes no sense, given that the narrator leaves with Bergotte. It is an example of Proust's careless correction of proofs: the scene, before he deleted some of it, was originally to end with the narrator accompanying Gilberte and Bergotte to Saint-Cloud.

57. Bernardino Luini: (1480?–1532), a pupil of Leonardo.

58. "Rachel, when of the Lord": the nickname derives from the first four words of a famous aria, *"Rachel / Quand du Seigneur la grâce tutélaire ..."* (act IV, scene v, *La Juive* [= The Jewess], by Fromental Halévy, 1835).

59. Mlle Lili: a series of illustrated storybooks published by P.-J. Stahl between the 1860s and the early 1900s.

60. Julie de Lespinasse: having been befriended by Mme du Deffand, then banished by her in 1764, she formed a circle of *philosophes* and *Encyclopédistes* including d'Alembert and Condillac.

61. Henry Gréville: the pen name of Alice Durand (1842–1902), many of whose novels are set in Russia.

62. "Well, that's how history's written, isn't it?": the allusion is to a saying coined or adapted by Voltaire (in a letter of Sept. 24, 1766), about the unreliability of accepted accounts of things: *"Voilà comme on écrit l'histoire."*

63. As La Bruyère says, "... without wealth": Jean de la Bruyère (1645–96) is remembered for a single book, *Les Caractères* (1688). The quotation is from IV, 20: *"Il est triste d'aimer sans une grande fortune."*

64. As both Joseph and the Pharaoh: see Genesis, chap. 41.

65. Ice Saints: the expression, also known in the form "Frost Saints," denotes three saints whose days fall in "the blackthorn winter"–i.e., the second week of May.

66. Good Friday Spell: the allusion is to the end of the first part of act III of Wagner's *Parsifal.*

67. like Hypatia ... measured tread: the French sentence contains an unretrievable echo of "Hypatie," one of Leconte de Lisle's *Poèmes antiques* (1852): "*Et les mondes encor roulent sous ses pieds blancs!*"

68. "... Sagan ...": Charles-Guillaume-Boson de Talleyrand-Périgord (1832–1910), known as the Prince de Sagan, an arbiter of elegance, may be the source of some features of Charlus and of the Duc de Guermantes.

69. Antoine de Castellane, Adalbert de Montmorency: like Sagan, Antoine de Castellane (1844–1917) and Adalbert de Montmorency (1837–1915) were real people.

PART II: *Place-Names: The Place*

1. Mme de Sévigné ... "the Pont-Audemer": Marie de Rabutin-Chantal, Marquise de Sévigné (1626–96), is remembered for her many letters, almost 800 of which she wrote to her daughter, Mme de Grignan. With some of these place-names in this sentence, Proust reproduces Mme de Sévigné's seventeenth-century usage: "L'Orient," for example, is now Lorient.

2. Céline and Victoire: in "Combray," these aunts are called Céline and Flora.

3. Balbec-Plage: roughly, "Balbec Beach."

4. Anne of Brittany ... book of hours: *Les Heures d'Anne de Bretagne*, the work of a French miniaturist, Jean Bourdichon (1457?–1521).

5. "Regulus was accustomed ...": a form of words modeled on one of the *Lives* of Plutarch.

6. "I'll have to draw ...": this quotation, like many others, is very approximate (letter of Feb. 9, 1671).

7. Mme de Beausergent: a fictitious writer.

8. Mme de Simiane: Pauline de Simiane (1674–1737) was a granddaughter of Mme de Sévigné.

9. "I could not resist ...": Proust quotes (approximately) from the letter of June 12, 1680, in which Mme de Sévigné describes uncanny optical illusions caused by the moonlight. The italics are his.

10. Minos, Aeacus, and Rhadamanthus: sons of Zeus who became the three judges of the shades in Hades.

11. Duguay-Trouin: Proust borrows this statue from Saint-Malo, the birthplace of René Duguay-Trouin (1673–1736), an admiral and privateer who left memoirs of his exploits.

12. **Cardinal La Balue:** Jean Balue, or de La Balue (1421?–91), was imprisoned for eleven years by Louis XI (1423–83). Modern historians tend to doubt whether he was held in a cage.

13. **for the Duc de Guise to have been assassinated in:** the Duc de Guise was assassinated at Blois in 1588 on the orders of Henri III.

14. **Saint Blandine:** one of the first Christian martyrs in Gaul, put to death in Lyon in 177, remembered for her serenity under torture.

15. **First Presidents . . . *bâtonnier:*** a First President is a leading magistrate; the *bâtonnier* is the president of the lawyers attached to a French law court.

16. **Cour de Cassation:** supreme court of appeal.

17. **". . . They're the *de* Cambremers, aren't they? . . .":** in many French names, *de* is a vestige of noble birth.

18. **". . . half of my Estate?":** the quotation is from Racine, *Esther,* line 660: *"Faut-il de mes États vous donner la moitié?"*

19. **"so sumptuous that you starve":** letter of July 30, 1689.

20. **the Cimmerians:** in the *Odyssey,* Homer speaks of the mythical Cimmerii, who dwelt at the western edge of the world, by the deep-flowing Ocean, amid perpetual mists and darkness.

21. **Archduke Rudolf . . . still alive:** the Archduke Rudolf of Habsburg (1858–89), the son of the Austrian Emperor Franz Joseph I, was found dead in a hunting lodge with his mistress, Marie Vetsera.

22. **"Each time I receive your letter . . .":** letters of Feb. 1671.

23. **Gustave Moreau's Jupiter . . . mere female mortal:** the reference is probably to Gustave Moreau's *Jupiter and Sémélé* (1895).

24. **". . . Baronne d'Ange!":** the title assumed by a courtesan in the play *Le Demi-monde* (Dumas *fils,* 1855).

25. **Mathurin Régnier and *Macette:*** Régnier (1573–1613) was a satirical poet. His character Macette is a reformed bawd.

26. **Glauconome:** a Nereid, often depicted as all smiles, one of the fifty daughters of Nereus and Doris.

27. **Esther or Joad:** characters from Racine's last two tragedies, *Esther* (1689) and *Athalie* (1691), written for Mme de Maintenon's school for young noblewomen.

28. **"like a flight of raptors . . .":** Proust quotes from Leconte de Lisle's tragedy *Les Érynnies,* after Aeschylus: *"tel qu'un vol d'oiseaux carnassiers dans l'aurore";* and *"de cent mille avirons battaient le flot sonore."* See also p. 481 and note 106 to pt. II.

29. **Molé . . . Daru:** many of these men, politicians or members of the

Académie Française in the early nineteenth century, dabbled in history or left memoirs that the critic Sainte-Beuve admired. Proust here gives to Mme de Villeparisis something of an admiration that he deplored.

30. **". . . As M. Sainte-Beuve used to say . . ."**: Proust's novel grew out of a projected essay on Sainte-Beuve, which criticized the critic for letting his judgment of writing be influenced by his knowledge of the writer. The superiority of Bergotte the writer over Bergotte the speaker is another reflection of this criticism.

31. **"The moon . . . august and solemn"**: the quotations, two of which Proust has slightly misremembered, are *"Bientôt elle répandit dans les bois ce grand secret de mélancolie"* (Chateaubriand, *Atala*); *"Pleurant, comme Diane au bord de ses fontaines"* (Vigny, "La Maison du berger"); and *"L'ombre était nuptiale, auguste et solennelle"* (Hugo, "Booz endormi").

32. **Hernani:** the first night of Hugo's verse drama, in 1830, was a controversial event in the development of the new Romanticism.

33. **". . . the Duc de Nemours . . ."**: probably the second son, also known as the Prince d'Orléans, of King Louis-Philippe.

34. **". . . Bagard . . ."**: César Bagard (1639–1709), a sculptor from Nancy, whose work figured in certain fine houses in Paris.

35. **". . . the ill-fated Duchesse de Praslin . . ."**: the daughter of General Sébastiani, married to the Duc de Choiseul-Praslin, was "ill-fated" because in 1847 her husband, having abandoned her for the governess of their ten children, then stabbed her (and poisoned himself when arrested).

36. **Doudan . . . Joubert:** Ximénès Doudan (1800–1872), an administrator and civil servant, whose correspondence (*Mélanges et lettres*, 4 vols.) was published in 1876. Charles, Comte de Rémusat (1797–1875), a minister in governments between the 1840s and 1870s. Joseph Joubert (1754–1824), a moralist and friend of Chateaubriand, known mainly for a posthumous selection from his notebooks, *Pensées, maximes, essais*.

37. **Doncières:** an invented name.

38. **Proudhon:** Pierre-Joseph Proudhon (1809–65), a theorist of French socialism, one of whose most celebrated statements was "Private property is theft."

39. **"intellectuals"**: the use of *intellectuel* as a noun became widespread in 1898, an acute phase of the Dreyfus Affair.

40. **Boieldieu or Labiche:** François-Adrien Boieldieu (1775–1834), a composer of songs and light opera. Eugène Labiche (1815–88) wrote about 100 comedies.

41. **". . . La Belle Hélène . . ."**: a comic opera by Jacques Offenbach, first staged in 1864.

42. **". . . rue d'Aboukir"**: a street in the 2nd arrondissement of Paris, a noted Jewish quarter.

43. **Concours Général . . . *universités populaires:*** the Concours Général is a competitive public examination in different subjects, taken by only the best pupils in each *lycée*. The one taken by Bloch and Saint-Loup would have been in French literature. The *universités populaires* were private adult-education establishments set up in the late nineteenth century with the aim of promoting knowledge and technical qualifications among the working classes.

44. **". . . 'lyfte' . . ."**: referring to the elevator boy, Bloch mispronounces the English "lift," as though it rhymed with "knifed."

45. **"common sense that is the commonest . . ."**: Descartes's ironic dictum *"Le bon sens est la chose du monde la mieux partagée"* is here slightly misquoted by Proust (*Discours de la méthode*, I).

46. **Barbey d'Aurevilly:** Jules-Amédée Barbey d'Aurevilly (1808–89), a Catholic dandy and polemicist from Normandy who wrote novels of provincial life in a belated Gothic-Romantic and derivatively Balzacian vein.

47. **"by the Kroniôn Zeus, keeper of oaths"**: here, as elsewhere, Bloch borrows tags from Leconte de Lisle's poems and translations from Greek.

48. **Samuel Bernard:** (1651–1739) a financier who lent much money to Louis XIV and Louis XV.

49. **". . . Menier of the swift ships . . ."**: it has been suggested that Bloch's Homeric reference is to the family of the chocolate-maker Gaston Menier, whose yacht *Ariane* was well known.

50. **Heredia:** José Maria de Heredia (1842–1905), a poet who began as an admirer of Leconte de Lisle and became, like him, a major poet of the Parnassian group.

51. **". . . a few of his friends . . ."**: Proust himself did the same thing with the Poulet Quartet during the Great War.

52. **". . . *Passavant . . . Combraysis* . . ."**: *Passavant* is made up from the verb *passer* (to pass) and the adverb *avant* (before), the utterance meaning roughly "Forward!" *Combraysis* is a word of Proust's own coinage, suggesting the lands around Combray (or perhaps the inhabitants of them).

53. **". . . Carrière . . ."**: Eugène Carrière (1849–1906), a painter of portraits (including those of Mallarmé, Alphonse Daudet, and Anatole France), family scenes, and works of religious and allegorical inspiration.

54. **". . . Gustave Moreau . . ."**: (1826–98) a painter of mainly symbolic, mythological, and allegorical subjects.

55. **". . . Île-de-France . . ."**: see note 43 to pt. I.

56. **Lebourg and Guillaumin:** Albert Lebourg (1849–1928) and Armand Guillaumin (1841–1927), minor painters from the fringes of impressionism and fauvism.

57. **Fénelon:** François de Salignac de la Mothe-Fénelon (1651–1715), an archbishop, remembered for educational works and as the tutor of a prince, the Due de Bourgogne, who, though he did not live to reign, was to be the father of Louis XV.

58. **Mme de Grignan:** see note 1 to pt. II.

59. **"... in La Fontaine ... the other pigeon ...":** Jean de La Fontaine (1621–95), a writer of fables and stories. The fables cited here are "Les deux amis" (bk. VIII, xi) and "Les deux pigeons" (IX, ii).

60. **"... 'This separation ...' ":** Proust conflates and misquotes two letters of Mme de Sévigné to Mme de Grignan (Feb. 18, 1671, and Jan. 10, 1689).

61. **"... 'so slight ... ever notices them' ...":** an approximate quotation from Mme de Sévigné (May 29, 1675).

62. **"... 'To be with those ...' ":** another misremembered quotation, La Bruyère, *Les Caractères*, "Du cœur," 23 (see note 63 to pt. I).

63. **Le Nôtre:** André Le Nôtre (1613–1700), a landscape designer who became "king's gardener" to Louis XIV. Among his gardens are those of the Tuileries and Versailles.

64. **"... Clara de Chimay ...":** a reference to a rich American, Clara Ward, who married the Prince de Caraman-Chimay in 1890, then eloped with a Gypsy violinist.

65. **"... Petit Trianon ... English garden in front of it":** this actually refers to Le Hameau, a pseudo-rustic dwelling built at Versailles in 1783 by Marie-Antoinette, near the mini-châteaux of the Petit Trianon and the Grand Trianon.

66. **"... hilarious and undeserved Christian name ...":** the Christian name Charlus refers to is "Aimé," which means literally "loved."

67. **"À Saint-Blaise ... Adriatique":** these lines from Musset's *Poésies nouvelles*, so fragmentary as to be barely translatable, speak of places: Padua, Le Havre, Venice, etc.

68. **Mme Cornuel:** of Anne-Marie Cornuel (1605–94) Saint-Simon says that on her deathbed she said to Soubise, of his forthcoming marriage to an heiress, "Oh, monsieur, what a fine marriage that will be in sixty or eighty years!"

69. **"... he's not my father ...":** a sexual innuendo and catchphrase, from Georges Feydeau's play *La Dame de chez Maxim's* (1899); a young woman of no

great chastity, speaking of men, says it throughout the play, giving an unambiguous suggestiveness to her activities.

70. **"the Duc d'Aumale's double"**: the Duc d'Aumale (1822–97) was a son of the last king of France, Louis-Philippe.

71. **Gramont-Caderousse**: Proust may be referring to Charles-Robert de Gramont-Caderousse (1808–65?), the prodigal son of a noble family.

72. **". . . your Villiers or your Catulles . . ."**: Auguste de Villiers de l'Isle-Adam (1838–89), a minor writer of some note, from the fringes of late Romanticism and early symbolism. Catulle Mendès (1841–1909), a prolific minor writer, associated with movements such as Parnassianism, Decadence, and Wagnerism.

73. **". . . Peter Schlemihl"**: the central character in the novel *Peter Schlemihls wundersame Geschichte* (= *The Marvelous Story of Peter Schlemihl*, 1814) by Adalbert von Chamisso de Boncourt (1781–1838), in which the hero sells his shadow to the devil.

74. **Mme Dieulafoy**: Jeanne Dieulafoy (1851–1916) was a French archaeologist, notable especially for the reconstruction of Mesopotamian friezes held by the Louvre.

75. **". . . Sardou, Labiche, Augier . . ."**: well-known writers of light comedies of the second half of the nineteenth century. On Sardou, see note 41 to pt. I.

76. **". . . Menander, Kalidasa"**: Menander was an Athenian comic writer, fourth century B.C., whose works were later adapted by Plautus; Kalidasa was a Sanskrit poet of the 5th–4th centuries B.C., whose drama *Sakuntala* was translated into French in 1803.

77. *agrégation:* a public examination, a qualification for teaching in secondary and higher education.

78. *Journal officiel:* the government gazette.

79. *Ancilla Domini:* Proust may have in mind Dante Gabriel Rossetti's *Ecce Ancilla Domini* (1850), though many religious paintings, from the Middle Ages onward, bore the words spoken by the Virgin Mary to the angel announcing her divine pregnancy: "Behold the handmaid of the Lord" (Luke 1:38).

80. **the little gang**: the expression *la petite bande*, handed down from the sixteenth century, originally meant François I's seraglio of mistresses.

81. **Peri**: Proust may have in mind a poem by Victor Hugo, or *La Péri* by Paul Dukas, danced in Paris by the Russian ballet in 1912: the Péri, an evil fairy in Iranian folklore, disappears back to paradise, having seduced Prince Iskander, who had stolen her lotus flower, with its power to bestow immortality.

82. **Pisanello . . . Gallé**: Antonio Pisano (1395?–1455?), a painter and engraver,

some of whose bird sketches can be seen in the Louvre. Émile Gallé (1846–1904), a French artist in stained glass and wood.

83. *Harmony in Grey and Pink* after Whistler: Proust may have had in mind Whistler's portrait of Lady Meux, also known as *Harmony in Pink and Grey*, shown in Paris in 1892 and now in the Frick Collection, New York.

84. Dreyfus was guilty, totally and utterly: between late Oct. 1897 and the summer of 1898, one of the Dreyfus Affair's most eventful phases, there took place the court-martial and acquittal of Esterhazy, the publication of Émile Zola's open letter *"J'accuse . . . ,"* the trial and exile of Zola, and the suicide of Colonel Henry.

85. Pauillac lamb: renowned for its red wines, Pauillac, a small town on the Gironde estuary, also grows fine lamb from salt meadows.

86. the builder in the fable: Amphion's lyre moved stones that Zethus then built into walls. In Ruskin, Proust found several allusions to this legend, recorded in the *Odyssey* (XI, 260–65) and in Horace (*Ars poetica*, 394–97).

87. King Mark . . . Forest of Broceliande: in the legend of Tristan and Yseult, King Mark is the husband intended for the latter. The Forest of Broceliande appears in the legends of the knights of King Arthur.

88. ". . . Redon . . .": Odilon Redon (1840–1916), a sculptor and painter of sometimes symbolist sympathies. Elstir's reference may be to the set of lithographs *L'Apocalypse de saint Jean* (1899).

89. *Sacripant:* deriving from the character Sacripante in *Orlando innamorato*, a poem by Boiardo (1441–94), the word *sacripant* had taken on a sense close to "naughty boy" or "rascal." See also the next note.

90. Miss Sacripant: *Sacripant* is the title of a comic opera by Gille and Duprato (1866). The hero appears disguised as a woman (and the part of the hero was acted by a woman). Works by Renoir, Whistler, and Manet have been suggested as possible sources for Elstir's watercolor of "Miss Sacripant." See also the preceding note.

91. ". . . something that surpasses them": here Proust noted on his manuscript: "This is all badly written; perhaps I've put it better elsewhere."

92. ". . . Arvède Barine . . .": the pen name of Louise-Cécile Vincens (1840–1908), who was instrumental in introducing Ibsen, Spencer, and Tolstoy to a French readership.

93. a goddess, a table, or a bowl: Proust here adapts a line from La Fontaine's fable "Le statuaire et la statue de Jupiter" (bk. IX, 6), in which a sculptor wonders whether his chisel will transform a block of marble into *"dieu, table ou cuvette"* ("god, table, or bowl").

94. "My duty . . .": Bloch combines pedantry and ignorance by ascribing to Voltaire ("Master Arouet") a couplet deriving from Corneille (*Polyeucte*, III, ii): *"Apprends que mon devoir ne dépend point du sien; / Qu'il y manque, s'il veut; je dois faire le mien."*

95. restful: editors disagree on whether Proust wrote *reposant* ("restful") or *passionnant* ("exciting").

96. the First President: on page 373, it was "an old banker" who was subjected to this indignity.

97. ". . . Conseil Général . . .": the elective governing body of a *département*, roughly "County Council."

98. ". . . *Cavalleria Rusticana* . . .": Mascagni's one-acter dates from the early 1890s.

99. ". . . they've gone and taken down the crucifix . . .": the symbolic removal of a crucifix from a public building is a symptom of the anticlericalism of the Third Republic and of the growing divorce between church and state, to be consummated in 1905.

100. " '. . . Alceste or Philinte?' . . .": men characters in *La Misanthrope*, a comedy by Molière (1666).

101. ". . . *Le Gaulois* . . .": an anti-Republican newspaper of the moneyed right, much read by the well-bred and fashionable (1868–1928). In younger days, Proust had contributed gossipy pieces to its social column.

102. ". . . Fortuny . . .": Mariano Fortuny y Madrazo (1871–1949), a painter and designer of Spanish origin. During the Great War, Proust became interested in designs of Fortuny's modeled on paintings by Carpaccio. If this first Balbec episode is set in the late 1890s, Elstir's reference is anachronistic.

103. ". . . Callot . . . Doucet, Cheruit . . . Paquin . . .": couturiers of the Belle Époque, mostly established at fashionable addresses on or near the rue de la Paix or the Place Vendôme.

104. ". . . Saint-Augustin . . .": a large church, imitative of Italian Renaissance and Byzantine styles, built just off the Boulevard Malesherbes by Baltard during the 1860s.

105. ". . . Les Creuniers . . .": Proust borrows this place-name from cliffs near Trouville in Normandy.

106. "Gone are the kings . . .": from Leconte de Lisle's *Les Érynnies*, after Aeschylus: *"Ils sont partis, les rois des nefs éperonnées, / Emmenant sur la mer tempétueuse, hélas! / Les hommes chevelus de l'héroïque Hellas."* See also p. 287 and note 28 to pt. II.

107. Combray-in-Champagne: Combray was originally not in Champagne, east of Paris, but to the southwest, near Chartres. Proust later relocated it, with Roussainville and Méséglise, to Champagne, so as to place them in the battle-fields of the Great War.

108. Bellini's musical cherubs: Proust saw cherubs by Gentile Bellini (1429–1507) in the church of Santa Maria dei Frari in Venice.

109. " ' 'Tis this passion ...' ": the couplet is from Boileau's *L'Art poétique* (1674), canto III (on tragedy), lines 95–96: *"De cette passion la sensible peinture / Est pour aller au coeur la route la plus sûre."*

110. "... Robert Garnier ... Antoine de Montchrestien": Garnier (1544–90) was a poet and dramatist, the most important playwright of his day. Montchrestien (1575–1621) was a minor poet and playwright.

111. "... 'not just the masterpiece ...' ": Voltaire, without apparent irony, more than once expressed this view of Racine's *Athalie*.

112. "... Merlet ... Deltour ... Gasc-Desfossés": in the second half of the nineteenth century, all three wrote schoolbooks on literature. Proust may have borrowed some of Andrée's words from Gasc-Desfossés.

113. Trianon: see note 65 to pt. II.

114. "... Laura Dianti's ... Eleanor of Aquitaine's ... Chateaubriand's sweetheart ...": Laura Dianti (1476–1534) was Titian's likely model for *Flora* (Uffizi, Florence) and *Girl with Mirror* (Louvre), paintings showing a figure with long hair. Eleanor of Aquitaine (1122–1204) was Queen of England and mother of Richard the Lion-Hearted; she was celebrated for her long hair. Chateaubriand's sweetheart was Delphine de Sabran (1770–1826), a descendant not of Eleanor of Aquitaine, but of Marguerite de Provence.

115. those figures by Michelangelo: the reference is to the figures representing Genesis on the ceiling of the Sistine Chapel.

116. Panama Affair: a political and financial scandal revealed in 1891, marked by ruin for many thousands of investors and corruption among politicians, much exploited by antiparliamentarians and anti-Semites.

117. Leucothea: a goddess of spindrift, mentioned as Ino in the *Aeneid* (V, 823).

118. Jules Ferry: a politician (1832–93), best known for educational reforms in the 1880s. Perhaps the narrator has confused him with Gabriel Ferry, a very minor playwright?

119. *Spinario:* A Roman bronze of a man pulling a thorn out of his foot (Museo del Palazzo dei Conservatori).

120. the First President from Rennes: hitherto, the First President was from Caen, the *bâtonnier* from Cherbourg.

Synopsis

PART I: *At Mme Swann's*

New versions of Swann—Odette's husband, "a vulgar swank"—and of Cottard, eminent man of science (3–6). The Marquis de Norpois: his career (6), conversation and manners (9–10).

Father and Grandmother disagree on whether I should go to the theater (11). Norpois's first opinion on literature as a career (12). Expectations of a revelation about nobility, grief, and Beauty from La Berma (13). La Berma and *Phèdre* (13–16). A great disappointment: La Berma in *Phèdre* (17). Françoise's preparations for Norpois coming to dinner: the "Nev York ham" (17–18).

I meet Norpois (23). Norpois on literature (24–25) and investments (26); he reads my "prose poem" (27). Norpois on La Berma (29), on Françoise's cooking (30). Norpois and style (30–31). Norpois on King Theodosius and "affinities" (32); on Vaugoubert and foreign policy (32–35); on Balbec and its church (36–37); on Mme Swann (37); on "Svann" and the Swanns' marriage (38–39).

The Swanns' marriage (40–42). Swann's daydreams about his daughter meeting the Duchesse de Guermantes (43).

Norpois on the Comte de Paris (44–45); on Odette (45); on Bergotte (45–47); on my prose poem (46). I had no gift for writing (47). Norpois on Bergotte's "ignominy" and "cynicism" (48–49); on Gilberte (49). Norpois would never mention me to Mme Swann (52).

A review of La Berma's performance in *Phèdre* changes my mind about her (53–54). Words spoken by my father destroy two illusions: that life "was about to start the very next day"; and that I lived outside Time (55–56).

My parents on Norpois (56). Françoise on Norpois (57); on restaurants (58–59).

New Year's Day: family visits and a letter to Gilberte (59). A photograph of La Berma and romantic dreams of her (60). I realize New Year's Day is not the first day of a new life (60); the New Year's Day of older men, who no longer believe in the New Year (61). A joy is seldom paired with the desire for it (62).

The palaces of Gabriel, my very first glimpse of beauty (62).

I forget Gilberte's face (63). My love for her is a new love every day (63). Gilberte tells me of her parents' adverse view of me: untrustworthy and a bad influence (64). My long letter to M. Swann protesting the innocence of my intentions, my purity of conscience (64–65). A smell of damp walls in a public lavatory (65). Françoise's "countess" (66). A tussle with Gilberte: I "shed my pleasure" (67). I recognize the remembered smell: that such an insignificant impression should fill me with such bliss confirms my inability to be a serious writer (68).

Illness (69). My grandmother: alcohol and sympathy (69–70). The physiological realism of my display of symptoms to my grandmother (70). Cottard's cure: *olé!* (71–72). Gilberte's letter (73). Delayed awareness of happiness (74). Our ignorance of the causes of sudden happiness (74). An untruth of Bloch's about Mme Swann serves me well (76).

The Swanns' household opens to me (76). Gilberte's hair (77); her tea parties, her notepaper (77, 78). My parents and the Swanns' "genuine antique" staircase (78–79). Mme Swann's perfume (79). Destruction of Gilberte's Ninevite cake-castle (80). Tea makes me tipsy with excitement (80). Mme Swann's at-homes (81). My "nurse" (82). The Swanns think I am a good influence on Gilberte (82). Swann shows me his treasures (83). Mme Swann's boudoir, her visitors; "Now, . . . that's a *lovely* story!" (84). Swann impressed by mediocrities (85). Gilberte mentions "that Albertine" (86). Naïve snobbery of the Guermantes set (87). My mother on Mme Swann's new acquaintances and on Mme Cottard: "Strangers to Speak in Sparta" (89–90). Mme Swann shunned by fashionable ladies (90). An effect of the Dreyfus Affair on fashionable society (91). Shift in the patterns of the social kaleidoscope (91). Swann's indifference to Odette's ignorance and social howlers (92). Swann's experiments in the sociology of entertainment, at the expense of the Cottards and the Bontemps (95). Swann close to indifference toward Odette and his former jealousy, but his curiosity remains (97–98). His jealousy now inseparable from his love for another woman (99). When his love for Odette ended, the desire to show her his love had ended had also disappeared (99).

Invitations to lunch and outings with the Swanns (100). Deprivation of the feeling of loving in the presence of the beloved (103). Mme Swann plays the phrase from the Vinteuil sonata (103–4). Music and memory: impressions gradually gather in the mind as recollections (104). Music is carried away by habit out of reach of our sensibility (105). In music, the beauties one discovers soonest are also those that pall soonest (105). The artist, present disfavor, and posterity (105-6). The work of genius creates its own posterity (106). For Swann, Vinteuil's sonata is full of leaves; it shows him things he once paid no attention to (107-8). The Swanns banter about Mme de Cambremer (108-9); their story of Mme Blatin at the Zoo (110); their view of Gilberte's rare virtues (110). Gilberte's considerateness and professions of love for her father (111). The Swanns favor me (112). I can never grasp my happiness (113). The former outcast among the emblems of the Swanns' special existence (113-14). Mme Swann's changing style in interior decoration (114); her tea gowns, our outings (115). Princesse Mathilde (116-19). Gilberte's surprising petulance toward her father (119-20).

Bergotte (122). Bergotte's appearance obliterates the man I had imagined (122). Names draw poor likenesses (123). Bergotte encumbered by his name (123). Bergotte's voice (124). Bergotte's spoken and written styles seem very different (125). The beauty of a stylist's sentences is unforeseeable (125). Bergotte's pronunciation (127); his siblings (128); his influence on younger writers (130); his ways of praising and receiving praise (130-31); his moral contradictions (132). The artist's answer to the moral question (133). Bergotte on La Berma (134); on Norpois (137). Swann's view that a man should choose a socially inferior woman (138). Contrast of Mme Swann and Gilberte (139). Gilberte's twin likenesses, to her father and mother (139). Two Gilbertes (140). Bergotte's mistaken view of my pleasure in intellectual things (144). Bergotte on Cottard (145); on Swann, "the man who married a trollop" (146).

My parents' view of Bergotte (148). My reluctance to invite Gilberte to tea (149-50).

Bloch takes me to a brothel (150). A Jewess: "Rachel, when of the Lord" (151-52). I give the madam some of my aunt Léonie's furniture, "dear, defenseless things" (153).

Flowers for Mme Swann (153). My parents wish I would start becoming a writer; my inability to do so, my resolve, my best intentions, my coming achievement (154-55). Mme Swann's view of Bergotte: a better writer since he has taken to journalism (156).

In love, happiness is abnormal; love secretes a permanent pain (157). A tiff between Gilberte and me (157). Misunderstanding, a furious letter (161). I decide to stay away from Gilberte (163). The daily torment of hope, looking forward to the mail (164). I give up Gilberte forever, condemn myself to separation (165).

Visits to Mme Swann (166). Her "winter garden"; her flowers, her "five o'clock tea," her tea gowns (167–71). Mme Cottard, Mme Bontemps, the Prince d'Agrigente, Mme Verdurin (171–83). Mme Bontemps mentions her cheeky niece Albertine (173). The pleasures promised by Mme Swann's chrysanthemums are not realized (183).

A painful New Year's Day (183). No letter from Gilberte (184). Renunciation as seen by those in love (185). Slow suicide of the self that loved Gilberte (186). The temptation to write to her (187). My laborious sacrifice undone by well-meaning or ill-intentioned people (188). Regret, like desire, seeks satisfaction, not self-analysis (189). I foresee my indifference to Gilberte (190).

Mme Swann's change of style, the importance of the word "sham" (190); her renown as a high-minded woman (192). She has grown much younger; her face is her own invention: a model of eternal youth (192–93). Swann still sees her as a Botticelli (193). Young men see her as a period piece (195). Her "afternoon jamborees" (195).

I persist in my resistance to Gilberte's invitations (195). The reposeful promise of my foreshadowed forgetting of her (197). Resignation is a mode of habit (197). I think I see Gilberte with a young man in the twilight (199). The stem of a single event may bear counterbalancing branches (199). The fate of all our joys: happiness can never happen (200). Happiness: a psychological impossibility (200). I decline to attend a function at which Albertine was to be present: the different periods of our life overlap (202). The happiness that comes too late may not be the same happiness for which we pined (204). We are no longer our former self (204). A painful dream about Gilberte (205). Calm returns: even grief is incapable of permanence (206).

I stop visiting Mme Swann (207). Pleasure in the thought of a visit to Florence or Venice (209). Mme Swann: a "Symphony in White major"; the Guelder roses (210). Mme Swann's Sunday-morning walk (211). The "Hard-Up Club"; her retinue (211). Noblemen's and clubmen's homage to a woman their mother or sister could never meet (216). The life expectancy of memories of poetic sensation: my heartbreak over Gilberte has faded forever, replaced by Mme Swann's sunshade (216–17).

PART II: *Place-Names: The Place*

Two years later, my grandmother and I leave for Balbec; almost complete indifference toward Gilberte (221). Love revives and offers itself to another woman (221). Habit weakens all things; memory's broad daylight fades the past, which becomes irrecoverable (222). Things that remind us of a person are those we have forgotten: memory exists outside us, away from our mind's eye (222). Railway stations: tragic places, depriving us of the familiar; the Gare Saint-Lazare (224). My body's objection to this journey (224). Mama's avoidance of the sorrow of leave-taking (227). Françoise's hat and coat; her doglike eyes (228). Alcohol-induced "euphoria": gazing at a Holland blind (230–31). The letters of Mme de Sévigné (232). Sunrise seen from the train (233). The beauty of a milkmaid (234). The surprise of real beauty and happiness incarnated in an individual, contradicting abstract images (234–35).

The name of Balbec; the church at Balbec (237–38). The tyranny of the Particular: the Virgin of Balbec is a little old woman in stone (239). Balbec's name now empty of poetry, refilled with trite realities (239–40).

The stops on the Balbec line wound my homesick heart (240). The pain of arrival: the Grand-Hôtel, its staircase, its manager, my grandmother's haggling with him (241–42). Lack of habit made more agonizing by the sight of people in their element (242). The "lift" (244). "My" unbearable room, unfurnished by habit (245). Rescued by my grandmother (246). Knocks on the wall (247). The analgesia of habit; the death of a former self (250).

The sight of the sea, the starched towel (251). Variations in lighting alter the outlook of a place; the hours' changing landscape, the strangers (252–53). My grandmother lets in the breeze: contempt, outrage, and dishevelment (253). Eminent provincial personalities (254). Aimé the headwaiter (255). The King of the South Seas and his mistress (255). An old lady in a black dress and bonnet, her carriage exercise, her servants (256). M. and Mlle de Stermaria, their arrogance (258). An actress and her friends (259). Obscure onlookers gloating from the outer dark (260). Legrandin's brother-in-law's wife's garden party (261). I want to be liked, anxious for the esteem of all these personages of local importance (262). Mlle de Stermaria, the more desirable for being possibly unattainable (262). The Marquise de Villeparisis (263). My grandmother's principle: on vacation you sever relations with people (265). M. de Cambremer and the eminent provincials (265). I watch Mlle de Stermaria (267). The visit of the managing director (270). Françoise's contacts (271).

My grandmother and Mme de Villeparisis meet at last (273). Françoise forgives Mme de Villeparisis for being a marquise (275). Mme de Villeparisis's kindness (275). My indignation at my grandmother's notion that Mme de Villeparisis might be a Guermantes (277). The Princess of Luxembourg (277): her Second Empire gait (278); her loaf of rye bread (279). Mme de Villeparisis's surprising knowledge of my father's journey (280). The eminent provincials and the Princess of Luxembourg (281–82). Middle-class misconceptions about aristocrats (282–83).

Daily seascapes from my window (284). Outings in Mme de Villeparisis's carriage (284). Mme de Villeparisis's familiarity with the arts; her watercolors of flowers; her advanced opinions (287–89); her family memories of writers (289–90). Glimpses of girls from Mme de Villeparisis's carriage: desire for something we cannot possess (291). A disappointment: a letter from Bergotte rather than from a milkmaid (294). The church at Carqueville; I attempt to impress a village girl (295). Three trees near Hudimesnil: an unsolved mystery of memory (297). The old back road to Balbec, in reality and in memory (299). Mme de Villeparisis on Chateaubriand, Vigny, Hugo, and Balzac (301); her excess of politeness, her professional mannerism (303–4); her anecdotes about the simplicity of the great (304–6). A conversation on life and death with my grandmother (307).

Mme de Villeparisis's nephew, the Marquis de Saint-Loup-en-Bray (308). I imagine being his best friend (308). My first impression of him: insolence and callousness (310). His apparent unfriendliness (311); his handshake like a challenge to a duel (311); his tastes in art and ideas (313); his father (313–14). My grandmother's liking for Saint-Loup (314). Misgivings about the virtues of friendship (316). I enjoy viewing Saint-Loup as a work of art (317).

An anti-Semite bemoans the presence of Jews in Balbec: Bloch (318). Bloch's mispronunciations of English (319). Balbec's Jewish colony (321). Bloch on my "snobbery" (319). Our friends are inseparable from their faults (323). Bloch's apology: that of the ill-mannered man (325). Bloch speaks ill of me to Saint-Loup and of Saint-Loup to me (326). Bloch's "Jewish streak" (327). A first glimpse of Bloch senior (328). M. Bloch and the stereoscope (329).

Saint-Loup speaks of his uncle Palamède's infatuation with nobility, liking for the working classes, passion for women (329–32). I am struck by the behavior of a stranger: a madman or a spy? (332). The Baron de Charlus, Saint-Loup's uncle (334). Revelations about the Guermantes family (335). My grandmother delights in Charlus (337). Charlus's ideals in nobility, art, and women (338–39); his invitation to tea with Mme de Villeparisis; his strange behavior (339); and penetrating eye (340); his dislike of effeminacy in young men (342–43); his liking for Mme de Sévigné (343); his voice (345); his anti-Semitism (345). Two strange encounters with Charlus (346–48).

Dinner at Bloch's (349). M. Bloch senior's way of knowing people "without being acquainted" (351). Bloch's sisters (351). M. Bloch on Bergotte (352). M. Bloch "the Duc d'Aumale's double" (353). M. Nissim Bernard (354). M. Bloch's "champagne"; his "Rubens" (357–58). Bloch's remark to Saint-Loup about Charlus (358). Bloch's "nice ride" with Mme Swann on the suburban line (359). Françoise's disappointment with "M. Bloch" (360); her admiration of Saint-Loup the "hypocrite" (361). Saint-Loup's class-consciousness and prejudice against society people (361). Saint-Loup's mistress, her influence on him (362); her torture of him (364). Saint-Loup's sacrifices for her (364); her fiasco at the house of Saint-Loup's aunt (365–66).

Saint-Loup offers to take a photograph of my grandmother (367). My scorn at this suggestion, and at Françoise's mode of sensibility (368).

First appearance of the little gang of girls (369–70). Their scorn for the esplanade walkers (370). Their shared beauty; my inability to individualize them (371). One of them jumps over an old man: "Oh, what a poor old guy!" (373). A girl with a toque; are they the girlfriends of racing cyclists (374)? Intimations of their immorality (374). My desire for them is full of pain, because I sense it is unattainable (376). The bicycling brunette: not the one I like best (375–76). The alteration in social proportions characteristic of life at the seaside (378). These girls' fascinating perfection in suggesting the unknown and the desirable (379).

Familiarity of the hotel (380). The "lift" and his conversation (381). First mention of "the Simonet girl" (382). The changing paintings in the window frame (384). Aimé and "the whole truth" about Dreyfus's guilt (388). The list of new arrivals: *the Simonet family* (388).

Dining at Rivebelle with Saint-Loup (389). Beer, champagne, port, rushing waiters (391); the planetary system of the tables (392). The art of cross-sectioning things rids them of their customary appearances, enabling us to see analogies (392). The restaurant full of music, women, and their promises of happiness (393). The insignificance of all things in my drunken exhilaration, even Mlle Simonet and her friends (397). The women and "young" Saint-Loup (399). The hotel bedroom has stopped being hostile (400). Drunken dreams, sleep's narcotic, waking (401–2).

Inquiries about the girls (404). A glimpse of their earlier childhood (404). Chance encounters with girls and seeming beauty, illusions of destiny's purpose (405).

First appearance of Elstir (406). The girl with golf clubs; her resemblance to the one in the toque but much prettier (409–10). I assume she is Mlle Simonet (410). The passionate astronomy of my uncertainty about the girls' lives is enough to make me be in love: the sadness, the feeling of the irreparable, the anguish that accompany the onset of love (412–13). Loving them all, in love with none (413). My reluctant visit to Elstir (414). Elstir's studio: the laboratory from which would come a new creation of the world (415). Elstir's metamorphosis of things, analogous to metaphor: removing names, he renews our impressions of things (416). The metaphor of the harbor at Carquethuit (416). Elstir makes himself ignorant in order to paint (420). Elstir on the church of Balbec (420).

Appearance of the young cyclist (424). The beauty mark on her chin (424). Elstir says she is Albertine Simonet (424). The importance of spelling Simonet with one *n* (425). My later familiarity with her was to prevent me from ever seeing her again as I saw her then (426). The watercolor of *Miss Sacripant* (427). Mme Elstir's unobtrusive beauty (430). The attitude toward beauty of Swann implicit in the expression "the beauty of life," a phrase almost devoid of meaning (432). Encounter with the girls: I contrive not to be introduced (435). Miss Sacripant: Mme Swann before marriage (440). A painter's eye dismantles the factitious woman (441). Elstir is "M. Biche" (443). My desire to know the girls can be postponed, now that I know it is a possibility (444).

Saint-Loup's gratitude to my grandmother (445). The "little Slowcoach" (446). Bloch and Saint-Loup's invitation to Doncières (446). A letter from Saint-Loup (447). Elstir has shown me glimpses of poetry in everyday things (448). At Elstir's I meet Albertine (450). My acquaintance with her proceeds by subtraction (452). The unremarkable and touching Albertine with whom I chat and the mysterious Albertine by the sea (454–55). The beauty mark on her cheek (455). Albertine's way of speaking (456); her beauty mark comes to rest forever on her upper lip (457). My difficulty in meeting her friends in the little gang (457). Octave, the "also-ran" (457). Albertine thinks Bloch "quite handsome"; her anti-Semitism (459–60). I meet Andrée, the tall one who jumped over the old man (461). The d'Ambresac sisters (463). Elstir's taste influences Albertine's (463–64). Andrée's lie (465). I meet Gisèle and assume she is in love with me (465–66). I wonder about the flavor of Albertine's cheeks (467). I plan elopement with Gisèle (468). I meet all the girls; I spend my days with them (469–70). Today's young buds; a glimpse of future ugliness (470); the present delights of them, desire's artful plundering of their fragrances (471). I neglect Mme de Villeparisis, Saint-Loup, and Elstir (471). Wet days in the Casino (471). Andrée's kindness (472). Albertine's fascination with outings and parties (472). Our curiosity about the woman we love reaches far beyond her character (473). Andrée's generosity to Albertine (474). Françoise's rigmaroles, her thought processes (475). Elstir's sketches of yachtswomen and racecourses (476); his views on women's clothes and Mlle Léa's parasol (478); his watercolor of coolness and shadows at Les Creuniers (479). My view of Balbec and the sea is now transformed by Elstir (480). Albertine's view of Bloch's sisters and Mlle Léa, an actress whose tastes do not extend to gentlemen (482). Picnics on the cliff top and children's games (482–83). The unleavened flesh of young girls (484). For the artist, friendship is a dereliction of duty, but not the fancying of young girls (485). Saint-Loup's friendship deprives me of the power of self-realization (486). Charm and character in the girls' ways of speaking (487). Albertine's note: *I like you* (489). Gisèle's composition (490). I simultaneously love several girls (494). The disparate stylizations of the remembered and the real (495). Our slightest impression slides down memory's slope; what is called remembering is a process of forgetting (495). A game of ring-on-a-string in a little wood (497). Andrée's hands, Albertine's hands (497). I spoil the game; Albertine says, "Next time, we'll make sure he doesn't come" (499). Andrée takes me to Les Creuniers; a childhood memory from a hawthorn (500). Andrée's indulgence toward Albertine (501). Les Creuniers (503). Knowing I love Albertine, I take precautions to prevent her from knowing it (503). I pretend to prefer Andrée (505). Andrée's reactions to my professed indifference to Albertine (506). Albertine to spend the night at the Grand-Hôtel (507). Albertine's cheeks (509). Albertine is doing her hair the way I like it; she suggests I come to her bedside (509). Expectations of happiness (510). I attempt to kiss her; she rings the bell (511–512).

My dreams forsake Albertine when I lose the hope of possessing her (512). Albertine's background (513); Andrée's mother's attitudes toward Albertine (514). Albertine's popularity, willingness to please (515–16). Semblances of selflessness (516). My speculations about her virtue (518). She and I talk about virtue and the attempted kiss (519–20). My feeling for Albertine lies latent within me, a toothing stone for a future extension (520). Andrée is an inadequate replacement for Albertine (521). Misconceptions, misreading of appearances (521). Incipient love for each or any of the girls (522). My desire drifts from one to another (523). The girls' faces, similar yet dissimilar (523). Albertine's faces (524). My assumptions about the girls' unchastity are now seen to be completely wrong (526). The girls' imagined charm is now replaced by the memory of delight in their company (527–28).

The end of the summer in Balbec; the girls leave (528). Brief friendships in the Grand-Hôtel (530). My resolve to return one day (531).

My lasting memory of Balbec: the morning moments of shade and solitude, imagining the sun, the sea, and the presence of the gang of girls (532–33).

Suggestions for Further Reading

Beckett, Samuel. *Proust.* New York: Grove Press, 1931.

Carter, William C. *Marcel Proust: A Life.* New Haven and London: Yale University Press, 2000.

Milly, Jean. *La Phrase de Proust.* Paris: Éditions Champion, 1983.

Painter, George D. *Proust: The Later Years.* Boston: Atlantic–Little, Brown, 1965.

Proust, Marcel. *Within a Budding Grove,* trans. C. K. Scott Moncrieff. New York: Modern Library, 1930.

———. *A Search for Lost Time: Swann's Way,* trans. James Grieve. Canberra: Australian National University, 1982.

———. *À la recherche du temps perdu,* ed. Jean-Yves Tadié, vol. 1, *Du côté de chez Swann* and *À l'ombre de jeunes filles en fleurs* (first part). Paris: Pléiade, Gallimard, 1987.

———. *À la recherche du temps perdu,* ed. Jean-Yves Tadié, vol. 2, *À l'ombre de jeunes filles en fleurs* (second part) and *Le Côté de Guermantes.* Paris: Pléiade, Gallimard, 1988.

———. *In Search of Lost Time,* vol. 2, *Within a Budding Grove,* trans. C. K. Scott Moncrieff and Terence Kilmartin, rev. D. J. Enright. New York: Random House, 1992.

Shattuck, Roger. *Proust's Binoculars: A Study of Memory, Time and Recognition in* À la recherche du temps perdu. New York: Random House, 1963.

———. *Proust's Way: A Field Guide to* In Search of Lost Time. New York: W. W. Norton, 2000.

Tadié, Jean-Yves. *Marcel Proust: A Life,* trans. Euan Cameron. New York: Viking, 2000.

White, Edmund. *Marcel Proust.* New York: Viking, 1999.